NEW
HEBRIDES

FIJI
ISLANDS

NEW
CALEDONIA

TH PACIFIC OCEAN

FRIENDLY
ISLANDS

Kororareka

Auckland

New
Plymouth

TARANAKI

Wellington

NEW
ZEALAND

Christchurch

N
W E
S

TOMMO & HAWK

ALSO BY BRYCE COURTENAY

The Power of One
Tandia
The Potato Factory

TOMMO & HAWK

BRYCE COURTENAY

McArthur & Company
Toronto

McArthur & Company
322 King St. W. Suite 402
Toronto, Ont.
M5V 1J2

Canadian Cataloguing-in-Publication data

Courtenay, Bryce, 1933 —.
Tommo & Hawk.
ISBN 1-55278-003-1
I. Title. II Title: Tommo and Hawk
PR9619.3.C59 8T65 1998   823   C98-931678 5
Typeset in 12/14.5pt Sabon by Post Pre-press Group, Brisbane
Illustrations by Philip Holliday
Map for endpapers by Craig McGill
Magpie feathers on jacket supplied by the Museum of Victoria
Jacket and internals designed by Penguin Design Studio
Printed and bound in Canada by Transcontinental

10 9 8 7 6 5 4 3 2 1

 PRINTED IN CANADA

For Alex and Brenda Hamill

ACKNOWLEDGEMENTS

To Benita, my wife, who is first to read my work and who endured, mostly with good humour, the painful process involved in a partner writing a work of fiction.

Owen Denmeade, who helped in a thousand ways with small and large chores. Margaret Gee, who constantly combed my manuscript for errors of form and function and always improved upon it. Bruce Gee, who undertook the task of major researcher and never failed to find both the important facts and wonderful tidbits that give a novel both veracity and colour. Christine Gee, my indefatigable publicist.

Adrian Collette, Adam Courtenay, Tony Crosby, Alex Hamill, Alan Jacobs, Sylvia Manning, Lisa Mills, Essie Moses, Phyllis Pike, Roger Rigby, Sardine, Dr John Tooth, and Dr Brent Waters. Professor Terry Sturm at the University of Auckland, who read those sections dealing with the Maori Wars. The Tasmanian Museum and Art Gallery, The State Library of Tasmania, The Sydney Maritime Museum, and the inestimable State Library of New South Wales and in particular the staff of the Mitchell and Dixson Libraries for their unstinting and generous help. My abiding gratitude to the hundreds of past writers of books, newspapers, magazines and historical pamphlets from whom I learned both narrative form and fact and whose prior work made mine possible.

To my publishers, Bob Sessions and Julie Gibbs at Penguin Books Australia, who never flagged in their efforts to help me meet my deadline. Finally, my editor Clare Forster who, together with editor Laurie Critchley, worked long and hard to take my words and make them sing. What a joy it has been to work with you all.

I have a boy who cannot speak

and a boy who will not speak.

Both I love with all my heart

but do not know how to keep.

MARY ABACUS

CONTENTS

BOOK ONE

Chapter One

TOMMO

It ain't long now before Hawk comes to fetch me, to scrape his brother off the floor of Brodie's sly grog shop.

Funny that, when you're mostly scared in life you feel things brave folk don't bother to feel. I know he's coming. I can hear his big footsteps coming down the hill two mile away. When you've been listening to fear as long as me, you can't never be fooled. Fear is always the little brat in you, ears pricked, heart thumpin', listening to what can't be heard, knowing what's gunna happen by the way your arsehole is puckering like a rabbit's nose. No matter what you learns in life, the fear in you never grows up.

That first fear, when you was seven and stolen from your family and took into the wilderness, that first big begetting of fear in your life becomes a part of every fear you has ever afterwards.

Fear builds up, like rust in a metal water pipe. Its beginning, its first trickle, is always about being alone. Not loneliness, but being alone and helpless, with no one what cares, no one what gives a fig, what will flick an eyelid if you lives or dies. You're a small creature alone what has no

3

defences of its own and so is the natural prey to a world full o' hungry mongrels.

It don't matter if you grows to be big and strong, and cunning as a shithouse rat. It don't matter if you can defend yourself with fisticuffs or use an axe or knife like nobody's business. Fear don't take notice of them things, it just don't grow up and start being brave. It stays with you, so you can't put faith in nothin' and nobody. If you can't trust, then it stands to reason you can't love, 'cause if you does, you'll become some mongrel's prey.

There is always someone watching you in the tall timbers. You learn to feel him like an itch under your skin. Like a chill breath on the back of your neck. You knows in your thumping heart it's a wild man comin' for you, a mongrel with harm in his heart. You can't see nothing, but he's lurking, creeping, minding his feet so his steps don't warn you. He's moving closer, one foot raised like a kangaroo dog, but you don't know where or which way to run. The wind roars in the treetops like waves crashing against the shore, killing the small sounds, the snap of myrtle thicket, the sudden flutter of a bird, all the things you depends on to catch him out.

You pull the air through your nose, sniff deep, testing for the sour smell of a grown man, but the early morning sun's sucked the perfume from the eucalypt, the sassafras and King Billy pine, filling the frosty air so you can't smell nothing behind the sweetness at the end of your nostrils.

You begin to tremble. You know what's coming. If he gets you he'll bugger you. Put his thumb and finger to his nose and snort his snot onto your back as he swives his cock into your arse. Then he'll hold you pinned, and whistle over to his mates to come. If you struggle, he'll pull back your head, twist and snap your scrawny neck like you was a new-born pup. Other mongrels comes over, charging through the undergrowth, brushing aside the fern, boots cracking twigs, urgently pulling down their breeches, tripping as their pants fall to their ankles, laughing. You stretched over a felled Huon log what has its bark ripped off, its lemon-yellow naked, just like you, your face kissing the damp, dark, musty earth.

'Eh you, dog shit!'

'Yes, boss?' Your teeth chattering.

'Ya ain't seen nothin' now, ya hear?'

'No, nothin', boss! I ain't seen nothin', no one!'

'Wha' are you then?'

'Dog shit, boss.'

'Louder! Say't loud, boy!'

'DOG SHIT!'

'Tha's better. You'll say naught t'no bugger, yer understand? Tell and we'll come agin, kill ya, cut yer froat ear t'ear!'

'Yes, boss.'

Then the crash of myrtle twigs as they melt into the trees, ghosts in the morning mist. You alone again in the forest. The bellbirds begin to call again, the sound of an axe striking deeper into the bush. You snivels a while, and try to wipe away the blood from your arse with a bunch of green leaves, then you scrapes the muck from your back and what's running down your legs with a strip of bark, ashamed. Nobody you can tell what cares. You shit bright red for a month after.

That's the all of it. It never changes, one fear begets another, but it's always the same fear. The same small brat in you facing the same mongrels. Once fear gets a hold of you, you can't trust no one no more, not even yourself, 'cause you know they be right – all you be is dog shit, and all they wants to do is bugger you so you never forgets what you is.

I got to drink down fast, get a few into me. Brother

Hawk don't countenance me staying on no matter how much I plead at him to let me be. I'm not afraid of Hawk, just of Hawk coming. I'm afraid of Mary. Of Sunday dinner. Of meself.

'Mr Brodie, sir! Another snort o' acquadine!' I hold up me last shilling, won yesterday at euchre. Got to find a game today, but it ain't so easy on the Sabbath. 'Ere!' I twist the silver coin to catch the lamplight. 'I got the money, now quick, Mr Brodie, if you please!'

Brodie shuffles over, sniffing, stepping over bodies, spilling some of me precious tot. He grins toothless and puts the little glass down. 'There ya go, Tommo.' He grabs up me shilling in dirty woollen mittens what's got no fingers. Then he holds up sixpence change he has ready in his other hand. 'Shall I fetch t'other half then?' He twinkles the sixpence.

'Why not? I got to go soon. Bring it right off, will ya?' I nods.

Brodie smiles, a smarmy smile on his ugly gob, like he don't believe me and he makes a fuss of fumbling at the front of his waistcoat, pushing the sixpence back into a greasy pocket, his dirty fingers dancing like spider's legs over his pot belly.

The acquadine don't hit as hard as it should. Barely tickles me throat. Bastard's watered it down, doused the fire in it to make it last longer, though it's better than the Cape of Good Hope brandy he serves to most of his Sunday drunks. More like Cape of No Bloody Hope, all the good hope in it watered down to make a gallon of misery out of half a pint of trooper's joy.

Don't suppose I blames him, human nature being what it is. Fair enough, I reckon, the pubs are closed Sunday, so we're in his hands, ain't we? He's got us drunks all to himself. Brodie milking a few more pennies from the slops of Saturday night's barrel and charging us double for the privilege. Daresay I'd do the same. Can't feel too sorry for a Sunday drunk, can ya?

The sun should be well up by now, if it ain't raining outside. That be Hobart Town all right, sunshine, then rain, snow, hot, cold, calm and blow, all in the course of the same morning. Not that I mind, used to it, the wilderness be mostly rain and wind and bone-snapping cold. It could be nearly noon, though who'd know here in the oil lantern darkness. The shadows be the same now as if it be always midnight in the world.

I comes in early, not much past dawn, with the mist still hanging on the river. Birds just beginning t' chitter, currawong, kookaburra, green rosella calling and silver gulls wheeling. They be the early risers and the noisy buggers. Then come the little uns, scrub tit, scarlet robin, yellow wattlebird and blue wren, kipping in a bit, then starting to talk with the sun. Tide coming in, slapping, spiffing and spuming on Salamanca beach. I couldn't sleep no more, even though I were sozzled last night and should've been well able. But me restlessness is getting worse. Time to move on. Hawk knows I ain't gunna stay in Hobart Town now he's back from England. But he still talks of us joining Mary, of being a proper family again and doing brewery work up at Strickland Falls. 'It would be our fortune made, Tommo!' he reckons.

Ha bloody ha! A fortune in me hands would be poured down me throat, or lost at the dogs and horses. Can't make a copper penny stay long enough in me pocket to even gather warmth.

Hawk'll be here soon. Silent, bending double to get through the door, a great dark shadow hunched over, his head bumping against the rafters. Him so black the lamplight don't show nothing but the whites of his eyes, the silver sheen of the scar on his neck, and the shine on his nails where he holds his fingers to his nose. A nigger for me brother though I be as white as one o' Mary's best Sunday tablecloths. Hawk be twice my size too though we be born of the same mama. Different from the start, Mary reckons, from the day she set eyes on us, two mewlin' orphans in a basket. Even more different now. Hawk wouldn't be caught dead down here if it weren't for yours truly, even the stink's too bad for his well-raised nose.

But I don't smell nothin' no more. Don't take no notice. Not even of the farts from the drunks lying at me feet or curled up in the dark corners, snorting bubbles in their spew or seeing things terrifying what ain't there.

Reckon that'll happen to me soon enough. A few more years on the grog, then some mongrel like Brodie'll add too much acid to give a kick to his watered down spirits and that'll be the end of dear little Tommo. Over I topples, a nicely pickled feed o' flesh for the waiting worms. Or it'll be the horrors. I seen it happen to some younger than me, holding their ears and closing their eyes and screaming for the snakes to be took away. You'd think I'd be shitting meself. But I ain't. Truth be, I'm more scared of Hawk coming to fetch me to Mary's Sunday roast! More feared about sitting at her clean white tablecloth and chewing through a plate o' mutton with Mary's green eyes watching on me, so's I want to jump up and make for the door and keep running until I don't feel the disappointment in her eyes no more.

There be so much I've forgot in the seven years since I were snatched from Mary's tender care. Seven years I've been in the wilderness, but I never forgot Mary's white cloth spread on the kitchen table for Sunday dinner. She'd spread it like forgiveness, like whatever we done wrong in the past week was forgiven when we sat 'round her Sabbath table. Mary's white tablecloth religion was most accommodating of our weekly wickedness. You'd sit down a sinner and rise up with a full belly and a clear conscience, not a holy word spoken neither.

When I were left to mind Sam Slit's whisky still beside the river, cold, wet, starving, drunk and alone in a timber getter's bark hut, I'd recall into my mind Mary's kitchen of a winter's Sunday. The same wind churning the river and howling in the Huon pine. I was that wind, battering at Mary's kitchen door, rattling on the glazed windows of her cottage. And then, when it couldn't find no way to come into the warmth, howling its protest high up in the eaves. 'Wind off the Antarctic sea, the banshees howling be the widow ghosts o' dead sailors,' Ikey, picking his teeth with his pinkie nail, would say when it got particular furious outside.

Inside Mary's warm kitchen there were no need to heed the rain beating on the steamed-up window glass like a boy's tin drum. We was seated there at her Sunday table, snug as a bug in a rug. Mary at the head o' the table, Hawk and me at either side, and at the end, tucking in like there was no tomorrow, Ikey Solomon, what handed us over to Mary's care when we was born. It were Ikey what give us his name too though he weren't our papa nor Mary's husband neither. Ikey died before I found me way back, but he comes to me mind often. When we knew him, he was just Ikey. But before he got nabbed, he were the most high regarded villain in all of London Town. The Prince of Fences they called him, with a finger in every pie. I've heard say that he and Mary were in the brothel business together. But Mary be a ticket-of-leave now, and owner of The Potato Factory brewery, and she don't like much to dwell on the past.

So there we'd sit, a small, strange family. In front of us, on a big white oval plate with a picture of blue willow trees and two Chinamen on a little bridge, were a huge leg of hot roasted mutton. The very best butcher's hogget, with Mary standing over it, big fork in one hand, knife in t'other, carving onto each tin plate, then pouring on a rich, steaming river of gravy. Little pearl onions glistening and swimming in the bright brown gravy what covered the thick slices o' tender meat. Mary always putting the same on my plate as Hawk, her full knowing I could never eat all of it, that Hawk would polish off what I left, then eat Ikey's left-overs and then what meat was still on the bone. It were her way of feeding Hawk while not showing me up to be a runt.

And that's where I always supposed God would be on a howling winter's Sunday. He'd be seated at our kitchen table sharing our leg of mutton, with Mary's best sharp knife and fork in His almighty hands, His holy elbows on the snowy white tablecloth of forgiveness, fork stabbing at great chunks of meat, champing away like nobody's business. He, Him, the nabob of heaven, there with us 'stead of presiding over all the God business going on down at St David's church, where the true merinos, free settlers and lags what should've known better be praying and hymn-singing and freezing their bollocks and titties off. Them in church thinking they be earning extra points in heaven for going out in all the flurry and howl of a winter's blustering morning, and meanwhile God be sitting at our kitchen table all cosy-like, getting a good feed of Mary's best mutton and enjoying Hisself.

'Touch more gravy, God?'

'Don't mind if I do, Tommo, m'dear.'

God polite as you like while I pours Him more gravy, little onions tumbling out of the jug. God ever so grateful to be out of the devil's breath weather what comes roaring and snorting down the mountain.

I'd lie there in the forest hut wrapped in me wet blanket, coughing and shivering, dreaming of Mary's Sunday kitchen. 'I'll come back, Mama,' I'd cry, teeth chattering fit to break. 'You just watch and see, little Tommo'll be back sure enough soon as I can find me way to Port Davey and stow away aboard a timber ketch.'

But now since I come back, me appetite's quite gone. Nothin' tastes good no more. Sundays were always me best days in them old days. Now they's bloody purgatory with me afraid to look into Mary's sad face. Me here drinking Brodie's sly grog, scared shitless because Hawk's gunna make me sit down to Sunday dinner with our own mama. How can I face Mary when I've forgot how to deal with kindness in me life? Hawk with his hands moving thirteen to the dozen, trying to make cheerful conversation, and me with me eyes on me plate, not wanting none of it 'cept to get up and run for me life.

Though Hawk can't talk no more with his voice, I can still hear him in my head. When he speaks with his hands I can hear him clear as a bell. All them years away and I never lost the sound of him. I promised meself when I were miserable that I were going back to my mama's Sunday dinner and to my brother's deep, sweet voice. Now it's gone. His voice what was always a comfort to me when I was away, always steady, unafraid, Hawk's beautiful blackie boomer voice is gone, rubbed away by the wild man's horse rope. Even then, in the wilderness, I had most strange feelings like something were trying to choke out Hawk's voice, but I tried to put it out of me head, for remembering was all I could hang onto.

Mary's told me what happened to Hawk when we was both kidnapped on the mountain and later became separated. A wild man took Hawk and starved him and led him behind his horse by a hide rope around his neck until his voice was rasped away. All he's got now is his necklace of scars. I've asked Hawk about this time, but he says with his hand language he can't remember anything except that we was took on the mountain by four men and afterwards nothing. I can't remember the early part either. I can remember how it were with Sam Slit, but I don't want to talk about it. Maybe one day we will.

I suppose I should count meself the luckiest cove in the world that I were spared the terrible thing done to make Hawk lose his voice. But I don't think meself lucky. Poor dumb Hawk, he's the lucky one. He didn't stay away long enough from Mary to learn to be afraid. Fear never took him and introduced him to the mongrels. He can still feel things. I've seen the tears brimming when he tries to ask what happened to me in the wilderness, his confusion when I shakes my head because I can't say for the bitterness inside of me.

I can see my brother's concern for me. But I don't feel it. Can't feel the love I know Hawk has for me. I could do before I was took. I could feel everything he were feeling, like we were two fingers on the same hand. Shit, now I don't feel nothing no more. Not for Hawk, not for Mary, not for meself. That's what the wilderness done to yours truly. It took all the feeling out of old Tommo and left only the fear of the mongrels what's always lurking in the tall timbers waiting to get you.

I calls for another shot. Brodie brings it, but before I can pretend to search for a sixpence I know I ain't got, a drunk on the floor begins to shout and jerk, taking a fit. Brodie curses and forgets to ask for me money. He goes over and kicks the poor sod in the head. Brodie knows his stuff – when a man's took to fitting, a kick in the head sometimes'll bring him to calm again. I suppose it be the shock. I can feel Hawk is close. Better drink up quick, Tommo.

Hawk says we got a purpose, him and me. Me, quick and nimble with a mouth full o' cheek. Him, strong and thoughtful and silent. It's a right rare combination what could work together, he says. Mary says we are her team to build up the brewery she started soon as she was freed. It's up to us now to gain folks' respect, be someone what our kind has never been before, what them merinos think the likes of us can never be.

'It's the world's best opportunity for the taking,' Hawk says. 'We'd soon be proper toffs, and your children, Tommo, they'd be true merinos!'

But old Tommo here knows that's crap. There's no purpose, no opportunity for the likes of me. You can't make nothing good out of nothing.

Take a look at me, will ya? Mary's little lamb is become a drunk, a useless scum what wakes up and needs a drink. Somebody what can't think of nothing but a bottle to leach the anger and the hate out of his rotting guts. What's I gunna do? Wear a clean collar and learn clerking? Sit in a high chair with a green eyeshade, sharpened quill and blacking, working at profit and loss? Mary's precious little bookkeeper, Tommo X Solomon, beer baron in the making? Load o' rubbish, if you ask me!

I ain't clever but me hands, now, they's a different story. Dog-baiting and fist-fighting and timber-getting and burns from Sam Slit's whisky still, that's what's made 'em look bad. Every finger and knuckle looks broke or dog-bitten, and what's skin for other folk is scars for me, scar-tissue what can take most kinds of pain. They don't look much chop but they be good hands, even if I do say so meself.

That's the difference, see, they ain't like Mary's hands what are black and twisted and broken and I think most painful of movement. That's me one big secret, hands what looks battered but are sly as a fox.

Other broadsmen see me holding cards at cribbage or the Yankee game of poker what's catching on among the troopers and gold miners, and they thinks: 'Here's a go, little bugger can't do nothin' nasty with the flats using them poor sodding little mitts.' Ha!

What they sees is timber getters' hands, bashed in the

sawpit, calloused on the axe handle, cut, broken, burnt. Hands what ain't capable of handling a deck or palming a card in broad daylight so that the most suspicious sharper can't see what's going on right in front of his very own eyes. No danger in them pathetic, scarred and sorrowful little paws. No sir, not them!

But that's where they be wrong! That's their biggest mistake! What Ikey taught us at cards, me hands took to natural, like they had a mind of their own.

Ikey himself were most complimentary about this. 'Most elegant and nimble, full o' guilefulness and most diabolical of purpose, flippers tailor-made by the devil himself to belong to a broadsman o' most superior talent. Congratulations, my dear.'

Ikey were right, me hands has a pure and natural ability for winning at cards by means of cheating. They's good enough kept on the straight, mind – they hold their own and more in any honest game, if such an event be possible. But they is most amazing on the cross. Sometimes they do things with a deck o' flats what can even astonish me. Never's the day they don't earn me grog enough to dampen down what's ugly and frightening and burnin' inside me. There's always some mouth who fancies himself at cards and who's got a silver sixpence to lose in a hurry. Or a trooper with the Queen's florin he wants to double or treble and who grows most confident when he watches Tommo's clumsy little hands busy at spreading the cards around the table.

That be me only asset, hands what are up to no good, good only for cheating at cards, fist-fighting, dog-baiting and being most fast and nimble when they are clasped around the handle of a small lopping axe, like the one I always carries on me belt in case of mongrels.

Them's me total credentials, me hands. Hawk says he'll learn me reading again, the trick of which I've long since forgotten. But I'm not so sure I can pick it up again. 'Look,' he says, 'you learned Ikey's hand language soon enough again. Reading is the same, you'll soon be schooled back to it again.' But reading be a thing of the head, and Ikey and Hawk's hand language be a thing of the hands. That's the big difference, me head's fucked but me hands ain't.

Nastiness is the only thing what I'm well schooled in now. Mary's nicely brought up little lad, Tommo, what even at seven years old had some book learning and writing, is now everything what's deemed bad. But Mary and Hawk expects that with a bit of plumping up, kindness and affection, what I am become will go away again. That the niceness is still inside me, only for a moment drowned out by me wilderness life, that with a bit of gentleness and love and a few gravy-soaked Sunday dinners under my belt, it'll all bob back to the surface, like a cormorant what's been fishing. And there I'll be, good as new, floating merrily down the river of happiness and contentment.

How the hell, I begs to know, does I do that? For seven sodding years I had the living daylights kicked out o' me by mongrels the like o' Sam bloody Slit! Now I'm supposed to pretend all is forgiven and the world ain't no longer a bad place. Can't them two see that ain't possible? That what's inside me is all screwed up for good?

A large hand come down on the back of me neck and squeezes. Not so it hurts but firm enough. Crikey, it be Hawk! I didn't see or feel him come in, so lost am I in me own stupid misery.

I grabs at the tot in front of me and tries to knock it back, but me head won't go back because Hawk's holding me neck and I spills most o' the precious liquid onto me blouse. 'Damn!' I twists away angry and looks up. Sure enough, Hawk's got his finger and thumb pinching at his nose, lamplight shining on his fingernails. I can't help but smile.

Hawk lifts me from the bench by me scrawny neck. He

don't do it rough but he don't intend to have no protest from me neither. I could still twist and kick him in the bollocks, double him up, then head-butt him as he's coming down – I'll take on any cove what's up to a foot higher than me and bigger yet if I be drunk. Besides, I got me axe. But I don't, of course. I don't fight Hawk, who's like a band of iron around me neck. It ain't him what's making me angry, so I lets him steer me towards the door.

Brodie shouts I owe him sixpence.

Hawk lets go my neck, digs in his coat and flips him a shilling. Then he touches me lightly on the shoulder, directing me once more to the doorway. Brodie claps his mittened hands together but misses the spinning coin and curses as it clatters to the floor and two wretches, growling like a pair o' pit bitches, come alive and scramble for it at his feet, tits falling out. Brodie jumps aside dancing a jig, then kicks out wildly at the two soaks, screeching like a demented cocky-parrot.

Outside the sunlight be so bright I'm blinded and Hawk waits while I hold my hands up against my eyes and rubs. He can't say nothing to me 'til I can see proper, 'til me eyes adjust to the sunlight. So he stands and rests his big hand soft on my shoulder.

We stand outside with all the tiny lights flickering in front of my eyes, little stars and explosions floating in blackness. Hawk's hand on my shoulder feels safe. It feels good. Jesus! He's coming back to me, coming back into me heart! But then I thinks, maybe it's only Brodie's crook grog what's pumping through my veins giving me a drunk's false hope. So I rolls me shoulder and shrugs off his hand. No point him imagining what ain't true.

I can see clearly again and I note it's well past noon by the position of the sun. Hawk is standing waiting. Now he has his arms folded and clasped to his chest, looking down at his boots. His dark shadow cast in the dust is nearly twice the size of my own.

'Mary, is it?' I sneer. 'Commanding yours truly to Sunday bloody dinner?'

Hawk looks down sideways at me, his eyes narrowed, then he shakes his head slowly and spits to the side of his boots. 'Come,' he signals to me, 'our ship is leaving on the afternoon tide.'

Chapter Two

HAWK

Hobart Town
July 1856

Tommo's come back to us bad. The wild men have made him bad, taken his niceness and smashed it. His blue eyes are hard, the laughter in them gone.

'Tommo's come back to us damaged, Mama,' I say to Mary with my hands, the language I now use between us. 'He's lost himself somewhere.'

'Hush, you hear!' Mary says. She doesn't like what I'm saying. She looks at me accusingly. 'You're still good despite what you've suffered, so why not him?'

I shrug. 'It's not the same. I'm a nigger, niggers aren't supposed to have feelings.'

She leans forward across the table. 'Nonsense. Now you listen to me, Hawk, he'll come good. All he needs is a lot of loving.' She purses her lips. 'I'm not much good at mothering no more, a bit old for all that malarky, but now he's back, he'll get lots of good food and proper care. Least I can do!'

'Yes,' I say, trying to look more hopeful than I feel. 'He'll get that and more. I hope you're right, Mama. The wilderness took a lot from our Tommo.'

'Not more than it took from you!' Sudden tears well up in her eyes and Mary points to my neck, to the rope burns, the permanent scars that ring it in a band of silver tissue an inch wide against my black skin. 'The wild man took your voice.' Her lips are pulled thin as she wipes her mouth with the back of her hand. 'Nothing could be as bad as that, now could it?'

She has never said anything about my voice before. Never spoken about it since it happened, since the day she found me in the mountains. Now I can see that it's more than she wanted to say, that she thinks it's come out wrong. So she thinks a moment, then smiles, brushing away the tears, trying to brush away the horror she's felt all these years at what was done to me.

'It were such a nice voice, Hawk. You was just a little un but your voice were already deep.' She smiles at me. 'Did you know that, son?'

I nod and she continues. 'Lovely it were, like a melody. Folk would listen when you talked, even when you were a sprat. The wild man took that, there's no making up for that.' She shrugs, eyebrows high, mouth twisted. 'You've come good. Tommo's got no lasting damage, a little to his hands but not like what happened to you, not like that.'

'It's inside, Mama.' I think about how Tommo's afraid. 'That's where he's broken, something's broken inside him.'

Mary looks strangely at me. She doesn't tolerate folks who feel sorry for themselves. When she speaks her voice is sharp again. 'Whatever it were what happened to Tommo, it were no worse than most of us gets in life. This poxy island be full of past suffering. Sadness be a part o' this place. Suffering beyond the wildest imaginings of them what's not like us. Tommo's still young, only just growed up, plenty o' time for him to settle down. Work will fix what ails him.'

She says all this quickly as if she has thought it all out. Mary mostly keeps things to herself. Thinks them out, then keeps them, holds them tight to use only when needed. Now I sense she's worried about my brother too. When you've lost your speech and must talk in hand language you learn to watch people more carefully. Ikey always said, 'Listen with your eyes, Hawk, it be your eyes what's your best ears,' and he was right.

I don't want to say it but I must. 'Mama, I don't think Tommo will want to work in the brewery.'

Mary draws back sharply. 'What's you saying? What's you talkin' about?'

It is late Sunday morning with a high blue sky over the mountain and the winter's sun polishes the river like mirror glass. Mary's kitchen is bathed in sunlight. The window panes reflect bright squares that burn out the colour where they make a pattern on the dark brick floor. Specks of dust, turned to gold, dance in the shafts of light.

Tommo has gone down to Wapping to drink at Brodie's sly grog shop. Since he's been back he does a lot of walking on his own, learning Hobart Town that's grown and changed so much since we were kidnapped. He walks then stops off to play euchre or poker in a pub or grog shop, coming home late and drunk. Sad drunk. A fifteen-year-old who finds no cheer in the drinking he does.

Mary and I are sitting at the kitchen table, which is covered with a white cloth. On Sunday, Mary always spreads a white cloth on the kitchen table. Damask, she calls it. It's like her Sunday altar. We don't go to church. Mary doesn't believe in it and Ikey, the closest thing we had to a father, was a Jew. So was our real mother, or so he said. He used to tell Tommo and me that we were too.

Mary says she doesn't know anything about that. All she knows is our mother was Sperm Whale Sally, a whaleman's whore. She says Ikey made up a lot of things to suit, like the X he put in both our names. Ikey added it on the spur of the moment when the government man said it wasn't Christian to have only one name and demanded a second be given. So Ikey scratches his noggin and thinks a moment then says, 'Israel and Moses,' and the man says they aren't Christian either and he isn't going to write anything down until Ikey comes up with good Christian names for seconds.

'Tell you what,' says Ikey, 'I'll put X and then they can both choose a second name to their own liking when they've grown a bit.'

The government clerk thinks for a moment, scratching his head. 'Fair enough, all right then, X it be.' He can't immediately think of a reason why X is not Christian, it being a sort of cross and all, and he doesn't really care. So now it's Hawk X Solomon and Tommo X Solomon forever after.

'Can't trust the silly old bugger to get nothing right!' Mary said when she first told us she wasn't our real mother, nor Ikey our father, even though he gave us his name with the X added.

'Probably gave you his name then got nervous that maybe it weren't quite kosher, so he cancelled it by adding the X. Nothing would surprise me with him.' Mary snorts each time the story comes up but she's got a smile on her face too as she thinks of him. 'Ikey always did have a bet each way.'

Mary also told us that Tommo and I are twins, the same but different, the same mother but different fathers. A fluke of nature, she said, that happens sometimes with whores. Tommo came out with white skin and blue eyes, small as a tadpole, and I as black as the ace of spades and big as a bullfrog! It's very confusing to other folk, but not to Tommo and me. We're twins in the heart and in the head. Whether Jew or Mohammedan, twins are their own religion.

Anyway, Mary isn't much concerned with religion. 'Tell 'em you're Church of England,' she says when we're asked. 'Don't suppose it matters, do it? God ain't got no religion, now does he? As far as worshipping goes, it's best not to take sides.' She decided for all of us when she pointed to the mountain towering above us, 'Best off worshipping that!' She was not jesting either, for she loves the mountain. 'God lives in that mountain, right above the organ pipes!' she told us once. The organ pipes are the shafts of rocks that form a steep cliff to one side of the top of Mount Wellington.

When we were little, Tommo and I always skirted well clear of those pipes when we climbed the mountain, just in case Mary was right and we should bump into God.

'What would you say to God if we should meet Him up there?' I once asked Tommo.

Tommo thinks for a moment then says right off, 'I'd invite Him to Sunday dinner.'

'Why?' I asked.

'Because that's the most holy place we got, silly!'

He was right, too. Once when Mary spread her damask cloth we asked her why, and she said, 'It be our way of giving thanks to Him what keeps our bellies full. It be our altar cloth.'

'We belongs to the White Tablecloth Religion,' Tommo once told the curate at St David's who stopped us in the street and asked why we didn't come to Sunday School.

As for not going to church, Mary always says, 'If folk don't like it, well, that's just too bad now, ain't it? Knowing right from wrong is all what matters and I've yet to meet the preacher on this Gawd-forsaken island what does!'

There is little doubt Sunday is important to her, though, and a special occasion. Almost every time she spreads the cloth she says, 'One day I'm going to buy us some silver, some Sunday silver!' But I don't think she ever will. Such a gesture would be much too flash for Mary and we're still eating off the same tin plates and using the most ordinary cutlery you can buy.

Since I have come back from England with Ikey's stolen fortune, Mary could have a crystal chandelier in the kitchen if she wanted, and bone china and silver cutlery heavy enough to sprain your wrist. But Mary doesn't want people to think she's a free settler or a toff, or that she believes herself better than the rest of the lags. She isn't ashamed of who she is, a convict who has earned her ticket-of-leave and had her freedom granted after serving her sentence.

'It's who you is when folk knocks at the door of your heart what counts,' she always said when we were young. 'Hide the past and it gives them what's jealous of you the power to bring you undone.'

I remember her telling us always, 'Never give no one the power to shame you. Keep everything clear and in the open. Hiding from the past be the main business o' this cursed island, people trying to pretend they's better than other people, when they's dirt, the scrapings o' the barrel, just like what we is. Hannah Solomon be the prime example, putting on airs and graces, talking like a toff and trying to be a free settler, what she ain't and never can be.'

Hannah was Ikey's lawful wife, but all she did was try to do him harm. Now she and Ikey's children live with a cove named George Madden in New Norfolk. Mama once taught three of Ikey and Hannah's brats, David, Ann and Sarah, when Hannah was a prisoner seamstress in the Cotton Factory. 'They was bright too, those young uns,' Mary told me.

Mary doesn't care much for the free settlers here. 'Who'd come to this miserable place even if it were free, 'less they was third-rate to begin?' is what she says. But she is not being altogether truthful about her feelings. She'd not return to Blighty even if the governor granted her free passage. Mary loves this island, it is where she found the chance she was always looking for. Tasmania is what saved Mary and gave her back her character. She doesn't pine for the good old days like Ikey did.

'Blimey, what good old days was they, then?' she'd say sarcastically when Ikey got to reminiscing about London Town. 'For the likes of me they was shit!'

'And this ain't shit, my dear?' Ikey asks, sweeping his arm to include the whole island.

'Yes, but there be a difference,' Mary snaps back. 'There you was buried permanent in it, born in shit and drowned and died in it, no bleedin' hope o' rising above it. Here if you pushes 'ard enough you can get your 'ead up through the surface.'

'And when you does, my dear,' Ikey cackles, 'all you can see is arseholes!'

But Mary would not give in. 'Life's too bleedin' short to be frightened o' what's already been,' she'd say. 'Can't get yesterday back and change it, now can you?'

That is why Mary can't see what has gone wrong with Tommo. She won't ever look backwards. When we were put to bed as young uns she'd often say, 'Today is all we got, ain't it? I mean, who knows, tomorrow we could all be dead.' She'd take Tommo's hand and mine so that we were joined to her. 'Be honest, fair, listen, keep yer gob shut. Anyone can get through one day at a time. It's light and then it's dark and then it's bleedin' over, ain't it? Persistence, that's all what gets you there in the end. Believin' in yerself and persistence!'

Then, after she'd made this little speech, she'd let go our hands and tug at the chain about her neck and produce from her bosom the gold Waterloo medal Ikey gave her. She'd hold it tight in her fist. 'What's it say?' she'd demand.

'I shall never surrender!' Tommo and I would shout

together, that being the legend written on the back of Mary's talisman.

'And don't you never forget it,' Mary would say. 'Persistence and character!'

That is everything Mary believes – never give up no matter how painful the journey. Overcome and persist. I know that in her heart she can't understand Tommo, how he's sorry for himself and won't forget the past now that things are good again. Drowning his sorrows in grog, not showing grit in his character, that's what she can't abide in my twin. I can sense she sees too much of Ikey in him. Not the Ikey of London Town, not the successful fence and forger much admired amongst thieves and villains and even accorded a grudging respect by policemen and magistrates; but the broken Ikey, the Ikey who was brought to his knees by hard convict labour and trained to obedience with the warder's whip.

Now I've told her Tommo doesn't want to take up her legacy of persistence and character, to work at her beloved brewery. She looks down at the white damask cloth and begins to smooth it with both her poor broken hands. A little frown forms, her top lip covered by the bottom one, then she begins to speak quietly without looking at me, like she's thinking out loud.

'Course he'll want to work at the brewery! Tommo never were a lazy boy. He'll do his share. He'll come good,' she says, as though she's trying to convince herself, as though she secretly fears she might not be right about my brother.

'Mama, it's not that. He isn't ready to come back to us yet.'

But Mary will not look, doesn't want to see my hands, and continues. 'We'll buy all the new land in the Huon Valley we can get. We'll do it through Mr Emmett, so nosey parkers what can't mind their own business don't catch on.

Surprise the buggers! We'll grow all the hops we need for the use o' the brewery and maybe some for the new colony of Victoria.' Mary lifts her chin and her eyes narrow. 'We'll not be caught short again because some bastard beer baron tries to put us out o' business. Not never again!' She grips the sides of the table, then she looks up and becomes aware of me again. 'Hawk, you'll not talk to no one about the money, Ikey's money, ever, you understand?'

I've been back from England three months and this is the first time Mary's talked about what we'll do with the fortune I took from his and Hannah's old Whitechapel home. Ikey's stolen treasure had lain there for years, hidden in an Austrian safe, for though Ikey and Hannah knew half its secret combination each, they never trusted each other enough to tell each other their half. Hannah believed she and her brats deserved the lot and sent her son David to claim it, but with a little luck and cunning, I got there first.

'You know I won't tell anyone, Mama,' I nod.

'Not even to Tommo, you hear!'

I look at her, shocked. There is nothing I have ever hidden from Tommo. 'Mama, Tommo's my twin!'

Mary gazes down at the table. 'Tommo's been away, we don't know where, he won't say!' She looks up, her eyes steady. 'You hear me, Hawk Solomon, don't you *never* tell your brother until I say!'

There is a part of Mary that's hard as granite, that won't brook any contradiction. Her mouth is drawn in a thin line, the skin seeming to barely conceal the hardness of the skull beneath. Mary has a look that can frighten me and now she's used it against Tommo, her dearest Tommo whom she loves with all her heart.

She lowers her eyes again. 'You know about growing hops, you learned it in England. That will be yours to concern yourself about. The Huon Valley, what we can buy of it, will be yours, Hawk. Tommo can work with me at Strickland Falls and prove himself, prove he may be trusted. He must learn what you already know about brewing. Catch up like, be an apprentice boy.'

I bang my fist on the table so she is forced to look up. 'Mama, Tommo won't, he won't come back, not yet!'

But she's too quick for me. She doesn't hear the half of it because her eyes are squinched tight closed and she can't see my hands speaking to her, though she's heard the smack of my fist and knows full well what I'm trying to say.

'The Potato Factory,' Mary says fiercely, her eyes still closed, like it's a holy catechism, 'comes first!' She opens her eyes and spreads her crippled hands against the white of the cloth, fingers splayed as wide as they'll go. Then it comes to her what she has just said and she adds, 'That be after you and Tommo, o' course.'

'Mama, we've got Ikey's stolen fortune, you don't ever need to work again if you don't wish!'

Mary is silent a moment, then she says, 'That be the whole problem. We has to make what's been stolen honest again.'

She can see that I don't understand her. She shrugs. 'All Ikey's money's been gained on the cross, not one penny comes from honest toil. It all comes from fencing, forging, laundering money, brothel-keeping and having his brats at the Academy of Light Fingers pickpocket for him. As for Hannah Solomon, hers comes from running scams in bawdy houses. All right, I put in me time in such places too, but I never cheated nor used poor kids what can't defend themselves. We has to put the money to decent use and make it clean.'

'But, Mama, *I* stole that fortune! *I* opened Ikey's safe using the combination we worked out from Ikey's riddle. We've no more call on that money than the Solomons have.'

'Hawk!' Mary shouts in protest. 'You know it's not the same. Ikey gave you the riddle that held his three numbers to the safe. He were as good as saying that if you be the clever one to crack the riddle what opens his half of the safe, then providing he could also find out Hannah's set of numbers, what were in it be ours, his to share with us!'

'Mama, Ikey didn't say anything of the sort! He didn't know you already knew Hannah's half of the combination! You never did tell him, did you? Ikey always thought it was just a clever riddle he'd given me to test my wits.'

Mary purses her lips. 'More fool him, then,' she says, but softly. 'He were a fool to underestimate the both of us, you in particular.'

'But even if I'd cracked Ikey's part of the riddle he knew it would give us only half title to the money.'

She smiles. 'If Ikey were alive he'd be proud, most proud that we beat the wicked cunning of that bitch, and her miserable brat, David Solomon! They were his natural family, but he saw them for what they were.'

She gazes at me fondly now. 'I were right to send you to England, to learn the growing of hops. Heaven knows we didn't have a penny to spare at the time, not for sending you, nor for purchasing land when you returned to do the growing. But I always knew it were the right thing to do,' she claps her hands suddenly, 'and look what happened, you returned with Ikey's fortune and the knowledge we needed. Now we can buy the whole Huon Valley if we wants!'

'Mama, perhaps we could argue that if Ikey hadn't died before the safe was opened, he would have left us the part of the fortune that was his to give. But half of what came out of that safe rightly belongs to Hannah Solomon! Ikey was willing she should have her share, he always said so. But Hannah demanded more, much more, and that's what stopped him giving her half in the first place – the thought that she wouldn't rest there! That, and the fact that he didn't trust her to do right by him, stopped them from dividing it fairly in the first place. They were both ruled by greed. But what was Hannah's wasn't Ikey's when he was alive! Nor is it for us to have now that he's dead!'

'Her half share be our compensation for the kidnapping of you and Tommo.'

'Mama, we can't prove she and David Solomon were behind the kidnapping!'

'Ha! And Hannah can't prove you opened Ikey's safe before David arrived in London either! That's two can't proves! We're quits then, ain't we?' Mary looks smug. 'Far as she's concerned, you were waiting in London with Ikey's half of the combination, and the two of you opened that safe together and found it empty.' Her expression turns grim. 'I *know* it were them,' she taps her chest with her finger, 'in me heart. I know it were David and Hannah Solomon what kidnapped my boys!' She points her finger at me, shaking it. 'All the bleedin' dosh in the world can't bring back your voice or undo what's been done to Tommo! They've *got* to be punished!'

Mary suddenly realises that she's shouting and looks around. She lowers her voice to almost a whisper even though there's no one about to hear us. 'Besides, if Ikey were alive and you'd brought him back the whole fortune from London, do you really think he would have divided it in half and given Hannah her share? Not bleedin' likely he would! I'll tell you something for nothing, he wouldn't 'ave given her a farthing! Not a brass razoo!' Mary folds her arms across her breasts. 'By keeping the lot we're only doing what Ikey would have wanted most!'

I shake my head slowly. 'Mama, we don't know that. It isn't a decent thing that we're doing.'

Mary's face reddens. She is suddenly furious. 'Don't talk

to me about decent! Decent be what decent does. That bitch done nothing decent in her friggin' life! I ain't giving that whore nothing, you hear? Over my dead body! Not a bleedin' penny, you hear me? Me conscience be clear on the matter!'

I've never seen Mary so fierce and Ikey's words come back to me. 'Out of a clear blue sky, my dears, with not a cloud o' contention to be seen, not a fluffy puff o' ill humour on the far horizon, Mary can evoke a hurricane in minutes. She don't give a tinker's cuss for the consequences to herself of her malevolent tongue. Mary has a temper what can turn the sweetest harmony, the calmest waters into a raging storm at sea greater than that what wrecked the Spanish armada!'

There is nothing more I can say in the face of her anger. I shrug, but Mary's not finished yet.

'You think Hannah's going t' be happy with 'arf? She'll be off to the law in a flash if she knows we've got Ikey's money. Besides, who's to know what's hers and what were Ikey's?' She stabs a finger at me again. 'You going t' let her decide? Let Hannah Solomon tell you what's her fair share? Eh? You going to do that? You barmy or somethin'?'

What Mary says is logical. Hannah will never be satisfied until she has the lot, but Mary knows Hannah won't go to the law. When Ikey was sentenced to transportation for purchasing stolen goods, the Old Bailey ruled that whatever could be recovered of his stolen goods was the property of the Crown. Ikey always said that if we recovered any of the money we should never speak of it. 'The law has big ears, my dear. Ears what can gather taxes and fines like a dredger gathers mud! When it comes to money, stay stum, the less known all 'round the better, know what I mean?'

I remind Mary of this, knowing full well that she doesn't need reminding. 'Mama, you *know* Hannah won't go running to the magistrate. She won't want to draw attention to herself. Besides, she'd have done it before if she'd thought it an advantage to her. She already suspects we've got Ikey's money.'

Mary frowns, then shakes her head. 'Suspecting and knowing for certain ain't the same thing now, are they? Once Hannah and that son of hers knows for certain, they'd be after us. David Solomon wouldn't never let up. The humiliation of him knowing it were you what tricked him would be enough, he'd kill you!'

I shrug. 'Mama, you recall I left a ring in the safe with a little note that purported to be from Ikey: *"Remember, always leave a little salt on the bread."* It seemed a good joke at the time. David still thinks Ikey outsmarted them. He thinks the fortune was taken when Ikey was still in England and that the note was intended for Hannah. As far as he knows, Ikey had the money and couldn't spend it before he died, so it must be here.'

'No!' Mary says. 'There's no proof of it.'

I shake my head. 'Listen, Mama, David *must* conclude that Ikey left the money to you. That would be a natural enough assumption, don't you think?'

'Assumption? Assumption ain't proof! That ain't knowing!' Mary snaps, still protesting.

'Ah, but if you buy the land in the Huon Valley he'll know soon enough, won't he?'

Mary thinks a moment then sighs. 'You be right.'

'But Mama, what if we tell them we wish to make peace? If we admit that Ikey left you *all* the money but that you wish out of the goodness of your heart to do the right and proper thing and give Hannah her half?'

Mary looks at me astonished. She's lost for words so I continue quickly. 'Mama, it would wipe away the wrongs done, and guarantee our safety. Ikey always said: "Mutual greed can make the worst o' enemies the best o' loving friends.'''

Mary sighs and looks at me despairingly. 'Hawk, you is always trying to fix what can't be fixed between folk. This ain't a peace what can be bought. Them lot is filth, they won't abide by no goodwill, no conditions!'

'But don't you see, Mama? We'll make it so they *must*! We'll leave a sealed envelope with Mr Emmett. They know he's the governor's chief clerk as well as being your good friend and so can't be corrupted. We'll give him instructions that it's only to be opened if harm comes to any of us and they're involved. The note will tell the authorities about Hannah's possession of Ikey's money that rightly belongs to the Crown. Then we'll tell Hannah and David about the letter lodged with Mr Emmett.'

'Ha! Fat chance o' pulling that off! What about our money? The law would confiscate that, too!'

'What money?' I smile. 'We'll say Ikey left instructions before he died to give Hannah *all* his money, that when I came back from London I only acted as courier for a small commission. You were his executor, entitled to ten per cent that you're now perfectly prepared to rebate to the Crown.'

Mary shakes her head and tut-tuts. 'You've gone barmy, Hawk.' But I can see she's thinking. Frowning and drumming her fingers on the white tablecloth.

'Tell you what,' she says at last.

I shrug and spread my hands. 'What?'

'Get Tommo to stay put, to stay at 'ome with us and after he's been sober one year and worked with me in the brewery, we'll do it. We'll give Hannah a quarter share. That be more than what rightly belongs to her!'

She looks closely at me now, reading my consternation. 'And you still can't tell Tommo about Ikey's money neither.

You hear me now, Hawk Solomon, you've got to stay stum!'

I shake my head. 'Mama, I must give Tommo a reason to stay! I *must* tell him. Helping to protect you from any harm might be the only way to convince him to stay. Please, Mama!'

'No, Hawk, he's not to be trusted yet!'

'Mama, Tommo would do nothing to harm us!'

Mary's lips are pursed. 'Be that as it may, you're not to tell about the money. Nor about David and Hannah hating us. Tommo ain't no fool, he'll want to know why.' Now Mary looks directly into my eyes. 'I'm worried he's going to run away from us. You'd not scarper too, go with him, would you, Hawk?'

My heart sinks. She must be able to see how distraught I am, how my throat aches with concern for her. Mary is counting on me and now, with Tommo returned, him also. She knows, though, that the brewery can get along without Tommo, but it will be harder without me.

'Mama, I can't leave my brother. I swore that if Tommo came back to us I'd never leave him again. If he goes, I must go too.'

I can feel the tears running down my black face now. I sniff, my hands working fast. 'Please, Mama! I beg you to understand. You must let me get the badness out of Tommo! Then we'll come back to you, I promise!'

Mary says nothing. Instead she pulls at the chain around her neck to bring up her Waterloo medal, which she clasps tightly in her fist. When Mary holds her good luck charm, it means she's not going to budge an inch. She will never surrender.

I feel defeated. Telling Tommo about Ikey's money was the last card in my deck, my only chance to make him stay. I was willing to compromise Tommo's peace of mind for the greater good, believing truly that he would be best off here at home with us. But now Mary forbids me this. She expects me to let Tommo go away on his own again. She's making me choose between my love for Tommo and for her. Mary, whom I love with all my heart. Mary, to whom Tommo and I owe our very life, who made us her own when Ikey brought us home in his tobacco basket, two brats of a whore died in childbirth, rats already eating the birth mess when he found us in the early morning sunshine.

I know what Mary has done for us, Tommo and I saw it often enough when we were small. Each morning at eight o'clock, after the Reverend Smiles had eaten lamb's kidneys and fresh eggs, with his napkin still tied about his neck, he'd take up his prayer book and come out to the churchyard beside the foundling home to bury the newborn dead. He would say what passes for a prayer for the unwanted infants left to perish in the churchyard or on the docks, under bridges and in ditches. In a hurry of words too fast for their meaning to be understood, he'd bury what the scavenger cats and dogs and the dock rats had not eaten. 'Dust to dust, ashes to ashes, rubbish to rubbish,' he might as well have said, for it makes no difference when there's nobody to mourn.

Tommo and I would have been in that graveyard if Ikey had not found us and Mary taken us in. They weren't man and wife, nor even living as such, but they became our mother and father. And Mary raised us up properly. She tutored us in reading and writing and sums until we were more advanced in these skills than other children and even most adults on the island. She loved us with a great fierceness, scolded us, bathed and bandaged our cuts and scratches, dried our tears and taught us how to be on our guard against a hostile world. Each night she held us tenderly. 'My boys,' she always said, kissing us on the cheek, 'my lovely little boys.' It was the last thing we heard every night.

Then when we were kidnapped, she went into the wilderness to look for us. She went on her own where no woman had ever been alone before, her life a hundred times endangered in the process. When she found me, she killed the wild man who'd captured me.

Now we are back together and all she asks of Tommo and me is that we stay and share in everything she's built with her own hands. That we stay and build her precious brewery now that Ikey's fortune makes it possible. That we become rich and happy and give her grandchildren to rock on her knee in her old age. But we will not. We cannot. Tommo's broken inside and needs to go away, and if I let him go alone, I know he'll never come back. Tommo doesn't think his life's worth a pinch of shit and it's up to me to help him see otherwise. If he'd never come back from the wilderness perhaps I could have eventually lived my life. But I grieved him every day he was away, and I always knew he wasn't dead. He was in my head first thing on wakening and last thing at night and a hundred times in between. Whatever should come to pass, I can never let Tommo go out of my life again.

The silence grows between Mary and me until it is almost unbearable. I sit at the table, looking out the window through my tears with nothing I can say. And Mary waits. Finally I cease blubbing.

'Tommo comin' 'ome for dinner then?' Mary asks at last. 'There's a nice leg o' mutton in the oven.' She says it quietly, then when I don't answer, she asks, 'Wapping, is he?'

I nod, grateful that she's left the topic of our conversation, but dreading she'll return to it.

'Drunk again, I suppose.'

She looks up to see my hands reply but I keep them in my lap and say nothing.

'Me old man were a drunkard,' she says quietly. 'How long's Tommo been drinking?'

'Since almost when he was taken into the wilderness. Six years, maybe more, he doesn't say exactly. The timber getter he was with ran a still.'

Mary sighs and shakes her head. 'Don't make sense. He can drink all the beer he wants here at 'ome!' She looks up and gives a bitter laugh, her eyes bright and wet. 'His mama owns a bleedin' brewery. Tomahawk's the best drop o' beer in Tasmania!'

'Mama, it's spirits he's taken to. He says it's the fire that's needed to kill the cold inside him.'

'Jesus!' Mary is suddenly angry. 'He even talks like a drunk! Drink don't drive away the demons, only character can do that!' Mary clucks her tongue. 'You can't make excuses for him, son. He'll promise you everything but he'll let you down, Hawk. Tommo'll break your heart before it's all over!' She stabs her finger at me. 'Mark me words, if Tommo don't stay, you won't cure him by being with him. Love never cured a drunkard! Hard work and watchin' over him like a hawk, that be the way, if there be a way at all.'

Watching over him like a hawk, that's funny, but Mary doesn't notice the pun. She leans over and touches my hand. 'Listen to your mama. If he stops here with us, at least we can both watch over him, keep an eye on him. We can see he don't come to no harm, maybe even bring him eventually to a cure.'

'Mama, Tommo's afraid. He's scared that if he stays he'll shame you, spoil things here.'

Mary looks aghast. 'Shame me? Me what's been the lowest of the low! Shame *me*? How do you propose he can do that? Tommo don't even begin to know what real shamin' be!'

'Tommo knows most folks think highly of you here in Hobart Town, Mama.'

'And you think I care? You think I'd put them miserable lot before my boys, before little Tommo?'

'Mama, it isn't what *you* think, it's what Tommo thinks.'

'Thinks?' Mary is growing furious. 'Drunks don't think anything but where their next drink be coming from. I know, I were practically one meself! Me old man were one! Christ! Don't tell me about drunks. I seen it, been it! I been broken like Tommo, let me tell you!

'See these?' She holds up her terrible hands. 'I got them broke by men, clerks looking for a job at bookkeeping. There was a job down the docks, see, East End. We waited, 'undreds of us, lined up to apply. All men, 'cept me. I gets the billet, out of all o' them I'm chosen and it's the happiest day of me life. I walks home, it's misty and you can't see nothin' down the wharfs. They's waiting for me, dozens of the bastards, waiting in the mist. "Woman taking our job," says they. "Clerking ain't for women, understand, bitch?"'

Mary begins to weep softly. 'They threw me down and raped me, then they held me and stamped on me 'ands 'til every finger were smashed and every bone were broke and more.' She places her hands into her lap below the table. 'That's how I become a tart. It were all I could do, me 'ands being useless and all. Then I were in a brothel and had a fight and run away and they sent the acid man after me, the slasher.' She turns her head slightly, showing the scar which disfigures her pretty face.

'I know how the bottle tempts you, numbs your pain when you's hurting. For a long time that were all I had, no hope for the future, nothin'.

'Then I hears on the grapevine that Ikey Solomon the fence be looking for a bookkeeper what'll keep their gob shut. I goes to Ikey and he gives me a job clerking, then later, running a bawdy house. Ikey were the one what first gave me a chance to come good, when nobody else would.'

Mary sniffs and jerks her chin upwards, knuckling the wet from her eyes. 'And that's what we'll give Tommo, a chance to come good. To make something of himself and forget what they done to him! To stop feelin' so bleedin' sorry for himself and get on with it! Begin a new life, just like I done. Believe me, there's not too many gets that chance given!'

'But Tommo is not strong like you were, Mama! He's not the same cheeky boy we loved, full of fight and vim.'

Mary's eyes soften at the memory of how Tommo was, then grow sad. 'He don't hardly say boo to a goose! He's been 'ome nine months and he ain't laughed proper once, just answers me polite-like, "Yes, Mama. No, Mama." He don't never meet me eyes.' The anger has now gone from her voice and she speaks barely above a whisper. She looks up, appealing to me. 'What's wrong with 'im? What's I done wrong to Tommo?'

'Nothing, Mama. I told you, Tommo loves you but he's shamed. Scared he's not good enough for us. He loves you, but it can't come out. It's stuck inside. He's forgotten how to bring it out.'

Mary's face grows hopeful now. 'Then we'll teach him! Me and you, Hawk! We'll show him how we both loves him. Show him there ain't nothing in the bottom of a bottle what can help him!' She jumps up and waves me away with the back of her hands. 'Go fetch him!' She's laughing. 'Garn, scarper, be gone with you!' She moves over to the hearth, wiping her hands on her pinny. 'I'll get the cabbage cooked, roast'll be ready in 'arf an hour. Tell him I done little onions and brown gravy too. Always liked a nice drop o' gravy, did our Tommo.'

Mary hasn't yet given up on the prospect of keeping Tommo or she doesn't want to face what we both know to be the truth, I don't know which. I smile sadly and shake my head, then I rise and go to where she's standing beside the hearth. Mary's head comes to not much above my waist. I'm fifteen years old, six feet and four inches tall and no beanpole. I stoop down to kiss her. It's not something I do often, and it's most clumsy.

Mary brings her hand up to her face and touches the place where I kissed her. A tear runs down her cheek and disappears into the notch between two fingers. Then she buries her head against my waist and clasps me tight.

'Don't leave me, Hawk. I loves you with all me heart. You won't leave your old mama, will you?'

I can feel my heart pushing up into my throat, filling my lungs so I can't breathe. Oh God! Mary is begging me. Mary, the hardest rock I know, is crumbling.

Suddenly I hate Tommo! Hate the ties that bind me to him. Hate him for spoiling all our lives. And I hate myself for my disloyalty to Mary. Mary is crying, sobs coming out of her breast so soft they're scarcely a whimper. And now I can't see her for my own tears. I am crying not because she's forced me to choose between her and Tommo, but because I love her so very much. I put her gently away from me.

'Mama, please, I beg you,' I try once more. 'Let me tell Tommo about Ikey's money. Perhaps he'll stay, if I tell him about the threat you face from Hannah and David. Perhaps that will be the difference to make him stay on.'

'No!' Mary shouts. 'No! No!' She bangs her fists hard against the kitchen wall, then turns to me again. 'You'll not dare tell him about the money!'

I can barely move my hands to talk for the pain in my chest. 'Then I must go with him, Mama,' I sign to her. 'I can't let him be parted from me again!'

Something snaps inside of her. I can see it, a dark thing that bursts out of her. I've seen Mary angry, her temper is well known, but I've never seen her like this. Her whole body begins to tremble. There is fire in her green eyes.

Suddenly she charges at me, pushing me in the belly. She's screaming and hammering her fists against my chest. 'Go! Go! Go to hell, the both of you!'

These are words I've never heard from her and they break my heart. 'Mama, please?' I clasp her wrists. 'Mama! Mama!'

She pulls away, but I hold onto her wrists and she spits in my face. 'Lemme go, you black bastard!'

So I let go of her and cover my face, weeping. She's beating against me again. 'And don't you call me Mama! You both come from a whore's cunt, a nigger and a drunken runt, you ain't no part of me! You ain't no sons of Mary Abacus!'

I hold out my hands to her, pleading, sobbing.

Mary pulls back suddenly and grabs at the medal hanging from its chain around her neck and holds it in her fist in front of her furious face. 'I been on me own before! It ain't nothin' new!' Her skin is ashen and her voice grown cold. She is breathing hard, talking in short bursts, hissing out the words, her chest heaving. 'You hear me, Hawk! If you go with your brother the two of you will not be back! Not never again! Not to this house. You'll not get what's mine. I swear it!' She pauses a moment and shakes the fist holding the Waterloo medal. 'What's swore on this can't be took back, you hear me? Now fuck orf! Get out o' my 'ouse, pack your bag and get out! I don't want to see neither of you never again!'

I am weeping again, though it is not for Tommo and me that I cry, but for our mama. I know on the morrow or the day after, Mary will beg our forgiveness. She loves us with all her heart and mind and soul. But, like Tommo, what's happened in her life can't be banished despite what she's always said. All her own hurt comes flooding back when she's backed into a corner, and she knows only how to snarl and claw her way out to safety or perdition. She's the small brat who's never been loved. She's on her own and, to her own mind, when she's crossed, all she's got is herself to depend on.

In her heart of hearts I know Mary's lost hope in Tommo and doesn't think he'll ever come good. But she won't come out and say it, she *can't* say it of her own son. If she does, she'll be admitting she loves me more than him, when before we were taken it was always slightly the other way. When we were brats, Tommo always made Mary laugh, he was just about the only one who could. Mary has always blamed herself for not finding him, not rescuing him as she did me.

And now he's come back, she's once again lost what she wants most to love. To realise Tommo doesn't want her, has no place for her in his life, must be more than she can bear. And so she fights and orders us away.

She has made me choose between her and Tommo. Either I go with Tommo, for he will not stay here with me, or I lose him forever, and that I cannot do.

I rise slowly from the chair and without signalling another word to our beloved mama, I leave the kitchen, not sure if I shall ever return but knowing that I will ever love her.

Chapter Three

TOMMO

The Pacific Ocean
November 1856

We's been at sea for three and a half months, sailin' North on the Yankee whaling ship, *Nankin Maiden*, what be out of New Bedford, Massachusetts. The master is Captain Mordechai O'Hara, a fearsome pious man.

The *Nankin Maiden*'s an old ship, a barque, but a good un, one hundred and fifty feet from stem to stern with a beam of thirty foot, three hundred tons and well known these thirty years in the Antarctic, Southern Ocean and Pacific waters. She is after sperm whale and we was quickly told that the Yankee sperm whalers are the toughest there be on the seven seas. From the looks of it, there ain't many Yankees aboard 'cept for the three mates, the ship's carpenter, the cook, blacksmith, cooper, sail maker and, o' course, the master himself. That's only nine out of forty-two men. The rest is all volunteers, like Hawk and meself, rough men of every colour and shape from sea ports in the Indies and the Caribbean, Cape o' Good Hope and the islands of the Pacific Ocean. There is also a few Limeys, Irish and Dutchies, mostly picked up in Rio.

Though Hawk were brung up better than me, here he's

treated as a nigger. There is four others, but they be true niggers, two from the Indies and two from the Cape. Hawk's bigger than all on board, except for one of the Maori and I am glad to have him about.

There be another black what's not counted a nigger, an Aborigine from the Stoney Creek tribe, name o' Billy Lanney. Hawk says he must be one of the few Tasmanian natives what's not been shot as vermin or what died when they was took to be settled on Bruny Island. Lanney keeps to himself, though he is friendly enough when you talks to him.

Lanney is a small man, no bigger than meself, though his head seems larger than suits the body what carries it. Under his canvas breeches, what is rolled up for deck scrubbing and the like, he has sparrow legs, thin pin-like sticks. He's built narrow o' chest too, but he seems amazing strong for such a little fellow. He wears a beard of tiny curls, close to his face, and his hair is a thousand or more tight, springy curls clung to his head, though quite different looking to Hawk's. He has deep-set eyes and most pleasing white teeth when he smiles.

This bloody ship is owned by a Rhode Island syndicate, all of 'em Quakers what have vowed it a 'dry cask afloat', meaning that grog ain't permitted on board while she's at sea. The past three months and sixteen days have been the worst of me life. Not a drop of grog has passed my lips. Any breach of this rule is punished most cruel, as we witnessed a week out to sea with Billy Lanney the victim.

Lanney, a regular crew member much experienced in the whaling game, come back on board ship in Hobart Town and brung with him a quart bottle of Cape brandy. He knew he would be punished if it were found, but he didn't care. Sure enough it were found, by the first mate, Mr Crawlin Nestbyte. We were just three nights out to sea when he found Billy Lanney drunk as a lord, dancing a merry jig in the fo'c'sle and singing a bawdy ditty.

To my mind, the real tragedy of the whole affair is that only a quarter of the bottle were consumed before the first mate found out. The sentence would not have been a single stroke more had Billy drunk the lot, as I'd surely have done! In the presence of the lot of us, the rest of the precious brandy were poured overboard by the first mate, while me tongue stuck to the roof of me miserable mouth.

Nestbyte, like the master, is a Quaker and told us that the Lord in Heaven did not propose to show any mercy to the feckless black; nor should we expect any from the highest authority on earth. This authority turns out to be Captain O'Hara himself who, it seems, knows all about the will of God.

Five days later, at ten o'clock on Sunday morning, we be called on deck to hear Billy's sentence. The captain, in best black cloth suit and white lace bibby, stands on the fo'c'sle to address us. Billy Lanney is made to stand before him, his hands clasped to his front and his head bowed as though in prayer. Nestbyte stands beside him with one hand on Lanney's shoulder and the empty brandy bottle in his other hand.

'The Christ within us lives in you all, because something of God exists in every man,' O'Hara begins in a most reasonable voice. Then he says to Billy, 'Even in thee, an ignorant savage.' He turns to us and goes on, 'In thee also, in every man here, there is the inward light if he should take it into himself and illuminate his heart in Christ Jesus' name.' He brings his attention back to Billy. 'This inward light is a guide to us of good and evil, in thee and me. In thy case, Billy Lanney, I have sought to discover the Will of God by deliberation and by the illumination of that same light in me.' The captain pauses and stares towards the topmast in a sort o' holy-looking way. Then he fixes his eyes on Billy again. 'It has been made clear to me by divine revelation that thou art to be most severely punished. Evil exists in all of us and we have witnessed it now in thee. In bringing strong drink aboard we have seen clearly the spirit of Satan confronting the spirit of the Lord Jesus Himself. It is written that thou shalt take no strong drink and thou hast disobeyed, and so this evil must be punished. Billy Lanney, whaleman on the good vessel *Nankin Maiden*, in the name of Our Lord Jesus Christ our Saviour, I pronounce sentence of one hundred lashes.'

There is a gasp from the crew, for a hundred lashes with the knotted rope be severe punishment. The captain then picks up a book what he explains to us is the articles of the ship. I can't remember the exact words, but it more or less says that the *Nankin Maiden* be under the tender and loving care of the Lord Jesus and be therefore, according to the Holy Scriptures, 'an empty vessel, to be filled with the Spirit of the Lord'. The Captain is responsible for interpreting the word of God in all matters requiring discipline and for delivering punishments with his own hand in the name of Christ Jesus, Amen.

This means he can punish Billy any way he likes. When they strips Billy naked and ties him to the mizzen mast, his back be so scarred from past floggings that the rope at first can't cut through the flesh beneath. Billy don't take no leather strap to bite down upon, and all the way through the terrible beating he don't make no sound except a grunt as the wicked whip strikes him deep to flay the meat from his ribs and backbone.

When all's done, the captain stands bent over with his hands clasped upon his knees, sweat pouring off and him panting like a bitch on heat. O'Hara wears a gold signet ring on his right hand with a flat top the size of a shilling. Now a piece of Lanney's flesh is stuck upon it, so that it looks like it's set with a large ruby.

There is smiles of wonderment among the crew at the

way Billy's taken his flogging. Some says that even if Billy be a black, never a braver man has put to sea, and all vows they would man a whaleboat with him any day o' the week. This is rare praise on board a vessel where it's every man for himself. The many languages the men gibber away in keeps 'em apart, and English is spoke only to give instructions, organise the whale hunt or give out punishment. But when the hunt is on, the six men who crew together in each of the four open whaleboats share a common destiny. They knows their lives to be in mortal danger and they stays close the better to survive. A crew member what's shown his mettle is not forgotten and Billy Lanney's courage under the captain's lash will hold him in good stead. This be even more true after what happens when he is cut loose from the mast.

When they cuts Billy down he stands unsteady, with the blood running down his open back to his scrawny bum and forming puddles o' crimson at his heels. Then he straightens, and faces out to sea, sniffing the air in great draughts. We watches silent, thinking that perhaps he's about to jump, when from deep within him comes the howl of the wild Tasman tiger dog, a long, mournful sound that I've heard a thousand times at night in the wilderness. Two Irishmen immediately crosses themselves and others is astonished, not knowing what to make of the strange noise so foreign to the human voice.

Then Billy turns slowly to Captain O'Hara and gives him a most gentlemanly bow, pointing to the master's white Quaker bibby which, with the rest of his blouse, is stained with Billy's blood and flecks o' skin. The black man gives a smile of tender sweetness and says, 'God bless thee, Cap'n, you be washed in the Blood of the Lamb and forgiven.' He says this in perfect English, which I ain't never heard from him.

O'Hara gasps and takes a step backwards. 'Blasphemy!

Thou hast blasphemed!' he yells, shaking his finger at Billy. 'A heathen savage hath taken the name of the Lord God in vain!' He orders Billy tied back to the mast and hands the blood-soaked lash to Mr Nestbyte, who gives him another fifty lashes.

When they cuts Billy down this time he don't howl like the tiger dog but stands at the ship's rails and looks out to sea, his hands fluttering as though he's trying to calm the waves. Then he turns to Nestbyte and points at him. 'Plurry big fish come get you, Boss!' He draws his finger slowly across his throat. 'Aarrrrk!' he says, like a man choking.

The crew moves back at this. Whalemen be superstitious by nature, but they knows this to be beyond mere fancy. Billy Lanney has put a curse on Nestbyte, right enough. Nestbyte turns away with a sick sort o' smile on his gob. 'Pagan nonsense!' he spits. 'God will punish you.'

Mary be right about religion. Them what's given themselves over to it, and what pronounce upon the rest of us in Christ's name, is more cruel than any other.

This is the first time since the age of eight years, when I were first made to tend Sam Slit's whisky still in the wilderness, that I've been without me daily drink. It's only today, fourteen weeks after I were took by Hawk from Brodie's sly grog shop, that I be feelin' the least bit better. The terrible sweats what come down upon me a day or two after I stopped drinking went away in two weeks and at about the same time, me gut settled down and me shit stiffened to normal. But the craving for strong spirits never stops. And yet, as I stands here on the cross-stays looking out for the whale, I be aware for the first time in many a year of the wind in me face, and the dancing of the white caps, like toy sailing boats stretched to the horizon.

The sky has clouded over since this morning when I climbed up the mainmast. What Hawk tells me in our lessons is cumulus cloud, now brooding against a grey horizon, has nudged aside the mare's tails what stretched across the horizon when me watch began. The sun, up above the gathering cloud, beats down warm on me back and it's excellent weather for a spotting of the whale.

Hawk and me ain't yet witnessed a hunt, though we've been among the blue whales twice. We did not give chase as they's too fast and strong to be harpooned. It is the sperm whale, the next largest in the sea, that we hopes to find.

I'm eating a bit more these days, though a whaler's daily ration ain't much good: hard biscuit what's a weevil's feast, a pound of salt beef or greasy pork or even horse, and two pound of plum duff on Tuesdays and Thursdays. This dreary lot is washed down with longlick, a mixture of tea, coffee and molasses, and three times each week a portion of lime juice for the scurvy. By decent folks' standards, the food is pig's swill, no man ashore 'cept a starving beggar would touch it. Hunger got me in the end, and I suppose the dead cockroaches in the molasses adds to its taste well enough!

Fancy dreamin' about eating possum stew again! It would be fair delicious right now, and the thought of a plump mutton bird split and flattened, then roasted on a fire of live coals, is enough to make me drool. I'd eat me own Sunday dinner as well as Hawk's at Mary's table, 'cept she don't want us there no more. But I can't think about that, and anyway I'd give up every morsel of food on earth for a single snort of Brodie's watered-down Cape brandy.

I'm a drinking man by nature, I know that now. From the very first taste of the hot whisky coming drop and trickle from the copper tubing of Sam Slit's still, I knew I'd found me true love. I did not come to drunkenness from despair, though I haven't said this to Hawk, what believes I am become a drunkard because of what happened to me in the wilderness. And without the whisky jug to fuel me through the bitter cold and rain of them days, the loneliness and the mongrels, I'd have surely died. But I sees it clear now – if I'd been born a prince, I'd still be a drunk. Now I'm just plain thirsty! Desperate for a drop!

I got a plan, though. I been collectin' raisins from the plum duff. On good days, there be as many as twenty a serve, and in not too many weeks I'll have a handy store. I'm gunna dry them and soak them, and then when I'm on galley duty, which is often enough, steal some of the yeast used for baking the skipper's bread to add to 'em. Sam Slit be of value to me at last! There were nothin' that bastard did not know about the fermenting of grog and I reckon a tolerable good brandy will come from these raisins yet. Yours truly shalt not be denied his grog by these God-gobbing Yankees.

Hawk is much pleased that his little brother eats more now. He is patient and tender to me when I sulks, dreaming of the drink. In our spare moments, he teaches me to read and write again from books and a slate he brought aboard with him.

Hawk is a fine teacher to me. When he hears something it remains in his noggin forever after. He can remember each and every word spoken by Captain O'Hara when he pronounced sentence on Billy Lanney. He's made me a copy of the captain's sermon on his slate as a means of me learning to write again, which is why I can now recall it word for word. Hawk reckons I must write to be educated and read so me mind might be alive to the world beyond the inside of a brandy bottle. The fact that I don't want to see nothin' but the insides o' that bottle don't worry him! Anyways, Hawk likes to teach me and I likes to learn from him. And on board ship I finds out something else – I can be a great help to him too, translating his hand language to the other men, though they's picking up a bit of it anyways.

Because Hawk is dumb, there's many reckon him deaf as

well, and they shouts and hollers at him, so that I needs remind 'em he can hear as well as they. But being mute, he can't much talk to no one in his language save me, so we've asked to work together. To me great sadness, though, we ain't allowed to man a whaleboat together because I were declared too small to row with the strength of t'other men. I fights back on this, as I've rowed since childhood and also on the Gordon and the Franklin when I were in the wilderness. But the fourth mate, Mr Seb Rawlings, takes one look at yours truly and that be bloody that! 'No whaleboat for you, lad,' he says right off.

But with Hawk it were different. A week out to sea, Seb Rawlings set a whaleboat over the side with a crew including Hawk. This were to see if Hawk's amazing size and strength would serve him well with the harpoon.

All of us what watched from the deck could see that Hawk were quite steady in the boat with the twenty-five-pound harpoon held above his shoulder, even though the sea were less than calm. A barrel with a white circle painted on it were cast from the whaleboat with a light line attached, and allowed to drift away, bobbing up and down amongst the waves. Hawk were then told to aim the harpoon at the barrel while standing full upright in the bow.

At first the crew laughed as Hawk launched the harpoon and were thrown on his back again and again, and once even up-ended into the sea. But Hawk don't give up easy and with a little instruction, he soon improved.

By Hawk's fifth outing, we watched as he threw the harpoon a good distance. He were most accurate too, often spearing the dot painted on the barrel and never so much as missing by more than the few inches allowable for the hunting of the sperm whale. Mr Rawlings pronounced himself satisfied and Hawk were appointed a standby – what sees that the whaleboat's equipment be all ship-shape before launching and what can be called upon to crew if someone be ill or unable to take their place for some other reason.

It's a terrible disappointment to me that I can't hunt whale with me brother. Hawk ain't happy neither, and makes me say this for him to the mate. Hawk tells Rawlings of me previous life as a timber getter, where I gathered strength in me arms and back. But Rawlings only laughs. 'A whaleboat be no place for a boy of your size, lad. I would not have you on my conscience nor as a danger to the other crew.'

'Tell him I'll be responsible for you,' Hawk signals to me with his hands.

I translates once again and Rawlings smiles thinly at Hawk. 'Are you now the captain of my whaleboat?' I can see his patience is sore tried and he dismisses us with a backward wave of his hand. 'Go on now, be away with you!'

So here I is, Tommo the brave, standing on two wooden rungs at the top o' the mainmast on a two hour watch, searching for the spout of a whale but not allowed to join in the hunt. And me without a drink for one hundred and six days. If I does see a pod of whale, I've a good mind to look the other way. But that would be stupid. Two other men, one on each of the other masts, are also set to looking and the first to spot a whale receives a week's extra rations. It's food Hawk would relish, as he never seems to get enough to eat.

I'm forever worried about Hawk's hunger and have set about trying to satisfy it with fishing. As little lads, before we was took, Hawk and me were good fishermen, but he lost the skill of it when Mary put him to book-learning and clerking, and then sent him to England to learn about growing hops.

Hawk still talks o' London Town sometimes, though he sees it through different eyes to Ikey's. He were in Kent, studying the art of agriculture, with little money. He'd pen letters for the farm workers, many of 'em Irish, Tipperary men and the like, wanting to send word to their colleens or dear parents at home. For sixpence a letter, he'd write the most tender love letters, though he knows nothing of love or women. His letters be so sweet the eyes of his customers would fill with tears, and it got so that before a note were dispatched, it would be read to the whole gathering for their enjoyment. So successful did Hawk become with his flowery phrases that most of his Saturday afternoons were spent in this pursuit, and it made him sufficient coin to go up to London Town by train of a Sunday.

With sixpence for a cup o' tea and a sticky bun, and another for a pint of ale, Hawk would take the omnibus to the East End and Whitechapel, visiting all the places Ikey told us of. In our childhood dreams, London Town were a place o' palaces and broad streets where everyone were a toff and Ikey much respected, a prince amongst men! Alas, Hawk found the palaces and grand houses but these was outnumbered a thousand to one by the hovels of the poor and unfortunate what crawled like ants in every dark corner. Yet these was the very places Ikey meant when he'd spoke to us of the throbbing heart o' the great city.

'Ikey's corner of the world was mostly rags, poverty and drunkenness,' Hawk reckons. He tells of how often in winter it never grows light, the smog from the coal fires and factories closin' out the sun. When the weather got warmer the stench were unbearable and attacked his delicate nostrils long before the train pulled into Waterloo station. The fumes made his nose drip and his lungs wheeze, so that after a few hours he longed to be back in the fresh countryside. In winter, walking the streets in the cold, wet and dark, the terrible stench were gone, swallowed by the frost and snow. But this were a time o' despair for our big-hearted Hawk, when he'd see barefooted children wrapped in newspapers and rags, begging a penny and near to perishing. He'd take as many as he could to a pie shop and empty his pockets of all he possessed. It was common enough, he says, to find their little corpses under the bridges when they did not survive the cold of the night.

Hawk made many a visit to Petticoat and Rosemary Lanes and found them not much changed from Ikey's tales, though it were the same poverty witnessed everywhere. Sometimes he'd drink a pint of ale at the Pig 'n' Spit, the public house what was once owned by our true mother, Sperm Whale Sally, or as she were known then, Marybelle Firkin. Hawk tried to find Ikey's old coves, Sparrer Fart and Bob Marley, but to no avail. Some knew of Bob Marley, what they claimed had taken the boat for New York. All had heard of Ikey Solomon, though only some knew what had happened to him. Only one person remembered Sparrer Fart, and it were thought he'd been transported to Van Diemen's Land or New South Wales, not long after Ikey himself.

Hawk visited Ikey's Whitechapel home o' course, and though boarded up at the doors and windows, it were most impressive, a veritable mansion when compared to the rows of miserable houses for the poor what surrounded it, all stuck together with common walls.

Though Hawk talks often of the poverty he saw, he sometimes recalls London in spring, when the sky above Hyde Park were duck-egg blue, the sun warm to the back o' the neck and the larks singing high in the sky. Daffodils, crocus and bluebells were poking up everywhere in great patches through the green grass of the park; the squares fronting the big houses were ablaze with peach, pear and plum blossom, and the rich folks' window boxes filled with tulips.

Then he tells of lovers sitting hand in hand, and old people clapping to the beat as they listen to the military bands play their stirring marches in the parkland rotundas. He recalls the wonders and delights of Vauxhall Gardens and the pretty girls everywhere. But always his conversation turns back to the never-ending traffic, full of carriages, hacks and conveyances of every conceivable kind, where the tooting and whistling and whirring of rattles continues twenty-four hours, day and night, like a great living machine driven by some unknown hand.

'Tommo, London is every type of misery and despair though it is filled with delights beyond your imaginings,' he declares. 'But still, I missed the simplicity of Hobart Town, with folks stopping to greet you and pass the time of day.'

Hawk also remembers his constant hunger while he were in Blighty for he never got enough to eat. He's been near starvin' on the *Nankin Maiden* too and so I've started to fish for him. In exchange for me kangaroo skin coat, the blacksmith has provided me with a long braided line, sinker lead and various sized hooks. The Maori aboard have showed me how to make lures from cloth and wire, and I've got an arrangement with the cook whereby he keeps half what I catches and the remainder be fed to Hawk and me.

The bastard cheats us often, claiming more bone upon cleaning and filleting my catch than a fish could carry. But what we get adds greatly to our rations. Some days I catch even more than we can eat or the cook can cheat us of, and this is shared with the Maori and islander crew. Apart from them, the men aboard will not eat fish or shark freshly caught, much preferring salt beef.

We've become friends of sorts with these kanakas, this being a word from Hawaii what means 'man'. Our friendship with the Maori be especially strong and they welcome Hawk and me to be amongst them sometimes.

Though their faces be every inch tattooed so that they appear to be primitive savages of great fierceness, they's a jolly lot and often laughing. They cannot say Hawk's name but call him Ork, what be good enough! Already I've some handy words of their language which Hawk also begins to understand. They show great delight when I make a word or string together a sentence in their tongue and are at great pains to correct me when I get it wrong.

And so my time when not on watch is well taken up, and not only with new learning at reading and writing. Billy Lanney has taken to showing us some of the many knots and hitches to be found in the seaman's trade. Splicing be the hardest, but I am learning to turn a neat splice, though Hawk with his big hands is making less progress. Sometimes I play cards in the fo'c'sle but it ain't the same without grog. It's fishing what is me most important daily task, almost more than gathering raisins. Fish ain't always plentiful and days may pass without me catching anything. I frets for Hawk when this happens. But though I don't never want to be parted from him again, I doubt that me love of Hawk is stronger than me love of grog!

It's near time for me to be called down from this bloody watch. Two hours spent standing on wooden rungs, me eyes peeled for whales, and the breeze stiffening and growing blustery in me face is most tiring work, and I'll be glad to be back on deck. But just as I'm thinking this, I sees a whale blow. At first I ain't sure, but then another whale breaks the surface and this time I sees the spouting clear.

'Thar she blows!' I yell at the top of my voice. 'Thar she blows!' I scream, pointing to starboard, my throat hoarse. Now I see them again, a pod of at least four, and big uns too. One begins to sound and I see its great fluke hit the water with an explosion like a small cannon fired against the wind.

What I've seen I takes to be sperm whale, though of course I'm no expert. But then the two men on the other masts see the pod as well. 'Sperm!' one shouts. 'Four of them! To starboard!' shouts the other. But the call is mine, the first sighting belongs to yours truly, Tommo X Solomon!

I am too excited to go down the mast straight away. Me heart is thumpin' in me chest and ears. I am needed below for it's every hand to the task when a pod be sighted, but me knees are gone to jelly and shaking beyond me control.

Below me on deck, there is a frenzy of activity, men running everywhere in great confusion. Our ship turns slowly to starboard, men adjusting the sails so that we might close the distance between the pod and ourselves.

The mates are shouting and waving their arms. The crew prepare to lower the whaleboats by means of the falls – a block-and-tackle arrangement which sets the boats to swaying in the breeze as they fall loose from their davits. Captain O'Hara on the bridge shouts, 'Where away!' for these be the words spoken when a hunt is on. From where I stand all is bedlam. I looks for Hawk but now the ship has turned, I cannot see the whaleboat on the starboard quarter which be his.

A whaleman has climbed into each of the three other whaleboats on the port side, making the harpoon and rope barrel ready and checking that the oars and all else be ship-shape and in their rightful place. The ship is making good progress in the stiff breeze, sailing towards our prey, which seem not to notice us.

Then the falls drop the whaleboats some two feet below the level of the main deck, and the remainder of the crews jump in. They takes their places at the thwarts with the oars and the steering oar shipped ready. At last the three boats are dropped into the ocean with a foamy splash.

As soon as the boats hit the water the five oarsmen in

each, including the harpooner, begin to row at a frantic pace, with the mate at the steering oar. The hunt is on! The stiff breeze makes my eyes water as I scan the waves, trying to see the fourth whaleboat and if Hawk be in it.

But it's all hands on deck when a whale chase is on and I got t' get down where I'm needed. I scramble down the mast wishing I'd been chosen to man a whaleboat with me brother beside me. But at that same moment I has a second wish, and I pray that Hawk has not been chosen and that he be safe on the deck below me. He'll not be in the crew 'less someone be indisposed, and I tell myself there is nothin' to worry about. Then suddenly me heart is full of fear. I am back in the wilderness, caught in the tall timbers, and I can feel that *they* are near. Tommo has smelled the mongrels coming, but this time they be after my brother Hawk.

Chapter Four

HAWK

The Pacific Ocean
November 1856

I am seated in a quiet corner of the poop deck, my watch completed and two hours to myself. I am here because I can't bear being in the fo'c'sle, a hell-hole where those who are not on watch congregate for smoking, conversation and sleep.

It's worse than Brodie's sly grog shop, a cabin about sixteen feet wide and as many again from the bulkhead to the foredeck and so low that a person of my stature must bend almost double to walk. Around the fo'c'sle ladder are sea chests, greasy pans, pieces of rancid meat and soap kegs belonging to the crew. Along the walls a dozen small berths are piled high with evil-smelling bed linen, consisting of old foul weather clothes. The one small consolation is that few fleas, lice and bed bugs are to be found. This is not because of the lack of dirt and human ordure but because of the prevalence of cockroaches. The cockroach is a hunter of these vermin and eats them with relish, being particularly partial to the flea, which it will chase with an insane ferocity.

As you lie awake at night in the fo'c'sle with not a stitch of cover except a lather of perspiration, you can hear the cockroaches at work, their wings clicking away busily. All too often an army of them will climb up your arms and legs and scurry across your stomach in pursuit of some flea, or congregate to lick the sweat from your body. Though rats are more numerous on a whaleship than on any other vessel at sea, and it is common enough to see them gnawing at the calloused soles of some sleeping kanaka's feet, they are but a nuisance compared to these vermin.

The cockroaches are described in jest as being as big as rats and the rats as big as cats. If this is an exaggeration, it is not by so very much. There is a shanty I've heard the men sing:

> *And the rats, oh the rats,*
> *be as big as dockside cats*
> *And the roaches in the fo'c'sle*
> *as big as Sally's flats.*
>
> *Row, row, whaleman*
> *Pull now at your oars,*
> *We're sailing off to hunt our prey*
> *wherever there be whaling*
> *from 'round the Cape to Boston Bay*
> *and down to the Azores!*
>
> *Row, row, whaleman*
> *Pull now on your oars,*
> *The skipper's docked your pay away*
> *with provisions from his stores*
> *with . . . pro-vis-ions . . . from . . . his . . . stooooores!*

In this weather the fo'c'sle is insufferably close. It is seldom cleaned and the dirt and stench are overpowering. But the men seem to prefer it to the clean breeze and sunshine on deck and there is always a game of cards going, the players' pipe smoke fugging the atmosphere so that the cards can scarcely be seen in the dim light cast by a whale-oil lamp. It is a place of much joshing and cursing, and every hour of the day it seems a fight is about to start. The knives come out at the slightest provocation. Yet it is the nearest a whaleman has to a home, and the men seldom come to blows.

It is mid-morning and a stiffening nor'easterly brings some relief from the heat. Tommo is on whale watch up the mainmast, a task which suits him well as there is still much of the solitary in him. He spoke once of how, in the wilderness, he would sometimes escape from his drunken master, Sam Slit, by climbing high up into the branches of a river gum. Slit, violent and angry, would fire a musket charged with birdshot to try to bring him down.

Tommo laughs at this memory. 'Them trees be too high for most of the shot to reach me and I be too well protected by the mighty branches.' I sometimes think of Tommo as a small child who climbs into the branches of a grog tree to escape his own miseries. I wonder how he shall become a man while still he seeks this escape.

But then I wonder, am I yet a man? How may I tell? How do we move from the state of childhood to manhood?

There must be a moment when we pass over into manhood. We are now sixteen, but it cannot simply be a time set by others when we are said to come of age. It is, I should imagine, a moment of the heart and of intelligence, or even, if there is such a thing, of the soul. But perhaps we can also lose our childhood too soon on account of suffering.

Tommo is an example of this. He has suffered too much and has been cheated out of his rightful share of childhood, its natural expectations and excitements. He has grown up too soon and thus is bitter and cynical.

But what of the others like him, the street urchins who hunt in feral packs around Hobart Town? Those brats who look at you with snotted noses and old, tired eyes, their only ability calculating the gain which might be made from your presence amongst them. Are they still children? Unlike Tommo, they are neither bitter nor cynical, for they expect nothing of life, only their certain death at the hands of others like them, or at the end of the hangman's rope. Perhaps the moment of manhood or womanhood is the moment when we give up hope for ourselves?

The feral children of Hobart Town are the flotsam on the tide of humanity. If the clergyman, judge, teacher and merchant – those four wise corners which frame our noble society – are to be believed, there is no hope to be held for any of them.

In the eyes of the clergyman, they are lost souls, doomed to a short life of no virtue and a pauper's grave. The judge believes it is his bounden duty to punish such delinquent brats for the sins they commit against their fellow man. To the teacher, they are simply the dull-minded infants who pay no heed in lessons and are quickly left behind. To the merchant, they are an easy source of stolen pennies, to be set upon by dogs when they beg for charity.

Yet if these pitiable slack-jawed children had been granted a childhood of love, decency and some useful learning, they might well have passed naturally into maturity and proved themselves as good as any other person. Even poor Tommo had the early benefit of love and teaching before we were kidnapped. Whilst I was fortunately returned to Mary quite soon thereafter, receiving her love and with it the opportunity to learn, Tommo spent his next seven years amongst some of the vilest of the human tribe. He has retained his intelligence, which was early formed, and is now only backward in its application. What he has lost is the ability to love and trust.

I fret for those lost children of Hobart Town and every

other town, and I fret for my brother. I feel saddened and somehow responsible that I was saved, while my twin suffered. It's perhaps one reason why I am with him now, forsaking Mary. It is to care for Tommo and teach him what I know so that together we might turn back the clock and restore the love and trust he has lost.

At times, though, I wonder whether I am rescuing Tommo or he is rescuing me. Have I run away from Mary? Since rescuing me from the wild man, she wishes to know my whereabouts at every moment and seeks to direct my efforts at every turn. Mary loves me with all her heart but thinks me disadvantaged in two ways: I am only a black man and I have no voice to speak for myself. She sees herself as my protector and as my voice, and it would be ever thus had I remained with her in Hobart Town.

How then should I test myself? How then should I come to know my own character, whether I am good or bad, strong or weak? Do my dreams for the future exist only because I am a privileged creature and have no knowledge of the true nature of men? All these questions I think of on our voyage.

In the end, I confess that I have longed for an adventure such as this. When I heard that the *Nankin Maiden* was in port I was already well aware of Tommo's discontent. I believed that if only Tommo and I were on an American whaling ship which did not permit grog, then he would be safe, and we would both be embarked upon a grand adventure. When Mary bade us gone, I acted on this notion.

Perhaps whaling is in our blood? This is a question I also hope to answer. Our fathers were whalemen – Tommo's a giant Red Indian by the name of Tomahawk and mine an even bigger black man by the name of Black Boss Cape Town.

Ikey had told us how we were conceived as a result of that legendary night when the two harpooners wrestled for the singular favours of the giant whore, Sperm Whale Sally. Our mother was said to be imbued with the spirit of the whale, and those who coupled with her won good fortune for their vessel on the hunt. Yet only two men had succeeded in bedding her and sailing under the 'True Blue' flag which bestowed her blessing. These men were Tommo's father and mine. When the whaling season brought both their ships into port at the same time, each man was determined to claim her for his own. But in the end, neither man alone was strong enough for Sally and, to heal the rivalry between them, she gave herself to both. It is from this loving that twins were born, one white and the other black, one tiny and one huge, one Tommo and the other me.

When we were born and Ikey adopted us, he wrote to the Royal Society in London, hoping to gain some fame from this remarkable birth. They replied that while the fertilising of the one female egg by seed from two different males is most unusual, it was not unknown to happen among whores where numerous and near simultaneous couplings took place, and that it was not a matter of sufficient interest for their record books. Ikey always said that if our mother had been a duchess instead of a whore they'd have taken more notice and we'd be famous.

Knowing our birthright, it was only natural that I should choose a whaling ship for Tommo and me to sail on. All on board the *Nankin Maiden* have heard the legend of Sperm Whale Sally, and some old salts claim they know the two giant whalemen, though none has heard of, or seen, either for several years, and none knows we are their sons.

I am lost in these recollections when there is a shout from high above me. It is Tommo, high-pitched and much excited, shouting that he has seen a spout. 'Thar she blo-o-o-o-ows! Thar she blo-o-o-o-ows!' he bellows down at the top of his voice. Then the other two lookouts start shouting as they too see the whales.

For a few moments nothing appears to happen, then the whole ship springs to life, like a dozing animal suddenly surprised. My recent thoughts tumble into oblivion as I jump to my feet to play my part in the whale chase to come.

Seb Rawlings, the fourth mate, has not yet included me in the crew of the whaleboat he captains. Instead he has selected William Lanney to serve as the fifth crewman along with four Maori whalemen led by Hammerhead Jack, an impressive giant of a man.

I am the 'stand-by' and must ensure that all the equipment needed in the boat for a whale hunt is kept in good working order and made ready. Now I climb in while it is still attached to the davits to make one last inspection before the crew is lowered into the sea.

I check everything thoroughly, though there is scarcely time. The fast launching of the whaleboats is of great concern to Captain O'Hara. Quickly I scan the two-thirds-inch manila rope in the aft barrel. Only yesterday I examined every inch of this line for fraying before folding it back myself, so I know all two hundred fathoms to be in good order. My secret mark is still upon it which means it has not been tampered with. Below me on deck I hear Hammerhead Jack lead his men in some sort of savage war cry, a ritual of theirs.

I check the splices to the two harpoons which will be attached to the line by means of short warps, and then look over the harpoons themselves. They are of the new double-barbed Temple iron which rotates ninety degrees within the flesh of the whale to form a T-shape which will not pull out. I examine the three lances and the five pulling oars, the steering oar and the paddles. I check that they are sound and that the rowlocks are well fixed. I make sure that the boat piggin is not holed, that three gallons of drinking water in a canvas bag are on board for the men, and that the two boat knives which are attached to marlin line are stowed. Finally

I see that the small lug sail is in place with a spare roll of canvas. All is ship-shape. There are over forty articles in a whaleboat and I cannot inspect them all now, though I have done so as part of my watch on the previous day. I am climbing down from the davits in haste when I hear Billy Lanney beseeching Hammerhead Jack.

'I go crew, Jack! Me back be tickety-boo, number one!' Billy says in some anguish.

'Let me see your back then, Billy!' a voice demands from behind us. To my surprise it is not Rawlings' and I turn to see the first mate, Crawlin Nestbyte, standing in front of the little Aborigine.

Billy Lanney shakes his head vigorously. 'You no must see, boss! Rowing me can do! No plurry problems!' He swings his arms about like a windmill to show that they are not troubled by the wounds to his back.

As I drop onto the deck where the whaleboat crew are gathered, Hammerhead Jack grabs me by the shoulders and pushes me forward, smiling at Crawlin Nestbyte. 'Him, Ork, him good! He be crew, boss!'

Nestbyte hesitates. Hammerhead Jack releases me and, after removing Billy's hat which he drops to the deck, he grabs Billy's canvas blouse. He jerks it roughly over Billy's head and then lifts Billy bodily, spinning him around in the air and planting him down again so that his naked back is facing the first mate.

At the sight of Billy's back Nestbyte grins broadly. 'Ah, a spine well worthy of God's wrath!' he says happily, leaning forward to make a closer examination. ' "I am not mocked, sayeth the Lord," ' he pronounces proudly, and steps back well satisfied.

My horror at what I see must show clearly upon my face. Billy's back is a great yellow and purple suppuration with maggots among the deep furrows of his infected wounds.

Hammerhead Jack shakes his head in commiseration, jerking his thumb in Billy's direction. 'Him, Billy, brave man!' Then he clucks his tongue twice. 'Not come, boss, too much sick to row boat!' He says this firmly, stabbing a large finger at Crawlin Nestbyte's chest, and pointing to me. 'Ork, him come!'

Nestbyte does not much like Hammerhead Jack's demand, and anger clouds his expression. His fists bunch at his side. But then he seems to think better of it and his hands unclench. Though the first mate is by most standards a big man, the Maori is more than a head taller than he. Besides, there is not much time and the other boats to portside have already been launched.

'Watch thy tongue, kanaka bastard!' is all he says to Hammerhead Jack. Then he turns to me. 'Well, well, if it isn't Mr Rawlings' fine nigger pupil! High time to see if thou art a good nigger or a gutless one, eh? Mr Rawlings hath the tropical fever and Captain O'Hara is himself indisposed. It will be my privilege to break thee in . . . or break thee – which shall it be, I wonder?'

I smile, though I have a great desire to smash Nestbyte's teeth into the back of his throat. It is just my luck that both Rawlings and O'Hara are indisposed!

'Him good! Ork good nigger,' Hammerhead Jack says and laughs happily, not in the least concerned by the first mate's admonishment. He slaps me again on the back.

Hammerhead Jack is truly a huge man. He is taller by four inches or more than I, and is also wider of girth and in the barrel of his chest. He has a long face and square jaw which are off-set by the height and flat surface of his protruding brow. This already extraordinary visage is framed by two great sweeps of hair which rise upwards and then hook down at the back. They are separated by an inch-wide scar which runs like a roadway from the front to the back of his skull, giving his hair the appearance of the claws of a carpenter's hammer, which is where Hammerhead Jack's name comes from.

At our first meeting Hammerhead Jack was much taken by the scar about my neck, pointing to his own scar and then running a finger around my neck, carefully tracing the silver ribbon of tissue. Then he shook my hand vigorously to indicate that we had in common a mutilation which, it was plain to see, he regarded as most handsome in appearance.

Our whaleboat is being lowered and we scramble overboard and into its bows as it passes the level of the top deck. Hammerhead Jack and myself are the last in, following the first mate.

The men working the falls lower us into the water with a great splash. Without thinking I take my place on the thwart, on the far side of the boat immediately behind Hammerhead Jack at the bow. He turns and gives me a great grin, pleased as Punch. 'Good Ork!' he says. The other three Maori laugh. 'Good Ork!' they shout, welcoming me to the crew and ignoring the scowling first mate who has taken up the sweep oar to steer us.

I would have felt more honoured if it had been Seb Rawlings who had chosen me. Mr Rawlings is no angel, a hard man, but he is fair in most things and respected by the men.

Nestbyte, on the other hand, is a proper bastard, a bully-boy who is much disliked for his harsh punishment of the smallest offences. It is said he is an expert with the blade and he carries an American bowie knife on his belt. If someone should so much as challenge him, he will pull it out and fight them.

'I'll take the bastard with me axe any day he wants,' Tommo boasts, but I have never seen my twin fighting with his axe and it is my earnest hope I never shall.

Sometimes the first mate is referred to as 'Creepy

Crawlin' as he will frequently creep around the decks at night with a whale-oil lamp, hoping to find men at sodomy. When he catches two men at it, he has the permission of Captain O'Hara for a most heinous punishment. First the offenders are held down and a spoonful of ground Chinese chilli peppers is inserted up their arses. Their hands are then tied behind their backs and they are allowed to go for the night. If any should render them aid in their agony as the peppers burn their insides, they too will receive the same treatment. The following morning at muster the offenders are given fifty lashes, inflicted by the first mate's own hand. Then, with their backs open and bleeding, they are made to walk the main deck with huge bags of salt tied about their necks by a cord. The bags rest on their backs, leaking salt into their open wounds by means of small apertures. Their wounds aflame, they must walk until they drop from exhaustion. Nestbyte repeats this torture of chilli and floggings every day for a week, with the victims still required to complete a full watch each day.

After this, each offender is issued with a brass neck-plate bearing the inscription, 'A Son of Sodom' and under this the words, 'I am not worthy of God's redemption'. Those who have been caught are named Brass Bimbos by the rest of the whalemen, and there are half a dozen or more on board who wear this attachment. They do so without shame, as if it is a badge of honour, hard-earned – which, I suppose, is true enough!

Crawlin Nestbyte is a cruel braggart who talks endlessly of his exploits and derring-do with the whale. There is an old saying on a whaling vessel which goes thus:

That which the coward brags he will do,
The whaleman true goes silent to!

68

It must be said in fairness, though, that those men who have shared a boat with Nestbyte admit that he is not lacking in courage. He is known to be reckless and because of this no one who has previously voyaged on the *Nankin Maiden* will volunteer to his whaleboat, choosing any other by preference. While he takes delight in inflicting suffering on others, he is not afraid to take on a man his own size even without a knife. That is all that can be said in his favour. The crew are hard men who would turn like a pack of wild dogs on one of their own kind caught stealing or cheating. But they take little pleasure in witnessing Nestbyte's numerous cruelties to whalemen whom he believes have offended him or have been neglectful of their duties.

Though his Quaker mouth is full of God's words, his dark soul is in the possession of the devil himself. Nestbyte employs only two expletives, 'Bastard' and 'Damn', explaining to all that both words are not a blasphemy or foul language. The first is but the name for a child born out of wedlock and the second a shortening of the word damnation which is to be found frequently in the good book itself. If both words are innocent, then never was there a man who could inject more venom into them!

I have been out to sea only half a dozen times in a whaleboat, on practice runs while we were becalmed to learn the harpoon. Now the atmosphere is charged. I sincerely hope that I do not let my companions down, for I don't know what to expect. Seb Rawlings, on the last occasion he took me out, pronounced himself satisfied that I have the strength and skill to throw the harpoon. But as we rowed back to the ship he said, 'Ah yes, lad, but do ye have the courage to stand up to the whale and will ye use the lance correct?'

Do I have the courage? I now ask myself. Will I prove a coward? I cannot answer. I must wait for the moment to come, when I must throw a harpoon into a live whale and not a bobbing barrel, and use a lance at which I've had no practice. I am thankful that Hammerhead Jack is the harpooner in our crew, and I hope by watching to learn much from him.

Seated on our thwarts we are perilously close to the harpoon rope. This runs from the barrel at the stern, down the centre of the boat, to the crutch on the starboard bow where it is spliced to the two harpoons in front of where Hammerhead Jack is seated. When the rope is running to the whale it becomes sizzling hot. Should we suddenly be thrown against it, or move carelessly, it will in a moment cut inches deep into our thighs or slice our arms down to the bone, cooking the flesh it ravages.

We cannot see the other three whaleboats and our late start has caused some anxiety in Nestbyte. 'Row, row! Row, row!' he repeats urgently. 'It's first to the pod for us, or I'll see ye flogged and stretched to the mizzen! Row! Row! Row, ye cannibal bastards, row!' His voice grows ever angrier as he envisages us lagging behind the other boats.

I am not sure how much of this call is understood by Hammerhead Jack and the rest of the crew. Their faces show nothing beyond the strain of pulling at the oars and they do not quicken their stroke at the mate's admonishments. My arms ache and I wonder how much longer I can keep up.

The breeze seems to me to be stiffening and the seas beginning to rise. Nestbyte, who steers the boat from the stern sheets, counts the breeze insufficient to hoist the lugsail and we must perforce row on. As we come over the lip of a large wave, I can see there is new cloud boiling up from the horizon. A sniff of rain is in the air.

I have been told whalemen hunting in the Pacific Ocean are not concerned by a squall at sea. The Yankee whaleboat is well constructed from half-inch, white cedar clinker planking and difficult to capsize. If it should up-end, or be swamped, it will continue to float or even right itself. If the sea is moderately calm, it is no great hardship to clamber back in. But in the Southern Ocean around Cape Horn and towards the Antarctic it is an altogether different proposition. If a boat should be overturned by an errant wave, the crew will often freeze to death.

'Pacific whaling be a treat, lad,' Rawlings once confided at harpoon practice, 'with naught to bother about except for a mishap with the whale.' Then he grins. 'Mind,' he says, 'should the great fishy tail smash down upon you and you be thrown into the sea and not killed outright, with your boat smashed to smithereens, then naught awaits except drowning or being taken by the sharks who gather at the smell of harpoon blood and tear at anything that moves.'

Nestbyte hoists the lug sail and I am much relieved that we can ship our oars and turn to see where we might be going. The whaleboat takes smoothly to the waves and we are soon making good progress. It is pleasant not to hear the first mate's harsh voice urging us on. Hammerhead Jack calls for water. We are all streaming with sweat and the sun overhead is as hot as Hades.

'A mouthful each! No more, hear ye?' Nestbyte orders. The canvas bag is passed to Hammerhead Jack, who hoists it to his lips and takes a long drink. 'Enough! No more!' Nestbyte yells. 'If the hunt is long, ye'll beg me for it later!'

The big Maori hands the bag to me and I take a mouthful, then pass it back. 'That's enough! That's enough!' Nestbyte keeps saying before we've brought the mouthpiece to our lips.

The wind changes direction and the lug sail begins to flap. 'Man the oars!' Nestbyte shouts, though we have seen the change and already set to rowing.

71

'Backs! Put your backs into it, ye kanaka bastards!'

I begin to wonder if Nestbyte's constant yapping will ever stop. Then we rise over another wave and I damn near die of fright!

Not forty feet to port a sperm whale surfaces. The sea around us boils and our boat begins to rise and rise until we are fifteen feet above the highest waves. Nestbyte yells to ship our oars. With a thunderous roar of falling water, the giant fish surfaces from the depths. It is a bull, a monster, a creature a hundred times bigger than anything I have ever seen before. Its malevolent eye, which appears to gaze straight at me, is bigger than a pudding plate!

Suddenly we are drenched, as the spray from its spout pours down like a waterfall upon us. We are too close and I prepare myself to die in the moments left to me. Terrified, I glance at Hammerhead Jack to see what is to be done.

Hammerhead Jack is seated calm as you like, his hands gripping the edges of the thwart so that he might steady himself. He has his back to me but he must sense I seek him, for he turns his head and there is a grin upon his much-tattooed face. His head and shoulders stream with the spray from the whale's spouting. His lips appear to move but there is too much noise to hear what he is saying. I think it must be, 'Good Ork!'

We are suddenly plunged back to sea level as the wave caused by the whale's breaching rolls away and subsides beneath us. The boat begins to spin like a cork in the foaming water and Nestbyte works with frantic energy to steady it by means of the sweep. Then, the very moment the boat is more or less on an even keel, he yells at us to grab our paddles and to row towards the great creature.

Row towards? He must be mad! We are practically embracing the monster! Hammerhead Jack ships his paddle and the boat rocks as he goes to stand at the bow. I look up to see him take up one of the harpoons. He stands darkly silhouetted against the sky. It is him against the whale, St George and the dragon, Neptune and the sea monster. For a short moment I gain courage at his immense calm and resolve as we row towards our certain death.

We are no more than fifteen feet from the great fish and I can see a multitude of barnacles, scratches and scars upon its black carcass, deeply wrinkled aft of its flippers. Then Hammerhead Jack, with a shout, delivers the harpoon into its side. The harpoon's head is buried a full three feet into the whale's flesh.

He has aimed for the heart, just forward of the small dorsal hump not far from the whale's great head, which looks to me entirely composed of a nose with a whitish whorl at its end. At first the harpoon seems to penetrate cleanly, in the manner of a neat dart, but a moment later a huge gush of blood spurts from the side of the whale as though a pipe has burst. Then, just as quickly, the blood stops to a trickle.

Nestbyte screams to Hammerhead Jack, 'Another! Quick, the second! Damn thee, man, thou hast missed the vital part!'

But it is almost as though the whale itself has heard the first mate's shouts. Before the giant Maori can lift the second harpoon above his shoulder, the great beast raises its flukes and crashes them down against the surface of the sea. Rolling away from us, the whale sounds – diving down into the depths beneath us. There is another rush of water and then all hell breaks loose in front of my very eyes.

'Aft, come aft!' Nestbyte yells. He has already wound the manila rope around the samson post, putting a drag on the line which immediately begins to pay out and is soon screaming through the bow chocks. We are now being taken for a ride, towed by the mighty fish at breakneck speed, faster even than any good four-in-hand upon the macadam road to New Norfolk. Our whaleboat skims the waves and Nestbyte is still yelling at us. 'Come aft! In the name of Christ Jesus, *aft*, ye bastards!'

We rise from our thwarts and stumble over each other as we crowd to the rear of the boat, careful to avoid the zinging rope. We crouch in the stern so that our bow may rise high and stay clear of the waves, for should it follow the downward direction of the whale we will all be dragged under. The eldest of the Maori crew has taken up the piggin and is dousing the whale-rope with sea water to keep it from bursting into flame. But the moment he goes to take another scoop of water, the line starts to smoke again as it whirls about the samson post.

We now come across the other boats and wave to them desperately for help. But all three boats are attached to a smaller cow which sounds at that moment and they are too occupied to see us.

'Damn!' Nestbyte cries. 'We are alone with the monster! This old bull will prove too much for us!' He cups his hands to his mouth again and yells for one of the other boats to cut loose from the cow and come to our aid, but they are by now too distant to hear.

I am shaking like a wet dog in a cold wind, though whether from fear or excitement I cannot tell. The rope is paying out at a great rate from the barrel and, despite its turn about the samson post which is intended to slow the whale by adding our weight to its drag, we are tearing across the water at a great rate of knots.

I cannot believe the speed at which we move. It is as though the whale is a clipper fully rigged caught in a sudden gale, and we the float on a boy's fishing line suspended from its stern – a mere bobbing cork dragged helplessly through the angry seas. How can any creature in nature be possessed of such enormous power as is the whale!

The manila line within the barrel is not attached and should the whale take it all up in its dive, it will be free of us. Nearly the full two hundred fathoms of line have gone, and we begin to think we must soon lose our prey. My silent hope is that we do! Then the rope suddenly goes slack and we are at once becalmed. Thank God! I think. We are saved!

But it seems this is the very moment we've been waiting for. 'Pull in! All hands to the rope!' Nestbyte calls. We begin, hand over fist, to gather the rope back into the barrel.

It is the hardest of work and soon my hands are bleeding, but there is no respite. The task must be done quickly and we must be ready for the whale when he breaches. We pull at the rope until it is no longer slack and so we know it is attached to the whale lurking somewhere below us.

The very moment the rope is gathered, the Maori move back to their thwarts. I follow, scrambling to take up my oar behind Hammerhead Jack.

'We go!' he says happily to me. 'Whale come,' he makes an upward movement with his hands and then blows through his lips, 'Phiff!' which I take to mean that the whale will soon surface spouting again.

We have been occupied with the whale for two hours since the first harpoon and the sun is fierce upon our backs. I have heard how such fights may last six or more hours until, with the coming of the dark, the line must be cut and all is to no avail. I cannot imagine how we will sustain ourselves at our present pace if this old bull fights through the long afternoon.

Within fifteen minutes, the giant whale surfaces about a hundred yards away, and we must follow the rope now toward him. At almost the same moment we run into a squall, the rain belting down so fiercely we can see only a few feet ahead. The raindrops hit like bird shot but they are welcome enough for we have become heated pulling in the line. With the sheeting rain I am once again afraid of our proximity to the giant fish which we can no longer see.

Then, with the rain coming down and the sea misty, we come quite suddenly upon the whale. It is like coming upon a galleon through the fog, its huge shape looming unexpectedly in front of us. It would seem we have arrived midships as both the head and flukes of the Leviathan are lost to us in the pelting downpour. We take up the paddles again so as not to cause unnecessary noise.

Nestbyte looks for our line so that he can determine the whale's head from its tail, for when the old bull sounds again, its flukes could destroy us if we are too close to the tail-end. I can hear my heart beating in my chest as we paddle quietly towards the whale's head and heart so that Hammerhead Jack may make a good shot.

Then we see our line and, a moment later, our harpoon sticking out neat as a needle in a ball of tapestry wool. The old bull seems strangely oblivious of our presence.

Hammerhead Jack takes careful aim, as much as that is possible in the torrents splashing off the whale's back and cascading into the boat. He gives a shout and makes a mighty throw not five feet from the whale. Nestbyte wraps the line about the samson post and screams, 'Row, row! Row, row!' We are scarcely thirty feet away when the bull begins to roll to windward of us.

There is a sound like thunder as the whale's flukes smash down onto the waves, lifting the whaleboat clear into the air. I have no time to think of death as I grip the thwart, expecting to be thrown from the boat at any moment.

But by some miracle the whaleboat remains upright and comes down again with a mighty splash into a cauldron of roiling water. As the bull dives, its huge tail towers above us in the air and then with a great rushing of spray and sea, it sounds, and we spin madly in its foamy wash. We have barely time to make it aft as the whale dives only a few fathoms down before levelling out and surfacing a hundred yards away. Then we are off again, hanging on for dear life with the whaleboat bumping across the waves and the rain like sharp pellets peppering our faces as the whale tows us through the briny.

The wet rope seems to pay out even more quickly this time and the whine of it through the bow chocks pitches high above the wind from the squall about us. Despite the rain, we must still douse the rope as it smokes.

We are a hundred fathoms through the rope when the rain stops. All that may be heard is the bumping of the bows against the glassy waves and the high whining of the line. Then the rope goes slack. The whale has been lost to sight in the rain and now Nestbyte scans the sea to find him.

'Good shot!' Nestbyte says, plainly excited. 'We begin to have him!'

Again we begin pulling in the rope and the blisters which have formed on my hands are soon broken and bleeding. Whalemen who crew the boats constantly soak their hands in brine and piss to harden them, but mine have undergone no such preparation and the coarse manila rope has torn the flesh from my palms in bloody scraps of meat.

I recall now why Nestbyte is so well pleased that only half the line has been spent on our second ride across the waves. It means the whale has been struck well and is bleeding copiously from its spout. The blood will coagulate and prevent the whale from easily breathing. At the same time, the beast is weakened and will soon be forced to the surface to try and draw breath. But this does not mean the fight is done. A wounded whale can still move furiously fast upon the waves and can tow a boat beyond the reach of help.

With the line gathered a full sixty fathoms or so Nestbyte turns us to the south-east. 'Haul in the rope!' he screams. 'Put your backs into it, bastards!'

Hammerhead Jack sighs deeply and I look around to see him shaking his head woefully. Then, to my surprise, he says something in his native tongue and all but myself rest their oars.

'What means this?' Nestbyte asks in anger.

I am forced to ship my own oar as the giant Maori turns towards the first mate. He makes a tumbling motion in the air with his hands and points in the direction Nestbyte would have us row. I follow his direction but I can see nothing out of the ordinary.

Ignoring him, Nestbyte shouts, 'Take up the slack, ye bastards! Damn thee, Jack Kanaka! Pull!' I sense that his hot voice is not simply fuelled by anger at being challenged but also defiance, as though there is something else afoot which is beyond my ken. I wonder what it could be between the two men. 'Haul in the rope, bastard! Or it is the mizzen mast for thee!' Nestbyte threatens again. Hammerhead Jack shakes his head adamantly.

I search amongst the many whaling incidents I have heard of for an explanation. Ikey knew much of whaling from his nightly sojourns to the Whaler's Arms Hotel and would often regale Tommo and me with stories when we were young. And then I realise that Nestbyte has chosen to row us into the weather.

No whaleman will take a boat to the weather side of a big bull if it can be helped, for it is as close a thing to suicide as might be done in hunting a wounded whale. When a bull whale is struck and comes to the surface he always rolls windward, and if the whaleboat should be close enough to use a lance he will roll on top of it, killing all within. Even if the boat is further away, the wash from the bull's roll will almost certainly capsize it, spilling all into the sea. A mate must always approach a wounded whale from the leeward side.

But Nestbyte, who must know this well, will have none of it and insists we row weatherward. 'Ye'll all be flogged, ye kanaka bastards, I swear it in the name of Jesus!' he screams at Hammerhead Jack. 'Ye'll not get away with this disobedience! Haul in the rope, ye cannibal bastards!'

Hammerhead Jack shrugs his shoulders and spits over the side, then says something to the Maori crew. Reluctantly, they begin to take up the slack of the rope as Nestbyte, his face contorted with anger, steers us directly into the wind. The rope has begun to play out again, though not so rapidly; the whale, wherever he is, is moving sluggishly.

Nestbyte's calculation is proved accurate again for we see the whale breach three hundred yards from us about half an hour later. We sail towards the bull and as we close in on him we see that he is spouting, a spray of rosy water rising high into the sky from his great square nose.

'We have his chimney almost afire!' Nestbyte yells joyously, pointing to the bloody spray.

We have been going four hours and I am bone weary, my hands hurting beyond any pain I have felt since the wild man lassoed my throat behind his horse. If we must fight this beast much longer, I am not sure I shall bear up. Death, should it come, no longer seems such a bad thing!

Hammerhead Jack's tattooed face is most serious, his lips pulled tight and his eyes narrowed. The others also appear unhappy. Nestbyte takes no notice, steering the boat directly towards the whale, which barely moves, its flukes slowly slapping the water. I am mindful of an angry man drumming his fingers on the table as he considers his next action. It is as though we are being forewarned that there is still much power in this beast, which must soon take vengeance on us or die itself.

All at once I am above my own miseries, aware only of the tension and the sense of death that prevails in the air about us, though whether it is ours or the old bull's, I cannot say. Judging from the expression on Hammerhead Jack's face I know that we are in mortal danger from this monarch of the deep. The sun, now out again, is warm enough, yet suddenly I am cold and a shiver passes down my spine.

We approach the bull from its windward side and from behind, keeping as quiet as possible so as not to alarm him. He seems unaware of our presence, his head facing away from our boat. He moves along slowly, spouting the rosy water we have seen at a distance. Under sail, we are well able to keep up with him, moving ever closer to the point where we might fasten. We are fifty yards away when Nestbyte pulls down the sail and instructs us to take up the paddles for a silent approach. We have only the three lances to make our kill, then we must ride it out or cut loose.

Now the whale turns on his side as though he is waiting for us, and all the while our boat draws closer and closer. Its left side is facing us, the side much favoured by the harpooner as it gives him a better chance to reach the aorta valve within the heart. The first mate turns the line in readiness about the samson post.

'Right up! We probe!'

Hammerhead Jack, who has taken up a lance, shakes his head vigorously. 'More blood! We wait some!' I take him to mean that the whale must lose more blood, that it is too soon to fasten.

'What have we here, a coward?' Nestbyte says.

I do not know how much of this Hammerhead Jack comprehends but he is plainly furious. We stop paddling and Nestbyte screams, 'Paddle, ye bastards! We must go close, ye damned cowards!'

For a moment it seems as if Hammerhead Jack will fight

Nestbyte, for he has taken up the razor-sharp lance and they stand glaring. Each has his eyes locked to the other's in rage, Nestbyte with one hand on the bowie knife at the side of his belt.

'Coward!' Nestbyte taunts and spits over the side.

It is this single word which seems to defeat Hammerhead Jack and with a shrug he turns away. By now, we are but thirty yards away. I cannot believe what is unfolding before my eyes. Nestbyte has chosen to take us right up to the whale so that Hammerhead Jack might use the lance as a deep probing blade.

The lance is not a natural spear, but a razor-sharp two-sided blade, more like a surgeon's scalpel, spliced to a long wooden handle. It is best used once the whale is substantially weakened through loss of blood. Only then will a whaleboat fasten to the whale. The harpooner's task is to insert the lance and probe for a vital spot, seeking the heart or lungs or major artery to start the final massive haemorrhage.

Not only are we on the windward side, but rowing right up to a whale that, far from giving up the fight, is more dangerous now than ever before. It can only be concluded that Nestbyte has gone stark mad, for he is taking us right into the jaws of death!

'Ship paddles on the whale side!' Nestbyte commands. This is my side and I am sweating with fear.

'Stand off!' Nestbyte cries, meaning that I and the young Maori behind me should stop the boat from bumping the whale by means of our paddles held against its great carcass.

I have never touched a whale before, leastways one which may kill me for being so bold as to dare. My hands go out at one point when we go closer to the great sea beast and I feel its wet hide, soft to the touch under my palms.

Hammerhead Jack turns quietly to me and motions that I should take up a lance. I do so, but I am shaking like a leaf and he can see the fear in my eyes. 'Good Ork,' he says quietly.

He seems calm as he makes his inspection of the whale's flank. Then he indicates a place on its side and points to me and to the lance I am holding. Moving a foot or so away, he swiftly inserts his own lance, which seems to cut through the beast's flesh like a hot knife through lard.

Numbly, I follow suit. I am astonished at the ease with which the blade runs through the whale flesh. Hammerhead Jack twists and probes, churning the malevolent knife to find the blood pipe he seeks, grunting with the effort. I do the same, though I feel sick as my blade buries into the great beast's body, not knowing what it is I seek to find.

Suddenly a great arc of crimson, ten inches wide, sprays out from where I have made my cut, and both Hammerhead Jack and I are deluged in the sanguineous gush.

'Push away and stand off!' Nestbyte yells.

I am not certain how, in my bloody state, I find my oar, nor do I recall pushing away from the whale. But we are a full twenty feet away when the bull begins to roll towards us and his great flukes come up and smash down in a mighty explosion which rings my ears almost to deafness. He barely misses us as he prepares to dive. It is as though a mountain is falling on us and I am certain we shall be crushed to death.

Somehow the bull's huge bulk misses and we escape his crushing weight upon us. But with a roar of rushing water, a tidal wave overtakes us, and the boat goes over. I am under water yet can hear the scream of the line as it pays out. I struggle to free myself, knowing I have only moments to reach the surface before I must tangle in the line and be cut in half.

I come clear of the boat at last, gasping and taking great gulps of air. The water about me is stained red. A paddle floats past and I grab it. It sinks beneath my grasp and then I see that I am clutching a man's severed arm. I drop it from my frantic grasp and swim the few strokes towards the whaleboat, which has by some miracle righted itself. It is not yet moving, though the line is still paying out with a high-pitched whistle.

My terror spurring me on, I lift myself into the half-submerged boat. I rest a moment, sucking in the wondrous air, before looking about me. In the water around me other heads have surfaced and they swim towards the boat where I pull each aboard as best I can, three of the Maori and Nestbyte, but Hammerhead Jack is missing.

Then I see him twenty feet away. He is threshing the water with one arm, his head coming up and going down again in a foam of scarlet.

A moment more and I am sure my courage would have failed, but I am in the water before I know it and stroking out towards the wounded man.

'Leave him! Damn thee, nigger! Leave the bastard!' I hear Nestbyte gasp from the boat, but I continue to swim. Tommo and I have been strong swimmers since childhood and in a few strokes I am upon Hammerhead Jack. I grab him about the chest and he has the good sense not to struggle or perhaps he has passed out, and I am able to pull him towards the boat.

As I reach the side, which is half-submerged in the water, a strong hand encircles my wrist and I grab back to make a better purchase. But at that very moment the line zings and stiffens, and the boat begins to move away. The whale, which has dived straight down, is now levelling off and pulling away again.

'Cut the rope! Cut the rope!' I am shouting, though only in my head of course.

'Leave him, nigger!' Nestbyte screams at me. 'Let go the damned cannibal!' Then he brings his boot up and, aiming it at Hammerhead Jack's head, kicks viciously downwards to separate him from me, or both of us from the boat, in order to chase his whale.

'Damn thee! The lance is perfect set, the whale is ours!' he screams.

I have my hand about the wrist of one of the Maori whalemen on board and my arm hooked through Hammerhead Jack's good arm and about his chest, my chin clasped to his neck. I will not let go, nor will the young Maori who is holding onto me. Blood drips onto my shoulder where Nestbyte has crushed Jack's right eye and nose with the heel of his boot. The water around us is stained crimson with the whale's blood, as well as that from the harpooner's severed arm socket.

I am hanging on for dear life as the whaleboat gains speed. Then I see the flash of a blade as Nestbyte brings his bowie knife down into the back of my hand. At the very same moment the whale finds a surge of strength and the boat's bow is pulled down and we jerk forward. The first mate, already off balance from his downward strike at me, loses his footing and with a cry of alarm is pitched over my head and into the churning sea. He is at once gone from sight.

How I am able to maintain my grip about the Maori's wrist and still hold on to Hammerhead Jack while the boat is moving I cannot say, for my palms are minced from hauling in the line. But somehow I do, and with the boat beginning to skim the waves, the two of us are finally pulled aboard. I reach for the boat knife so that I might cut the whale-rope and save Nestbyte. Before I can grab it, my arms are held by a Maori on either side of me, and I have not the strength remaining to resist.

The whaleboat is flying along and there is no turning back. Nestbyte will be drowned long before we can cut the line and return to search for him. Anyway, without oars, we have no way of rowing back to where he fell into the turbulent seas.

Nor do we have time to think about the whale. From a large artery at the junction of Hammerhead Jack's shoulder, blood is spouting to the beat of his heart.

I pull off my blouse, stained scarlet from the bull's blood now mixed with Jack's. What little I know of binding such a wound I have learnt only from a brief description in a book I once read about the Peninsular Wars. The wounds from a cannon shot cannot be much different to this one and though I am panicked, I try to recall the exact procedures advised. I cut and then tear some canvas into narrow strips and, taking twine from my pocket, cut a length and tie the pumping artery along with the smaller ones which are still bleeding.

Hammerhead Jack's arm has been torn clean out of his shoulder socket. This is fortunate as it means the socket hole is clean and the arteries protrude so the ties are easily made even though my trembling fingers are sticky with blood. Using the remainder of my blouse I make a pad to swab the socket hole and tie it as best I can to the unconscious man's shoulder by wrapping a strip around his chest.

I rinse my hand in the bloody water in the bottom of the boat and I see that my hand is bleeding from Nestbyte's knife wound. I look about me and see the weapon lying on the bottom of the boat where it must have fallen when Nestbyte did his fatal tumble. It is a handsome bowie knife, long-bladed with a fine ivory handle, the first mate's initials C. W. N. inlaid in copper. I put it in the stern, safe above the water.

I check the wrist of the Maori who hauled Jack and me into the boat, anxious to see if Nestbyte's blade penetrated through my own hand and injured him. But he shrugs and indicates a cut where the point of the bowie knife entered which has long since ceased to bleed.

'Good Ork!' he says.

It becomes clear to me what has befallen Hammerhead Jack. When the whaleboat overturned and we were caught under it, the whale line kinked and took Hammerhead Jack's arm with it, tearing it from its socket as the whale sounded.

It can only be supposed that the giant Maori, in the split second left to him, kept his nerve and hooked his good arm about the thwart. By holding on, he knowingly sacrificed his captured arm, else he would have travelled downwards with the whale to be drowned.

Still unconscious, Hammerhead Jack is now held by the eldest of the Maori, his head resting on the man's lap. The older man sits in the stern, his legs and most of Hammerhead Jack's torso submerged in the water-filled boat. He weeps as he tenderly protects Hammerhead Jack's damaged eye with his cupped hand. His tears spill down his purple-patterned face, splashing onto the unconscious giant's chin. All the while he moans and wails in a strange manner which I take to be the savage way of sorrowing.

The two other Maori, both younger men, have begun bailing water out of the boat with the piggin. Thankfully, this is always attached to the whaleboat by means of a marlin line and so was not lost when we overturned. They too are sniffing and moaning but remain busy at their task. They work hard and our risk of sinking diminishes as this wild sea ride with the whale continues unabated.

It is then that I see what has become of Hammerhead Jack's right eye. It is a terrible mash of jellied orb held by a tangle of bloody veins and sinew, now resting on the lower part of his tattooed cheek.

I have no time to think, or the task will be beyond me. Using Nestbyte's bowie knife I cut the tangle of sinew high up so the eye and socket entrails fall into his blood-soaked lap. Then with my thumb, I push what's left back into the empty cavity. There is now little blood as I pull the bruised and swollen eyelid over the mess. Hammerhead Jack looks to me to be more dead than alive, so I hope not to have done him much more harm than he has already endured.

I bend down and carefully scoop the eye from his lap and am about to throw it into the sea when the old man grabs my wrist and then cups his hands to receive the tangled mess. He calls his companions from their bailing and they stand beside him as he begins to chant in a wild high-pitched voice, the two young Maori punctuating the oration with great belly grunts, deep as a big military drum. Then, when the chanting is finally done, the old man leans over the side and submerges his hands to just below the water so that Hammerhead Jack's eye floats away into the waves as the three of them sing a strange but beautiful melody, filled with harmonies and a sense of great tenderness.

The whale has been forced by its bleeding to surface quickly and now is some distance ahead of us pulling the boat at a steady rate of knots. The mast has been snapped off by the whale-rope when we overturned, and the lug sail lost along with the oars and paddles, so we are captured, prisoners in our own whaleboat, tethered to a great sea beast which may eventually stop or simply continue onwards until the rope runs out. Either way, we are as helpless as small children lost in a snow storm on Cradle Mountain.

We have not had a drop to drink for six hours and before then only a mouthful. My head is light and the horizon dances in front of my eyes. Our hats were lost when the boat capsized and the sun will surely addle our brains.

After what seems like more than an hour, the rope slackens; the old bull turns and, in an arc, heads back in our direction.

Now, I think, he has come at last to take his revenge. It is better so, more worthy that we should die this way than any other. We are done for anyway, there has been no sighting of the other boats or the ship and we are lost at sea. In an open whaleboat we will go through the night well enough, but we will not last long without water. Hammerhead Jack will be dead before the sun climbs to its zenith again and we who are left will not see too many sunsets after that. Better this quick death at the hands of a worthy foe than a slow and lingering one, lying cooked in the bottom of a whaleboat.

I think of my death, not in terms of my own demise, which is now certain. No, what worries me is the question of who will take care of Tommo. My thoughts go to him at this moment. Dear Tommo, who I think is slowly mending his ways – though he is winning too often at cards and the men are becoming suspicious. He has collected nearly twenty Yankee dollars and various rings, knives and scrimshaw as his winnings and he will even play for the raisins from their next ration of plum duff. I can only suppose he craves the sweetness for it is a most curious prize to win at cards.

I have told him his gambling must stop soon.

'If they catch you at cheating they will kill you, Tommo!' I plead.

'But I don't need to cheat with these duffers!' he protests, most indignantly. 'I swears it, Hawk! It is all done above board and on the square!'

I am unconvinced. But then again, it would be just like Tommo's luck to be killed at *not* cheating. What would our poor mama think?

No day has passed on our voyage that I do not think of Mary. What will become of her, on her own? I ache to talk to mama and I have written many pages of letters telling her of our adventures. But now she shall never receive them unless Tommo thinks to send them to her when he reaches port, and who knows what state he will be in then.

My heart is heavy for Mary and for Tommo as I prepare

to meet my death. Not fifty yards from us, the great monster
slows his approach and I see that his chimney is spouting
thick black blood. We wait terrified – a dying whale is most
dangerous until the final moment when he rolls over. The
sperm whale has the largest brain of any creature in the
universe and this old bull has no reason to spare us. As
ninety feet and over seventy tons of malevolence bear down
upon us, I can see from the sombre expressions on the
Maori's faces that they too are aware of our approaching
doom.

However, as we draw ever nearer, the creature seems
unaware of our presence. We are now no more than thirty
yards apart, with no means of controlling our path. The
whale's giant mouth opens, blood falling like scarlet ribbons
from his upper jaw, missing the great rows of teeth
contained in the long, narrow lower jaw. This monster,
should we come much closer, will crush our boat to tinder
between those scrimshaw molars. Miraculously, the wind
shifts direction a fraction and we drift a little further away
again.

More than an hour passes in this way, as we drift in close
proximity to death. The whale moves more and more slowly,
his chimney frequently spouting blood and gore in a great
scarlet spray. His flukes have grown lethargic, and they slap
the surface, making no more sound than that of the wind
snapping at bed-sheets on a backyard washline.

I think, after all, that our grand opponent is aware of our
presence and, with none of his own kind around him, desires
to be near us. This Prince of Fish does not wish to die alone.
Ho, Great Fish! We will meet again at Neptune's tavern, for
we will not be long behind you.

The sea about us is crimson, bubbling and seething for
two hundred yards in the bull's wake. The blood pours from
him like mud running down a mountain side after a storm.

Sharks circle, snapping at the floating, bubbling gore, their fins cutting through the surface in ever increasing numbers.

Then, as the setting sun turns the western sky into a fiery blaze, and the sea grows so burnished the waves' reflections turn us into glowing red men, with a great roaring and sucking of water, the tormented beast rolls over, fin out. There is a sudden silence; the Prince of the Deep Waters is dead.

We are too tired for joy and must now pull the line in, a task which seems altogether too much for us. But we cannot risk drifting away in the dark and losing our line, for we count it safer to be tethered to the dead bull all night than drift helplessly at sea. If the *Nankin Maiden* comes a-looking in the morning, a dead whale will be easier to spot from the mainmast than a lone whaleboat lost at sea.

Though hope springs eternal, our rescue seems an unlikely event. With the three other boats having fastened onto the sperm cow, she was a certain capture. Captain O'Hara must tether her to the starboard of the ship, strip her of her blubber and boil it down for oil without delay. There is little chance that he will risk losing this valuable prize to come looking for us.

The supposition that an old bull sperm whale would prove too much for one boat to handle and the natural assumption following it, that we have perished under its flukes, is a most reasonable one. Our only hope is that we may be downwind from the ship so that sailing in search of us would not be an arduous task. It is to be hoped that the master places a great value on his first mate, Crawlin Nestbyte, for he would not search even to the bottom of a bucket of sea water for four kanakas and a nigger.

All the while the sharks have been gathering. They are now in their many hundreds, bumping their snouts against the belly of the whale and tearing upwards at his hide so that the old bull looks to be still alive but for the great fin sticking up into the air and the white patch now turned red on his underbelly. These jackals of the sea have the only true victory.

It is ended and, for what it is worth, we have won this bloody contest, even though the triumph of it will be short-lived before we die.

I sit upon a thwart, my hands dripping with fresh blood from hauling in the line, but I no longer care or feel the pain. It is almost dark, with only a sliver of the sun's brassy coin still showing above the horizon. I am weary beyond all endurance, yet there is something pestering at the back of my mind.

'Scratch around, look in the dark corners, clear the cobwebs, unlock the doors and open the windows, my dear,' I hear Ikey's voice say clearly to me. He would say this when I had lost track of an idea he had previously explained. 'If it is something you have thought or known before then it will still be there, stored in the old noggin box, to be retrieved when you should need it most. But when you look, my dear, do so in an orderly manner and all will be yours soon enough.'

So I go to thinking, letting this nightmare of a day pass once again through my mind and then, at last, I recall what it is that has been troubling me.

When I held Hammerhead Jack in the water and screamed to Nestbyte to cut the line, I swear I heard my own voice, not only in my imagination but out loud. Yet I know this cannot be. I have not uttered a single word since Mary rescued me from the wild man. I touch my throat, then swallow. It feels tender, raw, though this might equally be from lack of water during the long afternoon. Have my ears deceived me? I open my mouth to attempt to make a sound.

Chapter Five

TOMMO

The Pacific Ocean
November 1856

If I've spoken against the God-gobbers what owns this ship, or Captain O'Hara, the master, I now hopes desperately that Christian fidelity might save me brother's life.

It's near sunset and the other three boats returned to the ship two hours ago with a sperm cow in tow. They says they saw Nestbyte and his crew attached to a monstrous sperm bull what they at once judged too much of a handful for a single boat. The whale were ninety foot if it be an inch, with a ton to every foot. They was all made fast to the cow and none could let loose to follow Nestbyte and his Maori, though all felt sure that the first mate would be forced to cut the manila rope or that it would run out soon enough. They was sure that the giant sea creature would not find one whaleboat much of a drag upon himself and would easily out-run the two hundred fathoms of harpoon line.

But now it's close to dark and Hawk's whaleboat still ain't returned. Most now believes that the bull's got the better of them. It ain't unusual, though, for a whaleboat to stay out overnight if another hour might bring the kill and the moon be bright enough to see by. There is fresh water on

92

board and a lantern-keg with a little ship's biscuit and salt beef, even clay pipes and a quid of tobacco for comfort in the dark hours. But all this I'm told as the very tag end of hope by the second mate, Tom Stubbs. If they hasn't returned by sunset it is likely that the crew, including me brother Hawk, be lost at sea or dead.

The men know Nestbyte is reckless. Many in the fo'c'sle reckons he has taken one too many chances, that his luck has finally run out. It's five months since the last taking of a whale and it's just such circumstances that make a man careless.

Seb Rawlings has come from his cabin where he were confined with the tropical fever. It be his boat what's missing and he feels to blame for not going out with his crew. He's shaking with the fever and his eyes is bright as agates, lips cracked and teeth chattering, but he seems to have his senses about him. He asks that I be allowed to take the watch from aloft, where I can look out for Hawk's boat. He says that as the light grows dim in the west, my young eyes might prove better than those of an older whaleman.

There's great to-do on the ship. The cow is thought to be some twenty tons and a good catch after such a long time without a sighting. She's already chained to the starboard side ready for flensing, when the blubber will be cut from her for boiling down in the try-pots. Her oil will be enough with what's already been took to fill half the ship's barrels. This is a most important event, for the first half of our cargo will pay the costs of the voyage and the second half will pay the whalemen and the owners. Whale oil burns clean, without smoke, and is used for lamps throughout the civilised world. It be a precious commodity. Not a drop of oil from this cow must be wasted to the sharks or spoilt by the weather, and the sooner the trying out is underway the better.

There's been no talk among the mates of going to look for Hawk's whaleboat, and the men is clearly against it. Only Billy Lanney and meself wants a search party and we holds no sway at all. Billy calls for a whaleboat to go, with him and me as crew. 'Shut yer gob!' several shouts at him. 'Abo bastard!' someone else growls.

The other kanakas and the niggers don't want a search neither. The islanders hates the Maori, and the four black men, though from different parts themselves, don't sees Hawk as one o' them. Nestbyte is hated by one and all and his loss thought a good riddance. Four kanakas and a dumb nigger ain't worth keeping the flensing and the try-pots waiting for. 'Let the cutting in begin!' they cry. None wants to see a drop of their precious booty wasted.

Unchaining the cow from the ship and anchoring her at sea while we searches for the missing whaleboat would let a full night pass with a thousand sharks tearing at her carcass. Meanwhile, getting all ready for the flensing to be done by dawn's light tomorrow would save much of her bulk from being destroyed. Already the water around the boat is full of these mongrels of the sea. If a man fell overboard he wouldn't last ten seconds before his flesh-picked bones would sink to the ocean-floor.

Whale blubber spoils fast in the tropics. After less than a day and a half in the sun, it turns rancid and its oil loses value. There be little loyalty on a whaling vessel greater than the promise of coin at the voyage end, and still less if the lost crew be niggers and kanakas, even if it does include me brother. Me old feelings of love for Hawk are starting to return, like blood coming back into a limb what's been deprived, and with him lost, I'm at me wit's end. It's Captain O'Hara what must make the decision to search, and me only hope is that he be a true Quaker, what's a religion of conscience, so it's said. Nestbyte's also a Quaker and the brother of O'Hara's wife. Perhaps this family tie, if nothing else, will make the master order a search.

But in me heart, I knows that feelings of family ain't as strong as feelings of greed. O'Hara is a New Englander and they is notorious penny-pinchers. It's conscience against greed and I ain't yet seen care for one's fellow man hold out against rapacity. As Ikey says, 'It ain't religion what makes the world go round, 'tis everlasting avarice, my dear.'

My mind is filled with anxiety as I climb up the mainmast to the highest of the watch stays. I stand on the cross-stays, holding fast to the masthead hoop. The sun's heat is weakening though the sky is not yet turned to saffron to make visibility difficult. It's fortunate that the hunt took place in a nor'easterly direction so that I need not face direct into the setting sun. It's good fortune, too, that it took place downwind from the *Nankin Maiden* so the sailing conditions be good. Tonight is a full moon and the earlier clouds have cleared. A sighting in the moonlight is by no means impossible.

I want to pray, but I'm not sure how. I ain't had much practice since the age of seven at bedtime, and then it were only to repeat at Mary's knee the words she give us to say.

> *Gentle Jesus, meek and mild*
> *look upon this little child . . .*

I forget how the rest goes.

The only God I knows is the one what comes to sit at Mary's table of a Sunday to escape from the cold and the wind moaning in the organ pipes on Mount Wellington. But I doesn't think our White Tablecloth God of the warm brown gravy and the roast mutton is the sort of cove to find a whaleboat what's a thousand miles out to sea and bring my brother back safe to me.

'I wonder if you'd mind very much going out and finding me twin brother, God?'

'And where might he be, son?'

'Whaling, Sir. His whaleboat be lost or took by a whale.' Then I adds for good measure, 'The master be a Quaker and very pious.'

'Whales, eh? Sperm, is it?'

'Yes, Sir,' I nods me head.

'Sperm whale be my particular pride and joy, Tommo. Biggest creature of all 'cept for the blue whale, what's just a bit too big for my liking, not quite perfect-made like the sperm. There be no other creature in the heavens, on the earth or in the waters like the sperm whale. Did you know that I gave that creature a brain five times the size of man's? The largest brain of any creature on earth? Did you know that, Tommo?'

'Yes, Sir, Hawk told me.'

'Well then, why d'you suppose I done that?'

'Dunno, Sir.'

'Well you see, Tommo, every creature's got its mongrels and the sperm whale, what don't do no harm to no one, has got *you* lot, the terrible-est bunch o' mongrels of all! Sometimes, if you've got sufficient brains, it is possible to win against the mongrels.'

'Yes, Sir. Thank you, Sir. It's just that I was hoping . . .'

'Pass the salt,' God asks and then adds, 'No day can be judged until night has fallen, Tommo.'

'Yes, Sir,' I says, not knowing what that last remark's supposed to mean. There is no arguing with the Almighty and I am more troubled than ever. I fears that God is on the side o' the whale and me brother forever lost. What God done for Jonah it don't seem likely he's gunna do for Hawk.

There is nothing to be seen out there 'cept an albatross what's been following us for two days, and the endless waves stretching to the horizon. A gold colour starts to spread in the sky and if a search don't begin before sundown it's unlikely to begin at all.

Old Tommo's on his own again, just when I were beginning to feel like a twin, knowing there be somebody else what's connected invisible-like to me. First I thinks Hawk a fool for wanting me back, wasting his life over yours truly. Then he become a nuisance, watching me, fetching me back home when I were drunk, looking sad-faced at me. Then, when he brung me aboard this ship, I think it better than staying with Mary, who made me feel so bad, like a naughty child. Later, I planned to jump ship as soon as we were in some port, piss off and leave Hawk to go home where he be needed by our mama. Yours truly would be alone again with his cards and a bottle, what suits me just fine! But now Hawk feels a part o' me again, creeping back into me heart and mind like when we was brats. Mind, I don't know how I'll feel when I gets me hands on a bottle again.

When I came down on deck this mornin' to find Hawk gone as crew in Seb Rawlings' whaleboat, with Crawlin Nestbyte in command, I were full o' fear. The feeling of the mongrels being near, what I had when I were aloft, come back so strong it took all me courage to stay on deck and not climb back up the mainmast, to hide up there, like the mast were a river gum and I back in the wilderness again.

All day I've felt Hawk be in danger and that's how I know our twinship is returning. It's like it were meself what's suffering. All day me hands hurt awful and I thinks at first they's becoming like Mary's. They is rough and battered from the years in the wilderness. But I know it's more than that, it's something bad to do with Hawk.

If by nightfall Hawk ain't returned, I'm gunna jump to me death from where I now stand. I ain't staying another day on this bloody ship without Hawk. If he dies I won't even have the black bottle to comfort me. Alone on this ship at sea, I'll be in a wilderness not much better than the last. Sooner or later I'll get in a row over the cards, or a brass bimbo will come for me in the dark and I'll use me axe on him, and that will be the end of yours truly too. It all be as certain as the sun coming up in the mornin'.

Suddenly I hear the rattling of chains and I look down to see men scrambling to the starboard. I can't believe me eyes! They's unchaining the cow from the side of the ship and two whaleboats has been lowered on the port side to tow her away and anchor her at sea. My heart thumps as I watch the men climb the rigging to unfurl the sails and the *Nankin Maiden* turns to catch the wind. The sun is setting in a blaze o' glory and the sky is afire as the search gets underway.

We sail for an hour and a half, and the moon is now well up. The sea is cast in bright moonlight and if I had with me one of Hawk's books I could read it as if it were daylight. It is then that I see the whale, a dark shape looming in the water to starboard.

'Whale-o! Whale-oooooo! To starboard!' I shouts. Me heart is beating so fast it must burst from me chest any moment and drop to the deck below. Then I see the whaleboat moored not fifty feet from the dead monster but I can't see nobody in it.

'Oh God! Please, God, Sir, let me brother be safe!' I looks upwards through the topmast to heaven. 'I promise I shall return to Mary if he's saved!' Then I think, 'Oh shit! Me and my big mouth, I should've waited until we got a bit closer!'

In the pouring silver of the night, I see a head raise up above the gunwale of the boat and then it stands up and I know it's me lovely twin brother and I begin to weep like a stupid little brat!

We lifts the whaleboat back on board and sets to towing

the monster whale behind the ship. It's the biggest bloody whale killed in the history of the *Nankin Maiden* and Tom Stubbs reckons it be the biggest whale ever took by a single whaleboat. There is much cheering on deck, the whalemen having forgot that they was against the search. They's counting only their share of the oil, what now means profit for us all.

But I am only concerned to see me brother again. Hawk is the first to climb from the boat, and the Maori follow, carrying between them the limp weight o' Hammerhead Jack. It's clear they's been through a terrible ordeal. The boat is now empty, and we sees that Nestbyte is not among them.

Captain O'Hara ain't a happy man when he realises the first mate be missing. He's tall and frightening to behold, his eyes glowering from beneath midnight eyebrows, what meet across the bridge of his nose. As soon as they has lain Hammerhead Jack on the deck, he calls the four survivors to his cabin for an explanation. But o' course, none is possible. The four Maori got no English and, without Hammerhead Jack to talk for 'em, they is staying stum. Hawk, being dumb, can't say nothing without me. Finally O'Hara says he'll deal with the matter after we gets the cow, and gives orders to sail back to where she's waiting.

This is most lucky, for it gives me the chance to find out what happened. As we sails back, Hawk tells me the story of their hunt and I becomes afeared again.

'They won't believe ya, Hawk!' I says, after he explains how Nestbyte lost his balance and fell into the briny.

'Why?' Hawk says, moving his fingers slowly 'cause of the pain. 'It is nothing but the truth, Tommo.'

'It's a truth what will get you all hanged from the yard-arm!' I cry.

Hawk is wrung out. His hands is swollen to twice their size and is all red raw flesh. I've had me hands hurt from the pit dogs and the crosscut saw, and blistered once when Sam Slit's whisky still exploded, but never like this, never as terrible as this. He is nearly asleep as he speaks to me, his eyelids closing. Yet his great concern is not to tell me what happened nor that his hands be looked after, but that the skipper should give him medicine to care for Hammerhead Jack.

'He will die, Tommo,' he signals wearily to me. 'Then it will be my fault!'

'*You* will die!' I says. 'They will say you pushed Nestbyte if you tells it how it was. They won't believe you, Hawk!'

Hawk shakes his head. 'I am too weary to lie, Tommo. The truth will stand us in good stead.' He can't touch a finger to his palms without wincing with the pain and soon he gives up, too weary to use his hands or lift his arms to talk any longer.

I thinks to let him sleep awhile. I will hear him out again later, and talk a plan into him, once we is anchored alongside the cow.

It is nearly eight bells when we gets back to where we left her. In the bright moonlight there is so many sharks feeding on her that it be almost like watching a school of mackerel in the shallows of Salamanca beach. But the whalemen is much less worried now about losing bits of her bulk. The bull is good compensation, three-and-a-half times bigger in blubber than the cow. It's as though we has caught four whales.

We barely arrives when Captain O'Hara calls for Hawk and the three Maori. Seb Rawlings is also called from his sick bed, it being reckoned that they be his crew and perhaps he may get some sense from them. The fourth mate sends straight for me where I am working in the try-house to get ready for the flensing of the whales at first light. That I should be called upon be me deepest hope. With me translating for Hawk I reckon we has a chance to beat the mongrels.

'Evenin', Cap'n, sir,' I says, removing me cap as I stands at the door of his cabin waiting permission to enter.

O'Hara grunts. 'Come in, boy!' he barks.

Hawk and the three Maori is standing in the small cabin and the captain is seated behind a table with Tom Stubbs besides him. Seb Rawlings is also seated, being too weak, I suppose, to be on his feet. With all of us in the cabin there's scarce an inch to move and I find meself squashed against the oldest of the Maori.

The captain turns to Stubbs. 'Thou mayst go, Mr Stubbs, there is much to be done. Mr Rawlings will remain as witness.' We push aside to let Tom Stubbs pass.

O'Hara points to me without looking up from the ship's log which lies open before him. 'Thou wilt speak to thy brother, and he will tell thee what happened and thou us.'

'Sir, me brother has already told me the whole of it. It will be much the shorter if I speaks and then you asks questions what I shall put to him.'

Captain O'Hara looks up sharply, thinking me to be too forward, but I keeps me head down and me hands clasped humble-like. 'The sign language be most tedious slow, sir. This will be the quicker.'

'Is this the lad who saw the pod this morning?' O'Hara asks Rawlings.

'He is the one, Captain,' Rawlings says. 'He is reliable enough and not too stupid.' He points to Hawk. 'They claim to be twins, though how this can be I cannot imagine!'

'Most curious,' the captain says, but there is no curiosity in his voice and I reckon he don't care if Hawk and me be twins or the first two of the three blind mice. 'Speak, boy!' he commands.

I tell of the placing of the two harpoons and how Nestbyte

passed the other boats and shouted for help and then how, after being towed by the bull, they approached the whale from the weather side. I says nothing of the fight 'tween him and Hammerhead Jack. I tell how Nestbyte wished them to fasten to the whale while there were still much life in him, so's they might more quickly open a major blood flow, as the first mate did not think they could otherwise wear the bull down sufficient to take him with one boat.

'Mr Nestbyte did confide all this to them?' O'Hara questions.

'No, Cap'n, but it were clear enough to me brother.'

'Clear enough, was it? Your brother is an expert on the whale and whaling, and what actions to take in every circumstance?'

'No, Cap'n, but he didn't think Mr Nestbyte were going up to bid the whale the time o' day!' It were a stupid thing to say and I'm sorry the moment it come out of me big mouth.

'Hold thy tongue, boy!' O'Hara growls. 'I'll not take lip from such as thee!'

I drop my head. 'Yes, sir. Sorry, sir,' I says. Out of the corner of my eye I can see Hawk is trying to talk to me. I ignore him, not wishing at this moment to meet his eye, but Rawlings sees his movements, 'What's he saying, Tommo, what's your brother saying?' he stammers, all a-chittering and a-chattering o' teeth from the fever.

What Hawk's saying is that I should tell the story like he told it to me. He thinks the captain just wants to write it down for the record. Ho! I thinks. Hawk may be the smart one, but he don't know a mongrel when he sees one! Captain O'Hara here ain't just keeping his log, he's holding a trial. He wants revenge for his brother-in-law! I know this for sure. Old Tommo's nose for mongrels is working well.

'What does he say?' the captain demands to know.

'Yes, sir! He says that he's sorry for presuming to know

what Mr Nestbyte was thinking about what to do with the whale. He says I must say only what happened and should otherwise shut me big mouth.' I doesn't look at Hawk as I says this, and I can only hope he's got the nous to keep his hands to hisself.

'Continue!' O'Hara commands, a bit happier.

So I tells how the whale rolled to windward and capsized the boat. How only the Maori and Hawk come up again, with Hawk rescuing Hammerhead Jack from the briny after he had lost his arm.

'Did Mr Nestbyte do anything when the whale rolled to windward?' Captain O'Hara asks.

It's not a question I can answer. So I turns to Hawk, who gives me a most despairing look, like I've done them in. He has no way now to tell the truth and must go along with my tale. He signals that Nestbyte shouted they should ship oars.

'He said that they should ship oars, Cap'n,' I reply.

'Aye, aye!' O'Hara says impatient. 'But did he *do* something?'

'Do something?' I look to Hawk, who says he does not recall anything. Meanwhile the others' eyes are near closed as they tries to sleep standing up.

'Me brother don't recall, sir.'

'Do something with this!' O'Hara shouts, taking up a bowie knife from under the table and thrusting it, blade forward, at Hawk.

The three Maori jolt awake in surprise and pull back, falling over each other. I am pushed against the cabin door, where I bump me shoulder.

'Ha! I have thee!' the captain exclaims. 'This is Mr Nestbyte's knife and there is blood on it! Human blood!' He stands up and with the tip of his forefinger indicates a dark stain on the blade and points to Hawk, 'Thou didst murder him and then threw him to the sharks!'

I am took completely by surprise. Hawk ain't said nothing about Nestbyte's knife. I look at Hawk and see that he is smiling and shaking his head. He alone has not flinched when the captain thrust the knife at him.

'Well? Answer me, man!' O'Hara barks.

'You were right, Tommo, he wants a victim,' Hawk says with his hands. 'Tell him the truth. I used it to cut the mess which was Hammerhead Jack's eye. The blood on the blade is Hammerhead Jack's and that on the handle is from my hands.'

I says all this and Hawk holds up his hands to show their cruel state.

'How came he to be in possession of Mr Nestbyte's knife?' O'Hara demands. 'A man doesn't leave his own knife lying around, leastways Mr Nestbyte didn't.' He stabs down upon the table with the bowie knife so that it judders as he releases it. 'Thou takes me for a fool, boy! There is a boat-knife for the purpose of cutting! Why did not Hawk use *that* knife?'

'Tell him that when the whale rolled, Nestbyte took out his knife to cut the line but we were thrown out before he could do so. He must have dropped the knife in the boat where I later discovered it,' Hawk signals to me.

It ain't Hawk's fault he's so bad at lying – he ain't had much practice like me. Besides, he's weary. First he says he didn't see Nestbyte do nothing when the bull rolled, now he says Nestbyte were busy cutting the whaling line with his bowie knife and loses it from his grasp as the boat turns over. So, I asks you, how could that be? The boat capsizes, and by some miracle Nestbyte's bowie knife grows hands of its own to cling to the bottom of the boat so it don't fall out with everything else?

But the captain is waiting for me to translate what Hawk's just told me so I has to invent an explanation quick. Billy Lanney has recently shown us how to tie the short-warp to the harpoon rope and so I says desperate, 'He took it off from his lanyard and give it to Hawk to fix the short-warp to the harpoon rope, Cap'n, the boat-knife being tied to a marlin line in the stern of the boat and the warp to be fixed in the bow. Me brother then pushed the knife into his belt on account that they had to quickly man the oars. He thought to return it later to the first mate.'

'This happened just before the whale rolled?' the skipper asks. He must think me a fool to fall into such a silly trap.

I talks to Hawk as though I were asking him the question with our sign language, but what I am saying is that I'll tell the skipper that the knots were done just before the second harpoon were used. It were then that Nestbyte noticed the splice were not right on the short-warp. It's a feeble enough explanation what I gives to the captain but it can't be proved wrong, and it makes some sort o' sense. But O'Hara ain't yet willing to give up.

'Then why, I ask thee, did the kanakas grow most alarmed when I showed the bowie knife?' he demands, his eyes narrowed.

'I cannot say, Cap'n. They be savages and I doesn't speak their lingo.' Then I ask, 'Perhaps they thought you was going to do them in on the spot, like? Why, sir,' I rubs me shoulder, 'I meself jumped when you thrust the knife at me brother.'

Despite his fever and the sweat glistening on his brow, Seb Rawlings half-smiles at my reply, and I sees he has no love for the skipper.

Captain O'Hara pulls the knife from the table and lays it down, then takes up the quill again and dips it into the ink well. All is quiet as he writes in the ship's log and we can plainly hear his quill scratching upon the paper.

At last he looks up, scowling. He points the quill accusingly at Hawk.

'I feel there is more to this business than thou hast

admitted, Solomon. I warn thee, nigger, I will sniff out dishonesty! I shall pray to the Lord for guidance and then we shall see what we shall see. Thou mayst go, and thy damned cannibals with thee.' Then he turns to me, 'As for thee, boy, thou mayst be sure I shall find something to cool thy ardour and quell thy impudent tongue!'

We turns to go, the Maori shuffling out first, when Hawk signals frantically to me.

'Cap'n, sir!' I pipes up from the door of the cabin. 'Me brother pleads that he be allowed medicines for the injuries the harpooner got while most bravely killing the whale.'

'Hmmph! A nigger who cares about a kanaka! Miracles will never cease!' The captain turns to Seb Rawlings. 'We have here a nigger who cleverly turns Mr Nestbyte's whale kill to the credit of that damned savage, and turns himself just as neatly into a ship's surgeon! What think thou of that, Mr Rawlings?' He does not wait for the fourth mate to reply before looking at Hawk. 'But of course, I forget, thou hast already proved thyself most handy with a bowie knife!' He indicates Seb Rawlings with a flick of his head. 'Thou mayst issue a chit for medicine, though I think it much better for all if the savage should perish.'

O'Hara seems a little calmer, having rid himself of his spleen. He is well pleased with his crack about Hawk being a surgeon and with his last jibe about Hawk's supposed use of the bowie knife to kill Nestbyte. He twirls the quill in his fingers and muses aloud. 'The Lord's ways are indeed mysterious. I have the greatest need of a first mate on this ship and He hath taken my dear brother from me and allowed the devil to replace him with a cannibal savage, a useless kedger with one arm and one eye, who will draw from ship's rations and return me no profitable labour!'

He looks up at Seb Rawlings, his right eyebrow raised. 'Thou wilt charge the cost of the medicines to the kanaka's share of the lay, and he will be placed on half rations until he perishes or otherwise proves to be of some further worth to us!'

The captain is as good as his word and has found me a special punishment. I am working in the blubber room, where I must pitch up the pieces of blubber to be cut ready for the try-pots. These pieces is four foot long, and weighs nearly as much as me. Working them is usually a task for the biggest of the men. Two blubber-room workers in bare feet cuts the blubber with dangerous sharp spades and as a consequence of the deck pitching and rolling, one has had three toes sliced off and the other four, this being the badge of their trade. They is fierce men and don't like seeing the blubber they cut stack up. 'Git movin',' they snarls each time I forks another slab of blubber, 'we ain't got all bloody day!' I am soon knackered but there is no let-up. The deck is slippery with oil and whale blood and sometimes I near collapses under the weight of me blubber fork. 'Garn, move yer arse!' be the constant cry from the cutters.

Not one comes to me aid and some push me over when they see me loaded up so that I crash to the floor, falling on me face. Yours truly is a cause of great merriment to all in the try-works as I staggers to me feet covered in blood and oil. But it ain't the worst what's happened to me and I will not give in. No poxy bunch o' whalemen gets the better of Tommo X Solomon!

There be two hours to go and every forkful of whale blubber is stained with blood from me bleedin' nose. I feels a hand on my shoulder and I stops, expecting another shove. But it's Hawk, come to find me!

'I have been asleep and did not know of this,' he signals with his hands. They still be swollen to twice their size, yet he takes up me fork and begins to spear and lift the slabs o' blubber. Though the pain in his hands must be awful, it is as though he is shovelling straw into a hay-rick, such is his strength. One of the whalemen what has been amusing hisself at my expense now scoffs at me. Without turning, Hawk strikes him with the back of his huge hand, so that he flies across the try-deck and lands skidding in the whale oil.

It's the first time I've seen Hawk strike a man and it were like he was brushing away a fly. Then Hawk walks over to the whaleman, who is nursing a bloody nose, and with the fork pierces the greasy duck of his Norfolk breeches so that the tines fit under the man's belt. Hawk lifts him up and carries him across the room, depositing him on the blubber table in front o' the mincer. The mincer is a large man himself, dressed in a cassock made from the skin of a whale's penis, and he holds the blubber-room man down as though he's about to slice him to size for the try-pots, before letting him go again.

There is howls of laughter from the men watching. Hawk smiles his big white smile at the others in the blubber room and they ain't so stupid that they can't see that it carries a warning never to mock me again.

I am most shamed that me brother needs to defend me, though I be too tired to fight it. I tells meself that if it should ever come to an open fight, I'd even the score with me axe. But I know that Hawk's now a part o' me and that old Tommo is no longer alone in this world. And so I finishes me first watch in the blubber room.

The men is working 'round the clock to get the blubber into the try-pots so that it may be made into good oil, a most difficult task. The whale's tied by chains from its tail and head to the starboard side of the ship and the cutting platforms, hung from the ship's topside, is lowered to meet it. The cutting tackle is secured to the mainmast and also lowered so that the mates can begins the cutting in. With Crawlin Nestbyte dead and Seb Rawlings ill, two of the older, more experienced whalemen handles the cutting spades along with Tom Stubbs and Timbin Hollowtree, the third mate.

The men attaches the cutting tackle to the whale, using the blubber hook at its end. They cuts a long scarfing line about nine inches in width on either side o' the blubber hook. Then the hook is pulled upwards by the block-and-tackle and the mates frantically cuts the blubber to loosen it from the whale flesh. It's as though they is peeling a giant Spanish orange, though the blubber, if you can imagine it as orange skin, be about fifteen inches thick.

The power for the block-and-tackle is supplied by men working a windlass on deck, what is connected to ropes run down to it from the main top. The blubber peels off in a long, intact spiral what stretches from the whale right up to the topmast, pulling the whale's great carcass hard against the ship. The weight makes the vessel heel so that when the blanket of blubber is freed, the ship lurches violently back on her beam ends, as though buffeted by a stormy sea.

The long strips of blubber, what weighs as much as a ton, are then lowered by the tackle into the blubber room, where they's cut into slabs by the blubber-room men of the few toes. It is these self-same slabs of blubber which yours truly is required to lift and carry to the mincer. This cove cuts them into fine strips leaving only the skin attached so's the blubber now resembles the leaves of a book, known in whaleman lingo as bible leaves. These thin leaves, not much more than an inch thick, gives us the most oil. The bible leaves is placed into the bubbling try-pots and turned into oil, before being ladled into copper cooling-tanks and put into the cooper's casks.

If it all sounds simple enough, it seems to me a vision from the cavern of hell itself. At the cutting platform, not many inches from the surface of the water, the sharks is in a feeding frenzy, and the mates stabbing down at them with their cutting spades. This is no sport, for each shark killed means more blubber saved. A shark what's cut with the razor-sharp spade becomes the prey o' the other sharks, what's then distracted from the whale carcass as they turns to feed on their own kind.

Up on deck, the sails and rigging be completely clouded in black smoke while the deck is lit by the orange flames what keeps the oil hissing and bubbling in the try-pots. This fire ain't fed with wood for there ain't room enough on a whaler to carry timber. Instead the whale gives us the means to make its own oil. After the blubber is turned into oil, the skin and bits remaining, known as the fritters, is burned as fuel. The dense smoke makes it difficult to see. The men about the windlass be blackened by it, their faces like polished blackamoors' in the glare of the flames.

Every surface of the windlass and the decks, bulwarks, rails and try-works is covered in oil and slime from the whale. Inside the blubber room we is clothed in greasy duck and covered in oil, blood and blubber, as savage-looking a group of men as could be found on the face of the earth. The smell is beyond the ken of any landlubber. No abattoir or cesspool compares with the evil pong o' smoked blubber. This stink, once in the skin, can only be undone by weeks of scrubbing with lye. Us whalemen will be making our presence known to any what stands downwind for some time to come.

The *Nankin Maiden* pitches and rocks in the seas, like she's about to be engulfed in flames. And the rats is as many as ants at a picnic. They darts between our legs, feasting on the scraps 'til they's so bloated with blubber that they drags themselves along in the slime and may easily be kicked high over the ship's side as though they was footballs.

The final task is to take the precious spermaceti oil from the head of the whale. A hole is made in the whale's noggin and the spermaceti scooped out. This be a whitish, waxy liquid, what's five times more valuable than the best whale oil, and is used to make ointments and ladies' cosmetics. It makes the finest candles and incense what the Pope himself uses. The cow we took gives five barrels of this stuff and Hawk's large bull no less than twelve.

After me first watch I am too exhausted to feel shame that I would have collapsed had it not been for Hawk. But Billy Lanney comes up to me in the fo'c'sle and, patting me on the back, says in his peculiar lingo that I has done well. Such a job were for 'big pella' and the master be a 'plurry Kwaka Christmas sausage!' which I takes to mean, 'a bloody Quaker Christian savage!'

I crawls into me bunk and I has never slept more soundly in me life. I wouldn't have given a damn if the cockroaches had made merry over every inch of me body, though they was busy feasting elsewhere like the rats.

For two days and nights we works the try-pots and on my fourth watch, I am finally able to complete forking the heavy slabs of blubber without Hawk coming to my rescue. With a little help from his twin, yours truly has survived the ordeal what were meant to break him. Up yours, Captain O'Hara, sir!

At last we cuts the bloody remains of the whales loose and watches their blubber-stripped carcasses float away. The sharks still churn the water and tear ferocious at them, and ten thousand sea birds darts ever downwards for scraps. The top o' the whale carcasses look like giant rookeries with birds squabbling, wings flapping and beaks snapping for every available morsel o' flesh. In all the time we has been flensing the whales and boiling down their blubber, these birds has surrounded us with a screeching that has drowned out all other noise on deck and below, so that we must shout to be heard at more than a distance of three feet.

After the whales has floated far enough to the leeward away, so that they be two small dots on the horizon, I am amazed at the silence what surrounds us. It's like the great parties at the governor's mansion I has heard of, now finished and quiet, with every guest gone home again.

The first duty now, with the barrels stacked in the hold, is to wash down the decks and housing. This task is a tradition, a rite to bring successful hunts in the future. The men is knackered but they put great heart into the scrubbing of the decks, using absorbent cloths over their hands made from the tendons o' the whale.

Whale oil is most effective in removing stains of all kind and soon the vessel is ship-shape. But no amounts o' cleaning gets rid of the oily fish stink. Only the fo'c'sle, now lit by candles and whale-oil lamps, has a sweet smell. It don't take long though for the fo'c'sle to sink back to its former state, and who's to mind? Hawk is more particular about cleanliness than yours truly. Cards and sly grog is seldom found in clean-smelling places, and pipe smoke and spittoons is as much a part of a game of flats as the Joker in the pack. A little dirt don't hurt no one.

Hammerhead Jack is still alive. He is weak and in great pain, yet he never cries out. Under Hawk's tender care he is slowly mending. Billy Lanney has had a hand in this too.

The medicines Hawk got from Seb Rawlings did nothing to keep the Maori's shoulder socket from festering. His face were swollen mightily and his eye socket leaked pus and gore, despite Hawk cleaning it each day, along with the terrible shoulder wound. For days, Hammerhead Jack were in a constant fever and delirium. His men was ever at his side, never leaving, and it were clear they believed he would die.

It were Billy Lanney, ever the curious one, what comes over one morning to take a look, shaking his woolly head and clicking his tongue. Two days later he be back, carrying a small tin filled with live maggots. These worms does not come from his own back, what is now well scabbed, but were procured most cleverly.

After Billy sees Hammerhead Jack, he asks me to catch a fish and give it him. That afternoon when I comes off watch, I catches a nice-sized tuna, about six pounds. This I gives to him and he gets the cook to lay it on top of a salt-pork barrel in his galley overnight. By morning all the maggots in the pork has crawled out to find the fresh fish and Billy scoops them up and brings them to Hammerhead Jack, who is still fevered and unconscious.

Billy carefully makes two poultices of live maggots and puts one on Hammerhead Jack's shoulder and the other on his eye socket. He binds the shoulder loosely so's the maggots stays inside and covers the eye socket from the light. By the following morning the pus has gone, and the wounds be quite clean.

Hammerhead Jack is now making a slow recovery with no fevers to plague him. Billy's maggots does the task better than the captain's medicines what was bought at great cost.

It is two days after the cleaning and scrubbing of the ship and we has changed our course. It is said we be headed for New Zealand waters, the talk on board being that O'Hara hopes to pick up another ship's officer there to replace Nestbyte. No doubt he plans to make more trouble for Hawk once we reaches port!

The crew be resting up from the trying out and cleaning o' the ship. The hold is well over two-thirds full with barrels, and there's a feeling of calm. On Hawk's warning, I has lost several card games in the fo'c'sle and am telling the story of the killing of the sperm bull to as many as I can.

All seems well and so it knocks me for six when Captain

O'Hara sends Seb Rawlings and Tom Stubbs to arrest Hawk and the three Maori. He plans to try 'em for the murder of Crawlin Nestbyte.

I nearly panics but then takes heart, for the men's views has changed somewhat. Nestbyte is not missed and the fo'c'sle is a much calmer place for his death. I've been most careful to tell my cooked-up version of the hunt, making much of Hammerhead Jack's bravery and Hawk's courage in rescuing him when he were sinking in the briny in a foam of blood.

The crew already sees their bringing in a ninety-foot sperm whale as an awesome achievement, and Hawk, Hammerhead Jack and his Maori crew has become heroes of sorts. Although they's only a nigger and four kanakas, there is now a high regard for them, if for no other reason than each man on board will be more flush for their courage.

They has not forgotten, either, Hawk's backhanding of the cutter what scorned me. The man's name be Bob Jenkins and he's known to be a good fighter with a knife and unafraid with his fists. He's not small with it – fourteen stone and almost six foot, with good weight in his shoulders and nimble enough on his feet. News of Hawk's smashing him to the deck and then forking him up to the mincing man has spread throughout the ship. It has earned Hawk respect for his Herculean strength. The story grows more exaggerated daily. Jenkins is much shamed and vows he'll have his day.

When the master sends Rawling and Stubbs to fetch Nestbyte's crew and put them in chains, there is much unrest among the men. Hammerhead Jack is also brought into custody and on the Sabbath all is made to stand before the mainmast in front o' the entire crew.

Captain O'Hara is again dressed in his black Quaker suit with white lace bibby at his neck. Only his greasy stovepipe hat be the same as other days. He has in his left hand the Holy Bible which he holds against the pocket of his long coat. He looks 'round at us and begins to speak.

'We are gathered together here on the Sabbath and in the name of the Lord to witness that justice be done in the trial of the whaleboat crew under the command of the first officer of this ship. I have spent much time at prayer in the concern of the murder of Mr Nestbyte and have asked for higher guidance on the matter.' O'Hara frowns at the prisoners, what stand with their heads bowed before him. ' "I am not mocked, sayeth the Lord!" '

There is a groan from the crowd, for we has witnessed the Lord's word translated through the prayers of O'Hara before – and, o' course, through those of the recently deceased Nestbyte too. The Lord's instructions seldom turns out merciful to a whaleman. The crew be generally agreed that, if Christ Jesus were the skipper of a whaling vessel, there'd be none on board what would sign on with him, even though He could walk across the water to harpoon a whale.

'I have asked Mr Rawlings to speak on behalf of the prisoners,' Captain O'Hara now says, 'there being no one in their midst who can do so.'

'Me brother Hawk can, Cap'n, sir!' I shouts. 'If I may translate for him?'

The crew shouts their agreement. O'Hara has seen that the crew is of a contrary mood, and knows he's got to make his authority felt. 'We have heard sufficient of thy translations, boy!' he snaps. 'Thou and the nigger have not the sagacity to make a case for the defence!'

'Sir, I speaks only that me brother might speak. He is not without wit and is well learned at books. Has he not the right to defend hisself? May he be allowed to decide if Mr Rawlings be his defence or if he would speak for himself and the Maori?' I trembles at me boldness. But I must speak for Hawk, or die in the attempt.

'Oh, yes, thy brother we know already to be an expert at judging the whale after three months at sea, and he is a ship's surgeon too. Perhaps he is to be the judge and jury as well?' O'Hara says sarcastic.

'Cap'n, sir, it be one o' the rules of the sea that a seaman may speak in his own defence if he be accused.' I braves the mongrel once more, not knowing if what I says be true. But it becomes clear from the men's cheers that it is.

O'Hara's face grows red as I speaks and he begins to shake. 'Silence!' he roars. 'I am the captain of this ship and the law is mine to make while we are at sea! And make it I shall!' He draws breath. 'There is none amongst the kanakas who can speak English. Thy brother could accuse any of the crime and they could not defend themselves! Mr Rawlings will speak for all!' He turns and points to me. 'As for thee, boy, I will tolerate no damned sea lawyers on my ship! Another word from thee and it will see thee stretched to the mizzen mast. Thou art naught but a trouble-maker!'

The men is silent after this outburst. What shall become of Hawk? I despairs to meself. Then suddenly a weak voice is heard.

'Ork speak,' Hammerhead Jack croaks. He is being supported by the two younger Maori, for he is too weak to stand on his own feet. 'Him speak me!' He slowly raises his good arm and touches the two men on either side o' him, then points to the old man. 'Ork speak Maori all!'

O'Hara turns angrily to Seb Rawlings. 'What's he say? What's the savage say, Mr Rawlings?'

'He wants Hawk Solomon to speak on their behalf, Captain,' Seb Rawlings answers quietly, plainly gob-smacked. 'Perhaps, sir, it be best so done?'

O'Hara slaps the Bible to his knee. 'In the name of the

Lord Jesus Christ, have I not made it abundantly clear how we shall proceed! Thou shalt defend them and I prosecute.' He holds the Bible above his shoulder so that all may see it. 'The Lord God Almighty will be the judge!'

There is much murmuring and shuffling of feet among the crew but nothing further can be said. It be clear to all that Hawk and the four Maori is doomed. Me stomach grows cold. The mongrels is winning.

'I shall read from the book of Jonah,' Captain O'Hara thunders, opening the Bible. ' "And God created great whales, and every creature that moveth, which the water brought forth abundantly."

'God hath himself given us this abundance. The sperm whale is God's gift to us if we should observe His ways and be true to His faith. This we see to be near His first pronouncement in the book of Genesis, chapter one, verse twenty-one.' Captain O'Hara raises his head to look over us, for he stands on a small platform surrounding the mainmast what makes him taller than any man standing 'cept for Hammerhead Jack and Hawk, what's at eye-level with him.

'It is here we see that Jesus Christ our Lord created a special dispensation for those who hunt the whale. The great fish is His gift to mankind from the abundance He hath brought forth from the waters. He gave not permission to the fisherman to hunt the skipjack or the mackerel, nor to the hunter to hunt the deer or the mountain lion. But to the whaleman He gave the greatest creature upon the face of the earth, for hath He not made man in His image?'

O'Hara pauses and looks about, holding the Bible aloft. 'If you need proof of this, I shall give it you!' He has the Bible marked with a bookmark made of whalebone and he flaps it open and begins to read. ' "And the Lord spake unto the fish and it vomited up Jonah onto dry land." ' The master looks up and says with deliberate quiet, 'The book of Jonah in the Old Testament, chapter ten, verse two!'

I thought that Quakers didn't sermonise but said their prayers silent amongst themselves, but O'Hara is just like a preacher in his pulpit.

'Thus spake the Lord God,' he continues, 'proving that He places God-fearing man above the whale, that He hath given them dominion over the whale, causing the whale to vomit up upon dry land that which hath been taken against the will of God, the creator of heaven and earth!'

Captain Mordechai O'Hara glares at us for some moments. It's as though he wants one of us to challenge his Bible learning. 'Would any amongst thee dispute the word of God?' he asks.

Only Hawk among us would be able to do so, for he read the Bible twice-over on his voyage to England, it being the only book on board other than the *Apothecary for a Ship's Surgeon*, what he read five times. But he has his back to me so I cannot translate for him.

'Now comes the case for the prosecution,' O'Hara announces. He looks up to the top gallant as though for inspiration from on high. 'It is plain for all to see that God favours His Christian children in the contest between whale and man, or why else would He command the whale to vomit the prophet Jonah back onto dry land?

'I have been the captain of a whale ship a full twenty years and in that time have lost many a whaleman to the sperm, but only this once a Christian man! At all other times they have been heathens,' he points to Hammerhead Jack, 'like this kanaka! Niggers, cannibals and savages, or Papists from the godless South American ports or the Portugee, or men from Dublin. If not them, then heathen from the East Indies and godless Limeys.'

O'Hara points again to Hammerhead Jack. 'The Lord

hath clearly shown His direction in this when He took the arm and the eye of this hapless savage, intending him to drown – the arm which is used to throw the harpoon and the eye to aim it. God's message is abundantly clear. He took this heathen as the whale's sacrifice, knowing well that there is a Christian gentleman aboard!'

The master pauses. Well warmed-up to his mad notions, he looks about him, then points to Hawk. 'Thou rescued from the sea this heathen kanaka, and so did clearly transgress the will of God Almighty, Who had consigned him to his watery grave by removing his arm so that he could not swim!'

There is a grumbling among us what understands what the captain be saying, for many will be wounded in some future battle against the whale. Now we is being told that we won't be rescued 'less we is a Quaker Christian like our master. O'Hara takes no heed o' this muttering and mumbling from the men and continues to thunder at Hawk, shaking his finger at him.

'And then, when it behove God's servant, Mr Crawlin Nestbyte, to point out thy disobedience against the will of God, thou didst kill him with his own knife and throw him to the sharks!'

O'Hara speaks as though he himself has witnessed every part o' what took place. He snaps shut the Bible and with his free hand takes Nestbyte's bowie knife from his coat pocket, holding it high. 'This was the very knife used! The blood of human sacrifice is stained on the blade for all to see!'

There is a gasp from the crew, though most has long since lost the thread of O'Hara's reasoning.

'I rest my case,' Captain O'Hara says, most satisfied.

Seb Rawlings argues in Hawk and the Maori's defence. He tells Hawk's story as it were told that fateful night in the skipper's cabin, the version cooked up by yours truly. This he does most credibly, not missing much of the detail.

The men already knows the tale well and they nods in agreement as they hears it. Seb Rawlings be a plain speaker and it's clear they believes what he says to be true. They has all known danger while hunting the whale, and they knows the peril of bein' on his windward side. At the end of the mate's speech, the crew claps.

But their support has no effect on the captain. He steps forward. 'So be it,' he says, most abrupt. 'Now to the judgment of the Lord, who looks into all our hearts that He may find the truth!'

O'Hara drops to his knees on the deck and, clasping the Bible to his chest, raises his head towards the topmast and begins to pray, his lips moving silently. The men stands awkward, heads bowed, caps in hand, waiting, none daring to move, 'til a full five minutes later when O'Hara opens his eyes and rises, still holding the Bible to his chest.

' "I am not mocked, sayeth the Lord,"' he says in a deep, slow voice. Then he turns to Hawk. 'The Lord Jesus Christ hath spoken to me in a clear voice and I am commanded to say to thee: Thou, Hawk Solomon, and thou, Hammerhead Jack and your fellow kanakas, have received the sanction of the Lord Christ Jesus who hath sentenced each of thee to fifty lashes. Furthermore, from each of thee shall be confiscated that portion of the lay, the profit from the oil rendered from both whales most recent caught, when the final disbursement shall take place. This is the will of the Lord, till ye may be judged by temporal justice, the will of courts ashore.'

The men break into hubbub and O'Hara waits for them to quieten. The sentence is harsh, but those what stands before the mast of a whaling ship are brutal men. If they cares to give credit to a God at all, they counts His bounty by the number o' barrels contained in the hold. They praises Him if there be many and curses Him if there be few.

O'Hara now turns to the three mates. 'Mr Stubbs, Mr Hollowtree and Mr Rawlings, ye shall each administer fifty lashes upon the three Maori men and I shall fulfil my Christian duty by doing the same,' he points to Hammerhead Jack, 'to this damned kedger.' Then he pauses and looks over the heads of the men gathered about him. 'Bob Jenkins, where art thou? Come forward if you please,' he commands.

Jenkins, the blubber cutter what Hawk has forked to the mincer, steps out of the crowd.

'Yes sir, Cap'n,' he says, touching his cap.

'Thou shalt take the lash to the nigger!'

Jenkins grins widely. 'I shall do me very best, Cap'n.'

It be agreed that the mates shall go first, then Jenkins and finally the captain. The lashings is terrible and there is much yelling and groaning from the three Maori, what collapses to the deck sobbing when they is cut down. They are brave lads and the crew does not reckon them cowards for this. Fifty lashes with the knotted rope has been known to kill a man and there's very few like Billy Lanney, what be strong enough to accept such punishment in silence.

Then me brother's blouse is removed and he is tied to the mast. Jenkins steps forward, holding the bloody rope with a great grin upon his ugly gob. I vows that if ever we be ashore and I discovers where he is, I will take with me axe no less than three fingers from the very hand what holds the lash with such pleasure.

Jenkins flogs me brother, and Hawk jerks with each violent blow. Hawk makes no sound but, because he is dumb, the men don't see this as courage under the lash. Many winces though at the force Jenkins puts behind every blow. The blubber man grunts with each lash he places, and Hawk gets much the worst of the four beatings. My eyes smart with tears and I tremble with anger. The sod will pay for this.

At last it ends. They cut Hawk loose and he stands bleeding, though his head is not bowed. Slow tears squeeze from his eyes as he looks at me and sees that I too am weeping. Meanwhile, poor Hammerhead Jack is being lifted to his feet by the two mates, Tom Stubbs and Timbin Hollowtree. He is too weak to stand alone and when the Maori were beaten he was left to lie upon the deck. Now he struggles to rise with the support o' the two ship's officers. There is no fear in his eyes, though it's clear he has no strength left in his great body, and has lost much weight since the whale hunt. Through me tears I see that Hawk is talking to me with his hands and wants to address the captain.

I brush me eyes and step forward. 'Permission to speak, Cap'n, sir,' I says respectfully.

O'Hara stares at me. He has already taken the blood-soaked lash from Jenkins. 'What is it, boy?'

'Sir, me brother Hawk wishes to address you.'

'Hast thou not had enough then, nigger?' O'Hara scowls at Hawk.

Hawk speaks to me rapidly with his hands and I translates.

'Me brother wishes to accept the lashes on behalf of Hammerhead Jack.'

A murmur of shock passes through the crew and only then I realise what me lips have said. 'Hawk, no,' I protest, but he fixes me with such a look that I has no choice but to go on.

'The Maori is much weakened,' I hears meself say. 'He will die if he receives the knotted rope!'

'It is God's will that he should die!' O'Hara thunders. 'The Devil hath taken possession of thy soul, nigger! Thou hast once before disobeyed the Almighty in this matter, now, damn thee, thou wouldst do so again!' O'Hara is shaking all over, his fury risen to a pitch. The lash in his hands drips bright red onto his boot.

Now some of the crew what's been grumbling starts to shout. There is a growing anger amongst them for they realises that Captain O'Hara means to kill the giant Maori. Hammerhead Jack be only a savage but our good captain has gone beyond what even these port rats will stand. The islanders also have realised what is afoot and they too is growling, their fists held taut to their sides. Me heart begins to pound. The pack is turning on its master!

It is then that Seb Rawlings steps up to stand beside O'Hara. He has the captain's Bible and he raises it up. 'Silence!' he shouts. 'Be silent!' The men quietens down a bit. 'Silence there!' Rawlings shouts again, pointing to a small group o' Irishmen what still mutters angrily at the back o' the pack. 'Silence, you lot, or you'll have me to reckon with!' Finally all is quiet and he begins to speak.

'Captain O'Hara has already shown much of God's infinite mercy in dealing with this matter,' Rawlings says. 'I know him well enough to say that he will again put this matter to prayer so that God's will may be done.'

O'Hara jerks back in surprise at the fourth mate's words but he holds his tongue, allowing Rawlings to continue.

The fourth mate points to Hammerhead Jack. 'If God should intend this kanaka to die, He would have done so by means of natural causes abundantly available to him in the past few days. So, if the Lord God be our judge, as the captain has told us clear, and I be the defence, then I must ask Captain O'Hara to allow the Judge of Heaven to make a decision on this new request!

'I must most humbly ask, does God the Judge wish the kanaka to die at the hands of the prosecution? Or will He accept the plea for mercy from the defence? If He is the merciful judge, then I ask that He make the same judgment He made for the prophet Abraham – that Hawk Solomon, like the ram caught in a thicket near Abraham's sacrifice of his son, be allowed as a substitute to the taking of a poor man's life.'

I am astonished at Seb Rawlings' learning. His knowledge o' the Bible is even more amazing for he does not seem religious and is the only one among the mates what ain't a Quaker. Captain O'Hara suddenly shakes himself, as though Rawlings has called him from some sort o' pious trance.

'So be it,' he growls. He hands the lash to Rawlings in return for the Bible and once more goes to his knees on the deck. We all holds our breath as we waits for the result o' his silent prayer. Finally, after three or four minutes has passed, he rises and turns slowly to Hawk.

'There is something of God in all of us – even in thee and the savage whom thou dost wish to spare the lash. The Lord hath spoken to me and thou shalt take unto thyself the kanaka's punishment.'

Hawk's back already bleeds freely from Jenkins' flogging, and the top o' his canvas breeches is soaked full to his knees with blood. But he is calm as they ties him again to the mainmast. The captain takes up the lash and begins lashing me brother.

I can't do nothing but watch as Hawk silently takes the savage blows. The mongrels is back, and beating me twin. You bastard, I sobs to meself. I'll get you too, whatever the cost! You, O'Hara, and you, Jenkins, both shall taste the edge of my axe! I swear it or I die!

O'Hara pants with the effort as he completes his gruesome task, Timbin Hollowtree counting each lash. Hawk's once-smooth ebony back is ripped to raw and broken flesh, the runnels of one lash running into the others.

The captain's bibby is completely bloodstained, his dark coat wet to the front, and he has small scraps of red flesh caught up in his black beard. He strikes again and Hawk gives a soft moan.

At first I doesn't realise what I've heard. But another groan follows and yet a third, this time louder. I cannot believe my ears! Sobs catch in my throat. It is the first sound I've heard from Hawk's mouth since the day we was kidnapped.

Chapter Six

HAWK

The Pacific Ocean
January 1857

Tommo has spent all his gambling winnings on medicines for my back and for the Maori. This is mostly sulphur ointment and cheap enough ashore, though Tommo has been made to pay almost as much money as a whaleman would receive in wages after a successful two-year voyage. It is beyond all reckoning for the cost of medicines. Captain O'Hara has extorted this payment as further punishment and I have begged Tommo not to purchase the ointment, thinking we will heal as fast without it. But he will not hear of it.

'If I spends all I has it's in the best cause,' he replies and then grins. 'The lashes came hard, the winnings was easy.'

Our ship is sailing towards New Zealand waters from our position south of the Cook Islands. Captain O'Hara seeks a new first mate, or if not a first, then a new mate with experience, who has led a whaleboat crew.

There has been a robust migration of free settlers to the New Zealand shores, though not too many decent folk are among them. Even the missionaries are more concerned with buying up the land than preaching God's word. The

Europeans are largely from New South Wales, including escaped convicts and a great many ex-convict deserters from ships. It is estimated that there are three thousand of the latter scattered throughout the islands of the Pacific Ocean and half a thousand again in New Zealand. It's said that they have heard 'the wail of the wahine' and their bastard half-caste children may be seen on every island where there is a native tribe. This new generation is strong too, for they seem to be immune to the white man's diseases which now play havoc amongst the kanakas.

These new settlers have brought with them the European diseases of influenza, measles, small pox, venereal pox and consumption as well as other maladies. Measles has killed tens of thousands of islanders and as many again of the Maori. For every half-caste and white child born in New Zealand, ten Maori children have perished. This much I have learned from my reading.

It is amongst this motley crew that O'Hara hopes to find the man he needs. And so we sail to the whaling settlement of Kororareka in the Bay of Islands, a town long known as a centre of infamy and drunkenness, where at least three hundred whalemen reside.

The men are much excited about leave ashore, for they hope to encounter the 'dark, restless-eyed woman' as the Maori wahine is known amongst sailors. I cannot say that such a prospect does not excite me also, for I'm a man and so by nature weak of flesh. I have not yet taken a woman to my bed. I can only hope that the lighter, brown-skinned Maori will not see me as a nigger and despise me for the colour of my skin.

Six months have passed since we left Hobart Town and it will be good to feel land under our feet again. All the same, I would think O'Hara much better advised to sail on across the Tasman Sea to Australia, where he would more easily find a mate to suit his needs and meet our needs as well. Tommo and I intend to jump ship in Sydney or some other civilised port at the first opportunity.

We have grown weary of life at sea. Although it has provided me with a great adventure, this has been offset by a catastrophe and a brutal punishment which I did not deserve.

In truth, whaling is mostly an adventure to speak about at a later time, in the comfort of a warm parlour or in the company of men at an ale house. Mostly it is endless days of great tedium and repetition, with the hunting of the whale a rare interlude that we have encountered only once these six months.

We spent Christmas aboard the ship, a hot, sultry day with little wind. There was naught to mark it as a special day, save an hour-long sermon from the captain. Our rations were unchanged, salt beef and longlick, with not even a fish from Tommo to add to our repast, his efforts that day being unsuccessful and much curtailed by the captain's prayers.

For the Maori and islander crew, Christmas was a day as any other. But for me, it was a time of homesickness. Though Tommo and I are Jewish by birth, still Christmas was always observed in our family because of Mary, who made an occasion for yet another roast dinner. My thoughts turned time and again to our mama, home without her boys. I wondered if she had spread her white tablecloth out – probably not, she doesn't like to fuss over herself. Tommo was no comfort either that day. It being Christmas, the crew are merry enough and it is a grand opportunity for a game of cards in the fo'c'sle. Tommo does not share my sentiments, as there was no Christmas for him in the wilderness. When I came to sit with him at cards, the look he gave me made me feel more his keeper than his twin.

I am not yet fully convinced that Tommo has forsworn the demon grog. My hope is that his enforced abstinence may prove permanent and will rob him of the will to gamble, for grog and cards go hand in glove. With the one practised, the other must surely follow as night follows day.

The infamous settlement of Kororareka is just the place to test Tommo's resolve and I am ashamed to say I have great misgivings. I'm not at all sure that Tommo does not try to gull me with his claims that his need for ardent spirits has been quenched and that he will forsake gambling when we come ashore. He plays cards at every opportunity, now saying it is money for the medicine we need to cure our backs. He still wins too often for my comfort and each day I fear the men will flush him out in his use of relocation. But when I warn him he merely laughs.

'I ain't gunna relocate with *these* partners – they all be plough boys and dockside scum before they comes to whaling, half-wits and duffers! You insults me natural talents, Hawk, to say I relocate with them lot.'

Relocation was a favourite expression of Ikey Solomon's. In the beginning, Tommo's skill with cards came from Ikey's assiduous training. He taught us when we were small brats how to palm a card and a host of other nefarious tricks, each of which he would refer to as, 'One of life's little essentials, my dears.'

The idea of these 'little essentials' was that if a man should find himself in Timbuktu, broke and knowing nothing of the people, language or society, he could, through their use, earn himself a plate of food, a roof for the night and an ounce of shag. Ikey's 'little essentials' were a means of survival until the morning.

Ikey placed dexterity with a pack of cards as the topmost of these 'essentials' even before reading and writing. 'Every man on earth will gamble if he be given half a chance. The deck o' cards may be found from Bombay to Peking, Samarkand to Sydney, Cairo to the Cape o' Good Hope and London to New York. Like the roach, the flea and the bed bug, they are universally to be found wherever men congregate. The flats be a universal language, my dears, known to every level of society and transcending every tongue that man doth babble.

'There are rules to be learned by observation and, once mastered, to be broken. In any game o' chance, as much of the chance as possible must be removed. And success in any card game may be assured by placing a card where no card is thought to be. Relocation, my dears, that is it in a nutshell. And the most important requirement for relocation be dexterity, nerve, courage and a nimble mind.'

'Relocation? You mean cheating!' I once ventured when he talked of this.

'Cheating? Did I hear you say cheating, my dear?'

I nodded.

'Cheating be something what's done by them what's stupid and quickly found out. Cheating is in the dark, it looks over its shoulder, it pads on tender feet. It is a sneak, a dark thing. Cheating is not for the likes of you two, my precious little gentlemen. Relocation is the word, the word of princes and kings. Cheating is for beggars and vagabonds.'

'But is it not another name for cheating, then?' I asked again.

'Most certainly and decidedly not!' Ikey replied. 'Nimble minds, nimble fingers that never tremble and a look what betrays not the slightest beating of the heart go into relocation. All the skills of relocation depend on it taking place in the open, in the broadest daylight, completely kosher, cards seen by all who play with you.'

Ikey grabbed a pack of cards and shuffled it in a blur,

spreading it with a great flourish across the table, with every card in its right place and right colour. One to nine, ten, Jack, King, Queen, Ace of Hearts, Spades, Diamonds, Clubs and Jokers at the very end.

'Now that ain't possible!' he crowed. 'If a man should shuffle a deck a million times, and then a million more, it ain't possible for the cards to come out in the right colour, correct sequence and nomination. It ain't possible, but you've just seen it done, my dears. Right in front o' your very eyes, shuffled and spread, fair and square! That be the noble art of relocation.'

He pushed the cards together again and, in a flash, shuffled and spread them into a fan shape once more.

'What's missing, gentlemen?'

'The ten of all suits!' Tommo shouted gleefully.

'Very good!' Ikey said, pushing the deck together again. He shuffled and spread, and there were all the tens, sitting back in their rightful place.

'Now you see it, now you don't. But you don't know you don't see it, until it turns up in a flush or a straight where it's least expected.' Ikey scooped the cards into a deck and without looking he said, 'A Jack, is it? Snap!' Down went a Jack. 'Fancy a nine of hearts and diamonds to make a much-needed pair? Snip! Snap! Or an ace to make the trump? Snap!' Tommo and I stared open-mouthed as he laid down one card after the other, not even looking at the deck in his hand. 'What a lovely coincidence, don't you think, my dears?'

Then Ikey pointed a long finger at us, his eyes rolling. 'Never an extravagance, you understand. A royal flush or four of a kind be a most dangerous boastification. They must come naturally, by means of chance and skill, but *never*, you understand, by relocation. Winning at the flats must not be come at with a drum-roll, but with the timpani of fingernails on a velvet pad. Modesty of purpose, my dears, that be the golden rule. The card you need when you need it and sometimes, if the pot be a small one, a restraint even with the restraint already shown.

'The great knack of winning,' he continued, 'is to look as if at any moment you might lose. Touch the forehead with the finger tips, rub a little, sniff, click your tongue – but not too much. Nothing bolsters the courage of a punter more, or deadens the brain more effectively, than a little acted clumsiness and a downcast expression.

'Cards, my precious little gentlemen, will buy you food and shelter, a good cigar and a little companionship wherever you be on this mortal coil. Learn the flats well and they will be your friends forever.' Again he rolled his eyes and spread his long fingers. 'But one more caution. Never practise relocation when it ain't necessary. Relocation is a compliment to be paid only to those who be your equals in the game you play.'

From that moment on, Tommo took to the flats like they were an extension of his fingers. Even as a brat, he always carried a deck. He'd constantly finger the cards in his pockets, calling for me to name one and then producing it blind as though by some sort of magic. His skill astounded me for my hands were clumsy and my mind elsewhere, in books.

When we were kidnapped on the mountain, Tommo had in his pockets a deck of new cards that Ikey had given him for helping at the races. He later told me that without them he could not have survived, for Ikey was right – the gambler is to be found in every man, whether nabob or wood cutter. Even the damage done to his hands didn't stop him.

Ikey had been most pleased with Tommo's talents as a little lad. There was only one other his age who could match him, he said, a boy in London by name of Sparrer

Fart, also trained by Ikey in his Methodist Academy of Light Fingers.

'Sparrer Fart, if he should be here, would be too good even for you, Tommo, my dear. You must work harder to beat the Splendour of the Sparrer!'

And that, I think, is part of the trouble. Even in the wilderness, after losing all that you could call his life, Tommo took with him Ikey's challenge. Whenever it was bleak for him, which seems by all accounts to have been most of the time, he would seek the comfort of the cards. 'I'm gunna beat the Splendour of the Sparrer,' he would say to himself. This he has done. But his astonishing skill has brought with it a life that will destroy him.

Since Captain O'Hara's flogging, we have grown even closer to the Maori crew. Tommo, who is more clever than he knows, has begun to speak their language, and I to understand it. Hammerhead Jack confounds us all with the speed of his recovery and with Tommo feeding him fresh fish, he grows stronger every day. Tommo has been catching much tuna lately and Jack eats it raw, taken with a little salt and molasses which we save for him from our rations.

My back is healing well, though I never thought that I should learn to sleep on my stomach. As my wounds begin to bind, I often wake with a great itching to find a hundred cockroaches grazing upon the scabs like contented cows. At first, this disgusted me to the point of crying out. But Billy Lanney, who is an expert on matters of the lash, bade me be patient and led me to understand that these vile vermin do much good. Like the maggots in Hammerhead Jack's suppurating arm and eye, they keep the wounds clean.

We've learned that Hammerhead Jack is of the Ngati Haua tribe, though his hero is Hone Heke, leader of the Nga Puhi. Jack tells me that Hone Heke was the fiercest of warriors and also the first chief to sign the Treaty of Waitangi which recognised the sovereignty of Queen Victoria over the Land of the Long White Cloud, or Aotorea as the Maori call their country. Though Hammerhead Jack is too low-born to be a chief himself, he is most intelligent and a natural leader of men.

Hammerhead Jack has taken to walking about the deck again and the whalemen, whoever they be, kanaka, white man or nigger, have a new respect for the one-armed giant. His missing right eye makes him most formidable in appearance, so that grown men stand aside as he passes by.

If Captain O'Hara should happen along, then Hammerhead Jack will grin his big white smile, and be as pleasant as can be imagined in his greeting. But his smile does not soothe the Quaker master, who growls and scowls and sometimes, if he is close by, spits over the ship's rails. Never does he return the Maori's salutations.

Tommo has asked the other Maori what they might do when we make landfall in New Zealand. They shrug and point to Hammerhead Jack. 'It is for him to say.' Although he is not *rangatira* or noble born, they see him as their leader. But, of course, Hammerhead Jack will be put ashore without further ado. Captain O'Hara has bled him dry of his share of whale oil entitlements and regards him as a useless kedger not to be tolerated on board a moment longer. What perhaps he does not understand is that he loses all three Maori when he throws Hammerhead Jack aside. He will lose a whaleboat crew of much valuable experience, aside from me.

Tommo has grown more excited by the day as he coaxes a voice from my throat. At first I could make only a feeble grunt or two but he is wondrously patient and spends hours mouthing sounds he thinks I might produce, vowels in particular. I doubt he remembers that they are called vowels, but he offers these sounds as though by instinct. He works me until the pain in my throat is almost unbearable and then has me gargle with sea water. He insists I gargle every hour and when he is not on watch he attends to it himself.

Already I am making progress and hope in a week or so to say my first two words. These Tommo has decided upon as well as the following two. The first will be 'Tommo Solomon' and the next will complete the sentence, 'Tommo Solomon loves me!'

By the time we enter the harbour at Kororareka I am possessed of a voice that, while slow to form the words on my tongue, has a complete enough vocabulary of sounds. These sounds have grown familiar to my ear although my pronunciation is not always correct. The trouble is that while I hear the words as I have always done, my tongue can not yet form them clearly. But I am on my way and before long shall speak as a normal man, with perhaps a deep rasping that comes from a throat grown rusty in all the years I have been without a voice.

It is a strange sensation that I may now communicate without waiting for Tommo to cast his eyes in my direction first, and I am not yet accustomed to people looking upon me when I speak. It seems odd that their attention is not on Tommo, or Mary, as the case may be. I have grown so much a listener over the years that I doubt I shall ever be the main spokesman in any conversation.

Ikey would often say that I had been given a great gift in being without voice. 'Congratulations, my dear! You have been forcibly given the gift o' listening. That be very high up on the order as one of life's little essentials. Your ears be perfect tuned to savour the essence of every voice you hear. Mostly we drowns out listening with the need to hear our own voices. No man finds a voice sweeter to his ear than his own. But if you wants to know what's in a man's soul, listen to him, listen to his silences, they be louder than his words. Then listen to his speech, listen to what he's saying behind his voice. The conversation going on in a man's head be the one that tells you the most.'

By following Ikey's advice – though of course I had no option but to do so! – I have indeed learned a great deal about people. If the relocation of cards was Ikey's major gift to Tommo, then the skill of listening was his gift to me. Listening is my true language and I do not think I shall ever forsake it.

Kororareka is a settlement with nigh two thousand Europeans and numerous natives. The Maori to be found here are, for the most part, a poor-looking lot. They dress in flaxen mats or dirty blankets, though some who have prospered from port trade are in silk top hats and polished boots, with gold watches attached to chains looped across their large bellies.

A few quiet families are to be seen and children also, half-caste, Maori and European, many of them dirty and barefoot with snotty noses. It is a town well past its prime, though that itself was short-lived enough, I'm told.

Kororareka is a whaling town, possessed of five hotels, numerous grog shops, gambling hells and brothels. Drunkenness and lechery are everywhere to be observed, with the Maori man and his wahine consorts as bad as any whaleman. The dark alleys are filled with laughter and the grunts and groans of whalemen who have waited long enough to be serviced by the honey-skinned wahine at the cost of a silver shilling and a jigger or two of Bombay gin or sailor's rum.

It is in this very town that Hammerhead Jack's hero, Hone Heke, confronted the British some twelve years ago.

Grown tired of British duplicity, he withdrew his allegiance to the Crown and showed his contempt for the symbol of British sovereignty by cutting down the flagstaff from which the Union Jack flew. He then sacked the town. Most Europeans contend that the reason for the chief's outrage was that the British had imposed onerous customs duties on Kororareka so as to encourage trading vessels to call at the new capital of Auckland instead. This meant that the local Maori were deprived of their earnings from the port's trade in flax and ship's spars, pigs and potatoes.

But Hammerhead Jack refutes this. Hone Heke, he says, had come to the conclusion that the Treaty of Waitangi was most treacherous to the Maori people, for it was an attempt by the settlers to steal their land.

From our conversations with the Maori on board, we have learned of some of their beliefs. Paramount among these, as far as we can understand, is that by swearing allegiance to Queen Victoria and signing the Treaty of Waitangi, the Maori believed unequivocally that they had transferred merely the 'shadow of the land' to the British monarch, and that the substance remained their own.

'We cannot sell the land to the European, for it is not ours to sell,' explains Hammerhead Jack. 'One man, one chief, does not own the land. The land is owned by the Maori people and they would all have to come to one voice and one opinion if they were to give up forever their land.'

Hammerhead Jack waves his lone paw and makes a point too obvious to contest. 'Why would my people sell what is their *mana*, their spirit, their life force? Papatuanuku is our earth mother and we her children. Who would sell their mother? Land,' he explains, 'may only be gained by one tribe from another through war. Then it may be used by the victors, but it is still owned by the Maori. It keeps our *mana*, which is the same for all the tribes. The pakeha who wish to use the land may purchase its *shadow*, if the Maori tribe who control it agree. But though he may enjoy it and grow his crops upon it or graze his sheep over it, he may never own it! The *substance* must always belong to the Maori people, only the *shadow* of the land may be sold to the pakeha.'

It is a difficult concept for us who are not Maori, but it is Ikey again who helps me to comprehend the idea. For Ikey believed that property was also 'one of life's little essentials'. When telling me of the marvels of London, he would always explain how the English nobility are able to retain their fortunes and protect themselves against loss, even though they might spawn children who are drunkards and wastrels. The gentry build great terrace houses in the most salubrious parts of the city which may be leased for a period of a hundred years. If the purchaser of the lease wishes to vacate after only a few years he may re-sell what remains of the hundred-year period to another lessee, who may do the same again until the hundred years are up. Then the property reverts to the descendants of the nobleman who built it. They will then put it up for lease for another hundred years and, in this way, the aristocracy of England never lose the property they own, even if their sons prove profligate in the extreme and squander their inheritances.

I think upon this and decide that it is not so very different from the Maori selling the *shadow* of the land but retaining its *substance*. The British themselves have created a precedent and it would seem to me that those who own most of the land in Britain have their own kind of *mana*. They see themselves as the guardians of the spirit of their land, always maintaining the substance while leasing the shadow to any newcomer.

The great chief, Hone Heke, came to the conclusion that the *mana* of his land, its spirit and nourishment, had been stolen by Queen Victoria. The Maori people had become her slaves, for only the shadow has been given to them and the substance taken by the Europeans. Already twenty million acres of land have been purchased by the whites, who see this land as belonging to them for eternity. They see no cause for future redress to the Maori people, and what they have claimed, they will defend, if necessary, at the cost of Maori lives.

I am deeply saddened by this knowledge. If, as I have come to think, a good man must have a conscience, then the New Zealand Maori is much cheated by the rapacious white, who has shown no conscience whatsoever in his dealings with the land's original owners. Who amongst us is a good man, then?

As always, the church, which claims to be the custodian of the conscience of man through the salvation of Christ Jesus, is foremost among the greedy. It claims a large portion of the twenty million acres, some of which has been purchased at a cost of ten pounds for each four hundred acres, but most of which has been obtained for a few trinkets.

From the beginning, when in 1814 the Reverend Samuel Marsden, notorious chaplain of New South Wales, was instructed to establish the first missionary settlement in the Bay of Islands, Christ has become the major property owner in New Zealand. Jesus is now Hammerhead Jack's landlord.

There is no admission from the pulpit that the church owns only the *shadow* of the land. Instead these holy men give twice-on-Sunday praise to God that He has bequeathed them in perpetuity this new Land of Milk and Honey, this second Canaan, this green and pleasant paradise upon the earth.

It was this which caused Hone Heke to become disenchanted with the British since the signing of the Treaty of Waitangi. Queen Victoria, in return for dominion over Hona Heke's people, promised so much, but instead her rule has brought the Maori guns with which to kill each other in ever increasing numbers, disease, drunkenness, and a dependence on the white man amounting to virtual slavery. This is the real substance of her promises, so that the Maori are but a shadow of the mighty people they once were.

This is the New Zealand to which Hammerhead Jack returns, without one arm and one eye. A young whaleman who has been thus used by the white man is coming home for more of the same.

Since Hone Heke's vengeance destroyed the town, Kororareka has grown back in a most higgledy-piggledy manner and shows no promise of improving. The buildings, but for a very few, are rickety tin and timber affairs, with no sense of permanence about them. We are not anchored in the bay more than twelve hours before we learn that there is much foment among the Maori people. The great chiefs are once again on the warpath.

Our friendship with Hammerhead Jack is cut short when Captain O'Hara dismisses him from his service. It is a sad moment for Tommo and me. We have both grown most fond of the giant Maori, whose arm stump is not yet completely healed but which, he assures me, will soon enough be cured with the good medicine of his tribe.

Our friend will take with him only his few belongings, and a paper given him by O'Hara which shows how his lay has been fully and 'legally' used up with the provision of goods from the ship. Of course, there is no mention that these goods were, in every case, medicine to which he was freely entitled. The Maori is made to place his mark upon a duplicate and this is witnessed by Tom Stubbs. He will be rowed ashore on the morning tide.

I carefully explain to Hammerhead Jack in his own language that what has been done to him is unlawful and that he should complain to the colonial authorities, who may impound the ship while his case is heard.

But he scorns this. 'I am of the Ngati Haua. We do not go snivelling to the British! Their laws have robbed us of our *mana* and turned my people into drunkards.' He gives a bitter laugh. 'Look at me, Ork. Why should they take the word of a one-armed, half-blind Maori against the white captain of a whaling ship, who professes himself a Christian like Queen Victoria?'

I have long since known that Hammerhead Jack is not an ignorant savage and that he understands much more of the English language than he would admit to. I have also come to respect his understanding of the Maori situation with the pakeha intruder. He has often been surprisingly even-handed, admitting that much of what has happened to the Maori since the white man came is due to the wars they have waged amongst themselves, albeit with the use of the white man's gun.

'Our people must stand together against the white man or we are lost,' he has said often enough.

But I cannot convince him to pursue his case against O'Hara.

'If I complain against this madman O'Hara, then I am again a member of the British tribe.' Hammerhead Jack turns aside and spits his disgust. 'Accepting their justice and their ways in the past have not been good for my people. Why should I trust them to give me justice now?'

I search for words in my disbelief. 'You mean you will simply let this man go free, having beaten you and then robbed and cheated you?'

Hammerhead Jack throws back his head and laughs. 'With your new voice, will you complain for me, Ork?'

'Yes! Yes! I will go with you!' I insist. For a moment I feel almost confident that the law will prevail against the Yankee whaling captain.

'Don't be such a bloody stupid bastard, Hawk!' Tommo interrupts. 'It's bad enough a Maori complaining. What hope has a nigger got?'

I am at first hurt by my twin's outburst, but then I see the point and smile. 'You could do it, Tommo,' I reply, feeling brave. 'I will prepare an affidavit and tell you what to say. There would be no problems with the colour of *your* eyes and skin!'

'Me?' Tommo says, shocked. 'I trust them buggers less than Hammerhead Jack does! You can stuff yer affydavy up yer bum!'

Then, to my surprise, Hammerhead Jack, who gives no sign that he is listening, speaks to us in English. 'We do Maori way, Ork,' he says quietly.

The following morning with the six o'clock tide, Hammerhead Jack is lowered into a whaleboat carrying only a small canvas bag with his belongings. He waves his single arm at me as I stand much saddened by his departure. 'Ork good!' he shouts, then throws his head back and laughs. His laughter carries across the water and I am forced to laugh too.

'He be a good man,' Tommo says softly beside me. 'I hope we meets again.'

We are permitted to go ashore that afternoon. The whole crew has been granted shore leave, with the exception of the three remaining Maori, who are placed on watch by Captain O'Hara, under the supervision of Seb Rawlings. The skipper has refused them leave to go with Hammerhead Jack, though it is plain they wish to follow him. He says they must see out the voyage and guards them closely. O'Hara and the two other mates are also to go ashore, and a whaleboat will be beached for any who wish to return on board fifteen minutes before the midnight hour.

From the first of the morning light, Tommo has been anxious to go ashore. My heart is filled with trepidation that he will not be able to resist the first grog shop we come upon. There is nothing to do in this whaling town but drink and fornicate, and we have been told by the Maori that the pox is rampant among the wahine who frequent the grog dens, gin shops and brothels. 'You must not take these women!' Hammerhead Jack warns us. I am much afeared that Tommo will not be able to resist the temptation of hard liquor and so I conceal from him that I have money, hoping meanwhile that he has spent what coin he has won on medicine for our backs.

But, of course, I am deluding myself. The lack of money never vexes Tommo. He is a prime example of the value of Ikey's 'little essentials'. With a deck of cards and a space at the table Tommo can have cash in his hands in a matter of moments. Even if no card game is to be found, he will win the drink he needs by demonstrating his sleight of hand to the wonderment of all who watch. He can pluck a card from behind a whaleman's ear. He can make him shake the sleeve of his coat to watch the ace of spades he has nominated just a moment before fall from beyond the cuffs. He can even pluck one from the bosom of a doxy.

But Tommo surprises me when we come ashore. We visit many a grog shop and all five hotels and even a brothel, where we pass the time until the madam sees we are not customers and throws us out. Tommo asks me to buy two packs of cards, as he says his old ones are too well worn to be used on board and the others think he cheats by knowing every crease upon them. He picks two packs, one red and the other blue, both made by DeLarue & Sons, and asks me to hold them for him until we return to ship. And then it is onwards again. We enjoy the music and, at one hotel, the singing of six wahines who render love songs in a harmony to break any sailor's heart.

Tommo will not tarry long at any place but wants to see every hell-hole, grog den, gin palace, rum shop and hotel in this poxy whaling settlement. Card games are everywhere to be found. Men are going furiously at them in the one-shilling hells where they beckon him over and invite him to play. But Tommo shakes his head and grins. 'Too easy to take yer coin, lads!' It is as grand an exhibition of abstinence as ever I've seen and I am truly proud of Tommo.

In the course of the evening we meet every whaleman who has come ashore from the *Nankin Maiden*. At a hotel which is more salubrious, though only by comparison with the others, Captain O'Hara is to be seen seated in a private room leading from the main saloon. He is interviewing seamen to find a replacement for the late and unlamented Crawlin Nestbyte.

Several men sit on chairs outside this room with their knees held tightly together and their caps on their laps, in the manner of men anxious to make a good impression. They are a seedy looking lot, with raw faces and complexions which suggest that the rum bottle is a frequent gargle against the debilitating effects of inclement weather. O'Hara will be hard put to find a Christian gentleman among this scurvy assortment!

Tommo moves ever onwards from one hell-hole to another, but never a glass of spirits touches his lips nor a deck of cards his hands. His blue eyes dart everywhere and it is as though he is drinking in the sights and sounds he has missed for so long, that they are grog enough for him.

I am so proud of him, for he has been true to his word. I am already envisaging our happy return to Hobart Town and to our dear Mary, whose forgiveness I have begged for in a long letter telling of our adventures. This I posted as soon as we came ashore.

I am hard put to keep up with Tommo, for I am like a lumbering carthorse and he like a yearling with spirit. My back is not yet completely healed and hurts where my blouse sticks to it in the evening heat. After nine hours ashore I am anxious to return to the ship. I have not told Tommo that we have the means to pay for a doss house and a morning meal, eking out small coins for the ginger beer and sarsaparilla we are drinking. I fear he will have us up the whole night, visiting every nefarious establishment in town, though I believe we must nearly have done so already.

At last Tommo agrees to return to the ship. Before the midnight hour, we are back in the fo'c'sle, sober as two judges, with only the cockroaches and the snoring drunks who have made it back aboard to keep us company. Tommo has bought a bag of boiled sweets for the three Maori who have been forced to take the watch. He goes to give them their sweets. I can scarcely summon the energy I need to climb in to my bunk and am asleep on my stomach before the first cockroach climbs up my leg.

The following morning Tommo and I are summoned to Seb Rawlings' quarters and asked if we know the whereabouts of the three Maori. The watch, he says, has reported us as coming on board just before midnight, and being unusually sober as well.

He points to Tommo. 'You were observed talking to the three kanakas not much later.'

Tommo does not deny this, explaining about the bag of sweets, and I am quick to support him in this matter.

'I were back in the fo'c'sle not ten minutes past the hour, Mr Rawlings,' Tommo says.

'That is right,' I volunteer, though I have no way of knowing whether it is true.

'Besides your brother, who else saw you?' Rawlings asks Tommo.

Tommo shrugs. 'All who was aboard and not on watch were drunk and snoring in the fo'c'sle, Mr Rawlings. Only the night watch what saw us return in the whaleboat and the three kanakas would know we was aboard.' He shrugs again, 'As you already knows, Mr Rawlings, sir.'

Rawlings scratches his forehead with the tips of his fingers as though to smooth out the frown etched upon it. On a whaling ship there is not much that the crew do not know about the mates. It is known that the skipper remained ashore overnight and will spend tonight ashore as well. So too will Stubbs and Hollowtree. They have done Rawlings' duty watches while he was consumed with the fever and now, in return, he will remain on board and take their duties as well.

Rawlings is silent for some time. Then he says musingly, 'We have searched the ship, there is no whaleboat missing. They could only have escaped by monkeying down the anchor chain and swimming ashore!' He points to the town bathed in the early morning sun. 'It is a good two cables to the shore and this bay is well known for its sharks.'

It is not clear whether he says this in admiration or whether he thinks the Maori have likely been drowned or eaten for their trouble. At any rate, the three Maori lads have seemingly escaped the ship, and Seb Rawlings isn't happy. He has lost what remains of his whaleboat crew with only me, the new chum, remaining. Worst of all, he must explain this to O'Hara when he returns on board tomorrow morning.

'You two will be on watch today, and tonight you will be manacled to your bunks!' he barks.

'But why?' I ask. 'We have done naught!'

'You returned to the ship sober last night!' he retorts.

'Aye?' I say, my voice questioning.

'Six months at sea and you go ashore and return on board sober? I know you not to be religious. Do you take me for a fool, boy?'

'We are Temperance Union, Mr Rawlings, sir,' I attempt.

'Ha! You lie!' He points to Tommo but he is still looking at me. 'Your brother is a gambler and I have heard tell of how, when we were in Hobart Town, you were seen dragging him aboard from out of a notorious grog shop!'

'We were seen on shore last night by most of the crew, sir. They will vouch for us,' Tommo says.

'Christ Jesus!' Rawlings exclaims. 'No whaleman who ever lived returns from shore leave with a dry throat after six months at sea! They come back with sore heads and empty pockets, to a man!' He paces the tiny cabin and then turns abruptly. 'I shall know what you two have been up to, or I shall ask Captain O'Hara to strap you to the mizzen stays!'

Tommo meanwhile has his head bowed, but now he looks up slowly to meet the mate's angry eyes. 'We thought you was your own man, Mr Rawlings, but now we see that you is no different from the others.'

'Shut your gob, boy!' Rawlings shouts. 'You two were friends of the kanakas. I'll vouch you are all in this together!'

But Tommo, to my surprise, will not be quiet and now baits Rawlings still further. 'Oh, I see, guilty again is we? What will the Lord Jesus decide our punishment be this time, Mr Rawlings, sir?'

Seb Rawlings' face is close to apoplectic and he struggles to speak. 'Right! You will both be manacled and locked up below decks without rations until Captain O'Hara returns tomorrow morning!'

We have been alone in the dark with the rats and the cockroaches since yesterday morning. We have lost track of the time. Tommo, whose instincts are better than mine in such things, thinks it must be near to morning again.

We are in a dark hole amidships, a place where the harpoons and lances are kept under lock and key. No sound reaches us from outside and the only noises we hear other than our own voices are the creaking of ship's timbers, the squeaking and scurrying of rats, and the tic-tic-tic of cockroaches. We spend much time flicking off these last vermin as they clamber about our arms, legs and necks. This is a most difficult task with shackles and manacles on, and there is a rattle of chains each time we make the attempt.

The worst of it is the heat and our thirst, for we have had nothing past our lips but longlick, and that taken just before Seb Rawlings called us to see him yesterday morning. There is not sufficient room to lie down and we are forced to sit with our backs to the wall and our knees pulled up. My back is soon wet with blood and pus as I must lean against the wall, and my new-knit skin and the scabs covering my lashes break open again under the pressure. In all, it is a most uncomfortable situation, though we pass the hours at talk and I learn more of Tommo's lost time in the wilderness.

My twin has seen much in his seven years away. He never speaks as though he is sorry for himself, but is matter-of-fact and often humorous.

When I complain about our dark, cramped conditions, Tommo laughs and says, 'Ain't nothing compared to the cramped quarters known by Sam Slit when the timber getters turns on him.'

'Oh,' I say. 'So he finally got his come-uppance?'

Tommo has told me how Sam Slit would often give a drunken timber getter a pint of whisky from his still for the use of the man's half-caste Aboriginal woman or his little daughter. It was not so bad for the women, he said, who would get drunk anyway and not care what he did to them. But oh, how the little girls no more than ten or eleven years old would weep all the while and plead for mercy, to no avail. Sam Slit would have his way with them, then beat them unconscious, and rape them again and again. In the morning he would send them home to their huts in the forest, bruised and bleeding, with a flagon to soothe their daddies' hangovers.

'This time it were different,' Tommo recalls. 'This time he kidnapped a six-year-old half-caste called Gracie. Half-castes, particular if they be dark-skinned, be thought fair game at any age in the bloody wilderness. Ain't nobody what's going to make much of a fuss. But this time Slit picked the wrong sprat, for her daddy were a big fellow among the timber getters and not from a near settlement. He were most fond of his little black girlie. Slit took her without permission or in exchange, for he were drunk and liked the look o' this little urchin, and thinks he will square it with her papa later.

'But Slit, what's been drinking raw spirit, beats her and fucks her and kills her in the process.'

'Sam Slit was your master! Didn't you run to tell someone?' I ask, horrified by the story my twin is telling me. I cannot imagine he would stand by and let such a thing happen.

'Run to where? Tell who? This is the wilderness, ain't nobody to run to!' I can feel the bitterness in his voice. 'By wilderness laws what he done were normal enough. Besides, I weren't there, I were out setting possum traps and come back to find four timber getters at Slit's still.

'They has him slung on a long pole like an animal, tied wrists and ankles, and they are moving him out. He is moaning and groaning, but they've tied his mouth and his face is raw meat where they've beaten him. The little girl is slung over her daddy's shoulder like the two dead possums is slung over mine. I can see the dried blood around her mouth and nose where she's bled from inside.'

'Oh no, Tommo!' I exclaim. 'You need not say any more.'

Tommo is silent for a while then sniffs in the dark and I wonder if he is crying. He sniffs a second time and now I am sure he is. But a moment later he speaks. 'No, I'll tell you. After all, it's a story about cramped quarters.' He tries to laugh, but it comes out sad. Then he says, 'Besides, that little half-caste dying gave me the courage to come back to you and mama.'

Tommo draws a breath, then continues. 'I follows the men carrying Sam Slit most of the day, and that night they makes camp. I dunno how the little half-caste girl has come to be near Sam Slit's still, for these seem to be timber getters what are after Huon pine, for we has moved high up the Spring River, into the mountains where the big trees grow. I can only think they was on their way somewhere and made camp near Slit's, which in itself is deep enough into the wilderness for the law not to venture. But now these cutters takes Slit much further in than I've gone before.

'We more or less follows the course o' the river all the next day and that night, I camps sufficient far away and downwind so I can make a small fire and cook me two possums. One I eat and the other I put into my tucker bag with some berries I gather during the day.

'On the second day, we follows the river again, climbing up past several waterfalls. We are much higher up in the mountains, and it's late in the afternoon when we comes to a clearing. It's here that the timber getters has their camp.

'It's about an acre cleared and to me surprise they has several bullocks, which I know is used for dragging timber, but I can't think how they could be brought to such a spot. There is pigs and goats and a host of chickens, a proper village, like, with meat drying and a smoke house for fish, and three sawpits dug with platforms in working order, and in two of them a Huon log half sawn.

'I've heard of the deep-pine people and seen some from time to time when they passed along the river on the way to Port Davey. But I has always thought them lone men – or two or three together at most – ticket-of-leavers, debunked convicts, mostly Irish, who cuts the Huon pine high up on the Spring or Davey, and floats it down the river.

'Now I sees there is about thirty people what lives here, six men and four women. Two or three families sharing land is not unusual closer to settlement, but I didn't know that it went on so deep into the high timber. The men's white, but the women half-caste, all with babes to their breasts, 'cept for one: an old, toothless hag, bent over with her paps exposed and hair to her waist, but with a baldness to one side of her head. The rest is brats of every size and shape, light and dark. Some wears a worn wool coat or a knitted jumper much holed, but most are in possum and kangaroo skin, barefoot and snot-nosed dirty.'

Tommo laughs in the dark. 'I has only come to cleanliness since returning to Hobart Town so I don't know why I should remark on the state o' the children. They was no more dirty than I were meself. Anyhow, I finds a sassafras tree what looks directly into the clearing and I climbs high into its branches, where I is well hid.

'As soon as the men comes into the clearing, the brats and women run towards them, laughing and smiling. But their expressions change when they see Gracie's body. The children fall silent, the women begin to keen. One what I takes to be her mama, a scrawny half-caste woman, falls to her knees, tearing at her hair. The women reach out, lifting her up and, taking the dead little girl from her papa's arms, they all goes inside a hut. Sam Slit is still alive, Gawd knows how after such a journey. I'd have thought they'd make him walk and save themselves the trouble, but they has carried him, trussed, all the way and I thinks him dead.

'But he's alive all right, and with his gag removed, he is screamin' and cussin' and beggin'. He is tied hand and foot, and left to sit in a small enclosure surrounded by the bark huts of the timber getters.

'The children gathers 'round him, at first fearful and then bolder. They pokes him with sticks or throws dust at him 'til it gets dark. The night is cold and I climbs down when the camp grows silent and makes a small burrow to sleep in, eating some o' the possum. I wakes at dawn and climbs back into the tree, where I am well tucked away by the time the sun comes into the glade.

'Sam Slit is still lying in the enclosure. The pigs grunt about him and the chickens scratch and schwark and dash away, wings flapping, with each of Sam's outbursts. He seems to have gained strength, and is back to his caterwauling, yet I ain't seen him get food or water.

'I thinks how small and pathetic he looks, though in truth, he were a big man with a huge belly and hands like soup plates – hands that more than once near killed me. But now he's just a piece o' dog shit in the dirt, like he called me, and I wonders how he could have held me afraid to run away so long.'

I break into Tommo's story. 'I too have wondered this,' I confess. 'You were familiar with the wilderness and grown quite independent, and certainly big enough to leave. Yet you remained with this terrible creature? Why, Tommo?'

I cannot see Tommo's face in the dark, but I can hear him breathing. He sniffs, but remains silent for some time, so that I think I have upset him. Then he says simply, 'Grog. I couldn't leave the grog. I'd leave but be back in two days. The craving were too much for me to bear.'

I am glad I cannot see Tommo's face, for I can hear in his voice that he is ashamed of this weakness. I know that, but for the darkness around us, he could never have said this.

'Tell me more of Sam Slit,' I prompt.

'Well, another full day passes, where the children taunts him and pokes him with sticks, and some of the older ones spits or kicks at him. As for the men and women – well, it be as though nobody knows he's there. They pass him all day without looking, even when he screams and begs 'em for water.

'I've eaten all of the two possums and think that I must scavenge about if I am to stay put. So next morning at first light I find a nearby stream with the mist rising upon the water. It's a good hour for yabbies which be plentiful and I catches a freshwater crayfish as well. But I ain't game to cook these and risk the smell o' smoke. Piners wake early and is ever alert for the smell of a fire if it does not come from their own cooking fires.

'It's not long past dawn when I finds a new tree. Now I am hidden again, high up in a tall gum, where I has a better view into the clearing.

'Then I realise something's happening. It's still early morning but other folk has come to the clearing, small groups o' twos or threes with their children. They has the same rough look and most are men, though some be women, white and half-caste. By midday there's fifty or sixty counting the children, and folks keep coming 'til early afternoon.

'I ain't taken any water with me when I climbed me tree at dawn, and I have eaten the yabbies raw what's made me thirsty. But at about ten o'clock, it rains for half an hour and I am able to get a drop. Sam Slit has his mouth open to the rain and is covered in mud as if he were an old sow. His eyes are now great blue bulges where the bruises have formed from his beating and he be altogether a sight for sore eyes, so to speak!

'After the rain a large amount of timber is brought, great logs what will burn for many hours, as well as kindling and smaller wedges to sets them alight. A big fire is laid. Then two sets of poles, crossed at the centre about six feet from the ground, is planted on either side of the fire pit which be about twelve foot long and five foot wide.

'About noon the fire is lit and soon after, I hears the bellow of a bullock and much shouting from the children. Though I can't see what's happening further out in the paddock, it ain't too hard to guess. They is slaughtering the bullock and will have a feast tonight. The two cross-stays will support the pole on which the bullock carcass will be hung.

'Now I sees that four men are took to working one of the sawpits. It be as if they is at some game, for each pair competes with the other at sawing and there is much laughter and close examination of the cut. Then, when the log is cut through, I see that they has sawn a perfect plank, not more than an inch thick, fifteen or so inches wide, and twelve or fifteen foot in length.'

Tommo pauses. 'I know something of sawing and the sawpit, and what they has done with a two-handed pit-saw be masterful. The beautiful pine, what looks the colour of churned butter, is perfect cut to an even thickness. It bounces springy on the shoulders of the two men what carries it, catching the afternoon light as though it was some bright blade itself.

'About two o'clock of the afternoon, the bullock, fully dressed, is carried to the fire. It's fixed on a pole what goes through its centre and extends through the neck and out its arse. It is carried by ten men, five on each end. The bullock is placed carefully between the cross-stays so that it's suspended above the glowing embers now burning red and free of flame. To either end of the poles are attached two handles so that the beast may be turned to the needs of its roasting.

'An hour later the air rising up to me is filled with the delicious smell of the roasting bullock and me stomach growls at the thought of the feast to come.

'Night comes quickly in the wilderness and by four o'clock the shadows is long. The fire is spluttering and sends up puffs of smoke when the fat, rich juices of the bullock drips upon it. The beast is beginning to get nice and brown, having been turned from time to time by two men on either side of the spit-pole.

'Sam Slit is still sitting in the dirt, no doubt made as hungry as me by the smell of roasting meat. His clothes is now caked with drying mud and his face is swollen with the bites of insects. The children has grown weary of taunting him and he is silent and alone. He's too weak or weary to wail and has rolled on his side in the dirt, perhaps asleep. The pigs, goats and chooks has taken to snuffling and scratching about him as though he were part o' the scenery.

'With the parakeets quiet at last and the currawong took to calling the evening into coming, two men walks to a clearing directly under the tree where I'm hid. They carry long-handled spades and they beat away the bracken and the fern before they begin to dig a grave what I presumes to be the last resting place of the soon to be departed, Sam Slit.

'But after they's been digging a while, I see that the hole be much too small and I realise that it is for the little girl, who, I admits, I has quite forgot.

'Then I sees the coffin brought, and the men and women and all the children gathered 'round, now nearly a hundred in all. The coffin's been made from the pine plank I seen being cut and it is now placed within the hole. The folks all gather close and the little girl's papa speaks. He has the voice of a leader and it carries clear to where I sits high in the tree above the small grave. I remember what he says to this day.

' "We seem queer folk to others, though not to ourselves," he begins. "A people driven deep into the wilderness, though not by persecution, though God knows we have all seen enough of that, but by a need to be left alone. A need to be away from the Protestant and his shackles and his two hundred years of dominion over us.

' "We have no priest to bless us and our Latin catechism is all but forgotten. In God's eyes, we are His lost sheep, for we have not confessed our sins these many years. But we have ourselves and our freedom." He looks upwards as though he is lookin' for the Almighty and me heart nearly jumps out me mouth, for he is staring direct up at me in the tree and I'm sure I'll be found! But then he looks down again and continues talking. "Here in the wilderness no man and no law shall tell us what we shall or may do!" he says to all about him. "Nor where we shall go or what we shall be! And most of all, no man shall use his hands to take or use what be ours, hard won with the sweat of our brows or given as the seed of our loins!"

'He stops and looks about him, then turns his eyes to the small coffin. "We do not have much, but what we have is hard earned under a clean sky. It is honest bread. And most of what we have is our kin and our kith. If any of these be hurt or beaten or harmed, then we all be so hurt and beaten and harmed, and we must take into our own hands the means of justice required of decent men who live in the sight of a righteous and almighty God. 'Whomsoever harmeth one of my little children, harmeth me, thus sayeth the Lord.' "

'The little girl's daddy stops and looks around him again as though straight into the hearts of each of those what stands about the small grave. All is hushed, though the little girl's mama is heaving great, silent sobs.

' "Gracie were but six years old and she were harmed, she were broken, she were killed!" He points to the area near the fire and his voice thunders. "Damaged and broken and killed by yonder beast! He used her as meat for his fornication! He has the mark of the beast upon him and he must be returned to the beast. He will be sent to the devil, to Satan himself, to the very fires of hell where he will burn forever!" There is a long silence and then he says softly, "Amen."

'Throughout this sermon, the only other sound heard be the cry of a baby once and the night call of the mopoke. But now a fiddle plays the hymn "Abide with Me". The grave is quickly filled, with the soft, solid thud of earth clods hittin' the timber. None sings to accompany the lone fiddler, and the small community breaks up soon after. But they returns to the fire, where four of the women tend to the roasting of the bullock.

'What follows is a great feast, though not drunken as such affairs is known to be when wilderness folk comes together. There is now some hymn-singing and later songs of Ireland to which the fiddler plays a most melancholic strain. High up above, in the tree, I is starving hungry. I even envies the dogs what stand at the edge of the firelight, snarling and yapping over each bone tossed to them. Soon even the dogs has eaten their full. It is getting late and the smaller children has fallen asleep on their mothers' laps. What remains of the bullock is taken away and I thinks that I may soon be able to climb down from my tree as all takes their contented bellies off to sleep.

'But I am mistaken. As soon as it's quiet, the men what

have seen to the remains of the bullock return. They carries a fresh pole on which the head of the bullock, still attached to the bloody hide, has been arranged. It is trussed in the same way as Sam Slit were trussed when he was took away from the still, hanging downwards and tied to the pole by its hoofs and forelegs. They places the bullock hide besides the fire, though not so close that it catches alight. All the men now stand in a semi-circle around it. The night is very still and several men light beeswax candles, cupping the flame in their hands, so that with the moonlight and the blazing fire, I can see every detail.

'Then, from the darkness beyond the perimeter of the fire and candlelight, I hears Sam Slit screaming. He's brought into the lighted circle, carried by three men. His ankles and wrists is bound as before, and his legs has been tied about his knees with strips of green hide, so that they remain straight and he can't kick. They places him besides the bullock skin, holding him to the ground.

'Suddenly I sees the old hag with the half-balded head and bare titties to her waist. She breaks though the semi-circle o' men and steps to where Sam Slit is whimpering and gasping. She has a basket over her arm as though she be out shopping, and she places it besides Sam and removes a knife. She stoops over Slit, who is bug-eyed with bruising and, as he begs for mercy, she cuts away his clothing until he lies naked upon his own dirty swaddling. I am looking directly down on him and can see his great hairy belly heaving in terror, with his fat worm lying slack against the inside of his thigh. The old woman cuts a length of twine and ties it tight at the base of Sam Slit's cock as he screams and pleads.

'Then she takes up a clay pot from her basket and dips her hand into it. Her fingers is coated in white stuff what I takes to be animal fat. She greases Sam all over. When this is finally done, she begins to work the fat 'tween his legs. To my astonishment, I sees Slit grow until his great purple knob stands hard against his belly-button while he howls like a dog against the pain of the cord, what cuts deep into the flesh of his erect prick. The only sound from the men what forms the circle is a clearing of a throat or someone turning to spit at his own feet.

'Then, as though knowing the exact moment, the old hag grabs up her knife and slices off Slit's stiff cock. She holds it up a moment for all to see, then throws it into the fire where it sizzles, the animal fat catching fire, turning the embers into sudden flames.

'There is a small spurt o' blood and a terrible screaming from Slit, but the cord acts as a tourniquet and the blood soon stops. The old woman now makes a loop of twine and slips it over Slit's knackers. Again she pulls tight, to Sam's yells o' pain. She grabs his balls in her hand and pulls hard so that the skin stretches a full six or eight inches, and her blade slices again. This time, the twine has held so tight that there is very little blood at all.

'Sam Slit is now jerking, screaming and sobbing, snot running from his nostrils. The old hag beckons with a bloody claw and four men takes Slit up, two by the legs and two by the arms. As they raises him from the bloody bundle of clothes I see that he has shit hisself.

'Six men, three on each side of the bullock hide, pull open the bloody skin. Then Sam Slit is lifted over their heads and placed within the hide. The wet rawhide closes 'round him as he jerks and struggles, but it is a snug enough fit – cramped quarters, you might say! With his arms and legs bound, he can't do nothing but beg for mercy. The old hag takes a stick and lifts Sam's dirty clothes and drops them into the fire, where they smoulders a while before being devoured.

'With her bare paps hanging to the surface of the bullock's skin and the ends of her stringy white hair tipped with Sam Slit's blood, the old hag begins sewing up the belly of the beast with an awl and twine. She's busy as a pox doctor, barely aware of the men standing 'round her, as though it be a job not in the least unusual. When she finishes sewing, she takes up the knife again and cuts the rawhide around Slit's face so that he can see and breathe but make no other movement. The old biddy now puts down the blade and takes up Sam's knackers. Forcing open his mouth with the handle of the knife, she pushes them into his mouth so that both his cheeks is blown out with the two horrible gob-stoppers.

'The bullock skin, filled with a different beast, is now lifted on its pole and placed across the roasting coals, each end fitted into the cross-stays.

'I watches from my tree as the well-basted Sam Slit is steamed and then roasted inside the bullock. His full gob prevents him from crying out, so that he bakes in the silent flames o' hell.

'The moon is at the centre of the sky when I climbs down from my tree. All is asleep among the dogs at the fire or gone off to their bark huts. I am stiff from sitting up there for so many hours but now, as me feet touch the ground, I want to run and jump, whoop and do cartwheels through the moonlit bracken!

'It's as though a great burden's been lifted from me soul. Seven years of fear and hatred are gone. When Sam Slit first took me I were no bigger than Gracie, and could not fight back but only scream and sob as he used me. Then, when I grew older, he got me on the grog, so I were too weak of character and spirit to run away. But now, with the beast devoured in the flames of its own belly, I was free at last. I be no longer too ashamed to come home to you and Mary.

For the first time, I got some hope that the mongrels upon the earth can be defeated by decent men.'

Tommo is silent for a spell. Then he says softly, 'But always I'm reminded that the small and the innocent is the ones what gets sacrificed. Even me freedom from Slit comes at a price. A child named Gracie died for it. I vowed in her name that, as long as I live, I ain't gunna let the mongrels win against the small and the weak, against those what cannot fight back.'

I sit, stunned, in the dark. The pain of my back has been forgotten as Tommo talks, and now we are both silent. Then Tommo speaks again, quoting the words of Gracie's papa.

' "We do not have much, but what we have is hard earned under a clean sky. It is honest bread. And most of what we have is our kin and our kith. If any of these be hurt or beaten or harmed, then we all be also hurt and beaten and harmed, and we must take into our own hands the means of justice required of decent men who live in the sight of a righteous and almighty God." '

This is a different twin from the one I thought I knew. Tommo has led me to believe that he is uncaring and cynical, hardened in the ways of the world, too damaged to care about his fellow man, concerned only with where and when he may find his next drink.

Now I perceive in him an anger, one which he will not always use judiciously, as witnessed by his answering back of Rawlings and our subsequent incarceration in this dark hole. But I tell myself it is a much better Tommo. There is much of my old twin come back, the smart-mouthed though always caring little boy, whom I knew and loved so well before we were parted. The years in the wilderness have not destroyed him completely, I am sure. His abstinence ashore last night has given me great heart, and I am filled with optimism for our future.

Tommo reaches out in the dark and clasps my arm in both his manacled hands. 'O'Hara and Jenkins hurt and beat you and the lads, my kith and kin!' He adds quietly, 'And so I've remembered the words of Gracie's daddy and I have kept me vow.'

Chapter Seven

T O M M O

Kororareka
March 1857

Staying sober that night were the most difficult task of me life. At every gin palace, grog shop, brothel and hotel, temptation stared me in the gob. Two minutes at a game o' cards in a one-shilling hell and I would've had a brandy in me trembling hand.

If Hawk had known that I stayed sober only to make sure of the whereabouts of Jenkins and O'Hara so that I might keep me vow of revenge, he would have been happy to see me gutter-rolling drunk. Being stranded on these God-forsaken shores, sitting in a gaol cell at Kororareka is a bloody high price to pay for what we done. But our revenge worked even better than I'd hoped, and we are well rid of the *Nankin Maiden*, though she still waits in the bay for her master to return from the surgeon's hospital.

Twice in two days we've been manacled and put in custody, first by Seb Rawlings and then by the local constabulary. We is to go before the district police magistrate when next he sits, though who knows when that might be. The other prisoners reckon that we'll be taken to Auckland.

Hawk is still furious that I acted against O'Hara without

talking to him first. Now he sees how clearly I gulled him when we was ashore – he thought me show of temperance were from a new resolve to remain sober. I'll never get another drink in me lifetime if Hawk's got anything to do with it! I've even lost my raisin wine, the result o' nearly seven months of saving the raisins from me plum duff, and winning them from the rations of the crew when they lost to me at cards. I gave the cook five big mackerel for the yeast I needed to speed the fermentation.

Me ship-brewed grog were about a week off being ready when we was arrested and thrown into this foul nest. Now I won't never have the satisfaction of getting as full as a tick on board and thumbing me nose at Captain O'Hara and his pious Quaker owners with their bloody dry cask afloat. Never mind, I thinks to meself, our revenge on O'Hara and Jenkins be even sweeter than such a fine drop would've been.

We are sitting in this bloody cell where the vermin is as plentiful as on board ship. We has seen few rats and cockroaches but the fleas and lice are back and at night, the bed bugs, so that we is always scratchin'.

It is a good time to work with Hawk on his voice which comes along fine but is still very much on the rasp and low to the ear. I has to teach him to open his mouth and throw his voice wide. Honest, sometimes I dunno how me twin survived growin' up without me. Hawk has ideas what would make him the laughing stock o' men what know life for the misery it is. If those in authority ever knew his secret thoughts they'd arrest him for sedition. But, as I comes to think of this, perhaps they would not. He knows so little of the evil what lurks in men's hearts that those in power may well take him to be a harmless fool.

Since his voice is begun to recover, Hawk speaks much o' man's conscience and has the peculiar notion that men must form a brotherhood and act responsible, the each for the other.

'We have a new country, Tommo, why should we accept that we must follow old ways, old laws? Why must the poor be accepted as beyond redemption and not worth the smallest charity?' he asks.

'Because for the most part the poor be idjits!' I says.

'Only because they have no opportunity,' Hawk answers.

'Rubbish! Poor ain't an opportunity not given, it be how we looks at the world.'

He stares at me amazed. 'Bloody hell! You are right! *How we look at the world.* A way of looking at themselves and their own kind!'

It be the first time I've heard Hawk cuss with his new voice and I laugh at the sound. 'When I were took by Sam Slit, I were just a seven-year-old brat, cheeky though, and bright, with an answer for all and a bit of a joker, wouldn't you say?'

'You were all that and more, Tommo,' Hawk chuckles softly.

'But when Sam Slit beat me and abused me I become a different boy. Soon I were like a kicked dog. When me master called I'd come, me eyes filled with fear for the beating I expected. But I would still come. What else could I do? I were a child and in the wilderness with a wild man. So I gets accustomed to it, tries to please him and be a good boy. Soon I don't remember that I were ever any other way!'

'That's what I mean!' Hawk exclaims. 'You were taught to expect naught but blows and curses. That is what you received and soon you thought the world no different.'

'That's right!' says I. 'That's why your brotherhood of men won't work. Men ain't kind to them as they don't have to be – not in this hard old world.'

165

'No, no, that's just it! We must change the conditions of the world. Men of conscience must stand together and change the conditions!'

'Ha, what a load o' codswallop!' I says. 'There be only two conditions what exists in this world, Hawk, strength and weakness. The strong shall destroy the weak, that's how it's always been, and I'll vouch that won't never change long as we live. Your fine ideas o' conscience won't change anything, neither.'

'But you said yourself in the dark that you took a vow to defend the weak, to look after your kith and kin. That is the *conscience* in you, Tommo!'

'Bull! That ain't conscience! The mongrels kicks you, and you finds a way to kick back, like we done to O'Hara and Jenkins. That be revenge and well took too!'

'Tommo, you went too far! You and the Maori, what you did that night was not right.'

I look at Hawk and shakes me head. 'What we did were no worse than what they did to Hammerhead Jack, and what O'Hara and Jenkins did to you and the other Maori!'

'We could have gone to the law!' Hawk says. 'We could have had the vessel impounded and our complaint heard.'

'The law! You heard what Hammerhead Jack said about British law, well he were damn right! Four Maori and a nigger against the Yankee captain of a whaling ship what's known for his Quaker piety! The case heard by some drunken district magistrate! For God's sake, Hawk!'

I think about how surprised Hawk were when we was taken out of the dark hole and brought to a crew muster before the mainmast. First up Hawk thinks it must be the crew count before we sail. I ain't sure the plan has worked so don't know what to expect. We stumble out of the darkness into the brilliant morning sunshine and our eyes is blinded for a time so that we needs be led by the bosun what's come to fetch us from the hold. The shouting of the crew alerts Hawk that there is something new afoot. As we pass, some of the men touch us on the sleeve and some grin and wish us well under their breaths.

Our eyes begin to get used to the bright light and I sees the three mates, Stubbs, Hollowtree and Rawlings, standing beside the mainmast. O'Hara ain't among 'em and Jenkins too is missing. Good! I thinks. The three mates are grim-faced and all has their arms clasped to their chests, watching Hawk and meself.

I am glad Hawk don't know what we've done, for he's a hopeless liar and might give the game away. As for yours truly, well, the wilderness taught me all I needs to know about lying. I'm all innocence in appearance, though not *too* innocent, that be just the same as looking guilty. Instead, like Hawk, I has confusion writ upon my gob, as if I be silent-saying to meself, 'What's goin' on then?'

Several of the men are pointing to the mainmast, a foot above the heads of the ship's officers. Hawk looks up and I follows his gaze. He gives a gasp and this is followed by me own, for what I see is not expected. Hawk's horror be genuine as he grabs at me with both his manacled hands. 'Look, the mast!' he shouts in his rusted voice.

There, nailed to the masthead, is the hand of Captain Mordechai O'Hara, chopped off at the wrist with his gold signet ring still on his third finger. This time it don't wear the ruby of Billy Lanney's flesh as it did the day of his beating. The captain's hand has been nailed stoutly to the mast with a three-inch copper nail, the fingers pointing to the heavens as though giving praise to the Almighty. A thin line of dried blood runs all the way from the mangled wrist to the base of the mast and gives the evil appearance of a hand stuck on the end of a rod. Beside it, like two pale sausages nailed likewise with cooper's barrel nails, are a forefinger and middle finger, what I knows belongs to Jenkins, for the ginger hair below the knuckles glints in the morning sun.

I gasps and grabs back at Hawk's arm, feigning shock and horror. But inside I be pleased as Punch, silently singing the praises of Hammerhead Jack's lads, what has done so well! 'Gawd bless the Maori! To hell with British justice, this one's for Gracie!' I says to meself.

Well, o' course, it's presumed we be guilty and the bosun now pulls us roughly by the manacles to stand in front of the three mates.

It is Stubbs what speaks first. 'What say you?' he shouts, looking at Hawk.

What can Hawk say? He knows nothing. He is still shaking from the shock and I hopes that they do not think it is because he is afraid. But with Stubbs' question he seems to realise what might be afoot. Hawk is ever the optimist, but he ain't stupid.

'Say?' Hawk says, removing his cap. 'I am deeply shocked at what I see!' He gestures with his manacled hands to O'Hara's hand and the two fingers nailed beside it. 'Who has done this terrible thing?'

The men have crowded forward, straining to hear Hawk's voice.

'You are in this!' Rawlings shouts, pointing to Hawk and then to me. 'You two are part of this!'

'Part? How? You know well enough we be locked midships all of last night and aboard ship yesterday at your instructions.' I cough lightly then add, '*Sir*,' so as to show me disrespect, but not too much for I clumsily remove me cap from me head and hold it to me front. Hawk scowls at me. He's put two and two together. He knows I am up to my neck in it somehow, though how he still ain't sure. He knows Rawlings is a fair man at heart and does not wish to put him altogether on the captain's side. But Rawlings has little choice, he's got to take us to task as if he were O'Hara hisself. He is only the fourth mate, the most junior of the ship's officers, but he were in charge of the ship when the Maori escaped. And I doubts the other two, Stubbs and Hollowtree, will take the slightest share of the blame. Seb Rawlings is in big trouble and he must get to the bottom of this affair or be disgraced forever. No doubt there will be an official inquiry. Perhaps, I thinks, Rawlings can be pushed into saying or doing something foolish which might later be in our favour. Where the mongrels is concerned, yours truly is all for playing the crowd, and Rawlings is now on the side of the mongrels.

'You are in this, bastard!' he yells, spitting the words at me.

Now is the time to be humble. 'Mr Rawlings, sir, I begs your indulgence. As you know, the Maori took leave of the ship well after we returned the night before last. You yourself did muster us the morning following to ask if we did know their whereabouts. But, o' course, we did not,' I say innocently, and Hawk nods his head. We is now too deep into this affair for him not to go along with me and I sense that he knows what I'm up to with Rawlings. I continue, 'Then you locked me brother and me up 'til we be fetched but a few moments ago.' I turns towards the men. 'It is easy enough to ask the men if they seen Hawk and meself all the night ashore and also, if ever they did see us together with the Maori.'

There is a rumbling among the crew and some nods their heads. 'Aye, they be with us,' several call.

'Quiet!' calls Hollowtree, who ain't said a word until this moment.

'As a matter o' fact, sir, along with several of the men here, we was at the Whaler's Hotel at a late hour where we seen Captain O'Hara talking with some o' the locals there. I assures you, Mr Rawlings, sir, he were hale and hearty at the time we left to return to the ship!'

'Aye!' several of the men shout at once. 'That be God's truth! We'll swear to that!'

'Well then, what be this?' Stubbs shouts, holding aloft me kindling axe!

Hawk gazes at me in shock. It's a surprise to me too, but I quickly explains.

'Joshua Stokes, who were the watch, will be my witness that not ten minutes after me and Hawk come aboard from shore, I reported me axe stolen, sir. It were took from the fo'c'sle where I has me things and it were gone when we returned.'

Stokes steps forward. 'Aye, sir, that be right. The lad did address me on this matter!'

Stubbs steps two paces towards the mast and lifts the small axe and fits it to a deep cut within the wooden mast some four inches below Captain O'Hara's hand. The axe head sinks a full inch into the stout timber and fits snugly, so that Stubbs may leave it there. 'It were discovered here this morning at daybreak!' he says accusingly.

'Find who put it there and you has the man what stole it, sir!' I shrugs.

Now Hawk speaks beside me. 'I should be most grateful to have it returned to my brother, Mr Stubbs, sir!' he says in his gravelly voice. 'This is a ship full of villains as may be clearly seen,' he points to O'Hara's severed hand. 'I fear for Tommo's safety unless he may defend himself!'

The men falls to laughing uproariously so that the solemnity of the occasion is destroyed. There ain't a man on board what's sorry for the captain, nor for the blubber-room bully, Jenkins.

'Shut thy trap!' Stubbs shouts at Hawk and pulls me axe out from the mast. 'Thou and thy brother be in this up to your necks!'

'Which will soon enough feel the hangman's rope about

them!' Rawlings adds. 'There is blood on the blade! Human blood!' He points at it and looks darkly at Hawk. 'This is the second time human blood has been found on a blade of your doing. Last time it was Nestbyte's knife. Now,' he brandishes the axe above his head, 'this!'

The men grows silent. I should learn to shut me big gob, but Rawlings is after me brother and it comes out without me thinking. ' "I am not mocked, sayeth the Lord!"' I say for all to hear.

Well, Hawk and me is taken back to the dark hole, though it be plain to see the men ain't happy that this should happen. But this is a whaling ship and they ain't likely to mutiny over a spot of injustice, leastways for a sprat of a lad and a nigger. Most has been on board a full two years and the ship's hold is near full with oil. Besides, with O'Hara's hand lopped off, they probably think they will return to Massachusetts. There ain't a man among them what would sacrifice his share of the lay even if our lives be in certain danger.

As soon as we is back in the dark, Hawk ticks me off. He is fit to be tied, and I'm glad I cannot see his face and that his voice is not strong so that he must often rest as he shouts. But he grabs me arm with his manacled hands and shakes me 'til I thinks he will rip me shoulder out. My lip is bleeding from biting back the pain.

'Tommo, you are a damned fool! We are done for!'

'No! They got nothin' on us. We was locked in, snug as a bug in a bloody rug, here in this dark hole!' I protests.

'Your axe! They will say you gave it to the Maori! Don't you see, we are implicated!' Hawk yells again, his throat raw and hoarse. For a moment I wish he never got his voice back.

What he says is true enough, though. I did give me axe to the Maori when I told them where they might find Jenkins and O'Hara. But they agreed it should be thought they'd pinched it. I did not think they would return it.

'Tommo, my people will kill O'Hara,' Hammerhead Jack said to me several days before we reached New Zealand.

'No!' I tells him. 'We must cut off his hand!'

He pauses, thinking, then frowns. 'Why we not kill him?' he asks, puzzled.

'He's no warrior, he's a coward!' I says. 'He must live with the memory that he's a coward and a mongrel!'

'What is mong . . . ril?'

I don't try to explain, though perhaps I could have done for I has learnt a bit of the Maori tongue. Instead I says, 'Every time O'Hara lifts his arm, he's gunna remember that he cannot steal from a Maori, nor beat him when there is no just cause.'

'Nigger, too! He cannot beat Ork!'

'Yes! He must be punished for he is a mongrel!' I says again.

'Ha! Mongril!' Hammerhead Jack says. 'Mongril!' He sounds the word and seems to like the taste of it. Then he picks up me axe with his good hand. I were using it to gut a tuna when he comes upon me on the aft deck. He takes the axe head in his huge paw and tests the edge with his thumb, drawing a thin line of blood. He whistles in admiration, for I keeps it sharp as a barber's razor.

'Your hand has held this axe, Tommo,' he says in his own tongue. 'You must give it to us so a Maori hand may hold it when we find this mongril. This way we will share the pleasure of our *utu* with you and Ork!'

'You can have me axe, Hammerhead Jack!' I says, excited. 'But don't tell Hawk!'

Hammerhead Jack shakes his head and laughs loudly. 'Ork good! Not tell Ork!' he replies in English. He holds the axe in his hand as though weighing it. 'It has your *mana*, it

172

will come back with this mongril's blood upon the blade, Tommo.'

I can't say I didn't know what would be done with my axe, but when Hammerhead Jack nailed O'Hara's hand and fingers to the mast, he did so without me knowing. It were an act of incredible bravery what I greatly admires. I can see it were done in order that Captain O'Hara would forever know that it were the Maori what had wreaked their vengeance upon him. Tommo's 'mongril' has been punished at last.

I also know that Hammerhead Jack returned me axe thinking that, because it were reported stolen, the blame for what had happened would be placed squarely at his feet. Hawk and I would be innocent even if we was under suspicion, the axe the final proof that the Maori alone were guilty.

Now, with Hawk shouting at me, I realise that Hammerhead Jack is a warrior and don't give a fig for the British coming after him. I'd be surprised if he'd gone after O'Hara himself, though. He is too intelligent, and still too weak to take on the captain or Jenkins with only one hand. One of the other Maori must have done it and now that they has escaped back to their people, the law would have trouble finding the culprits amongst the tribe.

Hammerhead Jack would know little of the law, caring only that me axe, me *mana*, be returned to me and that his beloved Ork be safe. It takes some hours to convince Hawk o' this, and he still ain't completely happy with yours truly. But I think he is slowly coming to the view that British law would never have helped us out in New Zealand.

'Besides,' I point out, 'when Hammerhead Jack said he did not trust in the law you said nothin'. I thought you knew the bastard would get away with it and I wouldn't have the opportunity to keep my vow.'

Hawk stays silent and I think perhaps I have him. Then he speaks quietly. 'I have it written down, Tommo. Every word O'Hara said to us, every syllable. Sooner or later he would have come to port in Hobart Town and, with Mary's help, I would have him in front of the governor and brought to trial!'

I've learned something new about me brother. He is patient and has a long memory. 'Will you do so now? Now that O'Hara has lost his hand?' I asks.

Hawk gives a short laugh. 'You may be damned sure of that! I shall make the law work for small men as well as those who have influence. If we do not force the judge or the magistrate to do his duty then we cannot complain that we are hard done by. Poor men should have fine lawyers too!'

'Ha! And how's your penniless beggar gunna find such a lawyer?'

'We will build a land where Mistress Justice is once again blind, the way she is supposed to be. Alas, she has long since seen her blindfold removed so that she now judges those who supplicate in front of her by the cut of their clothes, the base or haughty accent on their lips, and the depth of their purse.'

I shakes me head in the dark. He's got his voice back, all right. How on earth can I make this big nigger see that he tilts at windmills?

It is late in the afternoon when, with a rattle of keys, we is brought once again on deck and handed into the custody of two police constables. Though we asks why we are arrested, not a word is spoken. The men gather around and there is some protest, but finally all our worldly goods is thrown into a whaleboat and we is rowed ashore. The only words spoken is by one o' the four oarsmen what stand on the shore as we is led away. It is one o' the Irishmen. 'God bless ya, lads! Don't let the bastard British grind yer down, keep yer Irish up, yer hear now!' he shouts.

This morning the gaoler comes in to see us. It is the first time we've spoke though we has been here a week. He is a big man dressed in a uniform much the worse for wear, with most of his recent breakfast on its front. He looks like a walrus, with a ragged ginger moustache and no beard, and his whisky-pocked and bloated nose is like a polished plum planted in a hairy red nest. His cap sits askew on his head, with hair like the straw of an old scarecrow poking out. His eyes are dull as raisins and his ears large and bright scarlet where the light shines through them. This is a deep-drinking, thirsty man, if ever I seen one.

'Mornin', lads,' he says in a mournful tone.

'Mornin', Sergeant,' we replies, standing up with a clanking of chains.

'Nottingham's the name, but not the sheriff o' Robin Hood fame.' If this be a joke it comes out flat. 'Best stand to attention,' he says, and we brings our feet more or less together.

'Well then, lads, you're off to Auckland,' he goes on. 'Your vessel be there now, sailed two days since with your one-fisted skipper aboard.' He looks up at Hawk. 'You're a big fella, ain'tcha? Nearly as big as Hammerhead Jack.' He scratches his chin as though he's thinking. 'Now there's a big fella in more ways than one, what say you?'

'He's a big fellow, very tall,' we mumbles without much enthusiasm.

'Big trouble-maker, too! Can't say I'm glad he's back. Been in the wars, from all appearances. Whale got him, was it?'

Hawk nods.

'Dangerous big fellas, whales. But not as dangerous as big black fellas, eh? What do you know of the savage?'

'Who?' we both says.

'Hammerhead Jack,' he says. 'What know you of this hand-lopping affair?'

Hawk speaks to me with his hands, though he does not look at me as I read them. 'Watch him carefully.'

I nods me head as though I am listening to Nottingham and then reply in sign language, 'Drinking man!'

'What say you then of this affair?' the Sheriff o' Nottingham asks again.

'Nothing. We know nothing, sir,' I answers quickly.

He points a stubby finger at me. 'You the one with the axe?'

'Axe, sir?'

'You know! The weapon what did the dastardly deed!'

'I'm sure I don't know what you means, sir. Does you mean did I own the axe?'

'Aye, and use it!'

'Use it, no. It were stole from me and used elsewhere by persons unknown.'

Our gaoler spins around, amazing quick for such a stout cove, and sticks his same podgy finger into Hawk's chest. 'And you be the one who murdered the first mate, ain'tcha!'

'Oh,' I says, quick and cheeky. 'All settled then, is it? We be guilty, is that it?'

'Would be if I had me way. Take you out the back, string you up the nearest tree together with the big Maori and call it a damn good day's work! One of each kind of villain, black, white and brindle, couldn't be fairer than that now, could it? Shame you can't just do it, these days.'

'Well, I'm thankful for that,' Hawk sighs softly.

'Now it's down to Auckland, magistrates on the bench growing haemorrhoids, jury sitting on their arses twiddling their thumbs and, when all's said and done, probably the same verdict: hanged by the neck until you dies. Goin' to Auckland be just a waste o' time and taxpayers' money!'

'And Captain O'Hara, what about him, Sergeant Nottingham? Has you thought that he might be the real villain?' I points to Hawk. 'Ask me brother to show you his back!'

Nottingham dismisses this with a toss of his hand. 'Could be, could be. Quite possible. But it ain't, see. 'Cause it wouldn't be right. Wouldn't be the decent thing.'

'What do you mean by that?' Hawk asks.

'It's all about sides, ain't it? Sides and ingredients! Yankee whaling ship skipper, Christian Quaker gentleman. That be one side. Ingredients on that side be a lopped-off hand.' He stops and looks at us hard. 'Four Maori, a nigger and a white man what carries a razor-sharp axe about his person. Ingredients here be the bloody axe what done the deed. That be t'other side.'

'What about British justice in all of this?' Hawk asks.

'Justice don't come into trials. White jury, Christian folk, or professed to be. Yankee whaling ships what come regular into port be good for business and ain't to be discouraged under any circumstances. And like I said, Quaker Christian captain with a ship what's a dry cask afloat, so the crew drink the port dry at top prices when they comes to land. That's more commerce. This be the case for the plaintiff.'

Nottingham sniffs and grabs his nose with his forefinger and thumb, wiggling it vigorously. 'Maori and niggers known to be heathen savages what can't see reason, don't have no discipline, 'less both be brought about by means of a good flogging before the mast. That be the case for the defence. What say you then, gentlemen o' the jury, guilty or not guilty?'

Nottingham says all this in a steady drone. Now he pauses and looks down at his naked big toe poking out of his broken boot. He wriggles it as though he's surprised to find it there. Then he shakes his head slowly and squints up at us. 'I might be a gamblin' man, but I wouldn't venture threepence on your chances. You be pushing wet dung uphill with a broken stick, lads. Best confess and be done with it, eh?'

'You say you're a gamblin' man, sir?' I asks.

'Could be, could be,' he sniffs through his tangerine moustache. 'Depends, don't it now?'

'Play the flats, then?'

'Been known to play a hand or two from time to time. Fancy yerself, does you? Didn't your daddy tell you never to play cards with strangers?'

'With friends? You play with friends?' Hawk asks.

'Poker, is it? Or whist?' I butt in before he can answer Hawk.

'Play the odd game in town now and then,' Nottingham says, without answering my question.

'What, in them one-shilling hells, full o' chumps and whores? I'll wager there's not a decent game to be found in this whole town!' I laughs.

'Look, lads, you be in enough trouble, don't go looking for no more. This town's got a poker school what's too rich for your blood!'

'Aye,' Hawk says, 'most wisely spoken, Sergeant Nottingham. On the other hand, there could be a quid in it for you.'

Nottingham looks at Hawk shrewdly. 'Cost yer five sovs to sit in.'

I whistle. 'Five pounds!' I has no idea if Hawk's got this kind of money. I look at him, showing me surprise, but he signals she'll be right. 'That be a big game,' I says to the Sheriff o' Nottingham.

'Too big for me, and I suggests too big for the likes of you mangy lot.'

'If you can get my brother into the game, we'll go fifty-fifty, what say you?' Hawk challenges.

A greedy look comes into the gaoler's eyes. 'You've got five pounds to wager?'

'Could be, could be! Depends, don't it now?' Hawk mimics him cleverly.

'Fifty-fifty?'

Hawk nods.

'And if you lose?'

'No onus,' Hawk replies.

'If we loses, you gets our confession signed, scaled and delivered. Feather in yer cap and all,' I says.

I can hear Hawk's sharp intake o' breath at this offer.

'A feather in me cap, eh? A written confession?' Nottingham removes his cap to show a bald, shiny red pate, spotted with bright brown freckles like stars in the night sky. Then he punches the inside of the dirty, misshapen cap with his fist. The crown flaps loose and three dirty fingers wiggle through the gap. 'Even with a feather it ain't never going to be much of a cap.' He grins, showing gappy yellow teeth. 'There's no more promotion for Sergeant Nottingham, this be my final patch, my last station o' duty!'

'You mean, you'd rather have the money?' asks Hawk, coming straight out.

'What do you think?' Nottingham grins.

'Well,' says Hawk, 'what I think is that *you* think my brother and I will be condemned whether we are guilty or not, would that be correct?'

Nottingham smiles a secret little smile and shrugs. 'That's about it, lads. Ain't no jury in this land what's gunna condemn your Captain O'Hara for a bit o' Maori and nigger flogging.'

I am impressed at how quick Hawk's grasped the situation. Nottingham be a man what's condemned by his own habits, a drinker and a gambler, and a failure at both. Shit! I thinks suddenly, that's what Hawk sees for me! He sees Nottingham. He sees his desperation, his despair, in me future.

That's the difference 'tween Hawk and me. I sees a mongrel clear as daylight. Not a very important mongrel, mind, but one what can cause us harm and what's got power over us. Hawk sees a man what's on the bones of his arse, what's closer to prisoner than to policeman, trapped by what he is and where he be. A man what's dying same as the town around him, sinking into nothin'.

Hawk is a fair man, fair in his heart and mind. He don't understand that fair be not understood by such as Nottingham or even, matter of fact, by such as me. Fair don't come into the reckoning of poor folk. Hawk sees someone to be pitied and yours truly sees danger. Hawk be about to mess things up proper by trying to get Nottingham to let us escape for five pounds. Hawk don't understand how a gambler's mind works.

'This game o' poker, we're in, then?' I takes up the question again.

'Fifty-fifty?'

'Fifty-fifty, solemn oath,' I shoots back.

'Remind me what happens if you lose?'

I shrug. 'You ain't no worse off and we still be Auckland-bound. But if we wins, what then?' I asks.

This is the moment o' truth. I sense that even Hawk knows this. I try to keep the smile on me gob, hoping that I haven't struck too early, that me smile means it don't seem too important to know the answer if I've read him wrong.

Nottingham don't know for sure if we've got the five sovs, but he's got to figure we must have, or there's no point. Thank Gawd Hawk ain't shown it to him. Then I thinks, Christ Jesus! What if Hawk don't have it and he is bluffing? Nah, Hawk don't have the gall, he's got the money all right. Nottingham has to figure he has, too. So what's his options? He can take it by force – there be three constables as well as himself and we be in chains and manacles. Five pounds be a lot of money. Or, he can gamble there's more to come if I can win at poker. It's time for all Ikey's lessons to pay off.

'Sergeant Nottingham, sir, if you'd be so good as t' remove me manacles for five minutes, perhaps you'd care to witness the skill what's being brought to *our* side.'

Nottingham looks me up and down and I guess he figures there ain't all that much to me and that even he might make a show of capturing me should I try to scarper. Besides, the cell is locked behind him. We waits and he don't say nothing. If he says no, we're done like a dinner.

'Righto!' he says and, taking the keys from his belt, opens me manacles.

Well, it's all sporting stuff. Ace where no ace should be. Ace, King, Queen, Jack dealt straight off after Nottingham has himself shuffled the pack. 'Take a card please, Sergeant? Any card.' I offers the pack wrong-side up and he selects a card blind. 'Turn it over and put it down,' I points to the four picture cards already spread face up. He turns his card and puts down the Joker, amazement writ all over his rough gob. Then he smiles and I know we has won. Greed be the most dependable of all human characteristics.

'Righto, you can count me in,' he growls.

'Just a moment, Sergeant, what about *our* winnings?' Hawk asks.

'Fifty-fifty!' he says, indignant.

'Ah! Not what *you* win, what *we* win?'

Nottingham looks puzzled.

'If we are Auckland-bound,' Hawk continues, 'and if, as you say, the verdict is already decided?'

There is a long silence as Nottingham stands thinking, looking down at his broken boots. Then he slowly raises his head and looks squint-eyed at Hawk. 'You means, what price freedom?'

Hawk stays stum.

The gaoler seems to be thinking again, and then he says quietly, 'Fifty pounds.'

'Fifty pounds!' Fuck! I'm took completely by surprise. Fifty quid, I'll wager, be near six months' salary for a police sergeant! But Hawk don't even flick an eyelid.

'How big is the game?' he asks cool as you like.

'Five, six with him,' Nottingham points t' me.

'Can't do it,' Hawk says firmly. 'Five-pound stake for each player, that's only thirty-five pounds. If each isn't prepared to lose more than his buy-in, we can't make the fifty. Even if Tommo cleans them all out, which isn't likely. Let's say twenty pounds, which will be hard enough?'

Shit, Hawk's got twenty pounds on him, I thinks. If Nottingham accepts, he'll offer him the money right off so that we can scarper, never mind the poker game.

'There's some what will be willing to lose more than their stake,' the gaoler says. 'They don't muck around.' He pauses. 'You scared, is it? Sorry, lads, but I ain't sticking me neck out for less than half a hundred.'

Hawk shakes his head. 'Sergeant Nottingham, it isn't reasonable.'

Nottingham laughs, his fat stomach wobbling like a jelly. 'It ain't a reasonable world, son. It ain't *reasonable* that the jury should hang you in Auckland, but take my word they will. Fifty pounds, that be my first and last offer.'

'You're on!' I says suddenly. With twenty pounds I can build a proper scam. But Hawk's right, to take fifty pounds from a single five-pounds-in game is damned nigh impossible if they's good players. Even if I does a whole heap o' relocation I'll need two games to set it up.

'But it's got to be two nights, two games. Over two games we've maybe got a chance,' I says to the gaoler.

Nottingham looks doubtful. 'Two games? I don't know if these gentlemen will like that.'

'Tell you what they won't like? They won't like playing with a stranger for one game only!'

Nottingham accepts this. He's said himself he don't play cards with a stranger.

'Fifty-fifty if you should not make the fifty pounds for your freedom?' Nottingham says again.

We both nod. It is sheer bastardry, but what can we do? 'Fifty pounds in your hand and you let us scarper, right?' I want it from his lips once more.

He clears his throat like he's even nervous to think of it. 'Yes, but I'll have to come after you, mind. Do me duty.'

Hawk smiles. 'By going in the wrong direction, I sincerely hope?'

'Aye, I'll do that by and by,' Nottingham says, still shifty.

'Two games, right?' I persist, bringing them two back to the business at hand. 'Five pounds on the table to buy into each game. The second five held at the end of the first night as surety for the next – right?' I points to Hawk, 'Me brother to hold the second game buy-in, in trust overnight. Oh,' I adds, 'and two new packs o' cards, DeLarue & Sons, no other, one blue, one red, we breaks the seals at the table.'

Hawk looks at me and I shrugs. In for a penny, in for a pound. Worst what can happen is we are transported to Auckland and strung up. I'm making a book on Nottingham's greed. He's a gambler himself, he'll be itching to sit in on the second game and I hopes to make it possible. Nottingham's a mongrel, and mongrels has to pay.

'Right, two games,' the gaoler agrees. 'I think I can arrange that all right. But,' he points at Hawk, 'I don't think they're gunna let a known murderer hold the stakes overnight.'

I see Hawk scowl and his eyes grow hard at Nottingham's accusation that he can't be trusted.

'Safer than a bank,' I pipes up quickly. 'We ain't goin' nowhere, is we now?'

Nottingham laughs, relieving the tension. 'Righto, the nigger holds the buy-in and the wee lad gets new cards, DeLarue & Sons. By the by, what's the ante?'

'Let's say five shillings.'

'Five shillings?' Nottingham thinks for a moment then nods, 'Fair enough, lad.'

'With the right to raise it before each hand?'

The gaoler hesitates then says, 'We'll let the others decide, though I can't see they'll object.'

We leave it at that and Nottingham returns the Queen's bracelets to me wrists. As soon as he's gone, Hawk asks me in strong lingo what exactly I think I'm doing.

'How much money has we got?' I ducks the question.

He hesitates. 'Twenty-five pounds,' he says.

I acts shocked. 'Shit, why didn't you say before? I thought I were gunna have to work with five! That I'd have to work a scam where we comes out square the first game so's we've got the deposit for the second. Twenty-five quid, eh? That's a king's bloody ransom! Now we can have a proper strategy.' I grin. 'With that much, the very best o' Ikey Solomon be possible.' I pretend to think for a moment.

'We'll lose fifteen right off! "Thicken the plot and sweeten the pot," as Ikey would say.'

'Lose? Fifteen pounds!' Hawk shouts, aghast. All these surprises is getting his voice up nice and strong.

I roll me eyes in the manner o' Ikey. 'Can't win in the first game, not kosher, my dears, not to be considered, quite out o' the question. Absolutely forbidden and not to be entered into!' I says, mimicking his voice. Hawk laughs despite himself, then grows serious again.

'What if we are taken to Auckland before there can be a second game and we've dropped fifteen pounds in the first?'

'Trust me,' I reply. 'Nottingham won't let that happen. He's a gambler what feels he's gunna get lucky!'

But I can't say I ain't worried. Any cove what plays regular in a five-pound buy-in is either cashed and most professional in his handling o' the flats, or apt to practise a little relocation hisself. Either way, such a cove don't much like losing to strangers and is likely to get violent.

'No grog!' Hawk says suddenly. 'Promise me, no brandy, no spirits!'

'Gamblin' can't be done without drinkin', Hawk!' I protest. 'Folks gets suspicious if you don't keep the tipple going.'

Hawk works his hands in the Ikey manner. 'Drink and think go together like boys, bishops and bedchambers – it has been known to happen but it is a most unholy alliance, my dears!' He can do Ikey even better than me.

I sigh and nod me head. At this rate, I ain't never gunna taste another drop.

The game takes place in the gaoler's office that very night, which leads me to think Nottingham ain't quite the innocent he seems. A high-stakes poker game don't come about this quick unless the players expect a pretty evening at someone else's expense. What, I asks meself, is Nottingham up to? It could mean two things. He's told the players we're easy fruit, ripe for the picking. But that be stupid 'cause he knows we ain't. So he's not going to shit on his own doorstep, is he? He's the one what has to live in this town. It might mean he's got a two-way bet – all the other players is in the game together against me, a case o' mutual benefit. Well, I thinks, there's no point in getting too clever at reading the bastard. I'll find out soon enough 'cause that's what the first game's for, ain't it?

Hawk is allowed in the room but he must be seated three feet behind me, and we is both shackled by the ankle to a chair leg.

It's a curious sort o' group, but no more strange, I suppose, than what's to be found in any sea port. Seated about the table is a Maori bloke, Hori Hura, what the whites rudely call the Hairy Horror. He is a merry fellow, what wobbles with laughter after every sentence. He can barely reach the card table for his big belly.

He is accompanied by Messrs Tate and Lyle. These last two are small, rough-looking gentlemen, though they wears good cloth-suits and clean linen with boots what have seen a shine. They is known as Maple and Syrup on account o' the fact that they's inseparable and their names is the same as what's on a Tate & Lyle maple syrup tin.

It turns out that both Tate and Lyle come to New Zealand as boys in 1844, transported on the *Mandarin* from Parkhurst Penitentiary on the Isle o' Wight, young felons to be apprenticed to settlers. But they soon ran away from their masters and took to living amongst the Maori to avoid the law.

This is how they met Hori Hura, himself only a young un. He is much taken with the pakeha boys, who soon learn Maori and teaches him English, including what Ikey would call a host of lively expressions fit to burn the ears off a church warden. They also teaches him the flats and now, for many years, they has become his partners in trading. Most curiously, there is no mention of what sort o' goods this trade be in. But they complains that much of their former customers is now took to Auckland, where they themselves wants to go. I reckons their 'trading' be of a gambling nature, with visiting sailors their patsy-mark. With so few ships now calling at Kororareka and most stopping off at Auckland, they thinks to move their shady operation to the larger port.

Maple and Syrup speak of their past with pride. Parkhurst boys is well known in Tasmania too. Such boys almost exclusively start out with a record as thieves. They is nurtured in vice and repeatedly convicted in the quarter-session courts of London Town until they finally appears at the Old Bailey. There they is given their free passage out to New South Wales or Van Diemen's Land or to New Zealand. Ikey told of how, when he first come to Van Diemen's Land, he would keep an eye on the Point Puer Reformatory near Port Arthur where the Parkhurst boys were transported, just in case the one and only Sparrer Fart did suddenly appear among 'em.

So, I says to meself, if these two bastards, Maple and Syrup, be on the straight and narrow as we're supposed to suppose, then our gaoler be the real Sheriff o' Nottingham, I be Robin Hood and Hawk, Maid Marian!

Then there is the Portugee, Captain de Silva, a small, dark man with a goatee beard and a most handsome moustache, waxed and curled high to almost touch his ear lobes. Nottingham introduces him to all, saying he has only come into harbour yesterday. When he went into the police station to post bond for his crew and pay his customs duty, he happened to enquire if there be a friendly game ashore.

The last of me erstwhile partners for the night is Mrs Barrett, what's in fact a man, thin as a rake, wearing a woman's dress and shawl, hose and boots. His grey hair is tied in a bun behind his neck and he has a long, black and very thin Jamaican cheroot in his mouth. His nose and cheeks is tattooed most unusual, an English rose on each cheek, one full blown, the other in bud, with the leaves and stems joined across his nose and his brow. It is a more friendly-looking tattoo than that of Hori Hura, who, like Hammerhead Jack and the other Maori aboard the *Nankin Maiden*, is covered in black squiggles and circles over every inch of his ugly gob.

Each player has brought along his preferred tipple. Hori Hura has rum, Maple and Syrup has Cape brandy, Captain de Silva drinks oporto wine and Mrs Barrett has Bombay gin. Me gut is howling like a dog at the moon with all these elixirs of heavenly transport placed before it. In their shining bottles they be so near to me yet so far from me reach. I has to concentrate all the harder for not drinking than if I were swilling it down, on me road back to drunkenness as Hawk fears.

To rub salt into the wound, Nottingham explains to all assembled that, because I be a prisoner of Her Majesty, I cannot consume ardent spirits. This be a ploy suggested by Hawk so me abstinence ain't thought strange. So, here I am dealing the cards for stud poker with a mug o' stream water which I am obliged to sip, to the constant chaffing and the pretended commiseration of all what sits comfortable and comforted with their favourite tipple at their elbows.

'Now the flats be a game o' two characters,' Ikey would say. 'It is popular thought that if you know the man you know the game he'll play, but that, my dears, be purest codswallop. Cards bring out the best and worst in a person and often the opposite to what's expected. Timothy Timid can play like a lion and Terrible Tim like a lamb. The flats be the other person in each of us; find this second person and you've got your patsy-mark.'

It's soon apparent that Hori Hura, and Maple and Syrup be skilled enough but lack true intelligence. Of the other two, Captain de Silva, the Portugee captain is a careful player – highly skilled but one who ain't prepared to venture too much. Mrs Barrett appears to be the one to watch. Cunning as a rat, he strikes like a cobra. A very pretty player o' the flats indeed but a mite too hot-headed, and I think he is working a scam, which I will soon enough locate.

I loses slowly but steadily to each of them, dealing them good hands each time it is my turn. I'm losing less than I had hoped to Hori Hura and his Parkhurst boys who are, towards the end of the evening, a little too drunk and do not take all the opportunities me generosity affords them. Each ends the evening with their buy-in still intact and a bit more besides.

Captain de Silva wins three pounds. Mrs Barrett is the winner for the night with seven pounds – three taken from the captain in the final hand when only the two are left in the game and de Silva is forced to see Mrs Barrett by matching his last bet or dropping out. I be surprised when he chooses to drop out as I know he holds a better hand than Mrs Barrett.

This brings me to the whole point of the night. While I has managed to lose nigh upon fifteen pounds, I has also been able to substitute both packs with me own, which I have previously marked. I have took in with me the brand-new red and blue packs Hawk bought me on the night we went ashore from the *Nankin Maiden*. These has been marked in Ikey's secret manner so it be almost impossible to discover. By the end of the night I has both decks substituted and I know every card on the table. This is why I know that if the Portugee captain had asked to see Mrs Barrett, he would have taken the pot. He's most cautious and this worries me some, for I also sees in him a hungry predator.

In all we are down fourteen pounds and sixteen shillings when the game finally comes to an end. With Mrs Barrett the big winner, local pride is intact and I has established that this fine lady-man is not in league with the other three locals, nor is he near as good as de Silva. I cannot be sure that he ain't in cahoots with Nottingham, but me final reading of him is that he cannot be relied on to win consistently. Nottingham would know this too.

As for the other three, they are clearly a syndicate, and Nottingham would, I reckon, be most reluctant to make a deal with them. Besides, he is all scowls at me loss and most hard put to show a brave face. I got to conclude that our gaoler has took us in good faith as a partner. But I still reckon there is something I has missed; something I has failed to speculate upon. 'Scratch around, look in the dark corners,' I hear Ikey saying to me. 'It will be there, stored in the old noggin box.'

Anyway, it be a neat enough evening's work and all are willing to put down their five-pound stake for the following night. It is decided, at Nottingham's suggestion, that we will play five-card draw tomorrow. Stud poker, the game we has been playing, is a great game for cheating if you knows what you're about. You has only to make sure you have the hole card you want and a good dealer can deliver the right card to make up a winning hand wherever he wishes to place it.

Poker is a game where cold decking is easily possible – that is, substituting a marked deck as I has done during the course of the game. It is a trickier business with five-card draw, though, and there is more chance to be discovered. I believe meself a good enough player with an unmarked deck and am confident I can hold me own with de Silva. If, in an emergency, I must substitute me own deck, I am a good enough mechanic to do it.

Hawk now asks Nottingham to put the two decks we has used tonight in the gaol-house safe. I has already removed me own marked cards and replaced the originals and so I am delighted when our gaoler refuses.

'We play with new cards tomorrow,' he says grandly. 'Captain de Silva has agreed that I should have the money from his winnings to purchase them.'

For my part, I am all brave smiles at my losses, just what might be expected from a good amateur what finds himself out of his depth but has too much pride and not enough sense to give it away.

'Better luck next time, eh lad!' they all says, patting me on the shoulder, pleased as Punch at the way things has gone.

Nottingham then collects the pot and makes Hawk give him five pounds so all can see we has the stakes for the next game. Hawk looks suitably long-faced when he hands over our five sovs and Nottingham is most unhappy that we have lost so badly but is trying not to show his anger to the other players.

Nottingham gives the thirty pounds to Hawk to keep and we is unchained from our chairs. 'See yer tomorrow night, lad. Could be yer night,' Syrup shouts as we is led back to our cells. We can hear them laughing all high and mighty.

When we is locked in again, Hawk sticks out his manacled hands. 'You said we'd lose fifteen pounds, we only lost fourteen pounds and sixteen shillings, where's the other four shillings?'

'Escape money!' I laughs, handing over the four shillings. 'I was keeping it for our expenses on the open road.'

'The open bottle, more like,' he says, a touch tetchy.

'That ain't fair, Hawk! Twice the Maori pushed his rum bottle to me when Nottingham weren't looking, "Help yerself, Tommo," he says.'

Hawk nods and grimaces. 'I wronged you, Tommo. I'm

sorry. It's just my own misgivings over the whole affair. The fat Maori and those two villains from Parkhurst, Maple and Syrup, I think they are the most dangerous.'

'I know,' I says. 'But they is poor mechanics and cannot match the play. Their cheating is only for chumps what know no better.'

'We could ask that they be seated away from each other?'

'No, that would alert them that we're on to them. Besides, it'll make no difference. I'll take them slowly tomorrow night, driving the pot up only at the end when they be well out o' the game. And what does you think o' Captain de Silva and Mrs Barrett?'

'De Silva is kosher, I think, and I only caught Mrs Barrett relocating once.'

'He done it seven times. He's got an apron pocket behind his shawl,' I laughs. 'He's quite good but not too quick on the draw.'

'Seven times, eh?' Hawk exclaims. 'Not much help then, am I?'

'Course you is. Poker games can turn nasty at any moment, and having you behind me be a great comfort in a room full o' villains. They will think twice about coming at us.'

Hawk laughs. 'Big and clumsy, that's me. I don't know how I'd go at fisticuffs! Never tried it. Besides, our legs are shackled to the chair.' He pauses and then asks, 'How are we going, then?'

'I know their second natures now,' I reply. 'The Portugee captain worries me. I left him out o' my favours tonight. He is an outsider like us, and there ain't no need to gull him, so I lets him play his natural game to gauge his skill. I didn't observe him to be relocating even the once and it be astonishing that he managed to come out ahead in a game where I gives the others so much help.'

I turns to Hawk suddenly. 'Watch him tomorrow night. Forget the others. Watch if de Silva does anything different when he asks to see someone's hand. Watch him when he folds. Anything, you hear? Clears his throat, touches his nose or ear lobe, crosses his legs, wiggles his foot, sniffs, bites his nail, touches his eyebrow, runs his tongue over his lips. The smallest thing! Fingers his moustache, twirls it, taps his knee or the table, if he does anything before he makes his play. It just could be we've got a wild card in our midst.'

'What if he doesn't do anything?'

'Don't worry, he will. He can't help but show his excitement, though he fights with all his might not to show it. Look for his gesture. I promise it'll be there, it always is. Remember what Ikey said, "The flats be the other person in each of us." Outside de Silva be the calm one, inside he's got Mexican jumping beans in his stomach. Now listen well, Hawk. The lamplight be behind you and throws the shadow of all of us against the far wall where your head is the tallest in the outline. When you sees de Silva make whatever sign it is, clear your throat once, wait a moment, then lift *your* hand to your head as though to scratch your noggin, leaving one finger in the air. I'll see your sign in the shadow.'

Hawk grins and I know he is glad he has a part to play. There's hope for the lad yet, I thinks. A little corruption will do him the world o' good. Something to lighten up that heavy bloody conscience he's always carrying around.

As soon as his guests have gone, Nottingham is in to see us and loses no time in telling us of his extreme displeasure at me performance. He calls me a wee lad what couldn't win at a game o' marbles. He cannot trust me to win and demands that he take me place at the table and play with our stake. Of course we refuse, but after much argument and cussing from our friend, Hawk agrees to advance him our last five pounds against the fifty promised if we should win, an outcome which Nottingham seriously doubts. He jumps at the offer of having a stake in the game and leaves us a bit happier.

I has not told Hawk that I thought Nottingham would demand to sit in on the second game, nor how well this would suit us. But he has worked it out for himself. The lad is definitely progressing!

'That were well done!' I says to him after the gaoler has left.

'What was?'

'Bringing the bastard into the game!'

'What do you mean? We had no choice!' Hawk says. 'He was threatening to cancel the game tonight and we are down nearly fifteen quid!'

I spoke too soon. Hawk will ever be an innocent. Nottingham, as I expected, be just arrogant enough to believe he may save the situation if he should take me place at the table. As Ikey were fond o' saying, 'A compulsive gambler always feels at his luckiest when he watches someone else lose and very soon convinces himself that it will go different for him. This be just the perfect time to invite him into your game, my dears.'

'Right,' I says, trying not to laugh at Hawk. 'You done well.'

Hawk knows he's got the wrong end of the stick but not why. He shakes his head. 'What is it, Tommo?'

'You don't know, do you?' I laughs. 'Letting Nottingham into the game were a stroke o' genius.'

'It was? How so?' He is even more confused.

'Before the night be out I'll vouch we will halve our debt to him,' says I.

I lies awake the rest of the night, trying to work out what is going on. Finally I reckons there is only one way that everything fits. I knows I got to be careful not to imagine what isn't, nor see coincidence for someone's clever and deliberate ploy, what's easy enough to do when playing cards. By morning I realise there can be only one explanation. The Portugee whaling captain and Nottingham are in a scam together.

This seems most strange, and I don't wish to explain it to Hawk, for there is too much speculation involved and Hawk is one to work with the facts alone. But in me mind I see it clear as day. Nottingham was harping on a bit too much about playing himself. At first I'd thought his whingeing about me abilities with the cards were 'cause he be a compulsive gambler who thinks he can do better. Nottingham *wants* me to think this, but his real purpose is in fact to *lose*, so that he cannot be seen to be in league with de Silva. He will lose to me because it is a debt he can deduct from what we already owes him, and still we will be in debt to him. Now I feels sure that the reason de Silva has agreed to pay for new cards is that he will first mark 'em for himself.

Nottingham, I realises, has never believed I can win. Me skills with the flats he has seen as simply a young lad grown over-confident and showing off some trick. The gaoler just can't bring himself to believe that a 'wee lad' can take on the great de Silva and win. Tricks I may have, but five-card draw, he knows, is much more than sleight of hand.

How Nottingham knows of de Silva's skill, I don't know. But I swears the other four, what are also locals, ain't in the know, for they treats him too obviously as a stranger. I remember how very careful Nottingham were when making the introductions to say he were newly acquainted with the whaling captain, what he claimed had sailed into Kororareka only the previous day. If de Silva cleans up, Nottingham will say he thought the captain were just another patsy-mark off a whaling ship and, at the same time, point out that he too has been a victim of this cunning poker pirate.

Captain de Silva is certainly the best poker player of the five, and, I expects, also a master at relocation if it be necessary, though I have not observed him at this. Last night he lay low and watched the other players, so as to take greater advantage of them tonight. This is the sign of a very good poker player and a professional gambler. If he is playing with a marked deck this will not harm his confidence either.

By losing last night, I've shown Nottingham that he were right about me, that I does not possess the skill to win the fifty sovs required for our freedom. He thinks of me as the fool in the school, but still with a stake o' five pounds to lose in the second game and also what Hawk has loaned to him. Mrs Barrett, he knows, is the hasty type, what will think he is going through a lucky streak and so bring last night's winnings back to the table. Hori Hura, Maple and Syrup will argue to themselves that, if they can win when they is not entirely sober, there will be easy pickings to be had when their heads be clearer.

Nottingham, I feel sure, thinks that before the evening is out the Portugee captain will take all Hawk's money and Mrs Barrett's, the Hairy Horror's and the Parkhurst boys' as well – a clean sweep. I'd wager that the plan is to let Mrs Barrett lose all he made last night 'cept for his original stake and perhaps a trifle more. Then, before taking this also, de Silva will allow him to be last to fold from the game. A local player will have had a series o' good wins, so proving the game straight, despite the visiting captain surprising us all with his amazing skill.

I takes me hat off to Nottingham. It is well thought out. He has made only one mistake in all this. He knows that in the first game de Silva has played to hide his skill, but he don't know that the same is true of me. The fact that he has managed to get Hawk to stake him the five pounds to partake in the second game will only convince him of our callowness. Nottingham must feel himself a pretty clever fellow all 'round. He will still deliver Hawk and me to the law in Auckland without tarnishin' his name as a policeman, gaoler and servant o' the queen. What's more, he will do so at a profit to himself!

Me only concern therefore regards de Silva. Will he buy Nottingham's theory that I be just a brash lad? Or does he see me as his equal and therefore dangerous? If this be the case, he will be most wary and on his guard tonight. I decides to continue acting the amateur and show too much excitement when I chance to win. There is one last thing: if the new cards supplied by Nottingham be marked it will confirm that Nottingham and de Silva be in this together.

Well the first thing I gets right is that I has picked Nottingham for a compulsive gambler. In our game tonight, he loses his five-pound stake in the time it takes me to win ten pounds. I makes a right fuss each time I win a pound, as if I am a silly child what can't believe his good fortune. I even lend Nottingham five pounds against his promissory note.

Meanwhile Hawk, what through his years of being dumb has developed the habit of keen observation, soon sees a pattern emerging in the Portugee captain. Each time de Silva holds a good hand or has relocated a card, he taps the tip of his left whisker. It be the tiniest gesture but it be there. Hawk clears his throat, pauses, then scratches his head and his finger rises above the shadow thrown across the wall in front of me. I soon gets the drift and refrains from calling de Silva whenever he has a strong hand.

Nottingham soon takes out another IOU from me and then another, 'til he owes me twenty pounds. I ain't yet certain that the decks are marked but know that if they are, Nottingham cannot read them and the marking method be de Silva's own. When Nottingham asks one last time for credit, I refuse and he is the first to be forced out of the game, amid much mockery.

I sense his fury, though I am still playing the lucky clown, with me tongue sticking out from the corner of me mouth like some country yokel. I win a little then lose it again and then win a little more, all the while holding me own. De Silva is winning slowly but surely at the expense of the four local lads and is gradually wearing down the weaker players. This is the ploy I would meself use in his position. My mission at present is simply to stay in the game and match me skill with the whaling captain, letting him slowly build his winnings at the expense of the others while I build me own.

Three hours into the game and all the locals is cleaned out. But the process o' taking their money has been played with much skill by de Silva and, if I may say so, yours truly. We raise 'em in small amounts to suck them in and so keep them in the game right to the end of their money. They has all committed considerable more pounds above their previous night's winnings and it is a pretty example of how to empty an opponent's pockets. I exclaims at each de Silva win so that the attention is taken away from me when I too win a hand. It is joyous clever poker, for each of the locals is made to believe that at any moment their luck will change for the better while they is being drained of every penny they possess.

I admires de Silva's patience and skill and he now has a large amount of gelt in front of him. Although I has been winning and losing steadily I am still only fifteen pounds ahead, so the remainder of the winnings sit in an untidy pile in front of the captain – by my reckoning, nearly fifty pounds. It is now only him and me as we continues to play. I am long since convinced the deck is on the straight and has not been shaved or marked. I'm playing against a very clever fellow, a master at the game o' five-card draw.

De Silva will challenge all me wits, but I am confident that me talents are sufficient to match his and perhaps a little more. I make sure that I seems no different in appearance and skill to the others, just fortunate to have lasted in the game as long as I have. I doesn't have the funds I will need to take him on if he should want to raise the stakes. But he plays me the same as them, raising me only small amounts.

Gradually, though, I starts to work up the stakes while sustaining some narrow losses to him, so that those what watches us groans and exclaims at me bad luck and grows excited as I win. I don't know if they see that I lose with a small bet and win with a larger one, for they's took to drowning their sorrows at their own losses. I reckon that if you asked them, they would say that it be only a matter of time before the whaling captain has me cooked as a plump bird, ready to be carved up and eaten for his dinner.

But I am playing well and have clawed back half of de Silva's winnings, though he is still much the favourite and has not yet lost his confidence. He is touching his whisker more frequently and Hawk is practically took to having a fit o' coughing. Any observer of his fingers would think the lice in his hair be biting most vicious tonight.

De Silva is just beginning to be of two minds about me. He is far from a fool and I know he will soon see that he is against a superior player, or at the least, a player to match his every skill. Then he will panic and try to end the game.

At last we reaches the stage where I feel that if de Silva

gets one truly big hand he will grow impatient and risk everything. I can see that he has finally worked out what is happening. He is angry at me for winning or losing each time by only a very small difference in cards and so encouraging his ignorance of me true ability. He thinks he deserves to win, so soon he will make his big move when he holds an unbeatable hand.

It is now that I must cold-deck him. The moment has come, there will never be a better one, to substitute the deck concealed on me person for the one on the table. The deck be already stacked and awaiting its chance. Up to this point Hawk's signals have kept me out of trouble and I has proved the better player, but now I needs extra luck, a deck stacked for me and not for the captain.

It's my turn to deal and, using the stacked deck, I deal de Silva a truly high hand, a medium running flush. I can almost hear his inward sigh of relief. God Himself has dealt him a hand he knows cannot be beaten. So the Portugee captain raises the pot by five pounds and I does the same; he bets another five pounds, and I raises him again. He would teach me a lesson, and puts down another five. I does the same. Now he can do nothing but fold or keep raising me. His temper is rising. He cannot believe his hand can be beaten and he *must* punish me. He raises again. Soon I have but five pounds left on the table in front of me and de Silva ten. De Silva's eyes are shining, he has lost his reason and now thinks only of the kill. He wants the lot, and with it my humiliation. He raises me five pounds. I has no option but to fold or see him, and I slowly pushes me last fiver across to join the heap o' money in the centre.

The moment me money touches the pile, de Silva is unable to restrain himself. With a huge smile what shows off his six gold teeth, and some fast babble in what I takes for Portugese, he puts down his medium running flush. His hands shake with the thrill 'cause he thinks he has won the night.

I stays calm, though I admits me heart is pounding. I lay down a running flush as well. Mine is only one number higher than his, but it is enough. One tiny little number different and the pot is mine. The game is over, yours truly has taken the loot. Every bloody penny! De Silva groans and the other five players cannot believe what they has just seen. I look at him and point to the five pounds in front o' him. 'What says you, Captain, another hand?'

De Silva shakes his head and slumps in his chair. He can scarce believe what has happened. He has been made to wager everything on one card, and lost. The emotion I know to be always contained within him now bursts to the surface like a dam wall breached by flood water. His face crumples and he buries his head in his hands and starts to weep, his shoulders heaving.

It is Ikey what comes to me mind again. 'When you wager everything and lose, show nothing. When you wager everything and win, show even less. Cards played well be a game as cold as ice, my dears!'

I reaches over and scoops the pile o' money to me side o' the table, close to eighty pounds. I picks up his hand from the table and then me own and calmly shuffles the deck. With a little relocation, I replace it with the original, so that my own marked deck is returned to me. If Nottingham and de Silva has marked the deck and should examine it later, they will see that it remains what they bought.

Hawk and me are away, clean as a whistle! I hands the deck to our gaoler, who is gone purple from rage. Alas, poor Sheriff o' Nottingham, Robin Hood has slipped through your fingers once again! I smile at the other players and thank them most cordially for the two games. Then I nods towards Hawk, but says nothing. Finally I turn back to the gaoler. 'What says you, Sergeant Nottingham, a bit o' luck for the wee lad, eh?'

Nottingham turns away from me, unable to contain his anger or to meet me eye. I silently apologise to Ikey for this transgression of his laws o' behaviour. It is the biggest game I has ever played, and also the neatest win. I would have liked to play de Silva clean, for in the end I was sure I had the better of him.

Nottingham's promissory notes, plus the five-pound stake money Hawk gave him, takes care of twenty-five pounds of our freedom money and, while we still has to give him another twenty-five to make up the fifty, we have Hawk's original twenty-five pounds back plus close to thirty more. Our freedom has come to us at a great profit!

I lean back and give the gelt to Hawk, who I am proud to say don't smile. He folds the notes carefully and puts them into his pocket and slips the gold sovereigns into his purse. I turns back to the table and suddenly the old fear rises in me like swamp mist. Here, in the smoke-filled room of Kororareka gaol-house, I sniff the early morning scent of the wilderness, smell the wet damp earth under my nostrils as I lie over the skinned Huon log with my breeches down around me ankles. My heart is beating furious again. The mongrels are here in this room and they has us trapped.

I turn quickly to see that Maple and Syrup have come to stand on either side of Hawk. I look 'round. The Hairy Horror is standing beside the window holding his rum bottle by the neck, his great, ugly, tattooed phiz smiling drunkenly. His tiny eyes is hard as black agates and I know Hawk and me is in danger.

The huge Maori smashes the bottle against the window sill. The bottle is not more than half empty and a shower o' dark rum splashes into me face and over me blouse, so that me eyes sting and for a moment I can't see nothin'. I am too frightened even to lick at the rum and when me eyes clear I sees Hori Hura moving slowly towards Hawk with the jagged green bottle neck clutched in his enormous fist.

'You give back me money, nigger!' he growls.

Chapter Eight

HAWK

I have just completed putting our winnings away when the two Parkhurst boys come to stand on either side of the chair to which I'm shackled. I am feeling most proud of Tommo, who has won us our freedom, and so I take little notice of Maple and Syrup. They are both small men, now somewhat tipsy, and I do not feel intimidated, though perhaps a trifle uneasy.

Nottingham seems most agitated by the events of the evening, and his complexion has gone from a rose to purple hue. This I cannot understand as he will soon be twenty-five pounds the richer. I suppose he is playing the bad loser. With the twenty pounds in markers that we have and the five-pound buy-in he owes us, he will no longer collect the full fifty.

I hear the sound of glass shattering and a shower of dark liquid hits Tommo in the face, splashing across his blouse as Hori Hura smashes his rum bottle against the window sill. He pushes the jagged neck and shoulder of the bottle towards me.

Maple and Syrup grab at my arms and of course my

ankle is shackled to the chair leg. Nottingham is grinning evilly and behind him Mrs Barrett and Captain de Silva have backed away in alarm, their hands and backs flat against the opposite wall.

'Hawk!' Tommo yells as the two Parkhurst boys cling tighter to my arms and the huge Maori draws closer. 'The chair leg! Break it!'

I am not quite sure what happens next, for I have never fully tried my strength, other than to lift a firkin of beer ten times above my head as a joke for Mary's brewery workers, and to punish Jenkins when he tormented Tommo. But I stand up as much as my shackle-chain allows and jerk my arms free, sending the two villains flying backwards across the room. Then I lift the chair and with my free hand break off the leg. With the chain, and the chair leg attached to it, still about my ankle, I face the Hairy Horror. He hesitates a moment, giving me just enough time to swing the broken chair at him before the neck of jagged glass slashes towards my face. Hori Hura takes the blow on his shoulder, staggering sideways a single pace, and the glass misses me.

From deep inside of me comes a rage so cold and hard that everything in the room seems to slow down. I drop the chair, which appears to bounce on the floor, and I watch as my left fist takes an eternity to swing through the air and connect with the jaw of the fat man in front of me. He too moves backwards, and I hit him again with my right hand, the bones in his nose smashing beneath my bare knuckles. The broken bottle drops from his hand and he starts to fall. His eyes roll to white as the back of his head hits the stone floor. 'Get Maple and Syrup!' Tommo calls out, and I turn.

It is at that moment that I feel a terrible pain in my own head and all goes black.

We are back in our cell and I am manacled and shackled again. My head throbs mightily and my back, not fully healed, is wet with blood. I imagine it has torn open again, though I feel no real pain except for my head. Tommo too is much bruised about the face and has lost his blouse. His torso is black and blue and one eye a persimmon shiner, now completely closed. His lips are swollen so that he looks somewhat like a parrot fish. If he is any indication, the two of us must be a very sorry sight indeed.

'How's you feeling?' asks Tommo.

'Crook,' I croak. 'My head feels broken open.'

'That's because it is,' Tommo says. 'You've blood on yer back from yer head where they hit you with the chair, but it's stopped bleeding now.'

I suddenly remember and grab at my pocket where I have put our winnings.

'Don't bother yerself,' Tommo says bitterly. 'Bastards took the lot!'

'Nottingham? Where's Nottingham?'

'Buggered if I know. Ain't seen hide nor hair of the sod since last night.'

'What's the time?' I ask.

'Past dawn, though not much, the birds ain't been singing long.'

'What happened, did you see?'

Tommo tries to grin through his bruised lips. 'I never seen a better left and right thrown. Bam-bam! You pole-axed him!'

'Did I? What happened after that?'

Tommo tells me that when I turned around to hit Maple and Syrup, Nottingham picked up the broken chair and smashed it down on the back of my head so that it was dicky-birds and bursting stars as I joined Hori Hura on the floor.

'Meanwhile there I is, trying to break the leg off me bleedin' chair, same as what you done!' Tommo attempts a cheeky grin and shrugs. 'Mind, it must've been a much stronger chair 'cause the bloody leg don't budge. Then the two Parkhurst boys rush over and beats the living daylights out o' me. When they's given me face a good going over they topples the chair and puts the boot in while Nottingham just stands by and watches! One o' the bastards kicks me on the side o' the noggin and I'm history. Next thing I knows I wake up back in here behind bars.'

'Did you see who it was who took our winnings?'

'Nah, must have been after. I woke up and it were black as pitch in here. Me first thought were to find you. My ankles are tied though me hands are free and so I feels about and finds your head and me hand comes away full o' blood. Jesus, I thinks, they's killed you. But then you moans, so I knows you ain't dead – yet! I were shitting meself until enough light come to see you was gunna live!'

'Only just,' I groan. I lift my manacled hands to touch my head and realise that I am swathed in a sort of turban. I sniff the sour smell of rum and realise it is Tommo's blouse torn into strips. My brother has taken the shirt off his back to bandage my head.

The sun is well up and pushing through the little barred window high up in the wall of the cell. I think I shall die of thirst at any moment. Then there is a rattle of keys and the door swings open. The dark shape of Sergeant Nottingham stands there, the daylight streaming into the cell behind his fat silhouette. Beyond Nottingham is another man. As our eyes adjust, I see that he is a constable, who carries two tin mugs and half a loaf of bread before him on a small wooden tray. He puts this down at Nottingham's feet and withdraws.

Tommo pulls himself over to the mugs using his arms. They have used handcuffs to manacle his ankles. He reaches out for the water but Nottingham's broken boot comes down on his hand.

'Not so fast, lad! Well, well, a touch thirsty then, is we?'

Tommo does not look up. 'Yes,' he sniffs.

'Yes, Sergeant Nottingham, sir!'

'Yes, sir,' Tommo says again.

Nottingham kicks at one of the mugs and it spills all of its water as it rolls across the cell floor to rest at my feet. 'One to go, lad. We must have proper manners now, show respect for our betters! It's not "Yes!" It's "Yes, Sergeant Nottingham, sir!"'

Tommo is silent a moment. Then he snaps, 'You're a mongrel bastard, Nottingham!'

Nottingham kicks the second mug over. 'Oops!' he says. 'Excuse I!'

'Where's our money, Sergeant Nottingham?' I ask.

'Oho! The nigger speaks! Money? What money?' He feigns confusion.

'We struck a bargain – fifty pounds for our freedom.'

'Money? Freedom? I'm sure I don't know what on earth you're on about, lad. Bribe, is it?' He throws back his head and chuckles. 'Oh, I see, a bribe, you're offering me a bribe? Fancy that! Fifty pounds?' Nottingham clucks his tongue several times. 'Fraid I can't give a known murderer freedom at the cost o' fifty pounds or even a hundred. Matter o' duty and respect to my vocation.'

'Sir, I am not a murderer!' I rasp. 'Mr Nestbyte's death was an accident which occurred while hunting the whale.'

'Nestbyte?' Nottingham frowns and touches the side of his bulbous nose with the tip of his forefinger. 'Oh, yes! Yankee from the whaler, wasn't it?' The gaoler shakes his head slowly. 'No, no, no, lad. Not him! This be *another* murder altogether. A *second* murder! I have arrested you for the murder of Hori Hura!'

He dusts his hands together and lifts his boot from Tommo's hand, then kicks him in the ribs with the toe-cap. Tommo goes rolling over but manages to bite back the pain.

'As for you, let's call it accessory before the fact! Aiding and abetting to the crime o' murder most foul.' Nottingham smiles expansively. 'The motive being attempted robbery, seventy-eight pounds took from five honourable gentlemen before you both were most bravely apprehended by yours truly with the help of Messrs Tate and Lyle. Attempted gaol-break valiantly prevented. Wouldn't be at all surprised if there's a commendation in it for me, and a medal from the governor presented to them two, for courage in the face of extreme danger.'

Nottingham farts loudly then pats his belly and burps, highly pleased with himself. 'This time the jury won't even be put to the trouble o' choosing between a heathen nigger and a Christian Quaker gentleman. This time there be five witnesses, all men of good repute, including a police officer.' He waves his hand airily and chuckles. 'The magistrate in Auckland will be delighted that he has been saved a long, tedious trial.'

I listen to Nottingham with growing consternation. The fat gaoler has tricked us out of our money and has me destined for the rope.

'It was self-defence, an accident, Sergeant Nottingham!' I cry. 'He was coming at me with a broken bottle, you saw it yourself!'

'Broken bottle? No sign of a broken bottle! No witnesses to a broken bottle! Nay, lad, that won't wash, won't wash at all!'

'You're a bastard, Nottingham!' Tommo spits again. 'I beat your scam and now you's robbed us of what's rightfully ours.'

Nottingham's mood changes quickly and he points

angrily to Tommo. 'You're a brash young lad, Solomon. I'd bite my tongue if I were you. Evidence is clear enough – you and the nigger escaped from your cell and come across the five of us playing a nice friendly game o' cards in my charge office.' He changes back to his laconic self. 'No harm in a game o' cards, now is there? Tried to rob us, you did, demands our money or else. Threatens us with a chair leg! Ripped right off, it were. Hori Hura bravely leaps to our defence and is knocked to the floor and killed before the rest of us manages to overpower the two of you.' Nottingham pauses, shrugs and grins. 'Except for Captain de Silva, who has sailed away to whaling on the mornin' tide, there are four of us what will swear to the truth of this in front of the judge.'

I look at Nottingham, shaking my head. 'Six into eighty pounds is only thirteen pounds and six shillings each. If you'd taken our side you would have earned yourself almost twice, twenty-five pounds, even after you redeemed your promissory notes. It makes no sense.'

'Don't you tell me what makes sense, nigger! What don't make sense is that the likes of you should escape Jack Ketch! I shall take pleasure in watching you dangle from the beam.'

'You never did intend to let us escape, did you?' I say.

'Ya tried to work a double scam!' Tommo shouts. 'A doublecross! It were the Portugee captain what was meant to take the night with a running flush!'

Nottingham doesn't deny this, but sends a gob of spittle to the floor. 'You'll be going to Auckland tomorrow, took by boat, full manacles and shackles,' he says, then he stoops and picks up the half-loaf of bread. 'Maybe you'll have better manners when you be a little more hungry and thirsty, eh lads?' With this he clangs the heavy door shut, taking the bread with him.

We look at each other, waiting until the rattle of the keys

dies away and we can hear Nottingham's footsteps departing.

'What on earth are we gunna do?' groans Tommo.

'We must try to get a message to Mary, have her call upon the governor so that he might intervene, talk to Governor Gore Browne over here.'

'It'll take too long for her to get here, we'll be dead by then.'

'*You* will not die, Tommo – only I perhaps,' I hasten to comfort him.

Tommo swallows. 'I wouldn't want to go on without you, Hawk.'

'Of course you would.' I try to remain cheerful. 'You could get drunk every day with nobody to nag you.'

Tommo falls silent for a while then begins to talk. 'More than once in the wilderness I wanted to give it away, toss it in, just walk out into the river and keep walking, but you were always there with me. I didn't know what had become of you, maybe the same as me, but I knew you was not dead, felt it in me bones. Long as I felt that, I could hang on.' He grins. 'I admits, I done it with the help o' Slit's whisky still. Without that,' he shrugs, 'I dunno.'

Then he says slowly, 'That were drinking with hope. The hope that one day we'd be together again. If the mongrels gets you now, strings you up, and leaves me here, that be drinking without hope. I'd sooner be dead, you and me together on the gallows, Tommo and Hawk together to the last breath.'

'Come here, Tommo,' I say.

Tommo crawls over to me.

'I can't hug you because I'm shackled, but you can hug me, little brother,' I say to him.

Tommo grabs my arm in both his hands and, putting his head against my shoulder, begins to weep softly. 'Oh God, I loves ya, Hawk!' he sobs. I can feel that he weeps not because of our predicament, but for all the years in the wilderness, all the loneliness. He cries for all the love in him that has dried up and shouldn't have.

'I love you too, Tommo,' I say. 'More than ever I can say!' And there we are, both of us bawling our eyes out.

It is Tommo who finally clears his throat to speak. 'Ya know what gives me the screaming shits most of all?'

'What?' I sniff.

'The fucking mongrels has won!'

'Only when the trap-door opens under our feet. We aren't dead yet,' I say, but there is not a great deal of conviction in my voice.

'Looks as though this time the Sheriff o' bloody Nottingham *did* get Robin Hood. What a turn-up for the books,' Tommo sighs.

I try to lighten the subject. 'Know what gives *me* the, er, shits?'

'What?' he asks.

'I never had a chance to know Maid Marian.'

'You still a virgin then? Well I never!' Tommo laughs.

I nod my head and grin, imitating Ikey. 'Absolutely and with certainty and not to be doubted, my dears, the wiles o' the fairer sex be most mystifying and bedding one what's not a whore is a most tricky set o' peregrinations and not always a journey o' the heart worth the sweat of one's brow!'

Tommo laughs again. 'It were the only nice part o' the wilderness, women wanting a taste o' liquor for a favour granted.'

I think to myself that I wouldn't wish it that way. Once perhaps, just to know what it feels like, but then I'd want something different. Not that I know anything about loving a woman. But I've seen how Mary looks at Mr Emmett and he at her. I don't think anything is going on between them –

their different stations in life don't allow it – but the softness you can feel between those two, that's what I'd like to have.

Tommo interrupts my thoughts. 'You ain't missed a lot, swiving's a bit disappointing really. Well the sort of stuff I has done, anyway,' he laughs. 'Knee-tremblers, sort of. Breeches still on!'

I try to imagine what he's talking about. I think of these knee-tremblers and my size and I can see in my mind it isn't possible. Besides, I'm a nigger – I don't suppose any woman would have me unless I paid for it.

'Tommo, have you, er, been in love? You know, like in the library books?' I ask. I don't like to admit to him that I've read everything in Mrs Dean's Hobart Town Lending Library, including the romances!

'Nah,' he says, 'I reckon love only happens in them stories.'

'I hope not,' I says.

I must have sounded wistful because Tommo shakes his head. 'Christ Jesus, Hawk! What's wrong with ya? First you want men to have a bloody conscience, now you want a woman what loves you! And you want to love her back! You got about as much chance o' finding a woman to love as you got o' giving mongrels like Nottingham a conscience! Better keep on pullin' your pud, that way you'll meet a better class of woman than what would think to mix with the likes of us!'

I laugh. Tommo as always is the practical man. I can well imagine the dainty little lass that I'd like for my own, but I can't imagine anyone like her agreeing to marry me. Anyway, it's all pointless, isn't it? Nothing but divine intervention will save our lives now.

I think of our beloved mama and her life's motto, 'I shall never surrender.' I cheer up a bit at this thought. Perhaps I can delay the trial. I have read a little of the law, Mary always being anxious to know her rights, and the other brewers in Hobart Town ever threatening to force her out of business by means of the law. In their opinion, a woman has no right to be in brewing and moreover to be successful at it. Subpoenas, it seems, are a way of life with the pure merino brewers. Beer and barristers go together like a horse and cart.

'What's that noise?' Tommo asks abruptly. His ears are all the sharper for his time in the wilderness. 'It's people,' he answers himself, 'coming our way.' We fall silent, both listening. 'A mob . . . marching,' Tommo says, 'coming closer, here maybe.'

Then I hear it, faintly, I cannot tell from what direction. We wait and by and by the shouting and marching grows louder. 'What do you think it is?' I ask.

Tommo shrugs. 'Buggered if I knows.'

The noise escalates until we are sure it's a very large mob, heading towards the gaol. Strains of singing float toward us, mingled with shouting. Tommo listens intently, trying to make out the words. 'Shit! They're after us!' he cries.

Now I hear it for myself. '*Utu! Utu!*' Revenge! Revenge!

'Maori,' Tommo says quietly. 'Oh no, they's after you for killing the Hairy Horror!'

We listen as someone shouts for silence, and there's a hush as someone addresses the crowd. It's Nottingham. But his voice is quickly drowned out by a great roar of protest as a thunder of stones rain down on the corrugated iron roof. '*Utu! Utu! Utu!*' The chanting takes up again, though some of it is lost under the rain of rocks. We hear cheering and the sound of running and more rocks being thrown. Then we smell smoke. Fire!

'They's burning us down!' Tommo cries again. 'The bastards is burning us out!'

Suddenly there is a rattle of keys and the cell door is flung open. Four Maori push through the door with others crowding behind them. Beyond them, I can see nothing but smoke. There is no one to save us. They drag me out of the cell, cursing and shouting. I struggle as much as I can, but the manacles and shackles restrain me. Two of them, both big men, have me by the legs and two about the shoulders and then others rush to join them until a dozen hands are attached to me. I hear Tommo yelling behind me but there is no way I can turn around. 'Tommo, get out, don't fight!' I scream and then begin to cough from the smoke.

I am carried out to the front of the gaol and there is a terrible baying from the crowd which surges forward, shouting, '*Utu! Utu!*'

The crowd is now all around me. My abductors lift me high above their heads while others push and strike at the howling mob, beating them back as frantic hands try to claw at me. If my captors let me go I will be kicked and torn apart by the angry mob. The posse abducting me force their way through the roaring crowd, shouting threats and using their fists, until we reach a horse-drawn cart. I am thrown into it while several of the Maori leap aboard, sitting upon my body and at the same time shouting and kicking at the crowd who now surround the cart, holding on to it.

Soon we are clear of the main mob though others continue to run after us and some to hurl stones. A shower of rocks hits the cart and also one of the Maori who sits upon my chest. He gives a gasp and is knocked senseless, slumping forward.

I am sure my end is near, but my most immediate concern is for Tommo. If the crowd gets hold of him they will tear him to pieces. I begin to sob for my twin, whom I shall never see again.

By now we are pulling away from the town of Kororareka. As we travel up a small hill I can see a great billow of black smoke coming from the gaol-house. The road is deep-rutted and the cart bounces badly so that my blouse, stiffened with the dried blood of the previous night, grates against my back which is soon again soaked. Tommo's turbanned bandage is also leaking blood which I can feel running down my neck. I have not drunk water since the previous night and know without it I will soon faint from exhaustion in the day's heat.

'*Kahore o wai? Homai he wai moku,*' I croak. Have you any water? Please give me some water! I beg in Maori, though I must repeat myself several times to be heard above the rattle of the cart. A bottle of water is held to my mouth and I drink greedily as it rattles against my teeth, but it is too soon removed. I feel much recovered, though sick at heart when I think of Tommo at the hands of the mob.

For over a week I am transported on the back of that cart, with no word of explanation from my captors. They give me food and water, but they do not engage in conversation with me. Fatigue and injury have dulled my mind and I am a passive enough prisoner. We have long since left the road and taken paths that lead through forest glades or cut through the tu-tu grass that often towers high above the cart.

For seven days we pass no human settlement but, as the shadows begin to fall on our eighth day, we come to a village beside a small mountain stream. The others climb down from the cart and I am left to lie alone. Soon children with big brown eyes and serious expressions come to look at me. They are for the most part naked. Each time I move in my chains they scatter like startled chickens. But they soon enough return to stare silently at me again. I daresay they have not seen a nigger before and I am to them as curious a sight as an unknown species of wild beast.

216

It is not long since the Maori have forsaken cannibalism and there is often talk that it is still practised in remote regions where the pakeha are afraid to go. Perhaps this will be my unhappy end, to be eaten at a great feast. I am almost resigned. The law will not find me here, and even if it should, the courts would treat me no better than the Maori. After the authorities have broken my neck they would feed me to the worms, which I think is no better than the cannibal's cooking pot.

In days past, the Maori believed that to eat your enemy made you strong. The chief must inherit the strength of the chief and all the others he has killed in battle and to do so he must drink their blood and swallow their eyes so that the spirits of his victims add to his power, his *mana*. All this Hammerhead Jack told me in the long days we spent together at sea. When my friend's eye was destroyed by Nestbyte, he explained that it was no great tragedy for it was the right eye and not the left. The godhead of a chief, and the spirit of the Maori, lives in the left eye. Had his left eye been destroyed, he would not have wished to survive, for he would have lost his *mana*.

From what I have observed of the white settlers and their soldiers and policemen, the Maori people will need all their strength if they are not to be reduced to the status of beggars and drunkards in their own country. I have seen what has been done to the Aborigines in Van Diemen's Land and hope that the same will not happen to the Maori.

Perhaps it is better after all that I be eaten in an ancient ceremony than die in ignominy. I would much prefer a warrior's sharp teeth to slow consumption by maggots. Despite my misery I smile to myself. After all, what Tommo calls Mary's white tablecloth religion is based on a good Sunday roast!

I can hear God sitting at the table of the Maori chief.

'Did you say a nice leg o' pork, my dear?' God asks the chief of the cannibals.

'No, Sir,' says the chief. 'This be a nice leg o' *Hawk*!'

But then my humour changes. I am too sore and uncomfortable not to feel pity for myself. I think about my neck, how it seems to have an affinity for the rope. I lift my manacled hands to touch the band of silver tissue, the bright scar caused by the wild man when I was seven years old. It is now a well-defined track where the hangman will neatly fit the final loop of hemp to break my neck, that is if Nottingham and his Auckland jury should catch up with me. What a sorry end I shall have either way.

When I took Tommo from Brodie's sly grog shop I was bitterly saddened by Mary's anger and banishment. And yet I had thought we might have a great adventure together and return to our mama with Tommo sober and both of us much experienced in the world. Now, in the late afternoon, with the shadows falling in a strange village, I think of how little luck poor Tommo has had. How his mongrels have followed us and how, through no wrongdoing of our own, our young lives will soon end: him burned to death in the prison or torn to pieces by a mob of angry savages, and me eaten by same.

The children are clambering more boldly upon the cart and some reach out and touch me, then pull their hands away quickly as though I have burnt their fingers. I ask for water and try to smile but they are completely taken aback at the sound of my voice. They leap wildly from the cart and scatter, the smaller ones fleeing helter-skelter, their tiny feet shooting back puffs of dust as they run, yelling in terror as if followed by a wild, black beast.

And then a large voice rings out. 'Ork! Ork good!' And this is followed by a great laugh which resounds in the gathering dusk. It is none other than Hammerhead Jack!

My old friend soon has me ensconced in a large hut

where a couple of plump older wahines minister to me. They cut away my blouse and gently remove the coarse linen from the broken wounds on my back, laughing every time I wince, as though it is a huge joke. They clap their hands whenever I find a word to use in their language.

The women make a poultice of leaves and sticky ointment which they apply tenderly to my skin, packing it in with black mud which is left to dry. Whatever the medicine is, my back is soon quite comfortable. Next they remove Tommo's turbanned bandage and shave the hair from the back of my head using the edge of a sharpened shell, which proves most effective. They laugh at my springy black curls, which one of the women gathers in her hand and cups to her thighs. After much cackling at this, they tend my head wound most caringly.

I drink what must be a gallon of water, and eat a large dish of yams and sweet potatoes with a little meat mixed in. Finally the kind women remove the poultices and bathe me, laughing all the more when I will not submit to the removal of my breeches. They carefully wrap a blanket around my shoulders.

It is well into the evening, with a three-quarter moon risen in a clear, clean starry heaven, when I am taken to the *marae*, the meeting place to attend a *hui*, a gathering of the men.

I am asked most politely to sit on a bright woven mat before the elders, the *runanga*, while the rest of the men are seated behind me. This, I surmise, is the *kawa* of the *marae* – good etiquette, which shows respect for me. Hammerhead Jack then addresses the gathering, speaking too quickly for me to understand everything he is saying. I soon realise, however, that he is telling of our voyage and the killing of the sperm whale. He points often to me, whereupon the elders facing me smile and those behind me murmur their approval.

My giant friend's arm socket is much improved and the skin, though tender in appearance, has no suppuration and is clean and healthy looking. The wound from his missing eye has healed up completely, the skin about the socket puckered like a Christmas prune. In the meantime, the left eye seems to have grown curiously larger and brighter in his huge head, and it is not so difficult to believe that his godhead lives there. This eye is most commanding. It opens wide and darts about as he talks, almost as though he is a cyclops.

Hammerhead Jack has the same air of authority about him as he did on board ship, while he still shows respect and pays obeisance to his chief. The chief is a man not much older than him, a tall solidly built *rangatira*, though somewhat smaller in stature than the whaleman. Finally, with a grand sweep of his good arm and a big smile, Hammerhead Jack points to me and says, 'Ork, good!' Then he bids me stand. After much poking out of his tongue and slapping of his thighs, he finally rubs noses with me.

Amidst cheering and clapping, the chief, whose name is Wiremu Tamihana, bids me sit again. He calls out and beckons to someone seated behind me. Presently a young Maori about my age comes to the front and, speaking in tolerably good English, translates the chief's speech of welcome to me. I later learn that Wiremu Tamihana speaks excellent English and has been well educated by missionaries but chooses not to use the invaders' tongue.

Chief Wiremu Tamihana first thanks me for saving Hammerhead Jack's life and says that his people are much honoured to have a brave man among them. He asks me to remove my blanket and show the lashes I have taken on behalf of his tribesman.

'Here is a man who has given his blood for the Maori

people! Is he not our brother and welcome in the Ngati Haua tribe?' the young translator declares.

The chief tells me I am welcome to stay and that they will hide me from the pakeha policemen who might come looking. There is no mention of the death of Hori Hura and it is clear they do not see me as guilty of any crime against one of their own people.

The Maori chief ends by saying that his people cannot trust Queen Victoria, who has taken their *mana*, their land, their prestige, and their substance, from them and left them only the shadow. They have twenty muskets and ammunition and the men are well trained in the use of the *taiaha*, the fighting stick which, during earlier skirmishes against the pakeha, proved much superior to the British soldier's bayonet.

At this the men show their delight, stamping their feet and slapping their thighs to make a thunderous whacking noise which reverberates through the dark night. The chief then holds up his hand to silence them. 'We cannot fight the pakeha. We are one tribe only and too few. We must come together. All the Maori people must speak with one voice.'

Some of the men voice their consternation when he says this and I can see the elders are not of one accord on the matter. But Chief Tamihana does not wish to discuss it and, instead, invites me to talk.

I am still not well and have only a little voice left, so I ask the young Maori who speaks English to stand close. I speak slowly, using as many Maori words as I am able, and thank them for saving my life. I offer my service to the tribe, though I have no training in firearms and admit that, despite my size, I am no warrior. I have never killed a man.

'We will teach you, Ork!' Hammerhead Jack shouts jovially. 'It is much easier than killing a whale!'

This is followed by much laughter from the others and I begin to wonder whether my offer was wise. When the merriment lessens, I agree with their chief that the Maori people must speak as one voice. 'Many voices speaking at the same time can only be heard as a babble,' I say. 'The pakeha have the governor who can listen to their many voices and speak for them as one voice. Their unity is their strength.' I do not take this further, for the chief has already made his point.

'I can read and write and have some knowledge of how the white man thinks,' I say, thinking this a poor substitute for these warriors' experience, but it is all I have. 'I have studied the methods by which the soldiers of Queen Victoria fight and this may also be useful. To know the mind of the enemy is always of some advantage.'

'And how was the mind of the enemy, Captain O'Hara, when we chopped off his hand?' Hammerhead Jack asks gleefully. It is clear they all know the story, because there is another wave of laughter among the men.

'I am not sure that it was a wise thing to do,' I say, trying to force a smile.

Now the men are completely silent and I can see from the expression on Hammerhead Jack's face that he is confused.

Then the chief addresses me in English, to my surprise. 'Ork, do you know much of the missionary talk?'

'Some,' I say. 'But I am not of their faith.'

'Me neither, though I know some of their ways,' he says, as the lad now translates his words back into Maori for the elders. 'Does it not say an eye for an eye and a tooth for a tooth in the missionary's black book?' I nod. Indicating Hammerhead Jack, the chief continues, 'Well, my blood brother has lost his eye and not taken the white man's eye in return!' He points at the shoulder joint which once held the giant Maori's arm. 'And the pakeha has taken my brother's arm and we have *only* taken a hand in return. Why is this not wise?'

'The pakeha have laws which, when they are disobeyed, lead to severe punishment. We should not take the law into our own hands but must wait for a proper judgment,' I reply, though it sounds rather foolish even to me.

But the chief does not at once dismiss this. 'Ha!' he exclaims. 'Then which is the more important, the laws of Queen Victoria or the laws of the pakeha God?'

'In theory, the laws of God.' The chief can see that I am struggling with my reply and raises his hand.

'We are told that we must obey Queen Victoria, who is the most powerful pakeha. But we are also told that even she must obey the Christian God. Is that not true?'

'It is true, but . . .' I begin.

The chief stops me. 'So, the laws of the Christian God say we must take an eye for an eye and an arm for an arm. When we take only a hand in return for an eye *and* an arm, and do not return the beating you took and the other Maori took to their backs, why will the pakeha whaling captain think we have acted badly?'

Tamihana pauses. 'I am told he is a Christian. Why, under the laws of his own God, should he not be grateful for losing only his hand?'

It is difficult to argue with the flow of his reasoning. I have read the Bible twice over, and there is much within it I have come to respect. To me, the stumbling block has always been that men piously preach God's laws on the Sabbath, but practise man's laws on the following six days. Any fool may see that the two are in direct contradiction – that in fact greed and corruption transcend charity and compassion in society.

'The Maori have much to fear from the pakeha laws but

we cannot defeat them by ignoring them,' I venture. 'We must learn to use their own laws against them.'

'Ha!' The chief points to Hammerhead Jack. 'Like my brother, the pakeha laws have only one eye. The other is blind and cannot see the Maori people. The governor never does anything if a Maori is killed – only when a pakeha is killed!'

I shrug. 'The white man will not leave New Zealand. They will not go away. Queen Victoria has the Treaty of Waitangi, the paper which is signed by many of the Maori chiefs.'

'Then we must tear it from her hand! She has stolen our *mana*!' the chief replies.

'It is said that since the Maori people have learned to use the pakeha guns, they have killed more than twenty thousand of their own people and as many have died from the white man's diseases. There are now as many pakeha as Maori in New Zealand.' I know this from reading the *Colonial Times* back in Hobart Town.

The chief shows no surprise at my words, and sighs. 'You are right, Ork. We are allowed to kill each other as we please and Queen Victoria does nothing to stop us. Only if we kill the pakeha must we go to gaol. Is this not strange? Did she not swear at the Treaty that the Maori and the pakeha would be the same under her law? Or do you think Queen Victoria likes us to kill each other so the white man will soon become greater in number than the Maori?'

'What can I say? I am young and not wise.' I take a deep breath and gather my courage. 'But you are right, Chief Tamihana, you will only be strong when you speak with one voice. Now you are single tribes and can easily be divided. As long as tribe fights tribe and Maori hates Maori, the pakeha will always win. Believe me, I am on your side, Wiremu Tamihana. The pakeha do not win because their laws are more just or their God is more powerful, but because they all fight for one Queen.'

The chief nods. 'I will think upon this. I am the *ariki*, the descendant of the eldest son of the eldest son of each generation since the Maori came here from beyond the clouds and the bending of the earth line. I will talk to the ancestors.' Then he asks again, 'You think the Maori must have a leader, like Queen Victoria?'

The notion is, I can see, a new one for Tamihana, who frowns as he thinks about what I have said. 'It is not for me to say, Chief Tamihana. I do not know the Maori customs.' I search for further explanations. 'But one big tribe which fights together under one leader will win the war over many smaller ones which fight alone.'

'Ah! One tribe, one war! You are a good man, Ork.' The chief smiles.

'Ork good!' Hammerhead Jack cries, amidst much cheering.

I wait until the noise has died down. 'I would like to ask something for myself?' I say to the chief.

Chief Tamihana nods, granting me permission to make my request. I turn to Hammerhead Jack.

'My brother, Tommo? Can we find out what has happened to him?'

The men laugh anew and I look about me in distress. How can they laugh at this? Hammerhead Jack knows we are twins and very close. He grins broadly. 'Ho! The little axe man!' His single eye grows wide and shines bright, as though it has taken in the light from the missing other. 'Tommo is Maori also! He will join you in two days, Ork.' He holds up two fingers. 'We will welcome him when he comes. We have taken him another way to confuse the pakeha policeman. He is with the old man and the others who were together with us in the whaleboat.' Hammerhead Jack takes a step towards me and puts his huge single arm about my shoulder. 'Tommo good! Ork good!'

I try very hard to restrain myself, but all can see the bright tears that run down my cheeks and the stupid smile upon my black face. Though we are fugitives, for the moment Tommo and I have beaten the mongrels.

BOOK TWO

Chapter Nine

TOMMO

The Land of the Long White Cloud
June 1858

We has been gone nearly two years from Hobart Town and has lived among the Maori for over a year. We's playing it safe even though there was never any warrant for our arrest. From what we've heard the authorities believe that the Maori attacking the prison was seeking revenge for the death of Hori Hura. No doubt we's thought to be well and truly dead! The government troopers wasn't too keen to come in search of us even if we *was* still alive, for there be a growing dispute between the white settlers and the Maori people over possession o' the land. A bad quarrel is brewin' as the settlers becomes more greedy for Maori land, and the Maori chiefs more suspicious and unwilling to sell.

To send troopers in search of them what's killed two criminals, what was going to hang anyway, weren't deemed in the best interests o' the colony. Instead, the whole business has been quickly forgotten in the name of diplomacy. Sergeant Nottingham were given the boot and retired on a government pension. We hears he has become another drunk, cadging drinks in Kororareka's hotels. Maple and Syrup has absconded to Auckland, while Mrs Barrett ain't been seen since the night o' the card game, his whereabouts unknown. De Silva, o' course, sailed happily away.

What a rescue it were! Smoke and shouting everywhere and I'm thinking it's all over for me and Hawk when he is carried out of the cell by four savages. Soon after, three blokes grab yours truly, and I expects we'll both be torn to pieces by the mob.

As they push me out of the cell, I sees Hawk through the smoke. He's being carried over the heads of his captors to the front of the gaol and I tries to follow him as they takes him towards the door. But them what's got a hold of me shoves me down a passageway towards the back of the gaol-house. In the corridor we come across Nottingham. He is on his hands and knees, with blood coming out his nose and mouth, coughing and wheezing from the smoke.

'Ya mongrel bastard, Nottingham!' I screams. 'Your scam failed, didn't it, you two-faced bludger!'

I suppose I should've saved me voice to pray for me life, but at that moment I hates the sod so much, I don't give a damn! Me brother's going to be killed 'cause of him and I only wish I had me axe so I could do the same to him. I hope the fire roasts the miserable pig like Sam Slit!

I can hear the crowd outside howling for blood. Strange, I ain't afraid for meself, only for Hawk. Without him there ain't no point anyways: might as well be back in the wilderness, or dead. I only hopes they make it quick. I don't want to die slow – hands clawing at me, feet kicking and stamping, me bones crunching under their sticks and stones. The mob is braying now. It's a weird sound. They must have Hawk, I reckons. I wish they'd kill me first, so I don't have to bear the pain o' hearing me brother bashed to death.

'May you rot in hell, Nottingham!' I screams as I'm bundled out the back door.

'Him mongril, Tommo,' shouts one of the Maori holding me about the shoulder, then laughs. I stares around in surprise. It is one of me mates from the *Nankin Maiden*! In me panic I haven't recognised him. What's happening here? I thinks. There's no one outside the back o' the gaol-house and them what's running me towards the bay are laughing like it's a huge joke.

Pretty soon we comes to a canoe well hidden on the beach, and we're off across the water and out to sea. We travels up the coast for several miles, then leave the canoe and head into the wilderness.

For over a week, we walks through mountains and valleys. Several times, we comes to a stream and we stops to bathe. It feels like we're goin' in circles and we does much of our walking in rivers to lose our footprints. Finally, towards the evening of the tenth day, we come to the *pa* of the Ngati Haua tribe and then into the village and there's Hawk sitting large as life with Hammerhead Jack.

Though me Maori friends has told me often enough along the way that Hawk would be all right, I were feared he could not make it through the mob unharmed. Hawk be just as happy to see yours truly as I am to see him and to me mortification, he lifts me high above the ground, swinging me up in his great arms as if I be some snot-nosed brat. But I can't wipe the grin off me stupid gob, as the tears roll down Hawk's cheeks. Hammerhead Jack roars with laughter and I can see he approves. 'We are safe from the mongrels here, Tommo!' Hawk tells me as he returns me to the ground.

And so we has been. But in the course of the year, I've learnt that life among the Maori can be as bloody difficult as life aboard ship. They has so many taboos, things they can and cannot do. They call this *tapu* and it is ruled over by the chief and the priests, the *tohunga*, what are the keepers of the tribe's history and lore. The *tohunga* are big men 'round these parts, second only to the chief himself.

Chief Wiremu Tamihana is not only the tribe's leader but also a kind of god. His *tapu* comes direct from the spirits and is the absolute law. All that the chief touches becomes *tapu* or, as white folk might say, holy.

We've only been in the village a couple of months when we sees how powerful this *tapu* be. Hawk and Chief Tamihana is sitting together, talking, with the chief smoking his pipe. By and by they takes a walk and the chief, not thinking, leaves his tinder-box behind. Four ordinary blokes happen by and, seein' the tinder-box, stops to light their pipes. But when they finds out whose tinder-box it be, they realise they has committed a terrible sacrilege by using it and they dies of fright. Truly, they dies! They is all stone dead, not twelve hours later, of the fear brought on by the *tapu*.

Tapu is most powerful in the chief, and he can get whatever he wants in the tribe just by saying it is his *backbone* or his *right arm* or some other part of his body. When the chief says this, he makes whatever it be sacred, so that no one else, includin' the owner, can go near it again. If a single drop of the chief's blood be spilled upon an object, then it is *tapu*, and can only belong to him.

In the common people, *tapu* is a more simple and practical thing. Say a man finds a piece of driftwood on the beach, he needs only cut a notch in it with his axe, and it becomes *tapu* and his property. What would Ikey thinks of this business, I wonders with a smile. A man can simply pull a single strip of flax across his doorway and no person can enter it until he returns to remove the *tapu*: a most efficient means o' protecting your property!

Of course for the white man, property be only owned by evidence of a government deed and protected by a gun. *Tapu* has often made it hard for the Maori to deal with the pakeha. Many white folks don't bother to learn the importance of their taboos and don't respect their rules. Living amongst the Maori, I has come to understand much about *tapu*, but I still makes mistakes. Hawk though has gone to much trouble to learn some of the complex *tapus* and laws o' the people. This has come in most handy in his dealings with the Ngati Haua tribe and many others. Me brother has become a big man among the natives.

Meself, I've had enough of adventures to last me a lifetime. I want us to move on, to find our way back to Australia. Being here ain't much different to being on the *Nankin Maiden* as Chief Tamihana don't allow grog in his villages, something what makes big brother Hawk happy, o' course! I am now almost two years dry, though not cured in the least of me desire for the fiery grape. Not a single day passes without me thirsting for a drop.

Hawk, meanwhile, is determined that we stay on in this dry place to repay our 'debt' to Hammerhead Jack.

'Debt! What's you mean, debt? We don't owe no debt! *You* saved *his* life!'

'You are wrong, Tommo,' Hawk says in his patient way what makes me want to kick him in the bollocks. 'I only helped him back into the whaleboat.'

'You saved him from the whale! And from being flogged to death!'

'Maybe,' he replies. 'But he saved both of us. Two lives! We owe him at least one, Tommo.'

'Me own, I suppose?' I says, sarcastic-like.

'No, Tommo, you needn't give up your life. But there is much we can do to help.'

Hawk reckons that a great injustice is being done to the native people by the white men. His conscience has got the better of him. But the world be full o' mongrels and now, with as many settlers in New Zealand as there are Maori, they's taken over this place and claimed it for their own. What can Hawk do to change this? Nothing! But he won't listen. And now he tells me that war is coming.

'War!' I shouts. 'War between the pakeha and the Maori? And you wants us to be a part of it? On the side of the Maori?' I scream at him. 'What can *we* do, a nigger and a skinny runt? For Gawd's sake, let's scarper while we still can!'

'Tommo, we can't, not now!' he says, pleading.

'What? Why not? You gunna be a general in the army or something?'

'Adviser, no more,' Hawk answers calmly. 'The Maori must unite. The tribes must be brought together or they cannot prevail against the government troops and the settlers.'

'You know what?' I says, truly angry now.

'What?'

'You're gunna get us killed, that's what!'

'Listen, Tommo! The settlers, with the connivance of the government, are stealing Maori land. As long as the Maori are divided they have no hope of impressing the governor. They have no collective power to claim their rights under the treaty.'

'Where'd ya learn all this rubbish, Hawk? Nobody has no power to exert against no British government! You think *we's* got power to exert? You think the Aborigines in Tasmania, what's practically all perished at the hands o' the government, had power? You think Georgie Augustus Robinson, the government man what was meant to protect the Abos, was their true friend? All he done was herd Truganini and her people into nowhere so the whites could take their land! What treaty is ya talking about, mate?'

'Waitangi. The Treaty of Waitangi.'

'Waitangi? That piece o' shit-paper! The Maori may as well wipe their arses on it for all the good it will do 'em!'

'It says the Queen will guarantee the full, exclusive and undisturbed possession of their lands and estates, forests and fisheries and other properties they may collectively and individually possess, so long as it is their wish and desire to retain the same in their possession!' Hawk quotes all this right off, so that I want to punch his face in.

I shrug. 'The government's changed its mind, then, like it always does.'

'No, there's more!' says Hawk, his eyes gleaming. 'It is in the rest of the treaty that they are boxing clever now, thinking to evade their responsibility with misinterpretation!'

'Misinterpretation, is it now? Shit, Hawk, wake up!'

'Listen, this is what the New Zealand Company say,' and he takes to quoting again: ' "We have always had very serious doubts whether the Treaty of Waitangi made with naked savages by a consul invested with no plenipotentiary powers . . ." '

'What's pleni-po-tentiary mean?' I asks. Hawk and his big words!

'It means someone what has been given the full powers of the government, like an ambassador.' Hawk answers. 'Where was I? Oh yes . . . "invested with no plenipotentiary powers, without ratification by the Crown, could be treated by lawyers as anything but a praiseworthy device for amusing and pacifying savages for the moment." ' Hawk stabs at the air with his finger. 'We *cannot* allow this to happen!'

'We? What's this "we"? Hawk, *we* is not Maori! *We* is supposed to be British, remember! Shit, *we* is supposed to be on the other bloody side, mate!'

'No, no, they are also British, the Maori!'

'British?' Now I'm curious. 'How come?'

Off he goes again and I think what a bloody bore he's gunna be if he ain't careful. ' "In consideration for consent to the Queen's government, the Queen will protect all the Maori people and give them all the rights and privileges of British subjects." ' Hawk looks at me steady. 'So you see, they are the same as the settlers in their entitlements, but their land be taken away from them with a clever ploy, a misrepresentation!'

'There ain't nothin' new in that! That's what governments do for a living, mis-bloody-represent!'

'Tommo, you must understand this thing! It is like we said on the ship, it's a matter of conscience, good men working for the common good of the common man!' He sees me doubtful face and adds, 'Not letting the mongrels win!'

I jerk my head and snort. 'The mongrels always win when they is the government!'

Hawk ignores me and if there were a tub nearby, I swear he'd have took to thumping it. 'The Maori do not possess the land individually like we do. Land is owned by the tribe, and if the individual should use it for his own, it is only by permission of all the tribe as represented by the chief. The tribe allows him to use the *shadow* of the land though the *substance*, the soil itself, belongs to all. It has been their way, their law, since time out of mind.'

'But it ain't our way, is it?' I insist.

'That's right,' says Hawk, 'but the British government understood this difference and recognised it. The treaty states that land can only be sold to the government with the full permission of *all* the tribe and its chief. Settlers may not buy land directly from any individual, only from the government. But the settlers are doing so, and the government is turning a blind eye.'

'There you are, what the eye don't see, the heart don't grieve over!' I claps my hands and laughs. 'Put down your spectacles, gentlemen, the little Queen in London Town owns all the aces in New Zealand! Can't expect her to see across the sea, now can we?'

'No, it's not right, Tommo!' Hawk shouts. 'It's deliberate cheating! It's Queen Victoria cheating her own subjects of what's rightfully theirs!'

'And so you wants to go to war against her? Ha! You must be mad!'

'The Maori people have a saying: "For women and land, men die."'

'And Tommo also has a saying: "We ain't got no women and we ain't got no land and so I'm telling you straight, we ain't gunna die for fuck-all o' nothing!"'

Hawk laughs despite himself. 'The Maori people *must* speak with one voice and Chief Tamihana wishes there to be a Maori king to bring all the tribes together. This he has almost accomplished. A new king will be announced in the next few months.'

'A king for them, a queen for us? You think *that* will solve the problem?'

'Tommo, Chief Tamihana has a most persuasive argument. He asks, "Is there not Queen Victoria of England, Nicholas of Russia, Louis Napoleon of France and Pomara of Tahiti – each a native monarch for their people? Each nation is separate, and I also must have a king for myself."'

'Sure, and *we* already has a queen. Why should we help him?'

Hawk looks hurt. 'Tommo, the Maori have always had their wars, one tribe hating the other. That's the government's strength, to encourage one against the other, to divide and conquer! Since the musket was introduced to them, the Maori have killed more than twenty thousand of their own people! I can help Chief Tamihana to make peace amongst the tribes.' He is breathing heavy now. 'They have agreed to a king of their own but there is still much dissension between them on other matters. If they may be united then they will be a force to be reckoned with. Their wishes cannot then be ignored by the governor.' Hawk grins suddenly. 'For the first time in my life my colour is useful. I am neither white nor brown, I am as black as the ace of spades, so I have no axe to grind. I'm no threat to either side. This makes me the perfect go-between.'

'That's right, it'll be no different to always! Everybody hates the nigger, so now everyone can hate the black go-between! You be perfect for the job o' being hated,' I says.

'Please let me do this, Tommo! I have been given my voice back and I must use it well. What better way than to stand up for what's right and honest, eh? Chief Tamihana is a good fellow, he wants peace and unity. He has shown us great charity, you know this. He has not spared his hospitality and his people have treated us like their own kind. We have so much to be thankful for.'

'Hawk! We can't live with the Maori forever!' I brings my face close as possible to his. 'We's got to go home soon!'

Hawk's eyebrows shoot up in surprise. 'Home? To Mary? You are ready to go home?' He has this big smile on his gob.

Hawk has been writing to mama and she to him. Chief Tamihana has arranged for our mail to be collected from Auckland. Mama writes all her letters to 'Mr H. Abacus' as the authorities reckon Hawk Solomon's dead and he'd soon enough be a wanted man if he weren't. Hawk's explained the need for secrecy to mama by telling her that we deserted the *Nankin Maiden* – he ain't said nothing 'bout her boys going to prison and escaping, though!

Hawk read Mary's recent letter aloud to me. She is well and the brewery's going nicely. He misses her and longs to see her again, I know. But I ain't ready yet for more of our mama.

'We got to get to Australia,' I says now. 'There's more gold been discovered in New South Wales, Mrs Barrett said so in the bloody poker game. And where there's gold, there be card games.'

Hawk looks disappointed. 'And grog?'

'Yeah, but I reckon I'm cured,' I lie.

'After this, after Chief Tamihana has managed to bring all the tribes together with the new king, I promise we shall leave.'

'And who will be this Maori king? Wiremu Tamihana, is it?' There is an edge of bitterness to me voice. I don't like this business of a Maori king, I'll wager nothing good will come of it.

'No, no, he does not wish it for himself. His ancestors are not powerful enough. The tribes have chosen Chief Potatau te Wherowhero to be crowned next month.'

'King Potato!' I laughs. 'Queen Victoria versus King Potato! What a contest that will be! Her ancestors, William, George, Charles, James, Elizabeth and all the bloody Henrys,' I say, mixing up all me kings and queens. 'Them against King Potato, Onion, Leek, Taro, Cabbage, Carrot and Beetroot!'

Hawk don't smile at my little joke. 'The Maori's ancestors be just as important as England's kings and queens, Tommo. Just as noble. But you are right, it is an uneven match. The Maori's belief in the malignancy of their dead ancestors adds a host of terrors to the *real* evils which beset them. It will be difficult to convince them to make the accommodations necessary for uniting the tribes.'

As Hawk predicts, Potatau te Wherowhero is announced King of the Maori in August. In the months what follow, I grows to admire me brother for his patience in trying to bring the tribes to one mind. My respect also grows for Chief Tamihana, who is much put upon by the other chiefs and the *tohunga*, the priests, of the various tribes, but who always listens to all points of view. In the end most of the tribes in the North are united. All that dissent are a few small ones and the mighty leader of the Taranaki Maori, Chief Wiremu Kingi.

By now Hawk and I both speak the Maori tongue well, and Hawk's voice has a deepness and calmness what makes men listen. But there is one thing left that he must do to earn the authority he needs, and I am much puzzled when he comes to me one morning.

'Tommo,' says he, 'they wish to make me Maori.'

'Might as well,' I quip, thinking to meself it means nothing more than what's already happened.

'No! You don't understand, they wish to tattoo me, to give me *moko*.'

'What?' I cries. 'Your gob and all?'

'Tamihana says if I do this the other chiefs will listen to us the better. They will name me the Black Maori.'

I look at me twin brother and shake me head. 'Hawk, you promised soon as they got themselves a bloody king we could leave this place! How'd you be at home with all them purple whirls on yer face?'

Hawk thinks for a moment. 'It isn't much of a face, by my reckoning, so no harm will be done there. As to what folks would think at home? They think I'm just a nigger anyway. Marks on my face will just confirm their view that I am a primitive savage!'

Hawk is smiling, but I sees the hurt of all the years underneath, the humiliation at being thought a black bastard. He is now seven feet tall and, at seventeen years old, near full grown. He is taller even than Hammerhead Jack and his strength be enormous. What he says about his gob makes me sad. I'm not sure I knows what handsome is meant to be in a man, but when me brother smiles it makes other men feel the world is good. The wahine, I've noticed, looks upon him with desire, which brings me to another matter what's troubling me. The Maori laws are strict about women and Tamihana has barred us from being with the tribe's wahines. Yours truly has been a mite frustrated.

'Will they give you the right to take a wahine?' I asks Hawk now.

It seems he's thought of this too. 'I have asked for us both and it is yes!' He smiles shyly.

'No chance!' says I, most alarmed. 'I ain't gunna have me gob scratched with blue lines for no bloody woman!'

'The *tohunga* and the chief will make a special dispensation for you, Tommo. If I become Maori, as my twin you are also Maori, even without tattoos on your face.'

'Without the tattoos, but still with the wahine?' I laugh, but me heart misses a beat.

Hawk nods, grinning as well. But I still don't want him to do it. 'I can survive. Pulling the pud ain't so bad. Don't let them bugger up your face, Hawk.'

'Like I said, it's not much to bugger up!' Hawk laughs, and turns serious. 'I would think it a great honour, Tommo. I have much love and respect for the Maori race.'

'Don't do it, Hawk!' I shouts, angry now. 'You'll be sorry forever!'

'No! You don't understand, Tommo! These will be the marks of my conscience!'

'To hell with your conscience! You be stark, starin', ravin' mad!'

'Please, Tommo, I *must* do it, show that I am not afraid

to be different, not afraid to fight for what's right and fair!'

'Your fight is gunna get us killed!' I shrug and look up at him despairingly. 'Nothing I say is gunna change your mind, is it?'

'No,' says he quietly. 'I love you, Tommo, but I don't seek your permission in this. I want only that you should understand.'

'I understand you're a bloody idjit!' I snort. But the anger is gone out of me voice and I gives up. 'Do what you like, it be none o' my business.'

Hawks grins. 'Thank you, Tommo. Perhaps I'll look the better for it!'

And that be the oddest thing. Hawk with all his Maori tattoos looks like a general. The blue swirls and markings are just visible on his black skin, but they seem to add to the strength of his face. Like I said, I don't know what handsome be, but Hawk is now a man what you is forced to look at with a lot of respect. He appears about five-and-twenty, and there is no mistaking him for a lad no more.

Life in the village is also gettin' better. There is a little wahine I've had me eye on for months, what looks at me the same. Most Maori women be too big for me, towering above, but this one be a perfect fit. After Hawk's tattooing, I talks to Chief Tamihana, and he gives the nod.

Maybe it comes natural with the Maori wahine, but it were never like this in the wilderness. My woman's name is Makareta and I am taken with her. She has a most beautiful disposition and laughs all the time. There ain't nothing she won't do for me and I be just as happy to care for her. I got no notion of what might be love, like Hawk sometimes goes on about, but whatever this be with Makareta, it will do me just fine.

We often goes walking together in the forest to gather

koroi, the beautiful scarlet and black fruit what grows at the top o' these giant trees. I shimmies up their huge trunks, jumping like a monkey from branch to branch as I done so often in the wilderness, and Makareta laughs and claps her hands. She says I do it much better than the Maori lads. Other times we gather berries what's so delicious that half is always eaten by the time we gets home. I know something of the way o' the wilderness from me past, but Makareta teaches me more. She loves the birds and they are of a great variety here, carrying on, shrieking, chirping and calling out, so's you can hardly hear yourself speak. I know the wren, the fly-catcher, the robin and the bellbird, o' course. She teaches me to recognise the calls of the pio-pio, the thrush what be different to ours, the popokotea, the piwakawaka and the riroriro. This last one's a funny name for a bird, though riroriro be somewhat like the sound it makes, like some small steam-engine starting up.

Makareta knows all the forest plants. She were taught by her mother what knows much about herbs. She can name all the ferns, maybe a hundred or more, also the many parasites and climbing creepers, their huge coils and slender vines festooning the massive branches. She knows every detail of their bright leaves, blossoms and fruits, what's to eat, what's poison, what can be used to cast a spell or stop a pregnancy. I've always thought the wilderness a dangerous place, but now I marvels in the infinite variety and cunning o' mother nature and sees the beauty of the lichen, moss, fungi and vines. The graceful clematis is everywhere, its white blossoms the shining stars o' the forest firmament.

Makareta takes great joy in teaching me what she knows and, in turn, wants to know everything about me. But the things I should tell her about meself I'd rather she didn't know. So I shows her some card tricks and tells her about

Mary. I even teaches her some o' the nursery rhymes, 'Three Blind Mice' and all the rest, as well as the songs Mary taught us when we were young uns. I tell her about climbing Mount Wellington and spearing yabbies and some of me and Hawk's boyhood adventures before we were took by the wild men. After that I don't say nothing and she soon knows not to ask, for she sees the look in me eyes.

I think Hawk is secret pleased about me and Makareta. He could have any wahine in the village, for he is now made *rangatira*, what best translates as a gentleman of high status among the Maori. But he has not yet taken a wahine for himself. I think even Chief Tamihana has took to wondering about him. He is always suggesting this wahine or that one, but Hawk laughs and says he will know when it's right and keeps busy with his work. There are some things about Hawk what's got nothing to do with our being twins.

After much fussing and shouting and to-ing and fro-ing, most of the objections of the other tribes are gradually sorted out. It takes many weeks, but at last the tribes agree to abide by the laws of the new Maori king. Our chief Tamihana is become known as the 'kingmaker' and 'peacemaker'. At last, I think, Hawk's work be done.

But Hawk is of a different mind. 'Not yet, Tommo. We have not yet got Chief Wiremu Kingi of the Taranaki to join the King Movement.'

'Then, after you's done that and all the tribes are united under your King Potato, *then* will you stop meddling?'

Hawk frowns. 'The pakeha and the government are most upset at the proclamation of a Maori king. Tamihana will need me at his side a little longer.' He looks at me appealing, 'Please understand, Tommo?'

And so we stays. I has been given the task of training five-and-fifty young Maori warriors in the art of the fighting axe, an art what's been invented by yours truly. It's one of me few talents. I've always been good with a hand axe, fast and accurate. Now I has worked out ways to fend off spears, knives and even bayonets with the axe handle. Chief Tamihana wants Hawk and me well instructed in the use of the *taiaha*, the Maori fighting stick, a weapon most formidable. In return, I'm to train his men with the fighting axe. This ain't difficult as the Maori are already skilled in using the hand axe for shaping their canoes and carving, and they quickly learns to use it as a weapon o' combat as well. Over many weeks I shows them how to throw it so the razor-sharp blade finds its target every time, but mostly we works on hand-to-hand techniques.

I calls me band o' merry men what I've trained, 'Tommo's Mongrel Killers'. The Maori can't pronounce this and so they has named us 'Tommo Te Mokiri', what I think sounds most pleasing to the ear.

It's no time at all before this new Maori king of ours has a flag, a magistrate, a surveyor, a council o' state, a police force and all the trappings. I be sure Hawk has had a hand in setting up all of this, though he denies it. The pakeha are not well pleased by these events and liken it to treason. There be a lot of hostility and some, even most, would march upon the new king to put a stop to such disloyalty to the queen of England.

Chief Tamihana, ever the moderate, says, 'The king on his piece, the queen on her piece, God over both and love binding them to each other.' I often thinks Chief Tamihana and Hawk both be idjits, birds of a useless, peaceful feather!

But Governor Gore Browne – a most pompous man, I gathers – thinks that the Maori will soon take to fighting among themselves. Hawk, who gets the newspaper from Auckland, reads the governor's opinion: ' "I trust that time and absolute indifference, a neglect on the part of the government, will teach the natives of the folly of proceedings undertaken only by the promptings of vanity and instigated by disappointed advisers.'"

Hawk laughs, setting the paper aside. 'I think we, along with Tamihana, are the *disappointed advisers*, what say you, Tommo?'

'I say governors won't deal kindly with *disappointed advisers* what stands up to them. Like I said before, it's time to scarper, mate!'

In truth, I has grown more content with life among the Maori, what with Makareta and all. But I sniffs trouble brewing, and sure enough, me instincts be right. Six months after Patatau's crowned king, a row breaks out between the colonists and the Ati Awa people of the Taranaki, which is where the settlers most badly want to buy land. Chief Wiremu Kingi declares his tribal lands is not for sale at any price. He ain't, he says, going to sell even a blade of grass or sod of earth or handful of dust to Governor bloody Gore Browne. He knows that all the government will do is promptly sell it to the settlers!

It's bad news that the first chief to tell the governor to go to hell is not of the King Movement and some thinks this is why the government has chosen to go against him. Chief Wiremu Kingi, though he be most powerful, now stands alone against the pakeha government.

Our chief, Tamihana, thinks this an opportunity to influence the Taranaki chief. He offers Hawk's assistance and the tribes agree that the Black Maori should go to the Taranaki to help in the negotiations with the governor's men. He can help with translations between the two parties.

For once the governor is feeling the pinch. Only seven of six-and-twenty million acres o' land in the North Island has been purchased by the settlers. So Gore Browne ups and says,

'The Europeans covet these lands and are *determined* to enter in and possess them, rightly if possible, if not, then by any means at all.' No 'Excuse I' or 'By your leave' or 'Does you mind?' What a mongrel bastard he turns out to be!

Well, Chief Wiremu Kingi ain't having a bar of it. He ain't selling and that's bloody that! So Governor Gore Browne starts to do a bit of re-interpreting of the Treaty o' Waitangi. He reckons that if a Maori, what tills or uses a piece of land he has inherited, desires to sell that land to the government, he can do so *without* the permission of the chief and the tribe. He can even do it over the chief's head, so to speak. It is the first time this be said official-like, by the Crown itself, which means Gore Browne intends it to become the law o' the land.

Soon enough the governor find a Maori turncoat by the name of Te Teira, who offers to sell the governor some land at the mouth of the Waitara. Quick as a flash, His Nibs agrees, provided a title can be made out.

But, with Hawk cleaning it up for the governor's tender ears, Wiremu Kingi sticks to his story. 'Listen, Governor! Notwithstanding Te Teira's decision, I will not permit sale of the Waitara to the pakeha. Waitara is in my hands. I will not give it up – never, never, never! I have spoken.' And he storms off in a proper huff, like Hawk says he should.

Things go from bad to worse when Mr Parris, the governor's district land purchaser, decides that Turncoat Te Teira's title *is* valid and the governor can buy his land at the mouth of the Waitara any time Te Teira cares to name a price. Parris sends in his surveyors to peg it, and a cove named Octavius Carrington marks it out neat as you like. 'This is the Crown's land now!' he announces, bold as brass to the applause o' the greedy settlers, what soon hopes to purchase it for themselves.

'Oh no it is not!' says Wiremu Kingi. 'This is my land and my people's land and my ancestors' land!' He then sends in the women of the tribe to pull out the surveyors' pegs.

'There's trouble coming, big trouble!' I says to Hawk. 'Time to back off, mate!'

'What?' says Hawk. 'Back off? Tommo, we've got right on our side! Tamihana thinks all the Maori will be willing to come together over this, and if he can persuade Wiremu Kingi to join the King Movement, this would be the first time we are a united front. The governor won't dare to go against all the tribes at once.'

'Just you watch him!' says I. Sure enough, ten days later the governor declares martial law and sends in the troops. 'So much for the king and the united tribes! Queen Victoria, it seems, don't give a fig about the Maori,' I says to me stupid brother with all his high hopes.

But Chief Wiremu Kingi is a man of his word and he don't frighten easy. He builds a *pa*, a Maori fort, on the disputed land. The governor sends in his troops and the two sides face each other. It be clear that the government has the better forces, with muskets and artillery at the ready.

'We're done for,' Hawk says bitterly. 'I blame myself. I didn't think the governor would go so obviously against the Maori. I have to persuade Wiremu Kingi not to fight or his people will be destroyed. This is a fight we cannot win.'

So Hawk sneaks off and, under cover of night, joins Wiremu Kingi in his *pa*. I am beside meself when I discovers him gone. Even when the game is up, me stupid brother won't save his own hide. I am all for going after him but Makareta begs me to stay. As she sees it, Hawk's gone to stop a fight and the chief will listen to the Black Maori. I hope she be right, and perhaps I have come to care for my wahine more than I thinks, 'cause I agree to stay with her, to wait and worry. The tribes of the King Movement are on the alert at the threat of war, and are watching the crisis most careful. Their informants be everywhere, so we hears all as it takes place.

With the government and Taranaki fighters facing each other, the governor sends an ultimatum to Chief Wiremu Kingi:

To the chief who obstructs the Queen's road,

You have presumed to build on Her Majesty's land, and to stop the free passage of persons coming and going. This is levying war against the Crown. Destroy the places you have built, ask my forgiveness and you shall receive it. If you refuse, the blood of your people will be on your own head. I shall order the men to open fire upon you if you not obey my order.

There ain't no road and there ain't no need for free passage. The land is not the queen's but is in dispute. Until this is resolved, it belongs to the Maori people, according to the treaty. But the governor's guns are pointed at Chief Wiremu Kingi's *pa* and Hawk, we hear, is desperate for the chief not to fight. Wiremu Kingi be no coward and it takes great persuasion. But at last he agrees and he leaves the *pa* swearing an oath of revenge as he watches the governor's troops destroy his fortifications.

In the six months what follow, Hawk tries to convince Chief Wiremu Kingi to meet with the governor. Ever the peacemaker, he argues that a forceful case may be made by the Maori, using the Treaty of Waitangi as evidence. They might yet save the day if they appeal to the colonial office in London or directly to Queen Victoria herself.

But Wiremu Kingi ain't in the mood to listen to Hawk's advice or any other. Instead he declares war against the pakeha. He explains his position in a most powerful letter to a chieftainess of his own blood:

> Peace will not be made, I will continue to fight and the pakeha will be exterminated by me, or by my younger brother Te Hapurona . . . It is well with your children and us, we die upon the land which you and your brothers left us . . . We are here eating the English bullets – My friends, my parents, this shall be my work forever. What though my people and I may die, we die for Aotearoa.

'Can we go now?' I beg Hawk when I hears of it. 'There's no more need for the Black Maori to stay. The war is declared and we has no part in it!'

As much as I care for Makareta, I'm afraid – afraid for my own skin, but more for me brother's. There is talk among the settlers of the Black Maori what be seven foot tall and speaks English well enough to trap the tongues of the governor's men. Hawk is thought to be a Maori of an extreme dark colour, for his tattoos are most correct and he is of the *rangatira* and so assumed to be high born. But his identity is a mystery. No one knows his true name and when he speaks to translate for any of the Maori chiefs or even for King Potatau himself, he's introduced only as the Black Maori. King Potatau has decreed that it is *tapu* to talk of Hawk to the pakeha, so his secret be well kept.

And so the rumour has begun amongst the pakeha that the Black Maori is the true power behind the tribes. It is he what threatens to destroy them, a new general who will come silent in the night and murder their women and children while they sleep. Hawk reads aloud from the *Auckland Herald* to me:

Black is the colour of the devil and the Black Maori has all the appearance and characteristics of Satan himself! His hair is black and close grown to his head and is easily likened to the devil's cap. His nose is large and his eyes dark as pitch and evil in every malevolent glance. If he lacks a pointed beard, it is only that his cunning has caused it to be shaved from his chin. His ears cannot be so well disguised and are pointed like a goblin's. He speaks with a most acerbic tongue, enough to burn the ears of any gentleman and not to be tolerated in the presence of the fairer sex. If a child should perchance come upon him unexpectedly, it would ever after be in a state of dreadful fright, the image of the devil burned into its memory forever!

'Hawk, you know what they says of you! They think you a danger to them and they will try to get you. Let's go now while we still can!' I plead when I hears this.

But Hawk ain't gunna be swayed. 'Tommo, I must see this through or I am a coward. I have done everything I can to avert war but the pakeha will not relent and are determined they should have land in the Taranaki, land the Maori do not wish to sell. If Wiremu Kingi relents it will not end there. This is the beginning, not the end, of the settlers' true rapacity!' He stops, scratches his noggin, then adds, 'Besides, there is something else.'

'What? Ain't you done enough?'

'It is the way the Maori plan to fight, the organisation of the *pa*.'

'The *pa*? But it looks like a most excellent fortification.'
The Maori *pa* is a fort, usually built upon a hill with
palisades o' logs, trenches, earth ramparts and underground
chambers, as well as a river or some natural defence on one
side. It is most difficult to attack and I don't know what
Hawk could be on about.

'The *pa* is about defence. This is fine for tribal war, but
in these battles, the Maori are often outnumbered by their
British attackers, who also have superior arms and
artillery.'

'But it has stood them well in the past. They talk of great
battles won, of fighting the British troopers to a standstill
from the *pa*.'

'Sometimes, yes,' Hawk agrees. 'But how well they
remember the victories and how soon they forget the defeats.
In the end, most attacks against the Maori *pa* were
victorious for the British. The Maori are brave men who
would willingly die for their land, but they are constantly
under siege when they fight from a *pa*. If not beaten at arms,
they can eventually be starved out.'

'But it be their way of protecting their women and
children. How else should they fight?'

Hawk looks serious. 'I do not love war but have read
much of it. Perhaps there is something to be learnt from the
wars of England and their military procedure in battle.'

'You're gunna teach the Maori to wage war from books?'
I ask. 'Hawk, they's warriors what come to it from
generations! And you hates violence!'

'Sometimes there is no other way but to stand and fight.
If we must do so, we might at least fight prepared with a
knowledge of the enemy. The Maori do not have this. They
have not designed the *pa* against the use of artillery. For their
own wars, where they use spears and fighting sticks, it fares
well. It may even be somewhat effective against the musket.

But it is defenceless against an artillery piece which can pound away remorselessly for as long as the pakeha likes, day and night.'

'So what is they to do?'

'They must avoid pitched battles,' Hawk answers.

'You means they should run away?'

'Well, yes, in a manner of speaking.' Hawk clears his throat and I resigns meself to one o' his lectures. 'During the Peninsular War under the Duke of Wellington – you know, the general who led the British and won at Waterloo where Mary's medal comes from?'

'Yes, I know who you means,' I say impatient. 'Mount Wellington be named after him.'

'Well, the Spaniards, fighting in their own country which they knew well, devised a new way of fighting Napoleon Bonaparte's troops. They engaged in "little wars", guerrilla wars, as they called it.

'The idea is to strike by surprise and then withdraw so the enemy never knows when you'll strike or where you are. You ambush them, keep on the move, never fight a pitched battle. In this way, much smaller forces can oppose much larger ones. Artillery is rendered ineffective and the battles are waged with muskets and hand-to-hand combat.'

'Hand-to-hand fighting?' I'm thinking of me fighting axe.

'Yes, small fast units that can do a maximum of harm in a very short time. The Maori have shown that with their fighting stick, they can combat the British bayonet. If they can be persuaded to fight this way, I think they will prove most effective.'

'With a fighting axe, too!' I says, excited. 'It be an ideal weapon for this kind o' war!'

Hawk nods. 'Yes. But I don't know if I can make Wiremyu Kingi agree to my ideas. The Maori are stubborn in their ways of fighting. I worry that their ancestors, speaking through the *tohunga*, could forbid it.'

He scratches his brow. 'You see, the Maori do not like to leave their land to fight. They think that they must hold the ground itself, defend it under their feet. I must persuade them that they might win the war with these tactics. That they can take their fight onto the lands the settlers have stolen, then return in peace to the land they still hold.'

Hawk's eyes shine as he thinks of how all this might be done. 'If the Maori adopt these tactics, they should attack the settlers on their farms and drive them into the towns, make them afraid to venture back onto their land. Then the Europeans would be under siege with no crops to harvest or livestock to slaughter.

'The troops would have to come out after the Maori to regain vacated territory and they would be ambushed, never knowing where the enemy was going to strike next. There are not sufficient of them to protect the pakeha farmers, to guard every farm, as well as the army's lines of communication. The Maori irregulars will strike wherever the governor's forces are not to be found. This will not be a war the British can win with artillery, using accustomed fighting tactics.'

Suddenly I see that what Hawk says makes sense. The Maori know the land and can move fast and silent across it. Their great war canoes can creep up the coast, attack and be away again. They be proven at close fighting. By drawing the British into the mountains, they could easily ambush them. If the troops remain on the plains, they could attack them at night, coming down from the mountains, where they hold their women and children safe.

'You think if the Maori do this, they can win?'

Hawk shakes his head. 'No, in the end, they cannot win, because the pakeha are not willing to leave New Zealand and there are as many of them now as there are Maori.'

'So, whatever method o' war the Maori use, it be a waste o' time!' I sigh, shrugging me shoulders.

'No, not at all. That is the whole point, Tommo. The Maori *must* resist, or they lose everything. If they fight from the *pa*, they will soon be defeated and their land confiscated by the government and given to the white man.

'They must harass the settlers, chase them with their women and children off their farms and into the towns. If the British troops can never engage them in pitched battle, then the war can continue, until the settlers' lands fall into decay and cannot be ploughed or harvested, until all their livestock is killed or captured, and until the towns are brought to the edge of starvation. When this happens, the government will call a truce.' Hawk grins and spreads his hands. 'This time the Maori will have power on their side in the negotiations, and the government will have to listen with some humility. This time we will hold most of the aces.'

'Has you put this method of warfare to Wiremu Kingi?' I asks.

'I have done so, and he has said he will think on it.'

I grab Hawk by the arm. 'Then, Hawk, please! Ask Chief Tamihana if I can join you with the fifty-five fighting axes from our tribe, the Tommo Te Mokiri!'

'No, Tommo! It isn't possible!' Hawk throws up his hands in alarm. 'You must not endanger yourself! I am but an adviser, and will not myself fight.' His eyes grow wide. 'You could be killed!'

'Hawk, if you won't ask him, I will find a way to do it. Tamihana is well pleased with our skill with the fighting axe. If he lends some of his trained warriors to Wiremu Kingi, then the chief will surely want to join the King Movement! The Maori will be a united force like you want.'

I know Hawk's got to see the logic in this. After a while

he says, 'I will ask Wiremu Kingi, but only if you do not fight with them.'

I laugh. I am no hero, but I'm never gunna get a better chance against the mongrels. I shakes me head. 'I trained 'em and I got to be with 'em when they fight. They will reckon me a coward otherwise!'

'Then I will not ask him,' Hawk says firmly.

'Hawk! I will find a way to fight, I swears it!'

'Tommo, if you get killed, why should I want to live?'

I look at him, furious now. 'Hawk Solomon, when you were in Wiremu Kingi's *pa* and the governor sent his ultimatum, tell me – if Chief Kingi had decided to fight, what would you have done? Run away?'

'I had resolved to fight,' Hawk says quietly.

'There! And did you think how I might feel? Here I am shitting meself that me twin is going to get killed!'

'Tommo! Tommo!' Hawk pleads, placing his hand on me shoulder. 'You don't understand. I don't want you to die for something I have done!'

'Well, we bloody near did in Kororareka gaol for something *I* done!'

Hawk sees I ain't giving in and changes tack. 'Right, Tommo! Let's go to Australia *now!* I will talk to Chief Tamihana. He knows nothing of my warfare plan. I will tell him it is time for us to leave. I'll say to him I can do no more for Wiremu Kingi and ask his help to get us onto a ship back to Australia.'

'Bull!' I says, jerking me shoulder away from his hand. 'You only want to go because of me!' I pauses and swallows hard. 'Of course I still wants to leave this damned place, sometime! But not as a coward and *not* because *you* wants to save me bloody useless life. And most of all, not so your stupid conscience be always troubled 'cause you ran away when you knows you should've stayed!'

I am shouting now and I wish I could punch his fancy tattooed gob! Smash his big white teeth in! 'Besides,' I yell, 'Makareta be expecting a baby!'

Chapter Ten

HAWK

The Land of the Long White Cloud
December 1859

Wiremu Kingi is set on war. He and his Ati Awa people
have reached the end of their tether. The governor and his
government will have no further discussions with the Maori,
such is the white man's greed for land.

Once again I am sent by Chief Tamihana to persuade
Wiremu Kingi to join the King Movement so that all the
Maori on the North Island might speak with one voice. I try
to convince the old chief of the advantages to be gained from
waging guerrilla warfare as well.

'What know you of this war, Black Maori?' he asks. 'It is
not the Maori way to leave their women and children. Have
you yourself fought by these methods?'

I have to confess to him that I know of these tactics only
through books.

'Ha! Books! Missionaries have books! What have books
to do with making war?'

I explain to him that the British are fond of writing about
their military tactics and methods of fighting. 'It is one of the
ways in which they have conquered the world – they learn
from history.'

This seems to impress the chief, but still he is obdurate. 'We have beaten the pakeha before. I shall build tunnels underground in our forts so that the big guns cannot harm us.'

I tell him that this is an excellent idea, but that a *pa* can only be defended for a limited time. 'If they cannot bring you out by means of muskets and artillery, they can starve you out, Chief Kingi.'

'That is true, it has happened before, but perhaps we will defeat them before it can be done?'

'It is possible that your fighters will be victorious once, or even twice, but the pakeha outnumber you in men and firepower. Sooner or later they will defeat you.'

At this remark the chief grows furious. 'Are you a coward to speak of defeat? We will kill all the pakeha. They cannot defeat us! This is our land, Maori land! Be gone. Come back only when you will talk of victory!'

I leave the *hui*, thinking that I have disappointed Tamihana. Expelled from Wiremu Kingi's presence and his tribe, I can do no good here. But it is late and I cannot travel until morning, so I prepare to rest.

Before I can close my eyes, a messenger, one of Kingi's warriors, enters my hut. 'Chief Kingi wishes to see you at once, Black Maori,' he says.

I wrap a blanket about me and go to the *marae* where the *rangatira* are still assembled. The old chief is silent a moment, then he points to me and barks, 'Black Maori, we have watched you now for many months. Why have you not taken a woman from our tribe? Is a Maori wahine not good enough for you? Answer, please!'

How can I tell him that I am a virgin? I have all the markings of the *rangatira* and though I have just turned nineteen, I look much older.

'I have had no time to look for a wahine,' I say, 'to find one who would take me willingly.'

'Willingly?' The Maori chief looks puzzled. 'I shall find you one!'

I thank him but say that I would like to choose her for myself.

His eyebrows shoot upwards at this. 'My choice is not good?'

'Your choice is most excellent, Chief, but it is a feeling I seek.' I put my hand to my heart. 'A feeling in here.'

Wiremu Kingi thinks this very funny, but after he has stopped chuckling he says, 'I have heard of this feeling, but it comes later, when a woman has been with you a long time and she has proved a worthy wife and given you many children.' He sighs as though he is talking to a young child. 'It is a good feeling to have for an old woman, who is a precious thing. How can you have such a feeling before you know what you are getting? When a wahine is still young and you have not tried her out?' Then, before I can answer, he adds, 'Perhaps she is barren, perhaps she cannot cook, or the milk in her breasts does not make your children strong. What if she is bad-tempered or lazy, cannot weave flax, or sings like a crow? What then of this feeling?'

'There is no Maori woman who sings like a crow,' I reply, smiling. How can I tell him that if I should love a woman, none of these things would matter to me? I shrug. 'It is something I cannot explain.'

Chief Wiremu Kingi looks at me shrewdly. 'Tell me, Black Maori, have you taken a woman to your bed?' The *rangatira*, who have been following our conversation with interest, wait tensely for my reply. I have never lied to the Maori but I think now is the time to do so. But Mary has trained me too well. 'No,' I say softly.

The assembled men howl with laughter and look at me in disbelief. Only Wiremu Kingi doesn't laugh. 'That is good, Black Maori. The Maori only die for two things, for women and for land. You will show us how to fight better for our land and I will show you how to choose a good woman to die for. A man cannot go to war without having known a woman! If you die now your ancestors would regard you with shame.'

'But . . . but . . .' I stammer.

'What is it?' The chief grows impatient.

'I am most honoured that you would choose a woman for me, Chief Kingi, but do I understand she is henceforth to be my wife . . . forever?'

This brings a fresh outburst of laughter and Wiremu Kingi shakes his head. 'There are a great many young widows in the tribe. I will choose one for you and she will bring her longing to your need. That will be marriage enough for the time being. She will not be your wife, Black Maori. We go to war and I would not have it that she be widowed twice over and so become bad *tapu*.' The chief waves me away. 'We will talk of your warfare after you have become a man.'

Some of the *rangatira* grin, but most nod their heads solemnly. I walk from the *hui* feeling small and ashamed, knowing all eyes are upon my back.

My heart is pounding as I try to think how it should be with a wahine. I have asked Tommo what it is like to make love, but his answers do not provide much enlightenment.

'Same as pullin' yerself off,' he offers. 'Only better and lots more happening upon yerself.'

'Like what?'

Tommo thinks for a moment. 'Softer, and her doing things back to ya.'

'What sort of things?'

Tommo looks a bit foolish. 'Kissing. Her tongue in your gob. You know, touching.'

'Tongue in my mouth, what for?'

Tommo grows impatient. 'It's nice, tongue in one soft place and cock in t'other.'

'Oh,' say I. Even though I have thought a thousand times about kissing, I have never imagined it as having anything to do with tongues. Soft, sweet lips touching my cheek or even sometimes my own lips, but I have never envisaged tongues anywhere but safely in their owners' mouths.

Watching me, Tommo suddenly gets a most mischievous look on his face. 'Not to mention sixty-nine.'

'Sixty-nine? What is sixty-nine?'

'Christ Jesus, Hawk! Didn't the blokes at the brewery teach ya nothing? Frenchies call it sixty-nine!' He grabs a twig and writes the two numbers in the dirt. 'Look! Can't ya see?'

I tilt my head to one side but all I can see are the numbers roughly marked. 'What's to see?'

Tommo looks plainly exasperated now. 'Your cock in her mouth and your tongue in her pussy!'

'Really?' I am taken completely by surprise and try to imagine such a thing happening. 'I am not at all sure I should like it,' I finally respond.

'Or just her doing it,' Tommo says.

'Just her?'

'Yes, sucking you, your cock in her mouth.'

'Oh,' is all I can think to say. This shocks me less than the idea of doing things to her with my tongue. 'What more should I know?' I ask softly, my heart pounding.

'Lots!' Tommo says. 'But I ain't telling you no more, you'll find out for yerself soon enough.'

We are both caught up in our own thoughts until Tommo breaks the silence.

'It's the softness,' he confides. 'Softness all over, and creaminess.' He has a faraway look in his eyes and a half-smile. It's a look I have not seen on his face before and it pleases me, for it contains none of the old bitterness. Perhaps it is the first sign of real happiness I have seen in him.

All the same, Tommo's description doesn't match the dreamy picture I've got in my imagination. My picture is a bit hazy, I suppose, and has the scent of roses about it, the rustle of crinoline dresses and someone very pretty standing on tip-toe so her ankles show. Her kiss is like a summer breeze touching my cheek.

And in my dreams, making love is something done politely, although I am not sure how. I know I would wish it to be most decent and allowing of every possible sensitivity. But exactly how to bring this about, I can't imagine. In my mind, it just happens and then is all over, beautiful and not spoken of, except with quiet looks.

Who would be the woman to let me love her so? As far as I can see, there are but two choices. At one end of the scale, there are the dockside whores, women damaged by life who would take a nigger the same as anyone else if he had the price. Then, at the other end of the scale, where I want to be, there is a prettiness pure as the driven snow. I don't rightly know what it would be like, loving all that purity, sort of like trying to touch a beautiful, perfumed ghost.

In the days following Chief Kingi's promise, I find myself looking at the Maori women, who are all most attractive. I can't help myself. I look at their lips. They have beautiful lips, soft and luscious, and I imagine them kissing me with their pink tongues inside my mouth and elsewhere too.

I try to put these thoughts from my mind. Nobody, I tell myself, is going to kiss a nigger that way, unless he pays extra for it with a whore. As Ikey always said, 'To brood over what you can't have be stupid, my dear.' On the other hand, he always added, 'But to believe you can't have something be even more stupid.' So I decide to keep the thought of it alive but tucked in the back of my mind, just in case Ikey is right.

It is my fourth sleepless night since my conversation with the chief, and the moon outside my hut is near full. The night is warm. Thoughts of softness and creaminess keep drifting about in my head, although I am tired and it is late. There is an owl hooting somewhere and soft laughter coming from one of the groups around the fires. I think of Tommo and Makareta, and how gentle Tommo is with her, though he does not say much. I think too about Chief Kingi and how I hope to teach him guerrilla warfare from the books I've read. He, a great warrior afraid of nothing, learn from me, who is afraid of a pop gun. I must be mad!

I must have fallen asleep, for I feel a stroking of my body. Soft hands glide across my chest and my belly. I am in a dream, a beautiful dream. I move. 'Hush.' It is a woman's soft voice. 'Do not open your eyes, Black Maori.'

I do as I am bid and feel a touching on my lips. A wonderful softness from her mouth seems to go through my whole body. My heart starts to thump, I can hear it: boom, boom, boom. Her hand moves down across my belly and her lips seem to melt over mine, opening my mouth. How this is done I cannot say, but there it is, the creaminess, as her tongue moves into my mouth and at the same time, her hand reaches me where I have grown hard.

I have already removed my coat and blouse the better to sleep, but now her hand works at my breeches, as her other takes my palm and places it on her breast. My fingers are hungry for her softness, and her nipples soon grow firm from my touch. I now lie naked inside my blanket. My eyes are still closed and I dare not open them for fear that I am dreaming.

The woman speaks to me, her voice soft but clear. 'Oh

Black Maori, I have wanted you so very long. I have eaten you with my eyes and I have tasted you in my heart a thousand times. I have moaned for you alone in my blanket and my mouth has cried out to hold your manhood. My breasts have grown hard from longing for you and I have brought pleasure to myself in your name.'

I am almost fainting with desire and her hands are everywhere at once. She places her lips upon mine and her tongue seems alive in my mouth. Then she draws back. 'Black Maori, open your eyes. I want you to see the woman who would make love to you.'

I open my eyes. Moonlight is flooding into the hut and throws a silver sheen across her skin. She is beautiful beyond belief, her breasts cast upwards and generous, and her stomach clean-curved as she sits on her heels beside me. Her thighs are strong, smooth and shining in the light, and I can see the curve of her buttocks and the narrowness of her waist. He dark hair falls across her shoulders, shadowing her eyes so I cannot see into them.

I open my mouth to speak, but she presses her finger to my lips. 'Hush, do not speak.'

Now she begins to kiss me across my chest and belly, moving lower and lower, and then her lips part and take me into her mouth. 'Oh, oh!' I cry. 'Oh!' I am in heaven. I fear I cannot last a moment longer as her soft lips stroke up and down, and each time seem to take in most of me. Then, when I am sure I shall die, she withdraws her lips from my trembling hardness. A moment later she is astride me. Her hand guides me so that I sink into a softness and a creaminess I have not imagined in my wildest dreams.

'Oh, God, oh, oh, oh!' I moan.

'Black Maori, you must wait for me,' she says, panting now, her voice urgent. 'Wait!' I don't know how she can believe I am in enough control to do anything. 'Wait, wait, I will tell you when,' she gasps. Her eyes are closed and her mouth half open, and I can see her white teeth and pink tongue.

I want to tell her I cannot wait a moment longer, but all I can do is moan as she moves up and down on top of me. Every part of her is pressed against me, her slender body caressing my skin. Now her lips are upon mine and her tongue is in my mouth. The softness and smoothness is everywhere and I must die for I cannot live another moment without release. Then she takes her lips from mine, and begins to moan. 'Now!' she says. 'Now, Black Maori! Hard, hard, I must feel your hardness! Now!'

With this permission I lift my body from under her and roll her over on her back, driving into her. Her legs clasp about me as she opens up so that my every inch is taken deep into her. I cannot stop the explosion inside me.

'More, more!' she screams, her nails raking my back. I feel nothing but the delight of her. 'Oh, oh, ohhhh!' she cries, and more and more of the same, which thrills my ear. She gives a loud and glorious moan and then a sigh. I drive the harder into her wetness as her voice dies to a whimper and her hips push back up into mine. Her arms come around me and she draws my head into her breasts. Then my explosion is over and, jerking wildly, the world collapses and me with it. I am emptied out and my youth has flown away.

We are gleaming sweat, panting together, our breath hot about our heads. I have never felt more a man, never more alive, more embraced by love and tenderness. I fear I shall not again in my life have another moment as beautiful as this.

'You are a warrior now, Black Maori,' the woman says at last. Pushing me gently away, she rises so that once again I see the length of her legs, the curve of her waist and the beauty of her glistening breasts. Her hair falls across her face as she kneels again. She brushes it away as she wraps the blanket about me and kisses me. 'Ah, you are beautiful,' she smiles. 'You are beautiful, and you waited.' Then she gathers up her own blanket and rising, wraps it about her and moves to the door.

'What is your name?' I call urgently, for I do not want her to leave.

She pauses at the door, the moon shining on her face. 'Hinetitama.' She laughs softly, then is gone in the moonlight.

'Will you come to me again?' I call, but there is no reply. I lie still, a great smile upon my face. 'Hinetitama,' I repeat. Flooded with happiness, I fall into a deep slumber.

In the morning I am summoned to the *marae* by Chief Kingi and the *rangatira*. When all are seated the chief addresses me, 'Five days ago, we talked to the boy but today it is to the man.' He grins. 'Did you dream well, Black Maori?'

I laugh. 'Better than I ever have, thank you, Chief Kingi.'

'That is good. Your ancestors will be most relieved.'

Laughter follows this reply, also applause, and then no more is said of it. The thing is done and I am welcomed. I feel as though something different has happened between these people and myself, something I cannot quite understand.

'We will talk of these small wars of yours,' Wiremu Kingi says. 'You will tell us all you know. Like the British, we too can learn from books, though blood is better!'

'Only when it does not belong to your side,' I reply.

'Ha! There is no shame in dying. If you have fought well it is an honour,' the chief replies.

I shrug. 'There is also no shame in living, if you have fought well.'

'Black Maori, keep your sharp tongue for the pakeha!' Wiremu Kingi rebukes me, but I can see from his eyes that he is not insulted.

'I have known a woman whom war has made a widow in your tribe, and all I can say is that the dead must grieve greatly for their loss.' I hope that this compliment makes up for my forward manner.

The chief laughs suddenly. 'Well spoken, Black Maori. You are right, our strength is more in the living than the dead. Already the Maori have done too much dying in these battles. It is not only the dead who grieve their wahine, the tribe laments the barrenness that is then forced upon them. You will tell us more of this new way to fight the British.'

I spend the remainder of the morning outlining the principles of guerrilla warfare and listening as the *rangatira* discuss it among themselves. This is a most equitable process and Wiremu Kingi shows a great deal of patience. The *tohunga* argue fiercely that the ancestors will frown on a departure from the practice of fighting from a *pa*, but the chief is most persuasive. 'In addition to this new way of fighting, we will build a great *pa* in the mountains where our women and children will stay with sufficient warriors to defend them,' he declares.

'Perhaps the tribe should build many forts in the mountains so the women and children can keep moving?' I suggest. 'Food may be stored in secret caves, for I have been told there are many such places and few are known to the pakeha. We can control the mountain passes so that they cannot penetrate. Then we can attack them on their own ground, always where they least expect us. The mountains and the forests are where we will hide.'

'The Maori always hold the ground under their feet. We cannot defend ground which is not our own,' proclaims one of the *tohunga*, an old man who is much respected.

'Ha! It is all our ground!' the chief snorts. 'Our land, which the pakeha have stolen from us!'

But the old priest will not be dissuaded. He has been most persistent all morning and much involved with the thoughts of the ancestors in the matter of this new way of warring. He shakes his head as I further my argument.

'The *pa* was a strong place from which the ancestors defended their land, a fort built upon their ground and under their own feet. But since the pakeha have brought the musket here, more than twenty thousand Maori have been killed defending their forts. These are not Maori who have been killed by the pakeha. These are Maori who have been slain by their own kind – those who have used the white man's gun to kill their own people! These traitors, who know the *pa* well, have defeated it with the gun. The British have even more guns – huge ones that can tear down the palisades and tear up the ground. The Maori *pa* cannot always withstand the British system of war. We must have another system.'

There is much concern among the *rangatira* at this denigration of the *pa*. Chief Wiremu Kingi is patient though firm and in the end, he rules that we will try this new kind of warfare. He turns to his younger brother, War Chief Hapurona, who has a mighty reputation but who has said little during the discussion, leaving the task of reconciliation to his brother.

'What say you, Hapurona? How shall we fight?'

All are silent as War Chief Hapurona speaks. 'The Maori are quick to fight and slow to learn, but I do not agree that we must give up the system of the forts.' The men murmur their approval at this, and my heart sinks. 'There are times in war to attack and times to defend,' the war chief continues. 'With the pakeha we have always defended, and sometimes this has been right and sometimes it has been wrong. Black Maori is right, we must use both systems to be effective in this war.'

Wiremu Kingi turns to me and nods that I should reply. I

have been so anxious to persuade him to embrace my new method of warfare that I have not seen the whole situation clearly as Hapurona has. 'War Chief Hapurona is our commander and what he says is right. It shames me that I have not understood this more clearly before,' I say, with my head bowed.

The old chief responds, 'You are not born a Maori, nor have you been a warrior, so you would not know the advantages of fighting a defensive action from a well-constructed *pa*.' He turns to Hapurona. 'Will you allow the Black Maori to be a general under you, to advise you in his ways?'

Hapurona walks over to me and places his hand on my shoulders. 'I shall prepare the feathers for a general's cloak.' He laughs. 'It is not often I must look up into another man's face. The women will need to gather many more baskets of feathers for the Black Maori.'

I tell Wiremu Kingi that I am greatly honoured but since I have not proved my courage in battle, I would be happy to be an adviser only.

The chief appears surprised at this. 'And if we should be defeated, who shall we blame? A mere adviser? Bah! We must have a general so that he is worthy of being put to death should he fail us – or of being honoured should we succeed.'

The *rangatira* laugh heartily at this and approve the appointment. Chief Wiremu Kingi then says, 'Black Maori, when you persuaded me not to fight the governor in the Waitara, that is something only a good war chief would do. You shall be a general for us, like those the British have, and we shall call you Black Hawk.'

And so I have been named General Black Hawk. I am a little afraid that I shall let the Maori down in this whole affair. Though they have agreed to fight small wars, they are

270

by no means unanimous, and the *tohunga* led by the old priest are against it. I shall have to prove myself very soon with War Chief Hapurona, or I shall be greatly shamed and Chief Tamihana will be disgraced by me.

I return to my tribe to tell my chief of Wiremu Kingi's decision. Of course, I must also tell Tommo.

Tommo is not amused. 'Have you gone crazy?' he screams, banging his fist hard down on the table. 'General Black Hawk, is it? You think the pakeha don't already want your head on a plate? Listen, mate, they'll string you up by your balls outside Auckland Post Office while singing the flamin' Hallelujah Chorus!'

'But you said you wanted to come with me. You and your fighting axes, Tommo Te Mokiri!' I say.

'Yes, but that was when it were just me and you! Me, a regular soldier and you, an adviser, safe in the background. Nobody'd know nothin' about us being there. Then, when it's over, or if it goes badly, we can scarper, piss off, slip into the night!' He pauses and glares at me. 'Now you're a fucking general. The flamin' pakeha will see it as treason! Remember we're escaped prisoners. They're gunna have your guts for garters, mate, if they ever puts two and two together and gets four. Mine, too! But I got to be with you, Hawk – I'm not letting ya go on yer own.'

'Tommo, please wait here,' I beg. 'What if something goes wrong or we are captured? Makareta is with child. You would not wish her to be a widow.'

'Makareta already knows we got to go away,' Tommo snorts. 'I've told her I'll come back some day to fetch her and the child. I'm coming all right, but that don't mean you ain't an idjit! Promise me when this is over, *if* we comes out alive, we're gunna get out of here.'

I nod my head.

'Promise, Hawk! Swear it on Makareta's baby!'

'I promise we'll go back to Hobart Town as soon as Wiremu Kingi's war is over.'

'No! I don't want to go back to Mary yet. We'll go to Sydney.'

'Sydney then, I promise!'

We are sitting in Tommo's hut and I am glad when Makareta comes over with some food. She will cool Tommo's anger. It's difficult to be angry with Makareta present. She has a mischievous grin, laughs often and loves Tommo with all her heart. She cannot help but touch him as though he is a part of her every desire. 'What will you name the baby?' I ask her, hoping to end the unfortunate subject of General Black Hawk.

'Icky,' Makareta smiles.

'Ikey,' Tommo corrects her.

I laugh. 'I'll wager he'll be the only Ikey Solomon who is Maori in the whole world or ever to come. But what if it is a girl, how shall you name her?'

Makareta frowns and looks downcast. 'I would want a son for Tommo. We have not thought of a name for a girl.'

I hesitate a moment, then venture, 'If it is a girl, may I suggest a name?'

'I know! You want to call her Mary, don'tcha?' says Tommo, now somewhat mollified.

'No, I had thought – Hinetitama?'

Makareta gasps and brings her hand to her breast. 'That is a name which may only be used for a Maori princess! It cannot be, Black Hawk! They will not allow it. Hinetitama is the daughter of Hineahuone, Woman Made From Earth, the first Maori woman. The mother of the earth called her daughter Hinetitama, the Dawn Maiden, because her cheeks were the same colour as the morning light.'

'That is beautiful, Makareta. If you should have a girl, I will ask Chief Tamihana if he will grant his permission to name her thus. I am *rangatira*, perhaps he will allow this honour through me.'

'He will not, Black Hawk. The *tohunga* and the ancestors would be angry. I do not want a *tapu* on my child!' She is most distressed, so I change the subject.

'It will be a boy,' I say quickly. 'There is a saying among the pakeha that a mother's beauty is stolen by a girl child in the womb, but if it is a son, the beauty remains.' I smile. 'And you, Makareta, are more beautiful than ever.'

Tommo sighs and rolls his eyes at this sentimental notion but I can see Makareta is pleased. Besides, her good manners do not allow her to show further disquiet. Her frown disappears and she laughs. 'You are right, Black Hawk. We will have Icky Slomon and save everyone much trouble.'

'Ikey,' Tommo repeats, 'I-key So-lo-mon!' He rolls his eyes, as though he has tried to teach her a hundred times and failed.

Makareta ignores him. 'Now you must eat,' she says, putting a large, steaming clay pot of fish and vegetables down in front of us.

'Ikey Solomon never saved anyone any trouble!' I laugh as I reach to fill my platter.

Tommo chuckles too. 'So, what's wrong with Mary?' he asks. 'It is our mama's name after all.'

'Nothing,' I say, 'Mary is a fine name, Tommo.'

'Well then,' says he, 'it's settled. Mary it is if we have a girl.'

But my thoughts have flown back to Hinetitama, and as soon as I return to the village of Chief Wiremu Kingi I try to find her. It is a large village of a thousand souls, perhaps more, but a widow of such beauty would, I feel sure, be well known.

My hopes are quickly dashed. All the wahine I ask about Hinetitama look anxious and shake their heads. 'We have no

wahine of that name, General Black Hawk, not in this tribe,'
they say. I come to believe it is a conspiracy, led by Chief
Wiremu Kingi, to keep me from Hinetitama and, although I
search widely, she is not to be found. I take to looking at every
woman's face I pass. There are many who are great beauties,
for the Maori are of the Polynesian race and perhaps the most
handsome people on earth. Though many are comely, none
could be mistaken for Hinetitama. I know from Makareta's
explanation that the chief has honoured me with a princess,
not just an ordinary wahine. But this makes it stranger still. A
disappearing princess is surely an odd occurrence. Perhaps,
after all, it was a dream? I have resolved, if ever an
opportunity arises, to ask Wiremu Kingi if he will let me see
her again. My heart is broken by her disappearance and I try
hard to concentrate on matters of warfare instead.

I am now so engaged with the Maori and their struggle that
I am too busy for thoughts of home and too occupied to
yearn for our dear Mary. Christmas passes unnoticed
amongst the tribes, although I send our greetings to mama.

I have not told Mary of my close involvement with the
Maori fight against the pakeha, informing her simply of
Tommo's recovery to health in Tamihana's village. If she
suspects I dissemble, she says not a word. Nor does she refer
to the bitter argument that preceded our leaving. Instead, she
writes of the brewery and of the loving thoughts she holds
for her two boys. I am anxious about how we shall ever get
to see her again, but for now we prepare for guerrilla
warfare against the settlers and my mind is much occupied
with this.

In great secret, War Chief Hapurona and I plan our first
attack against the settlers. But before we can carry it out,
martial law is again declared in the Taranaki by Lieutenant-
Colonel Murray, who is commander of the militia and the

Taranaki Rifle Volunteers, a mounted corps armed with carbines, revolvers and swords. The pakeha soldiers do not wait for us to come against them but immediately attack, looting and burning several Maori villages without warning. The war has begun in earnest, for it is now clear from these actions that the settlers will use whatever force is needed to occupy Maori land.

'We must drive the pakeha from their farms into New Plymouth,' I cry, 'empty the whole countryside.' New Plymouth is a town of some two and a half thousand souls, which depends on the surrounding countryside for food or else must obtain it by sea. War Chief Hapurona agrees and small units that can move quickly over the terrain are sent out in a series of daring night-time raids. In each are two or three of Tommo's fighting axes from Chief Tamihana and they prove most effective. Tommo has lengthened the handle of the axe so that it may be used to fend off a bayonet or even in the manner of the *taiaha*, the Maori fighting stick. In these raids we do not kill the settlers, but simply force them from their farms with their women and children, thereafter burning and looting their homes and taking possession of their livestock.

Soon New Plymouth has become the only safe haven for all the pakeha in the district and the countryside is empty save for the Maori. The soldiers have fortified the town and created a citadel on the site of an old Maori *pa*, now known as Marsland Hill. From here they plan to defend New Plymouth against our attack. We are well pleased with this development, for we have no intention of attacking the town but only plan to contain the pakeha within it.

It is now that War Chief Hapurona and the old chief show their great skill as leaders. Hapurona commences to build a *pa* about nine miles from New Plymouth. He has studied the trenching systems the British have used to fortify the town, and he constructs his *pa* with a double row of palisades containing rifle pits and similar trenches. We also have underground passages to protect us from the British artillery.

The *pa* holds one hundred fighting men, whom Wiremu Kingi places under the command of War Chief Hapurona and his chief aide, a Maori war leader named Tamati Kapene. Though one hundred men is not much of a fighting force, we hope that it sends a direct challenge to the British militia to come out of New Plymouth and get us. We trust they will think this small force presents a great opportunity for a victory, and an easy one at that. 'They will think it is the old times when the Maori fight on the defensive,' Hapurona explains, 'and it will give them great heart. This is the way they *think* they know how to defeat us.'

After much debate, I persuade Wiremu Kingi to purchase a hundred double-barrelled shotguns. At first the *rangatira* and even the chief are in great doubt about the wisdom of this, thinking the new rifled muskets to be much the better weapons. They have long used shotguns to shoot duck and small game and have even fought with them before, but they have only a few in their armoury. It is my plan to use the shotgun as the main weapon of defence, to entice the British near and greet them with a hail of buckshot at close range.

Though I know little of guns, my argument is simple enough. A shotgun charged with buckshot is deadly when used close-up, which is the way fighting occurs in the *pa*. It has double the barrels and hence twice the fire power of a musket. The fact that the shot will pepper widely is to be recommended in close combat, and at ten or fifteen yards, it will kill more effectively than the *pu* – the musket – with its single lead ball.

As I point out to the war council: 'We will have the shotgun and the long-handled fighting axe as well as the *taiaha*, the spear, and the musket. All the enemy will have is the musket and the bayonet. At close range, when the British storm the *pa*, we will be the better armed.'

'Oh, so now General Black Hawk would be an expert on fighting in a *pa*. Do I not recall he was altogether against it not so long ago?' It is the voice of Hapurona's aide, Tamati Kapene, who from the beginning has opposed me in almost every endeavour. He is against guerrilla warfare and would return to the old methods if he had his way.

Tamati Kapene is in charge of organising the defence in the forts and though he is most talented, he is vainglorious for a man not more than twenty-five years of age – even I, at nineteen, can see this. As the son of a chief he has risen quickly and he is said to be a brave man. I do not contradict him but simply answer that we are no worse off with the shotgun and the axe, for we still retain all the traditional Maori weapons as well as the musket. 'We have added the shotgun and the axe without losing anything,' I point out.

My argument carries the day. But although in favour of the shotguns, War Chief Hapurona has decided that I shall remain an observer when the Maori fight in a *pa*, until I am well enough acquainted with the Maori fighting system.

Meanwhile my brother is also preparing for war. Tommo's men have not yet been tested in open warfare with the long-handled fighting axe, which the pakeha have come to call the tomahawk, after the American Indian weapon. This is, of course, a coincidence and not intended as a compliment to me and Tommo. However, it is not lost on the Maori warriors who think the pakeha must fear the new weapon to have named it in our honour. I explain the real origins of the axe's name to Hapurona, for of course the pakeha do not know about Tommo and still think of me only as the Black Maori. But he laughs. 'General Black Hawk, it is our luck that the men think it so. They will follow you and Tommo the better for it.' In Hapurona's *pa* there are fifteen axe fighters from the Tommo Te Mokiri and among them is my twin, so that I am secretly most afraid for his life.

We are still waiting for the British to come after us when Hammerhead Jack turns up. 'I have come to fight with my brothers,' he says simply. 'I have one eye and one arm, but one eye is sufficient to see the British. My one arm will use a fighting axe and my eye will see it find its mark between the two eyes of the British soldiers.'

I ask if Hammerhead Jack might be my aide and it is agreed. Tommo is greatly pleased by this. He has spent much time teaching Hammerhead Jack the fighting axe, and knows him to be a formidable opponent who will do much more than his share in any fight. He is much reassured that he will be by my side in the event of close combat.

A few days later, in early March, we hear that the British have moved out of New Plymouth with a contingent of four hundred officers and men, as well as a naval detachment with artillery. Although they have only nine miles to go, they come with a long baggage train of wagons and carts.

I send out a small war party to reconnoitre and they report that the column is exceedingly well guarded by the 65th Regiment and that the navy is well equipped with heavy artillery. It is as though they expect to be attacked at any moment, for horsemen constantly patrol their flanks. This is not surprising as the surrounding country is wooded, scrubby terrain criss-crossed by ravines and gullies, with giant flax providing plenty of cover. Given their surveillance, it will be difficult to catch the British column by stealth. Moreover, there is little hope of cutting off their supplies. The Maori do not have much respect for the British regular who fights in the ordered and predictable manner of

Waterloo and the Crimea, but I believe it will be a tough battle.

The British build a large redoubt overlooking the river and this becomes their base. War Chief Hapurona and Chief Wiremu Kingi decide our forces are too few, and their reconnaissance patrols too well armed, to attempt to ambush them. So, in the time-honoured manner of the Maori, we wait for the enemy to come to us. In the meantime, we send urgent word to Chief Tamihana and several other chiefs asking for their support against these superior odds. My chief, Tamihana, has already sent fifteen axe fighters with Tommo but he sends a dozen more, and encourages the Ngati Maniapoto, the Waikato and the South Taranaki tribes to also come to our aid. Though we are still greatly outnumbered, our overall strength is much increased by the time the British attack.

It is the seventeenth day of March 1860, a bright morning without so much as a cloud in the sky. A rain-storm last night has made the approach to our *pa* heavy going. At last Tommo and I are at war, though I very much doubt that I have the stomach for the killing of men. As the fighting gets under way, I quickly become accustomed to the crack of musket fire and the whine of bullets, even the swish of an artillery canister or the boom of cannon shot. We are mostly underground when the firing from the British lines is at its heaviest and we fire back at them whenever the occasion allows. The explosions produce much sound and light, but little harm seems to be done. Some of our palisades are damaged, and much mud and soil is kicked up from the cannon fire. Once, a roof catches alight, though this is quickly doused.

Tommo is most impatient. 'When will they come?' he asks repeatedly. Like me, he is a greenhorn, anxious not to make a fool of himself.

Towards afternoon, a shot from the British cuts the rope which holds our flag, a red banner, more there so that we should have a flag like the British than for the purposes of any loyalty. The Maori die for women and land, not for this piece of bunting which we name the Waitara flag so as to annoy the governor.

The flag flutters to the ground, close to the palisades outside the *pa*, and we do not think to retrieve it. Then, in the late afternoon during a lull in the firing, we are met with an amazing sight. The British, ever the heroes, have sent two horsemen to capture our fallen banner. Up gallop these two cavalrymen, bent on glory. Up come our muskets, bent on destruction. Bang, bang, bang! One of them is dead, while the other is medal-bound, for he has scooped up the red flag with his home-made lance, turned his horse in a shower of mud clods, and galloped away again, showing us his horse's arse. I daresay they will one day hang the flag in Westminster Abbey as one of their battle honours – telling their children of the bright bunting hard-won from the ferocious Maori in a noble war of the Empire. Meanwhile, the first man in this battle lies dead in the mud and we are happy that it is an English trooper and not a Maori warrior.

'Do we have another banner to throw into the mud?' shouts Hammerhead Jack to much laughter among the men.

At sunset the British decide to cease fighting for the day. They have been pumping shot and cannon fire into us since the early morning and have by now done considerable damage to the *pa*. It is too dangerous to repair our fortifications and there is some doubt in my mind that we can take another day of bombardment. We have seen from the firing that we are greatly outgunned and that the British still have much the superior numbers. At the war council, however, there is some elation at the day's events. We have not lost a single man, our food and water supply is intact and our men remain in high spirits.

Tamati Kapene is the first to speak after the general has summed up the day. He is full of bravado and looks meaningfully at me. 'We have proved the value of the *pa* to all who may have doubted it. The British guns cannot harm us, their artillery fire is like flies on our skin and their cannons are no more than noisy mosquitoes. If these pests should come tomorrow or the next day, we will brush them off with contempt!'

War Chief Hapurona, who has observed that his aide's remarks are directed at me, now speaks. 'What say you, Black Hawk? Have you now observed sufficient of *pa* fighting to see its value?'

Chief Wiremu Kingi watches me closely. I nod before speaking. 'I can now see well the virtue of the *pa* – it is a most excellent system of defence, a brilliant fortification, War Chief Hapurona.' Then I am silent.

'Ha!' Chief Kingi snorts. 'I think there is more, Black Hawk. Your eyes say there are more words waiting in your head!'

I hesitate a moment. 'With great respect, has it been observed what the British artillery and cannon have done to our trenches and palisades?'

'Nothing!' Tamati Kapene shouts. 'Our palisades stand firm, they will hold the battle through.'

'In four places, the cannon fire has filled in our trenches sufficient to allow both horses and foot soldiers to cross them without difficulty,' I say. 'In six places, the first row of posts is knocked down and the second palisade is also damaged. With a little more cannon and artillery fire, we will be breached. Tomorrow, towards afternoon if I am not mistaken, the British will be upon us with their guns and bayonets.'

Tamati Kapene points to me and yells, 'This man is wrong! If they come we have sufficient defences. They will pay with their lives.'

'And we with ours,' I reply quietly.

'Coward!' Hapurona's aide shouts, pointing straight at me.

A deep silence follows and I hear Hammerhead Jack whisper beside me, 'You cannot accept this insult.'

We are seated in a circle. Tamati Kapene is but an arm's length away and I know he is looking to challenge me. I have my eyes to the ground and I do not look up to meet his. Suddenly, it is as if I am back at the gaol in Kororareka with Maple and Syrup holding my arms and Hori Hura threatening me. I am not sure where the anger comes from, but it is there, slow and cool, rising from somewhere deep within me. My right arm shoots out and I grab Hapurona's aide by the throat. In a trice, my left hand joins it and at the same time I rise to my feet so that Tamati Kapene is jerked upwards. The aide is a big man, but he now seems slight enough, for I pull him higher and higher until his feet are well off the ground and his head above my own.

I can see the young Maori's eyes as they near pop from his head. His arms flail and his legs kick wildly. Then they stop, as though the strength has gone from them. My fingers tighten and there is still more pressure I can bring. I would not need it all to kill him.

'Put him down, Black Hawk,' Hapurona says in a low voice.

I drop his aide, who falls to the floor unconscious. It is only then that I feel the strain in my arms from lifting a human of more than two hundred pounds in weight and holding him in the air as a child would a rag doll.

'Sit, General Black Hawk,' Wiremu Kingi commands and I sink slowly back to the ground. The old chief signals for two warriors to drag Tamati Kapene out of the way. With the heat gone from me, I wonder if I should apologise. I make to open my mouth but Hammerhead Jack squeezes my shoulder.

'Ork good,' he whispers in English. 'No talk.'

'We will leave tonight, before the moon rises,' is all Hapurona says. 'Tell your men to be ready.'

'What's going on?' Tommo asks as I tell him to make his axe fighters ready to move out.

'Nothing,' I say. 'Tomorrow the small wars start in earnest.'

'About bleedin' time!' he replies.

Before we leave that night, Chief Kingi calls me to him. 'So, Black Hawk, we live to fight another day, eh? Is it always so with you, to run in the face of a fight? Soon they will no longer call you General Black Hawk but instead General Back Off!'

I am mortified by these words. 'Chief Kingi,' I stammer, 'to die foolishly does not make a man a hero.'

The old chief looks at me a moment. 'You are right, General Black Hawk. Tonight Tamati Kapene would have died foolishly at your hands and he would not have been a hero.'

'I am sorry, Chief,' I say.

His eyebrows shoot up. 'Sorry? You are sorry? I am not sorry, Black Hawk. The Maori are a stubborn people, sometimes even boastful. We are given to exaggerating our prowess at war. If you had *not* acted as you had, there would have been no small wars for you. Instead, I would have sent you back to Chief Tamihana like a dog with your tail between your legs. We would have stayed to fight the British and we would have been soundly beaten.'

'I am most grateful for your support, Chief, but I am told Tamati Kapene is a bold warrior, and I have humiliated him. I have yet to know if I myself will behave with boldness in this war.'

'He is bold and stupid! We have many like him. Sometimes the Maori give their lives too quickly!' The old man begins to laugh. 'We will soon enough see what you are made of, General. We go to a place called Waireka, where we shall build a *pa*, but in the meantime you will harass Colonel Murray and his regulars. It is good country for your kind of fighting and then we shall see what we shall see of this campaign.'

We leave the *pa* while the British slumber. Later I learn that at first light, the British pound the *pa* with artillery fire, thinking to take it in the early afternoon. When after three hours there is still no return fire, they keep firing, thinking it is a ruse to lure them closer. Then, towards noon, they send in the cavalry with swords drawn and find that the enemy has escaped from right under their superior British noses.

We have melted into the surrounding countryside and now it is my turn to fight. I have sent out raiding parties, for we have news that some of the pakeha have returned to their farms, believing that Murray will soon finish us off. I know I must quickly put a stop to this. Fear of the Maori's power to strike anywhere at any time is a most important aspect of our campaign.

Over the next week, my men raid the settler farms, and we come by many horses so that we now have several dozen fighters mounted on horseback, myself sometimes amongst them. Our attacks are designed only to instil fear, and to make a livelihood impossible by destroying property and stealing livestock. It is only against the army that we wage war.

We enjoy good success against Murray's regulars, harassing, ambushing and killing several of his troopers. Our small wars are proving most effective, for the Maori take to it easily and are well disciplined in action. The broken-wooded country provides our warriors with ideal cover, and our ambushes are swift and devised more to disconcert than to take many lives, though some of the British soldiers give up their lives stupidly.

I have convinced the Maori that to destroy a supply wagon or ammunition cart is more important than taking a trooper's life. Soldiers, I point out, fight on their stomachs and we are making it as difficult as possible for Murray to feed his troops. Already, much of their food must come by sea. As a result, we have captured or destroyed several wagons. Murray has only one trump card, the Taranaki Rifle Volunteer Company, and this he uses badly. We seek to avoid these sharpshooters at all cost, and I later learn that they are the first British volunteer force to engage an enemy in the field.

It is curious, and yet another measure of British arrogance, that Murray and his Imperial officers much underrate these men and do not give them credit for their knowledge. Nor do they allow them the opportunity to come out after us. I thank God for this, for the volunteers are able to match us in almost every respect. They are the sons of men from Cornwall and Devon, and nearly twenty years of Taranaki life has moulded them into expert bushmen, familiar with the forest tracks and the terrain, and thus able to meet us on level terms. Some are on horseback and, being more skilled riders than we, are able to move swiftly to harass us.

Chief Wiremu Kingi and War Chief Hapurona know well the families who form much of the hundred-strong Rifle Volunteer Company. The Atkinsons, Smiths, Hursthouses, Bayleys, Messengers and Northcrofts are all respected as good frontiersmen and as hard, brave men. We know we would be in for a good fight if we were to come up against them. But while we have only to contend with Murray's slow-moving and often badly led regulars from the 65th Regiment, we enjoy the upper hand.

We are now based at a strong *pa* at Waireka, only five miles from New Plymouth, and it is from here that I direct my patrols to look for any brave settlers who think it safe to return. Each patrol is only six men – three axe fighters, two shotguns and a musket. Tommo commands one of the raiding parties, for I cannot contain him any longer. He must, he says, lead his men by example.

Only ten days have passed since our confrontation with Murray, when Tommo's band comes across a well-defended homestead and, for the first time, encounters serious resistance. He tells me later that there are four muskets aimed at them from a well-secured position in the farmhouse. These rifled muskets are most accurate and Tommo's band is pinned down behind a small copse of rocks and scrub. One of his shotgun warriors is wounded, though only lightly. They are not close enough to use the shotguns, while the warrior with the musket is no sharpshooter and provides little enough firepower against the four settlers.

Tommo instructs his musket to keep firing at the farmhouse. The wounded man too is told to fire his shotgun as a diversion. Tommo takes the remaining shotgun warrior and the two axemen and they creep up to the rear of the farmhouse while the others draw the settlers' fire.

Tommo is hoping that the settlers will think they have wounded or killed the other four Maori. He has commanded the two Maori left behind to fire as rapidly as possible for about ten minutes, hoping that the enemy will retaliate with equal determination. His ploy works perfectly. Tommo and his men reach the homestead when both sides are firing with gusto, and the noise allows Tommo to break down a door at the back of the farmhouse and enter.

What follows is simple enough as Tommo's band takes the settlers completely by surprise. The house is filled with smoke from the muskets and when they reach the room from

which the men are firing, Tommo and his men let go a blast
from the shotgun, further filling the room with dense smoke.
At the same time they rush in with their axes – Tommo in
the lead. It is over in a moment, and four men soon lie dead
at the hands of three axe fighters.

It is only then that Tommo discovers, to his horror, that
two of them are mere lads of ten or eleven years old, though
they stood bravely by their guns. Tommo is shocked and
deeply ashamed. The three Maori with him swear that with
all the smoke from the muskets and shotgun, it was
impossible to see well enough to gauge the age of the four
people in the room. Each of those four, they feel sure, would
have killed them with an easy conscience had the surprise
attack been the other way around. Nevertheless, Tommo
believes that his fighting axes have spilt bad blood and he is
anxious to go out again at the first opportunity to fight
Murray's regulars. 'Give us a go against the British bayonets.
I got no stomach for killing little boys,' he says sourly when
he returns that night.

I try to comfort him and remind him that in the
wilderness as a nine-year-old, he was deemed a man and
could as easily have been killed by any timber getter. 'I
know,' he says. 'But lads ten years old ain't yet mongrels in
their hearts.'

Like Tommo, I am already sickened by this war. I fear
Wiremu Kingi may be right and that I shall become General
Back Off whenever I may find an opportunity to avoid
bloodshed.

The British are enraged when they discover the killing of
the two boys at first light the next day, even though it is quite
clear that it was a terrible mistake. We fight only against the
volunteer militia and the British military. Our enemies are
those who have obtained Maori land without the permission
of the whole tribe, or who fight to gain even more. Ours is

a fight against greed, not against women and children. But the boys' deaths strike such terror that they cannot go unpunished and we wait for the soldiers to march against our *pa*.

We expect the British forces to attack us later that morning, but they do not issue forth from New Plymouth until one o'clock, a strange time to commence battle. We manage to keep them at bay, although their cannons and the artillery fire from their naval contingent keep us contained. For the first three hours it all seems to go in the usual way – the softening-up process by the British with us returning fire – and there is not much damage done except to a few palisades.

Then, to our enormous surprise, the British regulars from the 65th and the navy artillery contingent withdraw and set off to return to New Plymouth, leaving only the militia to hold us down. It is well before sunset and the volunteer militia, valiant and capable as they are, have only the old, slow-loading, smooth-bore muskets. As we will later learn, they have each been issued with only thirty rounds of ammunition to hold us for the night. Such is Colonel Murray's contempt for the Maori and disregard for the local volunteers.

For once the numbers are on our side and our weapons superior to theirs. There is great rejoicing in the *pa* and we send patrols out to harass the militia, intending to take them in a full frontal attack during the night when their muskets are least effective. They are not fools and retreat to a nearby farmhouse, where they construct a palisade. It is soon apparent that they cannot hold out against us. I am anxious to go in with a large force from the *pa* while daylight lasts, but this is an offensive under the control of War Chief Hapurona.

Hapurona decides to wait until nightfall. My fear is that these are settler militia who know the terrain and will use the cover of darkness to escape, as we did. It is here that I make a mistake of judgment which costs us dear.

So that they will not think to attempt escape, I use my men to harass the militia in the farmhouse and keep them pinned down. Unbeknownst to us, they have conceded that they must die in a night attack. With only thirty rounds of ammunition per man, they decide to use up all their firepower, hoping to intimidate my patrols before they perish, brave men all. For an hour they fire repeatedly as we wait for night to descend. Then Hapurona's warriors will go in with their shotguns and we with our fighting axes and spears against the settlers' swords and muskets.

A great many of Hapurona's warriors have assembled some distance outside the *pa*, ready to go against the enemy, when the navy suddenly re-appears. Later we learn that they have heard the gunfire and so have decided to disobey their orders to return to New Plymouth, choosing instead to march towards the sound of firing.

A terrible bloodbath ensues. We are trapped in near darkness between the militia and the *pa* by the naval artillery fire, and are cut to ribbons. Many of our warriors die before we are able to scatter into the night. What had seemed like a certain victory for the Maori before sunset, is by moonrise a dreadful defeat. The single initiative of a lone naval commander, who decided to disobey Murray's instructions, has saved the day for the British, at a great loss to the Maori.

If we had destroyed the volunteer militia here, it might well have made all the difference to the outcome of the war, for these volunteers are the most effective force the British possess. I am not blamed for pinning the militia down, so giving them cause to fire back sufficiently vigorously for the retreating navy to hear their guns. Nevertheless I blame myself.

During April, the British receive considerable reinforcements from Australia and many settlers return to their land, thinking the Maori defeated. The new forces, eager for action, lose no time in moving down the coastline, burning and pillaging our villages, hoping to starve us over the coming winter. We cannot meet them head-on for they are too well equipped with light artillery and grapeshot, and the most terrifying Congreve rockets. We must begin the old process of instilling fear in the settlers all over again. I send out patrols to burn every farm in those districts where we had not previously been and where the settlers have thought now to return. We carry off their cattle and horses and what food we can find, as the pakeha forces are doing to our people.

The governor, however, makes a great display of warning that we mean to kill all pakeha, including the missionaries. It must be obvious to him, though, that had we wished to do so, we could already have killed a score or more of the pakeha settlers. The Maori are upset by the governor's words, but I am not unduly concerned by them. I explain that it is the European way to build up hatred for the enemy. 'If the devil were to wage war with the angels of heaven, he would declare the enemy to be wicked and vengeful. It is in the very nature of warfare to make the enemy out to be monsters. Governor Gore Browne is only proving himself to be very good at it,' I advise the council.

'The ways of the pakeha are strange. Do not the enemy also deserve honour? Are they not also brave warriors?' War Chief Hapurona asks.

'It is called propaganda. They think it will aid their cause and will make their war seem righteous in the eyes of their own people.'

'War is only righteous when you defend your land, your women and your children. It is not righteous when you wish to steal another man's land,' Wiremu Kingi declares. 'We, the Maori, have fought each other for generations, hoping to take each other's land, make slaves of the other tribe's women and warriors of their children. But we did not call this a righteous war. We did not try to justify it as the British are doing!'

Murray promises to avenge the death of any white man killed, and the newspapers run lurid stories of those who have been tomahawked and scalped in the manner of the North American Red Indians! They have picked up the name of General Black Hawk, though they seem not to associate it with the Black Maori. They conclude that the Maori have recruited the famous Red Indian fighter, Chief Blackhawk, to teach them how to use the tomahawk on their pakeha victims. I am not sure such a man as Chief Blackhawk even exists. Perhaps he is simply the invention of a newspaper reporter with a fevered imagination. Nevertheless, there is much speculation among the pakeha population that more North American Indians have arrived by ship, landing higher up the coastline. The paper reports a reliable rumour that there are more ships en route, with whole tribes of tomahawk-wielding Indians bound for New Zealand!

This in turn fuels further fears that a legion of Redskins, led by the legendary Chief Blackhawk, will soon attack New Plymouth on horseback, whooping their dreadful war cries as they scalp women and children.

Rumours aside, if we can keep the soldiers at bay until the winter, we may become strong enough to achieve an equitable truce in this war. The onset of winter works in our favour. The heavy rains make movement of the large British baggage trains near impossible, the roads turn into quagmires and the rivers are flooded. We are less hampered and our guerrillas roam the countryside until we have driven all the settlers back into New Plymouth.

By June we have recovered our strength somewhat and,

working in difficult conditions, we construct two forts at Puke Te Kauere. I am forced to reconsider much of what I thought about fighting from a *pa*. I now realise the Maori have a genius for earthworks and fortification, and that we will need to meet the British head-to-head if ever they are to be brought to a truce. When this time comes, we shall need the forts to have some advantage in the proceedings.

The two forts at Puke Te Kauere are backed by heavy forest, the immense kahikatea trees. Wiremu Kingi takes Tommo and me into this primeval world of giant trees, ferns and damp. Tommo is at once at home.

'Ah,' he says, laughing, 'I knows this world of tall trees. If we was to fight in this I would become a general and we would surely win.'

Chief Kingi sighs. 'Not so long ago, much of my country was covered in great forests like this one. Now the pakeha have shaved us like a bald head, cutting down the trees which are older than our ancestors and have stood since time dreamed in darkness.' He turns away and spits to the ground. 'They cut them so that they might grow grass for their spotted cows. Once, there was the cry of birds in the morning, and the song of every kind of winged creature in the world filled the air. Now, where the pakeha have stolen the land, it has become silent and only the caw of the English crow is to be heard.'

He pauses and smiles sadly. 'If you listen with a Maori heart you may hear the earth trembling and weeping for the glory of the great trees. If the Maori do not hold onto their land, the pakeha will kill everything that is beautiful, so that they might make New Zealand like the faraway land of Queen Victoria, where there are no more tall trees to sweep the skies and brush the howling wind into whispers. The trees are the groves of life. Without them we are not ourselves, we are naked.'

I think of Tommo in the wilderness and our own sweet land of Tasmania, cousin to this one, where the giant gums grow as tall as the kahikatea. There, the timber getters harvest the Huon pine – and trees, a thousand or more years old, are bashed and beaten to the ground by the saw and the axe. I wonder how much longer they too will last upon this earth? Will our home become like New Zealand, a land shaved and broken by the plough of the white invader? Alas, we are of the same breed, and I cannot see how it will be any different. Perhaps, in our drier land, it will be even worse.

Looking at this forest, it is clear that we have placed the forts well, for no British column could think to gain access and attack us from the rear. To one side of the forts is a swamp. The water in some parts is well above waist height and it contains vast areas of sucking mud. To the other side is the heavily timbered country we can control. In the foreground, where the British will be forced to attack, lies thickly growing fern with abundant flax. It will make any approach, no matter how well organised, most hazardous.

We have built trenches and scarps twenty feet high and innumerable palisades. Both forts are a work of genius and give the defenders a great advantage against any assault by the British regulars.

After all is ready, we hold a final war council to discuss our tactics against the British. We have learned much of guerrilla warfare since the disastrous engagement at Waireka. With new regular forces coming from Australia, we do not expect that they will depart from conventional military tactics.

'These troops will not know New Zealand or the manner of the Maori,' War Chief Hapurona announces. 'Therefore we may fight them in our own way. What say you, Black Hawk?'

I am quick to agree, and point out that the terrain we

occupy is not only easy to defend but also allows us to attack the enemy's flanks. Hammerhead Jack, an excellent tactician, has suggested to me that we also use the swamp to our advantage. Now I put these thoughts together. 'Should we not also come at them from outside the forts? They will think that, as always, we will only defend ourselves and so they will leave their flanks exposed. If we can attack them from our positions in the woods, from within the flax and out of the gullies, and you are holding them down from the forts, they will make for the swamp, believing it to be good cover. That is where our axe fighters will take them.'

It is a bold plan and Hapurona is not sure we have sufficient men to both attack and defend. From their encampment less than a mile away, we know that the British have much the superior numbers. Finally it is decided that I should have command over the trenches outside the forts, and also have small roving bands with shotguns hidden in the forests, gullies and clumps of flax. Tommo and his axe fighters will be positioned in the swamp with their long-handled fighting axes, while others will wield fighting sticks to ward off the British bayonets. We have erected our flagpole in full view of the British camp. This time the flag is a black cross on a white field. We hope that they will once again seek to capture it.

We soon discover that Hapurona was right. The troops sent against us are plainly new regulars, greenhorns from Australia under British officers equally inexperienced at fighting our kind of war. The volunteer militia are nowhere to be seen and we are most grateful for this. I know that these local men are much too skilled to be drawn into attacking a position so well constructed and defended as our two forts.

After the disaster at Waireka, it is our turn for some luck. The British officers appear quite casual in their preparation and barely send out patrols to reconnoitre the terrain over which they must advance. It seems almost as though they expect some mild-mannered skirmish, a pleasant morning's outing for their men.

The British attack at daylight on the twenty-seventh of June, and are almost immediately in trouble. Our muskets start to pick them off from the trenches and the forts, and their advance is made most difficult by the heavily ferned terrain. The British think first to attack our flanking trenches and foolishly but valiantly charge with bayonets, but we simply retreat from the first line of defence, leaving them to face a second set of trenches beyond. Heavily loaded with equipment, they are exhausted, and now within reach of our double-barrelled shotguns. We begin to cut them to pieces with buckshot, so that they are soon forced to retreat. Not one trooper reaches us, though we shoot several at very close range. They turn to run with their entrails hanging to the ground and blood spurting from their mouths. They cannot even cry out, taking but a few faltering steps before they collapse and die. The British will later report that the storm of shot they ran into was worse than that of Balaclava.

As the soldiers withdraw, we come at them from the wooded flank and out of the gullies and flax, driving them towards the swamp where Tommo's men lie in wait. The black powder of the muskets creates a great deal of smoke, and we fight as though we are in a forest fire. It is Hammerhead Jack who directs this attack, for he seems to know every Maori position and when to employ it. It is he who is the true general and I will make this known to Hapurona lest I receive credit which I do not rightly deserve.

The retreating British regulars, thinking the swamp will provide cover and give them protection, are soon waist deep in water, and now Tommo's men attack with their fighting axes and *taiaha* sticks. It is slaughter of the most terrible kind and the cries of the dying are pitiful. Soon the corpses are so numerous that they float bumping against each other in the water, which has now turned the colour of blood. Those who manage to struggle back to higher ground are cut down by our warriors, who have emerged from the forts to attack the fleeing soldiers.

What remains of the attacking column is forced to retreat under cover of their artillery fire. The British have been routed and the Maori have established a new way of fighting.

I return to the *pa*, sickened at the sight of so much blood and death. Wiremu Kingi and Hapurona hail me as a hero, though I feel far from heroic. I have had enough. The Maori now know how to wage war differently and much experience has been gained. I can play no further useful part in their affairs. Tommo is right – it is time to leave.

Wiremu Kingi addresses me in front of the council of war. 'You have proved yourself, General Black Hawk, and your methods have changed the way the Maori will fight the British from now on. We owe you a great debt. Our ancestors will honour you as long as the Maori stand upon this land! Tonight we will celebrate our victory and you will be foremost among our many warriors.'

I know I should think this a great moment, but I am war-weary and most anxious to find Tommo, whose men have taken the brunt of the fighting in the swamp. The attentions of Chief Kingi and War Chief Hapurona and the other high-ranking warriors mean I am forced to remain with the war council until well after dark. In this time I am able to extol the virtues of Hammerhead Jack as a born leader of men, and I declare him a better general than ever I shall be.

I have already sent Hammerhead Jack to find my brother and expect them both to be waiting for me. Finally I am able to take my leave, and go to tell Tommo that our task with the Maori is complete, our debt repaid in full.

But Hammerhead Jack is waiting alone outside, and I see at once that something is wrong.

'What is it?' I ask in alarm. 'Where is Tommo? Where is my brother?'

'Ork, he has not returned from the swamp. Five of the axe fighters are not back, and he is among them.'

'Have you searched?' I start to shake him by the shoulder where his arm is missing. 'Have you sent men into the swamp to look for him?' My panic is growing rapidly.

'Ork, I have come out of the swamp to tell you. I have been in there myself with flax torches, and the others are still searching among the reeds.'

I notice for the first time that he is wet up to the waist. His breeches are covered in mud and he is shaking from the cold.

'The water is full of the bodies of the British and we have found three of our axe fighters dead,' Hammerhead Jack pauses, 'but not Tommo.'

'We must keep looking! I will come with you!' I turn to run out of the *pa* but Hammerhead Jack grabs my arm.

'Wait! It is full moon in an hour, we can see better then. You must eat first, you have not taken food today! You will have no strength, Ork. The swamp is freezing and treacherous with sucking mud. You will surely perish!'

'I must find Tommo!' I shout, tearing away from him. My heart is pounding and I think I will die of the fear that has taken hold of me. 'Oh God! Oh Mama! Ikey! Help me now!' I begin to run wildly towards the swamp.

Chapter Eleven

TOMMO

Puke Te Kauere
27 June 1860

I'm sitting up to me waist in a bloody swamp, near shitting meself. The redcoats are everywhere. There's smoke covering the battle so it's hard to see, but wherever there's a clear patch there's half a dozen British to be seen, loading, firing and panicking.

I had to open me big gob about the long-handled axe being better than the bayonet, but even after Waireka, I got me doubts. I've learnt a great deal from how the Maori handle a fighting stick, but it's different when a trooper with bad blood in his eyes is comin' straight at you – him with a reach o' six foot or more, and me with an axe what don't extend more than two foot. All of a sudden, it don't look too promising.

Ever since we took the farmhouse and them two young lads was killed, it ain't been the same for me. I've seen how the axe kills now. I've thought about that moment a thousand times. Could I have known they was lads before we struck them? The room were filled with smoke from their muskets and from the shotgun blast, so we couldn't see hardly nothin' at all when we entered. I know I axed someone, but who I couldn't tell. Just a neck and a bit of shoulder in the smoke and confusion. Our blood was up and running high 'cause we'd won the day. But when the smoke cleared, two young lads lay dead next to the two grown men. I don't reckon I'll ever get over that. So young and brave one minute, and then hacked meat at me feet. Oh Gawd! What would our poor mama think o' me?

We've been waiting here in the rushes for nigh three hours, having come into the swamp from the back. It's the middle o' winter and bloody cold! I'm thinking of Hawk in the trenches and worrying for him. But he says we're not to come out, we're not to fight in the open. Instead we must wait for the British to come to us. Let the swamp slow them down, then take 'em by surprise.

I know me lads, though. They can see the British be in a mess already on the higher ground and they'll want to go after 'em. I pass on the word, no one must move until I say. But these be young warriors, anxious to be blooded in battle. They won't like the idea of holding back, freezing their bollocks off while there's a hot fight going on.

How the hell does Hawk know the British will come? He's pretty new to the business of being a general. The lads have waited three months to have a second go at the British soldiers. They're spoiling for a fight. Me, I'm not so keen no more, not after Waireka and the farmhouse. When we comes back from that raid the *rangatira* called us heroes. Our attacks on the settlers be proof to them that we are of true value to them in this war. I'm not so sure. Waireka just about finished us off – Tommo Te Mokiri lost six good men that day. Now me boys are waiting for another chance to meet the British, and their turn will come soon enough if Hawk be right. He reckons the redcoats will run to the swamp for cover. I hope he's right. I can't hold me lads back much longer.

Suddenly it happens. I watch, hardly believing my own eyes, as the first soldier comes running towards the swamp. He's stumbling out of the smoke towards us, not charging with his bayonet, just running for cover, scared witless, fleeing the shotguns what's pumping hot. I pray the lads will wait, not take him at once in a rush and give the game away to the rest. I send out the word to let him come right up to us, right up to the bulrushes where we hide. The redcoat is splashing through the shallows, knees pumpin' high, trying to go faster, floosh, floosh, floosh. It's heavy going, 'cause his boots stick in the muddy, sucking bottom of the swamp, and he's panting and gasping, eyes popping.

Then they's all heading our way, coming thick and fast through the smoke. I can hear the Maori shotguns. Bah-bam! Bah-bam! It's a different sound from the muskets what sounds more like a ba-boom-whup. The shotguns are working fast and the redcoats are turning and making straight for the swamp. Any moment now there'll be ten or fifteen of them upon us and twice as many more behind. 'Hold it lads, not now, let them come in deeper, nearer, take yer time,' I orders under me breath.

My fear has left me, drummed out by the pounding of me blood. Next instant there's a face in front of me. It's black from gunpowder and almost comical-looking, the eyes red-rimmed and showing white eyelashes. The soldier's in up to his waist, with half of his musket under water. All he wants to do is get to the safety of the reeds and rushes. He's looking directly at me, but his eyes show no recognition of what they see. The axe in me hand seems to know its own way, and I feel the blade bite into the man's head, soft as butter. The poor sod don't have time to think, from the moment he sees me to the moment he's dead.

Now the British be everywhere around us. Some is trying

desperately to fire, but most has come into the swamp with their muskets unloaded and not ready to use their bayonets. They're belted and booted, and their shako caps sit high and awkward upon their heads. They be weighed down with their packs and most clumsy-like. With us bare to the waist and carrying nothing but our light fighting axes, it ain't no contest. The men at the front are forced towards us, as others come in behind them, pushing them forward in their haste to gain what they think is the safety of the swamp.

Another redcoat comes at me now. He's seen his mate die and he's got his bayonet at the ready. 'Bastard!' he shouts, and tries to run me through. It's clumsy stuff in the water and I brush the bayonet aside, hitting him on the jaw with the butt end of the axe handle. His head goes back at the impact of the blow, baring his neck with the strap of his shako biting into it. It's clear and clean-shaven, and me blooded blade finds its mark. It is all too easy, and he don't even have time to cuss again before he's a gargle of frothy blood sinking into the water. His eyes look sort o' surprised, though his neck is almost cut through and he's already dead before his head hits the drink.

All around me there's screaming from the British, and shouting and grunting and whooping from the Maori lads. The strange thing is that the redcoats keep coming. They can see us clear as daylight now – well, maybe not *that* clear given all the smoke – but they must not know that trouble lies ahead. They're at the edge of the mud, not yet in the water, but they doesn't turn back. They just keep coming, shoving on those in front as they line up to die at the hands of the Maori axe fighters.

And then I hear the shotguns on the flanks driving them towards us. Bah-bam! Bah-bam! If they keep coming like this, we'll soon be too weary to kill them all. We're fighting in the water and the mud is heavy going, and there's too many o' the dumb bastards for one afternoon's killing!

From the corner of my eye, I see a soldier coming at one of my lads from behind. The Maori don't see him 'cause he's fighting another trooper with a big yellow moustache what's trying to stick him. 'Die, nigger!' shouts the moustache. The redcoat behind has his bayonet ready to run me lad through his back. I got no choice and my axe leaves my hand. It flies through the air and takes the trooper in the back of his head, splitting his skull, and lodging itself tight. The other man sees this and stops for one second, and that's enough for the Maori's axe to take him.

I starts moving towards him, shouting to the Maori lad to grab my axe. The trooper I've hit has sunk slowly into the swamp. He is dead, but he must be resting on his knees somehow, his head still showing above the water. My axe handle pokes up out of the crimson water still stuck in his skull. But in all the noise the lad I've saved don't hear me and moves forward to take on another redcoat.

In the back o' me mind I think I hear Hammerhead Jack shouting behind the smoke on the higher ground. There are bodies floating everywhere, troopers' jackets stained dark from the swamp water with little air pockets of brilliant scarlet bobbing above the surface, bright lilies in a blood-red stream.

A few wounded redcoats try to beat a retreat in the shallows, but they don't last long. The mud sucks at their boots, and most slip and fall to their knees. The Maori lads has stopped their whooping and has turned into a killing machine. The axe kills more surely than the musket and more swiftly than the bayonet – its aim in a good warrior's hands is always to the head or neck.

I'm wadin' towards my own axe, its handle now only six inches above the surface. The trooper's head has gone under.

I hear a shot ring out and suddenly I'm knocked over. I'm down under the water, kicking out wildly, trying to catch me breath. Bloody hell! I've been hit. There is a terrible pain in my head and I tries to come to the surface, kicking and flailing my arms. The top of my head bumps against somethin' and I push against it. I try with all what's left in me to push me noggin past whatever's in me way but I can feel my strength failing. Then it's lights out for yours truly and I don't remember nothing no more.

When I come to, all is blackness and I can't open my eyes. Around me frogs is croaking and crickets chirping. I know I'm in water, suspended-like, not floating, though I'm not sure how my head comes to be above the surface. I am frozen stiff, so I can't tell whether me feet touch the bottom or whether I float upright. I try to force my eyes open but they's stuck closed. Perhaps, I think, they *are* open and I'm dead, or I've been blinded by the musket ball what hit me. Me head aches something terrible, but I have my senses about me. Only I can't move or see nothin'.

Slowly it comes to me. My eyes are stuck with blood, dried blood, my eyelashes glued together. In the distance I can hear singing. It's the singing what brings me back. The Maori is singing in the forts, singing their victory chants and shouting their fierce war cries. I must try to get my arm up, but it too seems stuck. How is my head held up out of the water? Why don't I sink? I try to work my eyes open again but cannot.

Then I hears me name. It's Hawk, shouting, 'Tommo! Tommo!' His voice is hoarse, as though he has been shouting a long time. I try to answer but nothing comes. Then I hear a swish of water as if someone passes nearby, and small waves lap against me head. Hawk is passing me! Calling for me and I can't say nothing! I can't lift my arm or kick or shout out or move me head. Inside, I'm screaming and, for the first time, I truly know how it must have been for Hawk when he were dumb.

An hour or more passes and then someone goes by again, calling out in a desperate voice. It is Hawk, still calling my name, though his voice be near gone.

Suddenly there is a bump as Hawk brushes into whatever is holding me. I hear a gasp and a great howl, like the cry of a hurt animal. Hawk pulls frantically at me, sobbing in big gasps as he lifts me from the water in his arms. 'Oh, Tommo! Oh, Tommo!' he bawls. 'Oh, Tommo, what have I done? I have killed you!'

He splashes out of the swamp and I hear others shout, then Hammerhead Jack's voice. I am laid down on firm ground and a head is put to me chest. It is Hammerhead Jack again. 'Tommo good!' he says. He starts laughin'. He can't stop and others join in. Then everything goes dark as I fall asleep or pass out.

When I awakes, I can see again. I'm lying beside a fire, wrapped in blankets, and my whole body aches as though it has been clubbed. But I ain't cold anymore, though my head still hurts fierce. Hawk is seated cross-legged beside me, his head on his chest and his hands in his lap. He is asleep. I am so tight-wrapped, I cannot move, though I can wiggle me toes and move me fingers. Best of all, I can see, but my throat's terrible sore from the cold and I doubt I can talk.

I look at Hawk sleeping and the tears run down me face. I dunno why, but I can't stop crying. Maybe it's relief 'cause I can see again. Maybe it's seeing Hawk. He has deep lines under his eyes and his mouth is pulled down from tiredness. Hawk and his stupid conscience got us into this bloody mess. Why can't he just be like other folk and not care, not give a bugger for naught, like his brother Tommo?

Then I think of Makareta and the baby what's due any day now. Maybe it's even come. God bless me soul, I could be a father already! Makareta were nearly a widow! With a shock, it hits me that I *do* care. I cares about the two young lads we axed, about Makareta, my unborn child, Hawk, even Mary! But, still and all, I don't know how *much* I care. Would I have done anything different if I'd known those two settlers were mere lads, even if one was pointing a loaded musket at me gut? Would I risk me life to save his? I don't think so. Hawk, he would. But not yours truly, that I doubts very much.

That's the thing about me brother – he don't measure how much he cares. If a man is kicking a dog he's gunna stop him, whether it be a flea-bitten mongrel not worth tuppence or a squatter's prize sheepdog. It don't bother the big bloke. Hawk just gallops to the rescue, bugles blowing, nostrils flaring, huffing full of indignation!

Hawk can't bear what's unfair in this world. I, on the other hand, knows everything's unfair. There ain't nothin' fair about this sodding world. The mongrels don't never go away. We has beaten the British but I know it's only *this* time. They'll be back. The Maori cannot win. The pakeha wants their land and they'll get it, come hell or high water.

Hawk opens his eyes and sees me looking at him, sees me tears. 'Tommo?'

I smile.

'Tommo, speak to me!' He reaches out and shakes me. 'You all right?'

I nod.

'Can you speak?'

I open my mouth and a small croak comes out.

'Throat sore? But you can speak?' he asks, anxious. I nod again and he smiles. It's Hawk's real big smile, what can't be resisted. I smiles back, me gob nearly as wide.

It seems I owe me life to a dead British soldier, the redcoat I killed when I threw me axe, as a matter o' fact. When Hawk found me, my head were jammed in between the dead man's legs, the back o' me neck tight against his crotch, my axe still sticking out o' the floating corpse. The redcoat's knapsack kept him floating and my feet touching the bottom of the swamp kept him level in the water. His big British bum were the resistance I felt when I tried to come to the surface. It ain't a pretty thought, my head up a soldier's arse for ten hours.

In two days I have me voice back. There's a wound to the side of my head where a musket ball grazed me, taking some hair and a bit of me skull as well. I guess I'm lucky. I could've caught pneumonia in the freezing water. All them years in the wilderness must have toughened me up. And now I'm just a bit snotty and chesty and has a terrible headache. But I'm alive and grateful and, best of all, it's the end of the Maori wars for Hawk and me.

'Sydney! We is going to Australia!' It's the first thing I says to Hawk when me voice returns.

Hawk is too relieved at hearing me speak to object, and he nods his head. 'Enough of war and killing, Tommo. We cannot do any more here.'

I know Hawk'd rather head for Hobart Town, but I don't want to go back to Mary, not just yet. I'm not ready for the brewery or for mama and her green eyes looking at me – even though I know she wants us back and will do anything to accommodate us. In her last letter she underlined the word *anything* four times! She's talking about me – she'll have me back however much trouble I be. She wants her precious boys home, she says. But I knows in me gut I'm not ready to see her again yet. We'll make our fortunes in New South Wales first, I'm certain o' that.

A gold rush be a gambler's paradise if you plays your cards right. For the man who can do a little relocation, there ain't no better place to be. I'm not intended for hard work of the digging kind. But with cards we can clean up. Then I'll return to New Zealand and bring back Makareta and me baby. Mary will have a grandchild and yours truly will be a respectable citizen, puffing his pipe and nodding his head and looking like he knows what he's doin' when he most probably don't.

I think about the grog. I ain't been near the black bottle for nigh on four years now. Perhaps I be cured of the drink at last. But I ain't been tested yet. Sometimes the craving still comes upon me awful. It gnaws at me gut, rips and snorts, and leaves me tongue hanging out panting for it! Other times it goes away for days at a time and I thinks it might be over. Perhaps having a woman and child to care for will help. I wants to get back to our village and see Makareta, to hear her soft, happy voice, to have her hold me tight in the dark and, if our baby be born and she be well enough, to make love to her again.

Now as I lies here and thinks of sweet Makareta, I realise how hard it will be to part from her and from all our Maori friends. They has been so good to me, Hammerhead Jack and the others on the whaling ship, with their axe revenge on Captain Mordechai O'Hara and our escape from the gaol at Kororareka. The one-eyed, one-armed giant is overjoyed at my recovery. This morning he comes to me and says, 'Always, Tommo, when we fall in the water, Ork comes to fetch us!' He throws back his ugly noggin and roars with laughter at his own joke.

But mostly I owes me thanks to Makareta, what loves me in every possible way. When I cries out in me sleep, she soothes me and holds me tight, or quietens me by letting me love her.

At last we take our leave from Chief Kingi and War Chief Hapurona, for I am strong enough for the journey back to our own tribe. There has been much praise heaped upon us and lots of feasting. Our fighting axes has killed more British than the muskets or shotguns and I am made *rangatira*. I am pleased for it means Makareta will have a higher status in the tribe of Chief Tamihana and when we're away, she'll be especially well cared for.

Chief Tamihana has grown in reputation among the Maori tribes, for though he is known as the kingmaker and peacemaker, he is also now known as a chief what is prepared to fight. His axe fighters has played a decisive role in the Ati Awa people's victory. Hawk, in particular, has been honoured for the work what he's done, and the honour is equally Tamihana's by rights and tradition.

In his farewell speech, Chief Wiremu Kingi says that we has both honoured the Maori people in battle. Hawk has proved he has the heart and *mana* of a Maori. There is nothing he cannot ask of the Ati Awa tribe save a chieftainship, what can only be bestowed by birth, though all says Black Hawk would make a very good Maori chief.

Hawk, as usual, don't ask for nothing. He just says it's been an honour to serve the old chief and his brother. Honour? I near loses me flamin' life and Hawk speaks of how privileged we be to serve! The chief says they want one of our ancestors to be included in the Maori tribe, to become an ancestor of the Ati Awa.

What ancestors? thinks I. Ikey Solomon be the only male what we knows, and he ain't either of our natural fathers. Ain't no good telling them about our true papas neither, 'cause we don't even know whether they be alive or dead. Maori can't have no female ancestors on their Council of the Dead, so we can't give them the fat old whore, Sperm Whale Sally, our true mother, or Mary, what I reckons might be of some use to them. More than them, we ain't got no ancestors to speak of. But to tell the Maori that would upset them something terrible.

'You must give the *tohunga* the name of your greatest ancestor and we will include him with our own, him you wish to sit beside the great ones. Will you tell us now who this shall be?' Chief Wiremu Kingi asks very solemn.

I can see Hawk don't quite know what to say. He can't insult the Ati Awa by giving no name, like we don't want our ancestor to be included in their tribal company. He scratches his head.

'There is one,' he answers, to my surprise.

The old chief turns to his *tohunga*. 'Black Hawk will give us this ancestor's name and he shall henceforth be in all your councils.'

The *tohunga* don't look too happy about this instruction. They don't seem to think it's a good idea, but they can't come out and say it, right there in front of us. Maybe later, among themselves, they will have the necessary arguments.

'Ikey Solomon,' Hawk says slowly.

'Icky Sloman!' all the *rangatira* repeat. 'Icky Sloman! Icky Sloman!'

'I-key So-lo-mon.' Hawk pronounces it carefully.

'We have it!' Chief Wiremu Kingi announces. 'Icky Slomon!'

I am hard put not to burst out laughing, but Hawk stays serious. 'I am most honoured,' he says, giving me a sharp look, 'and my brother is most honoured too that our venerable ancestor will commune with yours. Our ancestor's wisdom will always be available to the Ati Awa. On the affairs of the pakeha he is a great expert and will be happy to be on your side. I thank you deeply from my heart and on his behalf.'

'Tell us of this Icky Slomon,' War Chief Hapurona asks.

'To what tribe did he belong? What of *his* ancestors, what do you know of them?'

'A great deal!' replies Hawk. 'He belonged to the tribe of Israel and his greatest ancestor was a most wise king, King Solomon.'

'A king?' The old chief looks impressed. 'And this king, was he black like you?'

Hawk ain't gunna look at me in case he should laugh. 'No, he was like Tommo, like my brother, but it is said he took a black woman to his bed, the Queen of Sheba.'

'Ah, a white king and a black queen! So that is why you are black, General?' Hapurona nods towards me, understanding now how we come to be different, one from t'other. 'And Tommo is white.'

'Well, yes, it was not *quite* like that,' says Hawk, rubbing his chin.

But Hapurona don't hear, or don't want to. 'Then we are most honoured to accept the ancestor of a great king to sit with our ancestors,' he announces. I think he is glad we got a king, or someone what comes from a king, and is of the *rangatira*. Everyone, even the *tohunga*, now seems to agree that Ikey should be a Maori ancestor o' some prominence.

Hawk's turned two bastards born to a whaleman's whore on a beach into two noble princes. And there's old Ikey, peacefully dead in the graveyard in Hobart Town when, all of a sudden, without so much as a beg your pardon, he's whisked away in the middle o' some argument about who owes who tuppence ha'penny. Next thing he knows, he's sitting amongst a bunch of fierce cannibal savages what don't much care to be called 'my dears' and what thinks him more useful for the cooking pot than for his opinions on the art o' relocation.

I can hear Ikey in me mind as he expresses his alarm at being so abducted. 'Most strange and unusual, perplexing, astonishing, a whole sackful o' live rats and queernesses perpetrated upon a most properly dead and eternally slumbering soul, my dears!' Still and all, I reckon the Maori is probably more interestin' company than the dead of Hobart Town's cemetery.

Hammerhead Jack and the remaining of my troop of fighting axe men returns with us to Chief Tamihana's village. When we arrive at the *pa* of the Ngati Haua, we're greeted like heroes. We're escorted into the village and immediately taken to the *marae* for a ceremony to end the *tapu* what's been placed on us as warriors. This is conducted by the priests and makes us *noa*, that is to say, normal commonfolk once more.

Hammerhead Jack has told me that, not so long ago, warriors would feast on the carcasses of their enemies. This were known to be sacred food, *tapu* to any but themselves. In order for warriors to have the *tapu* lifted and become *noa* again, they was obliged to throw away the remains of the bodies what they'd been eating. Then the eldest female of the oldest hereditary stock, the *wahine ariki*, would eat the ear of the first enemy killed in battle. I, for one, be thankful customs has changed. I has already had me head up a dead redcoat's arse, but to have to eat him as well is asking too much o' yours truly.

Once we have been made *noa*, we gather at the *marae* for a great *hui* and there is much speechifying. I am made *rangatira*. Hawk receives a feathered hat and wears his black feathered general's cape for all to see.

Hammerhead Jack then tells the story of the battle so everyone might hear it first hand. He speaks of Hawk's wisdom and of my part in leading the fighting axe men. He tells of how I saved the young warrior's life, of how I were struck down and how I were rescued, giving it all in the most exact detail includin' how I killed the soldier and then got me head stuck up his arse. All assembled laughs heartily at this and one o' the elders points to the bandage on me noggin. 'Is that why you cover it?' he asks, to much merriment.

'So, Tommo!' says Chief Tamihana. 'Your new name shall be "The man whose face has seen the worst thing possible in battle."' I blush, for I thinks the chief is making merry again at my expense. But the Maori do not think this a joke and they nod sagely and clap at me new name. A warrior's name earned in battle be like being a knight o' the realm to the English. Then each of the axe warriors is named and honoured with a new song. Their names are took in by the *tohunga* and the dead is committed to their ancestors' care.

War Chief Hapurona and Chief Wiremu Kingi have sent a special envoy to Tamihana what now praises the tribe's warriors. The speech is long and boring and tells of the part each Ngati Haua warrior played in the Ati Awa's great victory. It is most flowery, but our *rangatira* takes in every word and I can see they be terrible proud of all us lads. Then we go to a great feast the women has prepared in our honour, with fifteen pigs slaughtered.

I am by now desperate to find Makareta, for I ain't been permitted to go to our hut. I had hoped to find her among the women what prepares the feast, but she ain't with them. Nor were she in the crowd what came out to greet us when we arrived. I can't leave the *hui* until I am given permission and it's very late at night before I can slip away.

I has only just left the edge of the great fire when I am met by Makareta's mother.

'Come quickly, Tommo. Makareta is birthing.'

'How is she? How long has she been in labour?'

'Since you came back, since sundown.'

'What! Why didn't you fetch me?' I cry.

Makareta's mother gives me a look. 'How may an old woman interrupt the affairs of men?' she says. 'Come, there is no time!'

Outside our hut, several women wait anxiously. 'The old women are with her,' says one as we approach.

'I got to see her.' I begins to shoulder my way to the door.

The women all draw back. 'It cannot be, it is bad *tapu* for the father to witness the birth,' Makareta's mother says sternly. 'You must wait, please.'

'Then tell me, how is she?'

But Makareta's mother goes into the hut without answering, and one of the women brings me a drink of bush lime fruit. 'It is a difficult labour. She is not well,' she tells me, then asks if I want something to eat. I say no, and sit down to wait. From inside I can hear Makareta groaning and crying out. The sound tears at me very soul and I keep asking to go to her, but each time I am most sternly refused. My hands are tied. It would only frighten Makareta to see me, because of the *tapu*. Another hour passes and the feast is still going on, with a great deal of singin' and merrymakin'. I wish Hawk were here, but I know he can't be. Chief Tamihana will want him to stay at the feast all night.

Suddenly I feels them. The mongrels are here. I rise, not knowing what to do. I can feel them crawling under me skin and the hair at the back o' me neck stands on end. I swipe at my arms, trying to brush them off, and beat at my shoulders. Makareta's mother comes out of the hut, shakes her head, and starts to keen. It is the terrible, shrill sound of women mourning. The others takes it up immediately. They do not even look to where I am sitting, and it is as though I do not exist. Death has possessed their throats and there be no place for a man within their heads.

I push past them and run into the hut. One of the old

women stands holding a small bundle what is squalling. Our baby! But Makareta is lying on a flaxen mat with much blood around her. She is breathing heavy and a rasping noise comes from her chest. Her lips is cracked and she is in a lather o' sweat, with tiny bubbles coming from her nostrils.

'Makareta?' I whispers, crouching down beside her. 'Makareta, it's Tommo! Tommo's come home.' There is no sound from her lips, only the rasping of her chest. I take up her hand and hold it in my own. 'Makareta, it's Tommo! Can you hear me? It's your Tommo, come home from the war!'

'She is dying,' the woman says. 'You have a daughter.'

I do not hear her at first. Then slowly it sinks in that she is talking to me as if Makareta be already gone. The pain in me heart starts to grow, not all at once but quick enough. It climbs up into me throat where it fills me 'til I know I'll choke with it. 'Oh God! Please don't let her die!' I hears meself say, though whether it be inside my head or out I don't know, for me fear and pain is blocking everything out.

I put my arms 'round Makareta, who is on fire to the touch. I bring her hand to my lips, and then crouches down and holds her in my arms. I rock her gently until my fear begins to fade, and I can breathe and speak once more. 'Please, Makareta, please don't die! I needs you! If you live I will stay here. I'll stay with you forever. Please don't die! Don't let the mongrels get ya, me darling!'

I feel Makareta's hand come up slow and touch mine. Her mouth moves painfully and she whispers once, 'Tommo!' She is too weak to say more, but I can see she is trying to speak. Her lips open, then close again, then open. She is trying hard to gather breath.

'What is it? I love you, Makareta!' I sob.

I feel her squeeze my hand again. There is no strength left and it is less than a child's hand putting pressure to mine.

Then a tear falls from her left eye. Another follows from the right, rollin' ever so slow down her beautiful, sweet face. They roll across her cheeks and over her chin. In a whisper I can hardly hear, she says, 'Tommo, it is a girl. I am sorry.' Then she opens her eyes and looks at me, and I sees the love she feels. 'Tommo, will you forgive me?'

'Makareta! It doesn't matter! Please, please live, me darling!' I am sobbing, shrieking, unable to hold back any longer. 'Please?' I am now begging her. But she gives a small sigh, and the life goes from her.

I weep and weep. I do not hear the midwife leave with the infant. I cradle Makareta in me arms and rock her, as though if I should hold on tight enough she may live again. Everything is still. Outside the women are keening. It is like a pack o' dogs baying at the moon. The mongrels have won again. Me head aches something fierce. My tears are frozen to the back o' my eyes, like shards of glass. Tommo needs a drink! Yours truly needs the black bottle!

Chapter Twelve

HAWK

The Land of the Long White Cloud
July 1860

Tommo has gone. He left before dawn's light. I retire from Tamihana's feast at sunrise, too weary to think, and am immediately met by the old woman who is Makareta's mother.

'Makareta is dead!' she announces the moment I appear.

'Dead?' I cannot comprehend what I hear. 'Dead?' I repeat. Death through violence has been around me for so long that a death unrelated to war seems somehow impossible.

'She died in childbirth,' her mother adds.

Now I am suddenly alert and cry out in alarm. 'Tommo! Where is Tommo?' I should think first of dear Makareta, but it is concern for my twin which comes crowding into my head.

Makareta's mother shrugs. 'He is gone. I have not seen him.'

I try to gather my wits. Tommo gone? He cannot go without me. He is grieving, I feel sure, and cannot be far away.

'I shall send some young boys to find him,' I say to her. 'What of the child?'

'It is a girl. We have found her a wet nurse and taken her away. She is small but healthy.'

I nod, and the old woman sighs and moves away.

So Tommo has a daughter. But his child has cost him the woman he loves. Why must my brother always suffer such misfortune? The mongrels, as he calls them, seem to abound in his life.

I have not slept for nigh on twenty-four hours and think the same must be true for my twin. Perhaps he has gone into the forest and sleeps there. I send several young lads to find him, though God knows how they will do so if he is in among the tall trees.

'Do not wake him if he is asleep, but come back to tell me where he may be found,' I instruct them, and the lads run off, anxious to do my bidding. Weariness overcomes me. After I have slept a little I must attend to Makareta and ask the elders and the *tohunga* to arrange the funeral rites.

When I awake shortly before noon, the young lads are waiting outside my hut. 'Have you seen him?' I ask anxiously.

'We have searched everywhere, Black Hawk. He is not to be found. Some of the women who rise early say they saw him leave the village before daylight and take the path north.'

'The track to Auckland?' My heart sinks.

'It is the same.'

'Thank you,' I say. 'Let me know if you see or hear anything more.' They chorus that they will do as I ask.

Slowly my suspicions begin to grow. The demon black bottle. Tommo has been pushed over the edge. My brother is back in the wilderness and wishes to escape into the oblivion of grog.

I must speak to Chief Tamihana, but he is still asleep and I must wait. I pace outside his hut impatiently, then go to sit under a shady totara tree. But I am too anxious to remain seated and soon resume my restless vigil by his door. It is mid-afternoon before he emerges.

'Why do you disturb me from my slumber, Black Hawk?' Tamihana frowns slightly.

I apologise and explain what has happened. Then I beg leave to depart at once, explaining that I fear that Tommo has gone to Auckland.

'Why?' Tamihana asks. 'Why would he do such a thing? He is *rangatira* now. He will have a good life with us.'

'It is a matter of the heart,' I explain. 'My brother will grieve much over Makareta's death and will think not to show this to the Maori.'

'Why can he not grieve here? We will understand. We are not savages, Black Hawk.'

'With the pakeha it is sometimes different. They wish to drink spirits to forget their grief.'

'And Tommo has gone to obtain spirits so that he may forget?' I nod and Tamihana continues, 'We will send a message to our people, they will soon find him and bring him back.'

'No, I must go myself. He is of my blood.'

Chief Tamihana laughs at this. 'You, the man they want most, would walk straight into the enemy's camp? The pakeha will murder you. You cannot go, Black Hawk. I forbid it.'

'Tommo will not go to Kororareka, where they might recognise us,' I say.

'My friend, they know who you are everywhere! Kororareka, Auckland, even in Wellington they know of you! They know of the American Indian, Chief Blackhawk, who fights for the Maori.'

'But I do not look like an American Indian! The townsfolk will think me just another Maori. They do not know me by sight.'

'Ha! There are no Maori who are so black and stand so tall as you.'

'Nevertheless, I must go. I must find Tommo before he comes to harm.'

'Sit,' Tamihana now commands, indicating a bench.

I sit, and a woman brings us food and drink. The chief's food and mine are the same, but are served separately as it is *tapu* to eat from the same dish as Tamihana. 'Eat, Black Hawk,' he says. 'I wish to talk to you as a friend. It is most foolish to go to find your brother. You must stay here and I will send others to find Tommo and bring him back to us.'

It is then that I tell Chief Tamihana that Tommo and I have decided to leave New Zealand and, with his help, return to Australia.

He is silent a long while before he replies. 'A man cannot be held against his will, but we will miss you greatly, my friend. We have come to look upon you as a Maori. Your blood is our blood.' He pauses. 'You have brought great honour to our people, Black Hawk.'

I struggle to reply. 'I have only used what I knew, that is all.'

'No, beyond that,' Tamihana says. 'There is one thing you have taught us we shall always remember. Do you know what it is, Black Hawk?'

I shake my head.

'Do you not remember when you lifted War Chief Hapurona's aide by the neck, after he called you a coward?'

I look up, shocked that he knows of this. 'I am greatly ashamed to have done such a thing. He is a brave man.'

'A brave man perhaps, but also a foolish one!' Wiremu Tamihana replies. 'What he did was a thing of tradition. What you did changed this tradition forever.'

'I do not understand. What did I do? It was over in but a moment and I thank God I did not kill him.'

'Let me explain. If you had not spoken against staying in the *pa*, no one else would have. When Tamati Kapene called you a coward, he was following tradition. To talk of defeat is to be thought of forever as a coward and no Maori would have had the courage to do so. There is even a *tapu* against expressing such a thought.

'When you lifted Tamati into the air with your bare hands, you challenged the *tapu*. If you had killed him, as any Maori would have done, the *tapu* would have remained fixed. When you threw him to the floor and said not a single word, all who watched knew then that it is not cowardly to think about defeat and to live to fight another day. They knew that the *tapu* had broken itself.'

Wiremu Tamihana spreads his hands. 'The victory the Maori have enjoyed against the British in this last battle was because you helped defeat this great *tapu*, the strongest of them all. We are in your debt, General.'

I am astonished at these words. 'But it is to your people that my brother and I owe everything. When we first came, we were hunted by the law and you gave us your protection and shelter.'

Tamihana smiles. 'You will always be welcome among the Maori, my friend. But it is too soon for you to join our ancestors. If you go to find Tommo now, you will not last one day before the pakeha have your life. This time they will not wait to put you in gaol so that they might hang you later. They will shoot you like a dog.' He looks directly into my eyes. 'Please, give us seven days to find your brother. I shall send Hammerhead Jack by ketch. He will reach Auckland before Tommo.'

It takes three or four days to walk to Auckland. By boat, it will take Hammerhead Jack less than half this time. It is a sensible idea. 'If after this time there is no news, I must try to find him myself,' I reply.

Tamihana nods. 'We shall find Tommo and put him on a ship to Australia!'

I am horrified at this. 'He cannot go without me!'

'No, of course not,' reassures the chief. 'We shall take you to join him and smuggle you on board at night. We will find a captain who may need our friendship should he ever return to New Zealand.' Tamihana points to the dish of yam and pork. 'Now eat a little. All will be well, you shall see.'

I take some yam and wonder for a moment how Ikey is getting along with the Maori ancestors, who are said to feast on unlimited amounts of roasted pork every day!

Then I pluck up my courage once more. 'I have a great favour to ask you, Chief Tamihana. It concerns Tommo's woman and the name of their girl child.'

'Name? What can it matter what she is called? A girl's name is not important.'

'I understand and would not usually make such a request. But when we leave, and with the child's mother dead, I would wish for this girl to be well cared for. Her grandmother's hut is *tapu* and has been burnt down as is the tradition. The old woman too is *tapu*, having been associated with the dead mother, and might not live much longer. Last night you made Tommo *rangatira*. I would not wish for his daughter to be forgotten.'

Chief Tamihana dismisses this idea with a wave of his hand. 'She will come into my household,' he declares. 'We will care for her. The old woman cannot come but we will see she is fed until her *tapu* is lifted, then she can join the child again. You need not worry, the infant shall be brought up as nobility.' I thank Wiremu Tamihana profusely, but again he waves this away.

'What do you wish her to be named?' he continues. 'We shall give her a Maori name, or is it a pakeha name you want?'

'It is a Maori name, but it is not an unimportant one.'

'What is it?' Tamihana asks, curious now.

'Hinetitama,' I say, preparing for the scowl to come.

Chief Tamihana keeps his expression blank, but it is some time before he responds. 'Do you know that this is a name we can only give to a princess? How can I justify giving Tommo's girl child the name of the Dawn Maiden, daughter of Woman Made From Earth? In our belief, to call a commoner or even *rangatira* thus would be blasphemy – unless she were, in her own right, a princess.'

'I beg your forgiveness, Chief Tamihana. I did not wish to blaspheme against the ancestors.'

Now the chief looks at me hard. 'You knew this was not possible, Black Hawk, didn't you? Why then did you ask me?'

'It was a most foolish thing. I had no right,' I say, feeling myself suitably chastised.

'My friend, you are young, but you are not foolish. Is it because of the widow who came to you in the night?'

'You know?' My face grows warm.

Tamihana nods slowly, then explains. 'Wiremu Kingi asked me why you seemed reluctant to take a woman. If you were to be killed, he did not wish you transported to your ancestors still a virgin. I told him I wished the Maori woman you took to be from the Ngati Haua but he said that while he was responsible for you, she should be from the Ati Awa.' Tamihana laughs, then shrugs. 'Ever the peacemaker, I suggested that she be from another Maori tribe, so that we need not quarrel. To this, the old chief agreed. But we wanted to be sure that this woman from another tribe was no less worthy than our own wahine, so we asked for a certain princess who is the young widow of a great warrior. She was ready to enter life again, to be made *noa*.'

I try to conceal my anxiety at my next question. 'If I should wish to find her again, would you tell me how?'

Tamihana shakes his head. 'It is a matter best left alone. We shall find Tommo and then you will leave for Australia.'

I know I should not persist but cannot help myself – the thought of lying with the widow princess again clouds my judgment. 'My chief, I have a great yearning for Hinetitama in my heart. Will you help me?'

Tamihana thinks for a moment, his eyes cast down, then he raises them slowly to mine. 'I will make a bargain with you, Black Hawk. You have two choices: you may find Tommo and leave for Australia. Or you may have this woman and the children she will bring you and stay with us. You cannot have a Maori princess and leave the tribe. Will you forsake your brother for her? You must choose.'

I look to Wiremu Tamihana and hope the distress I feel does not show on my face. 'There is only one possible answer. It must be Tommo. Will you send Hammerhead Jack to find him before much harm comes to him?'

The chief nods slowly. 'He will leave within the hour, and he will be in Auckland long before Tommo arrives on foot.'

It is a day later when I am summoned to the *marae*. I arrive to find many of the *rangatira* and the *tohunga* already assembled. I have no notion of why Chief Tamihana has called this meeting, unless it is to tell them of my leaving.

I take my seat, hoping that at some point I may be allowed to ask for a good burial for Makareta. It is my wish she might be given some small honour in her death for the sake of her mother and Tommo. Despite my pleas, I have not been allowed to see Tommo's newborn child because of the *tapu* created by her mother's death and Tommo's presence at her birth.

'We are here today to discuss the business of a girl's name,' Chief Tamihana announces.

There is a murmur of surprise among the *rangatira* and

the *tohunga*. I myself am in some shock. Tamihana pauses for a few moments before turning to speak directly to me.

'Black Hawk, we have heard that Chief Wiremu Kingi has taken one of your ancestors, Icky Slomon, to sit among their own ancestors. Is this so?'

I stand, though I am too nervous to look into the chief's face. 'It is true, Chief Tamihana. My brother and I have been greatly honoured by the Ati Awa, who have declared our ancestor Ikey Solomon to be worthy to sit among their ancestors.'

'And did you not explain that this Icky Slomon is of the tribe of Israel and directly descended from the great King Slomon himself?'

Chief Tamihana is missionary-taught and knows more of the Bible than I. He will most certainly be aware that King Solomon is an ancient King of Israel who can hardly be claimed as our direct ancestor.

I stammer slightly as I try to explain. 'Yes, I told Wiremu Kingi that King Solomon was a great and noble king of the tribe of Israel. It is also true that the name Solomon is given to the descendants of the great king.'

'You talked of the black queen, the Queen of Sheba, and of how King Solomon also took her and folded her into his blanket? And in this way, you explained how Tommo has come to be white while you are black? A white king and a black queen and ever after, the generations to come, both colours spawned?'

'That was the understanding of Chief Wiremu Kingi,' I reply, wondering at what point he will denounce this unlikely tale.

But instead Tamihana turns to the gathered assembly. 'As I have long suspected, both Tommo and Black Hawk are in their own right descended from a royal house. We of the Ngati Haua should recognise this along with our brothers from the Ati

Awa.' Tamihana is playing along with my story of our lineage! He smiles at me. 'Black Hawk, we too would wish to honour your ancestors. It is only right that we should do so.'

I hear a general hum of approval amongst the *rangatira*. Finally Chief Wiremu Tamihana puts up his hand to signal silence and when the assembly is once again quiet, he makes his announcement.

'Two nights past, Tommo's wahine gave birth to a girl child. The mother has died in childbirth and there is only a grandmother to care for the newborn infant. Her paps are dry and so I have decided this child should come into my household.' He smiles. 'My women grow lazy and fat. They shall be happy to care for the infant.'

I can see that the elders are curious as to why Wiremu Tamihana would even speak of this women's business, and the chief responds.

'I talk of this because we have not hitherto acknowledged the true status of Black Hawk and his brother Tommo and must now do so in the naming of this girl child.' Tamihana gazes about him for several moments. 'I am *ariki* and have communed with the dead on this matter and the ancestors have found a way. They would like this child to be named Hinetitama.'

All this is so very neatly put by Tamihana that there is only a short discussion about it and this mainly by the *tohunga*, who search for a precedent in ceremony which they might use to help fulfil this request. Ten minutes later they nod their assent to the chief. Tommo's daughter is to be called Princess Hinetitama Te Solomon and her ancestral claim to this title is to be the great King Solomon of the tribe of Israel. The Ati Awa ancestors may have gained the services of Icky Slomon but the Ngati Haua have acquired a royal princess of impeccable lineage.

I am again overwhelmed by the kindness of this great

chief, and my words cannot express the gratitude I feel for the honour he has bestowed on Tommo and me.

Chief Wiremu Tamihana then talks briefly of our wish to leave and explains that he will help us to gain passage on a boat to Australia. This news is received with the greatest regret by all. Several of the *rangatira* make speeches asking me to reconsider. Even the *tohunga* are most cordial for once, and the oldest among them expresses the wish that Tommo and I remain within the tribe when we depart.

'We shall always consider you Maori, for no Maori warrior could have honoured us more,' Chief Tamihana concludes. 'Black Hawk, in the name of our ancestors we salute you and wish you a safe journey across the sea. Our spirit goes with you always.'

I am once more overcome with emotion. I have nothing but love for the Ngati Haua, who have shown Tommo and me such care. I fear we shall never repay the debt we owe them.

I stand to address the chief and the elders. 'Chief Tamihana and all of the Ngati Haua tribe, you have been my brothers in peace and in war. Your counsel and wisdom have turned me from a callow youth into a grown man and as long as I live I shall cherish you in my heart.

'I would like to commend to you the man who first brought us here, Hammerhead Jack. I know that I am less a man, with both eyes and both arms, than he is with only one of each. I shall honour his name and his tribe as long as I have voice to speak of them. I know that if my brother Tommo were here he would say the same.

'We have left behind a girl child, the Princess Hinetitama Te Solomon. She is proof to you all that we love and honour your tribe and I hope that we may return one day. I ask that you keep a place on the *marae*, for my brother and me, where we may sit with pride among the *rangatira* and the

326

tohunga. I request most humbly that you keep our name and our lineage on the lips of your old women so that the Princess Hinetitama will learn of us and know that we left her with the people we loved.'

Much applause follows, until Tamihana holds up his hand for silence. 'Black Hawk, the women wait outside to sing and they have asked for a message to carry in your honour in some future song they wish to compose in your memory.'

I am close to tears and when the words come, they are the best I can manage. 'May you find peace and hold your land safe and secure for your children. Keep forever your pride in yourselves. I pray you do this in the name of your ancestors and your children yet unborn and their children.'

I bow to Chief Tamihana. 'I leave you knowing that whatever happens in my life, my spirit will always dwell among the great Maori people. Farewell, beloved friends. Until I return, I shall carry you in my heart always.'

We leave the *marae* and are soon surrounded by a great host of women who, except for the very foremost, are too close-packed to dance the *poi*. As we emerge they commence to sing a haunting lament and I am at once flooded with tears.

Chapter Thirteen

TOMMO

The Land of the Long White Cloud
July 1860

All I can think of is the black bottle. I doesn't think of
Makareta or even our baby. It be too hard. I must remove
Makareta from me head for I can't bear the sorrow. I got to
drown it, kill it, make it go away before it takes a hold o' me.
There is only one way I knows to do this, the black bottle.
It's the Cape brandy for yours truly.

That's all I think of as I leave Tamihana's village. Even
Hawk ain't in my mind. I can't think of anything or anyone
what might stop me from getting a drink. My head hurts
most terrible from the gun wound, and I don't care if I lives
or dies. I think I'm goin' mad.

I pass several Maori on the road what greet me and
seem to know who I am, but I don't care enough even to
reply. I walk for hours before I even think about where I
might be headed or what might happen to me if I'm
recognised by a pakeha. I wears a blanket and sandals in
the fashion of the Maori and would seem most odd to any
white man what looks at me for more than a moment. It'd
be stupid to go to a small town where I'd be recognised
before I even gets a drink, and so I decides to push on to

Auckland, where I can more easily disappear into a grog den or one-shilling hell.

I ain't felt the slightest hunger, me stomach craves only spirits, and there's a great gnawing at me guts. But by evening I knows I has to eat or I'll never reach me destination, the black bottle.

I stops in at a Maori village what I know ain't on the side o' the British as some 'round these parts are. It seems they don't know me, thank Christ. But I speak their language, obey their customs and wear their clothes and charms, and so they accept me. I ain't the first pakeha to take up the Maori style o' living and they are a generous-natured people. After feeding me they ask if I want a hut for the night. But I'm used to sleeping rough and now that I'm fed, I'm anxious to keep going. There is a clear sky for once and a bright moon, and no bitter cold wind blowing from the south.

On the morning of the second day I comes upon settlers twice. The first I sees is a lone man with a horse and dray, piled high with cabbages. The other is a man with his wife and family and all their worldly possessions packed on a bullock cart. I hides meself off the roadside as they pass by.

My head has cleared somewhat, and I realise that I can't enter Auckland dressed as a Maori and hope to sit down to a game o' cards. I should have bailed up the cove in the cabbage cart and swapped me clobber for his, though he were dressed as a farm labourer, a poor enough outfit for a man seekin' a game o' poker in the city.

Towards evening I spies a farmhouse set back from the road. The weather is fine but will soon enough close in, as it does most nights, and I need to find shelter. I'll watch the house and if the chance comes up, get inside and find me some pakeha clothes.

I follow a small stream up to the farmhouse and find a spot

from where I can see the comings and goings of the farm folk. Sure enough, I soon see two lads bringing in half a dozen cows. For one terrible moment I thinks of the two lads we killed. I remember how me darling Makareta used to comfort me in the nights when I were sick at heart with meself. When I'd wake affrighted, having dreamt of the wilderness again. But I must put Makareta out o' me head. From now on, it's just Tommo on his own again. I looks more closely at the lads. One is near me size, dressed in rags, and the other's smaller, perhaps three years younger, nine or ten years old. The house is neat and well kept with a bit of a vegetable garden at the back. They looks like poor but respectable folk, probably church-goers, and if so the elder might have a change o' clothes for Sunday best what could fit.

I starts to make me plans. Cows need milking in the early morning, requirin' all hands on deck. If there's a missus about then she'll be in the barn not long after dawn to see to the churning, and so the house will stand empty. The boys and the cows are followed by two border collies what might prove a nuisance. But dogs usually follow their masters and will no doubt be at the milking shed in the morning too for a dish o' milk or curds. The barn is upwind of the farmhouse and so they'll not scent me, and I reckon I can slip in from the back without being seen.

Shortly after I see the farmer coming in on a huge plough horse, the sort I've heard called Percherons. He's seated on its back without saddle or harness, a stout fellow, not too tall, though it be hard to judge with him sitting so high on the beast. Perhaps his Sunday best would suit me better than the lad's. Then a woman comes out the back o' the house and yells at the two lads to come in for tea. I reckons I has the family just about complete as there don't seem to be no farm labourers about.

I spends the remaining light exploring the creek, what I

crosses so the dogs will not pick up me scent. The brook leads to a small river and 'round a bend I discover an eel weir and with it a nice fat eel in a basket-trap. I gather dry timber, what makes only a little smoke, and I cook the eel under the shade of a tree what will help hide any signs of a fire. With a full stomach I goes back and builds a snug hide, well concealed, from where I can easily see the farmhouse. I'm hardly inside it when the rain comes down and darkness falls.

Some squabbling tuis wakes me at dawn. This be most fortunate because next I sees the farmer's wife carrying two silver buckets towards the barn, the dogs yapping at her heels. Her two sons follow behind, and then the farmer himself comes out, scratching his bollocks and sneezing twice. I wait for another sneeze but it don't happen and I wonder if this be an omen or something. Gawd, I thinks, I'm becoming a flamin' Maori, looking for signs and portents in everything. I waits several minutes before removing me sandals and wading through the freezing water of the creek towards the house. A thin mist hangs low over the paddocks and the air smells of more rain to come as I creep towards the farmhouse.

The kitchen door be open, o' course, and there's a small fire on the hearth. I smell a stew and am half-tempted to help meself. But I press on into the main bedchamber, where I finds a large brass bed, a cupboard and a timber chest against the far wall. I am drawn to the chest and open it – only to find within it a wedding dress, careful folded away. Again I thinks o' Makareta, and that we might have been wed. Then I kills the thought quick and tell meself I has no interest in wedding dresses. I am about to close the lid on the chest and the picture it brings to me mind, when I thinks to look a little further. Beneath the wedding dress, to me great delight, is a suit of brown tweed, smelling of camphor.

I pull it out and find it's an almost perfect fit. I can only guess it were the wedding suit of the farmer before his wife's cooking helped him to his present size. I thinks again o' the soup, what smells delicious, but I can't draw attention to meself by taking a bowl.

I place the wedding dress back as I found it, and close the chest. In the cupboard are three blouses hangin' upon a single peg. I takes the third what's hid behind the other two. It will do well enough, for it is made o' wool and has scarce been mended. Under the bed I finds a sturdy pair of well dubbined boots.

It will take until the Sabbath for the farmer to discover the loss of his boots and blouse, and months or years before he finds his wedding suit is missing. I am now possessed of a complete outfit. I am out the house in a flash with me booty under me arm and am halfway across the first paddock before I remembers a hat. Shit! I can't walk around with me head wound showing, and the Maori cap I wears won't look right with the pakeha clothes. I race back to the house.

In the small front parlour I find an old felt hat on the wall. It be too big for me and falls over my eyes but I am glad, as it will cover me wound without pressing down upon it. My heart is banging like a tom-tom as I flee across the paddock to me secret spot.

Long before the sun's climbed up in the sky, I'm back on the road in me new outfit. I has hid me sandals and Maori fighting axe in me blanket, and torn my old tattered blouse to make toe pads. These I stuff into me new boots so that they fits better. I does the same to the inside brim of my hat, leaving a small space so me wound can breathe and the lining don't rub against it. The suit fits well enough and, though the blouse is too big, I has it tucked in and bunched and knotted at the back.

I could hardly have done better for meself. The suit proclaims me a bumpkin well enough, but not one without resources. A yokel come to the city to chance his luck or spend his butter-and-cheese earnings on matching his skill at cards. There is a soft drizzle to the day but the tweed's thick and will keep the damp out. I strap me blanket roll to me back and it's away to Auckland for old Tommo.

I know well what to do. Thanks to me wilderness years, nobody can play the idjit better. With my hat close-pulled over my eyes, I look like the original patsy-mark what makes a wharf gambler rub his hands with glee. It's a thorough disguise and in the dim light of a hell or tavern, I'll be nigh impossible to pick out as Tommo X Solomon. I am well through my nineteenth year and has grown a tolerable beard. Me face still makes me look young, all the better to gull some greedy bastard bent on fleecing me.

I'd be all set up for an adventure if it weren't for the craving in my belly, the pain in my head and the struggle not to remember anything. Instead, I knows I'm only gunna play long enough to secure a black bottle and then another and another 'til I can no longer remember my own name.

I will need a coin or two to match the stakes. Even a shilling'd do to enter a small game in an alley or tavern, and I think to sell me tinder box which, frankly, ain't worth much more. Two shillings will buy me a bottle o' Cape and I'll be damned if I can't turn one shilling into two in any game o' flats!

I'm less than an hour on the road when I realise my feet be in trouble. Since living with the Maori I ain't used to wearing boots. Now Farmer Moo-cow's boots be rubbing my heels most severe and I feel sure there be blisters forming the size o' me thumbnail. I stop and remove the boots and put me sandals back on, tying the boots together by their laces and slinging them 'round me neck – the way folks do in the wilderness when they's travelling some distance on foot to a wedding or funeral.

The next day I'm offered a lift on a settler's dray. At first I think to say no but realise this be more dangerous than agreeing. No white man'd willingly walk twenty mile when he can sit on his arse and spit on the heads o' any passing Maori.

If me new-found benefactor notices me Maori sandals he don't say nothing. In fact he proves somewhat a clod, a slow talking cove by the name o' Timmy Dankmarsh. He's a farmer and fisherman with six sprats – four boys, two girls – and his wife be with child again. I ask him to drop me off on the outskirts of Auckland, saying I must visit a friend on a farm nearby. When he asks the name o' me friend, I says Jones quick enough – *Tom Jones* being the name of a most randy book Hawk taught me to read on board ship.

Mr Timmy Dankmarsh thinks about my friend's name for five minutes. 'Must be a new allotment. I doesn't know no Jones.' He thinks a few minutes more and shakes his head real slow. 'No, no Jones, I doesn't know him, that's certain.' Then he pauses again, so I swears I can hear him thinking. 'Not this side o' town anyways. No Jones this side o' town. Other side maybe, but not this side.'

'A trooper what's come with his family from New South Wales to settle,' I tries.

'Oh,' says Dankmarsh. 'Trooper, is it?' He thinks awhile then adds, 'Don't know no trooper fella lives that side.' But he don't say no more on the matter.

I walk the last two miles into Auckland and arrives as the one o'clock steam whistle sounds from the saw mill near the wharf. What a place! I had set me mind upon something different, perhaps like Hobart Town. I were expecting a proper town, with straight, well-paved, tree-lined streets, houses and cottages of a neat appearance of stone and brick, and shops with a good display of tempting merchandise.

This place ain't nothing of the sort! And it's the main port in New Zealand, the centre o' commercial life for the North Island! I can scarce believe my eyes. I comes across a main wharf what seems to be the centre o' the town. But the streets leading to it are mud tracks without a paving stone in sight and most with a trench dug to one side. I thought this were to channel the rainwater away, but later I hear it is to lay pipes for gas. I ain't never heard of a place what's got gaslights before paving stones.

The shops are mostly o' wood and brick, though dingy looking. Only one building o' grand design is to be seen. This be the Union Bank what's made of white stone, rising higher by three times than any other building. It has large columns from top to toe so it looks like one o' them Greek temples Hawk's told me about. I've never had no money in a bank, but I remember Ikey used to say that to own a bank and earn ten per cent on other folks' money is a most advantageous thing. On the other hand to deposit your own money and earn only two per cent is a terrible waste!

The town runs back from the water and up a steep hill, where the toffs live and where the troopers' barracks are. It's raining again, having stopped mid-morning, and the streets are muddy puddles, sprouting sudden wings o' wide brown water as the carts and sulkies go by. I has took to rolling up me breeches, and me feet are covered in red clay.

Now I see why that miserable sod, Nottingham, wanted us brought to trial here, for there ain't a shred o' kindness in any o' the faces around me. Still and all, every town has its bawdy houses and pubs and places what may usually be found with a little questioning. Muddied up to the calves, I walks along the waterfront hoping to find a suitable one-shilling hell. I see that other men has removed their boots, so I be no different to them. I enter a tavern, wipes me feet upon the mat at the door and puts on me boots. I don't even have the price of a glass of ale so must ask the publican straight out where a friendly card game may be had.

'Out!' yells the publican, pointing to the door. 'We don't have no truck with yer kind 'ere!'

Then I sees a grog shop in an alley, some ways up from the wharf, what's called the Scrimshaw Tavern. Two Maori whores stop me outside and make the usual offer. I tell 'em no, but politely and in their own language. Both laugh, showing me nice white teeth, and one says I can have it free if I want a knee-trembler behind the pub. The whores outside is good news. I got an instinct for places like the Scrimshaw, and I know at once things are beginning to go right.

I've seen two whaling ships moored in the bay and know there's a good chance o' finding some whalemen here. I'll strike up a conversation with them about finding a game instead of asking the owner. I hope there's none here what might recognise me ugly gob, but it's been well over three years since we was on the *Nankin Maiden*. Still I've no doubt that the tale of O'Hara's missing paw is by now a legend of the seven seas.

Inside, the Scrimshaw is crowded with whalemen, and I feel right at home. The tavern is a dark, smoke-filled cave what reeks o' rum and brandy, pipes and cigars, with a filthy floor, the daily sawdust barely covering the vomit. Here's a bloodhouse if ever I seen one and I be most delighted to have found it at last. I knows these men's lingo and it ain't long before I'm talking to an Irishman what works the try-pots on the *Cloudy Bay*, another whaling ship out o' New England.

'Tasmania, eh? Hobart Town? Bin there, know it well enough now, don't I?' he shouts when I tell him my home port. 'Got one o' your lot on board ship, a good man to be sure now. First class whaleman but always in trouble with the master. Likes a drink. Should be hereabouts soon enough, I would think.'

The Irishman offers to stand me an ale but I decline. Me lips are primed only for the taste o' spirits, for the sweet salvation of a bottle o' Cape brandy. A mug of beer ain't gunna do naught for what ails old Tommo. Besides, I has no way to pay him back.

'Suit yourself,' he says with a shrug, 'but I'll not buy you spirits, they be the ruination o' many a good man.'

'I ain't so sure I am a good man,' I says, then asks him if he knows of a poker game going. 'Later,' he says, 'around ten o'clock. Big game, five shillings to show, perhaps two pounds in the pot, you'll not be playing for a penny less, lad.'

'Oh,' says I. 'So you're not against the sport o' cards then, just ardent spirits?'

'Not at all, not at all,' the Irishman repeats. Bringing his frothy whiskers up from the mug he holds, he looks at me sternly. 'But they can't be mixed, now can they?'

'Cards and brandy? In my book they's part 'n' parcel o' the game o' poker,' I says, cheekily.

'Many's the ruination of the one by the other,' the Paddy says again, shaking his fat finger at me. 'Stay off the brandy, me lad!'

'This cove from Tasmania, decent bloke is he?' I asks, wanting to change the subject. I've grown tired of his 'many's the ruinations'.

'Aye, not too bad,' he says, then turns and walks away. But he spins around again and stabs a finger at me as if I might have forgotten so soon. 'I'll not buy you a drop, me boy, many's the ruination!'

I push my way through the crowd, feeling as out of place

as a fart in church. I'm lookin' here and there, as though I be seeking my long lost cousin Jack. Without a drink in your hand it ain't easy to look like you belong. I've been away too long from the company o' white folk, I decide. When I first come in, it brought pleasant memories enough. But now I feels somewhat uneasy in all the noise and the smoke. I ain't the old Tommo no more, the bright lad fixing his mark with a smile, full o' malarky and bluff. Instead, I feel meself a stranger. My head hurts and me tongue's hangin' out, rusty for want o' small talk, even whaleman's talk what I thought would come easy to my lips. I can barely speak the queen's English no more, if ever I could! Suddenly I hear the Irishman's voice boom from across the room, 'Over 'ere, Tasmania, your nigger brother's come!'

I nearly drops dead from fright. Hawk has come for me! He's found me already and I ain't even had a drink! I look up towards the door expecting to see Hawk standing two feet above most o' the whalemen in the room. But I don't see nothing of the sort. Then me name is bein' yelled out for all to hear. 'Tommo!' I nearly shits me breeches. A thin black arm comes pushing through the throng followed by the grinning gob o' Billy Lanney.

'Where you bin, eh?' Lanney asks, clapping me on the shoulder. He's drunk, but not hopelessly so. I'm facing the man what brought a flagon o' good Cape brandy on board the *Nankin Maiden* from Hobart Town, and then took his flogging without ever once crying out. I'm glad to see him but don't know what'll happen next, not with his shoutin' me name out and all. But Billy is all smiles, patting me coat up and down as though he's trying to make certain that it's me. 'Plurry good, Tommo,' he announces finally. 'Plurry first class, eh?'

'Billy,' I hiss, 'I'm not Tommo, ya hear?'

'You, Tommo!' he says, patting me again.

'Johnny,' I hiss. 'My name's Johnny!'

'Nah, it ain't!' he shouts back. 'It's Tommo!'

What's a man to do? Should I scarper, get the hell out o' the place? I look 'round to see who's looking at us. But the Irishman is way across the room, and them what's close by ain't the least interested. No doubt we can't be heard above the chatter and din o' the pub.

I take Billy Lanney's hand. 'How's ya bin then, Billy?'

'You wan' a drink?' Billy asks. 'Brandy?'

I nearly faint at the thought. 'I'm skint,' I says, pulling out the lining of me trouser pockets. 'I can't buy you one back.'

'Ha, Tommo, me got plurry plenty, what'cha wan' eh?' He pulls out his purse and shows me half a dozen gold sovs and as many Yankee silver dollars.

'Cripes!' says I, and place my hand over his purse while I look about me. 'Not here, Billy, too many villains in a hole like this.'

Billy ignores me. 'What'cha wan' eh? You take, Tommo.' He offers me his purse again. I close it and put it back into his jacket. Billy looks at me all solemn-like and puts his hand on me shoulder. 'Ya wan' a black bottle, eh, Tommo?'

It were always said he were a queer one, and when Crawlin Nestbyte went overboard, they all reckoned it were 'cause of Billy's prophecy. Now he's read me clear as a marked deck. He's seen right into my head, and spotted me cravin' for the black bottle. I'm tempted to answer yes, but I knows I'm gunna need three bottles, maybe more, and I ain't gunna steal from Billy. Billy follows the Aborigine way – if he's your mate, what's his is yours. He were most kind to me and Hawk when we come on board the *Nankin Maiden*. Some thought he were ten bob in the quid, but it ain't true. Billy's a proper gentleman and I ain't gunna sink to stealing from him, not now, not never. I ain't that kind o' drunk yet.

'Cards, Billy. I want t' play poker. Can you stake me?'

'Sure, sure.' Billy fumbles in his jacket and brings out his purse once again. He hands it to me. 'You take, Tommo.'

I take two gold sovs and an American silver dollar what be worth about five shillings. Then I put Billy's purse back in his whaleman's jacket. It's enough to get me into the big game and even to lose a couple of hands if I needs to set up some greedy bastard who thinks to take me.

I ask Billy what he's been up to, and he tells me his story, what be simple enough. After Hawk and me were took ashore under arrest, the *Nankin Maiden* sailed down from Kororareka to Auckland, where Captain O'Hara's stump were properly stitched up and took care of by the surgeon in the troopers' barracks. Then she sailed directly back to Nantucket, her hold being near filled. Billy gets paid his share when the boat reaches home port, and signs aboard the *Cloudy Bay*, what is bound for southern whaling grounds. But shortly after reaching Antarctic waters, the boat is damaged by an ice crush and must limp into Auckland harbour for repairs.

'This shit place, Tommo! No plurry good Aucklan', eh?' Billy shakes his head. 'Ya wan' a brandy, rum?'

I squeeze my eyes tight, but manage to shake my head. 'Billy, you're not to tell who I am.' I put a finger to my lips. 'I ain't supposed to be here, me name's not Tommo, ya hear?'

'Wha's ya name then, eh?' Billy asks, surprised.

I sigh. He sounds like he's three sheets to the wind but then again he always talks like this so I can't tell how drunk he truly is. I only hope he gets a handle on what I'm trying to tell him.

'Johnny Abacus. You calls me Johnny, right?'

Billy nods. 'Johnny, plurry good.' Then to me surprise he repeats perfect, 'Johnny Abacus.'

I laughs to meself. Billy, with his plurry this and plurry that, is easily mistook for being a bit slow, but he ain't nothin' of the sort. Billy's as good a man as you can have at your side and plenty smart with it.

It's nigh on ten o'clock when we is taken to an iron shed at the back o' the grog shop. Inside there's a table covered in green baize with three hurricane lamps hanging above to light it. Six chairs are set 'round the table and against the wall are two wooden benches. The room is warmed by a small pot-belly stove.

I takes a seat and when the owner asks what me poison is, I order milk.

'Milk!' he snorts. 'We don't sell no milk here, lad.'

The three other players what has come to sit at the table looks at each other, trying to hide their mirth.

'But I always drinks milk when we plays cards at 'ome,' I says, looking most disappointed. I pause. 'What be wrong with milk?'

The landlord sighs and looks to the ceiling 'Nothing wrong with it, lad, but we ain't got none here.'

'Oh,' I says all innocent. 'Then I'll drink water. Does ya 'ave water, sir?'

He turns away in disgust. The other players all order Jamaican rum which, in a joint like this, is likely to have more than a drop o' water added, with a dash of tobacco juice to give it a kick.

Billy sits on the bench behind me with a mug o' brandy and seems happy enough. I has me hat pulled down low, and with me long hair and beard, there ain't too much of me gob to be seen. It's clear enough to the other players that they has a bumpkin on their hands. When they sees I got two sovs and a silver dollar in my possession, they'll know me for the best possible patsy-mark.

I wait long enough for them to give up staring, then starts

up like Timmy Dankmarsh, the country clod what gave me a ride into town. 'Me pappy uh . . . er . . . he says, strong drink be the ruination o' . . .' I appear to be tryin' to remember what me pappy said, then gives up and shakes me head. I begins to giggle. 'He says it be the ruination o' something or other!' Then I take my hand out of my pocket and slaps down the two sovs and the silver dollar upon the green cloth. 'What's we gunna play then?' I ask, smiling cloddish-like again, not forgetting to leave me bottom lip hung open.

Suddenly I hears the scraping of the two remaining chairs. I look up from under the rim of me hat, and nearly falls off me chair. I feel the blood leave me face. If it ain't Maple and Syrup, them two bastards from the gaol-house at Kororareka what done Hawk and me in! It's the card-game all over again, and there's no way now I can make my escape. As if meeting Billy Lanney weren't coincidence enough for one night. Yours truly, I decide, is sailing very close to the wind!

The owner comes around and claims five shillings from all for the rent o' the premises and provision of the lookout. Gambling ain't allowed in Auckland. Billy ups from his bench, and pays it for me. 'Nigger yer banker then?' Syrup asks and the rest o' the table bursts into laughter.

'Aye!' I says slowly and grins. 'He can count better than me . . . and he don't use his fingers none.' I only wish my head didn't hurt so much – I'll need all me wits tonight.

The owner brings a new set o' cards and hands them all around for examination. I hold 'em up to the light. 'Why, they's all wrapped up!' I says. 'New, is they?' I lean back and hand the cards to Billy, 'Lookee there, Billy! Them's new cards an' all!'

Billy takes the cards and turns them around, shaking his

head in wonderment. He hands them back to me. 'Plurry good, Johnny, eh?' he says.

Well, the game begins and I lose the first two hands by being purposeful stupid, but not so stupid that I look completely out o' me depth. Then I wins and acts most excited. The next hand I lose again – all this with my tongue at the corner of my mouth.

Maple and Syrup are the best o' the five players at the table and I lets them win from the others as well as me. But by the skin of me teeth I stays in the game. Finally it's just the two of them with the money piled up in front of where they sit and me.

It's the same as Kororareka all over again. They ain't learned nothing and I sets them up one at a time and cleans them both out with eight pounds snug in me pocket before midnight. After I've cleaned out Syrup, he asks if I'll take his marker. I look at him sorrowful-like, 'Mr Syrup, me pappy always said, neither a borrower nor lender be . . . for loan often loses both itself and a friend . . . and I wouldn't want to lose your friendship, Mr Syrup. Hee-hee.' Syrup gives a sickly sort o' smile and then there were only Maple left, holding a couple of sovs in change. I think he'll fold, call it quits, but he stays in the game and in two more hands, I've took the lot.

I reach down and unstrap my blanket roll so I can get to my axe quickly if needs be. My head hurts terrible but I've done the whole thing without any relocation of the cards. I ain't lost none o' me skill over the years! I pick up me roll like it's still strapped and put it under me arm.

'Thankee, gentlemen, much obliged.' I touch the brim of my hat to Maple and Syrup and bows, then does the same to the other three players what's now sitting on the benches. 'Come, Billy,' I says. 'Time fer some tucker.'

Suddenly Maple is standing in front o' me and Syrup to

one side. 'I'm sure I seen you somewhere,' Maple says, pushing his finger into me chest.

'From Wanganui is you, then?' I says slow, but smiling like it's a nice surprise. 'Though I don't recall havin' seen ya.'

I can see he's trying to remember where he's met me before, but his head is rum-fogged and it ain't coming to him.

'I think you's cheated!' Maple accuses me now, and jabs my chest again, this time hard.

'Huh?' I says, open-mouthed. 'No, no! I'm a good Christian boy. Me pappy says . . .'

But I don't get no further, for Syrup has fastened on to me. 'Outside, you!' he says as Maple grabs my head under his arm.

'What's you mean?' I yells. 'I ain't done nothin' wrong!'

But both of them is dragging me away, back up to the pub and then through the front room of the Scrimshaw. 'Cheat! Cheatin' at the flats!' Maple yells to all what will listen. 'Him and the fuckin' black!'

When he hears this, Syrup cries out, 'Jesus Christ, now I remembers! Kororareka! The gaol, bloody Nottingham, you and the big nigger!'

'Billy, scarper!' I yell as Maple and Syrup throw me to the ground in the alley. There are whalemen tumbling out the door as fast as their feet'll carry them to witness the beating I'm gunna get. This is the moment I'm waiting for. I've hung onto me blanket roll for dear life. I rise from me knees as they comes close, and Syrup takes a kick at me. I duck and his boot goes flying over my head so that he slips in the mud and falls on his arse.

'Why, you bastard!' he says, angry now. He gets quickly to his feet while the whalemen laugh at him.

'He's a crook, an escaped prisoner!' Maple shouts and takes a swing at me. This time, the blow grazes the side o' me poor old head and ear, knocking me down flat again. I can see Billy held tight by the landlord and one other bloke. I get back on me haunches and tear at the blanket. In a flash I has the fighting axe in my hands. Syrup swings a blow at me but I catch his wrist with the handle of my axe. Then I bring the flat head around and pat him polite-like to the chin and mouth. Suddenly there is teeth and blood flying everywhere. He drops to his knees, both hands held to his face. I slams him again to the side of the head with the flat of me axe, and he pitches face-first in the mud. He'll see dicky-birds for some time after, I reckons.

Maple roars and comes at me with his bowie knife, the eight inches of blade aimed straight at me gut. I swing the axe blade 'round and knock the knife from his hand, taking the top of his fingers with it. Then I reverse with the butt and strikes him in the face. I feel his nose and cheekbone crunch. It's all over in seconds and the crowd has drawn back, pushing against each other so that Maple and Syrup are alone in the mud at me feet, out cold, like a couple o' stunned mullets.

'That's for me brother, ya rotten scum!' I pant. With the handle of me axe I point to Billy Lanney. 'Let him go, he be a whaleman! Come on, Billy, let's get the hell out o' this shit hole!'

Several whalemen turns on the landlord and the other cove what's got Billy, and they lets him loose quick.

'He's a whaleman! Plurry good!' Billy shouts. 'Me, too!'

'And any of you what follows us,' I point with my axe handle to Maple and Syrup, 'you'll get the same as them, ya hear?' I pick up my blanket and sandals and begin to walk away. Then I stop and turn back to the crowd. 'And I didn't cheat! I wouldn't insult meself cheating with shore scum like them two Limey bastards!'

There's a cheer from the whalemen in the crowd at this.

Then someone calls out, 'It be Tommo from the *Nankin Maiden*!' and there's a second cheer, this one louder. 'Go, Tommo, we'll see you clear!' another whaleman shouts.

'Plurry hell!' says Billy, coming to me side. Then under his breath, 'Tommo, we goes now, eh? Shit! Omegawd!' and he breaks into a trot.

'Don't run, Billy!' I grab his arm. 'Walk like you're not scared, then when we gets out o' sight, we'll run like the devil!'

We get to the end o' the alley and then take off, running as hard as we can away from the wharf. Soon we get to the outskirts of this miserable town. I stop, my axe and blanket and sandals feelin' bloody heavy by now, and farmer Moo-cow's shoes near killing me feet. Billy, who be fifteen years or more older than me, is well ahead. 'Stop, Billy!' I shouts. 'We ain't gettin' nowhere!'

Billy walks back to where I'm bent over, panting and dizzy, with my blanket and axe lying at my feet. There is something wrong. My head is now so painful from the running I am hard put not to cry out. The wound is bleeding, I think. I put me hand to me neck and my fingers come away bloody.

'Ya know what gives me the shits?' I says to Billy. 'I just won eight pounds at poker and I didn't even have time to buy a black bottle to drown me bloody sorrows!'

I dig into me pocket and takes out three pounds. 'Here's your stake and a bit more, Billy.' I add two sovs and ten shillings. 'And here's your share of the winnings.' I am left with just over three pounds and can buy enough gallons o' Cape brandy to keep me motherless for a week. 'Cept there ain't a grog shop left in this God-forsaken town I can go into without fear o' being arrested.

I hand him the money and am about to sit down to rest when I hears the sound of shouting coming towards us.

They're after us! 'You leave me, Billy, go back to your ship! You ain't done nothing wrong. Garn, scarper, mate, 'fore it's too late!'

Billy shakes his head, 'No, Tommo, me stay.'

'Billy, piss off. *Please,* mate! You don't want no part o' this mess.'

'You me mate, eh, Tommo.'

'Billy, they're gunna kill me when they finds me. You too! Garn, git!'

Billy folds his hands across his chest. 'Nah, me stay. Tommo, you plurry bleedin' in ya head,' he says anxious.

It's dark and I'm facing him. Me wound is to the back of my head, hidden by my hat. How the hell can he tell I'm bleeding? It's his strange gift again. Now we hear the footsteps of them what's chasing us. I look about for some place to hide, but the rain has stopped and it's bright moonlight. There's nothing but road and flat fields on either side, not even a ditch.

I hear the call of a mopoke, followed by a plover. Me name's yelled out, shattering the night's calm. 'Tommo!' Then it hits me – the two bird calls is used among Tamihana's axe fighters to signal danger to each other. Hawk sent 'em to find me. I start to laugh. 'Bloody Hawk, he ain't never gunna let me have a drink,' I says out loud and then my head hurts even more, and I begin to sob. 'It's too hard to be a bleedin' drunk 'round here!'

Four Maori come around the corner. One of 'em can't be mistaken – he's near big as me brother with only one arm and hair what sweeps back like a hammer. I quickly rub away my tears.

'Tommo, it's me, Hammerhead Jack!' the one-armed giant shouts. 'Why do you run away? We are your brothers. We searched everywhere, we looked for two days. Did you kill those two pakeha?'

'Nah, just messed their faces a bit and took a couple o' fingers off one of them's pullin' hand.'

Hammerhead Jack laughs. 'We couldn't hang around to look – too many pakeha.'

'How'd ya know it were me what done it?' I asks.

Hammerhead Jack laughs again. 'Maori women in the alley saw it all. Every wahine in town is looking out for you, man! One went to find us, the other stayed to watch and follow if you left the grog shop.'

I look at my tweed suit. 'But how'd they know it were me?'

'Whores know everything. Your hair, Tommo, it's cut Maori and your smell, they smelled you. You smell like Maori now!'

'How's Maori smell?' I asks.

Hammerhead Jack smiles. 'On the whaling ship Maori smells no different, but in the village they smell different from the pakeha. It is the food. Besides, you spoke to them. How many pakeha do you think speak Maori?' He looks at Billy. 'Who's this?' Then he breaks into a broad smile. 'Billy Lanney!'

Billy steps forward and pats Hammerhead Jack on the chest. 'Plurry good, plurry good, Hammer Jack, eh?'

I laugh. 'He's had a few. Didn't stop him running faster than me, though.'

Hammerhead Jack claps Billy on the shoulder. 'Billy good!' he says, sort of absent-minded. Then he turns to me. 'We must get you out, Tommo. You can't stay here.'

'I know that,' says I. 'Can't get a drink here anyways!'

'We've got a boat waiting,' Hammerhead Jack points across the field on me left to the coastline, 'not too far from here.'

'What about Billy? Can't leave him here. Could we take him back to his ship so he's safe?' I asks.

'He can come,' Hammerhead Jack says.

So off we sets across the field what's wet from the earlier rain and sown with rye about ten inches grown, so that we leave a dark stain as a trail for all to follow. One of the Maori has picked up my axe and blanket and is carrying it under his arm. I'm feeling more and more dizzy in my head.

Soon enough we get to a path down a small cliff which leads onto a pebbly beach where several fishing boats are moored as well as a small ketch. The mooring is in a cove away from the main wharf, on the Maori part o' the waterfront. Several Maori lads comes out from the shadows to greets us, yawning and knuckling the sleep from their eyes. Hammerhead Jack says something quiet to one of them. Three of 'em pulls a dinghy down to the edge o' the water and Jack turns to Billy and tells him that two of the boys will row him back to the *Cloudy Bay*.

Billy comes over to me. Swaying a little, he pats me gently all over to say goodbye. 'Plurry hell, cheerio, top o' the mornin' squire, eh, Tommo!'

Despite the pain in me head, I laugh. 'Where'd you hear all that, Billy? That be proper toff's language.'

His footsteps zig-zag across the pebbled beach to the dinghy where the two Maori lads waits with their oars shipped. He climbs in, the lads steadying him. Two of the lads on the beach push the dinghy off into the harbour. Billy waves to me, then, with a great grin in the moonlight, he shouts, 'Ikey Solomon, he give me my name in Van Diemen's Land, he teach Billygonequeer speak English most good, my dears, omegawd plurry hell!'

Chapter Fourteen

HAWK

The Tasman Sea
July 1860

We are on board ship, bound for Sydney, and Tommo is in a bad way. When Hammerhead Jack took him in the Maori trading ketch from Auckland, they sailed to the Coromandel. It was here that I met him and we boarded the topsail schooner *Black Dog*, under the command of Captain Joshua Leuwin.

Of Tommo's voyage from Auckland he remembers little. Not long after he was taken aboard by Hammerhead Jack he fell into a delirium. His wound had turned bad on the outside and his head was aching beyond endurance. He was soon lost in a fever, murmuring gibberish.

Hammerhead Jack told me of their fearful voyage. The ketch was a decrepit old tub, one of the many derelict vessels replaced in Australia by steam. It was no doubt purchased by some errant Johnny strike-it-rich from Sydney who sailed it in fair weather across the Tasman to sell to the Maori, who can seldom afford a new vessel locally made.

A head wind blew most of the way from Auckland, so that sailing the small ketch with its heavy flaxen sails was most onerous. The wind blew ceaselessly in the wrong direction and the boat punched into the waves, which marched forward in unending grey-green lines flecked with foam. The vessel lurched up and down from trough to crest, constantly leaning at twenty-five degrees away from the wind. The lee rail was often under water, a state of affairs which even for the hardiest man on board creates a great propensity for seasickness. Many lost the contents of their stomachs overboard, though the Maori are good rough-weather sailors.

To all this was added the crew's fear that Tommo's illness had been caused by the spirits of the dead. They knew he had run away from the tribe but had no notion of why, and thought that he must be in breach of some commandment. They believed he was being punished by the *atua* or ghost – the spirit of a dead kinsman which enters one's body and preys on some vital part. They would not approach him, nor touch anything he used, a dish or spoon or cup, for fear that he was *tapu*.

Even Hammerhead Jack, who has sailed the seven seas and seen the ways of the world, suggested bringing the priests, the *tohunga*, to our ship in the Coromandel. He proposed to delay our sailing several days so that they might come to cast out the evil spirit which dwelt in Tommo. He was of the most serious opinion that the spirit residing in my twin's head may have entered him through the arsehole of the dead soldier, whom Tommo had killed and then lain upon in the swamp.

Though I have become Maori in many ways, I politely declined Jack's kind offer, saying that I would nurse Tommo myself and seek further help when we reached Australia.

'Ha, pakeha medicine!' Hammerhead Jack snorted. 'Tommo spent much money on O'Hara's costly sulphur ointment, bought to heal our wounds, but what good did it do us? None!'

I acknowledged his point here. Superstition among the Maori produces some bad, but much good comes from it as well. By ascribing the protection of the dead to the chiefs, the tribes confer upon them an authority which they might not otherwise possess. This has created a remarkable sense of law and order within the community, and a respect for one another's property and rights.

It is a respect scarce seen in European societies, where greed among the wealthy together with crime and violence among the poor cause such great misery. In these societies, too, little punishment is meted by the law when the powerful cheat the weak, and the threat of prison or the rope seems not to deter those who would practise violence for gain. Alas, I fear we shall never learn to live differently. Most of those who have settled these lands of New Zealand and Australia have suffered in their mother countries of England, Scotland and Ireland. The Cornish tin miner, the Irish peasant and the Scottish clansman – all driven from their ancient lands by rapacious masters – now drive the Maori and the Aborigine from their lands. It is as though each man must have his turn against the fellow below him in the pecking order.

Somewhere, somehow, there must be some better system of justice which does not depend on superstition, religion or the rule of English law, for this last always favours the rich and powerful above the common herd. How this utopia might come about I cannot say, and who would help in this cause I do not know. As Ikey often opined, 'The poor be like mangy strays who fight in the dust over a dry bone but cannot think long enough to get together and raid the butcher shop, my dear. They may be relied upon to do as much to prevent an improvement to their circumstances as those who exploit their poverty and despair.' But perhaps Ikey may be proved wrong and some sort of brotherhood of those who are exploited could be formed against those who exploit them.

I confess myself too young and ignorant to know the answers, but the questions persist in my head and I shall not give up thinking upon their solutions.

I have dressed Tommo's head with sulphur ointment obtained from the skipper of the *Black Dog*, and have brought down his fever by placing poultices of vinegar upon his brow. Now, nine days out to sea, he is much improved, though he complains of headaches and constant nausea. His body has had a great shock and I can only hope that he will recover fully.

In my own passage to meet the *Black Dog* I was most fortunate. The Ngati Haua tribe owns several small coastal traders, in addition to the one which was taken by Hammerhead Jack. Included amongst these is a somewhat larger boat, a gaff ketch which is the sole property of Chief Tamihana himself. It is the vessel most prized for coastal trade, a carvel built in Tasmania and constructed of Huon pine, which is renowned for its strength and its resistance to woodworm and rot. Some of these boats, which were built forty years ago, are said to be still as good as when they left the shipwright's shed.

The equal of this ketch is seldom to be found in Maori hands and it was a great honour when Tamihana insisted I be taken in his vessel to meet my brother. We sailed in comfort to our destination and I was not once troubled with seasickness.

The *Black Dog*, on which we now sail, is of the best American design. Only ten years ago she worked as an opium clipper, making racing passages from Bombay to the Canton River. She has a long, low, narrow hull and the distinctive raked clipper bow. Her hull is curved back from the long bowsprit in a reverse curve to the waterline. She is painted black with a red strake and black masts. Never was such a fair ship more badly named. Though I confess myself romantic, should I own such a vessel with its great spread of billowing canvas, I would call her *Black Butterfly*.

Alas, there is little of the romantic about Captain Leuwin. He looks upon me with a most jaundiced eye and addresses me as though I am a nigger matelot. Of Tommo he has no opinion whatsoever and I do not believe he has said a word to him since we sailed. He has encouraged the four other Europeans aboard, the three mates and the bosun, a rough-looking lot, to act in the same truculent manner towards us. We are expected to sleep and eat with the crew and to draw the same rations. Luckily, because the voyage across the Tasman is a short one, these rations include some fruit and vegetables and, for the first three days, fresh meat.

I had greatly looked forward to talking with the officers aboard. It has been over three years since Tommo and I went to live with the Maori and there is much news to be caught up on and a thousand questions to ask. Instead I have made friends with the ship's hands, who are an odd assortment of Maori and Pacific folk from the Loyalty, Caroline and Marshall Islands. The *Black Dog* trades copra and cuts sandalwood for the Chinese market from all of these tropical ports, though our cargo at present is kauri timber from Arotorea destined for Sydney.

There is something strange going on amongst the men, which I cannot fathom. At the conclusion of each meal, Tommo and I are made to come on deck and remain there for an hour with one of the ship's officers standing beside the hatch to ensure we do not venture below decks. Even on the first three days, when Tommo was gravely ill and his mind wandering, Captain Leuwin insisted that I leave him below alone while I stood on deck. Despite all my protests, I would be kept on deck for an hour before being allowed back into the fo'c'sle to care for him. As soon as Tommo was conscious again, he was required to accompany me on every such occasion.

When I asked Leuwin why this was necessary, the captain replied that the crew had work to do, adjusting and lashing timber which had shifted in the hold, and that it was too dangerous for us to remain below. I knew this to be untrue. The crew made me realise this, for they avoided my gaze whenever they spoke, and I knew they were afraid to tell me the truth, whatever it might be.

We are expected to reach Sydney tomorrow, where I shall be most grateful to disembark. With the heavy timber cargo it will have taken us a full ten days at sea to reach our port. There has been little of interest to break the boredom of our voyage beyond the daily noon sightings to determine our course and the twice daily streaming of the log to gauge our speed. Even though I have offered to help with duties on board, I have been refused. At least the voyage so far has been a smooth one, free of winter storms. The greatest blessing is that each day Tommo grows stronger, and his headaches have grown less severe, sometimes vanishing altogether for an hour or two. ·

I am not sure how Chief Tamihana persuaded Captain Leuwin, a man of immense ill humour and impatience, to remain an extra three days in harbour so that we might be taken aboard. He may have offered him money but I suspect he recalled some past favour that needed to be repaid. Whatever his method of persuasion, Leuwin does not feel obliged to be courteous towards his two passengers. He summons us on this last evening to the wheelhouse and says that, if the weather holds and the wind persists fair, we shall be coming into Sydney Harbour in the early part of the morning.

'You will please leave my ship immediately the gangplank is lowered. You will oblige me by not talking of me, nor making reference to your passage under my care. If I hear that you have spoken to anyone of this, I shall report you to the authorities. Do you understand me?'

'And what is it you shall say of us to them, Captain Leuwin?' I ask, curious to find out how much he knows of Tommo and me.

'Aye, there is always something,' he snorts. 'Chief Tamihana said naught about you two, not even giving your names.' The captain stabs a stubby finger at my belly. 'That can only mean there is much to conceal!'

'I will tell you anything you wish to know, Captain Leuwin,' I offer.

'No thank you very much. I shall mind my own business and thank you to mind yours.'

'But we have nothing to conceal from you,' I persist.

'Ha! What do you take me for? You introduce yourself as twins, you taller than a bloody lamp post and broad as a barn and him, no bigger than a sprat. You, black as the ace o' spades and him, white. You both call yourself Solomon, which is a Yid's name. What do you take me for? A black Hebrew and a blue-eyed one?'

I shrug. 'It is the truth.'

'Truth, is it? Well if that be the truth, then we'll have no more of the same. I'll thank you to shut your black gob and not to include any further truth about your voyage on the *Black Dog*.'

Tommo, whilst in his delirium, often cried out for Makareta. Now that he is well again, though, he has not once mentioned her death or even spoken her name. He responds only with a nod of his head when I tell him of his daughter and her adoption into the household of Tamihana. I try to recount the tactics employed by our mentor Tamihana to persuade the *tohunga* and the *rangatira* to accept the child's name as Hinetitama, thus elevating her to high status within the tribe. To my regret, he shows no interest. His mind is closed, wandering, and he is once again the sad Tommo who came back to us from the wilderness.

'But she is your daughter, Tommo!' I venture, gently as I can.

'Who?'

'Hinetitama!'

'Oh . . . yes,' he answers vaguely. 'Why did you not call her Mary?'

I despair. It is as if he has forgotten, or rather, he wishes to forget his life with Makareta. With her death, I fear that the whole passage of their time together has become another closed chapter in the secret life of Tommo Solomon, buried where he keeps all the woebegone thoughts of his past. For him, the mongrels have won again and I, who could do nothing to prevent what has happened, feel guilty that I have somehow failed him.

I leave Tommo in the fo'c'sle, and turn my mind to happier thoughts. Sitting on the deck, I unfold the crumpled letter which Hammerhead Jack brought me from Auckland. I have read it many times, but news from Mary always brings a smile to my face.

It is a glorious morning as we enter Port Jackson between two high sandstone cliffs. Small white beaches may be seen on either side of the harbour, and beyond them lie steep wooded slopes. I have heard it said that Sydney Cove is one of the most sheltered and treasured ports in the world and this does not surprise me, for it is a beautiful sight.

A good breeze carries us easily forward and soon enough we begin to see life on the harbour. Hundreds of small craft make their way on the water and some larger ones as well. Though sail predominates, steam ferries and tugs weave their way through the small craft which are carrying every assortment of goods.

Soon we see a dozen small sailing boats rigged for racing speeding towards us. These must be the provedore's agents I have heard tell of, the young butchers' clerks from various establishments, anxious to win the captain's business. Once the signal station on Flagstaff Hill has received the semaphore announcing a ship's entrance through the Heads, the clerks rush to the watermen to hire boats. It is generally accepted that the captain of a vessel will award the first provedore's agent on board the contract for the ship's meat and vegetables and other victualling requirements. But this does not prove true in our case. Captain Leuwin will not allow them on board the *Black Dog* and sends them packing with a string of curses. To my delight, these young clerks are not in the least retiring and return the captain's greetings in no uncertain manner, each vying with the other to hurl the most colourful insults at the *Black Dog*'s master by means of several hailing funnels.

Tommo is much amused by this. 'I think I like Sydney already,' he announces, and I am glad to see a faint spark of his old spirit.

Soon the city comes into view, spread back from Sydney Cove and what I shall later learn is Semicircular Quay and the Rocks. We are met by a steam tug and begin our final berthing.

At last we are in Australia. Sydney is like a gracious lady, of a size large enough to conceal Hobart Town in the pocket of her apron and barely reveal the burden. It has been many years since I have been in so large a city and, though excited, I am a little nervous too at the prospect of being among Europeans again, having grown so long used to our Maori friends. I miss their company, especially Tamihana's and Hammerhead Jack's.

Shortly after noon we tie up at a wooden wharf which extends outwards into the harbour, just east of Semicircular Quay. The gangplank barely hits the surface of the wharf when Captain Leuwin orders Tommo and me to disembark.

'Be off!' he commands.

I do not trouble to take offence, grateful only that we have arrived safely. So I bid him farewell and thank him politely for our passage. But he stands at the top of the gangplank, thin-lipped, arms crossed about his chest, and will not speak again or even nod, his small, obsidian eyes fixed to the centre of my belly.

Tommo pauses at the top of the gangplank and turns to the skipper for his own farewell. 'You're a right bastard, Leuwin. The pox on ya!' he calls, then spits over the ship's side.

The bosun, a big cove called Red O'Shea grabs Tommo by the throat. 'Git!' he says through clenched teeth, which are black and blunted with tobacco stain and rot. Then with his free hand he lifts Tommo by the belt. He is about to throw him over the ship's rail and onto the wharf, a dozen feet below.

I have both our canvas bags slung over my shoulder, the rope ties held in my left hand, when I reach him. I tap O'Shea hard to the side of the jaw with a right and he crumples at my feet like a rag doll.

'Come, Tommo!' I shout and proceed to walk quickly down the gangplank. Tommo follows hard on my heels, but halfway down he turns to face the captain again. 'You're still a right bastard, a mongrel, Leuwin!' he yells again, not in the least quelled by his recent fright.

I am now at the end of my patience. 'Tommo! Leave it! Come on, let's go!' I grab him by his scrawny neck and propel him down onto the wharf. With my hand closing gently around his neck, my fingers meeting my thumb at his Adam's apple, I realise how tiny my twin is, and how much I love him.

The skipper of the *Black Dog* has now recovered from the shock of seeing his bosun lying at his feet and shouts after us. 'You're scum! I'll have the law on you, you hear me!' He points to me. 'Be gone, you piece of nigger dog shit!' Then he spits down at us, though thankfully it does not carry to where we stand.

Tommo laughs as I let go his neck. 'He's not gunna call in the law!' he declares. 'The mongrel don't want no constables snoopin' around below decks. Does ya now, Leuwin?'

'Be gone, scum!' the skipper shouts down at us again, and then turns to attend to O'Shea, who is half-standing with his hands on his knees, shaking his head to clear it.

But Tommo is now completely recovered, I see, and won't let it alone. He shouts as loudly as he can, 'Hey, Leuwin!' The skipper looks down at Tommo. 'It's wahines you've got in the hold, ain't it? You're bringing Maori women to work as whores in Sydney, ain't ya?'

'What's the matter with you?' I yell at my brother. 'We're here hardly two minutes and you're already making trouble!'

Tommo shrugs. 'Ah, to hell with him. Me head hurts. Bugger you, Leuwin, ya miserable bastard!' he shouts back over his shoulder at the skipper of the *Black Dog* and we go on our way. 'And bugger you too, Hawk,' he mutters under his breath, with scant gratitude.

We walk in sulky silence around the Quay, past the Customs House to George Street, and then turn left, away from the harbour. Though most of the merchant premises are still closed for lunch, the street barrows and the pavement shopkeepers are open for business. One, heaped high with silver mackerel buried in a glint of chipped ice, catches my eye. Beside it, pigeons and gulls squabble and squawk, ever hopeful that a fish might tumble loose from the slopes of the snowy mountain above. They barely manage to hop and flutter beyond the path of our feet as we pass by, afraid they might lose their place in this feathered queue of wishful thinkers.

The city streets are a fine sight, with the grand clatter of carts and carriages and the slower creak of a bullock dray coming out of Lyons Auction House, carrying a billiard table and a grand piano. A coach and four turns smartly into Bridge Street and charges down the road as if enjoying sole ownership of it. Everywhere, shipwrights, coopers, sail makers and carpenters, mechanics and those folk who are now termed factory workers, hurry off to an afternoon filled with hammering and clattering, pulleys, pistons, belts and steam whistles.

We are now well away from where the *Black Dog* is moored on the east side of Sydney Cove, and I have determined that we are not being followed. Tommo has never said anything to me about there being wahine captives in the hold and I still don't know if he accused the captain only to make mischief. But if the skipper of the *Black Dog* should have these Maori women trussed up among the timber, he must feed them at least once each day. This would well explain why we were made to come above decks for an hour after the evening meal. It would also explain the reluctance of the crew to speak to us for fear of the captain's retribution should the secret come out.

I realise that Tommo has indeed spoken the truth and understand too why he has said naught of this to me. It is possible that, with his sharp ears, he heard the women below decks, probably when he came out of his delirium after those first two days at sea. Tommo would know that, had I been told of it, I would have felt compelled to rescue these women, thus jeopardising our safety. It would have been easy enough for the crew to feed us to the sharks on a moonless night. Tommo has all the while sought to save me from dangers, and although I would have hoped to help those poor women, I cannot remain angry with my twin for his actions a moment longer. Besides, I am much pleased to be here in Australia, with a high blue sky stretched above me and the smell of steak frying in a chophouse nearby. All I want is to enjoy the beginning of our new life here.

'Hooray, Tommo, we're back where we belong!' I cry, clapping him on the back. 'A cup of tea?' We have reached a barrow sporting a tea urn atop a small brazier with a sign upon it: *Cup T 2d. Milk/Sug. 1d ex.* Even this crude sign makes me feel at home and I clasp the steaming cup I have purchased with pleasure.

Tommo does not seem to share my pleasure and his attention is taken by the barrowman next door who is hawking hot potatoes cooked in their jackets. 'Taties, steamin' 'ot taties!' the hawker yells at passers-by as he juggles a hot spud from one hand to the other. Then he throws it up in the air, a feat accompanied by a whole lot of oohing and ouching, blowing on his hands and dramatic carry-on.

Tommo's hand shoots out and grabs the potato from the air. I think he must fancy it for lunch, and it is good news that his appetite is returned. But then he asks, 'Excuse me, mate, where's a good pub?' and hands the potato man back his spud which, I realise now, is stone-cold.

The barrowman puts down the potato and squints at Tommo. 'There be 'undreds o' public 'ouses in Sydney to choose from, matey.' Then he points down Bridge Street. 'The World Turned Upside Down ain't bad. They cleans the cellar pipes at sparrer's fart every mornin' and you'll get a nice drop of ale on tap in there.'

'What's the name again?' Tommo asks, not sure he's heard it correctly.

'The World Turned Upside Down. It's a queer name, that I admits, but good as they come,' the barrowman repeats.

'Brandy? Does they sell brandy?'

'Course. Bit early, ain't it?'

Tommo grins. 'Never too early, mate. Brandy be mother's milk!' Then he turns to me. 'So?' he asks defiantly, anticipating my disapproval. He shrugs and looks down at his Farmer Moo-cow boots, before meeting my eyes again. 'Hawk, me bleedin' head hurts! I need a *drink*, all right?'

'Don't, Tommo, please.'

His eyes screw up and he starts to whinge, then changes his mind. 'Just the one. I *promise*, just the one.' He grins at me, the old Tommo grin. 'T' wet me daughter's head, like! A merry christening!' Then he steps past me and crosses George Street, darting in and out of the carts and carriages and into Bridge Street, not once looking back to see if I should follow.

Oh Lord, whatever shall I do now? Tommo has walked away from me in search of brandy and I know that if I try to restrain him, he will never return. His head wound has changed him. He seems lacking in patience of any sort and his temper rises quickly. But with his beloved Makareta dead and his little daughter lost to him, I cannot deny that he has cause to drown his sorrows.

I feel sick at heart as I watch him shoulder his way through the crowd and disappear into The World Turned Upside Down hotel. In my pocket is half of the three pounds he won from Maple and Syrup in Auckland. This means Tommo has thirty shillings, more than enough to get him rolling drunk if he chooses. Strong drink has not passed his lips in four years, and it is my forlorn hope that he will soon topple over and be shown out, with a boot planted squarely to his backside. I still have his seaman's bag and axe, so he is safe enough from himself.

I can only await Tommo's return, which I hope will be in an hour or two. There is nothing else I can do, and I feel myself at a complete loss. Despite my anxiety I am starving hungry, for I did not breakfast this morning, being too taken up with our arrival through the Heads. I must eat first and then I shall commence my vigil in the street outside the pub.

I must also find a slop dealer. I have reluctantly agreed that the first of Tommo's poker winnings will be spent on seeing me suitably dressed. My whaler's clothes are in tatters and my boots split and worn. Tommo still wears Farmer Moo-cow's tweed suit and boots, which could prove a little warm as the winter sun is far stronger here. But of the two of us, he looks passably respectable while I appear the vagabond.

Already I have noticed the stares of passers-by, some of whom laugh as soon as they believe themselves beyond my hearing. I cannot blame them. I am now seven feet and one inch in height, and nearly two hundred and eighty pounds in weight. My black face wears the *moko* of the Maori. I am probably a most peculiar sight on a bright winter's day.

My course decided, I take another mouthful of the tea which I bought from the barrowman before Tommo left me. It is the first I have drunk with milk and sugar for many years, and it tastes strange. 'Is the milk fresh?' I ask the barrowman, who has been observing me with interest.

'Struth, mate! Milked the bleedin' cow meself this mornin',' he replies. 'Orf a ship, is ya? Whaleman?' I nod and he shakes his head and smiles. 'Takes three or four cups before yer's used to it with milk again. It's always the same with whalemen, first cuppa after they been at sea couple o' years, they always complains the bleedin' milk's sour.' He points at the blue enamel jug. 'That's practically fresh cream, that is. Matter o' fact I oughta charge more for it, Jersey cow an' all.'

I suddenly find this a most curious conversation. There is Tommo down the road wetting his daughter's head with the first of what no doubt will be many Cape brandies, and here am I, discussing the qualities of a barrowman's milk. 'I'll let you know about that when I have had the fourth cup,' I say, and put the mug down beside the urn. 'Can you recommend a chophouse, please?'

The barrowman winks, then jerks his head towards the potato man. 'Don't fancy one o' Lenny's spuds then? Don't blame ya. They's last year's crop, them taties, spent a long time in the cellar!'

Lenny scowls. 'You're right to think the milk's orf, mate. Alf's missus pisses in it to make it go further.'

But the first barrowman pretends he hasn't heard and rubs his beard, as though he is thinking deeply. 'Tell ya what, how d'ya fancy a pound o' corned beef, thin-sliced and curled over, steamin' 'ot with the mustard o' yer choice?'

I think sadly of Mary's delicious meals, but at least this sounds an improvement on the food we were served aboard the *Black Dog*. 'Corned beef will do me a treat.'

'Good on ya, mate, yiz not chose wrong. Mr Smith's above the Cut, now there's an excellent eating-house and famous for mustard mixing. Can't miss it, right next door to the Rose of Australia, an excellent pub what the said gentleman and his missus also owns.'

Alf points back towards the direction from which Tommo and I have just come, explaining that the Argyle Cut is no more than a few minutes' walk that away. I hesitate, for it will mean losing sight of The World Turned Upside Down pub, and Alf grasps my dilemma in a second. 'Don't get yer knackers in a knot about the lad, mate. I reckon the little bloke'll still be there when ya gets back after yer feed, and

more likely to come quietly besides. What'cha reckon, Len?'
The barrowmen laugh uproariously together.

And so I put my fears aside and head up to the Cut, in
the area known as the Rocks.

Alf the barrowman's recommendation proves an excellent
one. At Mr Smith's eating-house I partake of one and a half
pounds of corned beef, though I cannot yet stomach the
spicy mustards, and I wrap up another half a pound in a
bandanna for Tommo. With half a dozen nice-sized potatoes
under my belt, and two set aside for Tommo, I have polished
off a delicious meal. I wash it down with three cups of tea
and, by the end, discover that the milk no longer tastes
rancid.

I am feeling decidedly better and somewhat cheered. I
reassure myself that the worst that can befall Tommo is
another headache and a bout of vomiting, both of which he
has experienced often enough over the past two weeks. I am
about to go into the backyard to wash my face and hands
when I hear a woman's voice cry out in a tone of amazement.

'Struth, will ya take a look at this!'

I look up from my plate to see a young lady staring
straight at me. She is dressed to the nines, in a satin gown of
palest blue, the bodice cut low to display a most ample
bosom. She is powdered and rouged, with her golden hair
swept up into a great knot on the top of her head. She wears
no bonnet, but several gay ribbons of different colours are
threaded through her curls. What appears to be a small
stuffed black-and-white magpie perches at the very centre of
her bun, as though upon a comfy nest. She is dressed as
though she is stepping out to a ball, yet it is not too many
hours past midday.

With this worldly creature staring at me, I am completely
flummoxed. I quickly avert my eyes, and stare down into my

empty tea mug. But I must act more manly! Collecting my scattered thoughts, I pick up my mug in both hands and pretend to drink quite casually from it. I gaze into the distance over its rim, so that she will think me not the least disturbed by her presence.

'Well, well, well!' the young lady says, standing with her hands on her hips. 'If yiz ain't the mostest nigger I've ever seen!' Then she floats over to where I sit and tilts her head, forcing me to look at her.

'Mind if I takes a pew, 'andsome?' Her lips, I notice, are ruby red.

I jump to my feet like a schoolboy and in my haste send my chair flying backwards. I grab the back of the nearest chair and pull it out for her. 'My, my, nice manners an' all,' she says smiling. 'Ta muchly.' As she sits, the silk of her gown pulls tight across, and I see that she has the nicest derrière to be imagined.

I retrieve my chair from where it lies, several feet from the table, and sit down. What I intend to say is, 'Would you allow me the pleasure of purchasing you a cup of tea, miss?' But what comes out is, 'Er, ah, tea, miss?'

'I don't mind if I do. Cuppa does ya the world, first thing, don't it now?'

I turn around and see the old woman who served me breakfast watching us. Too nervous to speak, I point to the empty mug and hold up two fingers. My mind is racing in circles, like a dog trying to scratch a flea bite on the tip of its tail. Once I penned love letters for other men to woo their sweethearts with, but now I am entirely lost for words.

'Cat got your tongue then?' my visitor asks. She looks me up and down, and I am suddenly conscious again of the fact that I am dressed in a whaleman's canvas breeches and jacket, all in rags and none too clean. But if she notices my ragged state, she does not show it. Instead, she reaches over the table and puts her hand over mine. It is small and feels cool and clean. My heart jumps into my mouth.

'We could begin by introducin' ourselves. What's ya name?' she asks me.

My breathing has stopped and I must swallow before answering, 'Hawk . . . Hawk Solomon.' My throat, with my heart still sitting in my mouth, feels as though the silver band of scars about it has been suddenly pulled tight.

'Garn then, Hawk, give us a smile?' she teases.

I smile and she brings her hand up over her mouth and giggles. I see how very young and pretty she is.

'Why do you laugh, miss?' I ask.

'You has such a stern face, but when ya smile, yiz beautiful!'

I try to keep my face straight, but I am forced to laugh. 'Men can't be thought beautiful,' I protest.

'Most ain't, but you is!' She points a finger at my face and makes a little circle in the air. 'Them whirls on yer face, you look like the prince o' the cannibals!' She laughs again and claps her hands. Then she tilts back her head and says suddenly, 'Do you think I'm beautiful?'

She has put me at my ease and now I look closely at her, noting her every feature. She is not beautiful but very pretty, with a small nose, big blue eyes and a mouth perhaps a trifle too big but which already I long to kiss. She returns my gaze with complete candour, not the least show of modesty in her scrutiny of me. There appears to be something resembling boot-blacking over her eyelids and she has darkened her lashes so that the colour of her eyes is intense. Her gaze is too direct for me to return and I am painfully aware of her abundant breasts at which I try not to stare. 'Yes,' I declare after a few moments. 'You are very beautiful.'

'Bull!' she exclaims. 'I'm pretty if I works bloody 'ard at it, but I ain't beautiful.'

I am not sure what I'm expected to say next, but she speaks before I am able to gather my thoughts.

'You could ask me name! A girl's not supposed to introduce herself, it ain't polite now, is it?' At this moment, the old lady shuffles up to bring our tea. 'Mornin', Ma Smith,' my companion says without looking up.

'Morning,' the old woman replies, and it is clear from her voice she does not approve of what's going on. She places down a tin tray on which sits a china teapot, two cracked cups, a milk jug and a sugar bowl with a piece the size of my thumbnail missing from the side. Then she sniffs and leaves.

The young lady arches one eyebrow at me. 'Stupid old cow,' she whispers, then giggles. 'Garn then, Hawk, introduce us. I can't hardly wait to make yer acquaintance proper.'

I'm not too sure how I should go about this. So I rise from my chair and do a little bow. 'I'd take it most kindly if you'd allow me to make your acquaintance, miss,' I say politely, once again aware of my poor rags. I feel a little foolish acting as though I'm dressed in a black tail coat and silk hat, when I look like a drayman's boy.

'Well, it's about bloody time, sir! I thought yiz was never goin' to ask! Maggie Pye,' she says, sticking out her dainty hand. 'Pleased to meetcha, Hawk Solomon.'

'Likewise, Maggie Pye,' I answer. Somehow she has taken my shyness from me. Then she leans over, and with her bosom practically popping out of the top of her gown, so help me, she stretches up and kisses me on the cheek. 'We'll be friends, Hawk,' she says. 'Good friends. What 'elps each other through thick an' thin.'

My heart leaps and bounces back up into my throat. It is as though my dream has come to life. A dainty, pretty girl is kissing me softly on the cheek. My shyness returns in a flood of embarrassment, and I blurt out the first thing that comes into my head. 'But how could a pretty miss like you kiss a nigger?'

Maggie Pye draws back and looks at me in mock-surprise. 'Well I never! You ain't a nigger, is ya?' She reaches over and picks up the teapot and begins to pour. 'I'm a whore and you're a nigger – there's a couple o' known facts we don't need to quarrel about no more. Now we can get on with what we don't yet know about one another but 'opes to find out.'

'I'd never have believed you to be a . . . one of them,' I stammer, unable to bring myself to say the word.

'A whore?' Maggie replies. 'Jesus, Hawk, where's ya been all ya life, under a flamin' toadstool? It's two o'clock in the afternoon, an' me dressed like this. Who does ya think I am, Cinder-bleedin'-ella?'

Since I've come in, the eating-house has begun to fill up with clerks and shop assistants, chatting and making a racket. Some have a pint of ale in front of them, which they've brought in from the tavern next door. From the sound of them, it isn't the first they've had today. A few have turned to watch this exchange between Maggie and myself, and I hope none has heard me.

'I beg your pardon, Maggie Pye,' I say. 'I should never have said what I did.'

'What ever do ya mean?'

'I should never have let it seem as though I should feel differently about you because of what you might be.'

Maggie sighs and puts her elbows on the table, resting her chin on her cupped hands. 'Look, ya silly, long-winded bugger, it don't matter what I am. It's *who* I am in me 'eart what matters, don't it?' She reaches out and touches my hand again, giving me a crooked smile. 'Besides, I ain't a common whore. I'm Maggie Pye! Just like you ain't a common nigger, you're Hawk Solomon! Now ain't that worth celebratin'?'

I don't dare ask her what she means by all this and she explains no further. But I can hear Ikey's voice as plainly as if he were next to me. 'Whores, my dear, don't come with soft hearts. Whores only has charms when their patsy-mark's got silver. They're hard as granite and not to be trusted under any circumstances whatsoever! A good whore be one what's robbed you of every penny you possess while you was sleeping but what ain't took your breeches as well!'

But then I think of Mary. Our own dear mama was once a whore – as was Sperm Whale Sally, without whom I would not be here to meet Maggie Pye! I decide that Ikey, who never had much luck with the fairer sex, might just this once be wrong in his advice.

'I think I understand what you mean,' I say to Maggie.

'Nah, ya don't, but ya will soon enough.' She points to my cup. 'You ain't drunk none o' ya tea.'

'Nor have you,' I say, grinning.

'Why's that, then? I love me tea. Maybe we's in love, Hawk?' Maggie tilts her head up at me again. 'Have you ever been in love?'

She asks this with such a serious demeanour that I don't know what to think. I have secretly counted myself in love with Hinetitama, but that now seems like being in love with a beautiful ghost who was half made of moonlight. I can hardly count such pinings as love, can I? At any rate, it isn't what I think Maggie would call love. Her notion of love, I'm guessing, would be loud and alive, with lots of laughter and sweetness in it. 'No,' I say slowly. 'No, I haven't.'

'Me neither,' she says wistfully. 'Many's the time I've thought I were, but it always turns out the same. Men just wants to fuck ya and women just wants to love ya, and the two things don't mix, do they?' She seems to think for a moment, then adds quietly, 'Well anyhow, if yiz a whore they don't.'

I've never before talked to a woman like this. But then I don't suppose I've ever really talked to a woman at all, except Mary. That one night in Wiremu Kingi's village when the moon was full and my manhood was taken or given, I didn't do much talking. Maggie, who's watching me carefully, can see that I am completely out of my depth.

'You'll need to visit the slop-shop,' she announces now. 'I can't be seen with you lookin' like Robinson bleedin' Crusoe, now can I?'

'Surely you mean Man Friday?' I retort, pleased I've still got some wits about me.

'That's clever an' all!' she laughs. 'O' course, I've always been of the opinion that Robinson Crusoe and Man Friday were up to a bit o' hanky-panky theirselves.' She grins wickedly. 'I mean, what else could ya do all alone on a bleedin' desert island?'

Most of what Maggie says seems to end in a question. Happily, I am slowly coming to realise that she doesn't expect an answer from me each time.

'Tommo will need to win at cards before I can hope for new clothes,' I say. 'And no slop-shop will have my size. It's a dealer I need.'

'Tommo? Who's Tommo, then?' she asks.

'Tommo's my twin,' I reply, realising that I haven't thought of Tommo in quite a while and that I must be getting back to Bridge Street to find him.

'There's two of ya?' Maggie exclaims in astonishment. She points a finger at me. 'Ya means to tell me there's two niggers your size in town?' She throws back her pretty head and laughs. 'Crikey! And they say there ain't no Gawd in heaven!'

I explain about Tommo and Maggie's face is a study in disappointment when I tell her that he is as little and as pale as she, and a gambling man.

'There's trouble!' she comments. 'Only one thing makes more trouble than men and whores and that's men and cards. Even worse if it's little men and cards!'

'Don't I know it!' I say, looking heavenwards.

'You a gamblin' man too, Hawk?'

I shake my head.

'More I hear, the better it gets. Does ya fart in bed?'

I'm shocked, but I also have to laugh. 'Only in the fo'c'sle to kill the stink,' I reply, using one of Tommo's jokes for my own, amazed at my own boldness. I'm glad I'm black, otherwise my face would surely show as scarlet as a trooper's jacket.

Maggie grins. 'You'll keep,' she says, and takes a small mirror from her purse. Pouting her lips, she examines herself carefully in it. Then she wets the tip of her forefinger on her pink tongue and runs it across her right eyebrow, before doing the same with the other. 'Don't I look a fright!' she says, pulling a wry face.

'Why, you look perfect, Maggie Pye,' I say, trying my hand at being gallant, for Maggie Pye is much to my liking and I wish her to like me too. But then I am troubled by a nasty thought. What if she only likes me as a customer?

Maggie puts back the tiny mirror and smooths her hair with both hands, finally touching the tips of the magpie's wings. 'Time for me to attend to business, Hawk,' she smiles, glancing up at me. To my surprise, she seems a trifle shy. A silence which seems to last forever stretches between us, and then I clear my throat and manage to blurt out, 'Will I see you again, Maggie Pye?'

'Christ, I thought ya were never goin' to ask!' she replies, her face lighting up. 'Hero o' Waterloo, six o'clock t'night.'

I move to get up from my chair. 'No, don't,' she instructs. 'If ya gets up, 'ow's I gunna kiss ya?' She rises from her chair and at her full height she's only three inches taller than I am when seated. 'Six o'clock, don't be late, Maggie don't like to wait even if she's late herself, what's more than likely, life being what it is, if you knows what I means?' It all tumbles out in one breath. She gives me a kiss on the forehead. 'Ta-ta then!' she says loudly and turns and walks out, her derrière moving like it has a life of its own.

As she saunters out, catcalls and whistles rise from the clerks and shop assistants and I am all at once angry. I rise from my seat. 'Be silent!' I shout, and bang the table with my fist so hard that the two cups of tea jump up and spill over, dribbling liquid to the floor. I see that Maggie's left a florin beside her tea cup.

As the sound of my protest dies away, the room is so quiet you could hear a pin drop. Everyone has their eyes downcast, staring at their cup or plate or beer mug to avoid my gaze.

Maggie Pye whirls around at the door and puts her hands on her hips. 'You low bastards couldn't afford to pay for what the nigger's goin' to get for free!' she announces. She blows me a kiss. 'Hawk Solomon, welcome to Sydney!'

I have never felt so embarrassed in my whole life. The tea drips onto the floor and onto my boots while the clerks and shopkeepers all look up at me with their stupid grins.

Maggie swishes out of the door like a princess. I pick up her florin, and walk over to where Ma Smith is seated beside the kitchen door and pay her. 'Thank you, ma'am, the brisket was excellent and the potatoes amongst the best I've tasted,' I say softly.

'Humph!' she snorts, handing me my change. 'You'd do well to stay away from that one!' Her lips are stretched so thin I think they must snap. 'She'll take every penny you've got and more!' She looks up at me with her rheumy, red-rimmed eyes and cackles, 'Why d'ya think she's called Maggie Pye, eh? 'Cause she collects bright little valuables for her nest, that's why!'

I laugh and look down at my tattered coat and blouse, my breeches, frayed and torn at the knees, and my poor old boots. 'Thank you, ma'am, I'll take care that she doesn't diddle me out of my riches!' I bow slightly to the old crone and take my leave.

I'm feeling good as I walk out the door with all eyes upon me. It isn't natural for me to enjoy such attention and yet I do! Then the men commence to whistle and clap and laugh. 'Welcome to Sydney, Hawk Solomon!' someone shouts and I can't help grinning. I feel light-headed and wonder if at last this might be love. It seems not such a bad idea. Maggie Pye and Hawk, birds of a feather!

Chapter Fifteen

TOMMO

Sydney
July 1860

When Hawk asks me if I wants a cup o' tea that first
morning it's the last straw. With me head hurtin' from the
musket ball more than I'm willing to admit, I can think of
only one way to kill the pain. I'm thirstin' for the black
bottle, for half a pint of the most glorious grape, me Cape
brandy, not a cup of friggin' tea!

Well, I've waited long enough for it, haven't I? Four
bloody years! My tongue is hangin' out so far that my boots
are fair tripping over it. So the moment I gets the chance I
tells Hawk I'm off.

I walks down Bridge Street not even lookin' back to see
if Hawk is following. If he tries to stop me, I swear I'll leave
the bastard forever. But he lets me be and I stroll into The
World Turned Upside Down pub. It's full with lunch-time
drinkers from the docks and the markets. With me sore
head, I'm in no humour to be among the yakking, 'baccy-
smoking, beer-swilling mob. So I make me way into the
saloon bar, what's nice and quiet, with only a couple of well-
dressed coves having a bit of a natter in the corner.

I walk to the bar and gives the bell a good thump. Soon

enough the barmaid comes through from the main bar. She ain't what you'd call young nor pretty and seems none too happy at the sight of me neither. 'Be 'appier next door, I should think?' she sniffs, indicating the main bar with a nod of her head.

'I'm fine right here, thank you, miss,' says I, then turns to the two men in the corner. 'Providin' these gentlemen don't mind?' A little bloke no bigger than me and a bit of a toff, though with the look of a weasel about him, nods friendly enough. The fat cove what's with him don't twitch an eyelid. 'Looks like I'll be stayin',' says I.

'Suit yerself,' says the snooty barmaid. 'What'cha want?'

'Brandy. A daffy o' Cape, thank you, miss.'

'A daffy?' she asks, one eyebrow raised most high and mighty.

'Fer goodness' sake, Doreen! Give the gent a nobbler of brandy and stop making trouble.' It's the little weasel bloke what speaks.

'Much obliged,' I says to him. 'Nobbler, is it?'

Doreen turns on her heel and she's about to vanish into the main bar when I shouts after her, 'Nobbler of *Cape*, miss!'

She soon puts down a glass in front o' me. I pick it up and sniff, waiting for the smell o' the precious ambrosia to hit me nostrils. I sniff and then I sniff again. 'This ain't Cape,' I says, looking straight at her.

She shrugs her shoulders. 'It be better than Cape.'

'Thanks, miss, but it's Cape I asked for and Cape I'll have! You know, brandy what comes from the Cape o' Good Hope!' Me head feels like it's gunna explode and I push the brandy away. Next moment the little bloke's besides me. He picks up the glass and sniffs at it.

'This ain't brandy!' he exclaims and pours the glass o' spirits into the brass spittoon beside the door. 'Now get this gentleman a Cape brandy, or I'll call Mr Hodges!'

'It ain't right!' Doreen cries. 'I tries to keep the saloon bar nice for the better class o' person like you and ye friends.' She sniffs and looks directly at me. 'Mr Hodges don't like it when the hobbledehoys comes in the saloon bar!'

Christ Jesus, I thinks, what is this? Ain't I ever gunna get a drink? If I had my axe with me I'd know exactly what to do with Doreen's saloon bar.

Anyway off she flounces and the little cove pats me on the shoulder. 'You'll get your brandy now, matey.' Then he sticks out his hand. 'Art Sparrow.' I take his hand a bit reluctant-like, for I don't want no company. I catch sight of the ring he's wearin' what sports a diamond the size o' me pinkie nail. Then he withdraws his hand and there, 'tween forefinger and next, is a small white card. 'My card,' he smiles, bowing his head.

It's a neat piece o' palming, not difficult mind, but nicely done. I take the card and read it, thankful that Hawk made me take up learnin' again at sea. It's very fancy lookin'.

F. Artie Sparrow Esq.

Special Arrangements
of a
Sporting Nature

The World Turned Upside Down
Bridge Street, Sydney

I dunno what makes me do what I do next, but I hold his card up, close me hand over it, and then open it again.

Where his card was, I now holds the ace o' spades.

'Well I never!' he exclaims. 'Use the flats, then, does you?'

'Some,' I reply.

He glances down at the playing card then he sticks out his hand again. 'How do you do, Mr Ace O' Spades?'

I don't feel much like smiling but it's clever enough said, so I oblige. 'Pleased to meetcha, Mr Art Sparrow,' I says, though me greatest pleasure would be for him to go away and leave me in peace.

'My friends calls me Mr Sparrow, and me enemies . . .' he pauses a moment and points to his card. 'Well, I'll leave that to yer imagination!' I looks at his name on the card again, F. Artie Sparrow. 'Frederick Arthur Sparrow,' the little cove says. 'I most sincerely hopes we can be friends and you'll call me Mr Sparrow?'

'Thank you, Mr Sparrow,' I says, though it's hard now not to think of him as Fartie Sparrow. I know a mag artist when I see one. But I think it best to humour him a while. Otherwise, he might see that Doreen here, or even Mr Hodges, sends me on me way without a drink.

'I ain't given you my proper name yet, Mr Sparrow,' I says.

He throws up his hands in alarm. 'No, no, don't! Leave it be, my dear. Ace O' Spades is a grand name for a young Irishman who plays the flats.' He cocks his head. 'That is, if you can play sufficient well to earn it as ye handle?'

Before I can tell him I ain't Irish, Doreen brings in my brandy and I goes to pay her.

'No, no, my dear – my stand,' Mr Sparrow insists. 'Make that two more. We have to celebrate Mr Ace O' Spades arrival in Sydney!'

'Cape again?' Doreen asks him.

Mr Sparrow grins. 'Now don't you be cheeky, my dear. It's finest cognac for me and rum for Fat Fred over there as you know well enough.' He nods to the corner. 'Bring your poison, Mr Ace O' Spades, and come over and meet Mr Fred. Perhaps you fancy a hand or two of poker? What say we play fer drinks, eh?'

'Much obliged, Mr Sparrow, but if you don't mind I won't today.' I points to the brandy in front o' me. 'I come in here to get a few drinks in me, and that is what I intends to do.'

'A misfortune or a celebration, my dear?' he asks, not in the least put down by me knocking back his offer. 'Celebration or misfortune, which is it then?' he repeats.

My head is aching so much I can't hardly remember why it is I wants to get drunk. Is it to mourn me beloved Makareta or am I wetting the head of me new baby daughter? I don't even know where the poor little mite is. Perhaps it's about coming to Australia, or perhaps none o' them things?

'Sort o' both, I suppose,' I replies. 'I'm best left on me own at the moment.'

Doreen brings Mr Sparrow's brandy and takes the other tipple over to Fat Fred. He's a hugely fat man with a very red face what has several spare cheeks and a spirit drinker's knobbly nose. I reckon he's about forty years of age and Mr Sparrow near enough the same. Fat Fred has his elbows on the small table in front o' him and his chins cupped in his hands, so that the flesh spills out the side most handsome. When Doreen puts down his rum, he makes no sign he's seen her, his piggy-eyed expression of darkest gloom unchanged.

'Cheerio, then!' Mr Sparrow throws back his head and swallows his drink in one go. With nary a glance in his direction, Fat Fred in the corner does the same, to the exact second, so that they bang down their empty glasses with a single sound.

Meanwhile all I has done is lift me glass and bring it close under me nose. The sharp fumes rises to my nostrils like an ancient memory. I close my eyes a moment. Then I takes a sip and damn near faints. The Cape hits me like a red hot poker down me throat. 'Bloody hell!' I gasp.

'What's the matter, lad?' Mr Sparrow asks most concerned, thumping me back as I choke and splutter. 'Doreen!' he cries. 'What's she done to yer brandy then?'

My eyes is watering and I can't hardly speak. 'Nothing's been done!' I croak. 'It's bloody delicious! But it's been a long time between drinks.'

'Oh dearie me!' he laughs. 'Whaleman, are yer?'

'I was.' I knuckle the tears from me eyes. The brandy is warming my stomach something wonderful.

'Harrington Arms be the pub for whalemen,' says Doreen, who's popped up from nowhere. 'T'ain't far from 'ere!'

'Right,' I say, taking another small sip. 'But I ain't a whaleman no more and intends to be a gentleman, if that be all right with you then, miss?' All it takes is a single sip o' the glorious grape and Tommo is back to his old self.

'*Course* you aren't a whaleman no more, it's plain for all to see you're a gentleman,' Mr Sparrow glowers at Doreen.

'It is, is it?' I grins. 'Could've fooled me!'

Doreen gives a 'Hmmph!' and stamps off again.

Mr Sparrow smiles. 'I like a man with a nasty sense of humour. And it's good to see you enjoy your brandy!'

I take another sip o' the blessed Cape. 'I'll be fine now, thanks. It's been a pleasure to meet you, Mr Sparrow, but I'd best keep to meself.'

Mr Sparrow looks at me with sympathy. 'Naturally, after all yer time at sea, you'll want to fully savour yer drink.' Suddenly his voice grows hard. 'But may I remind you, sir, it's your turn to stand a round.' He's smiling, but this time it's different and I sees the weasel again. 'Wouldn't do to neglect your stand, now would it?'

'Oh, of course, I begs your pardon, Mr Sparrow.' I dig in me breeches for coin.

'No 'arm done, Mr Ace O' Spades, it's not yours to know the local form. Tell yer what? I can see you want to be on yer own, so we'll spread the flats once each. You win and there's no need to shout me and Fat Fred and we'll leave you well alone. Can't be fairer than that now, can I?'

Mr Sparrow says he'll shuffle and then select five cards what he'll show. Then I'm to do the same, and if mine beats his, I win. Well, Tommo don't like to say no to such an offer. So Mr Sparrow picks up the cards and examines them most careful. I ain't shaved them none and they be in most excellent condition. He shuffles the deck a few times to get the feel and I'm interested to see how he does the relocation. He's very good, as I knew he'd be, and there's a pretty blur of the broads as he spreads them in a straight line across the bar counter. Then he picks five cards and turns up each in turn. Three queens and a pair of tens, a full house – the perfect poker hand.

'Nice.' I keep me voice steady. In fact it be most skilled and I can't understand why he's done it. A cardsharp as good as him don't play boastful with a stranger. I can see he thinks I'm a whaleman paid off in Sydney – a slip of a lad with a pocket full o' brass what a few games o' poker will soon empty. But why the big trick? That would do nothing but scare away a patsy-mark. It don't make no sense whatsoever.

Mr Sparrow takes a cigar from the inside pocket of his coat, bites the end off and sets about lighting it. He looks even more the weasel with his sharp little teeth bared, some missing to either side, and gold in three of 'em. I wait 'til he's got it going and the air about is filled with the rich smell o' tobacco smoke. Then I takes up the cards and shuffles, laying them down in a perfect circle with one card placed in the dead centre the way Ikey taught us. It's a trick, no more, and not to be used in any card game. But it takes hundreds of hours of practice to get it right, and few can do it well.

'Hmm!' says Mr Sparrow, chewing at his cigar. 'Card tricks, eh?'

I selects a card from the very top o' the circle and the next from the very bottom, leaving two gaps exactly opposite each other. I does the same to the left and the right so that the circle, but for the four matching gaps facing each other, remains perfect. Now I has four cards placed face down in front o' me on the bar. In a manner most casual, I turns them face up. King, then another king, then a third, then a ten. I reach out and take the card from the centre o' the circle and places it face up to show another ten. Three Kings and two tens. My full house beats his!

'I'll be damned!' says Mr Sparrow. 'If I hadn't seen it with my own eyes, I'd not have believed it!'

'I'd be much obliged if you'd let me be now, Mr Sparrow,' I says, upping me glass and drinking down what's left of my brandy. I do this so he can't see the big smile on me gob!

But Mr Sparrow's still staring at the five cards I've laid out on the bar. 'Ace O' Spades, there be only one man in the world what I've known can do that, and he's long dead.'

'Ikey Solomon?' I says. The cigar drops from Mr Sparrow's lips onto the floor. I lean down and pick it up. Then I put it carefully on the counter with the lighted part over the edge. 'You'd be Sparrer Fart, then, I presume?' I say, cool as you like.

'How the devil –' he exclaims. 'Who are *you*, then?'

'Tommo X Solomon, at ya service!' I says, sticking out me paw. 'Ikey said I couldn't never beat ya, but I bloody well just did!'

Mr Sparrow, alias the one and only Sparrer Fart, is too astonished to take offence.

'Yer Ikey's boy! Ikey Solomon! Prince o' London's Fences, sent to Van Diemen's Land?'

'One and the same,' says I. 'And you be Sparrer Fart, what Ikey considered the best pickpocket of all the lads he ever trained and a master o' the flats when you was ten years old.'

'I was, too!' Mr Sparrow muses. 'Thought I still was, until a few moments ago!' He looks me all over like he's looking at me for the first time. 'Glory be! Ikey's lad, eh? This is a most momentous occasion!'

I sighs. Me and my big mouth. I just never learns to keep me cleverness to meself. There's no hope of getting rid of Mr Sparrow now he knows who I am.

Mr Sparrow is banging the bell and the lovely Doreen appears once more. 'Ere, same again,' he calls to her.

I raise my hand to object. 'Mr Sparrow, please, we made a deal. I won, now I wish to drink me fill on me own!'

Mr Sparrow stops and gazes at me a long time. A tear escapes from one of his little red weasel eyes and runs down his cheek and across his small, sharp face.

'Son,' he chokes, 'I've waited thirty years for this moment. Ikey Solomon were the closest thing to a pater I ever 'ad. He give me a family – all the likely lads from the Academy o' Light Fingers. Ikey was our beloved kinsman. He found me when I were nothing but a starvin' guttersnipe. He taught me the most noble art o' tooling until I were the best pickpocket in London. He give me book-learnin' and writin' and taught me cribbage so that handlin' the flats became me second nature.

'Ikey Solomon gave me everything I am become, son. When Mr Dickens picked me character for the Artful Dodger in that book of his, *Oliver Twist*, I were the very finest example of the genius of Ikey Solomon.' Sparrer Fart pauses. 'Now I meets you, Tommo Solomon, alias Mr Ace

O' Spades, Ikey's lad!' Another tear escapes. 'And you tells me t' piss orf? I'm 'urt, 'umiliated to the uttermost!'

Fat Fred lets loose a gentle snore.

From the way he's talking, it's like Sparrer Fart's once more the little ragamuffin what Ikey found starving in Rosemary Lane. I don't know what rightly to say to his outburst. I know I'm being had, but also that some o' his declaration is genuine enough.

Ikey would always tell us, 'A good scam be from the heart as well as the head, my dears. Always find yourself something what you can say with a sense o' conviction, what makes you sad or happy or angry, then work it in like butter and flour. The result be most soulful and is as effective on your patsy-mark as mother love.'

Now Mr Sparrow has gave me a proper lesson in doin' this right. For a moment, I thinks I must cry for the memory of Ikey, which be most funny, for as far as I know ain't nobody much ever cried over the memory of Ikey Solomon. Mary might have shed a few tears what quickly dried, and so might me soft brother, but nobody else. It all goes to show the skill o' Sparrer Fart.

'You're right, Mr Sparrow, I've been most hard-hearted,' I says, even half-meaning it.

'No, no, lad!' He takes me by the arm. 'Tell you what? We'll 'ave a couple o' nobblers. My stand. Me and Fat Fred will nurse our drinks on our own, and leave yer free to take up the slack on your grief or celebration or bit o' both. Then afterwards, I want you to accompany us on a proper adventure. Put money in your pocket too. What do you say, eh, lad?'

'Adventure? What sort of adventure? Can't be better than getting shickered after four years!'

'Much better, a thousand times better, I promise. It'll fix whatever ails yer.' He bangs the bell and orders two nobblers each for us. I hasn't even touched the last one Doreen brought.

'But I ain't said yes, Mr Sparrow,' I protest.

He ignores me and retires to the corner as promised. He gives Fat Fred a shake and they talk quietly between themselves while I stand at the bar and tackle the three Cape brandies in front o' me. By the time I've finished the second, me head is spinning. It ain't sore any more but the saloon bar looks as wavy as if I were still aboard the *Black Dog*. I drink the third, spillin' some of the precious liquid on the front of me jacket. Then I take up the fourth.

All I remember after that is Mr Sparrow's voice murmuring. 'Steady now, take it easy, Tommo, there's a good lad.' Then he's talking to someone, what could be Fat Fred. 'We'll take him upstairs,' I hear him say. Then I don't remember nothing.

I wake up in a dark room and I'm lying on a proper bed with a blanket covering me. Me head hurts, but not too bad. I has a strange recollection of being waked from time to time and made to drink gallons of water, or so it seemed in me dreams. Now I'm busting for a piss. I lie a moment, listening for sounds, and see a thin strip of light coming in from the drapes. It's daylight and I can hear street sounds, but they is some distance below me.

I gets up and sees that me boots has been took off, along with me trousers and jacket. All I'm wearing is Farmer Moo-cow's woollen blouse. I walk softly over to the door and tries the knob, but it's locked. Then I goes to the window and pulls the drapes open. I'm looking down into a narrow lane, more a cutting between buildings than a passageway, barely wide enough to walk through. Two stray dogs are sniffing each other's arses, turning 'round and 'round, and bumping into the walls on either side. There's no sign of anyone else. I try to open the window, thinking I might piss out of it into the lane below, but it won't budge. What am I to do? Then I see a small washstand with a basin atop. I ain't tall enough to piss straight into it, so I put it on the floor and passes water for maybe ten minutes or more o' blessed relief.

I'm a new man when I lift the basin back up onto the washstand. Then I starts thinking about me predicament. Has I been kidnapped? How did I get here? Slowly, my memories of the pub comes back to me. Four brandies! Once I could've took ten and walked home. Hell, what time is it? Is it morning? Afternoon, I thinks, from the look of the lane. Is it today still or tomorrow? Where's Hawk? He'll be goin' spare!

I walk to the door and bang upon it with me fist. 'Anyone there?' I shouts. It don't take a moment before I hear the rattle of a key and the door is opened. Two lads, no more than ten or eleven years old, stand looking in at me.

'Afternoon, squire,' says one of 'em, cheeky-like.

'Where am I? What's the time?' I demand.

'It be just after noon, the post office clock just gorn not more 'n ten minute since, squire.'

'Don't call me squire! Who brung me here?' I ask.

'You was shickered, guv. Mr Sparrow said we should mind yiz. Been 'ere all bleedin' day, we 'as.' He jerks his thumb at the second boy. 'Him an' me, we's had no sleep and nothin' to eat all day, neither.'

'Where is he – Mr Sparrow? Can ya fetch him?'

'If you'll let us lock you back in? Strict instructions, we's got.'

'Where's me togs?' I ask.

'Dunno. Fat Fred took 'em this mornin'.'

They close the door and I hear the key turn in the lock.

Before long there are voices outside and soon enough in

comes Mr Sparrow, carrying a brown paper parcel tied with twine.

'How are we feeling, Tommo? How's your poor noggin?' He smiles, then reaches into the pocket of his breeches and hands me a small flask. 'Hair of the dog, lad. One sip only, mind. We got business t'night.'

'I've got to find me brother now, Mr Sparrow.' But I reach for the flask and take a long swig.

'Now, now! Steady on, we've got a long afternoon and night ahead, lad.'

I hand Mr Sparrow back the flask. 'Where's me clothes? I've got to go and find me brother.'

'The nigger?' he says straight away.

'Aye, Hawk Solomon, me twin. He'll be out lookin' for me.'

'Twin? Him? You and he be twins? T'ain't possible – he's pitch-black, a giant!' Mr Sparrow grins his weasel grin. 'Ikey knock up a black gin then, did he? Dirty old bugger!' Then he looks puzzled. 'But then that don't explain you, does it?'

'I'll tell you how it come about some other time,' I says, impatient. 'You've made Hawk's acquaintance then, has ya?'

'I ain't, but I heard he's been downstairs asking for yer.'

'Didn't that bloomin' Doreen tell him she'd seen me?'

'Doreen only sees what she's told to see. She's blind as a bat when she needs to be.' Mr Sparrow smiles. 'But don't you fuss none, Tommo, we've had 'arf a dozen of my lads following your brother. I daresay it ain't too easy to lose a seven-foot nigger. How's your head, then?' He grins again. 'We gave you plenty o' water on the hour.'

'Me head's fine, where's me clothes?'

'Be here soon, a new set for you.'

'What's you mean?' I cries. 'Where's me own clobber? Ya took me flamin' clothes!'

'Not took, replaced. You can't be seen to be the country

bumpkin where we're going tonight, Mr Ace O' Spades. I even took yer shoe size when you were asleep. Yer precisely the same size as me.' Mr Sparrow hands me the parcel under his arm. 'They be my third best set o' crabshells.'

I'm still holding this parcel when a lad comes to the door with another large paper package, his head and cabbage-tree hat barely peeking out above it. 'From Hordern's Drapery, Mr Sparrow,' he announces.

It seems Sparrer Fart is King of the Sydney lads. Apart from the two what were guarding the door, there's three more on the landing, and now this one's appeared. Not to mention the half dozen what's following Hawk.

'Help yourself, Tommo,' Mr Sparrow says proudly, putting the parcel on the bed. 'Best there is, short o' tailor-made!' Inside the parcel is a good worsted suit of clothes, three new blouses, a waistcoat and a fancy neckerchief of the kind toffs wear. There's even a hat of a sort I've never seen before.

Mr Sparrow picks it up, removes his own headgear and places the new one on his head at a rakish angle. 'Latest fashion, all the rage in London, most suitable and becoming for a young man about town like yerself.'

'Look, Mr Sparrow, I don't know what you're doing, but I don't want no part of it 'til you explains everything. What the hell's goin' on? All I wants is me own gear back so's I can get out of here and find me brother!'

'Steady on, lad,' Mr Sparrow soothes. 'You get dressed and I'll tell yer all about the grand adventure I've got planned for us tonight.'

'Oh, an adventure this very night, is it? No doubt a thousand times better than getting pissed, is it? I told ya already, I'm off!' I picks up a blouse and starts to undo the buttons when two young lads bring in a jug of hot water, steam coming out the top.

'Pour it in the basin,' Mr Sparrow instructs.

'What's that for?' I asks, suspicious. The lad hesitates and looks at Mr Sparrow.

'Don't suppose a wash be out the question, seeing you're near naked but for your woollen blouse?' Mr Sparrow says. 'Bit of a scrub up do yer the world o' good, plenty o' hot water and a clean towel, what do you say?'

I hesitate. Truth is, I fancies a bath. Hawk's put me in the habit o' cleanliness and I hasn't had a wash for longer than I cares to remember. But what's I gunna do? There in that basin is my own piss! It must stink something awful. 'Much obliged, Mr Sparrow,' I says, and turn to the lad holding the jug. 'Leave it here.' I set the new blouse aside and, rising from the bed, takes me time getting me old blouse off. Then I pick up the jug and walk over to the washstand. I pour the water into it and bend over as if to wash me face. Then I pause and sniff. I pull me head back in alarm.

'What the hell . . .' I exclaim. 'It stinks!' I point into the basin, then I looks 'round angry at the two lads. 'What's you brats playin' at?'

'What's wrong, Tommo?' Mr Sparrow asks.

I point to the empty jug. 'Some dirty little bugger's pissed in me jug of hot water!'

Mr Sparrow throws a conniption on the spot. He sends for another basin and jug of hot water, and soundly boxes the ears of the two boys, what jumps up and down, whining their innocence. Then, when me clean water arrives, he tells all the lads to scarper, so that we's on our own. He laughs quiet at me. 'I like a nimble mind. Piss in the basin, did yer?'

I grin in reply. He's a man after my own heart, I reckons. I bathe and dress and Mr Sparrow tells me about his plans for tonight. It seems that, amongst other things, he runs a regular game o' cards. It's mostly for rich toffs what wants to taste the entertainments of Sydney. 'Not just cards –

women, grog, a prize fight if we can arrange it. Delights of the Night, I calls it,' he says. He explains that Fat Fred is the manager of several prize fighters. 'Nothing like a prize fight to bring out the nabobs and open their purses, Tommo.' But while the gambling on the fights be a good earner when there's a big purse on, poker's the mainstay. Seems everybody's up for a game o' flats – merchants, squatters, barristers and judges, graziers, men rich from the goldfields, even the celestials what has learned to play poker out in the diggings.

'The Chinese from the goldfields?'

'Aye, they be very keen gamblers.'

'And they comes to yer poker games with the landed gentry?'

'No, once a month we play down in Chinatown and the landed gentry come to them. Very exotic it is, too. There be other attractions in Chinatown as well as a good game of poker. Matter o' fact, that be where we're going tonight,' Mr Sparrow smiles.

'We? I ain't said I'm coming!' I'm sitting on the edge of the bed lacing up Mr Sparrow's spare boots. They fit a treat and I has to admit I likes the feel of boots with hose again.

'Stand up and let's look at you, Tommo. Breeches fit, I can see that. Shoes?' I nod. 'Put the jacket on.' I does as he asks. 'Not bad, not too bad at all, a little bit o' fattening up and the fit'll be perfect.'

Suddenly Mr Sparrow takes a step forward and grabs me by the lapels of me jacket. He pulls me close. 'Look, Tommo, don't be a fool!' His voice is hard and he looks most weasel-like. 'If you're as good as I thinks, and if you're trained by Ikey Solomon, you'll clear a fiver tonight. You'll win a lot more, but the rest is mine until you're tested, then we'll split a bit more even. That's me best offer! Take it or leave it! Now make up yer mind, son!'

'A fiver, you say?'

'I'll guarantee it.'

'You're on.'

'You'll not regret it, my dear Ace O' Spades,' says Mr Sparrow, very pleased with himself. He points to the bed. 'Sit down. There's more to tell.'

In me new togs I feel my confidence return, and I like the sound of this adventure more and more. I sit back and Mr Sparrow starts to fill me in on the detail. 'Now, you don't know me from a bar o' soap, yer hear? That's the first thing you has to get into your noggin – we're strangers. You've just arrived from Tasmania and is looking for a game o' cards. You've got a quid or two – family has a sheep run and a good stand o' timber – but you're a bit of a cornstalk. This way, no one will get suspicious if yer can't answer their questions, seeing as you're from Tasmania an' all.'

'Well thanks very much,' says I. 'Wait 'til you meet Hawk. He's from Tasmania too.'

Mr Sparrow looks at me hard, not liking me little bit o' fun. 'Now listen, lad, we play straight unless we're losing bad. If I light me cigar and blow a single smoke ring, you may consider relocating your cards, but not a moment before, you understand?' I nod and he continues. 'The Chinese don't usually take to the flats, they's got their own ways o' gambling, but this lot's learnt in the goldfields. Don't make the mistake o' thinking them new chums to the game, though. If they think you're relocating, they'll have a knife in your belly soon as look at yer. I mean it, Tommo, no cheatin' unless I say. And yer name is Ace O' Spades. Incognito be well accepted around here. The chief justice himself be known as Tom Jones, and the attorney general as William Pitt.' He leans back and cups his hands about his raised knee. 'By the way, we've got a partner in this endeavour, Mr Tang Wing Hung. He arranges the game and the entertainment after and takes his cut.'

'From me fiver or from what I earns for you?'

'It don't work that way. What we earns in cash, we keeps. The celestials are back from the goldfields and they've got a lot o' gold dust. They'll play with coins or notes at first, but if they loses what they've got, and it's your job to see they do, most won't quit, they'll just think to change their luck by bringing out their gold.

'It's Mr Tang Wing Hung's pleasure to cash their gold nuggets or dust for currency at special rates, no doubt most onerous, it's not my concern. That's his profit and not to be questioned or shared with us.'

'I'll have to tell Hawk where I is,' I says. 'He'll be fretting that something's happened to me.'

'No, Tommo. This Chinese game be most private organised. There'll be some big wigs there what can't be seen in Chinatown. I can't take no chances of you tellin' anyone. There's reputations at risk. If the nabobs are seen to gamble with the celestials, heads will roll! You stay stum, not a dicky-bird to no one, you swear?' I nod and he says, 'Can you write?'

'A little. Me hand is very poor, though.'

'That don't matter, long as yer brother knows it well.'

'Well enough. He taught me.'

'Good! Then write yer beloved brother a note in yer own hand, telling him you're safe and you'll see 'im in the morning. One o' the lads will deliver it, I promise yer.'

After a moment I agree and he sends one of the ever-present lads standing outside the door to fetch pen, blacking and paper.

'Just one thing more, Mr Sparrow, to settle me mind. Why'd ya do that relocation this morning? That full house be a trick what a man of your skill with the flats would never reveal to someone he don't know. If you was thinking me a whaleman just paid out, ya would've scared me away with your tricks!'

'You insult me, my dear. I don't play with such bowyangs. Not my style, not my style at all.'

'So, why did ya waste yer talent on me? Easy to see I ain't no true merino!'

'I admit, when you walked in wearing those old togs, you had me fooled. But when I come over and took up the glass o' bad brandy Doreen gives yer, I take a gander at your right hand, and I see the calloused edge to yer thumb and forefinger. That comes from only one thing, my dear, playing with the flats, practising yer skill. It takes thousands and thousands of hours to build up that ridge o' skin and don't I know it! I saw at once you were no whaleman but a broadsman. I had to brave the next step, get you to show me yer form, see if you'd back off or not.'

'But what if I couldn't match your very superior piece o' relocation?'

'Matter o' fact, I was pretty certain you couldn't. But as the great Ikey Solomon would say, "Never take nothing for granted, my dears. The day you lose is the day you think you can't be beat. Sooner or later there's someone comes along what's younger and better than you. If you're ready for him, then you can delay the fall, make a deal, a partnership. But if you're not ready, then he will gobble you up." '

'And you supposed it could be me? That I could be the one what's younger and better?' I ask, amazed.

Mr Sparrow holds up his right hand, and with the forefinger of his left traces the calloused ridge on his thumb and forefinger. 'See that? It took me near thirty years to build and I'm getting older and slower, lad. It's rare to see a ridge what even comes close. I had to find out if you'd the nerve, the speed and the mind to match. If you were worth the training. I didn't think you'd best me. No, I thought when you saw what I could do, you'd want to learn from me.'

'And now?'

Mr Sparrow laughs. 'I can still teach you a trick or two, Mr Ace O' Spades! There's other things you'll need to know if you don't want to be found floating in Sydney Harbour with yer throat cut. We begin tonight with the celestials. I hope to make Ikey Solomon, may he rest in peace, most proud of the both of us. Proud of me fer listening down the years and you fer agreeing we be partners.'

'Ikey would've liked that,' I say. I thinks of him, stranded amongst the Maori ancestors, nothing to eat but roast pork three times a day. Old Ikey must be wondering what he done wrong to me and Hawk for us to put him into such a terrible predicament. 'I don't think Ikey's playing much cribbage where he is,' I confides to Mr Sparrow.

But wherever he is, I thinks, to meself, I hope Ikey's proud o' me for beating the Splendour of the Sparrer!

BOOK THREE

Chapter Sixteen

HAWK

Sydney
September 1860

Sydney is thriving. The houses of the wealthy merchants are most elegant, with not a lick of paint spared, and every brass doorknob highly polished. Many of them sit in pleasant gardens filled with native and English plants of all description, some even sporting fountains in this city short of water. The government and commercial buildings and the churches which, for the most part, are made of the local sandstone, are handsome and well maintained.

The streets are paved and have footpaths. Those running up from Semicircular Quay and across the length of the city are wide, though many a cross street is no more than a narrow lane. Hyde Park, a long strip of dust quite unlike its London namesake, is a popular area for promenading and recreation, a few minutes' brisk walk or a twopenny omnibus ride from the centre of town.

Only the Rocks, below the Argyle Cut, remind the curious of what the earlier convict settlement must have been like. It is a chaotic arrangement of mean huts, wooden skillings, slaughter yards, knackeries, cow pens, leather tanners, open sewers, broken fences, rutted streets, one-shilling hells and taverns, all crawling with rats and mangy cats. A hundred yards up from this sprawl, in George Street, the places where people go to drink are known as public houses or pubs, but here in the Rocks, such places are often called taverns, after the age-old tradition of the sea. Sailors drink at taverns when they come ashore and shall do so evermore. In the Rocks, these notorious bloodhouses carry names such as the Black Dog, which is also the name of Leuwin's schooner, though if there is a connection none I asked knew of it. Here one may also find the Brown Bear, the Whalers' Arms, the Hit or Miss, the Lord Nelson, the Mermaid, the Erin Go Bragh, the Cat and Fiddle, the Jolly Sailor, the Rose of Australia, the Hero of Waterloo, the Sheer Hulk, the Labour in Vain, the Sailors' Return and the Help Me Through the World. Tommo, alas, has become a steady visitor to The World Turned Upside Down in Bridge Street.

If the advantageous effects of the gold strikes may be seen in the upper reaches of George, Pitt and Macquarie Streets, and in the handsome houses of the well-to-do, here at the Rocks the discovery of gold has had quite the opposite effect. A great many working men have left good jobs to seek their fortunes at the diggings at Lambing Flat and Braidwood, amongst others. Most of these hard-luck fossickers find nothing but hard luck, and their women and children are left here without any livelihoods, so that misery, desperation and destitution are everywhere to be seen.

Many a respectable mother has been forced to resort to the 'purse between her legs' to feed her starving children. Some have forsaken their young and for a silver shilling are available in the Argyle Cut for a quick knee-trembler. The streets near the Semicircular Quay are over-run by tiny, barefoot urchins in tatters, begging for halfpennies. Others, boys and girls not much beyond the age of seven or eight, become child prostitutes and catamites to the sailors and many a so-called upstanding citizen. Most of these wild children die young. But if a boy should survive long enough to become one of the 'Sydney lads', he will be as tough a young specimen as you may find pound-for-pound anywhere in the world.

Here in the Rocks, the roads and the footpaths are so filthy and in such bad repair that no respectable person would venture down them. This matters little enough to the people who dwell here. They know themselves to be the flotsam of the human race, driven by poverty and despair to this dirty corner of the city. Some say that they are a tribe of their own but I don't think this is true: drink and poverty do nothing to unite a community. For those already in the clutches of the demon drink, the Rocks is the end of their journey and for those unfortunate enough to be born here, it is the beginning of a hard life.

There is also a Chinatown bordering the Rocks where large numbers of orientals reside, many of them on their way to and from the goldfields. These 'celestials' are treated with a contempt only surpassed by the treatment meted out to the 'niggers' or blacks as the Aborigines are called. I have noted that the Aborigines are also referred to in the *Sydney Morning Herald* as 'Sable Australians'. But this I believe merely reflects polite society's need to disguise the contempt it feels for the native Australian.

Those who live in the Rocks, even the poor whites whose existences are meagre, do not bother to hide their feelings towards the niggers of this squalid place. These poor blacks, who almost without exception dress in discarded rags, are mostly drunk from morning 'til night. Their women, known in the local parlance as 'gins', fight each other when intoxicated, with a screaming and caterwauling that would wake the dead. The men sit bleary-eyed in the dirt, their mangy kangaroo dogs panting beside them and their black bottles and clay pipes close to hand, taking no notice of the women's battles. Naked, snot-nosed children, with bloated bellies and flies clustering around their dark eyes, scream and dance in agitation as their mothers roll and claw at each other in the dust.

The gin-fight is so common a spectacle here that the regular denizens of the Rocks pause only a few moments in their passage to watch. It is the visiting sailors who are most amazed by these scenes, often betting on one or another of the women and then, at the end, tossing them a few coins so that they may drown their sorrows at the back door of the nearest tavern, for they are not permitted within.

I am black myself and know that men call me a nigger. Yet my lot is nowhere near as difficult as that of the Aborigines, who have suffered so much since the coming of the white man to Australia.

The corruption of the Aboriginal nature which has been brought about with grog is tragic. Each time I see one of their kind near dead from the drink, or one of their gins offering herself to a passing sailor for sixpence, I think sadly of our friend Billy Lanney from the *Nankin Maiden*. I know him to be a brave, generous and true-spirited man, who faithfully stood by Tommo in Auckland. I also now know him to be the much-loved Billygonequeer of whom Ikey spoke. Yet he too is the lesser man for the drink. But which man is not, black or white? I cannot let myself pass judgment on Billy, nor the sad people I see here, for my own brother is just as much a wretch when he takes solace in his grog-wilderness. Who then can blame the Aborigines for their plight?

While the Aborigines are abandoned to their fate,

efforts are afoot to save the white man from the temptation of the bottle. All over town this past week, I have seen posters telling of a lecture to be given by the Reverend Hannibal Peegsnit at the Congregational Church in Pitt Street this afternoon. His topic is most clearly announced:

———⇒●⇐———

WHERE GOD CAN NO LONGER REACH!

The death and disaster,
terrors and tribulations,
caused by
the pernicious celestial poppy.

———⇒●⇐———

The Reverend Peegsnit's special mission is to the drunks and especially the opium addicts of Sydney. And no story is dearer to his heart than that of his own salvation, which has become a tale all too well known in Sydney.

Peegsnit was educated at Oxford and came to New South Wales as an Anglican cleric. He soon took to the black bottle and sank to the depths of depravity. Cast out by his own synod, he became a dipsomaniac, visited in his delirium by serpents and hobgoblins – rats gnawing at his fingers, toes and nose, and monkeys jabbering into his terrified face, showing their tiny jagged teeth and sharp little claws.

Peegsnit's personal epiphany occurred when he lay drunk in the gutter outside the Town Hall on St Crispin's Day. Christ appeared to him, immediately banishing the simian creatures and assorted pestilences that plagued him, so that his mind was at once restored fully unto him. Then the Lord took his trembling hand and charged him henceforth to administer to drunkards. His Redeemer also warned him specifically of the pernicious influence of the Celestial Empire and 'the smoke of the scarlet flower, *Papaver somniferum*, on this Christian colony'. It was miraculous indeed that the Lord Jesus remembered the Latin in his warning against the opium poppy.

And so the Reverend Peegsnit asked to be returned to the bosom of the Anglican Church. But the Bishop of Sydney, the Very Reverend John Casper, was not convinced of the redemption of their prodigal son and refused. Denied the reversed collar by the Episcopalians, Peegsnit became a preacher in the Congregational Church.

The Reverend Peegsnit teaches that God's hands are always stretched out to sinners and especially to drunkards, no matter how wretched. But, he insists, there is one exception to Christ's ever-present promise of salvation: the opium smoker. I am curious about this man and his popularity, especially among the women of Sydney who see their husbands drunk most nights, and so have come to hear his lecture. When I enter the packed church, Peegsnit is already in full flow.

'We must stop this pernicious oriental influence before it destroys the noble British character!' he thunders, and expounds on his topic at length.

I settle myself comfortably against the back wall, for it is standing room only, and observe a sea of rapt faces drinking in the reverend's every word. I listen too but find myself wondering about this noble British character of which he so eloquently speaks. It was the English who created the opium trade. Even as the good reverend speaks, British merchants are buying the paste in India and sailing their fast clipper ships to the mouth of the Canton River. There, in the safe harbour of the island of Hong Kong, they exchange the opium for tea leaf which they bring to Britain for export to the colonies. Any Chinese addiction to opium, then, is a direct result of this noble British character and trade!

What's more, the colony of New South Wales is a chief beneficiary of the opium trade. The government here gains a tax of ten shillings per pound on its import and places no limit on the amount which may be brought in, despite the fact that the authorities are well able to gauge the amount needed for medicinal purposes. For those in pain, opium is a great blessing and it is called the 'Angel's Kiss' by those whose suffering it alleviates. But it is also called the 'Devil's Smoke' by those poor souls who are addicted to it.

While I am engaged in these thoughts, the Reverend Peegsnit has, through his fearful oratory, roused his audience to sobbing and strange excitement. Much of his passion focuses on the race whom *he* holds responsible for the corruption of our society. There is no doubting who they are – in his mind at least.

'The yellow-skinned, slant-eyed Mongolian presents our precious offspring, our sweet daughters and robust sons, with a pipe and a substance which allows them to indulge in an evil clothed in its most hideous form, until the nerves begin to wince and the frame to totter from excessive stimulation!'

Peegsnit thumps the Bible on the lectern. 'The Devil's Smoke renders them shameless and they are overtaken by an immorality which utterly beggars description. These are our beloved sons and daughters who, through opium, impair their mental, moral and physical systems beyond salvation and bring upon themselves the greatest of all vices.' He stops for breath and looks about him. 'The vice of *indolence!*' Peegsnit pauses again for effect, then repeats himself, thumping the Bible with an indignant fist. 'The vice of indolence! Once this is acquired, indecency and immorality follow closely in its train!'

Like the others, I feel myself affected by the Reverend Peegsnit's oratory. Once again, however, I am forced to consider that if indolence is the most heinous of opium's consequences, then half of Sydney's population must already be addicted and beyond recovery, for indolence is an affliction I have observed everywhere about me in 'European' Sydney. In contrast to this, the Chinese seem to be very hardworking. How is it, I now ask myself, that they are not also afflicted, if idleness is caused by opium? An article in the *Sydney Morning Herald* just the other day reported that out of every one hundred Chinamen in the colony, sixty-two are primary producers of wealth. Of every one hundred Europeans, however, only twenty are thus self-employed.

The thump of the Bible hitting the lectern startles me back to attention. Peegsnit's lecture has concluded with a bang, and with much relief I walk outside into the sunny day. It is several weeks since Tommo and I arrived in Sydney and, sadly, I already have reason to be preoccupied with the subject of opium and its effects. My little brother has taken up the pipe, and I am in two minds as to what I can do. Tommo is happy enough as a professional gambler in partnership with Mr Sparrow, and I cannot help but feel buoyed that some of Ikey has come back into our lives in this way. It is sentimental of me, I know, especially as I have some misgivings about Mr Sparrow's intentions as concerns my twin.

I have been warned that Mr Sparrow is a hard, even dangerous man, and that Tommo will not in the end benefit from the association. But he has taught Tommo much about gambling with the rich, and how to conduct himself in an acceptable manner with such people. This means that at least he is not forced to play with rough sorts in rough situations. These days Tommo is quite the dandy and he bathes and changes his linen twice a week. While he still craves the brandy bottle, Mr Sparrow watches him carefully, with one of his lads always on duty to see that Tommo does not drink during the day. At night, at the card table, he is permitted to imbibe, but only at a level which does not damage his concentration – and this only so he is seen to do his fair share of drinking with the other players.

As Tommo points out to me, no punter will play cards with him unless he is prepared to go along with the grog shout. It seems nothing is done here in Sydney without the 'nobbler' – the name used for a portion of spirits. Every merchant keeps a black bottle in his desk drawer to aid in his business with customers.

Drinking is seen by many as the mark of a man, and is certainly more prevalent than any sign of religion. Within two miles of Semicircular Quay, there are six churches and hundreds of public houses. The clergy may denounce the drinking habits of the citizens at every opportunity, but very few heed their call to higher things. People seem to live only for the present, not the afterlife or the past, for not far away are memories of the rattle of leg irons.

I am so taken up with thoughts of Tommo that I am almost run down by a carriage as I cross the street away from Peegsnit's church. I can think of no other place where the streets are in such a state of confusion. This includes London which, at the time of my visit, was said to be the most congested city in the civilised world. Here in Sydney, wheels are all-important. Those who in any other society could not imagine a means of locomotion beyond placing one foot in front of the other, here demand to be transported to their destinations. Such transport is provided by as motley a collection of doddering old horses as you can imagine. Most of these poor nags are long past their appointed hour with the knacker's yard. Every day I see some poor beast, its ribs sticking out like tent poles, collapsed on the street, with its owner kicking and lashing it in a vain attempt to raise it from the dead.

Carriages consist of contraptions of every sort, many of them most peculiar in construction, the work of some backyard mechanic. Even dogs are used to draw carts piled high with newspapers. These are led by news boys who dodge in and out of the traffic on the way to their accustomed corners. I feel sure that if cats or rats could be trained to the task, they too would soon enough be put into harness. There is even the story of a retired ship's captain who harnessed his African ostrich to a milk cart and caused the traffic to come to a tangled standstill as the bird panicked and rushed headlong up George Street on its way to Parramatta.

The streets here resound with the curses of cab drivers and cart men, who turn the air blue with their invective. Coach horns and rattles blast away and the drivers of bullock drays will even take their whips to other vehicles on the road. Every few minutes some form of accident occurs with its attendant altercation.

There is talk of a horse-drawn tram commencing next year which will run on tracks from Semicircular Quay down Pitt Street to Redfern Station. Today's *Sydney Morning Herald* speculates that once this is established, no Sydneysider with three pennies to jingle in his pocket will have to walk anywhere, bringing about the total collapse of the bootmaker's trade. It is claimed that the entire mile and three quarters of the journey will take no more than ten minutes.

The Sydney lads are as wild as the Sydney traffic. I have grown up with the wild youth of Hobart Town who, in concert, may become a dangerous mob but who, individually, lack wiles and nerve. The lads of Sydney are a different kettle of fish altogether. There seem to be two types of physiognomy amongst them. One lot are slim, dark-eyed, olive-complexioned, the other are carrot-topped and blue-eyed, with much accumulated dirt obscuring their freckles. The Sydney lad's hair – whether ginger or dark – is shiny with grease and falls across his brow, so that he is constantly brushing it away from his eyes. A cabbage-tree hat clings precariously to the back of his head, and from this a snip of black ribbon dangles like a rat's tail. The knees of his breeches and the elbows of his jacket are always covered in grease. If he is younger than ten years of age, he is likely to be barefoot. If older, he wears scuffed boots with no hose.

All are up to no good. The Sydney lad is insolent to everyone, particularly servant girls, police officers and new chums. He pushes and shoves his way along the street, not caring a whit for the small child, dainty female or elderly. He fears no one in authority and has no regard for any man, unless a cricketing hero or a challenger at chuck penny.

The Sydney lad is no coward and, at the least excuse, he will remove his cabbage-tree hat and greasy jacket, wipe the snot from under his nose with the back of his hand and 'have a go'. He will often take on someone older and bigger than himself, with a cussing and swearing that would take the paint off the Queen's mailbox. Should he have a halfpenny to spend, the lad will buy a thin black Mexican cheroot. This he will light immediately upon meeting an acquaintance and then, after taking a single puff and blowing out the smoke in a lofty manner, he will extinguish it so that it may be saved for his next assignation.

Sydney lads call all their female friends after the ships in which they arrived, hence Susie Blue Wren, Mary York Town, Jenny Memphis, Mary Armageddon. And they refer to all policemen as Israelites after a ship named the *Exodus* which brought a large consignment of English constables to the colony.

At the age of ten, the Sydney lad is out in the world on his own. By this time, he believes himself master of his own destiny and a man in all respects, earning good wages by some clandestine means or other, which does not involve manual work. By the age of twelve or thirteen, long before he has the slightest blooming of manly hair upon his grimy cheeks, he has tasted most of the joys and sorrows of existence. Mr Charles Dickens, the English writer, has much lauded the genuine cockney lad, but for shrewdness, effrontery, truculence and the affectations of manhood, the cockney lad pales beside the young gamins of Sydney.

Much of what I know of the Sydney lad, I have learnt from my brother. Tommo already knows many of these lads in their cabbage-tree hats. It seems that Mr Sparrow commands the nastiest of these scoundrels, which he addicts to grog early. They cannot be good company for Tommo, but of far greater concern to me is Tommo's wounded head and his increasing reliance on the Angel's Kiss, the dreaded celestial poppy.

Tommo insists he takes opium only to alleviate the pain of his injury, which certainly remains a serious condition. But I am much afraid that the Angel's Kiss will eventually turn into the Devil's Smoke and he will become addicted. He has been using the opium pipe since the first night we arrived.

I waited all afternoon for him outside The World Turned Upside Down that day, and then made urgent enquiries at the bar when he failed to emerge. But all who worked there claimed not to have seen him. Naturally, I was distraught and even close to panic. I searched the Rocks half the night and then went up to Hyde Park to see if he was there, perhaps lying under the gum trees with the other drunks. I missed my meeting with Maggie Pye, although I left a note

explaining my predicament, hoping she would not be angry
and that we might, with luck, meet again. I spent a most
miserable night looking for Tommo, only abandoning my
search when the currawongs called at dawn.

Hoping that Tommo might find me in the Rocks once
he'd recovered, I went back there to look for
accommodation. I soon found a decent enough room with
two mattresses and after paying the landlady ten shillings for
the first week's rent, I left our belongings with her and went
straight to the public bath house. There I paid a penny for
soap and another for the hire of a razor, and shaved for the
first time in a fortnight. I also gave myself a good scrubbing,
and washed my clothes, wringing them out as best I could
before returning them to my body damp. I spent a penny
more on two loaves of bread and went to sit in the sun,
watching the boats on the magnificent harbour as I
breakfasted. I meant only to stay until my clothes were dry
but I must have fallen asleep. I woke to hear two chimes of
the post office clock and realised with a renewed burst of
anxiety that it was past noon. As the last chime faded to
silence, I felt a small hand on my shoulder. My heart leapt
and I swung around, hoping to find Tommo. Instead a
scruffy lad with a cheeky grin stood before me.

'Yer name Solomon? Hawk Solomon?' he demanded.

'Why do you wish to know?' I replied, looking as stern
as I could.

'Ere,' he thrust a piece of folded paper at me. It was a
note in Tommo's unpractised hand, telling me that he was
well. I was to meet him outside the same pub in Bridge Street
at seven o'clock the following morning. Not content with so
little information, I looked up to question the lad further,
only to discover that he had disappeared.

I was furious with my errant twin. A night wasted in
worrying. It was then that I resolved to visit the Hero of

Waterloo, where Maggie Pye and I had agreed to meet. Maybe I could make enquiries and perhaps find my new friend again.

The pub, when I arrived, was crammed with customers and my heart, which had taken to thumping faster as I drew near, sank as I scanned the crowd. Suddenly, in the far corner, I caught a flash of black and white as Maggie's magpie bobbed cheekily up and down. I quickly made my way through the crowd, then I stopped short. Maggie was talking to someone – a customer perhaps? She looked up and our eyes met. With a big grin and a look of welcome, she waved me over.

I smiled and pushed my way through the crowd to her. 'I'd not have spotted you if it wasn't for the bird.'

'Me trademark,' she replied sweetly. Then she climbed up onto a nearby bench and promptly kissed me on the lips, a soft, welcoming kiss which made my knees tremble. 'Yiz better not be late again, Hawk, but I'll forgive ya this once! Now come and meet me friend. Mr Isaacs, this be Hawk Solomon what I told yiz about.'

Looking down, I saw a small, round man, neatly dressed, who was about fifty years old. His head was so bald and polished that his pate reflected the glow from the gaslight on the wall. He had a tape measure about his neck and held out a plump, well-manicured hand. 'Pleased to make your acquaintance, Mr Solomon,' he said.

'Mr Isaacs owns the slop-shop in Pitt Street. He's a tailor, do you up a treat,' Maggie explained.

'How do you do, sir?' I extended my hand.

'Hawk Solomon. Your name is Solomon? But surely you ain't a Jew?' The little man looked puzzled.

'I was christened a Jew,' I explained.

'Ha! Not possible! Jews ain't christened!'

I laughed. 'Pardon me, it's a figure of speech. My brother

Tommo and I were born to a Jewish mother, who died, then we were given the name Solomon by Mr Ikey Solomon, who was our father of sorts.'

The little man sniffed in disbelief. 'Well, he must have been colour-blind, if you'll forgive me saying. A schwartzer for a Jew, I ain't heard of that before!' As he talked, he measured me. Like Maggie when she kissed me, he stood on the bench to get the width of my shoulders, my neck and the measurement under my armpits, making me feel most foolish all the while.

'We wants the best, Mr Isaacs,' Maggie instructed.

'Maggie, it will have to wait.' I thought of the few coins left in my pocket. 'Mr Isaacs, I'm afraid I can't afford new clothes.'

'Who said anything about money?' Maggie grinned. 'Did I say anything about money, Barney?' She didn't wait for his reply but turned back to me. 'I have a long-standing arrangement with Mr Isaacs, Hawk, and none of it your business, sweetheart.'

Barney Isaacs had hopped down from the bench and, at Maggie's words, he shook his head forlornly.

'What?' Maggie had one eyebrow raised and her hands upon her hips.

'I can't oblige you, my dear,' Barney said, his face serious. 'Can't do it.'

'Why ever not?' Maggie demanded to know.

'Too much cloth and stitching, my dear. Mr Solomon 'ere be the biggest man I've ever been called upon for to fashion up a set o' gentleman's apparel.' The little man looked up from under his eyebrows at her. 'Couldn't honestly see meself doing it for less than . . .' he shrugged and spread his hands, 'three?'

'*Three!*' Maggie screamed. 'You dirty bugger! Christ, you've already had a down-payment an' all!'

'But he's a giant!' the little tailor protested. 'Biggest man ever I seen!'

Maggie took two steps forward so that her pretty face was right up to his. 'You tryin' t' cheat me? You got the wrong whore, Barney Isaacs! What if I says no, eh? Or I gets the nigger 'ere to wring your bloody neck? Or I even does it meself? How you gunna give me back what you already spent, answer me that?'

The tailor shrugged again. 'We could come to another arrangement – maybe a silk shawl, embroidered, from China? Or a new coat? What do you say, me dear? A nice warm coat for the winter, best worsted?'

'Maggie,' I interrupted, 'what's going on? I told you I can't pay. Send him away!'

Maggie turned on me suddenly. 'Oh, fer Chrissakes, will ya shut yer gob. This is between his nibs 'ere and me! He's tryin' to rook me!'

'Tell you what,' Barney added as though he hadn't heard anything. 'Make it three, and I'll toss in the blouse and hose?'

I had heard enough. I was halfway out of the pub when Maggie called out, 'Oi, where's ya goin', Hawk?'

'I don't need your charity, Maggie, especially not that sort!' I replied, angry now that I began to understand her method of payment.

Maggie sighed. 'Ah, Hawk, stop being so prim and bloody proper! Lemme sort this bastard out and then I'll explain everythin' to ya!'

She moved purposefully towards the tailor, who retreated until he bumped against the bar, holding his hands up to his chest to protect himself.

'Give him one, Maggie,' someone shouted. 'Kick him in the bollocks!'

'Maggie, come on now, he's seven foot tall and broad as a ship's mast,' Barney yelled. 'I swear it'll take twice the cloth and sewing and I'm only asking half again. Be reasonable, it's a most fair offer!'

Maggie stopped suddenly and tapped the little man on the chest with her finger. 'Righto,' she said. 'I admits he's a big bastard. I ain't goin' to fight ya and I ain't goin' to pay ya three either.' She took a step backwards and looked him directly in the eye. 'You've already had one fuck – that's fer the jacket. You'll get one more for the blouse and the hose and I'll go down on ya for the weskit. Two and a half, that's me final offer!'

Barney nodded eagerly, then pointed to my broken boots. 'Tell ya what, Maggie, the lad's going to need a new pair o' boots. What do you say, my dear, the other half and I throws in a pair?'

'Too late, ya bastard!' Maggie cried, clapping her hands happily. 'I already has an arrangement with the I-talian in Bligh Street, what's bootmaker to the governor!'

The tailor shrugged and departed and Maggie and I went to sit in a corner. She ordered a large gin and asked if I wanted something to drink. I declined and sat silently.

'What's the matter?' Maggie touched my arm. 'Cat got yer tongue?'

'Maggie, I don't want any charity, and I don't want you to keep me. I've always made my own way and always will. If we become friends or more, then it should be I who keeps you. I mean, once I'm back on my feet. I don't want you to do it to that man, do you hear me?'

Maggie leant over and kissed me. 'Hawk, that be the nicest thing what's ever been said to me. Lotsa men wants to fuck me, but ain't never been one what wanted to keep me.' She smiled. 'I don't blame them neither. I'm a whore, an expensive whore, but still a whore. But when all's said and done, darlin', Barney be a regular, and I always takes me just reward in kind with him.'

'Maggie, I don't want you to do that for me!'

'You'll be the same, Hawk. You'll see, once you've put yer big black snake into me, you'll want it regular too. Need comes first, then greed! First the free fuck, then the free dinner!'

'Maggie! Don't talk like that. It isn't nice,' I protested.

'Talk like what?' she tilted her head at me.

'Talk dirty like that!'

'What's you mean?' she asked, genuinely astonished. 'I'm a whore! Dirty? Talk dirty? Have I said anything what hasn't already crossed yer mind, Hawk Solomon?'

'Well yes, you have. It had not crossed my mind to . . . er . . .'

'Fuck me?'

'Well yes, that I admit. But not then to live off you.'

'Oh, what's you plan to do, then? Fuck me and piss off?'

'Maggie, I don't feel that way about you!'

'Yeah, o' course you don't – now. But after you've had it, that's when you can't get away fast enough. Take me word for it, darlin', and don't get too fussed. It's what I expects. You pays yer money, has your way and then ya buggers off!'

'Some might do that!' I protested. 'But not I! We will be more than that to one another. You said yesterday we could be friends. Good friends who help each other through thick and thin, that's what you said.'

'Hawk, it's me standard patter! I says that to all the punters. Men enjoy a lasting arrangement – providing it don't last much beyond when they get their breeches back on.'

Maggie made me feel like a schoolboy. In such matters I suppose I am. 'Maggie, I don't understand all this. I don't understand why you would do what you plan to do just to get me a suit of clothes. It makes no sense if I'm just some bludger like the rest of your, er . . .'

'Customers?'

'Yes, customers. I admit I desire you, Maggie. You're beautiful and I can't help what's in my nature. But I am no bludger and I would never exploit you!'

'Why not? What's ya goin' to do instead, pull yerself off?'

'Maggie, stop it!' I was suddenly angry. 'You don't have to speak like that! And you don't have to do it with that tailor fellow for my sake.' I looked down at my ragged apparel. 'I can get my own clothes, thank you! It will take a bit longer, that's all.'

'That's just it, see, I don't want t' wait.'

'Oh?'

Maggie grabbed my hand. 'Hawk, listen to me. There's a big prize fight Friday night and I wants yiz on me arm an' all! I wants a seven-foot beautiful black nigger on me arm.' She grinned up at me. 'I admits, it's t' show off! Me screwin' Barney ain't no charity to you, it's well worth it to me!'

'Oh Christ, Maggie, what's a man getting himself into?' I said, rolling my eyes heavenwards.

Maggie laughed. 'With a bit o' luck and a fair wind, you're getting yerself into the warmest little bed a man ever sailed into.'

I blushed and didn't know what more to say, so changed the subject instead. 'You like the fights then, do you Maggie?'

'Loves 'em, darlin'. All the crinoline cruisers will be there, the toffs, squatters, strike-it-rich-Johnnies, but I wants the best on me own arm.'

'Crinoline cruisers?'

'Whores, stupid!'

'Maggie, you don't have to buy me clothes and take me to your bed to have my company. I'll come to the prize fight with you anyway,' I said, though I knew full well that I secretly desired to make love to her more than anything in the world.

Maggie looked at me, her blue eyes blazing. 'You mean ya doesn't want me, is that it? You're too 'igh and fuckin' mighty t' be with a slut?' She was furious. 'Well fuck *you*, Hawk!' Throwing what was left of her glass of gin into my face, she stormed out of the pub.

The drinkers standing near were suddenly quiet. Then I heard one say, 'Go get her, mate! Beat the living daylights out of her!' This brought me to my senses, and I wiped the gin from my face. The fellow who addressed me was the same bloke who wanted Maggie to go for Barney Isaacs. He was a big fellow but I barely noticed this as I grabbed him around the throat. Lifting him off the ground, I threw him halfway across the pub, where he knocked over several stools before landing against the wall with his eyes glazed and tongue lolling. 'Watch your dirty mouth!' I growled, as I went out after Maggie.

I caught up with her halfway down the street, as she strode towards the Argyle Cut. 'Maggie, wait! Maggie, please! I didn't mean what you think!'

'Bugger off, Hawk!' she cried.

'Please, Maggie, listen to me?' I put my hand on her shoulder.

'Don't touch me, ya bastard!' She shrugged my hand away and started to beat her fists against my chest. How sweet and clean she smelt as she hit me, the magpie jumping up and down in its nest as if it were about to fly away, wanting no part of her temper tantrum.

I began to laugh at this, then I held her tight. 'I care about you, Maggie!' I said, surprised at my own words but also liking the bold sound of them.

'Leggo o' me, ya shit!' Maggie yelled, then started to weep against my chest. I stroked her hair carefully so as not to disturb the magpie. After a little while she pulled away. 'Bet I look a proper mess, don't I?' She sniffed and, taking a small handkerchief from her handbag, wiped her big blue eyes.

'By Christ, no. You're beautiful.' I held her by the shoulders and looked down at her.

She laughed and then began to sob again. 'Oh, oh, ya bastard! Ain't nobody said that ever before!' she bawled. 'It ain't true, you silly bastard, but I loves ya for it.' She sniffed and laughed and cried a bit, then laughed again and finally dried her eyes. Then she tilted her head and asked, 'Friends?'

'Friends,' I repeated solemnly.

And that's what we've been ever since – friends. Almost every afternoon we have a drink or a chat at the Hero of Waterloo, with no more said of me sharing her bed. Thinking of Maggie has nearly driven my worries about Tommo from my mind, and I am smiling as I enter the bar to meet her again.

Today Maggie is scrubbed of all her paint and dressed in a grey gown and black shawl, neat and clean. By contrast to her appearance most afternoons, she looks decidedly modest, and might easily be mistaken for a servant girl on her day off, except for her hair, which still sports the magpie sitting in its nest.

'Don't you look fine,' she says with a grin, after greeting me with her usual kiss. 'Has you eaten?'

I shake my head.

'Ya must be starvin', darlin'! Come on!' She leads me out of the pub and we stroll down to a chophouse just the other side of the Cut. I have never been here with Maggie before, though they all seem to know her and greet her most cordially. A young lass wearing a mob cap and an apron comes up and Maggie gives her a hug.

'This be Florence. Flo, this be Hawk.' Maggie's got a

smile like the proverbial Cheshire cat. 'What's ya think, eh?' she says to Florence.

Florence looks up at me and brings the tips of her fingers to her lips and giggles. 'Crikey, Mags, you gorn an' done it proper this time, ain'tcha?' she says.

'You betcha!' Maggie exclaims. 'One hundred per cent black magic! I told you so, didn't I?'

Flo giggles again and runs off.

I follow Maggie to a table and Florence soon reappears with a loaf of bread and two large soup plates, spoons and a ladle. She sets our places, trying all the time not to laugh.

'Don't be stingy now, Flo, Mr Black Magic 'ere takes a whole heap o' feedin',' Maggie instructs and then laughs. 'And, by crikey, he's gunna need all the strength he's got!'

'Is Florence your friend then, Maggie?' I ask.

'More like me little sister. Stopped her from cruisin' when she were twelve, and saw that she and her folks got work 'ere instead. Tom, the grocer's son, is gunna marry 'er.'

Just then Florence returns carrying a large pot of stew which she places on the table. 'Me papa reckons if the nigger can eat it all, it's 'arf price on yer tab, Maggie,' Flo winks. She looks at me, wiping her hands on her apron. 'He wants to know how tall ya is, Mr Hawk?'

'Seven feet and one inch, last time I was measured,' I reply. 'It isn't always convenient.'

'And it's all in proportion!' Maggie laughs, happily. 'The parts what can't be shown to an innocent little girl like you be just as big, I'll betcha!'

Flo's eyes grow large with surprise and she runs from the room back into the kitchen, where we can hear her laughing fit to burst.

'Maggie! You must be careful!' I admonish her, thinking how lucky I am to be black so that she can't see my own embarrassment. But still, I love being with her! Here I am in the middle of this noisy chophouse with a pot of stew in front of me and suddenly I realise that I love Maggie Pye. I sit stock still.

'C'mon, darlin', eat yer tucker! I got big plans for you after this, what will have yiz grinnin' like a butcher's dog!' Maggie leans over and, with the back of her hand, strokes the side of my cheek. It is so lovely I want to cry.

But even in love, I am ravenous and Maggie keeps filling my plate from the pot of mutton stew, which I must say is delicious. Soon enough, the pot is empty and I'm full as the governor's prize pig.

'Come, Hawk,' Maggie says, finally. 'I lives upstairs. Time to make yiz a nice cuppa tea!'

I follow Maggie upstairs to her home. She has two rooms and when she opens the door on her landing, I am almost forced to crawl into a small kitchen with a hearth. Even when I am seated at her small table, the ceiling is not much higher than my head. But Maggie can stand up straight and, as I look around, I see that her home is as neat as a pin. Everything is scrubbed clean, with pots and pans hanging from the wall and a flower pot on the window sill. A grey striped tabby, which she tells me is called Sardine, hops off the window sill and comes a-meowing the moment it sees her. Maggie feeds the cat with a scrap of stew meat she has brought from downstairs. Then she puts the kettle on the hob and lights a set of twigs and a bit of coal she's obviously made up earlier.

Now I'm starting to feel nervous. I don't know what's going to happen after the cup of tea, or what Maggie has planned, and I don't know how to behave. I'm not willing to tell her that I am almost a virgin, either. I well remember what happened that wonderful night with Hinetitama. But it may be nothing like whatever might happen with Maggie, should she decide to take me to her bed chamber.

Besides, Maggie has often made jokes about having her way with me, and I am not sure she isn't just joking.

I know what I would like to happen, but I'm not sure how to proceed even supposing Maggie wants to. I would like to treat her like a proper lady and not a tart, but is that what she'd expect? It's impossible for me to think of Maggie as a tart. She says she is one, but I can hear the sadness and longing for something else in her voice.

Suddenly I have a picture of Mary tucking Tommo and me into bed when we were little uns. 'I loves you, Mama,' Tommo says. Mary looks at the two of us and a tear rolls down her cheek. 'That's all I've ever dreamed of, Tommo,' she says softly and then kisses us. 'Just remember, all a woman ever wants is to be truly loved.'

'Are you truly loved by Ikey?' I ask. Mary smiles but doesn't say anything.

'Course not!' Tommo exclaims. 'Mama loves Mr Emmett!'

'Hush, Tommo! Don't you ever say that. Mr Emmett be a married man!' Mary admonishes him, but we both see that she's gone beetroot in the face.

Well, I now say to myself, I truly love Maggie. I know this is stupid, and that I barely know her. Yet I feel something which I suppose will some day prove foolish and young but now seems certain. If folks knew of it they'd probably laugh. Other men would no doubt wink at each other, thinking that only a callow youth could fall for a whore. Despite all this, Maggie makes my head spin. She makes my heart so happy that I don't even think of Tommo when she's near. Maggie claims me completely and I am besotted. She fills my being and even if I should try to cast her out of my thoughts I cannot.

How should I behave, then? 'Hawk, you are a gentleman.' Mary's words, which she has said so often to me, come into my head. 'Not a toff, not thinking yourself special, or putting on airs, pretending you be a true merino, which you ain't, but a true gentleman.' I have always tried to live up to my mama's words – Mary, who has seen and been everything but who wants me to be a gentleman. I sense there is something of Mary in Maggie, and perhaps it is this in her which I so dearly love already.

Then I have a shameful thought. Can a gentleman, even mama's sort of gentleman, love such a woman as Maggie? Hinetitama was different, a Maori princess, a ghost in the night. Maggie is so rudely alive, so loud and truthful and coarse. If Hinetitama were the shadow cast by the moon, Maggie is the blazing sunlight, every inch afire. Yet underneath, I sense, she is sad and wistful.

Perhaps I imagine all of this, I think now. Perhaps I should concede to Ikey's theory that there's no such thing as a good whore. What I do admit is that Maggie is altogether too much for me and I don't know what to do next. I feel like a bunny that should bolt down its burrow while there is still time!

Maggie has put the kettle on the hob and brings me a cup of tea. The cup is dainty and my big clumsy fingers can hardly grasp the handle. The tea is of the best quality and she has served it black with a slice of lemon. It is not sweetened, which I am unused to, but I find that it soon cleans my palate of the fatty mutton stew.

'Would you like a bottle of ale?' she asks. I am surprised at her voice, for it is suddenly shy and softer in tone. It is as though here in her home, she can be a different woman. 'Fetch you one from the pub on the corner, won't take a minute?' she volunteers.

I shake my head gently and she comes over and sits on my lap. A woman has never sat on my lap before and I am immediately overcome by the consequences. A terrible boldness grows between my thighs, as Maggie holds me tightly and kisses me all over my face and neck. I feel her sweet lips touch mine, demanding I should open them. And then, her tongue is inside my mouth! My whole body is aflame, and I find my arms encircling Maggie, drawing her ever in towards me. We kiss, she like an angel and I most clumsily. I think I must burst through the fabric of my breeches. She must, I am sure, feel the hardness under her buttocks, and she squirms about on my lap until I think I shall faint with the pain and the ecstasy of it.

I am beyond thinking when Maggie stops kissing me. Drawing back, she looks into my eyes. 'Come, darlin', into Maggie's nest.' She rises and takes my hand. I am afraid to stand up for the straining in my breeches, and am most grateful that the ceiling means I must remain stooped over as she leads me through into the other room. Here the ceiling is a little higher but not by much, and I am amazed at what meets my eyes.

I have never seen a whore's bedroom before, but this is unlike anything I have heard described by my companions at sea. Maggie has created a veritable Aladdin's cave in her tiny attic room.

The first thing that comes to mind is the 'palace o' purest pleasure' which Ikey and Mary once possessed in London. It was, Ikey told me, filled with Persian carpets, silks, brocades and erotic statuary, so that it resembled nothing so much as a maharaja's harem. But Maggie's boudoir has not entirely been taken over by the notion of titillation. There is a certain warm homeliness here as well. The room is very pretty, with lots of shiny bits, satin cushions and brocade curtains and a carpet, all in red. But there are white lace half-curtains to the single attic window, just like Mary's at home. It is the bed, though, which commands my attention and which I now observe with a mixture of purest terror and delightful anticipation.

Maggie's bed nearly fills the room and I cannot imagine how it could have been brought up here, unless it arrived in pieces and was built in the room. It is a large four-poster of the best cedar, resplendent with a red canopy, silk tassels hanging from each corner. There are no blankets, only red silk sheets and cushions to match. Lying at the centre, propped up against one of the cushions, is a golliwog doll with his round black rag face, red jacket and striped pants.

Maggie scoops the rag doll up into her arms. 'See, Hawk, I always were partial to darkies! Many's the night I've slept with him in me arms.' She holds the golliwog up so that its face is looking into hers. 'Ain't no secrets between us, is there, Golly? We've been lovers a long time now, hasn't we?' She shakes the doll's head so it appears he is agreeing. 'You can watch us, you're a good boy,' she says to him and props the doll against the bottom of the bed.

Maggie turns and smiles at me. 'Truth is, when I holds Golly in me arms and pleasures meself, he's the best fuck I've had all day.'

I'm shocked at this admission, which somehow seems more coarse said in this pretty room. But I'm also excited at the vision it brings to mind. I can see Maggie's slim little body naked as she hugs her little black Golly to her lovely breasts, her urgent finger stroking her pretty pussy as she arches in pleasure.

Maggie has removed her shoes but she is still dressed when she jumps onto the bed. She crosses her legs beneath her and pats the mattress. 'Come sit, Hawk,' she smiles.

I am still half-stooped over and I sit on the bed beside her, hoping she won't see my erection, though I don't know how she can miss it. It feels like a tent pole sticking up beyond my nose, a great tent of lust rising from my groin.

'Maggie, I haven't had, er, much experience of women,' I stammer. 'You know, making love to them,' I say, deciding I should come clean before she finds me out for the duffer I am.

Maggie laughs and stretches up to kiss me on the cheek. 'I ain't had much experience of loving neither, Hawk.'

'What do you mean?' I am surprised.

'I'm a whore, darlin', not a cheap whore, but a whore. I've been fucked 'undreds o' times, thousands, but ain't nobody's never made love to me.' She kisses me again and asks softly, 'You going to make love to me, Hawk?'

Maggie has the end of my belt and now she pulls against the buckle to loosen it. Then she turns me around and draws my blouse up over my head so I'm sitting with only my much-loosened breeches on. She throws my blouse on the floor beside the bed, and then suddenly yells, 'Oh me Gawd!'

'What? What is it?' I try to rise from the bed but Maggie has grabbed me by the shoulders from behind and has buried her head against my shoulder. She turns my head to look at her.

'Who done that?' she asks.

'What?' I ask, still mystified.

'Yer back! Who done that to yer back, Hawk?' A tear rolls down her cheek.

'It was a flogging on a whale ship, but it was long ago,' I tell her, not wishing to distract her from other things. She is stroking my back and kissing the scars which run like old wickerwork from my neck to my waist. I confess it is a wonderful feeling, Maggie caressing and kissing my back. I want to throw her on the bed and rip her dress off and make love to her. But I don't have the courage.

'Lie down, darlin',' Maggie says. The bed is big but not long enough, and my feet stretch several inches over the end.

'That's right,' Maggie says. 'Now lift yer bum.' Leaning over me, she grabs my breeches on either side of my waist and pulls them down. They get stuck on my stiff cock and I think I must die of shame. But Maggie laughs and takes hold of me. She pushes downwards, and pulls with her free hand, and down go my trousers. I have closed my eyes at her touch, praying to whatever gods there be. Now she pulls my breeches over my ankles and I am naked. 'Oh, Jesus, yiz beautiful, Hawk!' I hear her say. Then there is silence but for the rustle of a garment, and I must open my eyes to look.

Maggie has loosened her gown and it has fallen to her waist. Slowly, she pushes it down further still, until it pools at her feet and she steps out of it. She stands naked with only the magpie still perched on its nest of hair. 'Oh, Maggie,' I venture to say, my voice trembling. 'You are beautiful!'

'Nah. Only cute,' she says, stroking her lovely breasts and then running her hands down the curve of her slim waist and over her thighs. She touches her breasts again, pushing them upwards so the two little nipples look like rose buds. I ache to do the same, to touch and then lick them. I take a quick peek at the neat, little upside-down triangle of fur between her legs but I'm not brave enough to let my eyes linger.

'My, my, Hawk, that be a Maypole worthy of a dance or two,' she giggles, climbing onto the bed so that she is leaning over me. I hope she will kiss me again, lie on me and kiss me, but if she does I don't know how I shall hold out. I feel her lips on my chest and then my stomach, soft little kisses like a butterfly's wings touching against my skin. Then her hands reach out for my cock which lies hard against my stomach. She lifts it and her mouth closes over it. With her hands and with her lips, Maggie begins to stroke up and down.

'Maggie!' I gasp. 'Oh God, Maggie!'

'Shhh!' she murmurs. 'Hold on, Hawk!'

Just as I think I'm gone, she stops. 'A-ah, not yet, darlin', it's Maggie's turn. I wants some black magic! Show me yer tongue.'

Mystified, I do as I'm told and stick out my tongue. Maggie's leaning over me, and she and the magpie are having a gander down into my gob.

'Further!'

I stick it out completely, feeling foolish.

'Now wiggle the tip, up and down and sideways.'

I laugh, but do as Maggie says.

'That's good. Now put it deep into my pussy, darlin', right here.' She rolls over and lies on her back, guiding my hand to the triangle between her legs. I'm completely confounded. Tommo has told me about sixty-nine, but this is thirty-four and a half, a sum I don't know how to do!

Maggie grabs me by the hair and pulls my head towards her so I have no choice but to go down between her beautiful legs, not knowing what to expect. Well it doesn't take a moment to see why my tongue is needed, the way she begins to pant. I caress her with my tongue for all I am worth, not knowing if I am doing it right, but anxious to please.

'Gentle, Hawk. Talk to me pussy with yer tongue, talk soft, rub nice and slow and . . . oh yes, oh, oh!' I'm amazed at how soon I get the hang of it and how nice it is, Maggie's taste on my tongue.

I put my hands under her bottom and lift her gently to my mouth so that her back is arched and more of her is open to me. Soon her legs are gripped about my neck as I eat from her delectable dish, exploring her hidden places. She begins to moan and whimper as my long tongue moves and flicks over her. Then I find a little button, a sweet, hard little button which I begin to stroke with the very tip of my tongue. Maggie gasps, 'Hawk! Oh Hawk, yes, yes . . . ya bastard, yiz got me! Oh, oh! I'm coming home, darlin'! Oh Jesus! Ooooh . . .' Her hips grind frantically into my face and my tongue darts and moves deeply inside her, as she moans loudly and spills a great sweetness into my mouth, all the while whimpering and sobbing. Then she collapses back into my hands and I lower her gently to the bed, where she rolls away onto her side still moaning with pleasure.

My darling Maggie. I spoon her with my body, her back against my stomach, my hard cock resting between her legs and my arms about her so that my hand cradles her left breast. I rock her like she's a little girl, kissing the back of her neck where her hair is damp with heat.

Maggie rests a while, breathing hard. I can feel her heart beating under my palm. Then as we lie spooned together, her hand takes me by the stem and guides me deeply into her. She takes every inch of me as she moves her beautiful derrière against me, pulling the whole of me into her, then out again to the very tip, then sucking me slowly in again until I think I must die of ecstasy. It is all done slowly and firmly and tightly. She is panting again and I am too, as she leads me into a state of bliss I have never known before, not even on that night with Hinetitama.

Then she pulls away from me and turns to lie on her back. She takes up my glistening branch and feeds it slowly back into her softness, her hand holding my throbbing stem. I can hardly bear the pleasure of it. 'Me breasts, darlin', kiss Maggie's tits,' she says. I put my lips over her right breast, rolling her nipple on my tongue. In a moment it grows hard and her breast seems to swell and stiffen under my tender kissing. 'The other, kiss the other please, darlin',' she urges and I can feel her starting to pump against me as her legs wrap about my waist. I am trying to remember every second of it, in case this should never happen to me again. I want to touch and suck and stroke and make love to every part of her glorious body.

Maggie is now surging against me. It is magical what her pussy can do, and a miracle I have lasted this long. 'Now!' she says abruptly. 'Now, Hawk! Hard! Hard!'

I lift my head from her breast, and put both my hands on her shoulders. Arching my back and neck, I drive downwards so strongly that I fear she must surely split open or the bed must break. My body is drenched with sweat – it runs down my neck and chest, and into my eyes. I have become a wild animal possessed of some instinct which cannot be contained. Maggie is thrashing under me, crying out, and I cannot think but to ride her up and down, my urgent shaft driving with all my force. I am about to burst asunder when Maggie cries out, 'Take me, Hawk. Take my pussy. Fuck Maggie. Fuck me!'

I explode into her, thinking I must surely die, and that if I should, how happy I would be. Maggie cries out, panting and gasping, and I am laughing and crying, so pleased to have made her so happy. It seems to me that I have discovered something two people may do together which allows both to touch the face of a loving God.

And then I see it looking at me! Maggie has lifted her head and reached out her arms to me and I see her damned magpie still on its nest. Though her pretty curls fall every which way from their former neatness, somehow that blasted bird remains undisturbed. It looks at me with its hard, bright eyes, and I shudder.

'Maggie! That bloody bird is still upon your head!'

'Of course. Where else should it be? I told you it's me trademark, goes everywhere with me, Maggie Pye's magpie.'

I try to laugh, yet I don't like it one bit. 'But it's seen everything, you and me, us making love!'

'Hawk! That bird's seen more fucks than you've had hot breakfasts!' She laughs. 'It's a magpie, not a stickybeak!' She stretches out and grins wickedly. 'Don't worry, lovey, it's too busy on its own nest to be bothered with you on yours!' She points to the bottom of the bed to where the golliwog lies sprawled. 'He's the one what's got the dirty mind!'

'Maggie, is that all it was, you and me, just another trick, like another hot breakfast?' I am hurt, even angry, though I know I have no right to be. Maggie has been most generous. Why should I think I hold a special place in her affections?

Maggie looks at me and, for an instant, I think she is going to cry. Then she sniffs and brushes the underside of her nose with her forefinger. 'Hawk, I'm a whore. That's all I am, all I'll ever be. You hear me? Maggie Pye is Maggie Pye and don't you forget it.'

Chapter Seventeen

TOMMO

The Rocks
March 1861

Two things happen at the Rocks on the Sabbath what
always tells me it be Sunday, even when I has the worst head
after a heavy night. The first be the church bells, o' course.
They don't only call folks to worship but also, from the
crack o' dawn onwards, they toll for the week's dead. One
peal for a child, two for a woman and three for a man.
Though I dunno why a man gets three and a child one. I
reckons there ain't nothing what makes you any better than
anyone when you've snuffed it.

The second thing 'bout Sunday is the delicious smell of
roasting meat. It be the only time in the week when the
Rocks don't smell of the shit what comes from the houses of
the wealthy who lives above us in the big houses on the cliffs
above the Argyle Cut. Us lot, what live at the bottom of the
cliffs below them, receives gratis and free of charge the
sewage, what runs over the cliffs into our streets and homes.
There's talk of building sewage pipes to go out to sea but it
ain't happened yet. Maggie Pye, Hawk's sweetheart, says she
can't wait for them pipes to go into the briny, so's when the
rich eat a fine fish, they'll find it stuffed full of their own

432

shit! In the meantime, when the church bells toll, it is mostly for the poor.

Still, some folks here below at the Rocks like to keep up a bit o' decency. If they save a spare florin by the week's end, they'll have a proper Sunday roast. Few if any goes to church, knowing themselves to be of no consequence to God. Instead, while the rich kneel at prayer, the poor partake of the ancient ritual of the Sunday roast. The cottages and skillings here don't have no stoves nor colonial ovens, only open hearths. So the women buy a joint o' meat at the butcher shop and take it to Berry's Bakery, what on a Sunday turn their ovens over to meat-roasting.

Comin' home from me cards one Sunday morning, I happen to pass the bakery and I see women standing in a long line outside – each holding a baking dish with a piece of meat and lots o' taties. Some even has Yorkshire pud. They all be waiting to cook their roast, though it's no more than ten o'clock in the morning.

I stop to have a gander. Inside the bakehouse stand two tables what run the length o' the room and on these you can see two great rows of dishes with more than a hundred baked dinners in the making. Two bakers push the dishes deep into the oven with long poles. The women bring their roast in no later than eleven o'clock and call for them at one. Each woman is charged threepence and given a tin disc with a number on it. Another disc, what's got the same number, is stuck into the roasting joint.

Many's the fight to be seen when the time comes to collect the tucker. Some of the women has gone down to the pub to wait, supped a few drinks and lost their number discs meanwhile. Others remember their particular joint as bein' a much nicer cut o' meat than what they gets back. Often there's a bit of a set-to amongst the women, and the bakers are called on to sort it out. Then they make the offenders wait 'til last, in case they are just chancing their arm, hoping to steal another's dinner.

Mostly, though, waiting for the roast is a friendly time, with poor folk catching up on a bit o' gossip. And later every street and lane smells of mutton, pork and roast beef as the women hurries home to their families so's the joints still be steaming hot for their triumphant arrival.

After I sees this, I tell Hawk about it. What a damn fool idea that were. A do-good expression comes upon his gob, like God's touched him on the nose or something. 'Righto, Tommo,' says he, 'the first quid you win at cards on a Saturday night goes to the butcher and the grocer for meat and potatoes. We're going to feed the urchins with Sunday roasts!' I'm none too happy about this. Sometimes the first pound is hard-earned and then, quick as a flash it's purloined by Hawk, and I has to begin grafting and relocating 'til I've earned it back again. Knowing that if I don't take a quid right off them brats will go hungry is a bother I don't need at the card table. Hawk don't mind reminding me o' my responsibility neither. 'Don't forget my urchins, Tommo!' he always says before a Saturday game.

Hawk's bought ten roasting dishes and every Sunday, he's up at dawn peeling spuds. By seven o'clock he's at the butcher's, haggling like a fishwife over the size and quality of the meat, demanding with that big, scary smile of his that a portion o' cracklin' and basting lard be thrown in for free. By half-nine he's in line outside the bakehouse along with twenty or so dirty little ragamuffins, each pair holdin' a dish, with meat and potatoes set out pretty as a picture.

There's our Hawk, mother of the unloved and unwanted, standing two and a half foot taller than all the old biddies in line. They're teasing him about the size of his brood and what's in his breeches – all of 'em havin' a grand old cackle like people do when they's expectin' a good feed. Soon as it be ready, there's Hawk and Maggie Pye down by Semicircular Quay, carving meat for fifty or more little brats, what guzzles on the proceeds of me toils like a pack o' starvin' dock rats.

Mr Sparrow were anxious that we finds ourselves better lodgings as soon as we was able, in a more respectable part o' town, but Hawk would have none of it. He seems to want to stay here and look after his urchins – and me. All he agreed was that we should get better rooms, nearer the Argyle Cut, which is where we be now. Hawk loves his brats and they loves him, following him 'round like he's the Pied Piper, a ragged army of starvin' kids what he tries to feed best he can. Every chophouse knows him for he goes knocking on doors to beg for leftover scraps for his ragamuffins. In the evenings, down by the ferryman's wharf, he can be heard telling them tales o' derring-do. They listen enchanted and for a short time seem to forget the hunger gnawing at their bloated bellies.

Today, though, it's gunna be Flo what feeds them their Sunday tucker, for Hawk, Maggie and me are goin' up the Parramatta River to a prize fight. In the evening Mr Sparrow has arranged a game o' stud poker at the Woolpack Hotel. 'Some of the Irish gentlemen,' he cocks an eyebrow, 'if there be such a commodity, fancy their luck at the card table. I count on you to oblige them and to win 'andsomely.' He sticks a bony finger in me chest. 'So mind you do, lad.' I confess, there ain't much left what I likes about Mr Sparrow.

I ain't all that happy about Hawk and Maggie Pye being sweethearts neither. After all, she is a whore, or as the sporting gentlemen o' Sydney would call her, a crinoline cruiser. This is the name for a somewhat higher class o' slag,

435

but still a slag. Crinoline cruisers hang about sporting occasions where respectable women ain't found, like dog fights, bare-knuckle bouts, cockfights, card games, and the horse races at Homebush.

I has to admit though that Hawk seems a happy man these days. He and Maggie has been together more than six months now. When I warn him about catching the pox from her, he nods, with a serious sort o' look on his face, but I know he ain't gunna take no notice of me. He's talking about takin' Maggie back to meet Mary, for Gawd's sake! In fact, the two of them women ain't so unlike. Maggie's bright but also has a terrible quick temper like Mary, and a tongue to put many a tar to shame. But she's witty with it and good company.

Maggie likes her gin, though I be the last to judge her for that. After all, grog comes with the job for us both. Gin and women is often an ugly combination, though, and it don't seem likely to lead to connubial bliss. But Hawk, so sensible and solemn, won't hear no ill spoken of Maggie Pye and thinks the world of her. I tell him not to mention the prospects we has in Tasmania, for he is a man of potential wealth. He promises he won't, and I know it be most important to him that Maggie loves him for hisself. I just hope she ain't a gold digger looking for a life of ease at Hawk's expense. I'm gunna keep a good eye on that Maggie Pye!

As for yours truly, I can't say I fancy any of the women around here. Me darlin' Makareta has spoiled me for the average tart, I reckon, though I don't let me thoughts dwell on her much these days. Nor me daughter, Hinetitama, neither. My new mistress, the opium pipe, be a great help in that regard. It takes away much of me desire for female company too. It's a blessing that it does, for good women be thin on the ground in these parts o' the colony.

Any respectable girl what reaches the age of sixteen gets herself married quick smart. If you sees a younger girl on the arm of a man, you can safely guess she be a slut in apprentice, or one what's been on the game for a few years already.

The Rocks don't hold much hope for the bloke what seeks a lady's companionship. Instead, the Botanical Gardens is where the fashionables of Sydney's fair sex may be found. This be where young toffs go to meet the members of the opposite sex. For a laugh I go up there meself one day. Hawk tells me they ain't really Botanical Gardens – not like the Kew Gardens of London, what's a grand creation with exotic trees and shrubs o' great variety, growing in a green and watered landscape. What we has in Sydney is two rows of stiff gum trees in a long avenue leading into a wasteland of dusty ground. When it's dry, the slightest breeze blows up clouds o' sand and dirt.

But if you go up to these scrawny old Gardens today, you'll see many gay parasols surrounded by young coves dressed in their Sunday best. The female specimens beneath these bright sunshades only show themselves if you can push through their admirers for a closer look. Most has long since passed the summer of their life and make much use of powder and lip rouge and extravagant bonnets. They is expensively attired and bejewelled, their gold trinkets no doubt the gifts of admirers who've failed to make the final journey to the four-poster bed.

At Semicircular Quay, the boats from Europe are always met by scores o' young swells hoping to find, for the purpose of marriage, any single female within five years of their age. At card games and the like, I has heard many a bachelor say that there ain't much choice among Sydney's unmarried ladies. The demand is great, the supply small, and Europe a long way away, so that the poor specimens what does exist are quickly snapped up by the sons o' the goldocracy.

But like I said, I ain't much worried by all this. I'm busy with me cards, me pipe, and when I can get it, me bottle. The life I've taken up with Mr Sparrow don't let me drink during the daylight hours and only a little during my card games at night. Still, I usually glug down the better part of a black bottle before dawn. But I always keep my senses about me, 'specially now I has a new way to ease me pain.

I found the Angel's Kiss the very first night I played cards for Mr Sparrow, in a gambling den owned by Mr Tang Wing Hung. He's an important man among the Chinese what comes to Sydney from the gold diggings. He's tall for a Mongolian, six foot, and thin as a rake. He don't say much but Mr Sparrow reckons there ain't much business among the Chinese what he don't control, and says his bony yellow fingers may be found in many a pie concocted by a Sydney broker or merchant.

That first night in Chinatown, I did exactly what Mr Sparrow told me. I acted the country bumpkin, a wealthy settler's son from Tasmania, innocent of the ways of the world. There were no need for Mr Sparrow to blow a smoke ring so that I might resort to 'other' methods of winning – me skill proved sufficient. I cleaned up a pretty penny and earned five pounds.

By dawn's light, when the game finally came to an end, me head was so painful I couldn't bear it. When he heard about this, Mr Sparrow talked to Tang Wing Hung and I was took into a small room and given the opium pipe. The pain lifted at once and I came away most grateful to the Angel's Kiss.

Hawk is most worried about me new medicine, but I has assured him I use it sparingly and only when me head hurts. The black bottle is still old Tommo's first love!

I am now a solid member of Mr Sparrow's sporting fraternity and Hawk and me is well set up. I earn a fair bit from me card games most nights – though not always so much as five pounds. Mr Sparrow is talkin' of a partnership, now that I've learnt much about what he calls 'the predilections o' sporting gentlemen'. Mr Sparrow dabbles in sports of all kinds: horse races, dog races, cockfights, dog fights, gambling and o' course women and opium. He promises that I shall be a part of all of this if I play me cards right.

In all these months I ain't found a broadsman what can better me and it's grand to have a quid or two. After me first night at the game in Chinatown, I were very glad to see Hawk's smiling phiz outside the pub, as me note had asked. Hawk takes three pounds of the five I've earned. We goes off to a tailor in Pitt Street, by the name of Barney Isaacs. There Hawk pays for a suit o' clothes, two blouses, and two pairs of hose what he's had measured up for himself. He said somethin' about paying his own way, what's a bit of a laugh as it's my earnings what's paying for it! But I don't begrudge him none. As soon as his clobber were made up and boots bought from the Italian bootmaker in Bligh Street, Hawk gets a position as clerk at Tucker & Co. in George Street.

Hawk got the job 'cause of his experience in Mary's brewery and his knowledge of hops and beer. Captain James Tucker, the brother of the founder, William Tucker, is a wine and spirit merchant. Even though Hawk knows little of this side of the liquor trade, Captain Tucker seems pleased to have me brother in his employ. He were once a ship's captain himself and likes the fact that Hawk has been to sea. My twin has proved a careful bookkeeper and is always happy to help out, loading the drays and stacking shelves when times is busy in the warehouse. This counts for a great deal with Captain Tucker, what ain't a man to stand on ceremony and will himself roll up his sleeves when needed.

And so we've made our lives in Sydney. Hawk is still my keeper though I don't see that much of him – only at breakfast when I returns from a game, not always sober, and then again at supper. He puts me to bed after a breakfast of eggs and bacon or fish, and gives me a good dose o' Seidlitz powders so that when I get up on his return from work, I ain't got too much of a hangover. Often when it's just the two of us, he reads to me from newspapers and books. He gets me to do the same, so that I be ever improving, catching up on what I lost all those years in the wilderness.

This morning I ain't retiring to bed though, for we are on a family jaunt, making our journey up the river. The prize fight be organised by none other than Fat Fred, Mr Sparrow's henchman and the colony's principal procurer o' prize fights.

Mr Sparrow and Fat Fred can always depend on a big crowd as they are the only proper prize-fight promoters in the colony. Prize fights is against the law and most comes about as a result of a direct challenge from one recognised fighter to another. Then a venue is hastily arranged behind a pub or sly grog shop. When news of the fight spreads by mouth from pub to pub, the bookmakers and amateur oddsmen turn up and the betting begins, the odds changing constantly during the progress o' the contest. Often the ring is simply marked out with stones on the grass and the crowd what gathers around the fight surges backwards and forwards into the ring as the fighters advance and retreat.

Mr Sparrow, however, will tolerate no such higgledy-piggledy set-ups. He 'licenses' – some would say owns – all the bookmakers at his fights and rakes in a percentage from each, closing the betting after the start of the bout. At other fights it ain't unusual, if a favourite looks like he'll be beat, for some of the crowd to storm the ring and declare the fight 'no contest' so's to get their bets back. But Fat Fred has the rings well guarded by ex-pugs and bothermen what are prepared to spill considerable claret if a member o' the crowd comes too close.

A prize fight what's organised by Fat Fred be a most popular event, and despite today's fight being writ up for weeks beforehand in *Bell's Life in Sydney*, the police don't seem to know of it.

Maggie is much excited at the prospect of the fight and an outing in the country. She has packed a large basket of cold mutton, roast taties, a fresh baked loaf, three bottles of the best beer and some other tidbits from Flo's mum, what is a most excellent cook. Even if the fight be stopped by the Parramatta traps, Maggie promises we shall have us a lovely picnic.

Maggie never works the fights, even though they be a rich fishing ground for Sydney's tarts. Instead, she dresses up in her finest black crinoline with a black-and-white silk bonnet, her 'magpie' colours as she calls them. She takes a great deal o' pleasure from being seen on Hawk's arm at these events. Maggie Pye's become a right dolly bird, cocking a snook at the other girls as they shows their tits in their gaudy silks and wiggles their hips, trolling for a gold fish – what in their lingo means searchin' out a rich bloke!

We are all set to go upriver to Parramatta Town aboard one of the little Billy steamers leaving from the Quay. Maggie has persuaded us not to take the railway what has recently reached Parramatta Town but is still somewhat a novelty. Hawk reckons it'll be nice to be out on the water again and I don't give a bugger which way we goes.

Our steamer seems decked out as though for a festive voyage. She's brightly coloured with a copper funnel and a wide-rimmed chimney, and her shade awnings are of a bright purple and ochre. We're in for a merry time, the boat being full o' folk what's goin' to the fight, though we're calling it a picnic so's to fool any copper who's aboard in disguise.

Just as we're about to cast off, a great noise is heard from the wharf and we see a small tribe of blacks running towards the steamer. They comes on board panting, laughing and cussing, carrying and dragging small children. Several are pulling chains o' kangaroo dogs behind them. They are nearly all drunk and some of the passengers shout to the crew to 'off-load the niggers'. The newcomers climb up the ship's ropes and stumble about the decks.

We is hardly clear of the wharf when some of the black women take off their blankets and start fighting. They's cussing and screaming, rolling, kicking and punching, their blood and snot all over the deck. The kangaroo dogs are barking and the little black urchins are howling their heads off.

To the cheering and yoicking of the rougher folk amongst the white passengers, the women sets to hurting each other. They's pulling out tufts o' hair and one of 'em, a fat gin with breasts hanging to her waist, bites a large piece off her opponent's ear and dances about, holding it aloft for all to see. Meanwhile their husbands go 'round with their hats and begs tuppences off the spectators.

Some of the passengers reckon it's all a grand lead-up to the prize fight this afternoon. But Hawk puts a stop to it. He takes ten shillings from his purse and gives it to the bloke what looks to be their leader, asking that the women stop their scratching and caterwauling. There is some protest from the whites when they see what he is doing, but Hawk ignores them. One fat rowdy shouts, 'Garn then, nigger, leave it off! Let's have a bit o' sport from the black bastards!'

Hawk stops and walks over to this cove. 'What say you and I have a bit of sport, then?' he suggests, and a sick smile grows upon the bloke's phiz.

'Begs your pardon,' he says backing away, as the rest of his mates laugh at him.

The Aboriginal chief carries a large stuffed snakeskin coiled about his neck and seems most impressed with Hawk, what's as black as he is, twice as wide and two foot taller. Hawk ain't afraid to stand up to the white devils neither as they can see. Grabbing a big stick from one of the other men, the Aborigine beats the women over their heads and backs, shouting at 'em in their tongue, 'til they stop fighting and stumbles away to lick their wounds. The chief signals that he wants Hawk to take back his money and, for the sake o' peace, Hawk finally accepts it.

After this, the journey is pleasant enough. I look about the little steamer with interest as we make our way towards Parramatta. Dozens of live ducks, tied by their bright yellow feet, has been thrown upon several trusses of hay. Aft, four pigs grunt and snuffle amongst a pile o' cabbage leaves, and a donkey and two nanny goats are secured by their hind legs to the railings. In one corner I counts twenty wicker baskets of fish, some still alive, bars o' silver in the sunlight.

On either side o' the river the land slopes gently upwards, green from the recent summer rains. The gum trees what grew here not so long ago have all been rooted out and many a stump lies with its tangled roots sprouting like Medusa's head out of a great ball o' red clay. Along the river bank, poplar and willow has taken their place and the hand of civilisation is everywhere to be seen. Farmers have cleared the bush and tilled the land to beyond the horizon. Each farm is much like the one beside it, a homestead sat upon a farmyard square, the borders made up of a windbreak of fruit trees. These be lemons and oranges for the most part, though here and there I sees some quince and pomegranate. In every vegetable garden is cabbages, what must fetch a good price at market to judge by their numbers. Everywhere, there are rows o' green cabbages, each in its own nest of leaves. Sometimes there's a rose garden, what makes a circular patch of flowers at the very centre of the vegetable garden, and Maggie thinks this most romantic.

When we reach Parramatta Town, several of the passengers get off, including the Aborigine tribe. Yowling brats is taken by one arm and dragged off the boat by cursing gins, some still bleeding from their wounds. The old chief strikes willy-nilly at the brats and the dogs and the motley mob tumble together down the gangplank.

The rest of us continue two or three bends upriver, some four miles southwest beyond the town. Here we pulls into shore and the steamer moors beside a crude wharf made up of a few slippery logs.

The skipper announces that the Billy steamer can't go no further as the river ahead is silted up. We has to walk from here. The countryside about us is heavily timbered, scrubby terrain. The captain points to a small hill what has been cleared of trees, atop of which sit two fair-sized buildings – neither showing no sign of life. He explains these be a school and a church for the Irish navvies what's building the railway west to the Blue Mountains. Their camp lies beyond the hill, and cannot be seen from the river.

We're told to walk around the hill to the Katoomba Road, turning right to A'Beckett's Bridge and the Vauxhall Inn half a mile or so away. There we is to turn left into Dog Trap Road, what we're to follow beyond the Irish camp. And so we sets out with two or three dozen others to find the location of the prize fight.

Hawk and me is dressed in coats and collars and Maggie turned out in all her finery. We ain't dressed for a hike and are most uncomfortable trudging along. Soon our coats are placed on top o' Maggie's basket what Hawk carries, and our collar studs loosened. To our surprise, Maggie – never the sensible one – has brung old boots to wear until we gets to the ring. It's wet and muddy underfoot and by the time we reach the road the hem of her dress is soaked all the same.

The road when we gets to it is busy with folks walking from Parramatta Town railway station. Added to those of us on foot are the hacks, sulkies, drags, carriages and carts all headin' for the fight. A coach filled to the gunnels with merry punters passes us by. The coves inside laugh and joke at us what walks, and many an insult is hurled back in return.

It is only when we reach Dog Trap Road that we see the true size of the crowd. It be so full o' punters that we must walk at snail's pace. Mr Sparrow and Fat Fred has chosen their venue with a good knowledge of the district. The Irish are all around here and these merry punters pours out of their shacks to join the Sydney and Parramatta Town throng. There never were a keener sportsman than an Irishman with a dram or two o' whiskey in his belly and a week's wages in his pocket.

The navvies' camp on Dog Trap Road is a miserable sort o' place, with huts made mostly of slab and bark. Mangy dogs, snotty children and hard-faced women comes out to stare at us. Many of the smaller brats are naked and much in need of a wash. These are the people brought in by the government to meet the labour shortage what's been caused by the colony's men flocking to the goldfields. Some folks now reckon the bog Irish, as they's known, is lower than all but the Aborigines, but I wonder who they be to judge!

Dog Trap Road is rutted and rocky and the many conveyances what have thundered down the Katoomba Road are having trouble travelling along it. They hinder our progress and gets a fair amount o' curry from the mob on foot. The road ends suddenly, well short o' the spot where the fight will take place. The various vehicles can go no further, and the toffs and sporting gentlemen will need to huff and puff a good quarter of a mile through thick scrub.

The place Fat Fred and Mr Sparrow has picked for their fight is an inspiration. It turns out to be a sort o' treeless hollow, what Hawk calls a natural amphitheatre. The prize ring lies at the centre and there is room all about for several thousand folk to look down upon it. Fat Fred has built a roped enclosure directly about the four sides of the ring for the swells. It must have took a good many hours to get the place ready for the sporting gentlemen. Compliments of three red tickets given to me by me lord and master Mr Sparrow, Hawk, Maggie and meself is numbered among 'em.

As we make our way to the enclosure, Hawk with Maggie on one arm and the basket on the other becomes the focus of the crowd's attention.

'Who's the nigger on stilts?' someone calls out.

'It's two niggers, one atop the other, dressed in a suit!' some wit replies.

'No, it's Red Riding Hood and the big bad wolf!' cries another.

'Look, he's got his dinner on her bonnet, the last o' the four 'n' twenty blackbirds!' offers the first, all to the merriment of the crowd.

Hawk smiles but I know all this attention don't sit well with him. Still, the crowd is friendly enough. Hawk stands two foot taller than most, a black giant with Maori markings on his phiz and a young tart on his arm with a magpie nested in her hat. We must make a funny old sight as we join the fat sportsmen what's paid good money to be here.

Maggie has her pretty nose in the air and wears a big

smile. She knows she's watched by folks on every side of the enclosure and acts every inch the respectable woman. All the other working girls in their ribbons and bows is here to troll for sporting gents what might take a girl to one of the inns along the Parramatta Road for a glass and an hour or two o' dalliance. Today Maggie ain't working. When a gentleman sportsman tries to catch her eye, she ignores him, giving a superior sniff. I laughs, thinking to meself that her just being at a prize fight tells all there is to know about her. She's happy though, and as we take our seat, she flashes me a smile.

The ring is twenty-four foot square, roped in two spans and raised two foot from the ground so all can see. It's hard to believe the Parramatta traps could miss an occasion of this size, and I chuckles when I recalls Mr Sparrow saying how two of the three troopers responsible for law and order in town found an urgent need to visit Newcastle this very day. The one left in charge has had a severe attack of the trots and may not move further abroad than the shit-pit in the backyard.

Much of the excitement about today's fight is because it be between two heavies – most fighters being in the range of eight and nine stone, little fellas like meself. But today, Ben Dunn, the Sydney heavy, takes on a Welsh miner by the name of Thomas Thomas. The Welshman is but a week in the country, though *Bell's Life in Sydney* declares him a serious contender. He has eight fights to his credit and all of them won against well-known English opponents.

The betting is heavy on Dunn, for his form is well known. Among the heavies, there ain't no boxer in the colony that he ain't defeated, and several more than once. But some in the crowd reckon that the local heavies be soft, backwater fighters, and that Dunn has yet to face a real opponent. They think a bloke from the old country will give the currency lad a lesson in the art o' fisticuffs. Today's fight will prove them right or no.

The two fighters are called to the ring at three with the noonday heat now gone but with plenty o' daylight left. Mr Sparrow is ever present, clasping mawleys and spouting opinions, ever the jovial host. He is as busy with the nabobs and toffs as a one-legged man in a kicking contest and has no time to greet the nigger, the tart and the cardsharp.

Fat Fred is the referee and announcer and stands in the ring in a lather o' sweat. He holds a hailing funnel and constantly wipes his gob with a large, red, miner's bandanna. We all stand as the fighters enter the ring.

Maggie is on her feet at once, hopping from one leg to another. She's on tippy-toes with excitement, having given up all show o' respectable womanhood. Her bet of five pounds is on the Welshman, what's at long odds and I reckon a risky gamble. He is only a week off the ship and must be out of condition after the two-month voyage.

The two men is stripped to the waist and wear spiked boots to hold their grip in the ring. The fight is at catch weight so their weights ain't announced. The Welshman is much bigger than Dunn, what ain't large for a heavy, being estimated at around thirteen stone with no lard on any part o' him. This can't be said of his opponent what looks a stone and a half heavier and carries quite a belt o' fat about his waist. His titties wobble as he jumps about the ring to warm up.

'It don't look good for your man, Maggie,' I says. 'Ben Dunn be much the better lookin' specimen.'

'It's the heavies, Tommo. Speed don't count. Reach and power is what does it. The Welshman's got three or four inches on Dunn and he's a miner, ain't he?' She points to Thomas. 'Look at 'is arms – they can pump all afternoon!'

I has a quid on Dunn but there's something to what Maggie says. 'Nah, he'll not be able to take it in the bread basket,' I says hopefully, patting me stomach. 'Look at Ben Dunn, every inch the wild colonial boy!'

'Wild! Jesus, Tommo, he be about as wild as a nun's confession!'

'What d'ya mean?'

'Can't get it up for the girlies!'

I look quickly at Hawk to see how he takes this but in the middle of all the excitement he's sitting reading a book. He ain't taking no notice o' nothing 'til the fight proper begins.

'You'd know about that, o' course,' I says now, sarcastic-like.

Maggie ain't the least offended. 'Oath I'd know!' she agrees. 'I went to Johnny Sullivan's Sparring Rooms in Pitt Street. You know Johnny, the Champion of the Light Weights, we's good mates . . .'

'Mates? Ha, ha!' I laughs. 'Come off it, Maggie, yer talking to old Tommo here!'

Maggie stares at me hard. 'You know what's your problem, Tommo Solomon? You've got a dirty mind! Mates! That's all. Johnny and me grew up together, in the same bloody gutter. We're mates, and always will be!'

I takes another glimpse over at Hawk, to see if he's heard Maggie tellin' me off, but his eyes is fixed on his book. 'Sorry, Maggie,' says I.

'No need,' Maggie replies. 'If Johnny wants it from me, he can 'ave it for free any day 'cept Sunday when it belongs only to Hawk. Johnny's a champ o' more than fisticuffs!'

'So, what about him?' I asks, pointing to Dunn what's standing in the middle of the ring, throwing punches in the air and snuffling like a prime porker. 'What's he got to do with yer mate Sullivan?'

'Oh yeah, him. Well, he were working out at Johnny's rooms last summer, see, and I hears about it. At the time, he were my hero and I figures I'll drop by – see 'im in the flesh so t' speak. It ain't unusual for a tart to be seen 'anging around a prize-fighter. The cove at the door what knows I know Johnny says he ain't there. But I tell him I've come to see, you know, Ben Dunn, so he lets me in.'

Maggie stops and sniffs, as though she's about to tell what she'd rather not. 'I goes in and there's a few fighters sparrin' and workin' at the bag and so I sits at the back o' the room. Ben Dunn's in the ring, sparring with a big hairy bugger, a fighter what I've never seen before. Then after a while he climbs down from the ring and goes into the changing room.'

Maggie gives a little smile. 'It were stupid an' all, but you know me, nothing ventured, nothing gained, so I walks in behind him.

'"Hello," says I.

'He turns about. "Who are you?" he asks.

'"Maggie. Maggie Pye," I says smiling. "I'm one o' ya greatest admirers, Mr Dunn."

'"You a whore?" he asks.

'I'm in me glad rags, showing everything I've got, ribbons and bows, and tits near poppin' out. "Well, I ain't the governor's wife," I says cheeky, giving him another flash of me pearly whites.

'"How much?" he wants t' know.

'"This ain't a business visit, Mr Dunn. It's just that I admires ya very much and wanted to tell ya in person!"

'But Dunn's got a look in his eyes what I've seen often enough when a man's goin' to do something bad, and suddenly I'm frightened. He spits on 'is hands and rubs them together. By now I'm walkin' backwards towards the door. Quick as a flash he's moved 'round me and stands blocking the doorway.

'"Not so fast, Maggie Pye!" he says, smiling, but it ain't the right sort o' smile and believe you me, I knows every kind o' smile a man can give. "If you're not to be paid and you're here on a social visit, then you wouldn't mind obliging . . ." He wiggles his hips and thrusts 'em forward to show what he means, holding his hands out like he's hangin' onto me hips.

'"It ain't convenient. I don't do knee-tremblers, I ain't that sort o' whore!" I says. "Lemme go, please!" I try to push him aside so I can pass by.

'But he sticks his arm across the doorway and looks over his shoulder. "Lads!" he shouts. "Come 'n' get yer Christmas box!"'

Maggie looks up at me. 'Don't need to tell yiz the rest, do I? They rapes me, all ten of the bastards!' She is quite matter o' fact as she speaks, though her voice is soft. She points to the ring where Ben Dunn is still snuffling and punching the air, glaring at the Welshman. 'All 'cept him, your wild colonial boy. He's sittin' on a bench against the wall with his dick in his hand!'

'The mongrels – they's always there waiting,' I whispers to meself.

'What's you say?' asks Maggie.

'Nothing. He's a mongrel, Maggie. I put a quid on him but I hopes he gets the daylights knocked out o' him by the Welshman!'

Maggie laughs. 'Thank you, Tommo. But I ain't finished yet. You know what he says? After them what's raped me has scarpered, when I'm trying to put me torn dress in order?'

I shake me head. 'Please Maggie, you've told enough.'

But she goes on. 'He says, "Maggie, if you wants tickets to me next fight, come see me again."

'"Fuck off," I tells him. "I might be beaten, but I ain't broke."

'"What did you say, girlie?" he asks and grabs me nose

between his finger and thumb and twists it. His 'arf hard cock's still hanging out o' his pants.'

Maggie shrugs and grins. 'I know I should've kept me gob shut. I can either cry or lose me temper, so o' course I gets it wrong, don't I? I lose me temper.

' "Fuck off, arsehole, I wouldn't shit in your mouth 'case I got bit by somethin' poisonous!" I screams at him, scratching at his face. I feel the first haymaker to the side of me head and down I goes. I know well enough to stay down, and so I plays possum and he kicks me 'til he thinks I'm out to it.

'Then the big hairy bloke comes back in and Dunn fucks him from behind, right there beside me, the two of 'em grunting away while the blood runs down me head. It's been a long time since I've took a worse beating.'

Maggie sighs. 'I must've eventually passed out because Johnny Sullivan finds me an hour later. He's scared every bone in me body is broke. But it turns out that only most of me ribs are busted and two teeth at the back is missing. The rest is only bruises and blood, though I couldn't walk for two weeks nor earn a penny for nigh on a month. It were Johnny what looked after me.'

I wonder if Hawk's heard any of this sorry tale. Maggie has kept her voice low and there's a lot o' noise from the crowd anyway. Sure enough, me twin's still happily reading his book, as though he's sitting in some quiet library and not among five thousand screamin' punters. When Hawk carks it I'm gunna put a book in his hands and half a dozen more in his coffin, 'case it's a long journey to heaven!

Well, the fight begins and it's all bluff in the first round. The two heavies walks 'round each other, sniffing and snorting, and Dunn lands a good blow to Thomas's chest. This is returned a minute later, to the side of Dunn's head. Then

Dunn grabs Thomas and throws him to the ground. End of round one.

Round two is more of the same but this time the Welshman catches Dunn a tremendous blow on the chin and the local boy goes down. He's back up on his feet quick-smart. A knockdown means the round be over. It looks as though Maggie's picked the right bloke.

During round three, Dunn spends most of the time staying out o' the way. Still he manages to hit the Welshman two good blows to the stomach, and Thomas grabs him and pulls him down.

By round five, Dunn can see the Welshman is tiring so he steps up the pace. In return for three weak blows to the shoulders, he manages half a dozen of his own into his opponent's bread basket. Suddenly Thomas clutches at his stomach and Dunn unleashes a big uppercut, what knocks the Welshman sprawling to the canvas. It's clear to all that he won't get up, and his ring man throws in the sponge.

The fight's all over in five rounds. It's taken less than an hour, and the punters ain't happy. They boos and hisses, the toffs included. Many has come a great way and they wants more for their money. The booing gets louder and many around us shout that the fight's been fixed.

I puts an arm around Maggie. 'Bad luck, love, the good uns seldom win in this world.'

At this minute, Ben Dunn comes to the ropes near us and signals to Fat Fred. They talk a moment together, and then Fat Fred nods. Signalling to his minders to lift him into the ring, he grabs a hailing funnel and calls for quiet.

'Gentlemen and, er, ladies! Your attention, please!' He keeps at it 'til the crowd shuts up. 'Mr Ben Dunn, heavyweight champion of the colony, is aware of yer disappointment at the duration of today's bout and he agrees to fight anyone here for his purse won from Thomas

Thomas of one hundred pounds. The contender puts only five pounds down as a sign o' good will, winner takes all!' Fat Fred pauses, looking over the heads of the crowd and then, as though he feels he should add somethin' to his offer, shouts, 'The winner gets the title as well!'

The crowd bursts into laughter and more jeering. It's a joke of course. No man unless he be drunk or a fool will pay five pounds to have his head knocked off.

'Is there not an Irishman among you who's game enough?' Fat Fred taunts. I imagine there be plenty of Irishmen game enough but none big enough, them poor bastards being starved by the English for generations and this lot being the poorest physical specimens of them all.

'Have we got five pounds, Tommo?' Hawk asks suddenly.

'Sure, it's me stake for tonight's poker game,' I replies.

'Give it here,' he says, putting out his hand.

'Hawk, are you mad? You're not gunna . . . ?' I point to Ben Dunn what's dancing about the ring.

'Come on, Tommo,' he says impatient. 'Pass it over!' I hands him the fiver and he walks up to the ring and holds it out to Fat Fred.

It be the first and probably last time I sees Fat Fred smile, as he takes the money and holds it up. Over the hailing funnel he announces, 'Gentlemen and punters, we have a contender!'

There's a roar from the crowd as Hawk lifts himself into the ring. Maggie is sobbing and laughing and jumping up and down and biting her little clenched fist. She digs in her handbag and holds up a pound note. 'Who'll give me ten to one odds the nigger wins!' she shouts. The punters rush to the enclosure to take up Maggie's odds.

'Maggie, don't be a fool!' I yell as I climbs into the ring to be beside Hawk. Mr Sparrow follows me and we stands beside Hawk as he undoes the buttons on his blouse. He pulls it off and hands it to me, and the crowd sees him proper for the first time. He stands a foot above the heavyweight, and is six inches broader at the shoulder and six inches narrower at the waist. There ain't an ounce o' fat on his shiny black torso what's all power and muscle.

As for me, I'm plain terrified. He's gunna get the hiding of his life from the Sydney bruiser what's had more than fifty fights, with only four lost. Hawk knows nothing o' fighting with his fists and his size'll only make it easier for Dunn to hit him.

The fight begins, with Fat Fred the referee. Just as I expected, the champion of the colony hits me twin at will. I scream at Hawk to grab Dunn and bring him down so that the round may end. But Hawk don't hear me or don't care to listen, and they fight for fifteen minutes, though he barely lands a blow.

Dunn has a grin on his face as he smashes blow after blow into Hawk's body and head. Soon Hawk's left eye is closed and claret streams from his nose. But me brother won't go down. Nearly half an hour has passed and the crowd, what admires his bravery, is beginnin' to yell for the nigger.

Dunn ain't used to staying on his feet this long without a rest and he begins to slow somewhat. I reckon there's less strength to his punches but still he's making mincemeat out o' Hawk.

'Go down, take a rest!' I shout at him. But Hawk stands defenceless in the ring and won't move. I can't bear it no more and I look for the sponge to throw it into the air. 'Where's the bloody sponge?' I scream at Mr Sparrow. 'We got to end it now!'

Then I see Hawk starting to move around his opponent. It's like he's slowly come to life. Suddenly his arm shoots out and he hits Dunn on the nose. The champion's face seems to cave in as he drops to his knees, a look of utmost surprise on his gob. It's thirty-five minutes after the start of the fight and round one is ended. The mob howls with delight.

Hawk comes to his corner. 'We're gunna stop it, ya hear!' I yells at him. 'He's killin' ya!'

'Have you had enough, lad?' Mr Sparrow asks.

'Course he has!' I scream. 'We're stopping now! Where's the bloody sponge?'

Hawk is panting and don't say nothing. There's blood in his mouth and a steady flow from his nose and I still can't find the sponge. I takes up his shirt and, dipping it in the bucket o' water, washes his face. Then I squeeze water into his mouth for him to rinse. He spits out the water into the bucket and his breathing starts t' come back. Dunn has also tottered to his corner and sits there, glowering.

'It's all over, Hawk,' I says, patting his huge shoulder. 'You've fought good, mate, but ya can't go back in there for more!'

Hawk looks at me through his one eye. 'I must, Tommo, or the mongrels win. Tell Maggie the next round is for her,' he pants. 'I cannot last beyond it.' I shake me head at his stubbornness, for my body aches with his, and I know how bad he hurts. Sometimes, being Hawk's twin be a most painful affair.

The second round is called five minutes later and it's as though Hawk has it all figured out in his head. Dunn is recovered but is very cautious. Hawk walks around him, always stayin' on the western side of the ring – he won't let Dunn out of the eastern half. Then I realise what he's doing! Hawk's making Dunn face into the sun, what leaves him half-blind. He sets about him now. There ain't much polish to Hawk's punches, but they comes straight and hard. Each blow seems like it must break something inside the champion.

Dunn hits Hawk several times, but the strength seems to have left him. Hawk just walks through the champion's punches and keeps coming, sometimes hitting Dunn twice in as many seconds. The smack of his enormous fists into the flesh of the other fighter makes the ringside crowd wince and moan.

Dunn tries to pull Hawk down but Hawk's too strong and throws him off. Then, with the Sydney fighter slightly off-balance and his arms spread wide, Hawk hits him on the chin with a clean right-cross. It starts from way back and is so well timed and so hard that it lifts the heavyweight champion of the colony off his feet and, some will later swear, three feet into the air. Dunn's out cold before he hits the deck. His corner can't do nothin' but throw in the sponge. The fight is over. Dunn won't be rising to his feet again 'til well after sunset.

'Well now, my dear Ace O' Spades!' Mr Sparrow says to me, taking the missing sponge out o' his coat pocket. 'I think we've found ourselves a true champion!'

Fat Fred is laughing, and I don't reckon nobody in the history of the world has ever seen Fat Fred laugh. He grabs the hailing funnel and holds Hawk's arm up. 'Ladies and gentlemen, in a winner-takes-all contest, I give you Hawk Solomon, the new Heavyweight Champion of the Colony o' New South Wales!'

'And future champion of the whole bleedin' world!' Mr Sparrow shouts beside me.

I rushes up to Hawk and hugs him about the waist. Then I sees Maggie climbing up into the ring, crying and laughing as she too rushes into me brother's arms. 'Hawk, I loves ya! I loves ya,' she sobs.

The crowd is yelling and trying to reach the ring to shake

Hawk's hand. The minders kick at them wildly. It's all they can do to keep them at bay, for the mob is determined to carry Hawk off on its shoulders. The din is something terrible but I still hears what Hawk says to Maggie.

'Maggie,' he pants. 'Please, Maggie, next time stay away from Johnny Sullivan's Sparring Rooms!'

Chapter Eighteen

HAWK

The Rocks
May 1861

Life has become most tedious for me of late. Everywhere I go I am followed by the Sydney lads who see me as their hero. In fact, when one recalls that prize-fighting is against the law, it seems strange that there is hardly a soul in Sydney who doesn't know of my fight with Ben Dunn.

Merchants lift their hats as I pass and many a toff bids me good day. I have become a curiosity, well nigh a fairground exhibit, and I find it exceedingly uncomfortable being the subject of confabulation in every tavern. Every man now claims to know me. Only today I heard that the cove who insulted my Maggie in the Hero of Waterloo, whom I threw across the room, now boasts of our fight. He is enjoying a low fame accordingly.

Even *Bell's Life in Sydney* has waxed lyrical about my native abilities as a bare-knuckle fighter. It predicts that, with training, I could be a future champion of the world. This is quite ridiculous, of course, and I am amazed that grown men talk everywhere of such a nonsensical possibility. I am big and clumsy and know nothing of the art of fisticuffs. Moreover, things do not sit well with myself and

Mr Sparrow, who would arrange my life for me since that day at Parramatta.

After the fight with Ben Dunn, Mr Sparrow and Fat Fred were most anxious that I should fight again and that they should handle my career in this regard. I was then, and still am, most anxious not to enter the ring ever again. I have been stared at almost all my life for my size and blackness. To further encourage folks' attention is more than I can bear.

Only amongst the Maori did I feel comfortable about my size. Here it is a wretched nuisance. The average male in the colony is about five foot and three inches tall. Ben Dunn the heavyweight is considered a near giant at five foot and eleven inches. If he is a giant, then I am a freak of nature.

Fat Fred says I would make a fortune ten times over should I become a fighter. But I can see little sense in being knocked about for the sake of a few pounds. What's more I feel fairly certain that a great deal of money would end up in Fat Fred and Mr Sparrow's own pockets. As Ikey would say, 'If you cannot turn a man with words and you agrees to fight him and should win, you will have lost anyhow. The hero dies young on some soon forgotten battlefield, but a good coward dies in bed with his own bugs to bite him.' But Ikey's continued influence in our lives, in the form of Mr Sparrow, has caused me much aggravation of late. Perhaps there was more to Ikey than his gems of wisdom which I now recall.

I was bruised for a fortnight or more after fighting Dunn. I think he broke a number of my ribs, for I coughed up blood for several days after, and my sides and kidneys were particularly painful. My teeth seemed to rattle in my head and my nose was twice its usual size. My fists, which have never been cured in brine, were so sore that I could not hold a pen for four days. While my employer, Captain James Tucker, was most understanding, it is not my intention to let him down again. With Tucker & Co. I feel myself achieving

460

something, whereas I fail to see that my striking down of another man, or he of me, offers any valuable lessons in life's progress.

'Oh,' said Mr Sparrow when I told him that the purse did not merit the punishment I received from Ben Dunn and that I did not wish to enter the prize ring, 'that was only because you lacked the skill to avoid such blows. We will teach you the art o' fisticuffs so that you will take little punishment – at most a few rib-ticklers and pats to the jaw from the most belligerent pug. It's Johnny Sullivan's Sparring Rooms for you, lad. We'll soon have you ready to take on your first customer!'

Fat Fred nods most solemnly at this advice. I wonder how much punishment he himself has taken, other than the dozen meat pies and Cornish pasties I witnessed him eat after my fight with Ben Dunn. As for Johnny Sullivan, it was Maggie's visit to his sparring rooms which caused the whole furore in the first place!

Tommo, I know, is under some pressure from Mr Sparrow to persuade me to fight again but he will not speak on their behalf. I receive more than enough persuasion from Maggie, who wishes me to fight, thinking only of the excitement and believing me invincible, bless her bright eyes.

'You will be a hero, and me on yer arm!' she laughs happily.

'More likely a lamb led to the slaughter and you ashamed of me,' I reply.

'No, no!' she protests. 'I has it on the best authority you will be the champion o' the whole world!'

It is useless to try to put reason into her magpie head. Maggie has become quite famous after the fight at Parramatta, as well making a large amount of cash from my win against Dunn. She collected nearly fifty pounds in total from those who honoured their bets. A great many made themselves scarce, melting into the jubilant crowd as soon as she climbed into the ring to be with me after the fight. Thank God I was fortunate enough to win. At ten to one odds to all takers, had I lost, Maggie would have been on her back ten hours a day for the next ten years paying off her debts.

She has spent some of her winnings on a new outfit from Farmer's in Pitt Street. A great deal more went on a spectacular bonnet from Mr Israel Myer's emporium in George Street. She has had this hat fitted with a newly stuffed magpie, which sits resplendent amongst ribbons, bows and artificial flowers of every colour of the rainbow. But much the better part of her winnings was spent on me. She paid to have a solid eighteen carat-gold ring made for me, of the signet style. On the face is a magpie and inside is inscribed *Maggie Pye loves Hawk Solomon, Champion of the World*. It is the most beautiful gift I have ever received and I shall cherish it all the days of my life.

Maggie, who can scarcely read or write, does not see why I should wish to work eight hours a day at Tucker & Co. when I could earn fifty times my weekly wage with one fight. Of course she doesn't know about Mary and the brewery and how it is in my best interest to learn all I can of the liquor business before we return to Hobart Town. But although I haven't told her of my plans, I find myself hoping she may even accompany Tommo and me.

Meanwhile, Maggie weeps in my arms and begs me to take up prize-fighting. I'm afraid it will come between us if I cannot resolve the matter soon. Now, seven weeks after the fight, she plain refuses to make love to me and bursts into copious tears.

We have fed the brats their Sunday roast and have gone up to her rooms where it is our custom, after taking a meal downstairs, to make love. But she pushes me away when I would take her in my arms.

'No!' she says, her mouth turned down.

I have learned something of women and so ask her gently if it is her time of the month.

'No!' she says again, and a tear runs down her pretty cheek.

'Maggie, what is it? What have I done?'

'The girls mock me!' she wails.

'About me?'

She nods, unable to speak.

'Why? Because I'm big? A nigger? What is it, Maggie?'

'They say you're a coward!' Maggie wails. She flings herself onto the bed and begins to howl in earnest.

'A coward? How so?' I ask.

Maggie's eyes glisten with tears and she catches a sob in her throat. 'Cause you won't fight!' Then she buries her face in her arms and sobs fit to break a man's heart.

I sit down on the side of the bed and put my hand on her shoulder, but she shakes it off. 'Maggie, beating another man senseless won't make a man a hero. You should know that!'

Maggie sniffs. 'It be 'umiliating. The girls say you're a big black cock with a chicken's heart! Oh, oh, *oh*!' she cries, burying her head in a red satin cushion.

'A big black cock with a chicken's heart, eh?' I laugh. 'That is amusing. Maggie! Maggie! Come along sweetheart, you know better than that! It's obvious, isn't it? Mr Sparrow and Fat Fred have put this about. They've put all the tarts up to it, trying to get me to fight!'

'Johnny Sullivan says it, too!' she replies, looking up quickly.

'Maggie, surely you haven't been hanging about Johnny Sullivan's Sparring Rooms again?'

'Only the once, to see the Lightning Bolt, the heavyweight champion of all Ireland what's been landed a week from Belfast.'

'And that's when Johnny Sullivan called me a coward?' I shake her softly again. 'Look at me, Maggie!'

Maggie lifts her head from the pillow, then props herself on one elbow. 'Well no, he never said you were a coward.'

'What, then?'

'He says he could train you up to beat the Bolt, but he don't know if you've got what it takes.'

'What's that, then?'

'Internal fort-e-tood, he called it!' Maggie gazes up at me, her big blue eyes still wet with tears. 'Oh Hawk, you has got it, hasn't ya?'

I am forced to laugh again. '"Internal fortitude", I think, comes straight from the vocabulary of our friend Mr Sparrow, and not from the likes of Johnny Sullivan.' I look at Maggie, thinking how much I love her.

'Maggie, I'm no coward, but I'm no animal, either. Beating a man with your bare fists until he is half-dead, what does that make you?'

'Rich!' Maggie yells, jumping up on the bed and grabbing me around the neck. 'Stinkin' bloody rich! Oh, Hawk, you could take me to England to meet Queen Vic, or Lola Montez!'

I stifle a laugh. 'A hundred pounds to be beaten senseless? That's not rich, that's plain foolish! Anyway, what if I should lose? I'd be beaten stupid with nothing in my pocket!'

'No! Not a hundred pound! Johnny says there's *five hundred* pounds to be won. He reckons there's plenty o' folks what'll cover your stake, what's half of the prize money, with all the Papists betting on the Irishman and all the Protestants on you!'

'Maggie, I'm a Jew!'

'Them too,' Maggie answers, quick as a flash. 'Mr Israel Myer and them lot in George Street, they'll back ya.'

'To the tune of two hundred and fifty pounds, eh? That's a lot of money, Maggie. A lot of gelt to wager on a bloke who's had just one lucky fight!'

'Johnny says yiz a natural!' She pauses then adds, 'If ya has the internal . . .'

'Internal fortitude?'

'Yeah, that. He says you're fast for a big bloke and ya uses your noggin. He says your ploy with the sunset in Dunn's eyes were a stroke o' genius.'

'That comes straight from *Bell's Life in Sydney*. I read it to you myself, Maggie!'

'No, it's the truth, Johnny said it too.'

'The only sunset I'm likely to see against the Irishman is the sunset of my life,' I say. 'Mr Lightning Bolt is not only the Irish champion but the English as well. If you leave out the Americas that makes him practically the world champion.' I shrug. 'Maggie, can't you see? He's come out here to clean up the locals, to fight Ben Dunn and the like and take home a pretty penny, because the stupid colonials think their man can win!'

'That's right! That's what Johnny said, and Barney Isaacs . . .'

'And, no doubt, Mr Sparrow!' I interject.

'I dunno about him.'

'Maggie, you know there isn't a sporting venture goes on in the colony that he and Fat Fred don't have a finger in.'

'No, listen, Hawk, listen to me! It ain't like that,' she pleads, then jumps off the bed so she's standing up and has her face close to mine. 'The Irishman's gunna fight all comers. Ben Dunn and Fred Woods, Jack Robbins o' Victoria, Jimmy Shanks o' Queensland and whatsisname, you know, that bloke in South Australia what beat Jericho Joe, the darkie? 'Scusin' me. They's all coming here to fight him. The punters, them what's Church of England, will bet on the locals. And o' course the Tipperary men will bet on their man and be most chuffed at the sight of their own Catholic champion from the Emerald Isle beating the livin' daylights out o' the local proddie lads.'

'But wait a minute. Maggie, aren't you Irish too?'

'Yeah, I am an' all, a fat lot o' good it's done me!' she shoots back. Then without drawing breath she continues, 'When the Bolt's cleaned up, like, and thinks he's fancy-free, that's it, ain't it?'

'That's what?'

'That's when *we* challenges the bugger to fight for a prize of five hundred pounds. That's more than he's made beating the living daylights out o' the local lads. It's five hundred pounds to win against someone what's had only one fight. He can't say no!'

'So all the smart money bets on the Irishman and I get my brains boxed!'

Maggie draws back. 'Maybe Johnny's right, you are scared.'

'Damn right I'm scared!' I snort.

'Well if all the smart punters are gunna bet on the Irishman, how come there's some like Johnny what's willing to wager on you? Answer me that, Hawk Solomon?'

'Maggie, it's called a sting.'

'A sting?'

I explain. 'See, Mr Sparrow has most likely arranged a consortium of sporting gentlemen who are well known to the punters, a few toffs, merchants, squatters, to put the word about that I can take the Irishman.' I pause. 'By the way, where do they plan to hold this fight?'

'Johnny reckons one of the gold diggings, they can't say exactly where as yet, 'cause of the police.'

'Yes, the goldfields makes sense, somewhere where there's lots of money and stupidity, all of it available at short notice. It's perfect for a sting. What are the chances that the only bookmakers allowed to take bets are in the employ of Mr Sparrow and Fat Fred? The odds given on the Lightning Bolt would be,' I think for a moment, remembering what I've heard around the pubs, 'four to five on – short odds, so as to discourage your ordinary punter and to make sure the Irish don't win too much. Then on me it's ten to one!'

Maggie looks a little puzzled by all of this, but I continue. 'If I'm not mistaken, there will be a great deal of secret hullabaloo stirred up about me. You know, whispers into hot ears in pubs about my secret training – how I'm punching tall trees to the ground. An incident is reported where some man swears he's seen me lift a dray cart single-handed to rescue a child in Pitt Street and then wander away into the crowd so I can't be given the credit. I've been spotted pulling a four-in-hand drag down the street and all for a wager of a sovereign. It's said I can arm-wrestle six men, two at a time, all in a row. A punch thrown in training near kills my sparring opponent who, as a consequence, lies unconscious for a week.

'There'll even be a tale that when I was a brat some Irishman, believing me to be the very devil, put me in a sugar bag, tied the top, said a brace of Hail Marys and threw me into the river to drown. And to back all this up, there'll be the famous Parramatta fight, which by now will have me lifting Ben Dunn ten feet off the ground with a single punch that lands fifteen feet outside the ring!'

Maggie giggles. 'I've already heard some o' that sort o' thing!'

I chuckle too at my imaginings and at Maggie's smile. 'Well, anyway, enough of that nonsense. But what will happen is that all the miners and the little punters will be taken in by such stories and will bet heavily on me as a result. And there you have it: the sting is in.' I take Maggie into my arms so her head is tucked snug into the crook of my neck. It feels wonderful. 'Will you be there, Maggie Pye, to sweep up all the broken feathers of the dead Hawk and to watch the Sparrow fly away, with his fortune made?'

Maggie struggles away from me. 'Hawk, yiz wrong! It ain't like that at all! I trust Johnny Sullivan. We was brats together, he wouldn't do no wrong by me!'

'Not by you, my darling, by me, the big, stupid nigger.'

'But he knows I loves ya!' Maggie protests, most perplexed.

'Of course!' I say. 'Who better?'

'Who better what?' she asks.

'Who better to help set up the sting?' I say gently.

'You know somethin', Hawk Solomon, I'm glad I ain't got no brains. There's five hundred pounds going beggin' and you're full o' bullshit about a bee sting! Listen t' me, ya stupid bastard! I thinks ya can win!' She looks about her room, her precious home, and waves her arms to include everything in it. 'See this, it's took me four years on me back to get this. Four years to sleep in a decent blanket what's got no bugs and fleas, in a room where you don't wake up with rats running over yiz! It cost me two 'undred pound to make this place beautiful.'

'Maggie, two hundred pounds! Why, you could own your own house for a hundred.'

Maggie clicks her tongue at me. 'I ain't completely daft, ya know! I do, don't I? I owns this building and the chophouse below. How else d'you reckon I got jobs fer Flo and her folks?' She bounces on the bed. 'This bed once belonged to William Charles bleedin' Wentworth, or at least his fam'ly, one of his sisters. Now it's mine.' She knocks on the headboard with her fist. 'Pure cedar, that is!' She smiles at me and I am taken by the lovingness of her expression. 'I'd sell it all tomorrow and put every penny I gets fer it on yiz beating the Lightning Bolt. I means it, Hawk, every sodding penny!'

I hug her tight. 'Maggie, Maggie, you haven't even seen the Irishman fight. You'd bet on me without even seeing his form?'

Maggie grins. 'I seen *your* form, Hawk, and not only against Ben Dunn!' And she begins to pluck at the buttons of my blouse.

Later, when we're lying there together, I am reminded again of how big I am and how careful I must be holding her. But Maggie seems happy enough, content to be loved and in my arms. I know little of the fairer sex, but what I'm learning is that they need to be held and cherished, stroked and kissed long after you are empty of passion. This is when kissing has no other purpose but to tell them you love them. I have discovered that in the business of passion, a man's arms are just as important as what's between his legs.

'Hawk,' Maggie says suddenly, 'the Irish didn't really put you in a sugar bag and throw you in the river, did they?'

'No more than I pulled a four-in-hand dray quicker than a team of four thoroughbreds,' I laugh.

Maggie laughs too. She has a lovely laugh – a sort of tinkle, like a silver bell ringing. It's the kind of laugh you'd expect from the governor's wife, a toffy-nosed tinkle, soft as a sunlit morning.

'Hawk, how does ya know? I mean, that it be a sting an' all?' Maggie asks.

'Maggie, I took on Ben Dunn because I overheard you and Tommo talking. I was so furious at what he'd done to you, I don't believe he could have brought me down no matter what he did. He'd have had to kill me standing upright.'

Maggie kisses me, her lips soft against the silver scar around my neck. 'Ain't nobody done that for me nor will again. I ain't worth it, but I loves ya, Hawk Solomon.'

I smile, and my heart is full of love for her, but I cannot tell her I love her. Not yet. 'If I come up against the Irishman

I won't hate him, I won't feel anything. It'll just be one man against the other. The difference is that he's an experienced pugilist and a champion, and I'm just a big nigger with clumsy feet and fists.'

'But what about yer noggin? Johnny said you thinks real good.'

I grin. 'It doesn't need Ikey's brain to work out that a fast noggin and a slow body is not as good as a fast body and a slower brain!'

'But Johnny said, fer a big un you moves fast and ain't clumsy!'

'As fast as an elephant dancing the Irish jig!' I laugh. 'It would be no contest, Maggie. I'd get my teeth knocked through the back of my throat, and the little people would lose their shirts. Only Mr Sparrow, Fat Fred and various sportsmen, toffs and swells, including your precious Johnny Sullivan, would benefit.'

Maggie is silent a while and then announces, 'Hawk, I've changed me mind. Them bastards can't have ya, not even for five hundred pounds.'

But a mischievous thought has crossed my mind, an idea quite out of character. Perhaps Tommo and Maggie have encouraged in me a daring I never thought to have. 'Hold still a minute, Maggie. As Ikey would say, "My dears, one good scam deserves another!" I think we should talk to Tommo. On these sorts of matters he is much smarter than I am. After all, he's beaten Mr Sparrow at cards, which Ikey said was not mortally possible.'

Maggie looks perplexed but shrugs, and returns to her nap, leaving me to ponder. Should I raise with my twin the possibility of a sting within a sting? And do Tommo and I want to get into another scrape? What would our dear Mary think? Since we've been back in Australia, I have written to her every week, telling her of our various doings. I have given much thought to our homecoming and how Tommo and I would fare in Hobart Town.

Though he denies it, my brother is in the grip of opium. It is no longer the Angel's Kiss and I can feel the hot breath of Tommo's devils from the wilderness closing in again. I am beginning to think it could be time to leave Sydney, for there is no opium that I know of to be had in Hobart Town.

But Tommo, still struggling with his demons, says he is not yet ready to return home. Nor, I confess, am I. There's Maggie Pye to think of, for a start. I'm not sure she'd like Hobart Town. I would also like to try my hand at shopkeeping – a venture that is of my own doing, not Mary's – something which would allow me to feed the many hungry children who roam the streets in every place I've been. And I can see my little bower bird Maggie Pye doing very well in such an enterprise! If we could acquire the capital, we could open a shop, perhaps in the goldfields. I have kept all the one hundred pounds I won from the Dunn fight for this very purpose – though not without some argument from Mr Sparrow. When the money was handed over, he demanded sixty per cent of the purse.

'Wait on!' I said. 'Fair go! Sixty per cent, for what?'

'Expenses, my dear. You were fighting at my venue, engaged in fisticuffs with my fighter,' he replied imperiously.

'No fear,' I said, amazed at his audacity. 'You had a near riot on your hands because the Welshman couldn't fight. Though it was unintentional, I saved the day and saved your hide.'

'But this is the agreement I have with your brother. It's what Tommo gives me from his poker winnings as my commission.'

'Sixty per cent?'

'Aye, there are a lot of expenses to this game!'

'None ventured on my behalf, Mr Sparrow. I have no

agreement with you and you'll receive no commission from me!' I stood my ground.

'I see,' replied Mr Sparrow. 'In that case you can go to hell and your brother with yer!'

'What about the future champion o' the world you was so keen on an hour ago?' Tommo mocked.

'Business is business!' Mr Sparrow sighed. 'Didn't Ikey Solomon teach you nothing?' Then his mood grew darker. 'You know what, Ace O' Spades? You're getting too big for yer boots!' He pointed to Tommo's feet. '*My* boots! The nigger don't take care of you, lad. I does! You'd best remember that! You'd 'ave been nothing, a starving bloody drunk, without me and Fat Fred here!'

'And I'd be a lot less than nothin' without him, Mr Sparrow,' Tommo pointed to me. 'You gets sixty per cent of me card games, me twin gets one hundred per cent of me life!'

'We'll see how you go without me,' Mr Sparrow sneered. 'There's not a card game in this colony you'll be part of, son!' He flounced off and Tommo waved him away with a backward flick of his fingers. 'Toodle-oo, then.'

'We'll talk again, my boy,' Mr Sparrow murmured to me on his way past, wagging his finger. He didn't say anything further to Tommo but spat to the side of his boots.

Not five minutes later he came and apologised to us both, all smiles. Straight away I wondered what he was up to.

'It be the excitement of the fight, boys. Me nerves were on edge in case the police arrived and stopped it,' he explained. 'I lost my temper. You see, it cost me a pretty penny to stage. What I asked you for be the commission Ben Dunn would've also had to pay.'

'Shall I go and ask Ben Dunn, then?' I replied, not willing to accept Mr Sparrow's smarmy apology.

'No point,' he cackled. 'You took all the gelt!' He

brought out a Cuban cigar, bit the end in his yellow teeth and fussed about, lighting it up. Then, through a puff of smoke, he remarked, 'What a fight, eh? Worth losin' my commission just to see it, lad.'

But Mr Sparrow's eyes narrowed as he said this and I could see by the way he chewed his cigar he didn't like losing his commission one bit. I realised he was the type to sweep insults under the carpet in order to tidy up, but that he would come back to the dirt at a later time, never minding who got brushed aside then. I felt certain I had not heard the last of this business. I knew Mr Sparrow still intended to get the sixty per cent of my prize money, with a great deal of interest added, before he was through with me and Tommo.

But on the surface Mr Sparrow was all smiles and forgiveness. He wanted Tommo to sit back in on the poker game that night too. 'Plenty o' rich pickings, lad. The gold finders pay in kind, nuggets and dust. It'll be a most profitable enterprise!' I thought of Ikey, who would never have lost his temper and then come crawling back. Mr Sparrow is not a patch on his old teacher.

'I'll come, but only for an extra ten per cent of the action,' said Tommo, cocky as hell. 'From now on we shares fifty-fifty, including tonight. What's you say, Mr Sparrow?'

'Oh no, Tommo, I can't agree to that, lad,' Mr Sparrow murmured, nice as pie. 'I'm in business with Mr Tang Wing Hung and must first discuss everything with him.' He took a puff of his cigar and exhaled. 'You do understand me, don't you?'

I saw at once what he was getting at and my heart sank. More and more, Tommo had been visiting Tang Wing Hung's opium den before going to his poker game. Now I knew that Mr Sparrow had Tommo in his tiny claws. One word from him and the opium pipe would be withheld from poor Tommo. I closed my eyes and held my breath, ardently hoping that Tommo wouldn't give in to the threat hanging in the air. It wouldn't be the worst thing that could happen, should Tommo be denied the pipe. I would be with him, and would stay at his side however long it might take to rid him of his new addiction.

Tommo grinned foolishly. 'Sorry, Mr Sparrow,' he said quietly. 'I begs your pardon. Sixty-forty as always and no harm done, eh?'

'Ah,' smiled Mr Sparrow, 'that's much better, Tommo. I only wish yer brother could see it as commonsensical. A little co-operation and all's well with the world, ain't that so?'

I wanted to weep. For the first time, I saw how weakened Tommo was by his need for opium, for it had him grovelling to this overblown gnat. I could still taste the blood in my mouth from the fight, but I was almost overwhelmed by fresh rage. I wanted to crush Mr Sparrow and, for the moment, Tommo with him. I had an urge to wring Mr Sparrow's scrawny, miserable neck with my bare hands, and to put Tommo out of his misery too. I knew then that my brother had succumbed to his old despair, even though I would have done anything to prevent this.

'Tommo, tell him to go to buggery! We don't need him!' I pleaded quietly.

But Tommo looked down at his boots and stayed silent. I felt deeply ashamed for my twin. How was it that I wanted to kill him and love him and hold him and protect him all in the one moment?

'Tommo! Tell the bastard *no*, Tommo!' I yelled, the words coming from deep inside.

Tommo looked at me and I could see he was crying. 'I can't, Hawk, the mongrel's got me!' he wept, burying his head in his hands.

I turned to Mr Sparrow and grabbed him by the coat

front, picking him up off his feet. 'Leave us! Before I lose my temper, you bastard!' Then I threw him to the ground.

Mr Sparrow lay at my feet cringing. He covered his face with his hands, thinking I would kick him. Now it was not the great Mr Sparrow, a sportsman game as a fighting cock, but Sparrer Fart, little brat who was terrified. I leant down and took him by the collar, lifting him back up to his feet. He came no higher than my elbow and I could feel his whole body trembling.

'Please, Hawk,' he grovelled, 'don't hurt me!' He closed his eyes, expecting the blow to come. 'I'll give him fifty-fifty, whatever you wants.'

I let him go, disgusted. 'If any grief comes to Tommo, any harm, I'll come for you!' I growled. 'I'll see you pay, no matter what it takes!'

And so here is Sparrer Fart once again in our lives, become 'Mr Sparrow' as if no longer Ikey's little pupil. He's got Tommo in his clutches, and now he wants me. The sting is his revenge on our getting the better of him. He is using Johnny Sullivan, who is using Maggie, the innocent party in all this. I am pretty certain Mr Sparrow's vengeful mind is pitting me against the visiting Irish fighter so I can get my brains knocked out and he can clean up at my expense.

Ikey would see my idea of beating Mr Sparrow at his own game as an excellent way to get even, with a bit of solid business added. I feel in my bones that I am right and that it is not some crazed idea I have constructed out of my overheated imagination. How I have grown to despise Mr Sparrow. If he has learned his ways from Ikey, then I must think carefully about what this means for Tommo and me, Ikey's sons.

Sunday is usually Tommo's night off. On the Sabbath, the toffs, merchants and senior government officials, who enjoy the sportsman's life on all other nights of the week, generally settle down to Sunday roast with their respectable families. This is their time to pat the heads of their offspring and to grunt while their wives attempt polite conversation. They must also be seen at the evening service, for many will have missed the morning one because they were sleeping off hangovers gained from a night of gambling and carousing with the likes of Tommo and the ever-present Mr Sparrow.

I know Tommo will have risen at about five this afternoon. He will have gone to visit Tang Wing Hung's opium den, and will be returning shortly to have his evening meal with Maggie and me downstairs at the chophouse run by Flo's father. I will ask his opinion of my plan then, for Tommo has lost none of his wits.

This is the curious thing about opium. Whereas brandy will cloud the brain, the same is not true of opium which is said by some to promote great clarity of thought. Caleb Soul, my friend and colleague at Tucker & Co., is of this opinion. A pharmacist by profession, he speaks of opium's powers to promote intellectual thought and cites for example the work of Lord Byron, Percy Bysshe Shelley and de Quincy amongst other English luminaries.

This is still no reason to embrace opium, nor will I for one moment condone its use for anything other than alleviating pain. These days, Tommo cannot live without the Devil's Smoke, and it is my sad opinion that he could not give up the celestial poppy even if he most sincerely desired to.

Nonetheless, Tommo is in fine form when we meet for dinner, smiling and sipping quietly at a glass of his favourite Cape brandy. Though it tears at my very soul, I have accepted that he must drink. Accordingly, I have offered him the very best brandy imported by Tucker & Co. He will have none of it, preferring the rough Cape grape to all else. I have noticed that after taking opium he drinks less, though this only in degree.

'So,' Tommo says, when I raise the subject of Mr Sparrow's sting, 'have you decided to fight then, Hawk?'

I nod. 'Only this once, and only if we can think up a way for me to win and the money to be made is, as Maggie says, five hundred pounds.'

'Maggie's right,' Tommo says. 'Mr Sparrow is most confident of the winnings to be had. With the Protestants and the Jews against the Catholics, it be a holy war of sorts, he says. What a strange thing! Here we is, brought up with no religion to speak of, and you's gunna be promoted as a Jew.' Tommo chuckles. 'I reckon Ikey would have a good laugh at that! But Hawk, tell me. Why d'ya want to do it?'

'The gelt,' I say.

Tommo grins and shakes his head. 'Pull the other one, Hawk!'

I look at Maggie, who appears to be most interested in her bowl of Irish stew. 'It's true, I want the money – the reason being I want us to open a shop. You and Maggie and me. We could make a tidy sum from this fight – enough to set us up with a shop, perhaps at the goldfields where I've heard there's a fortune to be made.'

'Come on, Hawk! You're talkin' to me, Tommo, your twin! It ain't in your nature! Since when would you take up fisticuffs to earn money?'

'What's wrong with that?' Maggie asks sharply. 'Ain't nothin' wrong for a man to earn an honest crust at prize-fightin'!'

'Like I said, it just ain't in Hawk's nature, Maggie,' Tommo sighs. 'You've seen him with the brats. He'd rather give it to others than keep it for hisself! Besides, he's gunna take a terrible hiding in that fight.'

'No he ain't!' Maggie replies, looking furiously at Tommo.

'You can't win!' he says to me. 'This bloke's the champion of Ireland *and* England, for Gawd's sake!'

'*Hawk* could be the champion o' the world,' Maggie protests.

I cut across them both. 'You're right, Tommo, it's not just about the money. Though it's true, I'd like us to open a shop. In the end, though, it's not that.' I pause, not sure that even Tommo will understand what I'm going to say next. I take a deep breath. 'It's about getting Ikey out of our souls!'

'What? What about Ikey? What's all this got to do with him?'

'To my mind, everything!' I lean forward across the table. 'Don't you see, Ikey lies at the heart of our troubles!'

'Hawk, you're talkin' nonsense! What's you mean, Ikey's the reason for our problems? He's our father! Without Ikey's voice in me head, I'd never have come out o' the wilderness!'

'Without Ikey, you'd probably never have been taken there in the first place, Tommo!'

Maggie rises from her chair and picks up her bowl of stew. 'If you two are gunna fight I'm goin' into the kitchen,' she says, marching off.

We ignore her and I continue. 'Tommo, it all started with Ikey's greed over what was in the safe at Whitechapel – not wanting to share his half with Hannah and his children.'

'What the hell is you talkin' about, Hawk? What safe?'

In my excitement I've forgotten that Tommo knows nothing of the safe full of stolen treasure, which Ikey and Hannah had left buried under the pantry floor of their Whitechapel house. I'd also forgotten my oath of secrecy to Mary, though I suddenly recall her every sharp word as if it were yesterday. '*Hawk, you'll not talk to no one about the money, Ikey's money, ever, you understand? Not even to Tommo, you hear!*'

I look up at Tommo. He *has* to know. My loyalty to my

twin is greater than to Mary. And so I tell him the whole story of how Mama and I conspired to win Ikey's fortune for ourselves. How, while in England to learn about hop-growing, I found the safe and secretly emptied it of its contents, stealing the fortune from under Hannah and David's nose, and leaving only a ring and a note which said: *Remember, always leave a little salt on the bread.*

Tommo bursts out laughing, 'That were clever to use Ikey's favourite saying!'

I recall how David had fallen defeated to his knees, clutching the ring in his fist.

'Whatever can it mean? We are done for! My family is destroyed!' he had wailed. 'Ikey Solomon has beaten us all!'

'But it was Mary and I who'd beaten Hannah and David and the rest of Ikey's family. It was Mary's revenge for our kidnapping,' I confide to my astonished twin.

'Why'd ya never tell me this before?' he asks.

'Tommo, forgive me, but Mama made me swear I wouldn't tell you. When you came back from the wilderness and,' I pause, 'all was, well, not right between you two, she felt she could not trust you with the secret of Ikey's money, and so she asked that I keep it a secret. I didn't want to, but in the end I agreed. I'm sorry, Tommo.'

'Never mind, Hawk. You done the right thing. You didn't know how I'd be.' He smiles. 'I didn't know how I'd be meself. How rich is Mary?'

'Very!'

'All from Ikey's safe?'

'No, not all. She's done well for herself, as you know. But still the larger portion by far is Ikey's money from the safe. So now you know what happened, Tommo. It was greed that led to our kidnapping.'

I swallow. 'The same greed that made Mary take all of Ikey's money and then throw us out of our own home.

While David Solomon will never know what truly happened to Ikey and Hannah's fortune, I fear he may have concluded that Mary now has all his parents' hidden wealth. That's still the same greed working to destroy us. Even Mr Sparrow putting in the sting is more of Ikey's greed at work – Ikey, who taught him all he knows!

'It's like a curse working over and over again, from which we must somehow escape.'

I want desperately for my brother to understand, but Tommo isn't listening. 'You sure us bein' kidnapped were David and Hannah's work?' he asks abruptly.

'I can't prove it, but who else would do such a thing? Mama wasn't rich at the time, and there was no cause for anyone else to kidnap us.'

'But what happened to us, Hawk? How were we parted? Can you remember? I can't. I've tried a thousand times! I don't have no memory of what happened after we was took on the mountain.'

'I didn't either – at least not until I got my voice back,' I say to him. 'Since then it seems to have slowly come back to me, bit by bit, like pieces in a child's kaleidoscope. Of course, I don't know what happened to you after the wild man took me away into the mountains.'

Tommo leans forward across the table. 'Tell me, Hawk.' His voice is urgent and his eyes bright with hope. 'Maybe I'll get better if you tell me!'

I close my eyes and slowly draw back the past. Then I begin to tell my sorry tale.

'We were climbing down the mountain where we'd been to see the snowline when four men grabbed us. They blindfolded and gagged us, and stuffed us into hessian bags, after binding our feet and hands. Then they lifted us onto some sort of stretcher.

'They must have struck out across the mountains to a road where they had a cart waiting. All I remember is that when they take us out of the bags, we're both crying. They take off my gag and give me some water and a crust of bread. Then we're both put back into our separate bags and onto a horse cart. I must have slept some, because the next thing I remember is hearing a voice shout, "Stand to!" and the cart coming to a halt. Then there are four rapid shots and a man screaming and crying out for mercy. Then another shot, then silence.

'Soon enough a hand opens the bag and I'm pulled out by my hair. When the gag and blindfold are taken off, I can't see anything for a while. Gradually I make out a man holding me. Beside the cart lie three of our captors dead, and another further away a bit. All look like they are sleeping – all except one who lies on his back with his arms and legs sprawled and blood coming out his mouth. Already, there are ants around him. I begin to cry again and look about for you, but you're still hidden in your sack and I can't reach you. Then the man who shot them comes over and hits me on the side of my head. "Nigger!" he spits. Just the one word. "Nigger!"

'He is dressed entirely in kangaroo and possum skins but for a trooper's high-topped white cap, and he is filthy. His beard falls almost to his waist and his hair is wild and knotted on his shoulders. What can be seen of his face is dark with dirt, the skin weathered and criss-crossed with scars. His nose is flattened like a pig's snout and from it a stream of yellow snot trails down to broken and lopsided lips. His tongue constantly darts out, licking the snot. He is barefoot too, with the soles of his feet cracked and the long toenails all broken.'

'A wild man,' Tommo says, and I nod.

'Then I realise there is another man, mounted on his

horse. He is dressed in skins and ragged breeches and boots, ancient and cracked. He too has a ragged beard and his dirty face is deep-burned to a copper colour.'

'Was he bald?' Tommo questions me.

'I think not . . .' I think hard for a moment. 'No, he wore a hat, a bushman's hat. I remember, he took it off to hide whatever it was he'd taken from the dead men's pockets in it. He had dark hair and a deep scar across his left eyebrow, running into his hairline.'

'Well, it weren't Sam Slit,' Tommo says. 'Sam were bald and no scar.'

'It's most likely this bastard sold you to Slit, because he takes the cart and horses and you. You are still wriggling in your bag when the wild man takes me away.

'The wild man puts a rope about my neck and ties me behind his horse. I can't walk because my ankles have been tied and have lost all circulation. So he drags me along by my neck, me in the dirt and him not looking back. I'm screaming your name, blubbing and choking from the noose about my neck, stones cutting into me. I just want to get back to you.'

It is the first time I've spoken aloud about what befell us and now I begin to weep. Tommo reaches out and puts his hand on my shoulder. 'Hawk,' he says. 'Oh Hawk!' Then I see he too is weeping.

I am grateful it is Sunday night and well past dinner-time by now, so that the chophouse is empty. Tommo and I sit and have a good old cry over the past. I can hear the clatter of dishes and laughter in the kitchen as Maggie makes some joke. After a while, we're all right again.

'Can you remember the rest, when Mary come to find you?' Tommo asks, once our tears have dried.

I nod. This is the darkest of my memories and has only returned to me recently.

'Can you tell me?' Tommo gazes at me. 'Or don't you want to?'

'I do remember, and I will tell you,' I say gently. 'But first, you. Do you not remember anything of what happened when we were parted?'

'There must be something. Something what I remembers.' Tommo gives a bitter little laugh. 'Though I dunno why I want to. It were all so bloody awful.' He seems to be thinking and he looks up to the ceiling as he speaks, his blue eyes glistening with tears again, his voice unsteady.

'I remember going up the mountain, you and me, the first snow, racing up to the snowline.' Tommo smiles through his tears. 'Me winning, 'cause I were smaller and faster and you a bit clumsy on the rock and shale. Then coming down again, to return to Strickland Falls, to Mama.' Tommo stares straight at me for a moment, his expression so very sad, like a little boy who doesn't understand what he's done wrong.

'And then Slit. Slit and the sweet, sticky smell of the whisky still and the wilderness all about, stretching forever, darker and darker. It be as though I blinked me eyes, and everything changed. One moment I were playing with you on the mountain and the next I were with Slit in the wilderness Slit beating the daylights out o' me most days!'

'Tommo, poor Tommo, let's not speak of it any more,' I say, trying to comfort him. 'I'll tell you how Mary found me some other time, eh?'

'No, tell me now,' Tommo presses me. 'That silver scar 'round your neck, it haunts me. I needs to know!'

I close my eyes tightly and feel warm tears run down my cheeks. 'Every day the wild man led me behind his horse through the high mountains with the rough rope pulling tight around my neck, so that it bled and festered constantly. This went on for months until my neck was worn almost through. At night he'd tie me up, beat me, the rope still around my neck tied to a tree. I couldn't move away from his blows or I would choke myself. I hoped I would die. He was a monster worse than any in the books Mama read to us. Finally I lost my voice.'

Tommo is in tears again. 'I could feel it!' he sobs. 'In the wilderness with Slit, I could *feel* your pain, I swear it! When did you lose your voice?'

'Towards the end, just before Mama came. I don't know, five months, maybe a bit more. Why, Tommo?'

'I remember how Slit beat me for weeks 'cause I couldn't answer him. Me throat were closed up, shut tight. I knew I could talk, but then again I couldn't. It were our twinship, I s'pose.'

We both pause. 'But how did Mary rescue you?' Tommo urges.

'Well, we're climbing up a mountain one day – it's early morning and very cold. I was never warm in all that time, not once. I don't know where we're going, but the wild man keeps stopping and looking up at the track, a narrow path which seems to me all stones. He's sniffing, testing the air, his tongue darting out like he's tasting it. He sucks his finger and holds it in the air above his head, testing the wind. Then up we go, climbing the mountain. Suddenly he stops and turns his horse and we descend into a small box canyon.

'And then I see Mary. She is sitting up holding a blanket to her neck, and I realise that she has seen the monster and is filled with terror. Next she spies me, standing behind the horse with the rope around my neck.

'"Hawk!"she screams.

'But I've got no voice and cannot answer her. I just stand trembling in the bitter, cold morning. I raise my hands to confirm it is me, to tell her that I've heard her. I speak to her in the sign language that Ikey's taught us, and which Mary knows also.

"Mama!" I say.

'"Hawk! Mama's come!" she screams. Then she looks up at the monster. "He's my boy, my precious boy, give me him!"

'The monster jerks at the rope so that I am thrown to my knees. Loosening the rope from the saddle, he drags me to a rock and ties me to it. And then he drives his first into my face and I fall to the ground.

'Mama is still yelling at him, "You bastard! You fucking bastard!"

'I look up in my daze to see the monster, his tongue darting in and out and licking at his snot, ties his horse to another boulder and walks towards Mama. He's got her trapped, blocking her escape. He throws her to the ground and leaps on top of her, pulling his breeches down. He's grunting and puffing and tearing at her clothes and skirt, one hand around her throat. Then I hear the shot, and three more, and the wild man slumps down over Mama, vomiting and shitting himself. She's shot him.

'Mary is covered in guts, shit, blood and vomit but she pushes him aside, drops her pistol and comes running towards me, arms outstretched. She grabs me and howls like some primitive creature. Then she weeps and weeps, and I with her.'

I am exhausted at this telling and Tommo is once again reduced to sobs. 'Tommo,' I say, clasping my hand to his shoulder, 'Mama found me, but she never gave up looking for you. Not one day passed that she didn't try to find you! She offered a king's ransom if anyone should report your whereabouts. She put your likeness and description on the back label of every bottle of Tomahawk beer she sold. She questioned me for years about what happened and where you might be – all the time you were away.

'"Think, Hawk!" She'd shake me by the shoulders.

"Think, darling! The man what took Tommo, what did he look like? Can you remember anything, darling, the smallest thing?" But of course I couldn't. Not then.'

I grip Tommo's shoulder hard. 'It's all so clear now. I can see him, the man with a scar across his eyebrow. The scar went deep into his hairline, as if it had been done with an axe. Black eyes, dead like lumps of coal, another scar across his mouth, intersecting his bottom lip. That's who took you.'

'It weren't Slit,' Tommo mutters, and stares into the distance for a long time. 'So why must we get Ikey out of our souls?' he asks at last.

'Don't you see? Ikey's greed is at the root of all this misery. It wasn't his fault – he wasn't evil. But life was hard and that's how he survived. He had to be greedy just to live. That greed is still with us, it haunts us, Tommo!'

'But we're of Ikey's making!' Tommo says, wonderingly. 'He taught us everything, all we needed to know to survive.'

'We're of Mary's making too, Tommo. It was Mary who brought us up, who gave us decency and love.'

'But I loved Ikey,' Tommo says sadly, as if I'm taking away one of his few pleasant memories. 'Without him in me mind I couldn't have survived – not in the wilderness nor out of it, for that matter.'

'Me neither! There was much good in Ikey, Tommo! But we must also put his greed behind us! Ikey's greed lives on in Mr Sparrow, in the opium pipe he feeds you. It's going to kill you, Tommo!'

Tommo looks down, examining his nails. 'So now you wants to fight the Lightning Bolt, what'll beat you to a pulp, so's you can defeat Mr Sparrow and rescue yours truly. Is that it?' He speaks quietly, but is plainly angry.

I nod, knowing that I must step carefully here. But I can control my own anger no longer. 'He has turned you into his slave! He can't be allowed to do that. The mongrels *can't* keep on winning. Somebody must stop them!'

'Ho! That's my saying, Hawk, and it ain't got me nowhere. You *can't* win, Hawk. You can't win against the Irishman, and you got even less chance against Mr Sparrow!'

'Tommo, listen to me. I loved Ikey too but we must be rid of this curse once and for all.'

'How? By getting thrashed by an Irishman? That's precisely what Mr Sparrow wants, to see you killed and him get rich at your expense.'

'Tommo, you've got to think up a way I can win the fight! I *must* win. For all our sakes.'

I don't tell my brother the last reason behind my determination to take on Mr Sparrow and succeed. I have received another letter from Mary, in which she tells me all that has happened. The more I think of it, the more I know the time has come. If we are to make lives of our own, if my dream of a shop is to come to pass, Tommo and I must first make our peace with Mary. The time has come for Tommo, Maggie and me to prepare to go home.

May 8 1861

My dearest Hawk and Tommo,

I count each day you are away as though it be a year. Every morning when I rise, I go out into the yard and look up at the mountain. I have it perfect timed so I see a flock of green rosellas as they fly each day from the mountain across the Derwent River to some place too far for the eye to follow. How they screech and carry on as they pass overhead!

These emerald green parakeets have always been the birds of my good fortune. The very first morning I arrived in Van Diemen's Land, a flock flew over the ship's high mast and I knew then that I would survive. I clasped my Waterloo medal and swore that I would begin a new life and that the green birds would be my talisman.

This morning I waited for them to fly over, preparing to call out, 'Bring back my boys!' like I always do. They came, just as they do every day, but this time to my astonishment, they wheeled and came to rest in my garden – some on the peach tree what's in blossom and some on the washing line – screeching their hearts out.

'It's a sign!' I yell. 'A sign!' I clap my hands and with that sound they's gone, up and away, taking the same route as always.

This be the first time they've wheeled and stopped and I found myself crying, though for joy or sorrow I cannot say. Is it a warning? I fear for my boys – that one of you might be harmed. Or should I fear for myself?

David and Hannah have bought up the entire hops crop on the island this year – and our own planting has failed. There is word that David will start his own brewery soon and he vows to take away my business. Buying hops from the mainland makes my Tomahawk Pilsener and my Temperance Ale most expensive to brew and if I pass the cost on to my customers I fear it may lose me many a working man's custom.

Still, I shall manage, though I feel I haven't the heart if my boys don't soon return. Were you and Tommo here, we could buy land further up the Huon Valley where hop-growing is more reliable. I have also thought we might open a brewery in Melbourne or Ballarat to supply the diggings, and that you and Tommo could undertake this task in a year or two after you are once again acquainted with what is required.

David Solomon meanwhile spreads vicious rumours, ably aided by Hannah, that I have long been Mr Emmett's mistress and so have gained favours and concessions from the government. 'How else,' he asks, 'can a woman prosper over a man in the brewing business?'

This has caused me the greatest distress for, excepting my love for my two boys, I treasure Mr Emmett's friendship above all else. He has retired from the government and so David is now able to talk openly without fear of reprisal. There are plenty here too who are willing to believe him, even though I am innocent.

To make matters worse, Mrs Emmett has died recently and already there are those who say it was brought about by grief at the knowledge of our alleged association. I cannot protest, for to do so would give credence to this wicked accusation. Nor can I go to my dear friend and offer him comfort, for fear that it will be seen to confirm their gossip. Though I don't give a fig for their good opinion, I would not wish to cause Mr Emmett the least embarrassment.

I admit I did not care for Mrs Emmett one little bit. I find it hard to credit that a man so noble of spirit could have loved a woman so determined to look down her long and imperious nose at those she thought inferior, such as myself.

I hope and pray that dear Mr Emmett will forgive my not attending the funeral service but I am grown too old to turn hypocrite now. I did send flowers out of the respect I hold for him. I took to the mountain and picked wildflowers and made a wreath twined with the honeysuckle that grows there. I'll venture it was the only one of its kind among the pompous floral tributes on her grave.

My dearest boys, I think of you a hundred times each day and my heart aches with longing for your return. How I wish to hold you each by the hand as when you were young and tell you how your mama loves you.

Please write to me soon, I long for news that you are well.

Your loving mama,

Mary Abacus.

Chapter Nineteen

TOMMO

The Rocks
May 1861

When Hawk tells me he's going to fight the Irish champion, I'm most terrible worried. Hawk don't have the nature of a true fighter – he's a man of peace. If he takes on the Lightning Bolt, he won't be fighting the true object of his anger. In his mind, he'll be entering the twenty-four-foot ring against Mr Sparrow, and that ain't enough.

Hawk knows this himself. And yet he says I got t' help him win. He wants me to come up with a plan what will undo Mr Sparrow and his sidekick, Fat Fred. Somehow we also has to raise the money for the stakes – two hundred and fifty pounds in a prize of five hundred pounds, winner takes all – so that we won't have to forfeit any of what we makes to Mr Sparrow or his gang.

So far me plan is this. I'm gunna go to Mr Sparrow and tell him I have persuaded my brother to fight the Irishman. This will keep me in his good books as I depends on him for me living at cards and o' course for the favours of Mr Tang Wing Hung. If only it were possible to play in a Sydney card game what the bastard don't control, then I'd soon enough have the stakes for Hawk's fight with some to spare!

But how am I to tell Mr Sparrow that Hawk don't require Fat Fred as a manager and trainer, nor Johnny Sullivan's Sparring Rooms for training? It's gunna be awkward enough explaining that Hawk plans to raise the stake money himself, without me master's friendly involvement. I'll have to tell him flat that Hawk ain't yet buried the hatchet over Mr Sparrow demanding sixty per cent of his prize money from the Ben Dunn fight. Mr Sparrow will be miffed but, in the end, he'll accept Hawk's terms, knowing that me twin has little chance o' winning. Besides, the true profit for Mr Sparrow is in the betting ring, what he controls. And such a deal will make him a cleanskin. He may now promote the fight and fix the betting ring to his advantage. When Hawk, after much huffing and puffing, loses to the Irishman, Mr Sparrow can't be accused of arranging the outcome.

Maybe I'll say that the stakes for Hawk's side of the prize is being raised in secret by Captain James Tucker – Hawk's employer, what's known to be a sporting gent with the horses. This ain't something Mr Sparrow could go sniffing out the truth about, as it ain't proper for a gentleman of Captain Tucker's standing and a member of the Union Club to have an interest in an illegal fist fight.

I'm also gunna have to tell Mr Sparrow that I won't be keeping him advised of Hawk's progress. What worries me is that he'll withdraw me supplies of the Angel's Kiss. But I'll tell him that Hawk won't fight if he does this, and I reckon he'll give in to his own greed. There's big money to be made from this fight and nobody knows it better than Sparrer Fart.

That's as much as I've got planned at present and there's two questions still facin' me. How does we raise the stake? And how can I make Hawk a certain winner? What Mr Sparrow wants above all else is that Hawk gets beaten near to death. He reckons he's been cheated and humiliated by me twin. He wants his revenge, and he wants it at a profit. I ain't even begun to come up with a certain double-sting.

I think about this problem for several days on end but naught comes to mind. Me head wound, the pain of which never quite leaves me 'cept with opium, starts hurting something awful. And then the answer hits me like a flamin' bolt out o' the blue!

Mary! Our own mama!

Hawk has told me of Ikey's stolen fortune what's now in Mary's possession. If I could do a deal with Mary and get me hands on some of that money, I could offer the Irishman twice his winnings to *lose* the fight. For a sum of a thousand pounds, he'd surely do it. We'd set up what looks like a grand fight to the punters – a fight in which both men shows good scientific points and there's much ballyhoo in the ring – an excellent circus all 'round. We'd lodge the money in a trust account in England to be paid to the Irishman in the event of a deal well done. And if I was to offer him some cash up front, so that he could bet against himself at good odds, he'd be even further tempted. He'll take our bribe, let Hawk win, and go home happy enough besides!

The Bolt ain't a young man and he's well past his prime, though he'd still thrash our Hawk – no matter how strong me brother be. And he wants that prize purse bad. *Bell's Life in Sydney* reckons the Bolt's come to the colonies to get his snout into the money trough one last time. The Irishman talks o' retiring from the game and opening a pub in Galway, inviting all from the colonies to visit him. This be the ambition of just about every prize fighter what ever lived!

I've already seen the Bolt twice at the card table in Chinatown and has come to know a little about him. He's a fair enough player, game enough to win the occasional pot. He be just the sort to lose in the company of a player such as yours truly – and stupid enough to believe his loss has come about through bad luck on the night. On both nights Mr Sparrow told me to let him win enough to pay his grog bill and a bit more. I've also heard him boast that he ain't once had to pay for the pleasures of the sweet colonial lassies what visit his rooms above Mr Hulle's Shipman's Hotel at Brickfield Hill. Maggie says she'd bet London to a brick these girls works for Mr Sparrow, for the Bolt ain't no charmer to get it for free. What this means is that Mr Sparrow's softening him up. He plans to own all or a good part of all the Irish fister before he takes on me brother.

The Bolt's well-loved by the Tipperary men and they follows him wherever he goes. On Saturdays, the Irish navvies come in their hordes to drink all day in the Shipman's Hotel – just to catch a glimpse of the champion o' the Emerald Isle and conqueror o' the English bulldog. Some has even painted a large banner sporting a crude likeness of the Bolt standing with one foot upon the stomach of a bulldog, lying on its back with its legs in the air. The dog's tongue, what has the stripes of the Union Jack painted upon it, lolls out o' the corner of its mouth. Blood spouts like a fountain from its nostrils and falls into a glass held waist high by the champion, who's smacking his lips. This banner they raise on poles and carry about as proud as you like, with three men to the front, one beating a drum and the other two playing the cornet and fife, and any number of Irishmen marching behind.

If anyone mocks the Bolt, he's at once challenged to a fight by each and every Tipperary man within hearing. The Shipman's Hotel has become a dangerous place because of these shenanigans. The townfolks keeps well away from the drunken men what mills about the station at Strawberry Hills, waiting for the late Sunday night train home to Parramatta Town.

Imagine the hullaballoo when we declares Hawk's fight with the Irish champion! 'Hawk, the Black Jew, fights the blessed son of Erin who was baptised in the holy waters of the Shannon River.' What a banner that will be!

Now that I've worked out the sting I must get Maggie Pye's help to put it in place. Of course, it ain't worth a pinch o' shit 'less I get Mary's money to bribe the Irishman with. Without saying nothin' to Hawk, I writes to Mary in me best hand, what Hawk'd be proud of if he could see it!

Sydney

May 25, 1862

Our dearest Mama,

Hawk and me be in a spot of bother. Please come to Sydney and bring five hundred pounds. You can leave a message for me at the Hero of Waterloo in The Rocks.

Your obedient son

Tommo X Solomon.

I dunno if that'll do the trick – but I hopes so. I feel bad about keeping the sting a secret from Hawk but I tells meself it ain't worth bothering him with 'til I know if it might work. As Ikey says, 'First get the most important agreement, my dears, then use it to obtain any others you may need. It be most difficult to persuade a partner when you has nothing o' substance held up to advantage.' And so I'll wait 'til Mary agrees before I tell Hawk she's coming to Sydney.

In the meantime I try to come up with a way for Hawk

to beat the Bolt if Mary won't give us the bribe and we has
to do it kosher. Something comes to me in Tang Wing Hung's
opium den in Chinatown, though it's still mostly chancy.

Mr Tang Wing Hung has a place what's entirely for
opium-smoking two doors down from his eating house.
Those of 'respectable' European background goes to a
private room at the eating-house and escapes through a
hidden doorway into the alley behind. A signal is given from
two doors down and the opium den is opened.

Mr Tang Wing Hung's opium den is no filthy hovel
inhabited by creatures half-alive what slither and crawl
about in a dark and fetid atmosphere. His room is a grand
place, with six couches in maroon brocade what has dragons
leaping and twisting, and exotic flowers about the place. The
couches has curtains drawn about them for privacy. The
customer never gives his true name even if he be the
governor himself and known to all. Only Europeans what
can afford Mr Tang Wing Hung's price may enter.

I am greeted by an ancient celestial with a pure white
pigtail. He wears an oriental cap upon his head and a gown
o' silk down to his ankles. His long pointed beard flows to
his waist and his moustache droops downwards to disappear
into the fall o' his snowy beard. His yellow skin is creased
like crumpled butcher's paper and his narrow eyes show
barely a glint of light.

This is Ho Kwong Choi, what's always silent and always
ready to prepare the opium pipes. The pipe be a piece o'
bamboo cane about one inch and a half in diameter, and two
foot in length. The bowl is fixed about a third of the way
down from its end. It's broad and flat at the top, with a small
hole in the centre where the opium paste sits.

All is quiet here. Outside there's the call of children
playing, a hawker's cry, or the busy rattle of a hackney in
some nearby street. But these are dull and seem far away. A

small bowl o' paste is placed on a lacquer table beside me couch. Next to it is a lamp, its glass like an upside down bell, the shape of an Easter lily, so that the opening is pointed uppermost with the flame licking at its centre. I watch as Ho Kwong Choi dips a long steel needle into the bowl and quickly winds up a small amount o' paste what's somewhat like treacle on its end. This he holds over the flame until the precious pearl of opium begins to bubble.

Then he places the smouldering opium into the bowl of me pipe and I pull the glorious smoke into me lungs, letting it float in dragon trails through me mouth and nostrils. Each pearl o' perfection allows only three or four puffs before Ho Kwong Choi must roast another. He does this for near on an hour until I feels like I'm in heaven.

I'm here enjoying me smoke when the peace of the den is suddenly shattered. The door is battered open and six lads, much the worse for grog, charge into the room. There are three of us within, not counting Ho Kwong Choi, all drawn deep into ourselves from our smoke dreams what are now broken by these louts. They pulls out truncheons from their belts and one wields a rattle what makes a fearful racket. Then they sees Ho Kwong Choi as he comes from behind a curtain into the centre of the room. They storm towards the old Mongolian what stands alone and defenceless. I'm in a cloud o' confusion, not capable even o' standing up.

I ain't sure if what I sees is part of my opium dream or real but the old man seems to grow into some sort o' peculiar human spider, his arms and legs flashing through the air with grunts and hisses. He don't make no noise apart from a grunt or two when he delivers a few chops with the side of his palms to one of the fellows. Another he holds in such a way that his eyes roll back in his head and his knees buckle as he drops to the floor. In a few moments, all six lads is out cold or trying to stagger up. Ho Kwong Choi stands calm among them.

Four of the blokes slowly rise. They drag their two unconscious mates behind 'em, and the frail old man bows politely as they stumble out the door.

I am amazed at what I've seen. If I can get Ho Kwong Choi to teach Hawk, perhaps me brother might bring some o' the venerable Mongolian's skills to bear on the Irishman. This be our only hope for Hawk to win if Mary don't agree to pay for the fix.

It is also the plan I tells Hawk about.

'Within the rules of bare-knuckle fighting, is such a method permitted?' he wants to know.

'I'll lay a bet that such a thing ain't never been seen in a fight before!' says I. 'You can't forbid what's unknown now, can ya?'

'You mean it will come as a complete surprise?'

I nod.

'I must see this Mongolian method only as a part of my success. The other part must be competence in the true business of fist-fighting.'

'You be right in that,' I agree. 'At best we got three months to teach you the fighter's trade.'

'Three months? Can we do it?' Hawk asks.

'It's all we've got. That be the time it will take the Irishman to fight with all the big men coming here from around the country, includin' Ben Dunn. So you'd best start training, Hawk!'

'Yes, so I see! I told Maggie that we would not work from Jimmy Sullivan's Sparring Rooms and she is most concerned, thinking him the best trainer in the colony,' Hawk says.

'Hawk, your training's got to be a mystery, taking place in a hideaway so that we can build a frenzy o' rumour and speculation about your form. We has to make the punters think that you can win,' I says to him. 'That's what Mr Sparrow wants and that's what we wants also. Only difference is that he must be made to think you *can't* win, and we knows you can!'

'That should not be too difficult. Mr Sparrow already thinks I can't win. He just wants me punished.'

'Yes, but he's got to be absolutely certain you can't win.'

'How are you going to do that?'

'I dunno,' I says. 'I'll think o' something. The most important thing Mr Sparrow wants right now is to build up the expectations among the punters that you *can* win. I'm gunna make that very difficult for him!'

'How so?'

'Well, we're in secret training, ain't we? I ain't telling him nothing. So he's got no news coming out of your camp.' I spreads me hands. 'How's he gunna get the stuff to feed the punters about your prowess?'

'Make it up?' Hawk offers.

'Nah, that won't wash. The sportsmen will catch on that it's all bull. He's got to have a reliable source.'

'You got any ideas?'

'Yes. Maggie!'

'Maggie? That's ridiculous, everyone knows she's my sweetheart!'

'That's right,' says I. 'Here's the shot. Maggie goes to Mr Sparrow and offers to help him for five quid a week, pay on results end of each week. That way he won't think it's a scam and he'll still think he's in control.'

'And what exactly does Maggie do for him?'

'She starts rumours in the pubs about yer secret training. But she does this most reluctant, only letting a few stories slip out after a few drinks – never meaning to say nothing. Know what I mean?'

'That's fine, but how do we know that's what Mr Sparrow will want her to do? Why should he trust her?'

'She's a whore. He'd trust a whore to see an opportunity and make something out of it. It's how Mr Sparrow thinks hisself.'

'What if he doesn't?'

'Hawk, you got t' learn to think like a confidence man! It's obvious, ain't it? Maggie's on the inside. She knows what's happening in your training. She agrees to spy on us and he tells her what rumours she must spread when she's in the pub.'

'And the punters will trust her?'

'That's right! She's known to be your woman, but she's a woman all the same, what can't never keep a secret.'

'Tommo, are you sure that's how it will work?'

'It'll work better than that! Don'tcha see, Hawk? Maggie will tell Mr Sparrow how things is going real bad for you. You know – you ain't learning nothing, you've took sick, you won't work at training, you've broke two fingers on your right hand, that sort o' thing. That way, we build his confidence that you can't win.'

'And he gets Maggie to spread the *opposite* information! He'll ask her to drop little tidbits about my awesome prowess!' Hawk chuckles. 'And then close to the fight, Mr Sparrow offers very good odds against me winning?'

'You've got the idea!' I says, patting him on the arm. 'The excitement's been building for weeks and Mr Sparrow dangles great odds. All the punter fish, takes them hook, line and sinker, 'cept the Parramatta Irish.'

Hawk laughs. 'Tommo, I hope to hell you're right.' Then he looks concerned. 'But if Maggie agrees to cooperate, there'll be no harm come to her, will there? I mean, if we win the fight?'

'Can't see any likelihood of harm. If we wins it'll cost Mr Sparrow every penny he's ever owned. He'll be ruined and there's plenty waiting to see it happen so's they can put the boot in! Then he'll have no friends to protect him anymore.'

'Well, we must ask Maggie about all this herself,' Hawk says. 'If she's one bit worried, you're not to push her, Tommo!'

'You're on,' I says. But to meself I'm hoping our Mary comes in to save us. This whole ploy's too bloody risky for yours truly! I thinks what Ikey would say in such a situation and I can hear him clear as a bell. 'Never let no wrongs and rights creep into a deal, my dears. Who's wrong, who's right, that ain't the answer to the question. It's who profits at the end of the day!'

Now we's embarked on a scheme what's all about wrongs and rights and the money question only comes after. By Ikey's rules we've got it arse about face. I don't like it. I don't like it one bit.

On Sunday, after Hawk and Maggie has fed the wild brats their roast dinner down the Quay, I gets up from me bed to join them at the chophouse. I has a hangover to end all hangovers. Maggie tries to get me to eat a bowl of Irish stew but the thought of it damn near makes me puke. Hawk eats my tucker as well as his, and we puts the whole plan to Maggie. It don't take her long to agree.

'It'll give us another fifty pounds towards the stake too!' she says. 'All the better coming from his nibs, Mr Sparrow.'

'Maggie, it could be dangerous. He's a rough un underneath,' I warns.

'So's I, Tommo,' grins Maggie, 'and not too far underneath, neither! If Mr Sparrow buys it, we'll use the folk what live here in the Rocks. They's always in the pubs and will warm to the task o' spreading news from a most reliable source.'

'What reliable source will that be?' Hawk teases.

'Me, o' course!' Maggie laughs. 'Maggie the Mouth! What with women being notorious for gossip and me being well acquainted with fighters and their form, I'm a perfect choice!'

'Folks 'round here be most respectful of you, Hawk. They'll be 'appy to spread news about their hero!'

'Maggie, Tommo and I are only supposing how Mr Sparrow will react. Perhaps he'll not trust you after all?'

'He will,' Maggie says. 'He'd expect a whore to change sides for profit, just like he would himself.'

'The punters, will they not suspect Maggie?' Hawk now asks me again.

I sigh. 'You know what yer problem is, Hawk? You always think men is mostly intelligent when the truth is they's mostly stupid. 'Course they knows Maggie's your doxy! That be why they'll question her! She'll pretend to know nothing, naturally, bein' the very picture o' female innocence. But, ah, wait! With her tongue loosened by a shout or two o' Bombay gin, she'll tell 'em just a little. With each drink, she'll tell 'em a little more. Until, by the end o' the evening, the dullest dunderhead in the pub will feel sure he's heard it from the horse's mouth. Men's always willing to think women is stupid and can't keep a secret.'

'Tommo's right!' Maggie says, smiling at us both. 'There ain't a man in the world what don't underestimate the intelligence of a woman. Two o' them's sitting right here in front o' me!'

We laugh. 'Maggie, we never doubted you for a minute,' says I.

'And my trainer, who will he be if not Johnny Sullivan?' Hawk asks.

'That's it!' Maggie exclaims, clapping her hands. 'That's who I'll get to front Mr Sparrow for me! Good old Johnny Sullivan will tell him Maggie Pye requires an urgent and confidential with Mr Sparrer Fart, Esquire.'

'Perfect,' says I. 'As to trainers, there be two of 'em. We've got the services of an Aborigine and a Maori, both top-notch fighters in their time.' Hawk and Maggie look startled at this news, but I continue. 'Just imagine the talk when it comes out that the Black Jew has an Abo and a Maori to train him! It'll set a thousand tongues to wagging.'

Hawk looks bewildered. 'Tongues to wagging, as may be, but will they get my fists to fighting? Who are these two men?'

'Bungarrabbee Jack and Johnny Heki. The Abo were a lightweight and the Maori a heavy. Both copped a lot o' punishment from white men and they's most anxious to help you out against the Bolt, Hawk.'

'And the old Chinaman, have you asked him?'

'He's said he'll train you on the sly on Sunday mornings when his opium customers are all at church with their wives. As long as Tang Wing Hung don't get wind of it, we'll be right.'

'I've seen him,' Maggie chimes in. 'Funny old bugger, looks like he's come straight out o' me nightmares.'

'Can he speak English?' Hawk asks.

'Not much, but his sort of fighting is show more than tell!'

Maggie's got to go. She kisses Hawk goodbye, then me, her lips soft on the side o' my cheek.

I waits for Hawk to ask the final question, the biggest of them all, and now he does.

'We have the one hundred pounds from the Dunn fight,' Hawk says slowly. 'That will do for a down payment but how will we obtain the rest – the other hundred and fifty pounds?'

'If Mr Sparrow pays Maggie a fiver a week to be his informer, that's another fifty or so. She reckons she can also get a loan of another hundred pounds on her property if she throws in the chophouse. With your money, that's all we need!'

'No!' says Hawk, shaking his head. 'Maggie must not get a loan on her property for my sake!'

'Hawk, she loves ya! She *wants* to give you the money.'

'No, Tommo!' Hawk bangs his fist on the table.

'She thinks you'll win. It's only a loan. Besides, she'll be bitter disappointed if you don't let her. She'll think you don't love her!' I jokes.

'It's because I *do* that I don't want her to risk her money!' Hawk shouts at me.

'Oh!' says I, me eyes wide open in surprise, 'loves her, does ya? Loves Maggie Pye?'

Hawk's eyes drop to his hands what rest in his lap, his hands what used to do all his talking. Then he looks up slowly and asks quietly, 'What if I do?'

'Nothin',' I shrugs. 'Me brother loves a whore, that's all. Nothin' wrong with that, I suppose.' I raises an eyebrow. 'After all, our mama were a whore, weren't she!' I don't know whether what I'm saying is good or bad, comforting to him or an insult, it's all mixed up in me head. But I'm shocked more than I can say.

I likes Maggie, it's true, but always in the back o' me mind is the thought that she's a gold digger. If ever she hears of Hawk's prospects at home she'll dig her claws in, she'll suck him dry.

'You hasn't told Maggie about Mary and the brewery, has ya?' I asks.

Hawk looks up at me and I see a tear run down his cheek. 'I haven't told her anything, Tommo. She doesn't know that I love her, nor does she know about Mary's brewery!'

'Hawk, you remembers what Ikey says about whores, don't you? Once a whore, always a whore. There ain't no good ones, no matter what.'

'Ikey!' Hawk yells, banging his fist down on the table. 'Ikey's dead, why must we always kowtow to Ikey Solomon?'

'Because he were a first-class villain what got most things right,' I says. 'Ikey knew more whores than you've had hot dinners!'

Hawk clenches his fists for a moment, then sighs. 'Look at me, Tommo. I'm a nigger. You know what white people think of a big nigger? They think I'm going to rape their wives or harm their children. They think I must be stupid or inferior and when they find out I'm not, they like it even less. Now here's a white woman who loves me for myself!'

'Hawk, if women knew about Mary's money they'd be linin' up for ya.'

'That may be, but it's not enough. I want someone to love *me*, someone I can love back!'

'And so you think only a whore could love you for yourself, is that it?'

'I think this one loves me, Tommo!'

'But you won't let her help you?'

Hawk glares at me. 'Do you know what it took for Maggie to buy her home and the eatery? Most of the brats she grew up with are dead from violence or drink or opium. She's survived, to get her own place, own a small business, make things nice. That was done the hard way, but she did it!'

'The hard way? She done it on her back!'

'How else *could* she do it? Our society doesn't educate Maggie's kind. How many parlour or kitchen maids do you know who own their own rooms and business? None, that's how many! Whoring was Maggie's only way out of the gutter.'

'So why don't she stop, now she's a person o' property? She's still a whore, ain't she?' says I.

Hawk shrugs. 'Maggie has the right to choose how she lives, Tommo. This is a good time for a young and pretty woman like her, providing she doesn't go to her ruin on gin or the poppy. The gold diggings has made many a poor cove rich and generous and many a rich man very indulgent. Maggie's taking advantage while she can, knowing it won't last forever. I understand this of someone who's had her difficulties in life. She wants to give up one day, though.'

'What then? After she's done her share o' gold digging, she'll retire the magpie off her hat and marry a squatter, or even become Mrs Hawk Solomon?'

'I haven't asked her, Tommo. I don't expect she would if I did.'

'Hawk, ask her. Garn, ask her to marry you!'

There's a method in me madness here. If Maggie hears the true story of Hawk and me before he asks her, we'll never know if she's said yes because of the money. If she says yes before she finds out, that be quite another matter.

'I can't,' Hawk says in a low voice.

'Why not? You just said you loves her.'

'It isn't possible right now.'

'Why? Because of me? What's you trying to say, Hawk? You won't marry Maggie because of me?'

Hawk folds his arms across his chest. 'Tommo, when you came back from the wilderness I swore I'd never leave you again, that we'd be together no matter what. If I married, I'd need to settle down and that would mean returning to Tasmania for good. No more adventures, not even a shop in the goldfields. It would break Mary's heart all over again if I were to stay away once I married.'

I look at my brother and think how much I love him. 'You know what your problem is, Hawk?'

'Yes, you just told me. I think men are mostly intelligent when they're mostly not.'

'And you are the stupidest of 'em all! You try to please everyone when it can't be done.'

Hawk smiles. 'Tommo, I *won't* leave you.'

'You're talking rubbish, Hawk! Ask her! Ask Maggie to marry you! If she says she will, then I'll go back to Hobart Town with you both!' I stares at him, furious.

Hawk stretches out his hand to me. 'Tommo, will you?'

I realise what I've just said, and stops short. 'You cunning bastard.' I grin. 'But I'll go back on me own terms, understand? I'll give it one more go, one year in the brewery. But if it's no good with mama, that's it. I'm off, and you stays with Maggie, that's the deal!'

The whole thing's bloody stupid. Hawk's fighting the Irishman to get even with Mr Sparrow for what he believes he's done to me. He thinks this will get the bad bit of Ikey's inheritance out of our lives. But Mr Sparrow didn't put the opium pipe in me mouth and Ikey didn't give me a thirst for brandy. Yet Hawk believes that what's happened to me is evil what started with Ikey and got carried on by Mr Sparrow. If he destroys Mr Sparrow, he thinks that somehow I'll be safe, that the bad stuff in me life will all somehow go away.

I want to tell Hawk here and now that I don't *want* him to fight the Irishman. Mr Sparrow *does* own me, Tang Wing Hung's opium owns me and the poppy is stronger than me love for him, stronger than anything. I'll go back to Mary like I promised, but it won't last, even if I can get opium in Hobart Town. I can't be trusted to do the right thing, not even by meself.

I wants Hawk to marry Maggie Pye so he'll leave me alone. Yours truly never was no good, never will be. But I knows Hawk. Once he gets an idea there ain't no shaking it loose. Deep inside me, I knows Hawk has to fight the Irishman, has to try to destroy Mr Sparrow. It's like a sign that all ain't lost with his twin, that I can yet be saved. If he don't go through with the fight, he'll never be able to live with himself, thinking forever that he's let me down. Why has I got to have such a big, dumb, stupid, wonderful nigger bastard for my twin?

'Tommo,' Hawk says, 'thank you for agreeing to come home. But you are not ready to go back to the brewery and nor am I. If we win the fight, we'll go to the goldfields – you to gamble and me to open a Johnny-all-sorts. Caleb Soul from Tucker & Co. says to be a shopkeeper at the diggings is where all the real gold is. I've always fancied being a shopkeeper. We could do it on our own – not with Mary's money and not with Ikey's. You and me, Tommo!'

'And what about Maggie?'

'Maggie wants to come with us.'

'Oh, *I* see, Hawk the shopkeeper, Tommo the gambler and Maggie the whore!'

'No, Tommo. As I said, Maggie wants to give up the game.'

'She does, eh? What about the chophouse?'

'Flo's family will take care of it. Maggie thinks maybe she could open an eating-house at the diggings. Caleb Soul says miners will pay good money for a simple meal.'

'Christ Jesus, Hawk, how long's it been since Maggie done a day's work o' that sort? She's like me, a creature o' the night. Can she cook?'

'Flo's mother will teach her.'

Hawk must be in love to be thinking such foolish things. Maggie a respectable woman, cooking dinners! He's a dreamer, that's all, and always will be. 'Hawk, we ain't even got the stake for the fight yet, and then, if we gets it, we still has to win it! You could lose your bloody shirt. Mine too!'

Hawk laughs. 'You're right, Tommo, but we could also make a go of it together, what do you say?'

I am silent a while. 'What do you say, Tommo?' Hawk asks again.

'You forgets one thing,' I says softly. 'Me head.'

Hawk sighs. 'Tommo, there is opium at the diggings. The place is swarming with celestials. The Angel's Kiss will be there for you.'

I don't say nothing. What Hawk doesn't know is that Mr Tang Wing Hung controls all the opium in the New South Wales diggings. If Mr Sparrow has a word to the Chinaman, that's the end o' yours truly. Without me pipe, I'll die. I know it.

'Now,' says Hawk, full of hope, 'let's think how we might find the remainder of the stake money.'

Well, if he wants to go on with it, I've got to help him. I've already thought of how we might get the money ourselves without Mary's help. But it's not certain that we will and, if we do, it will only be enough to make the stake. Hawk will have to win for real.

'Do you think Caleb Soul would let me go with him next time he travels to the goldfields?' I asks.

'Why?' says Hawk.

'I think I could win the difference at cards, playing on the diggings. There's plenty o' patsy-marks waiting to be fleeced there, so they say.'

'Would Mr Sparrow let you go?' Hawk wonders.

I shrug. 'He'll have no choice. Come the time, I'll just scarper and be back soon enough. He needs me at the card table, so it'll be all right.'

'And the poppy for your head?' Hawk asks slowly, like it hurts him, but he knows I've got to have it.

'As you say, there's opium to be found there. Or else I could try and take some with me.'

'Maybe you'd be safer that way,' says Hawk. 'Caleb Soul worked as a chemist when he were in the old country. He'll know how to get opium for medical supplies – he sometimes helps out in the dispensary at the hospital in Macquarie Street.' Hawk thinks for a moment and smiles. 'Tell you what, Tommo. I'll come with you. I feel sure Captain Tucker will allow me the leave.'

'That's it, ain't it?' says I. 'I'll tell Mr Sparrow we's going to the diggings at Lambing Flat to drum up interest in the fight! That be where he wants to hold it anyhow, or somewhere near. The place is full of Irishmen. I'll tell him it's a chance for the fossickers to see ya for themselves. That'll suit his plans. It'll encourage the proddie miners to bet big on you, come the day o' the fight. How long will it take to get there and back?'

'About a week and the same back if we take the two-horse trap. Then you'll need at least three or four days there to get the lay of the land and set up a game. Three weeks in all, near enough,' Hawk replies.

'How soon can we go?'

'There isn't much work at Tucker's this time of year. Captain Tucker might even let me go with Caleb when he makes his next trip. That's only a couple of weeks away.'

I'm worried, o' course, that Mary might come to Sydney while we's away. It's over a week since I've written to her, but there ain't nothing I can say to Hawk. I went to the Hero last night to see if there were a message from her, but so far nothing's come. Perhaps she won't help. If she don't come to Sydney or send the money, Hawk and me must be off to Lambing Flat and get back to Sydney in time for him to train with Bungarrabbee Jack, Johnny Heki and Ho Kwong Choi. We'll need another thirty pounds to pay for them lot, plus premises for training.

Next day, Hawk tells me that Captain Tucker said that he may go with Caleb Soul and he's given me the nod to go as well. As the time draws near and there's still no news from

Mary, I decides I has no choice. I has to tell Maggie what's happening.

I've thought a lot about her and Hawk and if he should marry her. I reckon that if she's a gold digger and not truly in love with me twin, it'd be better to flush her out now, rather than be sorry later.

I makes a time mid-afternoon to see Maggie at her chophouse, The Cut Below – there being another chophouse above the Argyle Cut called The Cut Above.

Hawk gets home from work at six o'clock, what gives me enough time to see Maggie and be back in me bed for him to wake me up later. Like me, Maggie don't start work 'til late at night. We meet at three, with the sun still shining bright as a new silver shillin' on the harbour.

'Gawd!' she says, coming into the eatery where I'm already waiting. 'I ain't seen a Tuesday arvo this bright since I were a brat begging ha'pennies in Hyde Park. You hungry, Tommo?'

'Nah, Hawk'll cook me something when he comes home from work. If I don't eat he'll fret. By the way, I don't want him to know we're meeting.'

'Oh?' Maggie says, suspicious.

'I'll explain soon enough.'

Maggie pulls back a chair and sits down opposite me at the small table. 'Yer know something, Tommo, yer brother's too bloody good fer the likes o' you.' She stabs a finger at me. 'Ya knows that, don'tcha? He's too bloody good fer me too – fer the both of us.'

Maggie smiles to herself as though she is remembering. 'The bleedin' Virgin must 'ave smiled on me the day we met at Mr Smith's eating house. Jesus, he were beautiful! Sitting there, diggin' into his grub like it were the first tucker he'd had in a week. Him in rags and split boots and no hose! But bloody beautiful with all them lovely circle marks on his face, like a savage what wants to eat you up! "Crikey! That's for me," I says to meself, "and it'll not cost the nigger a penny. Stay as long as he bloomin' likes!"' Maggie giggles. '"See if I care if he eats me up!" That's what I said.'

I laugh with her. 'You done Hawk the world o' good, Maggie.'

'Yeah, maybe,' says she. 'But it won't last.' Her pretty mouth turns sad and her eyes are downcast. She's a lovely little bird, all right, that I can see.

'Hawk be most fond of you, Maggie. Why d'ya reckon it ain't gunna go on? You ain't planning to leave him, is ya?' I asks, against me own self.

'Nah, I loves him with all me heart, Tommo. But sooner or later I'm gunna do somethin' stupid, chase him away, say somethin' he can't forgive.' She looks at me fit to break my heart. 'We's the same, Tommo, you and me. Hawk ain't like us, that's all. What's bad in us ain't in him. Two of a kind, whores the both of us.'

I nod. Suddenly a picture of Maggie in her bed chamber comes into me mind, and I wonders what her punters see. Then I put it quickly to the back of me mind. She's Hawk's woman, I remind meself. I clear me throat. 'Hawk don't give up easy, Maggie. He's stuck with me come what may. If you do something to hurt him, he's got a lot o' forgiveness in his heart. I should know!'

She sniffs. 'That's different, you're his twin.' For a moment I think she's gunna cry and then what'll I do? 'Anyways he's still a man,' she says, smiling brightly now, her eyes wet. 'Sure you don't want ter eat somethin'? Tea? Nice cuppa tea?' She touches me arm. 'Do you the world. Flo, bring us a nice cuppa, will ya, darlin'?' she calls out loud. 'A pot, two cups!' Then she turns to look at me. 'So, why's you robbin' me of me well-earned sleep, if I might ask? Why's we here without Hawk knowin'?'

'Maggie, have you seen Mr Sparrow yet?'

'T'morrer. Johnny's set it up, t'morrer, six o'clock at his place.'

'Do you think he'll fall for it?'

'Sure, why not? I'm a whore, ain't I?'

'Maggie, what does you really think Hawk's chances are of beating the Bolt?'

Maggie looks at me suspicious. 'What's you saying, Tommo?'

'I mean, you know about prize-fighters and their form. Do you think me brother can take the Bolt?'

Maggie looks at me strangely. 'Tommo, what's this nonsense?'

'Hawk's gunna take a fair walloping. He's gunna be thrashed!'

It's like I've smacked her gob with the back o' me hand. 'No, he ain't! No, he bloody well ain't! Jesus, what's you gettin' at, Tommo?'

I reaches over and grabs her by the arm. 'It's true, Maggie, the Irishman's gunna be too good for Hawk.'

'No! No!' Maggie shakes her head. 'You're wrong, Tommo. Look what Hawk done to Ben Dunn!'

'Maggie, the Irishman could take on Ben Dunn with one hand tied behind his back. Why do you think he's come out here? Let me tell ya, he's come out here to take up a collection for his old age. There ain't a heavy in the colonies what can match him blow for blow, even go five rounds if he's serious!'

'Bull!' Maggie shouts.

Flo brings the tea and hurries away, leaving a plate o' scones and jam.

'Maggie,' I urges, 'you says you loves Hawk. Do you want to see him killed? Be sensible. You know him – he'll keep fighting 'til he's mincemeat!'

Maggie's hands are shaking as she pours the tea. 'Tommo, I've been around the fights a good while, ever since I was a brat. First cove what screwed me when I were ten years old were a fighter – only a featherweight, thank Gawd! I know form when I sees it. Hawk be a champion. Maybe the world champion. The blow what knocked out Ben Dunn lifted him three foot into the flamin' air!'

'Maggie, I know, I saw it. In New Zealand he killed a Maori in a card game with just such a blow.'

'Well then, what's this talk o' him being made mincemeat?'

'Hawk were angry then, just like he were angry with what Ben Dunn done to you. When Hawk's angry 'cause he thinks something's unfair or evil, he can't be stopped, the devil hisself couldn't do it. But that ain't the case here. Hawk ain't angry at the Irishman, he's got no reason to hurt *him*.'

'Yes he has – Mr Sparrow, he's reason enough!'

'It ain't the same thing. Hawk won't see that beating the livin' daylights out o' the Bolt be the same as beating Mr Sparrow. He'll want t' win, sure enough. But without his terrible anger, he's got no chance to beat him! Hawk is a gentle soul at heart. He ain't naturally mean, and he ain't got the skills in the ring. Put together, that's a recipe for disaster.'

'He can learn to be mean,' Maggie says stubbornly. But her eyes show she sees some sense in what I've just said. 'Johnny Sullivan could teach him.'

'Johnny Sullivan be in cahoots with Mr Sparrow and Fat Fred. He can't train Hawk, not for a fair fight anyhow, you know that.'

'He's me mate, and I know him to be his own man. He'd listen to me I know, he'd change sides,' Maggie protests.

'He's a poppy head. I've seen him at Tang Wing Hung's. He'd be in the pay o' Fat Fred, and that's the same as being owned by Mr Sparrow.'

'Tommo, what's you saying? Are we gunna stop Hawk fighting the Bolt? Throw up the sponge before we even gets in the ring, forget the sting?'

'Nah, nothin' like that.'

'What then?'

'We got to *fix* the fight, get the Irishman to lay down.'

Maggie bursts into laughter. 'And how's you gunna do that? Jesus, Tommo!'

And that's when I tells her the lot, all that Hawk's asked me not to. I tells her about Mary and us, and about the brewery. And I tells her about me idea for Mary to give us the money to bribe the Irishman. Maggie listens, never taking her eyes off me own and then, to me surprise, she begins to blub softly.

'What's the matter?' I asks.

'I told yiz, didn't I,' she sobs. 'I, I . . . thought it'd be something wrong what *I'd* do, but it ain't me, it's him!'

'What d'ya mean, Maggie?' I says, confused. 'Nothing's wrong with Hawk!'

She sniffs, trying hard to stem the tears, knuckling them away from her eyes. 'Yes there is! He's *rich*, the bastard! That changes everything!' She gulps, then hiccups. 'Oh shit, shit, shit!' she howls.

'Oh, Maggie . . .' I puts me hand on her arm and tries to comfort her but I never was too good at that sort o' thing, even with me poor Makareta. Now I can see Maggie ain't no gold digger, she loves Hawk any which way. I can't tell her Hawk loves her if he ain't told her hisself – it ain't my place to tell her. But to me surprise I wants to. I sit helpless 'til eventually she calms down.

'Gawd, I must look bloody awful,' she says, blowing her nose. 'So what do you want me to do now, Tommo? Why did ya come here? Does I still see Mr Sparrow?'

'Nothing changes with Mr Sparrow. We've still got to get the punters betting on Hawk and I can't be sure Mary's gunna come good with the money. Hawk and me is going to Lambing Flat so's I can try to win the money at cards.'

'You think you can win what you needs to bribe the Irishman at the gold diggings?' She looks at me astonished.

'No, 'course not. If I'm real lucky, with a bit o' relocation, I may win the the rest of the stake and training money for Johnny Heki and Bungarrabbee Jack.'

'Poppy money, more like,' Maggie snaps. 'Ya mean Hawk'll have to fight straight if yer mama don't come good?'

I shrug. 'Well, yes, that's about it.'

Maggie smiles. 'Well, you forgot me one hundred pounds what I'd put in from the loan on this dump.'

I swallows hard. 'Maggie, Hawk won't take it from ya.'

'Ha! See, I told yiz! Rich man don't want to owe no favours to a whore, that's how it is!'

'Maggie, that ain't fair!' I protest. 'That ain't it at all. Hawk knows he might lose!'

Maggie shrugs. 'So? I been broke before, but I ain't never loved someone like I loves him.'

I've got no answer to this one, so I try to change the subject. 'Maggie, will you meet Mary? Look after her if she comes to Sydney when we're away?' I asks.

Maggie's eyes grow large. 'She's coming here? Oh, Jesus no!' She brings both her palms up to cover her mouth. 'I couldn't!' She shakes her head. 'Her, a rich lady, finding out her nice boy has been beddin' a whore what says she loves him! Ooh, can't ya just see it! Her dumpin' a bucket o' shit over me! No, Tommo! Anything else, not that!'

'Maggie, please, Mary ain't like that at all! If you love Hawk, you'll do it,' I begs.

Maggie begins to cry. 'Damn ya, Tommo!' she howls. 'He don't need his mama's money. Hawk could win on his own, I know it!'

Chapter Twenty

HAWK

New South Wales
June 1861

Tommo and I are on the road to Lambing Flat. We have been most fortunate, for we have been given permission by Captain Tucker to accompany Caleb Soul in the Tucker & Co. trap to the goldfields. With the right introductions from Caleb, who knows everyone of importance in the diggings, Tommo will be able to arrange a card game quickly. Our hope is to be back in Sydney in no more than three weeks.

Once I had told him about Tommo's terrible pains from his head wound, Caleb Soul kindly procured opium for my brother to take on our journey. I know that he will not talk to anyone of Tommo's addiction. I also hope Caleb will introduce Tommo to some of the big gamblers here and I do not want his reputation tarnished, so I ask Tommo to employ no relocation in his card games.

Tommo is, of course, most indignant that I would even think that he might use such tactics when playing with a bunch of miners.

'Tommo,' I warn, 'there are men here from all around the world. If there are not one or two cardsharps among them, I would be tremendously surprised.'

'And if there is, you still want me to play kosher?'

'If they're not on the straight then you must make up your own mind. It's just that I do not wish Caleb's good name hurt.'

Caleb Soul is of a sanguine disposition, a man who is most interested in sports. He doesn't know yet that I intend to challenge the Irish champion – unless the rumours already circulating in the Rocks have reached his ears. However, I shall tell him of my intentions further down the road and thus explain why we need introductions to a card game where the betting is high enough to earn us some of the stake money.

I must confess, I am full of dreams about the diggings, though I have no desire to search for gold. It seems to me that the true rewards are to be obtained by supplying the men with their needs. If we should win the fight against the Irishman, I have in mind to open a Johnny-all-sorts store, with Maggie and Tommo alongside me. How happy we should be!

Winning the fight is essential to my dreams for the future, although I do not like my chances against the Irishman. But, I tell myself, for all of our sakes, I must win. If Ho Kwong Choi can teach me the Oriental fighting art and if I can absorb sufficient of my opponent's blows long enough to keep me in the fight, I hope that my endurance will see me through. I need to learn enough skills to soften or side-step some of the Irishman's harder blows, until he tires and I can get a decent crack at him.

I am well aware that I won over Ben Dunn because he had already gone five rounds with the Welshman, while I came fresh to the fray. He is demanding a return bout so that he may regain his title. As he puts it, 'I will break every bone in the nigger's overgrown carcass!' For my part, I believe that the title belongs rightly to him and have said so publicly. But he demands an opportunity to earn both his title and his revenge honestly, and will not hear of taking the champion's belt. This I have returned to its makers, J.J. Cohen of George Street, asking them not to engrave my name upon it, but to keep it until Ben Dunn chooses to claim it.

I know that the Bolt, who is vastly more experienced than both Dunn and I, will come well rested to the ring. With the encouragement of the Parramatta Irish ringing in his ears, he will be keen to make a fool of me.

Tommo reports that the Bolt drinks deeply of Irish whiskey, each dram chased down with a pint of beer. He spends most of his nights at cards and thereafter with various of the women procured for him by Mr Sparrow. He has a drinking toast which he often recites to the amusement of all.

> *Your doctors may boast of their lotions*
> *And ladies may talk of their tea,*
> *But I envy them none of their potions –*
> *It's a pint of best Irish for me.*
>
> *A doctor may sneer if he pleases,*
> *But the recipe for keeping me frisky*
> *Is the physic that cures all diseases*
> *A bottle of good Irish whiskey.*
>
> *So to Colleen, Bridget and Mandy,*
> *You may prefer brandy or gin,*
> *But to make a good Irishman randy –*
> *Pour a pint of good whiskey in him!*

Maggie keeps a close eye on all the Bolt's doings at the same time as she prepares to talk up mine. Mr Sparrow has accepted her as his informer and she is already busy in the pubs laying the groundwork for tales of my prowess. I fear she herself may even begin to believe the outrageous stories she concocts in bed of a Sunday.

Her favourite is the story of my Zulu ancestry. It seems I am the true grandson of one of the greatest fighting generals of Africa, the mighty warrior Dingane – or so the legend goes! Now that I have decided on prize-fighting, to hear Maggie tell it, my natural instincts have come to the fore, and those who would enter the ring to spar with me should tremble in their boots. I can fight two at a time and such is my speed and ferocity that they seldom last two minutes before crashing to the ground, spitting out teeth as they fall.

In truth, I cannot hope to learn even the most basic rules of fist-fighting in the few months available to me. How will I defend myself against an opponent who is a wily old campaigner, seasoned in every dirty trick of the trade? While I listen with interest to news of the Bolt's slapdash training, I know also that he has more than sixty bouts against his name, some of them against the best prize-fighters in the British Isles and Ireland. Even if he is past his prime, for a purse of five hundred pounds he will be sure to give himself a good margin of safety when he enters the ring.

Stamina will be my only chance of success. My legs are often enough described as tree trunks. I hope they will see me through as many rounds as are needed. My strength and endurance must help me to survive in the boxing ring long enough to win.

With this in mind I have developed my own training schedule, quite apart from what I shall be taught by Bungarrabbee Jack and Johnny Heki when I return to Sydney. At Tucker & Co., much of the liquor is stored in a great loft and pulled up by pulley, with fifty gallon barrels of rum and whisky being hoisted by three average-sized men on the rope. Each afternoon, I lever the large casks up to the loft, working the pulley singlehanded, to strengthen my arms. Then I run up the inside stairs to this same loft, carrying two ten-gallon firkins of port each time, one on either shoulder. Every day I spend longer at these exercises.

Captain Tucker knows that I plan to fight the Irishman and has announced himself my keen supporter. He has even employed the services of a physician, Doctor Nathaniel Postlethwaite, to check my weekly progress and allows me to train secretly in the loft.

The road to Bowral and beyond, on which we now travel, is in very poor repair. Since the discovery of gold it has seen much more traffic than was ever intended by its original builders. We pass hundreds of men who are making the journey on foot. Most carry only a swag, although some are equipped with a pick and shovel as well. Moreover, I count fifty-seven drays and carts before we reach Mittagong. These are heavily laden with tents, sluicing rockers, mining tools, bags of flour and sugar, large tins of tea and all sorts of stores and utensils. The drays contain as many as eight men and there are seldom fewer than four aboard a cart. Most men bear firearms, having read in the newspapers that bushrangers abound in these regions. With their equipment, the men of each dray may set up a camp, from where they hope to earn an easy fortune from the generous earth.

Some of these gold getters look eager and impatient to arrive while others are thoughtful, or wear a dogged, abstracted air. A few men smile sheepishly as we pass, as if half-ashamed of their errand. These men tend to be of the syndicates with cash behind them. Their equipment is new, and their firearms look unused, the butts glossy with varnish. Their horses too are stout, and wear harnesses fresh from the saddler's hands. But as Caleb Soul observes, these smartly turned out men are no more likely to find luck than the humblest man they pass on foot.

Some of those on foot are still in their city clothes. They are clearly clerks and shop assistants, their coats over their arms and their once-white shirts grimy with the dust and dirt of the open road. It's as if in the middle of adding a column of figures, or while selling a customer an ounce of shag tobacco or a set of suspenders, they have cast aside the task at hand and set off to seek their fortunes down the Parramatta Road.

Others are working men, wearing trousers tied with a lace below the knee. They already seem hardened to the pick. No doubt they too dream of finding enough gold never to have to return to their previous station in life.

Several push wheelbarrows loaded with all their possessions and such miner's tools as they can afford. Those who have already adopted the clothes of the miner wear gay-coloured woollen shirts and comforters and Californian sombreros of every hue and shape.

All these men have one thing in common. In every head resides a dream of riches, of castles in the air with flags flying from the turrets. Alas, most will return to their homes poorer than when they left, to find their wives bitter and their children starving. All this I'm told by Caleb Soul, who has observed every aspect of life on the goldfields and has not yet been tempted to give up his job at Tucker & Co. for it.

In fact, as he reveals to us, Caleb has quite a different ambition. He hopes one day to return to the art of pills and potions, to work as a pharmacist as he was trained to do. 'Liquor makes 'em sick and my pills and potions will make 'em well again!' He'll work at selling grog to the goldfields until he has sufficient to start in the chemist business. He laughs. 'It's the same business but at different ends, so to speak!'

Caleb now suggests, though perhaps only half seriously, that we should both come in with him in the chemist business, as he knows a great deal about medicines and selling, but very little of keeping books. 'Hawk, you will be the bookkeeper. I hear naught but good things about your penmanship and accuracy. Captain Tucker says your ledgers are a veritable work of art.'

'And me?' jokes Tommo. 'What a partner I would make! Good for nothing but cards. I'm most grateful you got the poppy paste for me, Caleb, but that's about all I ever wants to know about chemicals.'

It seems as good an opportunity as any, and so I tell our friend of my decision to turn prize-fighter and the real reason for our journey. Caleb greets my announcement with enthusiasm, and my fight becomes the focus of many a discussion.

We move southwest on the road to Lambing Flat along with a vast troop of men. There are almost as many men returning from the diggings as there are going to them. Their clothes are tattered and they appear half-starved. They are sullen and withdrawn and seldom respond to our greetings. Occasionally one will shake his head and spit at the ground as he passes those headed for the diggings. Mostly they stumble on unseeing, too disillusioned to care about the many fools who follow in their footsteps. Still, I notice that not one of our gold-seeking compatriots turns back at the dismal sight of these broken men.

After six and a half days on the road, we are well past Goulburn and have entered gold country. We hope to arrive at Lambing Flat shortly past noon. In the morning, we travelled through forested countryside, but it is now as if we have taken a journey to the moon. Dirt mounds and holes abound and not a single tree can be seen. What was once a wilderness of green and living stems has been chopped down to become hoists, crude shaft-heads, sluices, cradles, cabins, rough fences – dry sticks doing service to man's greed for gold. It rained last night and the dust has settled which, from all accounts, is something to be most thankful for. I am amazed to discover that a town, albeit constructed mostly of shanties of canvas, has risen so quickly on what must have been a wild and sylvan landscape not so long ago.

There must be ten thousand tents here, some with crude huts adjoined to them, most with bark chimneys of every sort sticking out from the canvas. Some even have small yards with fences and chicken coops, while others are not much more than bark and flour bag humpies. A few shanties have walls of no more than three feet, made from stones piled up together with a pole at each corner, and a canvas roof. We pass a wattle and daub cottage with a single glass window set somewhat askew in the wall, the most solid residence to be seen.

For every tent or shelter, there appears to be a hundred holes in the ground. If you were to look down from one of the rolling hills which frame the valley, and which themselves are almost as pocked, punctured and scraped raw as the flat ground below, it might seem as though some ragged alien army is camped here.

The town itself is chock-a-block with miners in woollen shirts and Californian sombreros, these items of headwear being almost as numerous as the ubiquitous cabbage-tree hat. Visitors and newcomers are easily recognised, dressed as they are in their grey or black city clothes, looking as drab as a convocation of curates.

The main street – if the largest of Lambing Flat's bumpy thoroughfares may be so called – was churned to mud early in the day. Now the noon sun has baked it dry, and it is so rutted and crowded that we cannot proceed any further. Caleb Soul pulls up beside a large tent.

'We'll stay around here,' he announces. 'Find a spot to pitch our tent nearby. The tucker here is good and the helpings plentiful. It's only mutton and damper mostly, Hawk, but I know you'll fancy their bread pudding with plenty o' plump raisins. They also make an Afghani curry which is delicious taken with rice.'

'How do we reach the centre of town?' Tommo asks.

'Not sure there is such a place, lad,' Caleb Soul laughs. Then, understanding why Tommo asks, he adds, 'Tommo, you must allow me to find out about a card game for you. Don't do it yourself, or it will be immediately concluded that you are a cardsharp. A mining camp may look like mayhem, but it has its own rough kind of order that must be observed.'

Tommo has grown to respect Caleb Soul during the course of the journey and nods at this advice.

'Why don't you accompany me on my rounds tomorrow and get the feel of life at the diggings?' Caleb suggests.

He takes out his hunter watch and clicks it open. 'I will meet you back here for dinner at six o'clock. In the meantime, perhaps you lads could pitch the tent and tether the horses. I'll arrange for hay to be brought, as there's no green grass anywhere about! It will be a little cramped for the three of us in the tent, but we shall manage well enough if you can bear my snoring.'

He moves away, then turns back to us. 'Oh, mind you don't pay more than two shillings a night rent to the cove on whose claim we stay. Explain to him why we're here or he'll become suspicious.' He grins. 'Everyone in the diggings is suspicious of everyone else, and doubly suspicious of a couple of faces they don't readily recognise.'

'Such as a seven foot nigger and a little dandy?' I ask.

Caleb Soul laughs uproariously on his way as Tommo punches me hard in the stomach.

We soon find a cove nearby who agrees we may put up our tent on his claim and after some argument agrees to a rent of three shillings. I am about to pay him when Tommo stops me.

'Wait on,' he says to the man. 'Show us your claim licence, then.'

'What licence would that be?' replies the man cockily.

Tommo points to a board nailed to a small post which has a figure written upon it. 'The licence what shows that number.'

'Oh,' he says, '*that* licence. Me mate what's working another claim has it in his pocket. I'll show it to you at sunset.'

'Right, I see,' retorts Tommo. 'That must be the mate what struck it rich in the claim what he staked out the other side of sunset? Garn, piss orf, will ya!'

The man grins. 'It were worth a try. Couldn't lend me a shilling, could ya?'

'Bugger off,' says Tommo, 'before me brother belts ya one.'

So we wander on until we come across a woman outside a bark shanty. She's feeding a cat scraps from a tin plate and it's questionable who looks mangier, the cat or the woman. For two shillings she agrees we may pitch our tent and, for another, we may tether the horses to a stump on her claim. She goes in to fetch her claim licence and asks upon her return if we'd like a cup of tea. 'It's bush tea but not too bad if you closes your eyes and holds yer nose!'

We laugh but refuse politely. Our bones ache from

sitting too long in the trap and we are both eager to stretch our legs and look around. 'There'll be a cuppa here when you gets back, then,' she says. 'No sugar though, run out weeks ago.'

We set off and find what we take to be the centre of the town, though as Caleb has said it's hard to think of it as such. It's a hodge-podge of shacks and holes and people – many more people than I had ever supposed.

Caleb Soul has told us that Lambing Flat, known to all as the poor man's diggings, is the most profitable market for Tucker & Co. outside of Sydney. As he explained, almost every man who is prepared to work hard and who owns a pick and shovel can make a wage here and some, occasionally, make much more. 'In the grog business,' he observed, 'a lot of men with a little money in their pockets is much more advantageous than a few men with a lot. There are over fifteen thousand souls in this district, nearly all of 'em drinkers.'

Caleb does not have a very high opinion of the folks to be found here. He says Lambing Flat contains the human dregs from all the other diggings where fossicking for gold is more hazardous. Here, the easiest gold can be found at three feet or less, and the very hardest from sixty to eighty feet. Every soul in these diggings can make a go of his claim if he is willing to put in a good day's work.

Unfortunately, many are not prepared to make the effort. While the Chinaman is not afraid to bend his back and does not expect to come by his wealth easily, his European counterpart is not so fond of small earnings and hard work in the hot sun. Every day he looks to strike it big and will take up a new claim with great expectations. He works it for a few weeks, grows impatient at the small pickings and abandons the site for what he believes is a more propitious one elsewhere – whereupon the Chinaman, who seldom starts a claim from scratch, moves in to rework the ground the European has abandoned. When the European is again disappointed and returns to his old quarters, he finds the Chinaman has worked it at a nice profit to himself, and so he demands it back!

Their hard work has made the Chinese the subject of the white man's resentment and hatred. The *Miner's Gazette* scurrilously describes them as 'filthy, immoral, treacherous and quarrelsome, heathen celestials, who waste water, steal gold, ruin good digging ground, spread leprosy, and practise secret vices on the bodies of white women and white boys.' It is firmly believed by many that the Chinese rape white women and children at every turn, without an ounce of evidence to support it – although some men will swear blind they've seen them.

Caleb Soul takes umbrage at this. 'It is often enough said that the Chinese are lesser beings than the white folk, but I count them a better breed than most of the European rabble at Lambing Flat. This particular diggings has the worst class of men of any goldfield I've seen. It's crawling with adventurers of the lowest type,' he confided to us before we arrived.

'I had hoped for the worst class of man with a pocketful of gold to lose at the card table,' Tommo had replied. 'Poor men with a little to spend may be good for your trade, Caleb, but for mine they be a disaster!'

Caleb Soul laughed at this. 'There are sufficient here who've struck it rich to fill your pockets ten times over, lad. Some of these men did not once have five pounds, and are now worth thousands. Poor men who grow rich overnight are careless with their money.'

At my suggestion, Tommo and I go into one of the general stores, to see what the trading is like here. The shop we enter is a tent like any other, but a bit larger and squarer, with a flag flying from the tent pole to denote that it is a shopkeeper's establishment.

I am unprepared for the scene that meets us within. Laid out before us is a collection of every known object used by man in the course of living. How such an accumulation of contradictory merchandise may be gathered in a lifetime defies the imagination. Yet the storekeeper has obviously managed to bring them all together here, to one of the remotest regions of New South Wales, from all corners of the globe. From sugar candy to potted anchovies, East India pickles to bottles of Bass's pale English ale, slippers to stays, babies' booties to picks and shovels, every form of mining equipment, household essential, foodstuff and frippery is here. A pair of herrings hangs over a bag of sugar. Nearby lie raisins, dried sausages, saddles, harnesses, ribbons and bonnets. Cheeses in the round and loaves of bread are stacked on the floor next to bars of yellow soap. Tins of every conceivable type of vegetable, fish and meat, and even a crate of champagne, line one side of the tent. All this I see in my first casual observation. A closer inspection would reveal a thousand more of these et ceteras, I'm sure.

The shop is crowded with men swearing and guffawing, children bawling and squealing, and women wagging their tongues – their shrill voices rising above the buzz. Banter, blubbing, brouhaha, laughter and earnest talk fill the tent.

In one corner stands the storekeeper. He seems undismayed by the cacophony around him and is buying gold from a miner, no doubt using every trick known to cheat a free fraction of an ounce from the precious hoard for himself. The storekeeper has put a priority on dealing with the miner and ignores the crowd waiting to be served. Not wishing to buy anything, we take our leave.

Tommo and I visit several of these stores in the course of

the afternoon. They all have a great variety of merchandise, much of which I would never have thought necessary at a gold diggings. One shop has a tailor's dummy on which is displayed a dress purported to replicate Queen Victoria's wedding gown. It is of a cream-coloured taffeta silk and glorious to behold, with many pearls stitched to it, though I don't suppose these are real as in the original. It is a trifle dusty and soiled in places where curious fingers have plucked at the material, but still it wears a price of fifty pounds. A notice is pinned to the frock.

HRH Prince Albert's wedding clothes
are also available upon enquiry.
Alterations made within the week.

I am much bemused by all I observe and wonder how as shopowner I should ever know what to order beyond those things normal to every store. I purchase a pound of tea and the same of sugar for our new landlady and am shocked at the price! I perceive at once how a shopkeeper's fortune is so readily made. The profit is upwards of four hundred per cent on each item.

Tommo and I return to our landlady's shack and I give her the tea and sugar. She fumbles at the hem of her petticoat to find a small knot. 'I must return your rent, then,' she says. We refuse as gently as we can, whereupon she brings her soiled pinny to her eyes and, sobbing, rushes into her miserable little shack.

We walk down to the creek and have a wash. The water is muddy and cold. What appears to have once been a wide river is now the merest trickle – the miners have used up the water for sluicing in their long toms, cradles and panning dishes.

Tommo points to several tree stumps rooted out and

tossed upon the scarred banks. 'That's wattle,' he observes. 'It would have looked a treat flowerin' here once. Now it's nothing but mud and gravel.'

As the sun sets, it grows cold and I realise I am famished. I have not eaten anything other than two cold chops and a pannikin of tea at dawn. My twin, however, shows no sign of hunger. He sips from a black bottle he carries with him, one of several I have bought for him from Tucker & Co. Tommo has grown fidgety and his eyes take on a vacant look I have come to know when he craves opium. On the road to Lambing Flat, Tommo would simply take himself away from our camp and return in an hour or so. Now he will probably go quietly to the tent and light his little lamp, seeking salvation from his poppy pipe. When I suggest it is time for dinner he shows no interest.

'Bring me something,' he says absently.

'Will you be in the tent?' I ask but he is already walking away from me. 'I'll see you in an hour, then!' I shout, and he lifts his arm to acknowledge he's heard me. As he goes he rubs the tops of his arms as though his skin has a terrible itch upon it. His head is bowed and he has acquired a sort of shuffle, and looks weary of life.

There is a lump in my throat as I watch him depart. He is so small that his shoulder can snuggle under my armpit and so fragile in appearance that it seems as if he might blow away. In the past few nights, I have become aware as never before that Tommo cannot live without the dreaded Chinese drug.

I ache with the pain of knowing this, and my eyes blur at the sadness in him. I would give anything that my brother might be cured. I resolve again to do whatever it might take to win against the Irishman so that I can destroy Mr Sparrow and his vile greed. Surely then Tommo will escape the grasp of this evil addiction. Poor Tommo, I love him so very much and yet can do so little to help him. The more I try the more I seem to fail.

I think of Maggie, my heart's delight, who makes me laugh and who loves me. How very much I would like to take the magpie from its nest and place a bridal veil in its place. I sniff back my tears and chuckle at this thought – the white lace of purity and chastity for my Maggie Pye! It seems ridiculous, yet there is a purity and openness in her loving heart which I have not observed in anyone else. It is as though, having faced the worst in life, she has come through the flames and the dross has been burnt off, leaving only the pure gold remaining. But sometimes I think I must be deluding myself – that whatever virtue I ascribe to her, Maggie is still a whore. '*And once a whore, my dears? Always a whore.*' I beat back Ikey's words from my memory.

I love Maggie and wish to be with her all the days of my life. But not at a cost to Tommo. I shall never leave Tommo as long as he needs me. For the seven years he was lost in the wilderness, even Mary believed him dead. But never I. Every day at the moment of waking, I could feel him alive, the pulse of him within me. I could hear him breathing in the silence of my own breath and, when feeling my heart beat under my palm, I could feel two beats for every one – two hearts, his and mine.

It's just gone six when I reach the large tent where Caleb left us this afternoon. My friend is waiting for me in a long line of men. He indicates for me to join him, turning to those in the queue who grumble. 'He's the heavyweight champion of the colony. Would any of you lads care to have a go? Anyone game?' He points to one of the complainants. 'You, sir?'

The crowd laughs, and a chorus of voices bids me keep

my place, though I worry it is not fair. Some wag shouts, 'Will he pay double for the size o' the supper he eats, 'cause he ain't gettin' mine!'

'What's yer name, then?' someone else asks. 'Yer fighting name?'

I think for a moment. Hawk Solomon does not sound too exotic to the ear. 'Black Hawk,' I say on impulse, remembering my Maori name.

Caleb Soul looks delighted. 'Black Hawk, heavyweight champion of the colony!' he shouts so all may hear.

This is repeated by several of the men around me, and passed up and down the line. 'Who's you fighting next?' someone asks.

'The Lightning Bolt! The Irish and English heavyweight champion!' Caleb Soul answers for me again.

'Jaysus!' a voice nearby exclaims. 'You be the blighter what knocked Ben Dunn out the ring. Right over the bleedin' ropes into the lap of a whore! I read it in the *Gazette*.'

'Not quite,' I reply, surprised at how quickly the story has spread and grown. 'I was lucky to hit him at all.'

'Yes, with a sledgehammer!' Caleb Soul laughs and holds up my arm. 'Take off your jacket. Make a fist now, champ!'

I feel most foolish, but realise it is all for the good of the coming fight, so I remove my coat.

'Roll up your sleeve, let the lads see,' Caleb instructs.

I think to refuse but he's a decent sort and means well. I pull up my sleeve and clench my fist, bending my arm at the elbow. 'Holy Jeremiah!' someone shouts and all around us laugh and exclaim.

I am most relieved when at this moment a man comes to the entrance of the tent holding a large metal triangle which he beats with a bar. 'Tucker's up!' he shouts over the clanging. 'Pay at the door! Them what's weekly, show yer grub cards!'

'That was a good start, lad,' Caleb says as we move forward. 'News of your arrival will be all over the diggings by morning. Shouldn't be too hard to get a card game going for Tommo!' He looks concerned. 'He is coming to eat, ain't he?'

'I'll take him something, for his appetite is poor.'

'He should eat more,' Caleb worries. He has said the same thing to Tommo himself, every night on the road, with Tommo always replying with a little poem of his own.

> *I eats like a sparrow*
> *And drinks like a fish,*
> *Brandy's me water,*
> *Thin air's me tasty dish!*

Inside the tent I take my mind off my little brother, knowing that worrying will achieve nothing. Caleb points out two of the gold commissioners among those around us as well as several bankers, squatters and swells who have come to see the rush. The room is mostly occupied by diggers, sweat-stained and dirty. Shopkeepers, bullies and loafers are there too. The diggings is a great leveller of men and all mix happily enough together.

The kitchen is on the other side of a wall of logs. It is built like a cabin, with a porthole set at waist height through which the various comestibles are pushed. The cooks within scream out to the waiters as each plate comes through – 'Irish stew!' 'Liver and bacon!' 'Roast mutton!' This mingles with the clatter of plates, the rattle of knives and forks, and the sounds of hungry men demanding to be served. All over the tent plates are held aloft and voices are raised to the waiters requesting a return, which Caleb explains is a second helping.

I eat everything that is placed before me, leaving nothing for Tommo. As soon as my plate is wiped clean, I too hold it up and yell for roast mutton, this being the easiest food to carry away with me. Just as the waiter places my second helping down, a fellow at the next table takes the plate.

'Oi, that's not yours!' says the waiter.

'Is now!' retorts the cove.

'It is not,' the waiter reiterates and goes to grab it back. The cove smashes him in the face and down he goes. Two miners next to the plate-snatcher also jump up and kick at the waiter, one hitting him in the head. Another ruffian leaps from the next table and lashes out at the fallen man's ribs. Several more rush to the fray.

I rise from my seat. 'Stop it!' I yell, pulling some of the ruffians away, but more come, kicking and stamping on the poor wretch with evil satisfaction. The man on the floor is now in a state of insensibility, his features battered beyond recognition. Another heavy boot lands toe-first into his face and several teeth depart from his jaw.

I am still trying to pull people away, and now grow furious. With a roar, I land my fist into one villain's face and then again into a second man. Both drop to the ground but are immediately replaced by others. I hit them too. Five more men come running. I grab the first by his belt and neck and, lifting him above my head, throw him at the other four, sending them all sprawling. In the process, several tables and the people seated at them go flying.

It is all over and a deathly quiet falls over the room as I pick up the little waiter and carry him in my arms to the porthole. The other diners gasp as they see what has been done to him. He is taken by hands I cannot see and I walk back to Caleb Soul, stepping over the five ruffians who are either unconscious or playing possum.

'I think we should leave, don't you?' I say, panting slightly from the fight.

We turn to walk out when, almost as one, the men in the tent stand and begin to clap.

'Good on ya!' someone shouts.

'Well done, lad!' yells another.

'Hooray!'

A small door set into the log wall opens. 'Mr Black Hawk! Mr Black Hawk!' It is the chef, whom Caleb has told me is also the proprietor. He is hurrying towards us from the kitchen.

'Here's trouble,' I mutter to Caleb, thinking the man must want me to pay for the broken crockery.

But as the owner comes up, I see he is carrying a plate piled high with mutton and potatoes. 'You've not had your returns!' He proffers the plate. 'Here, lad, eat up!'

'I think we'd best leave, Felix,' Caleb Soul says. 'We've caused enough trouble for one night.'

'Trouble? No trouble at all, mate! I've been hoping something might happen to them bunch of bully-boys.'

'Is the waiter all right?' I ask.

'Not good, lad, not good at all. But we've sent a boy for Doctor Bullmore. Let's hope he ain't too drunk to attend.' Felix holds the plate of food out for me to take. 'Bring back the plate tomorrow, will ya, lad. You're welcome to come back anytime. Your grub's on the house.'

We walk out into the night. It is near freezing cold, with a full moon, fuzzy at the edges. I think there'll be a heavy frost in the morning, though the stars are amazingly bright. I wonder at the grandness of nature and the depravity of mankind. Why is it we reduce everything to greed and hate and try to settle all with our fists?

Caleb Soul chuckles quietly beside me.

'What's the joke?' I ask.

'By Jesus, if the mob didn't know before, they'll certainly know Black Hawk is in town by breakfast tomorrow! If we'd paid those ruffians, they couldn't have done any better for us.'

When we get to our tent, I can see no light from inside and I wonder if Tommo is asleep. But he is not there and I can only think he has gone some place else to smoke his opium.

The landlady's cat comes up and I feed it a slice of mutton. Then the woman herself appears, rubbing her eyes. 'Too late fer tea. No fire, I'm sorry, lads.'

It is bright moonlight and she can see the plate of meat and potatoes I hold. Her eyes grow big. I take two slices of mutton and a large potato as Tommo's share and hand the rest of the plate to her. She snatches it and scuttles back into her bark hut. 'Gawd bless yer! Gawd bless yer!' she murmurs as she goes. The tabby follows her back into the hut, no doubt thinking to get himself another share, though I don't like his chances.

It is not much past seven o'clock and I take some of the hay Caleb has ordered to the horses. Caleb joins me and we sit in the trap, while he smokes a pipe.

Since Caleb has learnt of my plan to fight the Lightning Bolt, he has become my most ardent supporter. He knows that we are on this trip in the hope that Tommo will raise the money for our stake at a card game or two, and that promoting the match will bring the punters to Tommo's table. My brother has arranged with Mr Sparrow that we be allowed to drum up interest in the fight – though this is normally his and Fat Fred's domain. He readily agreed – no doubt thinking it a sign of how vainglorious I have become. Caleb does not like to see anything approached in an ad hoc manner, even gambling, and he now turns his mind to how best to stir up interest in the fight before Tommo sets up a game.

'There's a cove who does printing in Yass. We'll have handbills printed!' he says eagerly, then leans back. 'I can see it now.' He enthusiastically describes it for me.

P R I Z E   F I G H T !
HEAVYWEIGHT CHAMPIONSHIP!

B L A C K   H A W K ,
heavyweight champion
of the Colony of New South Wales, to fight
T H E   L I G H T N I N G   B O L T ,
champion of all Ireland and Great Britain!

Time and location soon to be announced.

Caleb looks well pleased with himself and takes a puff from his pipe. 'That ought to get the tongues wagging. I'll take the trap into Yass tomorrow, get the handbills done and announce that you'll meet the punters on Sunday morning at ten o'clock outside the George Hotel.' Caleb knocks his pipe out against the heel of his boot. 'I'll leave before dawn. I'd better get some sleep.'

I clear my throat. 'Caleb, it is most kind of you to help us, but Tommo is in charge of all the plans. I'd be most obliged if you would discuss it first with him.'

Even in the moonlight I see the look of disappointment that crosses Caleb Soul's face.

'I feel sure Tommo will agree with your idea, Caleb,' I say quickly. 'And it will help us find punters for Tommo's cardgames as well, that is, if you see fit to take the handbills on as a project. It's just that I don't like to do things without my brother being involved.'

Caleb is silent for a moment. 'Quite right, Hawk. I didn't mean to interfere,' he says at last.

'Caleb, please, we are most grateful that you should care enough to assist us.'

My friend seems suitably mollified. 'I'll wake you in the morning, see what Tommo thinks, eh?' He climbs down from the trap and disappears into the interior of the tent.

There is no wood for a fire so I take my blanket from the carriage and wrap it around me. I sit on a tree stump, waiting for Tommo to come home. The cat appears again to keep me company, purring and brushing against my leg.

By nine o'clock, it is eerily quiet. As we have seen, the river has run near dry and its banks have been churned to clay, and so there are none of those sounds of the night which are usually heard near a stream. No crickets hum or frogs croak. I hear no hoot of an owl nor the throaty hiss and rattle of the opossum.

The miners, who work from dawn to dusk, are asleep only moments after they eat. The diggings are brutally hard work, and men spend most of their days up to their knees in mud and water. Bouts of dysentery caused by the poor water are common, along with a terrible eye condition known as sandy blight. Because their tents are roughly made – usually just a single tarpaulin held aloft by wattle poles – the miners often sleep in wet blankets, even in the freezing cold of winter. Some do not even trouble to remove their muddy boots, and footrot is a complaint common to all.

Though Caleb Soul assures me there is gambling and drinking aplenty in the grog shanties, brothels, eating tents and pubs, there is absolute quiet where we have pitched our tent. I go to fetch another blanket. I can do nothing to find Tommo, who could be anywhere – the diggings stretch five miles in any direction. The full moon's silver light spreads over the desolate landscape. As ten o'clock draws near, an idea comes to my anxious mind.

I go to the tent and waken Caleb. He sits up quickly.

'What is it?' he asks groggily.

'Caleb, how much opium did you give Tommo for this trip?'

Caleb Soul scratches his head. 'A few ounces – all I could obtain.'

'How long would that last?'

'Depends. For severe pain, a few days.'

'And for smoking? In an opium pipe?' I try to pull the answer from him.

'I can't rightly say, I have never smoked it.'

I think back on Tommo's state of agitation when he left me today. It can mean only one thing. Tommo did *not* have a sufficient supply of opium. The craving has come upon him and I would guess he has gone to the Chinese encampment to try to get more. I decide I cannot wait here any longer and must go after him. I have a strong feeling my twin is in danger.

I go to the trap and from among Tommo's things, I take his fighting axe. He has not used it since we have been in Sydney but still keeps it razor sharp. I push the axe into my belt and pull my two blankets over me. Then I set out in the bright moonlight towards the celestial encampment, which is about a mile to the north of the diggings and somewhat clear of the European settlement.

A heavy frost has fallen. The ground clunks under my boots and, though I now have both blankets wrapped about me, a chill seeps into my bones. I walk over a short rise and come upon the camp of the Mongolians. All lies perfectly still in the moonlight. Two Chinamen, about thirty feet away, guard the camp. They huddle in their blankets near a small brazier to keep warm. As soon as they see me, they leap to their feet, their blankets dropping from them as they flee, yelling strange imprecations at the top of their voices.

Soon there are people everywhere as they rush from their tents and humpies while I stand quite still, not knowing what to do next.

'Ho!' I say. 'Ho, there!' I lift my arm out from under the blanket. 'Don't panic!' I shout. 'I mean no harm.' It dawns on me how I must appear. I am just over seven foot tall, and the blankets drape about my shoulders like a ghost's cloak. My face is clearly visible in the moonlight, black with strange signs carved upon it. I must look like a monster!

Some of the Chinese have stopped a little distance from me – no doubt thinking themselves safe with plenty of time to run should this ghost devil suddenly advance upon them. I remove the blankets so they might see me standing like a human. 'Friend!' I shout. 'I am a friend of the Chinaman!' Nevertheless, some at the back of the throng start to run, perhaps seeing Tommo's axe stuck into my belt. But some of the braver souls hold their ground.

'Friend of the Chinaman!' I shout again. In the earlier panic, an old man has fallen on the path near me and no one has dared go to his rescue. I carry this ancient Mongolian back to where my blankets are and I cover him with one of these. 'Friend of the Chinaman!' I repeat as I rise.

One man breaks from the group and walks towards me, to the shouts of warning from those watching. He stops perhaps ten feet away and brings his hands together to his chest, bowing deeply. I can see that his knees are shaking.

'Friend?' he says, trying to smile.

'Aye, friend!' I assure him, smiling. He moves forward to shake my hand and in an instant I am thrown onto my back, my head hitting the ground hard.

It is some moments before I recover, to find six men sitting upon me and a dozen more crowded around. I think that maybe they will kill me. Curiously, I am not afraid and through my mind flashes an imagined bill poster:

GIANT NIGGER JEW KILLED
BY MONGOLIAN HORDES!

I start to laugh. After what Tommo and I have been through, this is a stupid way to die.

To my surprise the celestials crowded about me also begin to laugh. I get up and dust down my breeches – looking for the Chinaman who has thrown me to the ground. I pat him on the back and grin. 'Good! Very good!' Then I lift him into the air above my head and twirl him around, before putting him down again. This time we shake hands like gentlemen.

'Friend,' says he.

'Friend,' say I.

It is too cold to stand around and slowly the crowd disperses, but for four whom I take to be the leaders.

Now I find myself in difficulty. How shall I tell them I am looking for Tommo?

'Do any here speak English?' I ask. 'English, speak English?'

It is soon apparent that none do, even my new-found friend. One of them hands me a black bottle. I do not as a rule drink spirits but now I take a deep swig. I cough as the brandy burns down my throat and warms my stomach, and

543

hand it back with a smile. My hosts smile too. They give me back my blanket, the one I used to cover the old man. Still, I have no way of asking them how he is.

Then, from nowhere, a woman is pushed towards me. I can see she is European but cannot judge her age. She is wrapped in a torn blanket, and her eyes are sunk deep into her skull so that I cannot see them but for bright pinpricks within dark sockets. Her skin is drawn yellow and taut, and her nose is half eaten away. Her lips draw back in a snarl to show black, rotting teeth.

One of the Chinese prods her and jabbers something. 'Inlish!' he says to me.

'Do you speak English?' I ask the woman. 'What's your name?'

'Sally, sir,' she answers in no more than a whisper. Her face may be that of an old crone's but her voice is a young girl's.

'How old are you, Sally?'

'Twenty, I thinks, sir.'

I have heard how young women are caught up in the craving for the Devil's Smoke and how they come to the Mongolians for opium and then cannot leave, paying for the poppy with their bodies until they die in some wretched hovel.

I know full well that there are lots of Sallys, but this is the first of them I've seen. She is clearly beyond all hope of recovering from the addiction. I know I am speaking to someone who will soon be dead and that she seeks no salvation from me beyond the price of her next pipe.

I feel desperately sorry for the poor creature, but I am also relieved. Possibly she knows where Tommo is.

'I am looking for my brother who seeks to buy opium. Have you seen him, Sally?' I say gently.

'There's no nigger here, sir.'

'No, he is not black. A small man, not taller than you, fair hair and blue eyes.'

'I dunno, sir. I can't rightly say,' Sally shrugs.

'Can't say what? You have not seen him?'

'Sir, I needs two shillings to eat,' she whispers.

I take a florin from my pocket and hand it to her. Sally's hand comes out to grasp it, but the moment she takes the coin the Chinaman standing beside her strikes at her wrist and the florin goes flying. He picks it up and hands it back to me. Sally cowers and whimpers.

'I'll give it to you later,' I assure her. 'Have you seen my brother?'

'There's someone like what you said,' she replies. She is shivering, rubbing her arms, just as I've seen Tommo do.

'Can you take me to him please?'

She looks at the men around her as though to ask permission. So I point to her, then to myself, and then back to Sally. The Chinamen laugh. They must believe I want to sleep with her. They nod their heads, and I bow to each respectfully. Now I take Sally by the bony shoulder and she leads me through a maze of tents until we come to a miserable hut made of bark slabs and hessian sacks. She parts the sackcloth and I must stoop to enter a smallish room, the floor of which is covered in filthy rags. In the light of three wax candles placed on an upturned log, I see two naked females lying on the floor. Their carcasses are stripped so bare of flesh that I can see their veins through their translucent skins. Between them lies Tommo, also naked. One of the wretches is holding a pipe to his mouth. Though his eyes are closed, his lips make a soft sucking noise, like that of a newborn pup. White smoke curls slowly upwards from his nostrils.

'That him?' Sally asks, her voice now bolder than before.

I nod, unable to speak.

'Give us the money, then!' She holds out her claw and I give her the florin. 'More!' she demands. I am too shocked to resist and hand her a pound note, not caring.

As she takes the money, a bundle of rags and hair and ancient skin scuttles from a dark corner to snatch the note from Sally's hand. It is a Chinaman, or perhaps a woman, I cannot tell. It hands Sally a pipe and a small wad of opium and as quickly as it appeared, vanishes back into the darkness beyond the candlelight.

Sally unclasps her ragged blanket and I see that she too is naked. She does not look at me but sinks to her knees beside the candles. She begins to work a small dob of opium around the point of what looks like a steel knitting needle, then she holds it to the candle flame.

'Tommo!' I call.

Both hags look up at me but say nothing. Tommo does not respond. 'Tommo!' I say again, this time more gently, bending down over him. Pushing one of the wretches away, I kneel beside my twin and shake him. My brother is as limp as a rag doll.

'He dreams,' says one or other of the hags. 'He'll not wake in an hour or even two.' She reaches across and touches me on the shoulder. 'You want me? Two shillings!'

'Where are his clothes!' I say through clenched teeth. She shrugs and points. I rise and move into the corner she indicates, and now I see the creature there, toothless, its mouth open with fear. It holds out Tommo's clothes in its claws. I take them and search through the pockets for his purse. It is missing. I grab the creature and hold my hand out, but it does nothing in response. Then I see it has been squatting upon a small lacquer box, about twelve inches square.

I take up the box and force open the lid. Inside is

Tommo's purse. The rest of the space is filled with small parcels of opium tied in bamboo leaves. I scoop up two handfuls of the opium parcels and put them in my pocket, dropping some money into the now half-empty box in exchange.

Meanwhile Sally has fixed her pipe and is on her haunches pulling at it. The two wretches have the other pipe, which is spent, and now they pester Sally until she hands them the wad. They have forgotten I am here and can think of nothing but their craving.

I wrap poor Tommo, still unconscious, in both blankets. His clothes I stuff inside my shirt, stained and stiff with blood from the fight at the eating tent. I tie the laces of his boots together and hang them around my neck. Then I pick up my twin, horrified at how light he is. I push aside the hessian-sack door and carry him out into the night.

The moon is at its zenith and it is almost as clear as day as I begin to walk out of the camp. By some miracle I am not lost in the maze and soon find my way back from whence I came. To my surprise, the four Chinese are still standing beside the brazier and they rise as I approach. I put Tommo down, though he is light enough, and shake their hands. They now know why I have come and nod their heads in sympathy.

'Me, Wong Ka Leung,' says the Mongolian who threw me to the ground.

'Me, Hawk Solomon,' I say.

'Friend!' they all chorus.

It is not these men's fault, I realise, that Tommo suffers so. It is the fault of greed.

'Goodbye, Wong Ka Leung,' I say and shake his hand solemnly again. We both bow deeply to one another.

I pick up Tommo and sling him across my shoulders, walking over the small rise. As soon as I am out of sight, and beyond the hearing of the Mongolians, I burst into tears. Tommo breathes deeply, then sighs against my back. I think of Mary and all her hopes, of her love for me, for Tommo, for both of us – her two precious boys! 'Oh Mama, whatever shall become of us?' I sob.

Chapter Twenty-one

TOMMO

Lambing Flat
30 June 1861

It is early Sunday morning and we've been in the goldfields just over a week. I've slept badly and am up early, wandering through the diggings. The day's very still and several of the miners I pass reckons there might be snow in the air.

The Sabbath be the one day of the week the authorities don't allow work at the diggings, what's very funny when you thinks about it, 'cause the miners use this day to get themselves drunk as lords. Then o' course they fights and carouses for as long as they can. Sunday be the most *unholy* day of the week!

Just last Sunday a priest come up from Melbourne to hear confession and say mass for the Irish. They was given plenty o' warning of the good father's arrival and a church and confessional was specially erected out of canvas, but not a single bloke presented himself for the absolving of sins and the taking of the wafer and wine. Some wag reckons that the Pope, upon hearing of this shameful event, will rename Lambing Flat 'Sod 'em and T'morrer'. The 'sod 'em' is for not attending mass and 't'morrer', the day after the Sabbath, is when they'll all be excommunicated and condemned to hell.

Caleb Soul returned from Yass earlier in the week and brought with him the handbills announcing a meeting for the punters to see Black Hawk. The venue is the Great Eastern Hotel, as it's one of the few proper buildings of Lambing Flat. It's away from the diggings and the river, and is a favourite meeting place among the miners.

Caleb has arranged a rough timber platform for Hawk to stand on. Thank God, though cold, it's a day o' bright sunshine, otherwise my brother might be a little chilly! He's to strip to the waist and wear a bright red cummerbund so that all may see he's in the very best physical condition. To show his strength, he'll challenge anyone in the crowd to arm-wrestling, taking a new opponent every ten minutes. Hawk don't much like the idea, saying it be boastful, but Caleb and me told him that were the whole idea! Anyhow, he's agreed to do it.

We has put up the handbills everywhere – in the grog shanties, brothels and pubs as well as the chophouses and about the miners' fires where they cooks their meat and damper.

Already there's a strong rivalry among the men, with the Irish going for their own man, the Lightning Bolt, and t'others going for Hawk. Hawk's become somewhat of a hero after giving the ruffians a walloping the night they attacked the waiter. Turned out they was Irish and now all the Irish has made the 'Nigger' their sworn enemy. As Caleb Soul says, 'It could not be a better situation if we tried.'

Since that night, there's been some muttering about the Irish boyos taking revenge. Hawk's been warned to have a few stout men with him when he presents himself this morning. I'm a bit worried for him, but Hawk insists we goes ahead as planned. 'I can't scuttle away like a cockroach on the *Nankin Maiden* when they make the slightest threat! I must face this if I'm to face the Bolt!'

This morning's turnout promises to be a big un. The Miners' League, what has been formed to protest against the presence of the Chinese at the diggings, will be there. The League has as many as two thousand men in their membership along with a brass band, for they likes a bit of a march. I've heard how it's made up of different chapters, each with a banner showing the diggings they hail from. There's Blackbutt Gully, Tipperary Hill, Possum Creek, and the like.

They'll be marching behind their leaders and carrying their bright banners with pride, so the whole thing'll look like a bleedin' carnival. Caleb has even paid 'em to play a tune or two at Hawk's appearance!

One of the leaders of the Miners' League, Mr Cameron, told Caleb that if the payment were a subscription fee for the three of us to join, they'd play the whole morning for naught. But we has refused, being most wary o' those who are against the Chinese, what we thinks has done nothing wrong other than to be a different colour.

A special correspondent from the *Sydney Morning Herald* has come out here incognito to report on the Miners' League and their battle against the celestials. He's said to lurk about the diggings, making up scurrilous lies about the miners. Caleb reckons we should recruit him to our cause but we don't know who he is! Still, if we could encourage the special to add a few lines about Hawk and his fight, that would stir the possum nicely.

The special's pen has already struck some hard blows against the diggers, telling his readers that the Chinese ain't done nothing to the miners and is a most peaceful group. The special also points out that the rough element in the diggings is the real culprits behind the uproar. They make trouble with the Chinese and then steals their claims. Hawk reckons this a very fair point of view, but the mob don't like it one bit.

Meantime I has had meself two card games thanks to Caleb's introductions. The first were with the various shopkeepers, what's among the richest folk in the diggings, and the second were with the sly grog shop owners and publicans, what's not short of a bob either. Yours truly won at both!

Me winnings were ten pounds each time. Twenty pounds is bloody good wages but it falls far short of our ambition. These blokes ain't true gamblers and is too timid with their wagers. We still need another eighty pounds towards the stake – and that don't even begin to cover the cost o' Hawk's training. I got to get one really big game if I'm to have any hope of making this.

Tonight I've a game with the Irish. It ain't one set up by Caleb who has warned me against playing poker with these boyos. 'Tommo, there will not be an honest cove in the game and all of them broadsmen,' he warns. I can hardly tell him that I won't be adding even one per cent of honesty to the game meself! I'd rather take me chances and pit me own talent against villains than play with the duffers what he's lined up.

With only two games played, the word about Tommo is already out among the respectable folk and they's all gun shy, even though I didn't cheat once! At least the rough mob play for big stakes. Besides, I got no choice. We must leave on Tuesday morning to return to Sydney, so this is me last chance.

I first come across this mob I'm gunna play with while passing out handbills at a place called Possum Creek. They's not working a claim and they don't look like they intends to neither. They all sit outside a bark hut playing the flats. I put down a handbill and stop to watch them a while. They's playing whist and one of the players what's thrown his hand in picks up the poster.

'What's it say?' he asks, holding it upside down.

I read the handbill out to them and they all stops to listen.

'By Jaysus, that be clever an' all,' says one o' them. 'The Irishman cannot be beat!'

'Oh? Who says?' I asks.

'I says,' he replies. 'You work for the nigger, then, does yer?'

'Aye,' I replies. 'I helps Mr Caleb.'

Still seated, he grabs me by the shirt front so I'm standing up against him. I'm looking into his foul, grinning mouth of broke teeth. 'That black bastard be askin' fer a hidin', and my oath, he'll be gettin' one at the hands o' the Irish champ!' He shakes me. 'I'm inclined to give you a taste o' what he's in fer! How'd yer like that, eh?'

'Not much,' I admits. 'But I tell you what! If the Irish fight as poorly as they cheats at flats, your man ain't gunna win.'

'What's yer mean?' he growls.

I take out an ace of hearts from his sleeve and a Jack of the same from behind his collar and throws them down in front of his mates.

'Why, ya right bastard, Micky!' they chorus.

'Dunno why you bothered. Whose deck is that?' I point to the cards on the table. All eyes turn to another of the Irishmen. 'Well, it's shaved, ain't it?' I says.

It's a guess o' course. I can't tell from where I'm standing. But the moment I says it I see the sly look in the eye of the one they're all looking at, and I know straight away I be right.

'What's goin' on, then?' one o' the ruffians shouts, throwing his cards down and rising from the bark table to glare at his mate.

'Righto,' I says, me heart in me mouth. 'That's two of yer what's cheating. How about the other three, eh?' Each man looks at the other narrow-eyed. 'Tell ya what,' I suggests, 'let me sit in on yer game. I'll play ya all together, the lot of you against me! What say you, a shilling a point? But if I catches any of ya cheating, ya drops out of the game. If you catches me, I'll double any winnings on the table and it all be yours. Are you game, then, gentlemen?'

Me suggestion's just silly enough, and them's just stupid enough to accept. An hour later, three of them's been tossed out of the game. The other two I clean out too. They look fit to kill when I rise from the table, scooping the pool. Then I hand 'em back their money! 'Sorry gentlemen, but the nigger lover don't play with amateurs.'

The one what grabbed me in the first place has grown very red in the face. He balls his fist. 'Mind yer mouth, laddy,' he growls.

I pretend I ain't scared. 'Know a big game, then? High stakes?' I asks. 'Among yer mates? Someone maybe ya don't like, someone what owes ya? Or perhaps you wants revenge, eh? Tell ya what, gentlemen. If you has the nous to set up a big game, high stakes, I'll cut ya in on ten per cent. But it's got to be real big. How's that, then?'

'Twenty,' says one of 'em.

'Fifteen,' says I.

They agree and we shake on it. I share me black bottle with them and then goes off, telling them they can contact me by leaving a message at the Great Eastern. As I leave I yell, 'Oh, and gentlemen, take me advice, put yer winnings on Black Hawk!'

'Bullshit!' one of 'em shouts, but this time they laughs. 'See ya right soon, Tommo!' another yells after me.

Well, since then they've found me a game with the Callaghan mob, where the stakes are ten pounds in. It's to be held in the Great Eastern Hotel, starting ten o'clock tomorrow night.

Me and Jonah Callaghan, what's leader of the mob, made
the booking. Him and me went to see the proprietor of the
Great Eastern, Mr Makepeace Chubb. He's a little cove, fat,
bald and always with a coating of shiny sweat to his florid
face. We inspect a room upstairs, to the back of the hotel.
Each of us pays the publican a pound for the arrangements,
and then we arrange for him to get in two brand new decks
o' cards.

'I've got 'em on sale here,' he volunteers.

'Give us a look then?' Callaghan asks.

The publican returns with two packs of Mermaid Brand.

'What's this shite?' Callaghan growls.

'He's right,' I says to Chubb. 'They has to be DeLarue &
Sons.'

'Oh,' says Chubb. 'That serious, is it? I'll have to get 'em
in. Jeremiah Neep has them in stock as I recall.'

'We'll be in on Sundee mornin' ter inspect them,' Jonah
warns. 'Have pen and ink ready, much obliged.' Though
Jonah Callaghan's words seem mild enough, the way he says
them ain't at all pleasant.

So ten o'clock this morning, accompanied by Jonah
Callaghan, I goes to the Great Eastern. Makepeace Chubb is
busy out the back and we sends a message we wants to see the
flats. A few minutes later, he comes huffing and puffing to the
bar, and puts two packs down on the counter in front of us.

'Where's pen and quill?' Callaghan demands.

The publican sighs and leaves to fetch same.

I orders two nobblers of Cape brandy and when they
comes, I push one in front o' the Irishman and invite him to
inspect the decks. He looks down at the brandy in front of
him. 'What's this shite?' Before I can open me mouth he
pushes the drink over me. He throws his head back and
shouts to the barman, 'Oi, you! Irish!'

'Suit yerself. Only trying to be friendly,' I says, a trifle miffed.

'Yeah, well don't waste yer breath,' he replies. 'Two! With a pint o' best to go with it!' He knocks one nobbler o' whiskey back, chases it with half the beer, then the other Irish whiskey follows and the remainder of the beer. All of this is done straight off, no pause between. Good, I thinks, he'll be drinkin' whiskey and beer all night at the game. It's got to catch up with him unless he be made of cast iron.

Callaghan wipes his mouth with the back of his hand. He then picks up a deck and examines it closely, picking gently at the seals with his fingernail to make sure they's tight closed. He does the same to the second pack of DeLarue. Satisfied, he dips the quill into the ink pot and makes his mark across the seals. I does the same, spending even a little more time at examination before I signs.

We call for the publican and makes him sign across the front of each pack. Then we follow him out the back and into his office, where he has a small safe for miners to keep their gold in. He fiddles with the combination, groaning as he stoops down low with his back to us. With the safe open, he steps aside so that we can see it's empty, 'case we've got any ideas. He puts the two decks into the safe and closes the door, scrambling the combination once again. 'There,' he says, puffing, 'all safe and sound, lads.'

'You'll be sure to see there's plenty o' firewood and the hearth be well lit and the room warm?' I asks. 'We'll be playing in our shirt sleeves rolled up to here.' I indicate the top o' me arm. 'No hats to be worn either.'

'Eh? What's this, then?' Callaghan scowls.

'Just helps to know there ain't no handy sleeve or hat about. I've known cards what had a natural affinity with sleeves and hats. Hand goes under a hat to scratch a louse. Never know what it might find lurking! Could be the king or queen herself. Or an ace may pop out of a coat sleeve, know what I mean?'

Jonah turns and stabs a hard finger in me chest. 'Think we's gunna cheat ya, does ya?'

'It's been known to happen,' says I. 'But I'll find you out if you does.'

'Like hell yer will!'

'Steady on now, lads,' says Makepeace. 'There'll be no cards played in this house if yiz going to fight. A drink on the house with my compliments will settle youse down! Cape and Irish with a chaser, if I remember rightly.'

We follows him through to the bar and he pours the drinks. 'On the house!' he repeats, looking a bit pained. 'Oh yes, and the house takes ten per cent, lads.'

'What?' Callaghan grumbles.

Makepeace shrugs, safe behind his bar. 'As you wish, take it or leave it.'

'It'll be fine,' I says.

'Bloody hell it will!' Jonah growls. 'Fine is it? It'll be just fine for you to pay it, laddy.'

'Oh, and another five pounds to cover breakages. Returnable o' course, if nothing's damaged!' Makepeace adds.

After each of us puts down our share, Callaghan and me walks out into the bright, crisp sunlight and I sticks out me hand. 'See ya t'morrer, then.' He ignores me, spitting to the side o' his boots as he walks away. 'Charming!' I exclaims. 'Real nice to know ya, Callaghan!'

'Fuck off!' he says, not looking back.

Well, I thinks to meself, everything's going just right and dandy for yours truly. Now I'll go and see how Hawk's faring.

Hawk still worries about me too much, I reckon. When I tells him about me game coming up, he looks most worried. 'Tommo, Caleb Soul says these men are dangerous. They don't dig for gold but live by robbing others of their dust. Two of the brutes I subdued in Felix's eating-house were from their gang, or so I was told.'

I shrugs. 'Cards is funny. If you win against a villain and they think it's kosher, or they can't work out how you done it, you got their respect. It's sort of honour among thieves.'

'Do these men know this?' Hawks asks. 'I'd best come with you to make sure.'

'Hawk, let me go on me own!'

'What if something happens?'

'If you comes with me, o' course something *will* happen!' says I. 'This time you've got to stay a mile away. Them Callaghans don't know I'm yer brother, only that I works for Caleb.'

'What about today, then? They'll see you with me, won't they?'

'Caleb can handle the show with you. He'll love to spruik it. I'll just be in the crowd watching. Cheering you on, Hawk!' I can see Hawk ain't happy about letting me go alone to the game, but he knows that it's our best chance to raise the gelt.

'Tommo, be careful, won't you?'

'Course I will, big brother,' I say.

It's near noon, and already there's a big crowd outside the Great Eastern Hotel waiting to see Hawk, a brisk trade going on at the bar. It's about time for Hawk to meet the punters. He walks out and I can see his head sticking up nearly two foot above the crowd. His black shoulders, scarred from O'Hara's knotted rope, shine ebony in the sunlight. He turns and smiles, showing a row of gleaming white teeth. They be most unusual at our age when most men's teeth is yellow from tobacco-chewing and pipe-smoking. Hawk's Maori tattoos give him the look of a black prince or warrior.

As he wades through the crowd, I admire his huge shoulders and narrow waist. His legs is like tree trunks, but he is trim at the ankle and can move surprisingly quick for such a big fellow. He's bulging with muscle everywhere – a result of all his work hoisting barrels at Tucker & Co. And his stomach's like a washboard. I can't believe the Irishman won't tremble when he sees him in the ring.

Hawk climbs the platform to cheers and boos from the crowd. I can tell from their murmurs that they's struck with his massive size. Just as I walks up to join the mob, the Miners' League marches in and their band strikes up. I reckon there must be more than two thousand of 'em all up. They play a marching tune with cries of 'Roll up! Roll up!' from those behind the banners. It is a grand sight and everyone claps as they comes to a halt. A single drum marks time and at the command of each section leader, each group falls out.

Meanwhile Hawk stands on the platform like a black general surveying his troops. With blokes from the Miners' League joining it, the crowd is huge. Caleb Soul has got up on the platform beside Hawk. He brings a hailing funnel to his mouth and calls for silence. When at last the mob settles down, he nods to someone at the foot of the platform. There's the roll of a kettledrum.

'Diggers and gentlemen!' he proclaims. 'I give you the next world champion in the division of heavyweight – the inestimable, pugilistic, ferocious and *undefeated* Black Hawk, champion of the colony of New South Wales!'

The crowd cheers and then a voice near the platform calls out, 'Garn, tell us how many fights 'e's 'ad!'

'Only recently discovered, the Black Hawk has beaten the redoubtable and famous heavyweight, Ben Dunn!' Caleb bellows over the crowd's laughter, not missing a beat.

'Who?' shouts the same wag, to more laughter.

'You, sir,' says Caleb, pointing to the man, 'step up and let's see your form. Up here, lad!' he indicates the platform. A small man, not much bigger than me, climbs up, with Caleb lending him a hand.

'What's your name?' Caleb asks.

'Pat Malone.' The little cove grins.

'How about you arm-wrestle Black Hawk, Pat Malone? Five pounds to you if you win!' Caleb says.

The little cove don't back down. 'Can I stand up and use both arms?' he asks, quick as a flash. Caleb looks at Hawk, who nods. I ain't so sure it's a good idea. Though small, the man's a miner, hardened to manual work. With the use o' both his arms and his body-weight he won't be easy to beat.

The crowd grows quiet as Hawk sits at the arm-wrestling table. The miner takes up his position, his legs wide apart, and grasps Hawk's hand in both of his. Caleb holds up his bandanna. 'Take the strain!' The bandanna drops. 'Go!'

The little cove is no shirker and he keeps Hawk's hand vertical. Then me brother's arm starts to go down, and the crowd begins to shout their encouragement.

The miner is gaining on him and the mob thinks he's gunna win, so they shouts him on. Hawk's knuckles is about to touch the deck when he gives a great grunt and swings his arm up. He pushes the little bloke backwards so hard that the miner loses his balance and goes flying off the edge of the platform, into the crowd. It's an amazing feat of strength.

Hawk rises quickly to see if Pat Malone's been hurt. He pulls him gently back onto the platform. The little miner seems no worse for his fall, and Hawk lifts his challenger's arm as if declaring him the real winner. Then me big brother lifts Mr Malone high above his head and the crowd cheers at this show o' sportsmanship. He puts the miner down and they shakes hands like the best o' friends.

Caleb holds up a five-pound banknote for all to see. 'Five

pounds to Pat Malone for having a go!' he shouts. 'Let's have three cheers for the miners, lads!' The crowd is completely won over.

'Shit, that's another fiver I has to win,' I mutters to meself, but Caleb has done good. The band strikes up a rousing song.

Caleb now announces that Hawk will talk. 'Hear from the champion himself!' He hands the hailing funnel to Hawk. The crowd draw closer so that they hears his every word.

'Gentlemen! I thank you for your time. It's grand to be among so many friends.' There's more cheers and boos. 'Let me tell you about the Irishman, the Lightning Bolt.'

The fighter's fellow countrymen raise a great swell o' noise at his name and Hawk waits 'til they has quieted down. 'My worthy opponent is better known as the Bolt, because he can take a great hammering to the head and yet remain true to his metal.' The Irish like this remark and I can see they'll store it up to repeat a thousand times. 'He is the champion of Ireland and Britain and there is much speculation that he cannot be beaten by anyone in this colony or any other in the Empire! He is a most formidable adversary.'

Hawk points to Pat Malone, what's sitting on the edge of the platform. 'It is quite true, as my little friend here says, that I lack experience in the prize ring and my stamina has yet to be tested. Some say it was a lucky punch that knocked out Ben Dunn.' Hawk pauses a moment. 'Ben Dunn himself has been heard to espouse this theory!'

A roar of laughter goes up from the crowd and I can see they is warming to my twin. He waits for it to die down before continuing. 'I admit, Mr Dunn was most tired, having just fought five rounds. But those who speculate on these things and know better than I say that the Irishman will take

Ben Dunn with one arm tied behind his back and a glass of good Irish whiskey in the other.'

The Irish in the crowd cheers wildly. 'So, if you are an Irishman I will reluctantly accept that your wagers will not be placed on me. If, on the other hand, you are an Englishman, you may well be in two minds, not wishing the Irishman to win, but not too sure of the big nigger, either!'

Most know what Hawk says is true and they admires him for it. Hawk takes the hailing funnel from his mouth and smiles, 'til the laughter and clapping settles. 'But if you are an *Australian*, then you will know we are a new breed of men and not given to easy surrender!'

The crowd rises to a new peak of excitement at this and it takes some time to calm down again. 'In my favour, I have my size and, if you will allow me to say so, a great determination to win. I trust you to make up your own minds about me and not to be swayed overly much by the bookmakers' odds! I thank you for hearing me out. May your efforts reward you with gold aplenty!'

Thunderous applause and cheering follows as me brother ends, and the band strikes up 'The Wild Colonial Boy'. There's men about me what has tears in their eyes. It's a brilliant piece o' work. Hawk's pulled off what no amount of vainglorious bragging could do, for these ordinary blokes knows sincerity and the honest truth when they hears it.

Hawk arm-wrestles half a dozen or so miners, one directly after t'other, with no rest in between. He beats all six. But the seventh, a big man, wins 'cause Hawk is knackered. These are men what works hard with picks and shovels and ain't no milksops. 'Luck of the Irish!' Caleb shouts, as he hands over five quid. He thanks the crowd once more and the show is over. Now it is left to me to do the rest with Jonah Callaghan's mob.

The meeting of the Miners' League is to take place at

two. The men has been drinking steadily all morning and many is starting to fall about. Hawk wants me to rest in our tent for he sees how tired I am after my bad night's sleep. I don't say no. Sleeping during the day comes natural to me!

I stops at the butcher's on me way and buys two pounds o' chops and a quarter o' chopped liver. When I gets back to the tent I calls out to Lucy, our landlady. She be a widow what tries to make a living as a washerwoman. If she has a surname, she ain't giving it to us. 'Just Lucy,' she replied when we asked. 'Me husband were a right bastard when he was alive. I don't see I has to carry the burden o' his name now 'e's dead, does I?'

So our private name for her is Just Lucy. 'Lucy, I brought something for the moggy!' I shouts as soon as I gets back. She's out of her bark hut quick smart, carrying the mangy cat what seems to be her only company. 'Mornin', Tommo.' She squints up at the pale sun. 'Or is it afternoon? It's me day orf, no washing on the Sabbath, so I's kipped in a bit.'

'Here, chopped liver and chops for the tabby.' I hand her the meat and she lets the cat jump from her arms. She unwraps it careful, like it were a late Christmas present.

'Cat can't eat six chops, Tommo!' she says soft.

'Sorry Lucy, I doesn't know much about cats. You'll have to find some other use for them chops.' Just Lucy don't like charity. Since the tea and sugar Hawk bought her, she's been trying to do our washing and cooking.

'Yer a good boy, Tommo.'

'Nah, I just likes cats! They don't give a bugger for no one, like me!'

'A likely story! How'd ya go with the packs of cards at the hotel, Tommo?' she asks, dropping a lump of the chopped liver at her feet for the cat.

'Perfect, Lucy. Matter o' fact, couldn't have done better

meself.' I take out a pound and hand it to her. 'It's what I promised if it worked, so this ain't charity.'

'Ten shillings you promised, Tommo!'

'Ten shillings a pack!' I says.

Just Lucy shakes her head but takes the money and puts it in her pocket. I see her eyes getting a bit wet.

'No, no, don't cry, Lucy!' I says in alarm. 'It's yours well earned. How long did ya have to wait in Jeremiah Neep's shop?'

'All Saturday afternoon, almost. About five o'clock, in comes a young lad and asks for two packs o' DeLarue cards.

'"DeLarue, eh?" Mr Neep says. "Where's you from, lad?"

'"Great Eastern Hotel," the boy says. "Mr Chubb sent me, sir."

'"Must be an important game. Sold a couple o' the self-same packs yesterday. Don't get much call for DeLarue, too expensive, they is."

'"Dunno how come, sir," says the boy. "Mr Chubb just said they must be *them* cards, no other."

'I'm standing like you's told me, right next to the shelf where the playing cards is kept. I puts yer two decks where you said, on the top. Then Mr Neep comes over. "Here we are, then. Right on the top they is, the last two." He takes yer two packs and wraps them up proper and gives them to the lad, what pays 'im ten shillings. He sends the boy away with a bright red sucker from a jar.'

'And Mr Neep ain't suspicious, you standing in the shop all afternoon?'

'Nah,' says Just Lucy. 'He be a decent man. I asks him if I can stay there so as to ask customers if they wants their washing done.' She grins. 'I got two new customers out of it, too! Took Mr Neep's dust coat 'ome to wash, for his kindness, like!'

'Well it were nicely done, Lucy.'

Just Lucy looks at me. 'Tommo, why'd ya give Jeremiah Neep back the two packs o' cards you bought yesterday, them brand new and not ever been opened?'

I points to the moggy what's busy eating the liver. 'Cat's got me tongue, Lucy,' I says, laughing.

'Oh, sorry, always were a bit of a stickybeak. Too curious for me own good.'

'It ain't that, Lucy. What you don't know you can't be hurt by if someone should come asking questions.'

'You mean I didn't never go into Mr Neep's shop, 'cept to find new customers for washing?'

'That's right, Lucy. That's the bonus earned for keeping your gob shut.'

'Happy to oblige, Tommo. Fancy a nice chop fer ya tea?'

'Maybe when I wakes up. Got to get a few winks.'

'I'll see yer not disturbed,' she promises.

Well, I does get disturbed. About three o'clock Just Lucy herself sticks her head in and shouts, 'Tommo, it's the miners, they's marching on the Chinamen's camp!'

I dunno how, but I know straight away that Hawk's there and he ain't marching with the miners. I runs to the trap and fetches me fighting axe. 'Be careful, Tommo!' she shouts after me as I trot down the path to the celestial encampment.

It be a good mile or so to the Mongolians and I'm half running. As I draws near, I hears the mob shouting and the band playing, and some musket fire in the background. Smoke billows up on the horizon. The running has made me head ache real bad and it's near time for me smoke. But all I can think of is that Hawk's in danger. I can feel it in me gut and in the back of me throat.

I get to the camp to find half of it already destroyed, tents and huts up in flames, people's belongings strewn on the ground. Two Chinamen lies face down with several miners kicking at them, though I soon enough realise they're dead. I run towards the noise and suddenly I'm in the middle of the fray. Men on horseback are firing pistols into the air and running down celestials, what are fleeing in every direction, screaming for fear.

Two horsemen corner an old Chinaman with a scraggly beard. A mob of ten or so men runs over and drags him to the ground. They're yelling and laughing like wild things. Four men roll the Mongolian onto his stomach and two of 'em holds him down by sitting on his legs. The other two plants their boots on him, on each shoulder and each wrist. Then they both grabs a hold of the Chinaman's pigtail and, to the count of 'One, two, three!', they rips it out of the back of his head. The men all cheer as one holds it aloft, bright drops o' blood dripping steady onto his dusty boots. Then they begin to kick the old man to death.

I keep running, looking for Hawk, and pass several more dead Chinamen. All is lying on their stomachs with crimson patches to the backs of their heads, the blood still running down their necks and shoulders. One what I thinks is dead gets up and starts to stagger away, holding both his hands to his gut. But he gets only a few feet before he collapses again. Someone has sliced his gut open and his intestines spill out as he falls.

In the smoke, white miners shout excitedly as they comes across stuff they wants in the Mongolian tents. Some carries armloads of loot, piled up to their chins – lamps and picks and lacquer boxes and every manner o' thing you can imagine. One has a sack of rice over his shoulder. It leaks out the bottom, where some wag has stabbed into it, so that he leaves a white trail as he dashes this way and that. Up ahead I sees a mob of about fifty miners, shouting and throwing their fists in the air. I run through the smoke towards them.

I am exhausted by the time I get to the circle o' rioters. As I draws near, I sees Hawk standing right in the centre. Oh, shit! I force me way through the yelling miners, pushing them away with the handle of me axe 'til I gets to the inside.

There stands Hawk, with a white woman what's holding a Chink's baby. Four other Chinamen stand close beside him, three younger men and an older bloke. They's whimpering and shaking from head to foot – all 'cept for the old bloke, who stands calm to Hawk's back. Hawk is holding a pickaxe handle. Most amazing of all, he's calm and smiling!

'Come on, then,' he cries. 'Who's willing to die first? I'll take ten of you before you take us!'

I push through the last o' the crowd to join him.

'Tommo!' Hawk shouts. He reaches out and grabs the axe from me. 'Now it's fifteen! Fifteen men will die before you harm these people! Who will it be among you, gentlemen?' He points with the axe. 'You holding the pigtail, like to be scalped?' He hands the pick handle to me and whispers, 'Cover the side.' Then he raises the fighting axe and takes a step towards the cove with the pigtail. The mob tumbles backwards, falling over each other in their haste to get out of his way. The bloke with the pigtail drops it and runs.

Just then a man on horseback rides up, raises his pistol and fires at Hawk. His horse shies as the mob runs towards him and the bullet misses, hitting the ground. I use the pickaxe handle like a Maori fighting stick and a second later the bastard is on the ground, with all his teeth smashed and his nose missing. The pistol has gone flying as he falls and quickly I rush to pick it up. The horse gallops away, whinnying, and the cove with his face missing gets up and runs blindly into a hut what's burning fiercely. Soon his clothes are alight and he's screaming blue murder.

Hawk is moving forward with the axe and me with the

pistol. The woman and her brat and the four Mongolians keep close. There's smoke everywhere and not a tent or hut left standing. All around us, the miners say and do nothing as we make our way out o' the burning camp, passing dead men lying in the dust. In the distance, we hears the band playing 'Cheer, Boys, Cheer!'

The woman holding the Chink baby begins to sob. One of the Mongolians takes the child in his arms and lays its head against his shoulder. He puts his arm 'round the woman as we walks towards the Yass Road, with no one daring to follow.

When we reach the road, Hawk stops beside the stump of what was once a big river gum. It's been burnt and blackened but stands solid beside the track. 'Tommo, go get the trap and meet us back here. Whistle when you get back – we'll be lying low nearby.'

I hand him the pistol. 'Ere, gimme back me axe. I don't care for this thing. Reminds me of Sam Slit.' Hawk takes the pistol and gives my axe back. In my hands, the pistol felt big and clumsy and I doubt I could've fired it. In his fist, it looks like a child's toy.

Almost an hour later I'm back with Caleb's trap. It's turned dark and I whistles for me twin. Soon enough Hawk, at first a huge dark shadow, appears. He calls to the others.

'Tommo, I want you to take them into Yass. They'll be safe enough there. Then head back here as soon as you're able. It's a hard pull for the horses with six people but they'll make it well enough.'

'No sir!' I says. 'It's twelve hours to Yass and I've got a game o' cards to play tomorrow with the bloody Callaghan mob! I'll never make it back in time. Betcha boots they was in the front of the Miners' League this arvo!'

'Tommo!' Hawk exclaims, looking cranky. 'I'm the weight of two men. I can't go! It's too much to ask the horses to pull!'

'They're game enough. Good nags them two. Take it slow.' I fold me arms. 'I ain't doing it! I ain't gunna let them Callaghan bastards off the hook.'

'It isn't *safe* to play cards with them!' Hawk yells at me.

'It's safer than rescuing Chinks!' I yells back.

Hawk tries to argue some more. I shrug. 'I ain't had me stuff. I'll be useless in an hour.' Hawk stops, knowing he can't win. In fact, I had a pipe o' poppy when I returned to get Caleb's trap but I ain't gunna tell him that. Hawk calls to the Mongolians to climb into the trap. The woman and her baby, the old man and the smallest of the remaining men gets in the front. The other two stands on the back platform, what Caleb uses to carry a couple o' cases of sample liquor. Hawk climbs in and takes up the reins and I can see it is a tight squeeze. The woman ain't said a word all along and now she's feeding her brat by a tit what don't look too promising a source if you ask me. The baby's little mouth is working overtime.

One of the Chinamen steps down from the back platform. He comes over to me and bows low. It's the man what earlier took the woman's baby and put his arm about her. He looks up at me in the moonlight and smiles. 'Me, Wong Ka Leung!' He sticks out his hand and shakes mine up and down several times. 'Very good, sir.' He bows again, then climbs onto the back of the trap.

'I'll be back Tuesday!' Hawk calls.

'Yeah, see ya,' I says. He hasn't once mentioned the camp or what's happened, just gone about the business of doing what needs to be done.

I watch them move off. I'm about to turn and walk back to Lambing Flat when I sees him rein in the horses.

'Tommo!'

'Yeah, what?' I shouts back.

'I love you!' Then he's off in a clatter of wheels and hoofs down the rocky road.

Jesus! I thinks. Four useless bloody Chinks, a wore-out white whore with a half-caste Chinky brat, and me twin risks his life to save them! When is that big nigger gunna grow up some?

I begin to walk back to the camp and the card game. It's bloody cold.

Chapter Twenty-two

HAWK

Lambing Flat
1 July 1861

I return to Lambing Flat from Yass shortly before noon on Tuesday, having travelled through the night. As soon as I arrive, our landlady, Just Lucy, tells me that Tommo is still at the Great Eastern Hotel. Just Lucy enquired after him at ten o'clock this morning as soon as the bar opened for business. The barman said that Tommo and the lads were still upstairs. Some of the lads had ordered kidneys and hard-boiled eggs at dawn, but Tommo and Callaghan played on at stud poker.

This is somewhat alarming news. I unharness the horses and Just Lucy gives them a feed of hay. Meanwhile, I take myself off to the hotel to see Mr Makepeace Chubb. The publican is in a regular sweat when I find him. For the past eight hours, two of the Callaghan mob have been stationed in the passage outside the upstairs room where the game is taking place. They will not allow anyone to enter. The publican is afraid they are holding Tommo captive. Since midnight, several bottles of Irish whiskey have been ordered, but no Cape brandy, which he knows Tommo drinks. All the bottles must be left halfway up the stairs, where they are collected by the two ruffians guarding the door.

'Should we not call the troopers?' I ask, concerned.

'You won't find them, lad,' says Makepeace Chubb. 'They're all busy investigating the miners' riots on the Chinese encampment.

'Besides, I hasn't got a gambling permit and if the traps find out, I'll lose my liquor licence,' he adds. 'They'll put your little mate in gaol too, with his winnings in the pocket of some good officer.'

I thank him and return hastily to our camp. The road leading from the hotel is strewn with sleeping drunks. Others sit with vacant expressions, mumbling or shouting insults, each nursing a black bottle and often covered in their own vomit.

Back at Just Lucy's, I take the pistol gained on Sunday from the horseman in the Chinese camp. I reload it and place it inside my blouse where it cannot be seen. Next I find Tommo's fighting axe. It's where he usually keeps it, wrapped in an oil cloth in his blanket roll, together with his opium pipe and lamp. How I wish I could smash these last two objects and his addiction with them.

I take some comfort from knowing that Tommo does not have his axe with him. He is deadly with this weapon and could easily take four or five men at once with it. But under the circumstances, he is much better without it. On consideration I too decide to leave the axe where it is, telling myself the Callaghan mob would not kill him on the hotel premises. Tommo is safe enough while he remains at the Great Eastern.

And so I return to the pub and ask Chubb to direct me to the upstairs room. He takes me as far as the base of the stairway and points upwards before he tiptoes away. The short, narrow stairway is made of timber and without the benefit of a carpet, so there is no possibility of a stealthy approach. Instead, I prepare to bolt up the steps, hoping to take Callaghan's two guards by surprise.

I pull a large breath of air into my lungs and, taking the stairs three steps at a time, reach the top only moments before the two villains get there themselves. I knock them both to the ground and they go sprawling, their knives clattering from their hands. Picking up the knives, I kick one villain in the ribs and the other in the small of the back, hurling their weapons down to the floor below. Then I charge the door. The lock cracks from the door frame and it flies open.

Three of the Callaghan mob lie asleep on the floor while Jonah Callaghan and Tommo sit at the card table. Tommo has his back to the door and another member of the mob stands beside him holding a bowie knife. I smash my fist into his jugular as he turns his head at my sudden appearance. He staggers backwards, cracking his skull hard on the wall behind him, then slides to his knees and plunges forward onto his face.

A loud explosion fills the room. Jonah Callaghan has fired a pistol which is still pointing at me, though the bullet has missed. His hand waves drunkenly and he squints to aim a second time, just as Tommo pushes hard at the table. Its edge shoves into Jonah Callaghan's guts, spilling his chair backwards. He falls, knocking the back of his head against the floor. Somehow he still holds the pistol, which goes off again, the bullet passing through the ceiling. Tommo jumps from his chair and stamps on Callaghan's wrist, then kicks him hard in the jaw.

The three who were sleeping on the floor are now awake, but still drunk. They come to their feet dazed and unsteady. I pull my pistol and point it at them. Meekly, they put their hands upon their heads.

Tommo has now got hold of Callaghan's pistol. 'There are two at the door, mark them!' I shout to him.

'They's scarpered,' he replies. 'Bastards!'

I make the three men face the wall and put their hands flat against it. Tommo takes the bowie knives from their belts and as he does this, I see that each has a pair of Chinese pigtails hanging from his belt. No doubt Jonah Callaghan and the other cove who lies unconscious also have these gory trophies, ripped straight out from their victims' skulls.

'Tommo,' I say, 'take only what winnings are yours – leave what's rightfully theirs.'

Tommo seems remarkably sober though his eyes are bloodshot and his face pale from fatigue. 'It's all bloody ours!' he snorts. 'Callaghan took me winnings and made me play for them a second time at gunpoint.'

'Well if it's rightly yours, put it into my pockets. Take the cards as well. Call the publican and tell him to bring some rope so we can tie this lot up.'

Tommo is soon stuffing my coat pockets. To my surprise the loot feels very heavy. Then I realise he's stashing small bags of gold dust and nuggets. These are followed by a fistful of banknotes and gold sovereigns until both my coat pockets bulge. 'I've took the cards too,' he says, and goes off to call Chubb.

Puffing for breath as usual, the proprietor of the Great Eastern Hotel arrives with three of his men. He walks cautiously into the room, which is a sorry sight – the table upturned and the hearth strewn with broken whiskey bottles and plates, chop bones, eggshells, spent tobacco and Mexican cheroot butts.

Chubb takes in the scene and wipes his red face with a bandanna from his back pocket. 'It'll cost a pretty penny to set this straight. Lock's broke too,' he complains.

From downstairs, others have come to the doorway to peer at the disturbance. 'Leave it off, all of you downstairs, you've got work to do,' Chubb snarls at them, then he closes the door.

'Mr Chubb, I want you to call a trooper to place these men under arrest. But first tie their hands.' I point to the pigtails hanging from their belts. 'There is plenty of evidence to suggest that these men are implicated in the murder of several Chinese in Sunday's riots.'

Chubb frowns. 'What about the card game? I'll lose my licence, lad. Besides, miners drink here. They won't like it if I gets their mates arrested for a bit of rough and tumble with the celestials.'

'What card game?' I say. 'Do you see any cards? It's clear these villains have been drinking and have smashed up the room. You've broken down the door, very brave too, and made an arrest in the interests of law and order.'

Tommo laughs at this. 'Wouldn't be surprised if you doesn't get a medal for this, Mr Chubb. Anyways these men ain't miners, nor mates of them neither. They're thugs and standover men, Callaghan's mob – they'll get no sympathy from the miners.'

'Aye, I get your drift,' the publican says with a sly grin. 'They can be the troopers' scapegoats for causing the riots.'

One of the men with Chubb begins to tie up the villains, who are still standing facing the wall. Not a word is spoken as their hands are secured behind their backs. Then the same is done to the two lying on the floor, and their ankles bound for good measure. I think Tommo's boot must have broken Jonah Callaghan's jaw, for it has a peculiar lopsided look and blood runs from the corner of his mouth into his beard. The cove I punched in the throat is now making rasping sounds. I'm most relieved I have not injured him fatally. It is good, however, that neither man will be able to tell tales of what has happened for some time.

The publican is examining the table and the chair. 'Both broken,' he says mournfully, and he waves his hand vaguely about the room. 'Lot o' damage done over all, ain't there? A lot of repairs will be needed.'

There is probably not much that couldn't be fixed by a maid with a bucket and a mop, or a carpenter for a pound's worth of work. But I know what he is getting at.

'How much for the repairs?' I sigh.

Chubb looks around again, pursing his lips. 'Four quid would clear it nicely, I should think.'

I nod. 'What about my ten per cent, lad?' Chubb asks my twin.

'What ten per cent be that, Mr Chubb?' Tommo asks politely.

'The house takes ten per cent o' the winnings of the card game.'

'Card game?' Tommo queries ingenuously, scratching his brow. 'I thought you just agreed there were no card game, only villains what's murdered Mongolians. A respectable pub owner like you wouldn't take a chance on losing his licence for gamblin', now would he?'

Chubb looks down at his boots and shakes his head slowly. 'Aye,' he says, 'I can well see yer point.'

I hand the publican my pistol and Tommo gives his to the man who has supervised the tying up. The three Irishmen now sit facing the far wall.

'You'll be wanting to send a lad to fetch a trooper?' Tommo suggests to Chubb. 'Citizen's arrest – your name in the *Sydney Morning Herald* for sure.'

' "Brave Publican Arrests Irish Murder Gang!" ' I quip.

'Single-handed!' Tommo adds.

I pull out a handful of Tommo's winnings and select a

five-pound note, issued by the Oriental Bank, and push it into the publican's vest pocket. 'For the repairs, and a bit extra to buy the lads a drink. We're off to Sydney within the hour and I'm sure we'll not be needed at the enquiry. After all, you've captured the Callaghan mob all by yourself, isn't that so?' I pluck three more pounds from the bundle in my hand and give one to each of the hotel employees.

'Much obliged,' two of them say and take the money shyly. The third, who still holds the other pistol, grins. 'I'm gunna bet it on you beating the Lightning Bolt, Mr Hawk. In the meantime, we ain't seen you two, that I'll guarantee. Blind as a bat we is, eh, lads?' The others nod their heads.

'I'll thank you to call the police after we're gone. Give us ten, perhaps fifteen minutes,' I say to Chubb. He wipes his face again with the rag and smiles greasily. 'Another fiver would seal my lips, and a sov more to each o' the lads would settle 'em down nicely.'

'It ain't necessary,' the man with the pistol protests, 'not fer our part.'

Chubb glares at him. I dig in my pocket and give a pound to each of the men. 'That's so your men will not feel inclined to falsely report that a card game has taken place and so get their master into trouble with the police,' I say to Chubb.

'Much obliged to ya, Mr Chubb,' Tommo says. 'We'll be off, then.'

'Never trust a nigger!' I hear Chubb mutter as we leave.

When we return to our camp, we find that Caleb Soul has harnessed the horses again to the trap. 'I'm anxious to get going, lads. It's chaos all about – we must get back to Sydney.' He points to the horses. 'They're good for a stint before they're done for the day. Hawk, you don't seem to have pushed them too hard.'

I nod, for I'd taken them slowly knowing Caleb would be keen to leave upon my return.

'We'll camp a few miles out,' Caleb says, 'and let them graze the night. I've purchased provisions for the road.'

I think what a good man Caleb Soul is. He has already pulled down the tent and packed our belongings. Tommo and I do not have much gear – a blanket roll, a shirt or two, shaving tackle and the like – but Caleb has carefully loaded it all, ready to leave. Tommo goes quickly to the trap and takes out his blanket roll to check to see his fighting axe, opium pipe and poppy lamp are there. Poor Tommo, all that is precious to him is destructive.

We take our farewell from Just Lucy and Tommo gives her a fiver. She waves us goodbye, blubbing all the while. I note that her moggy is nowhere to be seen. It's most likely asleep in some sheltered spot, catching the best of the afternoon sunshine. Cats don't give a damn for farewells, even though this one's been fed like a king since we've been here.

As soon as we're on the road, I ask Caleb's forgiveness for using the Tucker & Co. trap to help get Wong Ka Leung and his family to Yass. But he is most kind, saying we are heroes for it. This I cannot agree with. Tommo is a hero, yes, for he fought a hostile mob to be at my side. But as for me, it was simply a debt repaid. Wong Ka Leung, or Ah Wong as he's said I may call him, helped me with Tommo. I owed him a good turn.

'What a day – look at that blue sky!' Tommo smiles as we move along. I am only grateful that he is able to see this glorious day and is not dead in a pool of blood in that stinking hotel. I know now that, in his drunken fury, Jonah Callaghan would have killed my twin without thinking twice about the consequences.

The brilliant blue sky reminds me of Maggie's eyes. We have only been away for just over two weeks but oh, how I long to return to her. She has found a place in my heart so that I think of her a hundred times each day. I do not think I could bear to be parted from her again. Every morning and every night I take off Maggie's magpie ring and read the inscription: *Maggie Pye loves Hawk Solomon, Champion of the World*. Then I kiss it and put it back on my finger. Soon enough I spy a magpie carolling away, high up on a dead branch of a gum tree, as we pass by. 'Maggie, I'm coming home!' I say silently to the bird. 'Tommo's got our stake and all's well, my darling.'

We have not been on the road long when Tommo takes to shivering. He complains to me in a whisper that his head wound is giving him merry hell. After a while, he drops into a fitful sleep, moaning and waking and falling asleep again. Though he is exhausted, I can see he is also in pain and will soon need his pipe. As he sleeps, I wipe the sweat from his face, though the air is cold.

'He's been up all night,' I explain to Caleb.

'Poor lad,' Caleb says. 'I know a nice place with a running stream. We'll camp there for the night. Not too far to go now – it will give Tommo a chance to recover.'

He asks me how the card game went, and I tell him more or less what happened. He cannot resist reminding me that he had warned Tommo against playing cards with Callaghan and his mob.

'They could've killed him,' Caleb says, nodding his head at Tommo's slumbering form. 'And most likely got away with it, leaving his body in the Chinese encampment. He would have been just another corpse – the lone white man to die in the riots.'

'What happened to the man who was burnt, a white man?' I ask, thinking of the horseman Tommo clobbered.

'He lives, though he's badly burned all over. There's some justice, though God knows it's little enough,' Caleb observes.

'Well, we were lucky. We got away, and got our stake to boot.' I take a small bag of gold dust from my pocket. 'Would you know its worth?'

Caleb switches the reins into one hand and judges the weight of the bag in his palm. 'I'll put it on the scales when we stop for the night, but I'd judge it at fifty pounds, give or take.' He hands the bag back to me.

'Well, Tommo's won six of them and three small nuggets as well. There's also some banknotes and gold sovs which I haven't counted yet.'

'Exactly the same size bags?' he asks.

'Yes,' I reply.

Caleb nods. 'Well, there's no doubt where Callaghan got these from. They're Chinese, see, made from rice sacks.'

I look at the small bag and see it has been neatly stitched with a drawstring pulling it tight.

'Open it, you'll see it's lined with silk. Gold doesn't stick to silk,' Caleb says.

I work the drawstring open and see that he is right. The gold dust gleams in the afternoon light. 'What are we to do now?' I ask, concerned.

'Nothing, lad. The true owners are dead or fled. Callaghan's mob looted it, but Tommo won it fair and square.'

I suspect that Tommo won the loot thanks to a couple of marked decks but I refrain from saying so to Caleb. Privately I resolve to give one bag to Ah Wong when we meet as arranged in Sydney.

'You must let me pay for all your expenses. We have enough,' I say to Caleb, holding up the bag again.

'I'll take a pinch tonight when we weigh it. It will pay for the handbills.'

'Yes, and what about the ten pounds you paid to Pat Malone and the Irishman who beat me?'

Caleb chuckles. 'Righto, seeing you're so flush, I'll

accept.' I pay him what's due and he jams the notes into his vest pocket with his thumb.

'There is much more we owe you, Caleb, I've kept a record.'

'No, no, Hawk, no more,' Caleb smiles. 'It's been a long time since I enjoyed such company. I'm in your debt for the good fellowship you've provided me on my last trip to the diggings.'

'This is your last trip?'

'Aye. It ain't been bad work and the recompense is fair, but it's a hard life too. For a start, I have to drink too much with the customers.'

'But I've never you seen intoxicated!' I exclaim.

'Not ever quite sober either.' He jigs the reins and the horses move a little faster. 'It's time for me to take out my pills and potions, time to settle down, have a family. I've put a fair bit away, and pharmacy is what I really want to do.'

I think on this. If Caleb is correct I calculate that Tommo has won about four hundred pounds, most of it in gold.

'Caleb, you asked Tommo and me once –' I hesitate '– if we'd be partners with you in your pharmaceutical company?'

'I did.' He looks at me. 'I'd be proud to have you in with me, Hawk. Your brother too, though I don't know quite what he'd do.'

'What would such a partnership cost?'

'I thought you wished to try your hand at being a shopkeeper at the diggings?'

'Caleb, like you, I think it's time to settle and have a family. But now I see that the goldfields are no place for a woman and children.'

'You're not wrong,' he says. 'Then you'd consider coming in with me?'

I clear my throat. 'Caleb, I haven't been entirely

forthcoming with you. Tommo and I must go back to Tasmania for a while – perhaps even longer than a while. I'd like to be your partner and maybe work with you later, but I would be joining you as a silent partner for the present. There's the fight and then there's my duties in Hobart Town . . .'

'Your lass? She's down there, is she?'

'No, she's from Sydney, but I'll have to present her to our mama. I must have her blessing.'

'Quite right,' Caleb murmurs. We don't speak again for fifteen minutes, then Caleb says, 'Hawk, I'd rather our partnership was fifty-fifty, with us both putting in equal amounts of capital and working together. But if you want a one-third share as a silent partner for now – with this to be revised to a half share should you come as a working partner within two years – it will cost you a hundred and fifty pounds.'

'Will you measure it out on the scales in gold dust tonight?' I ask. 'Plus, of course my share of the legal expenses – including the cost of drawing up the papers for Tommo and me.'

Caleb Soul leans over and offers his hand. 'You'll not regret it, Hawk. Two things are certain in this life. People will always need grog and they'll always need potions.'

So my course is set. I have resolved to marry Maggie and I must somehow persuade Tommo to return to Hobart Town with me. Mary's last letter was most unhappy – she misses us terribly and I know she fears she may never see her boys again. I sink back into silence, much preoccupied by how I shall bring together all my loved ones at last.

Our friend is true to his word and we camp by a pleasant stream late in the afternoon. I help him set up the tent while Tommo goes away to attend to his pipe. Later that evening, Caleb brings out his gold scales and, after considerable reckoning, he declares that we have, at the very least, five hundred pounds! When I ask him to accept a little more for the trouble he has taken on our behalf he adamantly refuses, requesting only that he might help with the preparations for the fight. This I readily agree to.

A week later we are back in Sydney, where Maggie receives me with joy and tears. I too am overcome. Oh dear, how very much I love her and, from her joyous reception, it seems she loves me too.

'Oh, Hawk, ya lovely bastard, I loves ya!' she says, jumping into my arms.

'Maggie, what would you say to giving up your work?' I ask her after we've made love.

'What's ya mean?' she asks, horrified. 'Become respectable-like?'

'Well, yes, sort of.' I cannot quite imagine Maggie completely respectable.

'Jesus, Hawk! What's you on about? Respectable? Is you ashamed o' me?' Her lips begin to tremble, but then she gains control and her big blue eyes come to fire. 'You bastard! You nigger bastard!'

I hold her tight against my chest as she yells at me in anger. 'Lemme go, you black shit! Lemme go!'

'Maggie, Maggie! Hush! I'm asking you to marry me! To have my children.'

Maggie goes totally still in my arms and I release her.

'Brats?' she asks.

'Aye!'

'Me own brats? Oh Jesus!' Maggie begins to sob.

I don't know what to do. I thought to see her anger or scorn, but not these tears. I pat her on the back. 'You'd like to have children, then?' I query, anxious that I may have said completely the wrong thing.

Her head buried in a pillow, Maggie nods. Then her sobs begin afresh. 'Brats,' she howls, 'oh, shit! Oh, oh, oh!'

I continue patting her and then begin to stroke her back and thighs. My hand wanders over her tight, sweet derrière to the inside of her legs, and I let my finger slide into her warm and creamy place. Maggie opens up to receive me, and I push her gently onto her back and enter her. Her sobs turn to whimpers and moans, and I think how beautiful she is and how much I love her. 'Oh, Hawk,' she cries, wrapping her legs tight about me. 'Oh darling, Maggie's coming! Oh, Jesus! You bastard, you lovely bastard! Brats! Me own!'

Afterwards, she sits up almost immediately. 'You wants me to marry you? Be respectable-like?' she wonders. 'I ain't never been respectable. Don't suppose I've got the knack.'

'You'll get the hang of it soon enough,' I laugh.

Maggie makes a pair of dainty fists and knuckles away another rush of tears. She's sitting cross-legged on the bed, her blue eyes red-rimmed from crying, but her pretty mouth is set firm. 'On your wages? No bloody fear, mate! Respectable takes money. I ain't gunna be respectable washin' the bleedin' floor, scrubbin' pots 'n' pans. I'm a respectable whore, not a bleedin' respectable scullery maid!' She looks at me fiercely. 'You can shove yer respectable up yer arse, Hawk Solomon! I'll work and keep ya 'til you makes somethin' out o' your life!' She stops and thinks for a moment. 'And not out o' fisticuffs neither, I ain't marrying a prize-fighter. O' course, you can fight this once against the Bolt!'

'Then you'll marry me? Oh, Maggie!' I go to embrace her but she pushes me away.

'Only if I stays what I am 'til we can afford better. I ain't gunna scrub no floor for no one! I loves ya, Hawk, with all me heart, but I ain't gunna go down on me knees for no bastard!'

'Maggie, it doesn't matter to me what you are. I love you with all my heart too.'

'Yeah,' she says, 'it don't matter to *you*. I know that now. I didn't never think it could 'appen to me. Oh sweet Mary, Mother o' Jesus, I loves ya, Hawk Solomon!'

I hold her for a while. 'Maggie,' I say eventually, 'now you must meet our mama.'

Maggie draws back. 'But she don't like me!'

'Of course she will. Mary will love you, you'll see!' Then I see Maggie has brought her hand to her lips and wears a look of consternation. I hear again her last words in my mind. '*What* did you say?' I ask slowly, my heart pounding.

'I said what if she don't like me?'

'Maggie! That's not what you said!' I frown.

'Orright,' Maggie says tremulously. 'We has met. I'll tell ya the whole story. Tommo think yiz gunna get beat. Hurt bad. He asked your mama to come up here!'

'What, here? To Sydney?'

Maggie nods and sniffs. 'We needed her help!'

'What for?'

'Oh, Hawk, don't ya see? There's only one way yiz can win. The Bolt's got to take a dive, least that's what Tommo thinks!'

'And you? Do *you* think that?' I ask her. Maggie drops her eyes but says nothing, her fingers playing with the corner of the pillow. I grasp her by the shoulders. 'Answer me! Is that what you think, Maggie?'

'Leggo, yiz hurting me!' she cries, but I continue to hold her. 'Please! Yiz bruisin' me, Hawk!'

I cannot bear the idea of hurting Maggie and all the anger goes out of me. I sigh. 'I can't possibly win no matter how much training I do, so Tommo's going to fix the fight! Is that it?'

Maggie's eyes grow big. 'Hawk, yiz the bravest man I've ever known. It's just . . .'

'Just what?'

'Well, Tommo says you can't learn enough technique in

585

time to fight the Bolt, no matter what. I know prize-fighters and I thought you could win but he's made me believe you're gunna get hurt.' She tilts her head at me. 'Oh, Hawk, I don't want them to hurt you! The Irishman will be too crafty and cunning. You don't have the skill to take him on! You said so yerself, remember?'

'Yes, but I've changed my mind.'

'That don't change nothing!' Maggie exclaims. 'Think the Irishman's gunna shit his pants 'cause you've changed your bleedin' mind?'

'You're wrong. It changes everything,' I say. 'We're going to set it up so that Mr Sparrow lays down all his money against me, and then I'll take on the Lightning Bolt fair and square and win – even if I get killed in the process.'

'But why?' Maggie pleads. 'I can take care o' yiz. And you'll soon get on in yer job, get a raise! We don't need to do this bloody fight!'

'Maggie, you forget what Mr Sparrow's done to Tommo! He's a mongrel. You can't let the mongrels win.'

'Oh bull!' Maggie exclaims. 'What's been done to Tommo he's done t' himself! There's always a Mr Sparrow. Get this one and another'll take his place soon enough. World's full o' bastards what you calls mongrels – always has been, always will be!'

'It's more than that, Maggie. It's what happened to Tommo and me when we were brats. Mr Sparrow's a part of that. It's time to change our fates.'

'I dunno what yiz talkin' about, I'm sure,' Maggie sniffs.

'Yes, well, be that as it may, Tommo's got to answer for himself, and so do I. Part of the answering is believing the mongrels don't always win. You can't just give in to evil, you have to fight it! If you don't, it destroys you. If I have to fight the Irishman to beat Mr Sparrow, then I shall. And I mean to win.'

586

'But you *will* win!' Maggie insists. 'That's it, ain't it? We bribe the Irishman to take a dive, and Mr Sparrow loses all his loot on the betting ring. Abra-bleedin'-cadabra! You've won!'

I sigh. 'Maggie, you have not heard a thing I've said. I can't win by cheating!'

'Shit, why not? What's wrong with cheating, all of a sudden? What's Tommo been doing these past weeks to raise your stakes if it ain't cheatin'?' Maggie asks.

'That's different! To bribe the Irishman to lose is to be just like Mr Sparrow. All the things that have destroyed us – me, Tommo, even you – are the result of good men standing by and watching, while mongrels like him corrupt the human soul!'

Maggie shrugs. 'Well, I shouldn't worry about it too much. Nobody's gunna bribe nobody. She ain't got the money.'

'She? Who hasn't?'

'Mary bloody Abacus!'

'Maggie, you've met our mama, then?'

Maggie sticks out her chin. 'Yes I has. Tight as a squid's bum, that one! I don't mean t' insult yer mama, Hawk, but Tommo said she'd be willin' t' pay the bribe.' Maggie pauses, then meets my eye. 'Well, it ain't so.'

'Maggie, what has Tommo told you about Mary?'

'He told me she were rich.'

'Oh Lord. And then?'

'I started t' cry, 'cause if she were and you also, then you wouldn't love me when ya went back to Hobart Town. Rich blokes fuck whores, but they don't marry 'em. But now I knows different. She told me she ain't got no money.' Maggie looks at me, still near to tears. 'She *don't* like me, Hawk. She said I were a whore!'

'Well, you are, aren't you?' I say, cuddling her. 'You say so yourself!'

'Yes, but the way she said it, it were different.' Tears begin to roll down Maggie's cheeks. 'At least she can't think me a gold digger if she ain't got no money to give ya.'

I can see in my mind what's happened. Mary's arrived dressed in a simple black dress, hair brushed tight under a dark bonnet, looking plain as a crow, hoping to seem a respectable working class woman. She's taken one look at Maggie and made up her mind in an instant. So she cried poverty, thinking to send the little gold digger away.

I sigh at these thoughts. 'Maggie, you aren't marrying Mary Abacus. You're marrying me, Hawk X Solomon!'

'I suppose,' she says doubtfully. 'But I'm glad she ain't rich after all. I can look after ya, Hawk, honest. I'll work harder. We'll save a bit, we've got me rooms and we won't starve.'

'How long has Mary been in Sydney? Does Tommo know she's here?'

'Tommo knows. She's at the Hero of Waterloo. She only came in last night. Mr Harris sent a lad to tell me. I got her a nice room, paid a week's advance meself, full board.' Maggie looks accusingly at me. 'She didn't even say ta!'

'I'm sorry, Maggie. Mary's pretty plain-spoken, that I'll admit, but she is not usually rude. She's a good woman, Maggie, you'll see. Did she truly call you a whore?'

'Good as! It were the way she looked at me. I wore my best outfit too and me new magpie hat from Mr Myer's Emporium. It were me red silk gown, what I bought from Farmer's after the Ben Dunn fight. I wanted to do ya proud, Hawk, so your mama'd think I were pretty enough for yiz! I even wore one o' them Chinee silk shawls what Barney Moses give me, so she wouldn't see me tits.'

I close my eyes. I can just imagine the set of Mary's thin lips when she first set eyes on my darling Maggie in all her finery. As to what she'll have to say to me when we meet, I am loath to think!

Chapter Twenty-three

TOMMO

The Rocks
July 1861

Hawk's flaming mad about our plan to bribe the Bolt. He says I've lost me marbles. He even threatened to get Caleb Soul to take charge of our side of the arrangements. I tried to tell him I didn't think he could win no matter what, 'cause he don't have the experience to fight a pug like the Bolt.

And Ho Kwong Choi's turned out to be no help to us. On me first visit to Tang Wing Hung's opium den, after we gets back from Lambing Flat, old Ho tells me he can't help us none. He said he couldn't remember nothing what could be useful to Hawk. But I reckons it's a set-up – he spoke to Mr Tang Wing Hung after all, what told Mr Sparrow, what warned the old man not to help Hawk.

I should've saved me breath, tryin' to persuade Hawk to my way o' thinking. Hawk's a stubborn bugger and once he's made up his mind he don't change it too often. He reckons if we win by cheating, we ain't beaten greed, greed's beaten us. And if it ain't a straight victory over the Bolt, then we'll still be in Mr Sparrow's power – and he'll have won after all. As usual he's done a measure of practical thinking about the whole set-up too. What he's come up with isn't half bad, even if it won't be of any use in the end.

Hawk points out that the Bolt has now fought and won against most of the champions of the various states. He's already beat Ben Dunn as well as Fred Woods and Jimmy Shanks, and all of them stopped well short of twenty rounds. Ben Dunn did best, lasting nineteen rounds before his corner threw in the sponge. *Bell's Life in Sydney* reckons the local champs have given the Lightning Bolt no trouble whatsoever – his ringcraft and cunning had them well and truly beat.

'The Bolt boasts that he hasn't done a lick of training and that against Jimmy Shanks he took a bottle of Irish whiskey into the ring to drink between rounds!' Hawk looks at me most earnest. 'Don't you see, Tommo? He's well cashed from the bouts and from betting on himself. He's ready to return home after one last easy fight. Maybe I can't match his cunning but I've got height and reach and strength. I reckon I can outlast him, wear him down 'til his legs give in.' Hawk smiles. 'The Bolt hasn't yet had an opponent who could do that. All of them have been old pugs, not one of them a day younger than thirty-five, and not trained for stamina.'

'Hawk, it won't come to that,' I argues. 'Bare-knuckle fighting's a dirty business. There ain't no rules for sportsmen! It's a free-for-all in the clinches. He'll stamp on your insteps, knee you in the bollocks and head butt you as he pulls you in. It ain't about stamina or about outlasting him. It ain't even about punching. It's about fighting cunning!'

But Hawk won't listen to none of what I tells him and so I've done me best to see he gets the right training. Most of the past two weeks I've been waking early so I can watch him spar before I goes for me smoke and night of poker. It ain't left me much time for Mary, what's been in Sydney since we got back from Lambing Flat. She's still at the Hero o' Waterloo and after telling me she ain't gunna get involved none 'til she's seen for herself what's goin' on, we've barely spoke – what suits me just fine, thank you very much.

Since he started training proper, Hawk's built his strength up and has shown himself a quick learner. Bungarrabbee Jack and Johnny Heki, the Aborigine and Maori blokes what's training him, are old-timers and knows all the dirty stuff what's likely to come his way.

Johnny Heki loves Hawk like a brother and they chatters away together in the Maori tongue for hours. Hawk has Maori tattoos of a very high order and so is much respected by Johnny, who imagines me brother is fighting for his people's honour. In a way that's true. I reckon Hawk's fighting for all of us what's been wronged – all what's been taken advantage of, as he sees it.

Johnny tells Hawk how the dirty fighting's done in the clinches, when the referee's to the back of you so he can't see what's going on below the belt. He shows Hawk how to stand with his feet wide-spaced, so that he can lean against his opponent and still keep him from getting too close. Johnny Heki and Bungarrabbee Jack reckons the Bolt will try to draw Hawk in, and that's where Hawk can do his best work. They teaches him how to use his knee in a groin and grab his opponent's bollocks. But it's not the kind o' fighting me brother takes to, it's too low-down and dirty for him.

Instead, Hawk must learn to avoid having these things done to him. So his trainers show him how to rest his head on his opponent's shoulder when he's pulled close to prevent a head butt. Hawk must keep his head above his opponent's shoulder at all times, 'cause if the canny Irishman can lower it to his chest, he'll surely poke his fingers into Hawk's eyes or get two fingers up his nostrils, tearing his nose so bad the fight must be stopped for the blood what's pouring out. Everything, Hawk's coaches explain, happens in the clinch, in the hugabug. So Hawk must use his reach and strength to avoid the clinch.

Both blokes teach Hawk how to defend himself from body blows and, in particular, from blows below the belt. They reckons Hawk can only learn one good combination punch in the time they've got, so they teaches him how to lead with a left and follow through with a right. Bungarrabbee Jack calls this the 'one-spot, two-shot, left-right, bang-bang!' He makes Hawk practise this combination over and over again 'til he can do it without thinking. Hawk's left can drive a man back several paces and the right hook what follows up and under the heart will lift his opponent's feet off the ground. The Aborigine slaps his palms together as though he is dusting them, 'Ten times, boss! One-spot, two-shot, left-right, bang-bang! Ten times one fight, all over – sleepy time!' Bungarrabbee Jack reckons if Hawk can land a good left and a right under the heart ten times during the fight he'll stop any man on the planet.

They also school him to keep hitting under his opponent's heart, what's much better than trying to hit him in his head, where Hawk could easily break his hand and leave himself defenceless.

'Same spot, boss!' Bungarrabbee Jack keeps repeating, as he drives his fist under Hawk's heart. 'Keep hittin' him same spot! Time come he can't stand no more. Same spot, eh!'

Then, just a few days ago, things really began to look up. Hawk were hauling barrels up to the wine loft as part of his training, when a boy apprentice comes to say there be a Chinaman at the gate. He hands Hawk a scrap o' paper what the man has given him. Hawk sees that the note is in his own handwriting and has his name and the Tucker & Co. address. It's the note he gave Wong Ka Leung – or Ah Wong as he calls him – when he left him in Yass after they'd fled from Lambing Flat.

Hawk goes immediately to the gate to greet the Chinaman. Me big brother is most anxious that Ah Wong should get one o' the bags o' gold I won from Callaghan. Yours truly argues against it. After all, I won it fair and square – it ain't the celestials' no more – and Hawk's done enough by rescuing Ah Wong and his family.

But Hawk as usual sees it quite the opposite. 'We've profited, but he's lost everything! He can't go back to Lambing Flat. He's skint, poor bastard, with a wife and child to support, and we're rich. It isn't fair he should suffer more while we benefit from his misfortune.'

'So what about the other five bags o' gold? They must've been took from the Mongolians too?' I says, just to make trouble.

Hawk sighs. 'There's an old Chinese proverb, Tommo. "Every journey of a thousand miles begins with one step." We don't know the others who lost their gold, but we do know Ah Wong. He is our first step to making things right.' Where Hawk's learnt a Chinese proverb I'm buggered if I know. Them books he reads go straight into his head and he don't seem to forget nothin'. Stuff comes out when you least expects it.

So Hawk goes to the gate to welcome Ah Wong, and gives him money for food and arranges to meet him later that night in Chinatown, at the scrag end o' the Rocks.

When Hawk gets there he finds Ah Wong and his family sharing a filthy cellar room with eleven other men. The property belongs to an importing merchant what has a godown on the wharf. All these men works eighteen hours a day just for food and a corner of the room.

Ever the bloomin' mother, Hawk takes one look and immediately buys food, clothes and blankets as well as all sorts of oriental paraphernalia, like chopsticks, cooking woks and bamboo baskets. He buys a bolt o' black cotton for clothes, boots for their feet and everything what's needed to set up Ah Wong and his family. Then he rents them a room what's only for them. After all this, when they's safely moved into their new home, he gives Ah Wong the bag o' gold to get him started out in life again.

Two days later an uncle of Ah Wong's family turns up at Tucker & Co. to see Hawk. He can't speak no English, so it's all busy hands and sign language between the two of 'em. Hawk can't make head nor tail of what the old man's on about. Suddenly the Chinaman takes a step forward and brings the fingers of his right hand up into the top of Hawk's throat and presses. Hawk feels the strength leak out of him and he sinks to his knees.

So now, with Ah Wong's uncle teaching Hawk the ancient celestial arts, we has our replacement for Ho Kwong Choi. And this time Tang Wing Hung and Mr Sparrow don't know nothin' about it. I begins to feel that perhaps Hawk *can* win the fight against the Bolt. It ain't much of a chance, but it's better than a kick in the arse.

Meanwhile Maggie's been going all out in the pubs and sporting houses. Anywhere people might listen she's letting drop her rumours, where they spreads and spreads. Her latest story is that Hawk's been running a hundred yards with a grown bullock across his shoulders, not even puffing at the end. Some o' the likely lads even swears they's seen it with their own eyes.

Most of the stories we come up with are so wild and ridiculous, you'd reckon people'd die laughing. But the punters lap 'em up and clamour for more! There's even tales what we didn't invent spinning about, each one stranger than the next. Mr Sparrow is delighted. He offers most attractive odds on Hawk while keeping them short on the Bolt.

The smart punters ain't took in by the brouhaha, of

course. *Bell's Life in Sydney* still rates Hawk as no chance against the Irishman. They ain't seen Hawk spar and so they concludes 'he is hiding the defects he plainly suffers as a fighter'. They reckons that he ain't game to be named for the mismatch they feel sure this prize fight will be and, given all o' this, rates me brother at forty to one.

The views of *Bell's Life in Sydney* don't seem to matter, to the little punters anyways. The average bloke is all for Hawk and Mr Sparrow's booking shop is taking a king's ransom in bets what favour him. Fat Fred is now claiming to be Irish and has opened another booking shop in Parramatta Town, where the Irish bets their weekly wages on their own champion, the Bolt. Meantime Mr Sparrow has his betting agents in all the goldfields surrounding the district o' Yass and forty miles beyond the Victorian border, where they's doing a roaring trade.

The Irishman is still taking on the local fighters to the tune of one a week. And each time he wins against the champions of the various colonies there's trouble. Extra police is called out to control the Irish mob what comes from all about to celebrate. When the story come out about the Bolt drinking whiskey between rounds, Tucker and Co. trebled their regular sales of the liquor. That were on top o' sales what were already doubled since the Irishman arrived in the colonies, and still the pubs has been drunk dry by midnight. The Bolt is the darlin' of the publicans, what has named a new drink for him: 'Irish Sunrise'. It's Irish whiskey and crème de menthe in equal measure took straight. 'The gold of the whiskey and the green of the crème de menthe be heaven's golden light upon the green and pleasant land of Erin', so I hears. I don't know how much golden light a bloke'd enjoy in the gutter after a dozen of 'em.

Maggie's been reporting back on all her doings to Mr Sparrow. She tells him most convincing that Hawk is at the point o' complete despair. 'He ain't got the nature to be a fighter,' she confides to me master. If our Maggie's to be believed, Hawk hates to go into the ring for sparring and the two broken-down pugs what's training him can hit him almost at will, for he's too slow to parry their blows.

Twice she has gone to Mr Sparrow seeming at the end of her tether. 'Hawk wants t' give it away,' she wails the first time. 'He don't lack the courage, mind, it's just he can't learn the craft of it. He's strong as a bull but just as clumsy. The Abo, what's 'arf his size, can put him down any time he likes and the Maori sits him on his arse a dozen times each sparring. He's took to speaking to no one and he seems most down in spirits.' Maggie brings tears to her eyes. 'He don't even want to take me to bed no more!' she howls. 'Mr Sparrow, honest, I don't think he's gunna hold up. What shall I do?'

Maggie reckons that's when Mr Sparrow started to tremble. 'You keep him in the fight, Maggie, you hear!' he shouts. He fumbles in his purse. 'Ere!' He hands her another pound. 'I don't care what it takes! You keep him matched up!'

The second time Maggie goes to him with the same story 'bout how Hawk wants to quit, Mr Sparrow don't even waste time trying to bribe her. 'You keep him in!' he screams.

'Don't know that I can, Mr Sparrow, he's that forlorn,' Maggie says, her blue eyes wide and misty. 'He don't listen t' me no more!'

Mr Sparrow speaks very low and calm now. 'Maggie, you keep the nigger in the fight. Don't let me down now. You know I hold yer responsible!'

'I'll try, Mr Sparrow, but I can't work no miracles, now can I?'

'Maggie, let me tell yer something.'

'Yes, Mr Sparrow?'

'If the schwartzer goes, *you* go. Know what I means?'

'No, Mr Sparrow.'

'Then I'll leave you to think about it, girlie.' Mr Sparrow points his bony finger with its big diamond ring at her, before bringing it back and drawing it across his throat. 'It ain't no idle threat, neither,' he warns.

Maggie gets a real fright at this. 'I ain't done nuffink! I only done what you asked, Mr Sparrow! It ain't fair!'

'*Life* ain't fair, Maggie. That's my last word. Keep him in, or you're done like a dinner!'

Poor old Maggie, she ain't having a great time of it. She don't say much but I'd guess Hawk ain't doing his duty by her in the bed chamber. He's plain exhausted by the time he's finished with his sparring and lugging o' barrels. He's still trying to do some clerking, even though Captain Tucker says it ain't necessary 'til after the fight. But Hawk's dead proud of his books and he don't want someone else messing up his ledgers, all marked up in his own beautiful hand.

On Sunday, when he and Maggie are together, Hawk can hardly get himself out o' bed to buy the roasts and take them to the bakery for the orphan brats at the Quay. He keeps falling asleep while he's waiting in the line, much to the amusement o' the housewives. Maggie's took to carving the roast herself, in case Hawk cuts himself.

Sunday be Maggie's only day off and she treasures it, for it's the only time she gets t' see Hawk properly. When they're through feeding the brats, they usually goes to The Cut Below. There they has themselves a late dinner before popping upstairs. But these days I reckon Hawk'd be asleep before he gets to the bedroom.

And now, to add to Hawk's load, our mama's decided me and him should have our Sunday roast dinner with *her* every week. Mary has arranged with the publican, Mr Harris, for a special room to be made into a dining room for her on

Sundays at the Hero o' Waterloo. She's even bought a snowy white tablecloth like the one from home, so's we can have our white tablecloth Sunday dinners again, or so she hopes.

This Sunday'll be the first of the new set-up but Mary ain't invited Maggie and Hawk says he ain't coming if she don't. The two of them, Mary and Hawk, are standing toe-to-toe and I can see Mary ain't gunna give in despite the fact her boy's towering over her.

'She's a slut!' Mary snaps at him.

'Mama, don't speak like that. I *love* Maggie.'

'Humph!' Mary snorts. 'Love! My son loves a whore!'

Quick as a flash Hawk replies, 'You were a whore, Mama, and I love *you*!'

I ain't never seen Mary so taken aback. Her jaw drops and she sits down with a bang, then begins to weep. But deep down she ain't upset – she's pleased at what he said in a funny kind o' way, pleased he loves her. Mary is still Mary, though, and underneath she's made of steel. Soon as she stops crying, she says, 'Hawk, don't throw your life away. Come home, lovey, you and Tommo. There's many a fine young lass in Tasmania what would be proud to call herself Mrs Hawk Solomon. Mrs Tommo Solomon too, I've no doubt! The both of you be most eligible young men.'

Hawk says firmly, 'Mama, I don't want any of those fine young lasses. I want Maggie!'

'And she wants your money!' Mary retorts. 'Mark my words, I know her sort. She'll bleed you dry then leave you for some pimp with a celluloid collar and a set o' gold teeth! That one ain't done a day's honest graft in her life.'

'Mama, she ain't like that,' I says in Maggie's defence.

'Oh, what would you know!' she snaps at me.

'That's not fair!' Hawk says. 'Tommo had his doubts about Maggie too, Mama.'

'It's true, Mama, but I've changed me mind. She's a

wonderful girl!' I blush at meself when I says this, but it's true, I reckon.

As soon as she sees she can't win this one, Mary changes tack and smiles up at Hawk. 'Please, Hawk, just this one Sunday, just the three of us, Tommo and you and Mama, like old times? Look, I've even brought me big gravy boat from 'ome.'

'Is God coming too?' I asks, trying to lighten the mood.

But neither takes any notice of me quip. Hawk shakes his head slowly. 'No, Mama, Maggie's my betrothed. If you won't have her at your table, then you won't have me. Maggie comes on Sunday or I won't!'

Hawk is laying down the law and Mary can see he ain't messing about. Still, she tries again. 'Oh Hawk, I've missed me boys something terrible. It ain't been easy on my own, with David and Hannah bloody Solomon on me back all the time. My arthritis is playing up something terrible. I don't suppose I've too long left, and I ain't seen much of you these last couple o' weeks.'

She looks at both of us with pleading eyes. 'All I want is for me two boys to be home again. I don't ask nothing more. I've got the brewery built to give you something in your life what's your own. I done it for the both of you. I've had a hard life, and you two boys has been the only joy in it. Come home, I beg you! I'm beggin' you on me knees.'

Mary strings all these reasons together, like if she can find enough of them we'll be convinced. But she don't go down on her knees like she says. I don't reckon Mary would go down on her knees for the Almighty Himself. She might make Him Sunday dinner, second helpings and all, but that's about as far as she'd go. In me head, I hears her putting Him in His place.

'Help yourself, Gawd, plenty o' mutton left, gravy and onions. Here, have another tater. Bleedin' cold up the mountain, ain't it? Soon be warm in here, that's a red-gum log in the hearth since mornin'. Soon warm the cockles of your heart.'

Then God says we ought to give thanks for our blessings before we tucks in.

'Hang about!' says Mary. 'Thanks to who? Who done all the bleedin' cooking then?'

'Well, *you* did, my dear,' the Almighty says. 'And very nice too. Nobody does them little onions in gravy like you.'

'Well then,' says Mary with one of her sniffs, wiping her hands on her pinny. 'Anyone going to give blessings 'round here can bleeding well thank me. And I don't need no thanks neither, thank you very much! Go on, tuck in and don't be so high and mighty!'

'Quite right, m'dear,' says the Father of Heaven. 'Couldn't have put it better myself. Would another slice o' mutton be out o' the question, do you think? Splendid! Pass the gravy please, Tommo.'

Afterwards God always says thank you most polite to Mary, in case He don't get invited back.

Now here's Mary, who ain't afraid of God Himself, saying she'll go down on her knees for us to come back. She won't, but even for her to say it is quite something, for she's the proudest person I've ever known.

'Mama, I love you, we both love you,' Hawk says softly, glancing at me. 'But I will not come home without Tommo and Maggie, and I will not come on Sunday without her either.'

Mary sighs. 'All right, then. I'll set the table for four. Don't be late. I've spoke to the cook, leg o' mutton be ready one o'clock sharp!' Then she manages a smile. 'Where d'you reckon I'll get them little onions around here?'

Mary may have given in but our first family Sunday dinner looks like it ain't gunna be the most pleasant gathering ever.

We're all in the saloon bar of the Hero. God's definitely missing, Mary's looking down her nose at Maggie and Maggie's scared to death about the whole thing. It all starts to come apart while we're still having our drinks before dinner. Mary's having a lemonade and Hawk a beer, me a Cape brandy and Maggie a double o' gin for Dutch courage. I've come to realise that Maggie ain't in fact a big drinker. She can nurse a single gin an hour or two and often she'll make it look like she's tippling by arranging with the bar for them to give her plain water instead.

Maggie's wearing a plain black dress made of what she calls bombasine, buttoned up to the neck. All the same, it's fitted tight to the waist and shows off what's hers to show up top. It's her hat what's the problem though. She's wearing a black bonnet – 'cept it's been fitted with a birdcage, like they sells down at the markets to keep your songbird or canary in. Maggie's got a young magpie in hers, and it's chirping and jumping and bumping against the wires, shitting everywhere. It clearly ain't too happy about it all.

Hawk, o' course, don't notice anything's wrong. He probably thinks his little magpie is very clever, but Maggie should've known better than to wear this trumped-up bonnet today of all days. It's all show, I reckons – she's frightened and this be her way of pretending she ain't. Maggie don't take no lip from no one but I reckon she were expecting a heap from Mary. She's done the magpie deliberate so's to get it all over with.

Now Maggie don't know it, but Mary has a special love for birds. She just about worships them green parakeets, and she can't abide birds being kept in cages. She once spent time in the dungeons of Newgate Gaol in a cage of whores, and she reckons that's exactly what a birdcage must be like for a little winged creature what's born to fly free.

'Stupid girl!' I hear Mary muttering under her breath when Maggie's back is turned. But she don't say no more and we goes into the dining room. Mary's already been into the pub kitchen to make sure the cook's done the leg o' mutton to her liking. Now she says that she don't trust him with the gravy and must make it herself. 'Them little pearly onions must be cooked just right – simmered in gravy made with the dripping from the roasting dish – just the way my boys like them.'

While she's away seeing to the gravy, Maggie downs another double o' gin. Hawk don't say nothing and I ain't game! By the time Mary returns, with the cook carrying in a monster leg of mutton and her behind him with a large gravy boat, Maggie's three sheets to the wind. During the dinner she giggles and snorts and whispers into Hawk's ear, making a terrible mess of her plate. There are drops of gravy splashed all over Mary's white tablecloth. Mama's forehead is as furrowed as a new-ploughed hill paddock and things definitely ain't going too good.

'Oops! *Pardonnez-moi!*' Maggie giggles in the Frenchy lingo as she spears at one o' the little gravy onions and it shoots off into Mary's lap. Mary stays stum and picks up the onion and puts it to the side of her plate. She's wearing white gloves to conceal her poor hands and now the finger and thumb's got a big, brown blotch on the tips.

But Maggie don't quieten down even at this. She's got the giggles again and stabs at the next onion on her plate. This time the whole plate wobbles, spilling more gravy. Two sprouts roll off and half a dozen little onions merrily follows across the tablecloth.

'Shit!' says Maggie, not speaking the French no more.

Hawk too is now scowling. Perhaps it's 'cause I'm anxious for him and Maggie but I'm pissing meself with laughter inside, and trying not to show it. A shame God ain't been invited. He'd get an almighty laugh from what's happening.

Maggie becomes aware there's silence all about her. 'What's wrong with yiz all?' she asks suddenly, jamming the handles of her knife and fork down on the table. 'It ain't my fault them stupid little onions ain't growed up yet! How's I supposed to eat them, the slippery little fuckers?'

I can't hold me laughter in no more and I bursts out and Maggie with me. She's shakin' her head up and down and the bloody magpie is chirping and fluttering and there's feathers floating down onto the table. Then the door to the cage flies open and out jumps the little magpie, straight into the gravy boat, landing in gravy up to its neck.

Out steps the birdy into the middle of the table and shakes itself like birds do after a bath. There's bloody gravy everywhere and Mary's face is spotted – it looks like she's got a bad case o' brown chickenpox! The bird tries to fly away, but it must have got gravy in its eyes or something, 'cause it's banging into everything. Maggie says, 'Oops! *Pardonnez-moi!*' again then gets the hiccups. We both goes after the flamin' magpie but we's laughing so much, we falls over each other, and the bird escapes our clutches. It's still flying about, leaving splotches o' gravy on the walls and everywhere. Finally I catches it, opens the window, and lets it go. Off it flies, dropping globs o' Mary's best gravy as it leaves. Maggie runs to the open window and yells after it, 'Come back, ya forgot the bloody onions!'

Then she turns and sees Hawk's face and her bottom lip begins to tremble. She reaches up and pulls off the bonnet with its empty cage and throws it to the floor. 'Oh, oh, oh!' she sobs and slides down, with her back against the wall. She starts to howl, her head between her knees.

Mary bangs her fist against the table so that everything rattles. 'She's a whore!' she screams at Hawk. Our mama ain't wiped the gravy from her face and it's gone pale with rage. The scar down her cheek be bright purple, and her beautiful green eyes is on fire.

There follows complete silence, 'cept for Maggie's crying. Slowly, Hawk gets up and walks over to Maggie. He takes her gently under her arms and lifts her to her feet. Then he swings her up so that she's got her arms about his neck and is sobbing into his chest. He turns to Mary. 'Perhaps she is, Mama,' he says quietly, 'but she's mine and I love her.' He carries Maggie out of the room, out of the pub, and down the street towards the Argyle Cut as I watches from the window.

Back in the room, Mary's still sitting like she's got the headmaster's cane stuck down the back of her black dress. I can't see her expression 'cause she's got her back turned to me.

'Mama,' I says, trembling in me boots as I does so, 'Maggie's a nice girl, truly. She don't drink much as a rule. She were scared, that's all, and took a drop too much.' I go to sit in my chair, though I feels like running away – scarpering out o' there like Hawk and Maggie. I looks up to meet Mary's eyes and, to me surprise, she's smiling!

'Hawk's got himself a good un, Tommo. Lots o' gumption, that Maggie, ain't scared o' life like most. Bit narrow in the hips though. Birthing won't be no picnic, but we'll get a good midwife to attend.' Mary's laughing now. 'Mr Harris says she's got a good head on her shoulders, owns her own chophouse and the building it's in.' She's laughing while she wipes the gravy from her face. 'A bit headstrong, mind, she'll need a bit o' straightening out, but I reckon she'll get there.'

'Mama, Maggie ain't easy to push around,' I say, starting to like Mary for the first time.

'Hmmph! I daresay we'll learn to live with her and her

with us.' Mary dabs the napkin to her lips then folds it carefully and puts it on the table. Her eyes fill with tears as she looks at me. 'Tommo, please come back to Mama? Come home, lovey?'

'Mama, I ain't no good for you!'

'Oh no!' she protests. 'You're good enough for the likes o' me, son. I weren't an angel myself!' Her eyes glisten with tears though she tries to smile. 'Ha! Fancy me, Mary bleedin' Abacus, calling Hawk's Maggie a whore. Me what's been the very same. That's funny, that is, me the respectable one!' Then she stops and clears her throat.

'I know about the opium, Tommo,' she says, very quiet.

I'm shocked. 'Who told ya?' I asks, tryin' to look like I don't feel guilty.

'Hawk. He made it a condition.'

'Condition?'

'Well, a condition if you were going to come back. Him too. If ever you was to come back, I'd have to accept that you're . . .' she thinks a moment, trying to find another way to say it, but Mary can't not call a spade a bloody shovel, 'addicted to the poppy.' Then she adds quickly, 'He told me about your wound, I mean, how it gives you great pain and you need the opium.'

'Mama, I *told* you I was no good,' I says. 'But Hawk ain't got no right to be telling you about the opium!'

Mary sighs. 'Tommo, he *had* to tell me. He won't come back 'less you do, he's said that to me, time and again since I been here. He's told me that if you two was ever to come back it would have to be on your terms, you'd have to agree and me too.' Mary smoothes the tablecloth in front of her with both hands. 'Well I do, I agree.' She looks into me eyes.

'Mama, how long would it last? I can't work in the brewery, I ain't the type. I'm a gambler, cards is me life.'

Mary reaches over and pats me hand, then leaves her

hand covering mine. I look at them together, mine all mangled from the wilderness, hers from the bad things what happened at the docks.

'Tommo, I ain't goin' to judge you,' she says, giving a bitter little laugh. 'Me, judge? I ain't got no bleedin' right, have I? I was addicted meself to the stuff once. Opium and a few other things what I don't care to talk about.' Her voice is very soft now. 'I love you for what you is, Tommo Solomon. What I done after you come back from the wilderness were wrong and I beg your forgiveness! But I never stopped loving you.' The tears are rolling down her cheek and I feel a lump in me own throat. 'Never for one moment, through all the dark years, did I ever stop loving you. "Tommo'll come back," I'd say to myself every morning as I woke and every night before I closed my eyes. And wherever you was, I'd always say, "Good night, Tommo. Mary loves you, darling."'

'Oh Mama!' I bursts into tears. I can't help it, it's like a dam in me's just burst and I can't hold back the flood. All the loneliness of the wilderness comes back – the cold, the beatings, what the timber getters done to me when I were a little brat. I blubs and blubs and Mary rises from her chair and comes t' hold me. Then she starts to cry and the pair of us is howling and hugging and I'm seven years old again and Mary's got me in her lap and I'm safe, Tommo's safe again.

Mary orders a bottle of Cape brandy for me and I has a drink as she begins to talk. It's like it's all been bottled up in her as well. We already knows from her letters that things were bad 'tween her and David and Hannah. But now Mary pours it all out like she wants me to hear it straight.

It seems old man Madden, what's now married Hannah, is stricken with the gout and crippled with arthritis, so he spends all his days in bed or in a bath chair. Hannah and David has took over his timber and wheat-milling business, with David proving a sharp businessman. It ain't long before he and Hannah sees their chance to make things difficult for mama by making it hard for her to get her supply o' brewing hops.

New Norfolk, where David and Hannah lives, be the best climate for the growing of hops and they buy up land and plant hops. They also purchase in advance, at guaranteed prices per bushel, the crops of all the other hop growers. They even gain control of all hops imported from New South Wales and Victoria. Soon Hannah and David have got a monopoly and Mary can't get her hops from nowhere 'less she imports 'em from England and sometimes from Cape Town, what's both unreliable and expensive.

Then David does nearly the same thing with Mary's supply o' glass by buying into the Tasmanian Bottle Co. Now Mama can only obtain her bottles from Melbourne, what adds greatly to their cost. He's even building his own brewery in Launceston to compete with her.

Mary tells me all this and shrugs. 'I've only got one pair of hands and none what I can trust or ask for advice 'cept Mr Emmett. I need my boys to come home. Hawk tells me you got a quick mind, Tommo.'

Well, o' course I'm pleased by this as well as worried for her. 'But Hawk says Mr Emmett's always helped you lots, Mama? Can't he keep an eye on David and Hannah? See what they's up to?'

'He did help me a great deal, it's true. But with the death of his wife, Gawd rest her pernicious soul, he's retired, so he can't no more,' Mary replies.

I knows Mary has a soft spot for Mr Emmett, what's always helped her from the very beginning when she were in the Female Factory. Whenever she was with him she were like a young girl, giggling and flirting. Even as brats, we knew that, beside us, Mary's only great love were for Mr

Emmett. She cared for Ikey too, but that were different. For days before she was going to see Mr Emmett she'd be in a regular dither, burning the porridge and dropping things. And her what's always rushing around would take t' standing about and daydreamin' with half a smile on her face, her head tilted to one side.

What with Mr Emmett being a true merino and a married man, and Mary thinking herself a common ticket-of-leave, there weren't much chance o' their friendship turning into something more. But now Mary's wealthy and Mr Emmett a widower on a government pension, so perhaps it ain't impossible after all.

'Mama, what about Mr Emmett and you?' I asks, screwing up me courage.

Mary goes quite scarlet. 'Tommo, mind your tongue!' she gasps, like I've just used a dirty word in front o' the vicar.

I laugh at her embarrassment. 'Well, you loves him, don't you?'

'Mind your own business!' Mary retorts, but she won't meet my eye.

'Why don't *you* ask Mr Emmett? No harm in asking, is there? Him alone and you alone, two lonely people. It don't make no sense not to!'

'You think *I* should ask *him*?' Mary ain't too sure she's heard me right. 'Propose to Mr Emmett? Me?'

'Aye.'

'Don't talk nonsense, Tommo. Mr Emmett's a gentleman and me common as muck! Chalk and cheese! It ain't possible for them two things to get together. The whole bleedin' island would sink under the shame of it!'

'Mama, Hawk says there ain't no one person better than another. It's how we lives what matters, not how we's born.'

'Hawk's right too, but try telling that to the governor's wife, what calls me *Miss* Abacus like some reptile hissing it out. The nabobs don't marry the thingumabobs in this world, Tommo!'

'All right, well at least put Mr Emmett on your board of directors. Hawk reckons ya should, least that's what he said to me. Ain't no harm in that, is there? It'll keep his wise head working, Hawk says.'

'Hawk said that?' Mary looks pleased and I can see she thinks it a fine idea.

Never in me life have I talked like this with Mary. When I comes out o' the wilderness, she thought me a bit of an idjit. She'd talk to Hawk about the brewery and the business but never to me. Now she's treating yours truly like she wants my opinion, and I must say I likes it!

'Perhaps, perhaps,' she says, folding and unfolding her napkin again. 'Anyways, that's quite enough nonsense about Mr Emmett!' She throws her napkin aside. With the finger of her glove she picks at a spot o' dried gravy on her bodice. 'Now listen, Tommo, I wants to talk to you about Hawk and the Irishman. The more I sees, the less I like of this fight. We must stop it at once, at all costs. How does we do it, Tommo?'

'Mama, we can't! Hawk's got it into his noggin that this be a fight between good and evil. He reckons the evil began with Ikey and carried through to Mr Sparrow, what's got me under his thumb now.'

'That Sparrer's bad news and no mistake. But Hawk blames *Ikey* for all this?' Mary asks, surprised.

'Not Ikey hisself. Hawk loved Ikey, we all did. It be what happened to us because of Ikey's greed. That's what Hawk says he's fighting.'

'Oh me Gawd!' Mary thinks a while. 'Ikey were not the only one who were greedy. Hannah were even worse and now David.' She pauses, then says softly, 'Even me.'

'That's just it! Like Hawk says, it's a canker, it festers and turns everything rotten. Greed destroys everyone it touches!'

Mary's lips are pursed as she listens. 'Tommo, let's not forget the hard things what happened to Ikey too. He were a creature of the times, a survivor. To be a poor Jew in London when Ikey were a child was to be treated as dirt – lower than dirt! The lowest villain there was would think himself better than a Jew and spit on him. That ain't no way to treat another human being, but Ikey survived all that and he beat all who would destroy him.' Mary looks at me. 'Don't forget how much he gave me and you boys. Ikey were a truly remarkable man, Tommo.'

'Mama, I've told Hawk that. It's not Ikey what's the problem. If it weren't for Ikey I couldn't have survived the wilderness. But Hawk says, if it weren't for Ikey we wouldn't have been took by the wild men in the first place. If Ikey *had* shared his fortune with David and Hannah, we wouldn't have been kidnapped and there wouldn't have been no wilderness for me and for Hawk.'

'It weren't quite as simple as that,' Mary protests, though I can see from her expression that this line o' thinking ain't entirely new to her. 'It were Hannah wanting more than she were entitled to! It were *her* greed more than anything!'

'Mama, how is we to know what Hannah really deserved? Who knows what went on 'tween her and Ikey?' I shrug. 'I'm just tellin' ya what Hawk thinks. When Hawk gets an idea in his head nothing's gunna shake it out. He thinks Mr Sparrow's another example o' greed destroying everything it touches. And he's got a point. Mr Sparrow turns everyone what works for him into addicts and drunkards, and when they's no further use, he throws them out onto the street to die.

'Now, with the fight, Mr Sparrow thinks to take all the little punters to the cleaners. He's tempting 'em to bet every cent they has with his odds, when he *knows* Hawk can't win. For him, Hawk losing to the Irishman be a certainty. If he thinks Hawk's got a chance, he'll do something to stop him. Hawk says it's always the little people what gets preyed upon.' I draws breath. 'He says *somebody*'s got to stand up for the poor and that if we expects it to be somebody other than ourselves, it ain't never gunna never happen. The villains will win again!'

Mary sighs and remains quiet a long time. 'We could still bribe the Irishman to lose? Hawk don't have to know. The poor *will* get their winnings, Sparrer Fart – or your Mr Sparrow as he now calls himself – *will* be ruined and Hawk won't be hurt too bad in the meantime!'

'Well,' I says, 'there's a lot o' "wills" in there, 'cept the one you ain't thought about at all. You *will* lose Hawk forever if he finds out. I sees that now. I were wrong even to think of it in the first place, Mama. Completely wrong! Wrong to ask you to come and wrong to ask you for the money to make the bribe.'

'I'm glad you did, Tommo. It's given me a chance to see you and Hawk again. And to help you, if I may.'

'Mama, if Hawk thinks you and me and Maggie don't believe in him, he would never get over it. He knows he's gunna need a miracle to win, but our Hawk believes in miracles!

'Matter o' fact, he works so hard at his training that I'm beginning to believe in 'em meself. He soaks his hands in brine every day and they be hard as mallets. He's training with Bungarrabbee Jack and Johnny Heki and Ah Wong's uncle, too. They's all saying that if Hawk can just stay on his feet long enough and keep out o' the clinches, he might win the fight.'

I can see Mary ain't convinced by this so I goes on. 'Best thing we can do is believe in Hawk – and hope,' I says. 'Hawk be the bravest man I've ever seen and he's awful strong, Mama.'

'I'm coming with you to the fight,' Mary says suddenly. 'If me boy's gunna be hurt, he'll need his mama.' Mary looks defiant at me, thinking I'm gunna object. 'And I want Hawk to know I does believe in him, with all me heart and soul.' She grabs her handbag from the floor beside her chair. 'Tommo, I want you to put five hundred pounds on our Hawk to win. Mind, you put the bet with our Mr Sparrow so it costs him dear and he knows it when the time comes. We want him to know the true price of underestimating the underdog, eh, Tommo?'

Mary snaps open her bag and digs into it. She brings out a roll of banknotes as thick as me forearm and slaps it down on the table in front of me. 'Now take me to Maggie. I'd best make things right with her and start making plans for the wedding and all. You'll be Hawk's best man and I'll ask Mr Emmett to give Maggie away! Let's be off!'

Chapter Twenty-four

TOMMO

New South Wales
August 1861

I walk around with Mary's five hundred quid stuffed inside me coat for near on two weeks before I figures what to do with it. I can't just do what she reckons and put the whole lot on Hawk. Mr Sparrow would smell a rat straight away! A hundred quid placed on the Irishman by a squatter or a big merchant would be all right. But if five hundred or even one hundred were put on Hawk, all the sporting gents'd want to know what rich fool made such a stupid bet! Or else they'd want to know what was going on with Hawk, in case they too should be stickin' their money on him. Either way, it wouldn't be wise to plonk the whole lot down on me twin at once. Finally I decides to get Caleb Soul and a few of his mates to dole it out for us in smaller bets of twenty quid or so. Even this be a big bet on Hawk and in the days what follow it causes noise enough.

The fight's just a week away but we must leave Sydney today to be sure o' making it. Its location's a secret so's the law can't prevent it, but we has to go to Yass, where we'll find out where it's at. Mary's hired a coach-and-four for all of us, with full provisions for the six days' journey. One thing's certain, the fight ain't gunna be at Lambing Flat. Since the riot there, the diggings have been crawlin' with about two hundred military men, marines and police.

We sets out on our journey and I reckon Mary and Maggie, what's made their peace together, would be enjoying themselves if it weren't for the flies. We've had a bout of warm weather and the flies are swarming *everywhere*. We take to startin' out early, to try and avoid 'em, but the moment the sun comes up, the little black flies comes to life again and they keeps up with us all day. They stick to the horses so that scarcely a patch o' horse hair can be seen beneath them. They gets in our eyes and noses and mouths. Luckily Caleb Soul, in his trap behind us, has brought along netting what Maggie makes into veils and attaches to our bonnets and hats, giving us all a most mysterious appearance!

But if the flies is bad, the blowflies is worse. They get into the woollen blankets by day and spoil 'em. They lay their larvae and in a matter of hours the blankets is covered in patches a foot square with maggots, what are at once fried by the sun and stick to the blankets. Again, Caleb saves the day by wrapping the blankets up in lengths of oilskin before sunrise and protecting them against the blowflies.

At first Maggie and Mary stay in roadside inns overnight, with us camped nearby. But soon they's complaining about the bed bugs and the noisy drunks, both of which be plentiful! They decides to camp with us, rough though it be.

The road is full o' people what's heard about the fight. Many reckons they'll go to see it and seek their fortunes in the diggings afterwards. Some have been walking for weeks to get to Yass. Lots of 'em cheer heartily when they sees Hawk. They run beside our coach to wish us well, stretching out their hands so that Hawk might touch 'em for luck.

I can see Mary is thrilled to see all the fuss being made

over her boy by the passers-by. But every now and then I catch her watching Hawk with an anxious, loving sort o' look, as if she's seeing terrible things happen to him at the hands of the English and Irish double champion. Some of the travellers around us ain't so pleasant, with a band of rough Tipperary men jeering insults at Hawk and his team, Bungarrabbee Jack and Johnny Heki, sitting atop the coach with Ah Wong and his uncle, Ah Sing. But Mary brushes off the insults and is back quick enough to her staunch old self, declaring that o' course Hawk will win!

Mary and Maggie is having a grand time together as we trundles along, which pleases Hawk very much, and me too! Maggie makes Mary laugh such as we ain't never heard. The two of 'em gossips from morning 'til night, swapping whispered stories about their work on the streets – at least that's what I gathers from the way they huddles together, and then bursts into giggles, like two naughty little girls! Maggie's even told Mary the rudiments o' bare-knuckle fighting so that she can follow the bout.

When we arrives in Yass our carriage is mobbed by every sort of human being you could imagine – women, young and old, men from the city, men from the diggings, men of all nations! There's as much booing as cheering around us. Our carriage can hardly move an inch down the street for men hanging off the harnesses of the horses. It's said that our welcome be every bit as big as that of the Irish champion.

The Bolt arrived the previous day and is now settled in at the Golden Nugget Inn. He's taken three rooms for himself and his six doxies, what I reckons be mostly for the look o' things.

With his doxies on his arms, the Bolt is already a great favourite with the crowd. We hear that last night in the pub, he challenged everyone there to down one drink to his two. He were the last man still standing at dawn, waving a whiskey bottle and singing *Mother Macree* and *Danny Boy* to the cockerels! They reckon he drank four bottles of Irish whiskey in all, followed by any number of beer chasers. The publican's made a fortune in drinks and out o' sheer gratitude has sent his wife to stay with a relative and given the Bolt their very own bed chamber for his visit.

We're staying with the manager of the Oriental Bank, a mate of Caleb's. Mary and Maggie will stay in the house with him and his wife. We'll camp behind the bank in the yard, what has a high wall to protect us from them what wish us well and them what wish us dead!

By nightfall several thousand visitors are in town. The diggings for a hundred miles around be just about empty o' manpower. The celestials has made their own camp a couple o' miles out, so as to avoid harassment by the drunken revellers. Ah Wong and Ah Sing has gone to join them and will make their own way to the fight.

At eight o'clock at night, a young boy arrives with a message from my employer. 'Mr Sparrow sends his compliments!' he says brightly and I brood darkly for a moment on what Mr Sparrow's idea of a compliment might be. 'The bout will take place at Black Billy Creek, about five mile out o' town on the road to Lambing Flat, noon tomorrer! Fighters to be there an hour before!' he tells us. Mr Sparrow must be bloody confident of the Bolt to make his man fight in the midday sun.

After that news, we all tries to settle in for a good night's sleep. But all night long, folks is arriving by whatever means possible, and making a lot o' noise about it too. It's hard to get a wink what with all the hullabaloo. Hawk seems calm enough and sleeps soundly all night. I've learned a long time ago that whenever Hawk's gunna face some manner o' danger, he draws into hisself. In the Maori wars, when every other bloke were shouting, singing and doing the *haka* to get a bit o' courage, Hawk'd be away on his own, sitting very still and silent. He be at his most powerful then and so it is on the morning of the fight. He ain't even got eyes for Maggie.

'What's up with 'im then?' she pouts as we climbs into the coach at nine o'clock to go to Black Billy Creek.

'He's gettin' ready to fight,' I comforts her. 'To win!'

'Ooh, I hopes 'e does!' says Maggie, smiling and squeezing her arms with anticipation. 'Then he might be ready to go a few rounds in the bed chamber again!'

'Maggie!' I look 'round to see if Mary's heard. But she just gives Maggie a little smile and I reckon I sees a wink there too!

The road is rocky and rutted, with a vast army o' men walking along, and others on horseback or in carriages, traps and drays. We even pass a one-legged man what's being pushed in a wheelbarrow. It takes us nearly two hours to cover the five-mile distance.

Mr Sparrow has a genius for picking locations, I'll give him that much. This one's right near a billabong and is like a natural amphitheatre in a sort o' half-moon shape. Several thousand men can be seated on the slope with the prize ring built below. There's plenty of water for the horses and men, though already the banks o' the billabong are knee-high deep in black mud and several men are trying to pull a mare out what's got herself stuck.

Rumour has it that Mr Sparrow's arranged for all the local traps to be called to Lambing Flat to meet with all the militia, navy and police forces what's gathered there. What a piece of timing! Even though he's our sworn enemy, I still can't help admirin' the way he operates. Me boss has his very own police, the fight stewards what wears red armbands and carries truncheons, and they ain't reluctant to use 'em either. It's their job to keep the drunks under control and break up any fights between the two sides. But the atmosphere here is mostly one o' goodwill, with lots o' loud singing and good-natured chaffing from both sides.

The crinoline cruisers are all here, parading about in their finery. Some be from Melbourne and others Maggie knows from Sydney. The rougher sorts from the brothels in the diggings is also trawling for business, and many an insult is traded between the city whores and the gold dust girls.

Mary's the subject of much curiosity as she walks in. She's dressed in a respectable black gown, with a black veil over her face, looking like a good Christian lady on her way to church! She sits herself down on the small stool she's brung with her, as prim as someone's maiden aunt what's turned up at the wrong place but won't admit it.

Maggie, seated beside her, is the only other woman in the ring enclosure. While Mary sits stiff as a musketeer's ramrod in her black dress, Maggie's as bright as a butterfly, in a blue silk gown what's displaying all the necessary. She wears a matching blue bonnet with her magpie roosting atop – a stuffed one this time. Maggie's nigh impossible to contain and keeps jumping up from her seat while we waits for the fight to begin, chirping like a bloody budgerigar.

From where I stands in the ring, I can sense both women's fears. Mary's silent and thoughtful, like Hawk, and Maggie's a regular chatterbox – but both are worried. Caleb Soul is with them and seems to be tryin' to keep 'em occupied.

Bungarrabbee Jack and Johnny Heki are with me in the ring. Johnny Heki is massaging Hawk's shoulders and torso with eucalyptus oil, and the Aborigine has a branch o' coolibah leaves what he's using to swish the flies away. Our corner is the red one, shown by a red bandanna tied to the ring post. There's a green one tied to the ring post where the Lightning Bolt will sit. Hawk also wears a sash of red to hold up his knee breeches – no doubt the Bolt will be wearing one of the best Irish green.

It's nearly half-past eleven, but the Bolt ain't yet arrived. Bloody cheek, I reckons – we've been sweating in the ring for half an hour. It could be a tactic o' course to make us anxious. Finally at ten to twelve, just before the bout is meant to start, the Irishman makes his way to the ring from a tent, followed by our dear friends, Mr Sparrow and Fat Fred. The crowd is on its feet and roaring.

The Bolt's gained nearly twenty pounds o' lard since arriving in the colonies. He's most flabby 'round the waist, his gut sticking out further than his great barrel chest. His knee breeches show the bottom part of his legs, the calves still thick, and the skin scarred from a hundred fights. Scar tissue what's built up on his shins shines pink in the bright afternoon sunlight. His nose has been broke beyond ever looking natural again, and his ears are half the normal size, bunched up like cauliflowers. His head's fresh-shaved and gleaming and his broad smile glints with gold teeth.

The Irish champion climbs up the crude steps and slips between the ropes and into the ring. He's followed by Fat Fred, what lumbers up behind. He's much too fat to fit through the ropes, and the Bolt has to come back and hold 'em apart for Fred to climb through. Once in, Fat Fred takes up the hailing funnel what a fight steward's given him. With Fat Fred as the referee, I wonder, what chance have we got? But I keep my thoughts to meself.

Mr Sparrow's perched high on a special timber seat built up so he can see clearly how the fight progresses. He don't acknowledge Hawk or me, though he smiles when the Bolt nods in his direction.

The crowd hushes. Only the melancholy sound of a crow cawing can be heard as Fat Fred starts his announcement.

'Gentlemen, sportsmen and punters, I welcome you on this grand occasion. Today is a tournament, the greatest bare-knuckle fight yet fought in the colony of New South

Wales. Two truly great behemoths contesting for a purse o' five hundred pounds – *winner takes all!*'

The crowd gives a good cheer, after which Fat Fred declares, 'This be the biggest purse in the history of the colony!' There is further clapping and yelling and Fat Fred waits for it to die down before gesturing to the Bolt, what's holding up his arms and waving to the largest group of his supporters on the centre of the hill. 'In the green corner, we have the champion o' Great Britain and Ireland! Undefeated in the colonies, the most remarkable pugilist in the known, civilised world – the one and only, *Lightning Bolt!*'

The Bolt jumps up and down as the crowd roars. Then he catches sight o' Mary and Maggie and he blows a kiss at Maggie. Maggie lifts her veil at this and the Bolt blows her another kiss before wiggling his hips and thrusting them at her. Hawk's kept his eyes well down so far but at the very moment the Irish fighter does this, he looks up and sees it. His whole body stiffens and he begins to rise, taking the three of us to restrain him. Maggie makes matters worse by giving the Bolt a knowing tap of her finger against her nose, as if to egg him on.

Hawk don't see this, as he's too busy staring at the Bolt, what gives another big thrust of his hips in Maggie's direction. Johnny Heki has his arms about Hawk's neck trying to hold him down, with Bungarrabbee Jack hanging on as well, but Hawk's too strong for them both and brushes them aside. He rushes towards the Irishman.

'Hawk! Come back!' I yells, but he hears nothing. Reaching the Bolt, he grabs him by the neck. He's holding him at arm's length and has started to squeeze. The Irishman's trying to tear Hawk's arms away but he ain't got a chance and his eyes is beginning to pop. Then Hawk throws him to the ground and the Bolt goes sprawlin'. Me brother bends down now and says something to him, though I don't hear what.

Then he walks calmly back to his corner. Mary's pulled up her veil the better to see all this, and has a huge smile on her face, what she tries to hide behind her glove.

The Irish fighter rises to his feet. He ain't hurt, but he's angry. If half a dozen ring stewards hadn't jumped into the ring to hold him back, the fight would've started then and there.

Back in our corner, Hawk's sitting down again but his nostrils are flared and his breathing's a bit fast.

'Calm, be calm,' I says. 'If ya fights him with temper he'll get the better of ya.'

He nods, and takes a few deep gulps of air.

Meanwhile the stewards have pulled the Bolt over into the green corner and his seconds have made him be seated. Fights are breaking out all over the hill and the crowd is screamin' and roarin', each side wanting blood.

Up gets Fat Fred, sweating lots and keen to get the preliminaries over with. 'Gentlemen, sportsmen and punters, in the red corner, we have the Black Hawk, New South Wales champion and challenger for the British and Irish title! May the best man win!' Before we knows it, the two men are facing each other alone in the centre. The fight against the mongrels has begun.

My heart is in my mouth as I watch Hawk prepare to meet the Irish fighter. The Bolt's also reined in his temper and smiles as he approaches Hawk. Like true pugs, they spends the next few minutes walking about each other, sizing each other up.

The Bolt takes the first move, a good kick at Hawk's ankle. But he misses and in that moment Hawk's left goes in hard, followed by the right. The one-spot, left-right, bang-bang is seated right under the Bolt's heart and it's plain to see Hawk's hurt him.

The Irishman draws back and circles 'round. Closing in, he plants a punch in Hawk's belly. You can hear the smack of his enormous fist as he puts the full weight behind it. He has hit Hawk a blow what would put most fighters to the ground or, if not, leave 'em clutching their bellies, so that they's opened up to the uppercut. But Hawk don't even flinch. Now the Bolt realises he's gunna need every trick in the book to win against this opponent.

He rushes Hawk, lashing out his leg. Over goes Hawk with a mighty thud. In an amazing exhibition of the fighter's craft, the Bolt manages to head butt Hawk at the same time and my twin lies dazed on the ground, his eyebrow split wide open.

Fat Fred begins to count, but Hawk is up by the count o' five, though dripping blood from the cut to his eye. The first round is ended after seven minutes.

The second round be a longer affair, as the Bolt's much more careful in his approach. Hawk manages to hit him several times, though mostly on the arms. Twice the Bolt lands good blows to me twin's ribs and stomach. The round has gone nearly fifteen minutes and I can see the Irishman's getting tired. Hawk's watching him most careful, expecting to be rushed and sure enough, in comes the Irishman. He grabs at Hawk, ready to deliver his head butt. This time Hawk's ready and in goes his fist – one-spot, two-shot, left-right, bang-bang – straight under the Tipperary man's heart again. The Bolt goes down like a sack o' potatoes but manages to rise unsteady to his feet at the count of nine. Fat Fred quickly brings the round to an end.

The next fifteen rounds goes along much the same lines. I keep me eyes fixed on me twin – not looking at Mary, Maggie, Mr Sparrow, or the crowd – as if by doing this I can somehow help him. The Irishman uses all his dirty tricks against Hawk, butting and gouging. Twice he knees Hawk in the groin as they go down. He is awful cunning and always has his back to Fat Fred so his actions can't be seen. Fat Fred ain't too eager to look neither. The Bolt's having a grand old time at Hawk's expense. Several of the toffs and sportsmen in the enclosure complain about the dirty play, shouting 'Fair go!' and 'Steady on!' but nothin' happens about it. I complains twice too, but Fat Fred waves me away. 'All in the game, lad. All in the game o' fisticuffs!' he says, smiling.

Hawk's shins are cut deep by the raking of the Bolt's spiked boots and his left knee is much swollen where the Irish champion's stamped upon it as he's pulled me brother to the ground. In round twelve the Irishman suddenly bites Hawk's ear and Fat Fred is forced to stop the bout. The Bolt is all innocence and points at the corner post, what has some blood on it where he's pushed Hawk's head against it. 'The post done it, I swear!' he protests.

Fat Fred accepts his explanation straight off and orders the fight to go on. Part of Hawk's ear has been completely torn away and we has great trouble stemming all the blood, though a doctor stitches it up with horsehair.

All the cloth rags we got is now soaked in blood. Between rounds Johnny Heki fetches buckets o' water and rinsing cloths. But, by the end of each round, Hawk's shoulders and chest is smeared crimson from the claret leaking from his ear and the cut to his eyebrow.

The Bolt don't seem damaged almost at all, though he's huffin' and puffin' and starting to wear out. In round twenty he manages to get Hawk into a clinch and he brings his head down to break me brother's nose with a mighty crunch. Now the whole crowd can see that the Irishman's fighting dirty and as the blood gushes from Hawk's nose, a huge cry o' protest goes up. It's the second time Hawk goes down himself to end the round and his bleeding's getting worse.

But the Irish pug ain't finished with him yet and, in the

very next round, he tries the same routine again. This time Hawk's ready for him. His hand comes up under his chin and I see him make one of the Chinee grips what Ah Sing's taught him. A moment later the Bolt's eyes roll up and he goes limp. Hawk lets go of him so quick that nobody sees what's happened. The Bolt begins to topple, his eyes wide open in surprise. It's like a mighty mountain crumbling. Now Hawk sees the spot clear and it's the one-spot, two-shot, left-right, bang-bang as the Bolt goes down. I can see the fear in the Irishman's eyes.

To me surprise the Bolt gets up again at the count o' six and in the very next round, gives Hawk a few more of his rotten tricks. He uses every pug trick in the book, gouging Hawk's left eye and biting his lip so that it bleeds into his mouth. He's torn Hawk's ear again and I can see me twin's losing too much blood. In every clinch what follows, the Bolt makes sure to tweak his nose hard to make it bleed the more. Hawk's knee is paining him too and the Irishman bangs his kneecap into Hawk's swollen cartilage at every chance. As a result, Hawk's knee has blown up like a balloon and he's dragging his leg behind him.

Now the Bolt's starting to hit Hawk more easily. If he weren't near exhausted himself he'd quickly finish me brother off. Only Hawk's top physical condition keeps him going. The Irishman goes into a clinch and brings his hand up to hook into Hawk's nostril with two fingers. But he's a slow learner, the Bolt, and Hawk's hand comes up under his throat with another Chinee grip. The Irish fighter's eyes roll up, his arms fall to his side and he tumbles backwards like a sack o' spuds thrown from a dray. I think Hawk's killed him! Even those standin' close by don't see what's happened, and they shouts at him to get up and get on with it. Most o' the crowd now favours Hawk, for they sees how the Bolt be fouling him cruel at every chance.

The Bolt stirs and gets himself on all fours but can't rise any further. His seconds rush to help him to his corner, where he stays for nearly ten minutes before the next round is called. Fat Fred's given the Irishman as much time as he can to recover – only the crowd's jeers to get on with it makes him announce the next bout. From the way the Bolt rubs at his throat, it's clear he ain't gunna risk fouling Hawk again for fear of another o' these secret manoeuvres. Even so, I fears Hawk has left his run too late. At the end o' round twenty-six, I'm weeping for him. He's hurt bad and bleeding everywhere. He can barely speak through his busted mouth. His nose is broke and spurting blood, one eye's been bashed and has closed up, his ear's almost ripped off, and the deep gash on his forehead's pulled open even more.

'Hawk, you has to stop,' I urges.

He shakes his head as I sponge the blood away. 'No. He's slowing down, tiring. He can't last much longer,' he gasps.

'You neither!' I cries. 'Let me throw in the sponge.'

Hawk looks at me through his one good eye. 'No, Tommo. If we throw in the towel, Mr Sparrow wins. We'll not get a second chance at the mongrels.' Hawk ain't forgotten why he's here. He tries to smile and nods his head towards the green corner. 'Besides, he mocked my Maggie!'

For the first time I realise that Hawk will truly die in the attempt rather than give in. If this be an example o' good versus evil, good seems to be getting much the worse of the deal as bloody usual. Fat Fred signals the fight to continue and Hawk rises wearily, dragging his bad leg.

Now we see the game change. Hawk begins to stalk the Bolt what's mostly trying to stay out of harm's way. His flab and lack o' fitness has finally caught up with him and he's all scarlet, puffin' like a steam engine. Hawk's waiting for the opportunity he knows must come to him. Still, the Irishman is cunning. Whenever Hawk comes too close he pulls him in and holds him tight, then drops to the deck to end the round.

Hawk follows him doggedly and, in the next three rounds, finds him time and again with the one-spot, two-shot, left-right, bang-bang! Now he's brushing off the Irish fighter's feeble punches like they was flies. The Bolt is on the run.

Hawk is stalking his prey like a lion. He moves forward but slips on his own blood. He grabs wildly at the ropes to keep his balance but as he does so, the Irishman kicks out viciously, landing his boot hard and deep into Hawk's crotch. Hawk gives a gasp and collapses in agony on the deck. Fat Fred counts to nine before Hawk somehow manages to rise onto one knee, his hands cupped to his bollocks. He can't stand up. It *must* end. I pick up the sponge and Hawk sees me. 'NO!' he screams. 'NO, TOMMO!'

We drag Hawk back to his corner. Fat Fred comes across and I starts shouting at him like a mad man. 'Foul! It were a foul, ya mongrel!'

'One more word from you, lad, and you're out of the ring!' Fat Fred hisses at me. 'Understand? That were no foul, his foot slipped. It were an accident, no more.'

'An accident! Listen to the crowd, they bloody seen it. Everybody seen it 'cept you, ya fat, useless bastard!'

Fred looks at me hard and points a sausage finger in me face. 'You'll keep, son. You'll keep.' He turns to Hawk, what's retching with the pain. 'Now, does you fight on or does you quit?'

Hawk spits out more blood and gasps through his broken mouth, 'I shall never surrender.' It's the words from Mary's medal! 'We fight!' he says.

I hold back a big sob. 'Aye, we fight on,' I says to Fat Fred.

'You sure?' he asks. I can see he's hoping the fight will

end now and suddenly me temper gets up. 'Tell the Bolt me brother ain't *begun* to fight yet! Tell him we're coming for him! Coming for all o' you mongrels!'

Fat Fred moves closer. 'We'll give you a thousand pounds if you throw in the sponge,' he whispers. 'You get five hundred, Tommo, and your brother gets another five hundred. You'll get a thousand between you. I swear it upon my mother's grave,' he whispers.

'Fuck you!' I snarls.

'Righto!' he shouts, straightening up. 'Yer man's rested enough, it's back in the fight!'

But Hawk ain't in no condition to go back just yet and needs another few minutes. The Bolt's been given ten minutes for much lesser wounds. 'Fair go!' I cries, hating the fact I has to ask him for mercy.

'Fuck *you*, son,' says Fat Fred and goes to the centre o' the ring.

Meanwhile the crowd's getting ugly – they can see what's going on. Fat Fred signals the fighters to come out o' their corners and Hawk, plainly half-dead, rises slowly. 'I need two more!' he says, as though to himself. 'Two!' he mumbles, holding up two fingers and looking at Bungarrabbee Jack.

'Two, boss! You get 'em!' the Aborigine shouts gleefully.

It is round thirty, over five hours since the fight began. I wants to blub at the sight o' me brother as he drags himself towards his opponent, barely able to stand upright. I'm sure Mary and Maggie would both be crying, though I ain't been able to look at 'em.

The Bolt hits Hawk with every punch he has at his command. Even so Hawk only goes down three times and each time to a foul what the crowd insists Fat Fred call. The stewards are looking worried – they knows they could have a riot on their hands. While Hawk can't last much longer, the real power is gone from the Irishman's blows and he's struggling. He'd hoped to finish Hawk off long before now and it ain't worked! When Hawk comes at him now he's dead scared and ready to run, if only his weary legs would carry him. Hawk manages to get in a one-spot, two-shot, left-right, bang-bang.

In his weakened state, the Bolt can't stay more than two minutes at a time for the next two rounds. He drops willingly to the ground after Hawk taps him, so as to rest a moment and regain his breath. Then I sees why. The patch under his heart is become a horrible purple bruise. At the same moment, Bungarrabbee Jack starts dancing beside me.

'One more, boss! *One*!' he is shouting at Hawk. 'One-spot, two-shot, left-right, bang-bang – *sleeeepy time*!' Bungarrabbee Jack is boxing the air, most excited. He's seating his left and then his right into an imaginary opponent like he wants Hawk to do.

'Open him!' I'm not sure if Hawk can even hear Johnny Heki. 'Now's the time! Hit him to the head to open him up!' Johnny Heki shouts at Hawk in Maori. Never before has I heard Johnny tell Hawk to hit to the head, so I knows something's up.

Then I sees it happen. Hawk's great fist slams into the Irishman's face, right into the flattened nose, crashing into his mouth and jaw. The Bolt's face appears to collapse under the impact. Bits o' gold teeth go flying and I hears the crack o' bone as the Irishman's jaw breaks – or perhaps it's Hawk's hand?

The Bolt begins to reel backwards and Hawk comes in again. Wham! Wham! Left! Right! Bang! Bang! The Bolt is lifted clear off the ground and bounces hard against the rope. Hawk grimaces in pain and I know his hand be broke.

Somehow the Bolt is still on his feet. But his knees begin to buckle as Hawk hits him again with a left, followed by a right, plumb on the deep purple spot under his heart. I can hear Hawk's howl o' sheer pain as his broken fist smashes into the Bolt with all the force he has left. The Lightning Bolt sails over the ropes and, after knocking several toffs over on the way, lands at Maggie's dainty feet. There he lies still. They be the two hardest blows I've ever seen struck.

'Ho! That bugger never fight again in this life, Tommo,' Johnny Heki says with deep satisfaction.

'Bloody beauty, eh!' Bungarrabbee Jack says, dancing about in delight. 'It work! It work!'

Maggie leaps over the unconscious loser and climbs into the ring, her petticoats flying. She is sobbing and laughing at once as she clasps her arms 'round Hawk's waist and buries her face in his bloody torso. 'Oh, oh, I loves you, Hawk Solomon! More than me own life!' she howls, her birdy bonnet falling to the deck as she hugs and kisses him all over. With the last of his strength, Hawk picks her up and holds her in his arms and the crowd erupts. They has a champion they will never forget as long as they lives. Even the Irishmen are crying, though it may well be for the money they's lost on their fallen hero.

Mary's standing with her gloved hands pressed to her face, looking down at the Bolt, what lies out to it. Then she looks up and gives me a watery smile as her eyes turn to Hawk and Maggie. She turns her face towards me and blows me a kiss.

'I love you, Tommo,' she calls out.

'I loves you too, Mama,' I calls back, me voice catching.

And now I realise it all be over. We has won. We's beaten the mongrels. And I am very, very tired.

Suddenly the hair on the back of me neck prickles. I glance up to see that Mr Sparrow has disappeared from his perch in the fading sun. My heart's hammering as I searches the crowd, hoping to see him. I turn towards the billabong, now dark against the surrounding bush. A currawong calls from the clump o' coolibah trees. And then I sees him. He hops into a carriage what moves away into the night at a fast pace.

'Wherever ya runs, I'll find ya,' I vows. 'This time Tommo ain't gunna let ya win, ya mongrel.'

BOOK FOUR

Chapter Twenty-five

H AWK

The Rocks
September 1861

Since returning to Sydney after the fight with Ben Bolt nearly three weeks ago, I find myself a hero beyond any possible reckoning. *Bell's Life in Sydney* has proclaimed the event to be one of the great fights in history. It must also have been one of the greatest hidings in history for I am somewhat of a mess. The surgeon has straightened my nose and stitched my lip, ear and the wound above my eyebrow – but I still look like a golliwog that's been run over by a cart.

Despite my appearance, people carry on as though I am an object of exquisite beauty. Maggie, Mary, Tommo and I have even been invited to a garden party held by His Excellency the Governor. The whore, the gambler and the nigger are now the toast of the town! Suddenly Maggie is called Miss Pye by shopkeepers and merchants who would have spurned her not so long ago. Their womenfolk still refuse to have anything to do with her, for she is well known as a whore, and we learn later that numerous members of Sydney society have refused the governor's invitation.

But Maggie is puffed up with pride for me, and takes no notice of such snubs. She parades down the street with her head held at a jaunty angle, her magpie perched high atop her pretty hair, and men doff their hats as she passes by. The Sydney lads think her almost as much a hero as they do me. I shall be most glad to return to Hobart Town where Mary thinks we should have the wedding – well away from all this fuss and bother.

Maggie and I are officially betrothed, our forthcoming marriage announced in the *Sydney Morning Herald*, and Maggie has given up working since Mary's come to town. She tells me of her decision to stop work the night after the fight, when we make the most tender and considerate love, and she uses her mouth gently so as not to hurt my many wounds and bruises. She kisses my face everywhere except the places that the surgeon has stitched.

'Hawk, yours be the only body I shall ever again give me love to. No other man will lay a finger on me again, even if you should die before me,' she says, looking solemnly at me with her big blue eyes. 'I swears this on me life, may Gawd strike me dead this moment if I don't tell the truth.'

Now she no longer sleeps all day and by mid-morning is out and about with Mary, shopping and fussing about the wedding details, or having afternoon tiffin in all the best tea rooms in town. The only thing she hasn't forsaken is the magpie in her bonnet. And when she doesn't wear a bonnet, the bird still nests in her hair.

David Jones' and Farmer's, the two great emporiums, are now well accustomed to Mary and Maggie's visits, and our mama has been on a shopping spree the likes of which she's never indulged in before. The Belgian lace and the ribbon and satin cloth for the wedding gown have all been purchased here and the various department managers fawn over the two of them as though they are the grandest of gentlefolk.

On one occasion, Mr David Jones himself came down

from his office to serve them and sent his compliments to the champion. He even donated five yards of the best French grosgrain ribbon with his good wishes. 'A small nuptial contribution, with my compliments,' he said fussing, 'to remember a great occasion.' He smiled when Mary shook his hand before leaving. 'Delighted I'm sure,' he beamed. 'Such a nice lady,' Mr Jones now tells all around him.

Barney Isaacs, who made my first set of clothes at Maggie's behest, now begs to make the wedding gown for the cost of the workmanship alone – provided, of course, that he can display the grand creation in his George Street window.

While Maggie and Mary spend their days together, we all meet as night falls. Tommo, naturally enough, is not working, for all Mr Sparrow's card games have come to a halt. But he remains a creature of the night and persists in his habit of sleeping all day, seeming to find games enough on his own. Because I have lost so much time with the fight, I have a great deal of bookkeeping to catch up at Tucker & Co. At six o'clock every afternoon when I finish work, we meet at the Hero of Waterloo to have supper together and to hear all the gossip from the two women. It comes mostly from Maggie, as Mary seems to enjoy the retelling as much as Tommo and I. Maggie is like a small child in her excitement, chirping, like the magpie she is, at every new experience and making an event or grand joke out of everything that's happened in the course of the day. It seems my great affection for her only increases every day, and I have come to love her with my very life.

How very much things have changed since Tommo and I arrived from New Zealand on the *Black Dog*. On that same day I met Maggie in Mr Smith's eating-house after I'd had my fill of his best corned beef. I recall with a smile to myself how I came here in my whaleman's rags and split boots with

Maggie leaving a florin on the table to pay for my breakfast. I have much to thank her for besides the special love she has brought into my life.

While Maggie and I are not exactly the cream of society, the *Sydney Morning Herald* is all a-twitter about the bride and groom to be. It has suggested a wedding in the Botanical Gardens so that the general population may turn out to support the champion of the world among the spring blooms. The *Herald* has even reported that the military band from the New South Wales Regiment would be pleased to attend, with Sydney's mayor, Councillor John Sutherland, handing us the key to the city at a reception in the Town Hall.

Meanwhile this same newspaper has been raging on about Mr Sparrow and Fat Fred. The editor has put on a 'special' who has lost no time digging out unsavoury facts about boxing's two worst scoundrels, as he terms them! Not a single penny has been paid out to the punters who backed me. Everyone is holding onto their betting tickets which entitle them to their winnings, but to no joy. Mr Sparrow is holed up with Fat Fred in his rooms above The World Turned Upside Down and will say nothing to the newspapers except that he is 'consolidating his assets so he can pay'.

'Assets!' snorts Mary. 'I'll bet me own gravestone he declares himself skint! I know his sort. Ikey were of the same mould. What he's got, and it be plenty you may be sure, he's got stashed. There'll be no bank account with money lying about in it. He lives in rented rooms above the pub and if he owns property it will not be in his name. The Sparrows of this world travel light. They keep their fortunes portable – of the kind that can be carried away in a saddlebag on a dark night or slipped aboard ship in a suitcase.' Mary pauses. 'Blimey, I should know one when I sees one! I lived with Ikey for Lord knows how many Gawd-forsaken years. We'll have to be on our guard or our Mr Sparrow will vanish.'

There's little chance of that. Mr Sparrow and Fat Fred owe the townfolk here a fortune. There's not a single street corner, a single laneway, where eyes are not searching for them and tongues telling tales. Every kitchen maid and barman, matelot and mechanic, hackney driver and barrowman is on the lookout should they make any move to leave the pub.

Bell's Life in Sydney and the *Sydney Morning Herald* have both leapt to the defence of the thousands of small punters who put their money on me. It is estimated that two thousand or so punters in the gold diggings alone have placed bets, and in Sydney nearly twice as many again. These are all small gamblers who placed their money on a local hero, much against the advice of the so-called experts, and won. That they should now bear the brunt of Mr Sparrow's outrageous efforts to defraud the public is terribly unfair.

The press also declare Mr Sparrow and Fat Fred ruined for life and vow they will keep a watch on these scoundrels. If Mr Sparrow doesn't meet his obligations, declares the *Herald*, then he must not be allowed to operate in any part of the sporting business again. A front page headline shouts:

F. ARTIE SPARROW BANNED FOR LIFE!

The *Herald* is particularly keen on this idea but points out that, because prize-fighting is illegal and gambling equally so, Mr Sparrow may get away with his monstrous confidence trick. They ask that, at the very least, he should give the money he has taken to the Orphanage Fund.

At Mary's white tablecloth dinner on Sunday I propose a toast. 'We have ruined Mr Sparrow and so defeated one of the world's worst mongrels. He will never again live off the profits of greed and corruption.' I lift my glass.

'Oi, I ain't drinkin' to that!' Maggie exclaims. 'It's the poor folk what's suffered again, not Mr bleedin' Sparrow. That bastard's still rollin' in it. What about all the money he took in the betting shops? Yiz told me yerself. The newspapers reckon it were nigh on twenty thousand pounds.'

'But he is ruined, Maggie,' I protest. 'Mr Sparrow and Fat Fred must find near one hundred thousand pounds to meet their creditors. The loss of folks' gambling punts is a small price to pay.'

'Small price! Hawk Solomon, what's yiz talkin' about? Many of the folk here in the Rocks bet a week's pay – hoping to win a month or more's wages. They's skint! Their brats don't have no food. Those that can get credit won't even be able to pay it back for months! No nice Sunday dinners for them and the rest is starving.'

'We's dropped five hundred pounds ourselves,' Tommo reminds her.

'But we're still eatin' our Sunday roast dinner, ain't we?' Maggie says sharply.

'Everybody's lost. Even Mr Tang Wing Hung,' Tommo sighs, thinking of his opium no doubt.

'Tang Wing Hung? But he's Mr Sparrow's partner, surely he's not been touched?' Maggie exclaims.

'Oh, he's been touched, all right,' Tommo says. 'Ah Wong told me about it, so's I knew who I were dealin' with. Seems Tang Wing Hung's the head of some sort o' Chinese secret society, called a triad, what's thousands of years old. Most of Sydney's celestials come from the same place in North Shanghai and they owes this triad for all sorts o' favours. In Sydney, Tang Wing Hung's the head bloke, the Dragon Master, as they calls it. All the fellows here has got to pay him a percentage of their profits, including what they makes gambling. In return, he's s'posed to look after them, if you knows what I mean.'

Tommo pauses and puts up his finger. 'Now, from what I can make out, Mr Tang Wing Hung went and told all the celestials they should bet on Hawk. If Hawk had lost, like he were supposed to, then Tang Wing Hung would've shrugged his shoulders and said he made a mistake. He'd have probably told 'em he'd lost his money too.

'But now they's won and Mr Sparrow won't pay. So Tang Wing Hung must get their money for them somehow – even pay it himself out of his own pocket – or he'll lose face. It ain't done for the head of a Chinese triad to lose face. Ah Wong says it be at least a hundred years of shame brought down upon his head!'

'Tommo, can we see this Mr Tang, er, whatchimacallit?' Mary asks.

'Tang Wing Hung, Mama,' Tommo corrects. 'He's a big nob so you has to use all three names.'

'Blimey, it ain't 'arf a mouthful!' Mary exclaims. 'Will he talk to us? I mean, him being Mr Sparrow's partner and all?'

'I dunno, Mama,' Tommo shrugs. 'What's you have in mind?'

'Well it seems to me,' says Mary, 'that Chinatown and the Rocks be the same kind o' neighbourhood.'

'Not if the folks in the Rocks can help it,' Maggie interrupts. 'They hates them Mongolians.'

'Yes, I know, I've noticed,' Mary nods. 'But what if they has sudden cause to like them?'

'Mama!' I exclaim. 'However do you hope to bring that about? Folk here believe our Chinese friends caused the cholera that broke out two years ago. They blame them for spreading leprosy and every imaginable type of disease, despite the lack of evidence that it is so. And they reckon the

639

Chinese are taking white men's jobs. They aren't going to suddenly take to the celestials and claim them as good neighbours.'

But Mary is adamant. 'I'd still like to speak with Tang Wing Hung, if it can be done,' she insists.

Through Tommo we are granted an appointment with the rich Chinaman the very next day. I must confess I am curious to meet the man who people say rules the life of every celestial in New South Wales.

We go to Tang Wing Hung's chophouse in Chinatown and are shown into a private room at the back. It is decorated in the Chinese tradition with opulent silks and painted lacquer furnishings showing cherry blossoms, dragons, colourful birds and peacocks. Tang Wing Hung sits on a couch of his own while we share two others of the same size. I take up almost all of one of them and Maggie must squeeze in beside me. I can feel her warm thigh, comforting against my own.

A servant brings jasmine tea which he pours into beautiful little bowls. We all watch as Tommo takes his up, sips at it politely and then puts it down. I then do the same and find that it tastes pleasant enough and refreshes the mouth.

A plate of little dumplings is brought to the table and chopsticks put about. Another plate arrives, this time bearing biscuits which look like small sea shells. The little dumplings smell delicious but we are not accustomed to using chopsticks and dare not try them. So we sit not knowing what to do.

'Them dumplings are most delicate to look at,' Mary breaks the silence at last.

The tall Chinaman smiles. 'This is dim sum – it means "touch the heart". You try, please!'

'Can't use them chopsticks,' Mary replies, forthright as ever.

Tang Wing Hung leans over and picks up a little dumpling between his fingers. He dips it into a small bowl of dark liquid. 'This soy sauce,' he says. He pops the dumpling into his mouth. 'You try, please.'

Mary takes one of the little balls and, as our host has done, dips it into the bowl of sauce. We all wait as she pops it into her mouth. 'Delicious!' she declares.

Tang Wing Hung looks at Tommo, Maggie and me, indicating the dumplings. 'Please,' he insists.

To my surprise, Tommo and Maggie pick up their chopsticks and, taking up one of the dumplings each, dip them into the sauce and bring them up to their mouths with ease. I know I could never use the delicate sticks as they have, and so I reach over and pick up one of the little shell-like biscuits. Just as I am about to put it into my mouth, it smashes to crumbs between my fingers and a piece of paper flutters to the carpet.

I am most embarrassed. Tang Wing Hung rises and stoops to pick up the paper.

'This is fortune cookie,' he explains. 'An American invention, but Chinese recipe. Very popular – mostly we have after food!' He looks at the slip of paper. 'You be very lucky, Mr Hawk. "*True love will come to you!*"' he reads. Then he glances at Maggie and smiles, 'I think this fortune cookie already too late, eh?'

Then Tang Wing Hung takes a cookie himself, putting his thumb and forefinger to each end and bringing it up to his mouth. He pulls his head back the moment he bites at it and the cookie falls apart in his fingers, its crumbs clinging to his mouth. He retains only the slip of paper between his lips.

'"*Today a fortunate opportunity will present itself.*"' He smiles at Mary. 'Perhaps we both get good fortune?' Then he calls the servant to take the plate of cookies away. Bowing, the man leaves but reappears soon enough with a plate of good English wheaten biscuits. 'You like better, I think,' Tang Wing Hung explains to me.

Turning to Mary, he asks seriously, 'Why you come to this humble place to see me? I not worthy, madam.'

'I am grateful that you would see us, sir,' Mary replies. She does not tell him that she knows of his predicament as Dragon Master of the triad. Instead she speaks about the bad blood that exists between the folk of Chinatown and the Rocks, and how both the poor celestials and the poor white folk have lost because they bet on me.

She looks up, appealing to Tang Wing Hung, her green eyes full of sincerity. 'Poor folk may have a different colour, but they have the same needs,' she pronounces. 'They are always trying to find enough money to feed and clothe their children. It is the same with Joe Chinaman as it is with Joe English. Now both have won by betting on my son. They are owed a small fortune and they stands never to be paid.'

'It is sad,' Tang Wing Hung shrugs, 'but what can I do?'

'Yiz can join us t' put the squeeze on Mr Sparrow!' Maggie blurts out.

Tang Wing Hung is somewhat taken aback by her outburst. 'How can I do this? A Chinese man cannot threaten a white man!'

'Ah,' says Mary, 'but white men and Chinese men can come together to fight a common enemy. Your people are owed how much in bets? Two thousand? Three thousand?'

Tang Wing Hung appears to be in deep thought for a moment. 'Hmmm . . . perhaps three thousand pounds,' he replies at last.

'Right! And we reckons the folk in the Rocks and us are owed about the same – if we don't take what we've won and only what we've bet.'

'You bet how much?' Mr Tang Wing Hung asks.

'Five hundred pounds!' Maggie answers, unable to contain herself any longer.

Mary frowns. I can see she is a trifle annoyed at Maggie. I know she feels that some things are best left unsaid but I don't know if my Maggie will ever learn this.

'Five hundred pounds! You very brave!' Tang Wing Hung exclaims, clapping his hands and affecting an expression of astonishment.

'No,' replies Mary. 'I have a very brave son.'

Tang Wing Hung nods and smiles. 'Too brave, perhaps.'

Mary ignores this. 'It were reported in the newspaper that Mr Sparrow took about twenty thousand pounds in bets and now owes one hundred thousand. Well, if he pays us – that be the folks in the Rocks and your folks here in Chinatown – back what we bet, that's only six thousand. We know he can pay us all from what he took all up.'

'There were other expenses,' Tang Wing Hung points out. 'To set up such a fight costs much money.'

Mary smiles. 'Mr Tang Wing Hung, I weren't born yesterday. I know what it takes in bribery and corruption and "miscellaneous expenses". That ain't my concern – though I'm sure he's got plenty.'

Tang Wing Hung brings the tips of the fingers of both hands together and touches the end of his chin. His lips pout slightly as he thinks. 'Madam, why I do this? I can make Mr Sparrow pay only the Chinese people – only three thousand pounds, much easier for him.'

'And a bleedin' sight more expensive for you!' Mary snaps. 'What do you think the white folk are going to feel about the Chinese folk then? They know you're Mr Sparrow's partner, or if they don't they'll soon enough be told by the newspapers. Imagine, if all the celestials get paid and none o' the Europeans. What you think's going to happen then?'

Tang Wing Hung laughs. 'You think clever like a Chinaman, missus.'

'Well, I'm plain-spoken by nature, Mr Tang Wing Hung.' Mary smiles. 'If we work together and the white folk of the Rocks know they got paid because the Chinese helped, everyone'll feel better all 'round.'

Tang Wing Hung rises, bowing very slightly. 'It's good plan – but what do you ask of me?'

'You must tell Mr Sparrow that you have bought all the betting tickets belonging to your own people and also all those belonging to the folks in the Rocks. Now you want full payment. Six thousand pounds in the next forty-eight hours.'

'And if he will not?'

'Then you will kill him!' Mary says.

'I cannot!'

'You don't have to do it, just say it!' Mary explains. She pauses and plays the ace in her hand. 'If the head of a Chinese triad should threaten Mr Sparrow, then he will believe he will die – and it ain't no use reporting nothing!'

Tang Wing Hung draws back in surprise. 'Where you hear about triad? I am businessman, madam.'

'It don't much matter to me what you calls yourself, Mr Tang Wing Hung. You're the boss of the Mongolians, ain't you?'

'I have a little influence maybe. Most Chinese come from same place as me, they know me.' Tang Wing Hung shrugs.

'So where does that leave us, then?' Mary asks bluntly enough.

Tang Wing Hung pauses. 'I will do it,' he says at last.

Mary smiles and so do the rest of us.

The Dragon Master raises a forefinger. 'But I do it because the Chinese owe your sons.' He gives a little nod to me and then to Tommo. 'For Lambing Flat when they help my people. They are brave men and so we will do this thing.'

Out of the corner of my eye I see Tommo squirm in his chair a little at Tang Wing Hung's thanks, but I do not look at him. We had been worried that Tommo might be banned from Tang Wing Hung's opium den on our return from the fight, the Chinaman being in cahoots with Mr Sparrow. Now I understand why this was not so. It seems the story of how Tommo and I rescued Ah Wong and his family is known among the Chinese of Sydney.

Tang Wing Hung pauses, then returns to the subject at hand. 'Not six thousand pounds, ten thousand pounds. We will demand ten!' He claps his hands and then bows to Mary, deeper this time. 'What is left we share.' Tang Wing Hung works a large gold ring from his finger. 'Here, you take.' He hands the heavy gold ring to Mary. 'It is a gift given to me by Mr Sparrow. Give it to him. Tell him it is returned – our partnership is broken forever. Tell him he must pay or he will die.' He grins. 'Mr Sparrow will understand.'

'But will you not tell him yourself?' Maggie asks.

Tang Wing Hung sighs. 'I cannot be seen to go near Mr Sparrow. There may be those who think I am still in business with him. No, no, you must go in my place.'

'I will then.' Mary puts the gold ring into her purse. 'It's been very nice doin' business with you, Mr Tang Wing Hung.' She pauses, thinking. 'But I need one more thing. I need a letter from you to Mr Sparrow to put the wind up him.'

'No, no, you do not understand. No letter. I cannot make threat to him!'

Mary laughs. 'You don't have to. All I wants is a letter written in Chinese. You can make it one of them poems by that bloke Confucius that Hawk's always quoting.

Anything you like, so long as it's written in Chinese letters and sealed with wax and a chop – any chop. Then on the envelope you must put Mr Sparrow's name in Chinese *and* English.'

Tang Wing Hung smiles and bows his head. 'Very clever. Mr Sparrow, he cannot read Chinese, and he will think this message a threat? Very clever! You give him ring and letter!' He claps his hands and the servant appears. He speaks to him in rapid Chinese and the man nods and is gone.

'You will have such a letter in half an hour. And I will make sure no Chinaman tell him what it means. You wait here, please. Drink tea? I must go now, thank you very much.'

Mary has managed Tang Wing Hung wonderfully. She has shown him how to avoid losing face in front of his own people and convinced him to serve our purpose as well. And it will not cost him a penny other than the gold ring. I am most proud of our mama.

'How do we know the bludger will come good, give us our share of the brass if Mr Sparrow pays?' Maggie asks as we make our way back to the Hero, where Mary has promised to buy us supper.

'Face,' Tommo says. 'He'll lose face if he don't.'

Mary sniffs. 'I don't know about face, but I know about business and so does our Mr Tang Wing Hung. We've just got Mr Dragon Master off the hook. We've made him look like the hero of Sydney's Chinese and he'll make a tidy profit to boot.'

Mary has clearly taken charge as the general of our campaign and means to see that the folks in the Rocks and Chinatown get their bets returned in full. Over the next two days, she sends Maggie around to all the pubs to ask the publicans to chalk up the amounts their customers show them on their old betting tickets. Soon we know that we'll have more than sufficient to cover the money bet.

Mary decides that the best way to get to Mr Sparrow is to see him herself. 'It's our best bet,' she announces. 'A woman's hard to deny and thought to be harmless. If I says I've been sent from Mr Tang Wing Hung and have proof,' she holds up the gold ring, 'Sparrer can't refuse me.'

'May I come too, Mama?' Maggie begs.

Mary smiles and nods. She's pleased when Maggie calls her mama. 'I want to see Mr Sparrow's ratty little phiz when he sees it's us what's got him well and truly nailed!'

'When will you go?' Tommo asks. 'Now?'

'No, first we must scare him somewhat, I think!' Mary turns to Maggie. 'Do you think you can get folks here to march on the pub and shout a bit? Make our Mr Sparrow fear for his miserable carcass? It'd be a way of softenin' him up.'

'Daresay I can,' Maggie says. 'The pleasure would be all mine!' She giggles with anticipation.

But both she and Mary draw the line when I say I'll go with her. Mary shakes her head, 'No, son, you and Tommo must stay well clear! If this business should end badly, the magistrate mustn't see it as an act of vengeance, with us taking the law into our own hands. Maggie be the ideal person to spread the word and she's happy to do it.'

'Happy ain't the word!' Maggie exclaims. 'I'd count it a great privilege to give them two mongrels a fright!'

Our mama has thought of every detail. 'Pick four strong leaders, men what won't lose their heads and start a riot,' she instructs Maggie. 'No stones or clubs, mind you – just drums, bull-horns and bugles. They're to make a lot of noise. Remember, this be a protest, an orderly but very noisy protest. The *Sydney Morning Herald* must describe it as an outcry by common folk what's been cheated out of what's rightly due them by a pair o' scoundrels.'

Mary now turns to me. 'See that the police are informed of the march so they're on hand when the mob arrives at The World Turned Upside Down. We don't want any in the crowd to get no fancy ideas of storming young Sparrer Fart's lodgings.'

Maggie is delighted with the task she's been given. That very night, she visits the Hero of Waterloo, the Rose and Crown and half a dozen other public houses. By the time she returns home, the march against Mr Sparrow is all set.

'Folk are only too happy to make their feelings known,' she tells me.

The protest is to take place the following afternoon when the men come home from work.

'We'll put some real fear into them upstairs. Make the little shyster and his fat mate think the mob's come to get 'em!' Mary laughs when she hears Maggie's news. I can't help feeling she is enjoying the whole campaign.

By the following afternoon the news has spread throughout the Rocks and three or four hundred men march on The World Turned Upside Down. Here they are met by three constables who tell them that Mr Sparrow and Fat Fred are not in residence in the rooms upstairs. Nevertheless the crowd makes a great deal of noise, banging on drums and blasting on bugles. Towards the end a rock is thrown which breaks one of the upstairs windows. But the protest is, in fact, quite orderly. Maggie has picked her leaders well – there's noise and threats enough hurled at the windows to frighten Mr Sparrow and Fat Fred, who we know are in residence no matter what the policemen say.

Mary and Maggie have Tang Wing Hung's ring and sealed letter with its beautiful Chinese characters and F. Artie Sparrow Esq. written on the envelope. As the protesters slowly drift away, they prepare to confront the villains.

Tommo and I wait downstairs in the saloon bar of the pub which has just this minute opened its doors once again. Tommo insists on wearing his axe in a shoulder holster under his jacket. These days the barmaid, Doreen, welcomes him like he's an honoured guest, bringing him a Cape brandy without his even asking. I order a glass of best ale and she does a sort of curtsy. 'Honoured ter serve ya, Mr Black Hawk,' she says, all smiles. Mr Sparrow has clearly lost the sympathy of the staff here as well.

At first the three Sydney lads guarding Mr Sparrow's staircase won't allow Maggie and Mary into the corridor that leads upstairs. Maggie kicks up a bit of a fuss and one of them goes leaping up the stairs. Soon he returns with a hulking lad in tow. This one has a runny nose and an ugly, festering scar down the length of his cheek. The newcomer sniffs and folds his arms across his chest.

'What's yiz want?' he says to Mary, as Tommo and I wait at the ready in the saloon.

'How'd you get yours?' Mary asks.

'Me what?'

Mary runs her finger down the red line on her own face. 'Your scar. Were you cut by a villain too, acid thrown in after?'

The boy looks impressed. 'Nah, just a fight. Weren't nothin' much.' He begins to pick absently at the weeping scab.

'Don't pick at it, lad. Give it a chance to heal itself, won't show so bad then,' Mary advises gently.

'Don't much care if it do, missus,' the lad grunts.

'Hey, I knows ya!' Maggie exclaims, pointing at him. 'Johnny Terrible! Yiz got a brother and sister, both little uns, twins ain't they?'

Johnny Terrible nods.

'They comes to our roast dinner on Sunday. One of 'em, the little girl – Alice ain't it? – once gimme sixpence for her dinner though we never asked. She said ya told her t' give it t' me!'

Johnny Terrible gives a little half-smile, and Maggie can tell he's pleased to be recognised. 'Want ter see Mr Sparrer, does yer?' he now asks.

'The very same,' Maggie grins.

'What fer?'

'Business that's to his benefit. Tang Wing Hung's sent us,' Mary says.

Johnny Terrible gives a deep sniff and wipes his hand under his nose. 'Tang Wing Hung? What proof's ya got yiz from him?'

Mary shows him the ring and holds up the letter with the Chinese characters. The boy takes the ring and looks at it.

'See what it says inside,' Maggie urges, then recites from memory, '"To Tang Wing Hung in sincere friendship, F. Artie Sparrow".'

'He won't see yiz anyway. He's in the wardrobe,' Johnny Terrible says, handing Mary back the ring.

'In the wardrobe? What's you mean?' Maggie asks.

'It be the riots, he's gorn panicky.'

'Does he often go into the wardrobe?' Mary enquires.

'He's took it up since the fight. Spent four days in there when he got back from Yass!'

'What about Fat Fred?' Maggie asks.

'He's drunk, shickered. Drinks a gallon of Portugee port 'fore noon each day, cryin' all the while that it weren't his fault, and that he only done what he were told. He'll be no good ter ya, Miss Pye.'

'Call me Maggie, darlin',' Maggie smiles.

'Well then, we'll just have to see Mr Sparrow in his wardrobe,' says Mary.

'Easier said than done, missus.' Johnny Terrible snorts

deeply and makes a loud noise sucking the phlegm down his throat. 'He's got the lock put wrong way round so he's got the key on the inside. Locks hisself in.'

'Can he hear ya when ya talks?' Maggie asks.

'Depends if he wants ter. Don't rate yer chances. Sometimes he hears but he don't talk to no one 'cept me. Reckon I'm the only one what can figure out what he's sayin'. But yiz can try.' Johnny Terrible brings two fingers to his lips and gives a sharp whistle. Three scruffy heads pop around the top of the banister. 'Take the ladies to see Mr Sparrow,' he orders.

'Ta, muchly,' Maggie says, giving Johnny Terrible a kiss on his dirty face. The three Sydney lads on guard laugh. 'Shut yer gobs!' Johnny Terrible snarls and they are immediately quiet.

'Extra 'elping comin' to ya little brother and sister on Sunday, Johnny,' Maggie promises. 'Come down yerself and I'll put some iodine on yer cut, do ya the world.'

They are halfway up the stairs when Johnny Terrible shouts, 'Eh, Maggie, is it true yiz gunna marry the nigger?'

Maggie turns and looks down at him. 'What if I am? What's it to you, Johnny Terrible?'

'Nuffink,' he sniffs. 'I think yiz done good. He be a great champion, the strongest man in the world.'

'You don't want t' believe all ya hears,' Maggie retorts. 'I can beat him up anytime I likes!'

What follows we hear from Maggie and Mary once we're back at the Hero of Waterloo. The two young lads make a great fuss of unlocking the stout door that leads to Mr Sparrow's lodgings, then ushers them into a parlour fitted with a red and blue carpet of Chinese design that covers most of the floor.

The room has two tall windows facing onto the street – one of them with a broken pane. The windows are draped with maroon velvet curtains, somewhat dusty, with tassels tied at the centre. It's clear that the drapes haven't been drawn in a long time. Indeed the windows seem the only source of light in the room as there are no gas lights and only two empty lantern brackets on the wall. Against the wall opposite the windows is a large, double-winged cedar wardrobe. But what first catches Maggie and Mary's eye is a long, horsehair leather settee, badly scuffed and worn in several places, that sits in the centre of the carpet.

Laid out upon its leather upholstery, so that in some places its worn springs nearly touch the ground from the weight of him, lies Fat Fred. He is heaving and snorting, his great belly making rumbling noises like a small volcano preparing to blast its contents out into the firmament. Six boys aged between ten and twelve all sit cross-legged on the carpet before him, playing cribbage. They jump up when the two women enter.

Mary and Maggie can't tear their eyes away from the supine form of Fat Fred. Though it seems hardly possible, the man has grown even fatter in the weeks since the fight. Little bubbles of snot come out of his nostrils. He wears only a pair of black Chinese silk trousers which are very dirty, and his huge, hairy stomach dominates the room.

Fat Fred's stomach has, as they tell it, become a creature in its own right. It resembles nothing so much as a live container in which secret and dangerous chemical concoctions are being mixed with other equally dangerous substances – causing an amazing series of oleaginous gurgles, sighs, splats and small muffled explosions.

Every few minutes the pressure within this amazing container builds up, resulting in an alarming tautness. Then the entire stomach holds dead still, but only for a moment as though it has reached a point where it might at any second split wide apart. At this point, it lets go a truly resounding fart so that the great belly wobbles and reverberates like jelly.

Each eruption of gas makes the lads snigger behind cupped hands. They seem to know the precise moment it will come. Eventually Maggie too takes to giggling. Soon they are all having a merry laugh, and even Mary joins in, though her finger and thumb remain firmly pegged to her nose.

With this intestinal factory commanding all their attention, it is some time before Mary and Maggie become aware of a series of soft and urgent whimperings emanating from the wardrobe. Later they realise it is Mr Sparrow asking, in his peculiar new way, who has come into the room.

Just then, as Fat Fred lets go another of his great and glorious farts, Johnny Terrible walks in.

'Play him, Johnny, garn, show the ladies!' one of the lads shouts. 'He's ready tuned, he's bin doing lots o' them big ones.'

'Yeah, garn, Johnny!' the others chorus. Whereupon a boy of about eleven rushes to pull up a Windsor chair, which he places in front of Fat Fred, as if before a pianoforte.

Johnny Terrible's face doesn't move a muscle. He walks over and sits down, laying his hands upon the enormous stomach as though upon a truly great instrument. He appears to be lost in thought as though considering a repertoire in his head. And then, to the astonishment of Maggie and Mary, he draws a great breath and, with a flourish, commences to push his fingers down into Fat Fred's belly.

Sometimes he plays hard, sometimes soft, his fingers darting to various parts of the great expanse. Each time he prods or pats the monstrous organ, Fat Fred lets out a fart of a different timbre, tone and length of duration – a sort of musical note. Some are short and sharp, others prolonged. Some are deep-toned, others high and squeaky. Johnny Terrible uses his fists for some notes, his thumbs for others, and his prodding fingers go deep into the hairy flesh for yet more flatulent harmonies. His hands flash and plunge in a truly virtuoso performance – his head bouncing as he performs.

'Can you hear it?' one of the boys shouts over the din. 'Can you hear it, missus? "Gawd Save the Queen", he's playing, "Gawd Save the bleedin' Queen"!' Indeed, after some concentration, it becomes apparent that this is precisely what Johnny Terrible is playing on Fat Fred's abdomen. It is a strange and discordant key, but the notes are accurate enough. A most positive and sustained trombone effect is created to honour the final strains of the anthem to Queen Victoria.

At the end Johnny Terrible rises from his chair to the claps and cheers of his companions. He does not smile as he bows to Mary and Maggie. It is as if he regards himself a true concert artist, and is merely receiving the accolades due him from an appreciative audience.

Then he turns to the boys in the room. 'Orright then, bugger off the lot of yiz! The miss and the missus here got business with Mr Sparrow!'

The six lads in the room troop out obediently. Johnny Terrible moves the chair from beside Fat Fred and carries it to one side of the wardrobe door. Then he fetches a second and places it to the other side of the door, before asking Mary and Maggie to be seated.

'I'll act as yer translator, Maggie,' he says.

'What's wrong? Can't he talk for himself?' Mary asks bluntly.

'He can, but he won't. I'll have to tell yiz what he's sayin'. It's his code what only I understands.' He nods his head for Mary or Maggie to begin. Mary nods to Maggie.

'Hullo, Mr Sparrow, it's Maggie Pye here, come to visit yiz! How's ya going, then?' Maggie waits for a response from inside the wardrobe. There is complete silence for a minute, then a few high-pitched whimpers are heard.

'He wants ter know what yer wants?' Johnny Terrible interprets.

Mary takes over now. 'Now listen 'ere, Sparrer Fart, it's Mary Abacus. You might remember me from London! I come with a letter of demand from Tang Wing Hung for ten thousand pounds.' Mary is shouting to make sure Mr Sparrow can hear every word through the oak panelling. But no sound, not even a whimper, is heard.

'It be Tang Wing Hung what's bought up all the celestials' betting tickets from the fight and some from other folks as well,' Maggie explains. But still there is no reply from inside the wardrobe.

Maggie looks at Johnny Terrible as if to ask if she should speak again. He nods and she says, 'Mr Sparrow, listen t' me! Yiz got two days, today, tomorrer and the next mornin' only – that be Friday mornin'! Forty-eight hours from now yiz got to come up with the readies, ten thousand quid! If ya don't, well Tang Wing Hung ain't gunna like it. He don't want to be no business partners with you no more. He says to tell yiz! You know what that means don'tcha?'

There is silence again and then a few muffled sounds which are followed by several knocks to the interior panelling. 'He says how does he know yiz from Mr Tang Wing Hung?' Johnny pronounces.

'I have proof. Mr Tang Wing Hung's ring that you gave him and a letter wrote in Chinese!' Mary takes a deep breath, adding, 'It be a death threat from the triad.'

There is the sound of a key turning and the door of the wardrobe opens a crack. Mr Sparrow's little hand with the diamond ring on its pinky comes out, the fingers twitching like spider's legs.

'Give him the letter an' the ring,' Johnny Terrible instructs.

Mary hands Mr Sparrow the letter first and it's snapped up and taken inside the wardrobe. A moment later the hand reappears in a cupped position and she drops the ring into it. Then there's the sound of the lock turning again.

'How can he see in there?' Maggie asks.

'He's got a bull lamp.'

Just then, the whimpering begins again. It's fast and high, and makes no sense to the two women. Finally, there are several knocks on the panelling.

'He wants seven days ter pay,' says Johnny.

'Forty-eight hours!' Mary shouts. 'That's all and not a minute more! It's what Mr Tang Wing Hung says – after forty-eight hours, your life won't be safe a moment longer.' She turns to Johnny Terrible. 'You be me witness, Johnny Terrible, that I delivered Tang Wing Hung's letter to Mr F. Artie Sparrow Esquire. I don't want his death to come as a surprise!' She takes out her purse and hands Johnny Terrible half a sovereign. He takes it, bites it to ascertain it's gold, then flips it in the air, grabs it and puts it into his pocket. He nods silently to Mary's request.

Another of Fat Fred's enormous farts resounds from the centre of the room, as if signalling that the interview with Mr Sparrow is over. Johnny leads them to the door. 'Yiz'll have ter go now,' he says. 'The Chinaman's comin' soon.'

'What Chinaman?' Maggie asks in alarm.

'The old bloke, Ho Kwong Choi. He comes ter give Mr Sparrer his pipe.'

'Opium?' Mary asks, surprised.

Johnny Terrible shrugs, his face blank as ever. 'Yiz got ter go now,' he repeats.

Mary walks quickly back across the room and leans close to the wardrobe door. 'Oh, and Tang Wing Hung says after forty-eight hours no more opium, ya hear? Your supply'll be cut off unless o' course you pays up! Don't make much difference I suppose – except, instead of dying happy, you'll die miserable with the shakes and pains!'

Mary and Maggie follow Johnny Terrible down the stairs to where the three boys are still standing guard. 'You was most harmonious on the stomach piano!' Maggie says giggling. 'Come Sunday to Semicircular Quay and I'll fix yer cheek. That wound could turn nasty on ya. Iodine's what's called for. Burns like buggery, but it'll fix yer cheek, 'andsome!'

Tommo and I roll with laughter when Mary and Maggie retell their story of the interview with Mr Sparrow. All of us imagine him crouching in the dark, hugging his bony knees. Maggie recounts the most of it and she tells it well. Even Mary is taken with a fit of laughter but then she stops.

'Maggie, that Johnny Terrible, he were sociable enough and done what we asked and all, but did ya see his eyes?' she asks abruptly.

'Eyes? Can't say I noticed. Brown, ain't they?'

'Yes, and dead. No light in them, no expression.' Mary shivers suddenly. 'I seen eyes like that before, on a man in the East End o' London named Bob Marley!' She runs her crooked finger down the scar on the side of her cheek. 'It were him what cut me and marked me with the acid. One moment funny and most clever and sociable, the next gone cruel and crazy. But his eyes were always the same, just like that Johnny Terrible today – dead eyes!'

I shudder, for Ikey had once told Tommo and me about Bob Marley, who would only work for gold sovereigns counted into his hand before a job. 'Always in advance and then always done what was asked of him, no matter what.'

Ikey had admired Bob Marley greatly. 'A true professional, my dears, only once half-nabbed by the constabulary and then got off with a marvellous alibi he'd worked out beforehand! Twenty-five years a thief and no form whatsoever, remarkable!'

But even as youngsters, we could tell that Bob Marley was also the only man who scared Ikey Solomon. 'When you can't reach a clever man with your wit or soften him with your tongue, then know him to be most dangerous!' I recall him saying.

Maggie, however, laughs at Mary's fears. 'Johnny Terrible? Nah! He's just a bad lad brought up rough. Thousands like him, proper hooligan. Ain't no real harm in him – he'll steal, fight, be cheeky, rob old ladies. I grown up with his sort. They only murders if they 'as to!'

Maggie now tells Tommo and me how Johnny Terrible played 'God Save the Queen' on Fat Fred's stomach. We are soon roaring with laughter again as Maggie imitates with her lips the noises that came from Fat Fred.

Suddenly I think that we've never been so happy since we were brats. Maggie's made us a family again. Mary's come alive – it's something more than just being happy to be with her boys. She's grown most fond of my Maggie, and it's as if she's found, in our upcoming nuptials, new hope and meaning in the future.

I smile at this, then return to the conversation around me, hearing with surprise of Mr Sparrow's addiction to opium. But Tommo just says quietly, 'That's how the bastard knows it can enslave others to his will.'

Mary reaches over and takes his hand in hers, patting it. 'You'll be all right, my boy,' she says, 'you'll be all right.'

Chapter Twenty-six

TOMMO

The Rocks
September 1861

I'm back in New Zealand, walking in the forest with Makareta, when a great noise brings me awake. At first I thinks it's part o' me dream, and a pakeha settler's fired his musket at us again, but then I realise I'm back in Sydney, me beloved Makareta's dead and it's someone at the door. The sun is streamin' in and it's too early in the day for me to be up, especially after me celebrations of the night before. Yesterday, Mary and Maggie put the squeeze on Mr Sparrow, what I now knows needs the Devil's Smoke as much as yours truly. I had a good night with the flats after that, and an extra bottle of the Cape besides, and I ain't too pleased about being waked up early.

I opens the door and sees Mary there. She is none too happy neither. Seems she were meant to meet Maggie this afternoon, but Maggie never showed. Normally, them two's together from early morning, but today, Maggie had some other business to see to. She and Mary were to meet at noon – when they were gunna look for a canteen of sterling silver, Mary's wedding present to Maggie and Hawk. Only Maggie don't get to the Hero on time. At first, Mary ain't too concerned. She's scolded Maggie plenty o' times about being late, but it's never done no good – Maggie simply don't have no sense of time.

But by two o'clock Mary's a little worried, so she walks down through the Argyle Cut to Maggie's rooms above the chophouse. There's no answer to her knocks on Maggie's door and so she goes downstairs to the Cut Below. Flo tells her that Maggie were in for a cup of tea and a fresh bread roll at about nine this morning, as is her habit now that she's up and about in the daytime.

'How were she?' Mary asks.

'She's always the same. Whether she be up all night or just woke up, she's ever cheerful.' Flo smiles. 'This mornin' she said she was gunna let me have a borrow of her wedding dress when I gets married.'

'And then she left?'

'Yes – no, hang on. Me papa come through from the kitchen and brung her a letter what he said were left earlier by a lad. I remembers 'cause the brat wouldn't say nothing 'bout who it were from – just gave him the letter and scarpered.'

'A letter? What sort o' letter?' Mary asks.

'Dunno. It were in an envelope, sealed with red wax on the back. I remember me dad handin' it to her with the blob of red wax uppermost. Then when Maggie turns it I sees the writing on the front's a bit scratchy and untidy-like, not nice like Hawk's.'

'Did she read it?'

'Nah, Maggie don't read too well. She can make out what's on the page but it ain't easy. She has ter take her time, like. So she laughs and says she'll read it later. Then she kissed me like she always does. "Be a good girl then, Flo, but if yiz can't, for 'eavens sake be careful!" She always says the same when she's leaving, ever since I were a little brat.' Now Flo looks anxious. 'Is somethin' wrong, Mrs Abacus?'

'No, girlie, she's late to meet me, that's all. So I thought I'd come down and fetch her,' Mary tells her.

'She's always late,' Flo points out hopefully.

'Blimey, don't I know and all,' mutters Mary and goes to take her leave. Then she stops. 'Did she wear a bonnet, like she were going out?'

'She had the magpie nested in her hair what she often wears instead of a bonnet,' Flo answers.

Mary goes back to the Hero and waits another hour. By now it's three o'clock and even Maggie ain't ever this late. So Mary has come down to where Hawk and I has our lodgings and woken me up. I don't waste any time and get dressed in a minute.

'Shall we fetch Hawk?' Mary asks as we leaves the house.

'Nah, we'll check the pubs first. Maggie said she were gunna thank the boys what led the march on the pub. Hawk give her money to buy them all a drink.'

'Maggie don't drink during the day, well, not with me she don't,' Mary says doubtfully. 'I has the habit of trying a different brand of ale or beer in Sydney every day 'case I comes across a blend I likes. She's never once joined me – always asks for sarsaparilla and a slice of lemon.'

'Maggie be unpredictable, Mama,' I says to comfort her. 'Never know for certain what she'll do next. We'll go ask around first before we tells Hawk. She'll turn up, you'll see. She probably took a gin or two too much and fell asleep.'

But Mary ain't convinced. 'She was that excited about the canteen o' silver, she'd not have got drunk!' she insists. Finally she agrees we should check the various pubs around the Rocks. Two hours and eighteen pubs later, we finds out that none o' the publicans – what all know Maggie well – have seen her today. It's nearly six o'clock by the time we gets to the Rose and Crown where the owner, Daniel 'Pinchgut' Lewis, tells us that Maggie were meant to have a drink with the lads here at eleven o'clock but never showed.

'Can't think what's happened,' he frowns. 'Maggie's always late, but she turns up in the end.' He chuckles. 'Matter o' fact it be good for business, Maggie always being late. Folk'll wait for her, guessing at her excuses, what be that marvellous inventive that it's worth the waiting no matter how late she be. And o' course they keeps buying drinks in the meanwhile!'

It's now well past six o'clock. Weary of soul and terrible worried, we hurries back to the Hero of Waterloo where we'll meet Hawk. We still holds out hope of finding Maggie there but it ain't much of a hope.

We hasn't yet reached the Hero when suddenly I stops. Mary can see that I be shivering with me arms clasped about me chest, rubbing and scratching the tops, near the shoulders, like I'm cold and itchy.

'Mama,' I says, 'I'll be just the half hour then I'll be back. Tell Hawk not to do nothing 'til I returns.' I looks pleadingly at Mary. 'Half an hour won't make no difference if Maggie ain't there.'

Mary nods. She's never seen me before when the craving for the poppy has took me, but she knows at once what it is. 'We'll wait for you, Tommo. Mind you come back quick now.' She's fighting to keep back her tears.

'I loves you, Mama,' I says, reaching for her hands.

'I love you too, Tommo, with all me heart,' she says, squeezing mine.

The sun is setting and there be a golden blaze across the harbour. The water has turned a deep red. As I starts to walk away, Mary calls after me and I stops and turns. 'What, Mama?'

'Tommo, you were the sweetest little boy,' Mary says, then smiles. 'You still is.'

Chinatown be only a few minutes walk from where I left Mary. I feel such a weak bastard, having to get me fix of Devil's Smoke. But in the past few weeks the pain in me head has been near constant. By nightfall I can't bear it no longer and am just waitin' for Ho Kwong Choi's pipe of blissful relief.

Hawk has often found me moaning with me head in me hands. He knows me wound's getting worse, for he hears me cry out in me sleep as I thrash about having nightmares of the most frightening kind. He's always asking about me head and when I tells him not to worry, gets angry.

'Tommo, you lie, *I* can feel it,' he says, touching his hands to the exact spot where the pain be.

But I says nothing. He is so happy with Maggie and if he knows how bad it is for me I fear it would spoil his happiness. I meself am happy for them. I have grown terrible fond o' Maggie meself and thinks what pretty children they shall have.

But my own pain has grown such that I has even lost at cards once or twice. This has mostly been in the early hours when me afternoon pipe has worn off and I am quite beside meself with the ache in me noggin. These days I've took to visiting Tang Wing Hung's opium den in the mornings before I returns home, as well as in the evenings. Without the relief of the poppy I'd go quite mad.

Sometimes a dizziness takes hold of me and I cannot see and must sit down in a hurry. I tell all this to Ho Kwong Choi, who nods and clucks his tongue as he prepares the paste for me pipe. It be stupid, I know, telling me troubles to a Chinaman what can hardly speak English, but he has looked into my dreams and heard me cry out. Sometimes, when I wake after a pipe, I find he has put a cool cloth to me head. He has seen poor bastards like me before and much worse, I reckon. He's a mate, in a way, but still I can't read the diamond pricks of light in them eyes what's cut like slivers in his paper-creased face.

Now, as I gets to the opium den, Ho Kwong Choi comes forward, his hands clasped together and his head bowed in greeting. I bow to him too.

'Ho Kwong Choi, you got to be quick tonight, then I come back later, maybe eleven o'clock, you savvy?'

He nods his head and shows me to a couch before shuffling away. He seems most solemn tonight. Me head is nearly took off by the pain as he prepares the pearl at the end of the needle, roasting it in the flame, before handing me the opium pipe. After the fourth or fifth puff, I starts to feel a bit better. By the time the pain is took away, not much more than fifteen minutes has passed. Soon I'm feeling bright enough, though slightly light of head.

Ho Kwong Choi brings me jasmine tea after my pipe and stands there waiting and watching as I sips it as fast as I can. Suddenly he says, 'Tommo, you go Mr Sparrow.'

'What?' I asks.

'Quick, quick!' He takes the bowl of tea from my hands. 'Now!' He is shaking slightly. 'Hurry up!'

'What is it, Ho Kwong Choi?' I grip him by the shoulders, even though he could kill me in an instant if he wished.

'Missy Maggie! She with Mr Sparrow!' He trembles under me hands. 'You go now, hurry, hurry!'

Still light-headed, I run from the opium den out into the back lane and then all the way to our lodgings, where I tear me blanket roll apart. I rip off the oil cloth what keeps my axe from rusting. Frantic, I take off the leather sheath that protects the head. I test the blade on my thumb and a tiny drop o' blood appears. It is razor sharp. I put the axe back in its holster what fits under me jacket and then I starts to run towards Bridge Street.

By the time I get to The World Turned Upside Down I'm

panting and has to catch me breath for a few minutes on the pavement opposite the pub. A watchman what's sitting there with a lantern beside him sees me and shouts, 'Move on, mate, I don't want no trouble.'

I duck across the street towards the pub, only I does it a little higher up so the watchman can't see me. I dodge between two hackneys and a toff what's drunk and driving his own sulky, lashing at the poor nag. The gaslight here is dim, so I'm in the shadows as I cross. I stay in the darkness as I make my way towards the hotel – waiting for the right moment, before nipping into the dark alley what runs alongside it. There's a door here what leads straight up to Mr Sparrow's lodging. I've used it often enough in the past, when I come to see him. This time though I'm gunna have to break it down with my axe, I thinks.

I put my hand to the door to find where the weakest spot in the panelling might be, and to me surprise it swings open. I push it a little further and peers into the dark passage. I can hear the faint sound of the drinkers in the public bar through the wall beside the staircase at the end. There's no light in the passageway and I can't see a thing. Odd there's none of Mr Sparrow's lads about neither. Is it a trap, I wonder? If some of his more vicious lads be hiding in the dark, I'd have no chance to defend meself if an arm with a knife were to suddenly appear.

I take out my axe as quietly as I can, and move forward slowly towards the dark stairway. My heart is boomin' like a drum and I'm terrified I'll be jumped any moment.

One hand on the banister, the other holding my fighting axe at the ready, I feel my way carefully upwards. The steps are wooden boards and creak at every step I take. I be certain Mr Sparrow's boys are hidden in the blackness of the landing, watching for me, waiting to cut me down.

At last I get to the top of the stairs and I wait a full

minute to steady meself before slowly going along the passage. My heart's thumping in my throat as if to jump clean out of me mouth. I has my back pressed to the wall and I hold my axe with both hands in front o' me face.

My shoulder touches the frame of the first door but I know it ain't the one I need and I pass across it. I reach the second door frame, what I knows to be the parlour door of Mr Sparrow's rooms. I decide it's the third door I want, and so I pass across the second also, quietly testing the door handle, what's locked.

When I reach the third door, I try the handle and it turns easily in my hand. Taking a deep breath, I push it open. It creaks like the timbers on a ship at sea and I near faints with fright. I wait for the count o' ten, but there's still no noise from within. I go through and am in Mr Sparrow's parlour.

I take two steps further and stand on the Chinee silk carpet looking about me. The curtains be open and one window pane is broken. There's a faint light coming in from the gaslight 'cross the road and, compared to the dark passage, the parlour seems quite light. A dreadful smell of shit hangs in the air.

Then I see the settee, a dark shape in the centre of the room. On it lies a huge form, what from its size looks like Fat Fred though it is too dim to be sure. I stand still, listening – but the noise from the street below is too loud for me to hear the rise and fall o' someone's breath.

I move closer to the couch. Swallowing, I put out a hand and touch naked flesh, hairy and cold. It is a huge body lying on its stomach, and I am touching its back. It's a warm evening yet the flesh is stone cold and dead still. It can be no other than Fat Fred – and he's carked it.

I'm sure I'm alone in the room, but I need light to find out what's happened. I look about, then run me hand across the walls to see if I can find a light fixture. On the far wall, what be in almost complete darkness, I touch a wardrobe. It be the one Mary and Maggie talked to Mr Sparrow through, I'm sure. Finally I comes upon two lamp brackets but with no lantern hanging from them.

Then I remember the night watchman across the street. I hurries downstairs again and, crossing to where he's sitting, and offer him half a sov for his hurricane lantern. It's five times what it's worth and he all but falls over himself handing it to me. This time, I climb the stairs as quick as I can. I go back into the parlour and turn the lamp wick up.

Fat Fred's monstrous carcass is lying on the couch with his great arse up in the air. He is dead and no mistake. The very moment folks die they shits themselves and I sees shit all over the back of Fat Fred's huge thighs, which is where the terrible stench comes from. His enormous stomach is sunk into the lounge so that the bottom of the springs touch the carpet beneath.

Then I see them. Lying on the carpet beside the couch are three black-and-white magpie feathers. Just three feathers. A grief takes hold o' me heart such as I've never felt before, not even at me darlin' Makareta's death.

The mongrels have come, and this time I heard no warning. I feel a most terrible pain as though I've been stabbed. I starts to moan like an animal, moving frantically 'round the room, searching for Maggie Pye. That Hawk's darling Maggie should come to grief at the hands of these bastards be too cruel a fate for anyone to bear. Then I see the wardrobe and suddenly I know what I must find inside it.

I rush towards it and see there are no knobs or handles on the door. It's been locked from the outside.

'Ya bastard, ya fucking mongrel bastard!' I scream and kick the door. Taking up my axe, I smash a large hole in the panelling around the lock. I cut the frame above and below the lock so that the door is free and open it. I can see the faint outlines of a body on the wardrobe floor and now I pick up the lamp and shine it into the dark interior.

Inside, trussed and gagged so that it be impossible for him to cry out or move an inch, is Johnny Terrible, one eye looking directly up at me. Such is my grief and fury that I immediately swings my axe to take his throat, before it hits me that he ain't the villain. I turn me wrist and the blade grazes his scalp, sticking into the wood at the back of his head.

With a grunt, I jerk the blade out. I've already cut free the centre frame of the wardrobe and now I fling open the second door. Johnny Terrible lies huddled at me feet. His legs have been bent backwards so that his boot heels are tucked into his bum and a rope has been lashed around the tops of his thighs and ankles. His hands are also tied behind his back and more rope coiled about his chest and arms. Even his head has been tied so it cannot move. His gag has been pulled so tight that the cloth fills his gob and cuts his mouth.

Johnny's face has been badly smashed. His nose is broken and caked with blood what has made a dark stain on the front of his blouse. One eye is completely closed and the scar to his cheek is tattered and raw, newly opened and filled with pus and blood.

I pull him out of the wardrobe by the ropes around his wrists and see that his hands have gone a deep blue from the tightness of the cord about them. He falls face down upon the carpet.

I cut the various ropes away with my axe blade. But though Johnny's free, he can't move. Bending down, I pulls his legs to straighten 'em and he screams at the pain. I does the same with his arms and then begin to rub his wrists until his fingers start to twitch. I have left his ankles loosely tied so he cannot jump up but must remain where I have dragged him, and I sit him up with his back to the wall.

Apart from his groans and screams as I pull his legs straight, Johnny ain't said a word. But now he begins to sob, though almost silently, the tears running down his face and splashing onto his blouse what's covered in blood.

I hold the three feathers right up to his eyes.

'Where's Maggie?' I says, with cold anger in me voice.

He tries to speak but his throat must be too parched. I take the lantern and goes into Mr Sparrow's bedroom, the same where he took me the first day we met. I grab the jug from the washstand what's half full and, going back, pours the water over Johnny Terrible's head and into his mouth, so that he nearly chokes.

'Where's Maggie?' I says again.

Johnny still can't speak but raises his hand slowly and points to Fat Fred.

'No! Damn ya! *Maggie! Where's Maggie Pye?*'

He points again to the dead man and a rasping noise come out of his throat. 'Unn . . .'

I clocks him hard on the cheek and me hand comes away messed with pus and blood. 'Where?' I yells.

'Unn . . . unnerneath!'

'Underneath?'

Johnny Terrible nods his head, but it ain't possible for anyone to fit underneath that couch.

Suddenly I go cold. I walk over to Fat Fred and shine the lantern light over his huge form. And then I see it. The tips of the fingers of a small female hand sticking out from under his shoulder.

Maggie lies underneath this mountain o' dead human flesh.

I scream and grab the dead man's arms. I pull and pull at him, but Fat Fred's body will not budge. 'Help me!' I scream to Johnny Terrible. He tries to get up but can't. 'Help me, ya bastard, help me!' I keep pulling at Fat Fred's arm, and I begin to blub. If Hawk were here he'd lift him off in an instant and Maggie'd be free!

'It's no good, Tommo!' Johnny Terrible's voice rasps. 'She's dead!' I am frozen in me grief, listening to him. 'Mr Sparrow done it . . . with the lads . . . before they scarpered.'

'What happened?' I whisper.

'They thought it be a great lark . . . yer know,' Johnny swallows, 'Fat Fred and Maggie.' He swallows again and his voice grows firmer. 'Mr Sparrow sent a note to Maggie tellin' her to come an' get the money what he owed ter Mr Tang Wing Hung. But he never meant fer her to 'ave it. Instead he told the lads to grab her soon as she got 'ere. Then they gags her and ties her to the couch with her legs spread ready. Fat Fred, what's only half drunk, climbs on top and fucks her.'

Johnny's hoarse voice chokes. 'Suddenly Fred raises his head . . . and . . . he gives a groan and grabs his chest. All the lads are clapping, thinking Fat Fred's had his pleasure. But he 'asn't, it's his fuckin' heart!' He takes a breath and forces the words out. 'Fred gasps and gurgles and falls over Maggie, so she can't breathe none. And all the time the lads just thinks it's Fat Fred enjoying hisself!'

Johnny Terrible's voice trails away and he just looks at me as the tears run down me cheeks. 'Then . . . when they finds out Fat Fred's took dead . . . they all scarpers. Mr Sparrow leaves with a big bag o' stuff, thousands and thousands worth, and him disguised like one o' the Sydney lads.'

'The fucking mongrel! Where is he?' I sob, hitting my hand to my pounding head in anger.

Johnny Terrible points to his mouth and begs in a croaking voice, 'Water.'

I splash what's left in the jug over his gob.

'Where is he?' I yell again, shaking with pain and rage.

'I'll tell ya. What's the time?' he asks.

I take my hunter from me pocket. 'A quarter to eight.'

'Tide turns at nine o'clock. He's on the *Morning Song* – a trading vessel, kanaka crew. She's bound for the Fiji Islands, sails with the tide tonight.'

'Tonight? Christ Jesus! Where's she moored?'

'Anchored midstream, in the harbour two hundred yards or so from Kellett's Wharf.'

'Are you sure?' I shout. 'How'd ya know he's there for sure?' I shove his leg with me boot in a wave of fury.

'I done the arrangements meself, paid the master one 'undred quid, the same to be paid again by Mr Sparrow when he comes aboard safe,' he replies sadly. 'Tang Wing Hung sent a message with Ho Kwong Choi this morning when he come to give Mr Sparrow his pipe. He said if he paid the ten thousand what he owed, he were free to scarper.' Johnny Terrible shrugs his shoulders, wincing as he does so. 'Mr Sparrow gave the old Chinaman diamonds and emeralds and other valuables and he went!'

'Why'd he not take you, then?' I snarl. 'You're his bleedin' right-hand man.'

To me surprise the tears run down Johnny's cheeks. 'I tried to save Maggie when Mr Sparrow wanted his revenge on her – for scheming with you lot against him. "Let me just beat her up bad, cut 'er tits, that be all that's needed," I offers him.' Johnny Terrible is now sobbing. 'But he said I'd changed sides on 'im – and that he couldn't trust me no more, and he set the lads on me and had 'em tie me up.' He wipes the snot from his bleeding nose.

'He were like a father to me, he were – the only one I ever had.' Johnny puts his head between his knees and sobs. 'I dunno why I didn't do what he said. She were only a fuckin' whore. Why should I care anyway?' He looks up at me puzzled. 'She were the first woman what's ever kissed me, and she said she'd fix me face up fer me!' Now he begins to howl like a little boy. Despite me pain and grief, I can't help feelin' sorry for the lad. He were only a pawn what the mongrel's used, and he saw the good in Maggie too.

'Johnny, I got t' go!' I says, though I want to howl meself. The fucking mongrels have taken Maggie and destroyed my brother's life. I would gladly die if only it would bring Maggie back for him. Sweet Maggie Pye, who Hawk loved so much. I feel despair overtake me.

Then Johnny Terrible speaks up. 'Mr Sparrow never did love me, I know it now, never at all!' he blubs. He swallows his tears. 'Mr Sparrow ain't got no heart, that's what!'

'Mongrels don't have a heart, that's why they's mongrels,' I hears meself say. And I start to get ready to go. I have but seventy minutes before the tide turns.

I put the axe back in me shoulder holster and, giving the lamp to Johnny, turn to leave. I'm already at the door to the passage when I hear him say, 'Tommo, they'll be watching out fer trouble 'til they sail. Don't take a row boat. Can yiz swim?'

'Aye,' I replies, I'd swim the seven seas to get the mongrel what killed Maggie. And there ain't a single doubt in me head that I'm gunna. Mr F. Artie Sparrow be as good as dead already – he just don't know it yet.

Suddenly, I remembers something what Mary told Hawk before he left for London, and what later he told me. 'Life is too precious that you should die for money. If you has to die, then die for love!' Up to now, it's always been Hawk what took on the mongrels. This time the fight's all mine. Old Tommo must be his brother's champion.

'Johnny, soon as you can walk, fetch Hawk. He's at the Hero o' Waterloo. Tell him everything what's happened. And tell him Mary must not be with him when he comes to fetch Maggie.' I swallow a sob.

'Tell Hawk everything and Mary can't come,' Johnny Terrible repeats.

I'm halfway down the passageway when I turn back.

'Johnny?'

'Yes, Tommo?'

'Tell my mama I love her – and tell me brother I loves him too. Tell Hawk I wish him a long life and ask him to look after me daughter.' I hand Johnny the three magpie feathers what I've held clasped, bidding Maggie a silent farewell. 'Tell him that by the time he gets these, I'll have took care o' the mongrel for him, and tell him now I finally knows what's worth dying for.'

'Righto, Tommo.'

I don't suppose Johnny Terrible will remember all that, but then I don't suppose it matters. Hawk knows yours truly loved him.

OTHER BOOKS BY BRYCE COURTENAY
AVAILABLE FROM McARTHUR & COMPANY

THE POWER OF ONE

Bryce Courtenay's first novel has inspired over one million readers worldwide.

In South Africa in the 1940s a young boy struggles to realise his individuality in a society divided by racial hatred and conflict.

A spellbinding story of cruelty, sadness, love and faith, filled with unforgettable characters, and told with great compassion and humour.

'The ultimate international bestseller!'
New York Times

'A profoundly moving book, it'll have you breathlessly burning the midnight oil!'
Cleo

TANDIA

Half Indian, half African and beautiful, Tandia is just a teenager when she is brutally attacked and violated by the South African police.

Desperately afraid, consumed by hatred for the white man, Tandia at last finds refuge in a brothel deep in the veldt. There, she learns to use her brilliant mind and extraordinary looks as weapons for the battles that lie ahead: she trains as a terrorist.

Then Tandia meets a man with a past as strange as her own. An Oxford undergraduate, Peekay is also the challenger for the world welterweight boxing championship – and a white man.

In a land where mixed relationships are outlawed, their growing love can only have the most explosive consequences...

'[Bryce Courtenay is] a brilliant raconteur
who piles up set piece after set piece.'
Sydney Morning Herald

THE POTATO FACTORY

Mary Abacus, tenacious, spirited and a woman of independent mind, has arrived in her new land under the most onerous of circumstances.

Sometime mistress of the notorious London criminal, Ikey Solomon, Mary has been transported to Van Diemen's Land for running a bawdy house.

She is soon joined on the convict settlement by Ikey and his wife, Hannah, herself a strong-minded woman, consumed by warring passions, a great love for her children and a loathing for her husband and his mistress.

Determined to survive their past and to shape a new future, the two women raise separate families – one legitimate, the other bastard, and both bearing the name Solomon.

Ruled by Ikey's greed, Hannah's hate and Mary's unswerving ambition, the families ride the brink of disaster as each woman sets out to destroy the other.

'Courtenay is unquestionably a master of a good yarn and he knows the power of myth.'
Sydney Morning Herald

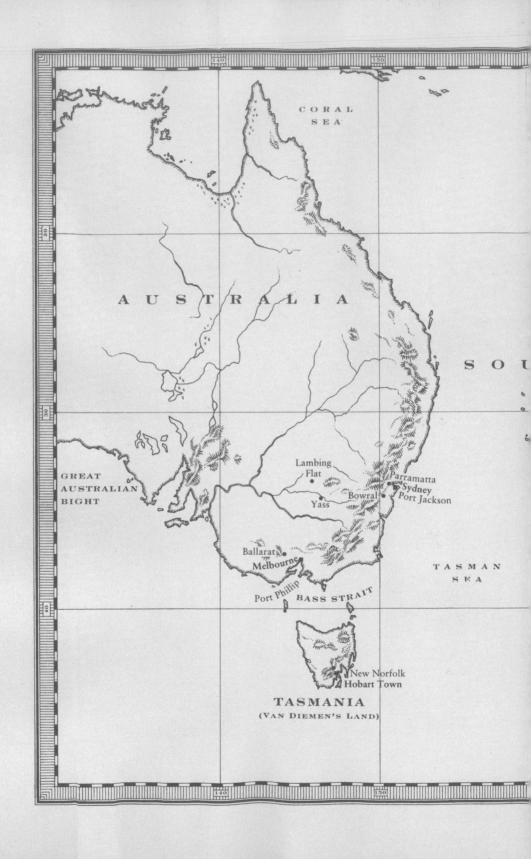